# A FAMILY AFFAIR

Also by Judith Saxton:

*All My Fortunes*
*Family Feeling*

# A FAMILY AFFAIR

*Judith Saxton*

ST. MARTIN'S PRESS
NEW YORK

A FAMILY AFFAIR. Copyright © 1989 by Judith Saxton. All rights
reserved. Printed in the United States of America. No part of this
book may be used or reproduced in any manner whatsoever
without written permission except in the case of brief quotations
embodied in critical articles or reviews. For information, address
St. Martin's Press, 175 Fifth Avenue, New York, N.Y. 10010.

Library of Congress Cataloging-in-Publication Data

Saxton, Judith.
    A family affair / Judith Saxton.
        p.    cm.
    ISBN 0-312-03966-2
    I. Title.
    PR6069.A97F35    1990
    823'.914—dc20                                        89-24151
                                                         CIP

First published in Great Britain by Grafton Books, a division of
the Collins Publishing Group.

First U.S. Edition

10  9  8  7  6  5  4  3  2  1

# ACKNOWLEDGMENTS

I owe a great debt of gratitude to the late Abraham Lomax, whose book, *Royal Lancastrian Pottery*, describing his revolutionary experiments and discoveries in colours and finishes, is an exciting experience in itself, and to his granddaughter, Nancy Webber, who also happens to be my editor, for suggesting I might find the subject interesting and subsequently lending me her rare copy of her grandfather's book.

On the practical side Stephen Roberts of 28 Glan Garth, Wrexham, a skilful and dedicated potter, explained all about potting in the early twentieth century and checked the MS for my errors.

Libby Ridgeway lent me a rare book on a small pottery which was most useful and the owners of the Castle Bookshop, Holt, ransacked their excellent shop for helpful material.

As always, Marina Thomas and the staff of the Wrexham Branch Library performed sterling work in running to earth both the books I knew I needed and the ones they realized I should require.

# Part I

*Adeline and
Arnold*

# CHAPTER ONE

## 1898

It was a cold morning. Adeline could hear the soft crunch-crunch as her boots crossed the frosted grass and it made her glance uneasily about her, for she had no wish to be seen or heard by another early riser as she made her way down the sloping meadow which led to the river.

Not that I've anything to hide, she reminded herself, the mist of her breath puffing out like white fog around her mouth. There's nothing wrong with meeting Arnold Haslington for a walk before breakfast. Why, I've known him all my life, pretty well. It isn't as if we'd anything to be ashamed of.

It had been Arnold's idea that their meeting be kept secret, or at any rate not talked about, and now, considering it, she was inclined to think he was probably right. After all, she was only seventeen, and had it not been for the fact that her father was looking forward to seeing his only child take her place beside him – for her mother had died a dozen years before – she would probably have spent the previous evening doing lessons in the schoolroom. Instead, she had attended her first grown-up dinner party and met Arnold on an equal footing for the first time.

She had enjoyed last night, but probably, had Arnold not been present, it would not have been such fun. After dinner the young people, as their host phrased it, had got up a bit of a dance and Arnold had singled Adeline out, treating her as the young lady he assured her she now was.

'Of course I've known little Adeline for years,' he said, when she had questioned his using the more formal title. 'But this is the first time I've met the delightful Miss Warburton, and I'm anxious to further the acquaintance.'

Childish admiration for her friend Bella's handsome elder brother had taken a breathtaking leap, then, into a far dizzier emotion, for there was no doubt about it: Arnold was the best-looking young man present, and it soon became clear that he found Miss Warburton's company more exciting than that of other, worldlier damsels. Because of her youth, Adeline had used few arts to attract. Her gown was not low-cut or striking; indeed it was a simple white figured cotton with long sleeves and a high neck. Her hair was up, to be sure, but secured in its bun with long, plain pins, not with Spanish combs, jewelled ornaments or hothouse blooms. Her eyes shone with excitement which owed nothing to bella donna and her delicate skin was neither concealed nor enhanced by face powder, its usual pallor flushed into rose by excitement and the heat of an over-warm room.

Arnold had danced with her twice and had sat beside her for at least half an hour discussing the recent Christmas festivities and the attractions still to come. Very correctly, he had not been in the least amorous, nor embarrassed her by dotting his conversation with fulsome compliments or innuendo. But there had been a warmth in his eyes as he spoke which made the most commonplace remarks seem special. Adeline had eagerly agreed to meet him for an early walk by the river, and had complied with his suggestion that they should say nothing about it to their respective families.

'For if I mention it to Bella she'll be sure to get up early for once. And I shan't get a word in edgeways,' he said, laughing, and Adeline laughed too because she and Bella were frequently accused of chattering like a pair of monkeys, to the despair of tutors and governesses.

Now, Adeline was across the meadow and plunging into the belt of trees which hid Saintley Manor from the river. Arnold had said 'early', but he had not mentioned a time and she did not want to be late or even, horror of horrors, to miss him altogether. When she burst out of the trees on to the towpath she was so breathless that she stopped short for a minute, a hand on her side. The air was so cold that running had hurt her lungs; she could feel the chill even through the beaver muff she carried, and her toes, snug in the button-up boots, were going numb at the tips. Even standing for a moment she could feel the cold encroaching, so she began to walk in the direction of Haslington Hall, whence Arnold would soon appear. She stopped again presently though, involuntarily, as the sun began to edge up over the distant blue hills, flooding the winter landscape with palest gold, setting the frost-touched trees sparkling and gilding the cat-ice which stretched its long fingers across the river, blurring the dancing surface.

The river here was always lovely to Adeline's eyes. It ran broad and swift between its banks, curving around the corner ahead so that it formed a sandy beach, frosted today and rimed with ice but in summer an inviting play-place for two small girls, a safe harbour for the creaky wooden skiff Adeline had learned to handle as soon as she could swim, for her father brooked no nonsense about girls not learning such essential pastimes.

'It may be unladylike to swim, but I'd rather that than see her drown,' Sidney Warburton had said firmly when her current governess had raised her brows at the sight of Miss Adeline being dunked in the river on the end of a rope. 'The river's deep here, and it floods in a hard winter. I want my daughter to be as capable in practical matters as the son I never had.'

So Adeline had learned to swim and to row and even to sail, and so had Bella, for Mr Haslington deferred to the Warburtons in such matters. The Haslingtons were industrialists, a good deal richer than the Warburtons but with nowhere near the same social standing. Adeline's family had owned the Manor for four hundred years or more; the Haslingtons had built the Hall a mere twenty years previously. Albert Haslington, Arnold's father, had been grateful to Mr Warburton for treating him as a friend when some of the county families smiled behind their hands and failed to invite him to their more intimate gatherings.

That would never have been Sidney Warburton's way, for he was an honest and generous man; perhaps a trifle eccentric, but a father, Adeline knew, to be proud of. Besides, after her mother died he had been glad of the Haslingtons' friendship and had happily sent his child over to the Hall to share in Bella's lessons and play.

'We never wanted an only child,' he told Albert Haslington, ruffling Adeline's curls. 'But it was to be, so I'm the more grateful to you, my dear sir, for taking my little one into your home the way you have.'

For though Adeline had her own governess she trotted over to the Hall a couple of times most days to share with Bella the services of a music teacher and a landscape artist, and the French and German lessons which were so much more fun with two of you.

Now Adeline, hurrying along the towpath, reached the stile which separated Warburton land from Haslington, and hesitated. She discovered that she did not want to be first at the rendezvous; it would look so forward! However, she could scarcely lurk here and wait for Arnold to arrive, since he had suggested they meet at the tower and she could not even see the edifice from where she stood because of the trees. If she did reach the tower first she had best lurk there, where she could watch Arnold's arrival.

It was the work of a moment to climb the stile and trot down the towpath until, through the winter-bare trees, she could see the Hall. It was a huge house, and to Adeline's eyes it was brash and bare, very unlike her own dear home. The Manor was built of red sandstone and turreted like the castle it had once been. Its walls were richly hung with creepers, wisteria clustered outside her bedroom in June and a deep red rose fought with an old cream and green ivy around the nursery. The windowsills were all feet deep because the walls were so thick, and on the landing and stairs the arrow slits, though glazed in deference to the modern dislike of draughts, were the original ones and very romantic she and Bella had thought them when they were playing at medieval knights and ladies, or chasing each other in a game of hide-and-seek.

The Hall, on the other hand, was built of grey stone, square fronted, with imitation Greek pillars forming a portico at the front. It was much warmer than the Manor and probably better run. It had a folly too, built from the stones of a ruined castle some ten miles away: the very tower at which Arnold and Adeline had planned to meet.

Mr Haslington was proud of his tower, and of his great house, but Bella had never made any secret of the fact that she infinitely preferred the Manor. What did she care for wide staircases, modern window frames and

11

neat little fireplaces? She wanted romance, beauty, and a garden to play in which had trees in it that the young Adeline assured her had been there for hundreds of years.

But the tower is fun, even though it isn't really old, Adeline said to herself now as she saw it looming up on her left. She bent under the willow which wept right in her path, then pushed through the undergrowth and reached the tower the wild way, not by following the track which would have led her to it by a more roundabout route.

One glance, however, told her that Arnold was not there. She walked all round it just to make sure and then hesitated. Should she stay here, or walk towards the Hall and see if Arnold was in sight?

Adeline had never been one to wait passively around when she could be acting. She left the tower and followed the path between the trees until she could see the Hall . . . and there was Arnold, in his city suit, his hat in his hand and his overcoat open, coming fast towards her.

Adeline's heart quickened its pace; should she retreat into the trees once more and pretend she had only just arrived? But it seemed rather silly, and acting a lie which wasn't necessary was a shabby sort of thing to do. Instead, Adeline walked forward.

They met at the fringe of the trees, shook hands formally, though both with such warm smiles that formality seemed foolish, and then he took her elbow and steered her back to the towpath by the river.

'Well, Miss Warburton, and how did you enjoy your party last night?' Arnold's dark eyes were tenderly teasing. He was very handsome, a tall man with dark brown, wavy hair, dark eyes and a classically straight nose. '*I* enjoyed myself very much indeed; I met such a pretty young lady! She had hair black as night, skin like milk, big blue eyes . . .'

'What nonsense you talk,' Adeline said, feeling her cheeks warm. 'My eyes aren't really blue at all; they're too dark. People sometimes think they're dark brown or black!'

'Anyone who thinks that is blind, or a fool,' Arnold assured her. 'But I don't mean to embarrass you. How did you sleep after your first proper party? You were certainly up betimes – and what a lovely day you've brought with you. Sunshine for a change.'

'Yes. I watched the sun rise,' Adeline said. 'It was beautiful. I think this is the most beautiful country in the world, don't you, Ar . . . Mr Haslington?'

'I think now that we've met socially, we might return to using each other's first names,' Arnold said, smiling down at her. 'As to this being the most beautiful country in the world, how can either of us tell? We've no experience of other countries to judge by, though I hope very soon to be able to persuade my father to let me visit some big cities . . . Manchester, Leeds, even London.'

'I don't need to go anywhere else to know that this is the most beautiful place,' Adeline said obstinately. 'It's *my* place, it's a part of me and I of it. You must surely feel the same.'

'Ye-es, but my family's only lived here for a generation,' Arnold pointed out. They turned right along the towpath and began to walk slowly beside the river. 'Have you time for a half-mile or so? I want us to get to know one another a little better, Adeline.'

'Oh yes, lots of time,' Adeline said rather breathlessly. 'I want that too, Arnold!'

Making his way home along the towpath half an hour later, having seen Adeline as far as the open meadow between the manor gardens and the river, Arnold felt pleased with himself. Odd, that he had known Adeline for so long and had simply never thought of her, save as Bella's little friend, until the previous evening. At first he had not even recognized her, except as a remarkably pretty girl, and when he had he had wanted to get to know her, just as he had teasingly told her. She was a lovely creature, slight but long-legged; she had kept pace with his stride easily and he knew from Bella that she swam and rode a horse and bent to her oars when she was in a boat with as much vigour and enthusiasm as most boys. She was popular too. 'A broth of a girl', the head groom at the manor had called her once, and 'a pretty, independent lass', his own father had said. Arnold, even in the time he had been with her, had realized that there was more to his young neighbour than a pretty face. She spoke her mind, laughed when amused, and could skim a stone along ice and water with the strength and skill Arnold himself possessed. She had a good sense of humour, as well. Once she got over her initial shyness she had relaxed and laughed with him over one of her tutors, boasted that her watercolours were actually recognizable and talked of her horse, her dogs, and her three brindled kittens, offspring of the housekeeper's old she-cat, as though she had known him all her life. Which, of course, she had, Arnold reminded himself. Only with three years between them they had scarcely ever met, had probably only exchanged half a dozen words a month, if that. Between twelve and fifteen, too, there yawns an enormous crevasse which, between seventeen and twenty, is easily bridgeable. And I'm eager to build that bridge, Arnold thought, striding out. How good it is to know her, how warm the memory of her will lie in my mind as I go round the pottery this morning!

For the Haslingtons owned a large and thriving pot-bank twenty miles away in the town of Langforth, and Arnold was, at the moment, working there every day to learn the business. His father had started with pots but had gone on to other things. A bank, a chain of hardware shops, a biscuit manufactory and his latest whim, a small saddlery which had come on the market because its owner had died. None of his later interests made much money but the pottery went from strength to strength. Arnold regretted that they made such mundane objects – chamber pots, jugs and ewers, thick white cups and saucers and dreadful ornaments – but mundane or not people bought them by the hundred, and then presumably broke them and bought more.

Sometimes Arnold dreamed of producing fine china for people who liked nice things and could afford to pay decent prices, but at twenty advancement in the world of business did not seem so important as excelling at tennis, riding to hounds, or simply finding a girl who, with batting eyelashes and simpering smiles, would Give her All. This last, to Arnold's chagrin, had not proved easy to attain. He was far too well reared by his parents to consider an alliance, of however brief a nature, with one of the girls who worked for him, far less a servant at the Hall, yet it was obviously out of the question to approach a young lady with such a proposal. As for Adeline – his heart swooned in his breast at the hateful indelicacy of the thought – she was far above things like that. She was the sort of woman he wanted to marry, not . . . not experiment upon!

Arnold reached the house and shed his coat and hat, then went along to the breakfast room. His father sat at one end of the big oval table, knife and fork poised over the sort of plateful the doctor had warned him against. Not that he'd taken the slightest notice, save for a day or two after the seizure which had so terrified him last year. His son already knew the uselessness of reproaches, so he went over to the sideboard, lifted the lid from the first of the big silver dishes, kept warm by a spirit lamp, and helped himself sparingly first to bacon and kidneys, then to a fried egg, and lastly to mushrooms and a bulging brown sausage. Only then did he return to the table and sit down by Albert Haslington.

'Morning, Father, want some more coffee whilst I'm pouring mine?'

His father put a fork, heavily laden with provender, into his mouth, chewed and then answered, grease running down his chin and plopping off the end of it on to his plate.

'Eh? Ah, coffee . . . yes please me boy. Out early again this morning eh? Going to the pot-bank, of course?'

'That's right.' Arnold poured the coffee, added a dash of hot milk to his own and a generous slurp to his father's, and pulled his cup towards him, trying not to look censorious as his father piled sugar into the cup, grasping the silver spoon with one hand whilst the other carried another giant forkful up to his hopefully opening mouth.

'There are some good lines coming along,' Albert Haslington said, when he could speak. 'Oh I know you say it ain't quality, but it sells, boy, it sells.'

'I know. We've some biscuitware, though, that's a bit out of the common run. I'm hoping you might let me take samples over to Manchester or Leeds, see if I can get any of the big stores interested.'

Arnold stopped speaking. Albert was not listening. Fried bread was being quartered, piled with bacon and sausage, deluged in the gleaming gold of egg-yolk and lifted to his father's mouth.

Arnold finished his own breakfast, wiped his mouth on his napkin and pushed back his chair. Useless to expostulate, useless even to expect a serious answer to a serious proposal whilst his father ate. Breakfast was now the most important event in his father's life because his wife did not come down for the meal, preferring a tray in her own room. Lunch would be presided over by her and Albert would eat what he was given. Dinner at night was the same. Only at breakfast could he really make a pig of himself and he did so unhesitatingly, day after day.

'Off so soon?' Albert clawed his coffee cup towards him, lifted it and drank. 'Where's the toast? As you pass the bell, lad, give it a jerk, would you? Mary knows I like my toast hot; she won't bring it through until I ring.'

Arnold nodded, bade his father farewell, and jerked the bell on his way past it.

Now that he did not have his father's gross eating before him he could think, once more, of Adeline. He made for the stableyard a happy man.

For her part, Adeline found coming down to earth after being with Arnold very much an anti-climax. She went home, had coffee and toast for breakfast, saw her father off to see his legal adviser about some land, conscientiously practised the piano for half an hour, did some work on her French verbs, and then picked up her sketch book and announced to her erstwhile governess, Miss Palling, that she was off to visit Bella and possibly to sketch a little if the weather proved sufficiently clement to allow her to sit outside for half an hour.

'Still life does not appeal, my dear?' Miss Palling suggested hopefully. Sketching a summery scene in warm weather was one thing, but perching on a wall in the freezing cold drawing the icicles hanging from a filthy cowbyre did not, in her eyes, constitute ladylike behaviour. However, she was very fond of Adeline and waved her off, telling her that she herself would spend the morning darning linen until it was time for luncheon. If there was any reproach in the words Adeline did not let it worry her, for Miss Palling was now employed as a sort of superior housekeeper and Adeline herself, though willing, was useless with a needle.

The sun was still shining as Adeline trod the path she had used earlier in the day and the frost was lifting. Trees were diamonded with drops now, the cobwebs on the gorse bushes were pearled with them and the sheep, placidly grazing, steamed gently as the sun warmed their wet and heavy fleece. But Adeline noticed nothing, for she was rehearsing just what she would say to Bella. Her friend would think her evening had been tame indeed, she realized belatedly, if she said she had spent most of it talking to Bella's elder brother. The three years which separated Adeline and Arnold separated Bella and Arnold too, but how different they seemed! Bella was for ever pestering Arnold, hiding his hairbrushes, using his pomade to smooth down her own lively locks, telling him – Adeline blushed for her friend – that his feet smelt or his sock had a hole in it. A

15

brother cannot, Adeline realized, be a hero to the sibling next to him in age.

However, it would be another year before Bella was officially 'out'. Mr Warburton, a much respected landowner, might flout the conventions and bring his daughter into society a year early because he had no wife to accompany him to parties, but it was a different case entirely for the Haslingtons. Bella's mother was very much alive for one thing, and for another people might well say the Haslingtons were upstarts, and pushing, if Bella came out before her eighteenth birthday next September.

Despite Bella's frequent quarrels with Arnold, though, she was fond of her elder brother. If she was vowed to secrecy, would she abide by her word? But Adeline knew, at heart, that she could not confide in Bella; without meaning to do so, Bella would somehow manage to let Arnold know she was in on the secret and Arnold would not be at all pleased.

It was a pity, in fact it was a wretched nuisance, for Adeline had been longing for the fun of displaying her new-found happiness to her best friend. But it would only be a matter of time, she was sure, before she and Arnold could confess their friendship to everyone, and by then perhaps Bella, too, would be 'out' and able to admit that Arnold did have a great many charms. If I were to ask her now she'd merely say he trimmed his moustache lopsided, Adeline told herself bitterly.

What a good thing the party had been a nice one, though. She would be able to chatter about that and try to push into the back of her mind that exciting early walk and the walks which were to come.

'We'll meet each morning, shall we?' Arnold had said, as he helped her over the stile which separated their estates. 'Rain or shine, eh? It'll be fun even in the rain if we're sharing an umbrella.'

He was so romantic! Adeline had agreed breathlessly, of course, but could not imagine that rain would fall on her and Arnold; they were destined for endless sunshine!

Adeline reached the point on the towpath where she should strike up through the trees to get to the Hall; she took the sensible path, which was well marked and clear, but cast an affectionate glance at the tower through the trees. Tomorrow, she told it in her mind. Tomorrow I'll be waiting.

As she reached the Hall and went in through the side door, tugging off her coat, casting down her muff and trying to kick off her boots without bothering to undo them – a vain task – she heard footsteps scampering across the floor and then Bella was upon her, wisps of fair hair standing on end despite two tight braids which reached nearly to her waist, dark brown eyes shining with anticipation. Bella was a pretty girl, smaller and more compactly built than Adeline but with a puppylike charm all her own. Her nose was retroussé, her mouth wide and her nature affectionate. Adeline's father often remarked that she would be popular with the gentlemen one of these days and his daughter believed him. Breathless Bella, Arnold had dubbed her because she was always chattering and rushing somewhere, but even Arnold admitted that Bella was bound to marry young. 'My mother will dress her up and let her loose and she'll charm some poor johnnie out of his right mind and he'll propose,' was actually how he had put it, but Adeline interpreted this as a compliment, as indeed it was meant.

'Dearest Addy, what happened? Tell me at once! Oh no, hold on a tick, here's the brat . . . don't say a word until I get you all to myself in the upstairs parlour.' Bella turned to the Haslingtons' youngest child, eight-year-old Bertie, who combined the looks of a cherub with the nature of an imp from hell. 'Go on, get away. You should have been in the schoolroom with Miss Pratt hours ago!'

'Miss Pratt's a stupid old bat,' shrieked Bertie, grinning widely and crossing his eyes with masterly ease as soon as he saw Adeline. 'Oh we've got a *visitor*! With her hair *up*, it must be a young lady!' He pretended to scrutinize her more closely, still with crossing and uncrossing eyes, and then said in a relieved tone, 'Oh no, it's only ugly Addy from the house next door!'

'I'll break every bone in your body,' Bella shrieked, lunging for her small brother. 'You're a nasty, spoilt, rude brat and it's about time someone taught you a lesson.'

Used to such outbursts from his volatile sister, Bertie merely ran to the stairs and continued his insults from there, but as Adeline and Bella advanced towards him he decided that discretion was the better part of valour and made off, singing a song which Adeline devoutly hoped he had learned in the stables and not from his elder brother.

'That child will be the death of me,' Bella said as Bertie disappeared round the top of the stairs. 'How Miss Pratt puts up with him I can't imagine, and mother's no help; she just says he's full of high spirits and will calm down when he goes to school. Only whenever I ask when he's going to school, she says he's got a weak chest, or a tendency to sore throats or some such thing.' She slipped her arm through Adeline's. 'Oh, I can't wait to hear about last night!'

'When we reach the parlour you shall,' Adeline promised. She revised her thoughts rapidly as they ran up the stairs, along the corridor and into the parlour. It was a pleasant sitting-room, used just by the two of them at the moment, though Dorothea, Bella's sister next in age, was showing an alarming tendency to consider herself quite grown up enough to join them when her studies permitted.

'Now tell!' Bella demanded when they had crossed the room and thrown themselves down on a chintz-covered sofa. Adeline looked thoughtfully round the room, wondering where to start. There was a fire blazing in the hearth, a round, faded carpet with sprigs of roses all over it and a wide window which opened, in summer, on to a sizeable balcony with a stone balustrade round it.

'Shall I start with the room? It was very smart. The flowers were done specially, you could tell. Crimson, pink and cream carnations from the Oxenhams' hothouses to go with the crimson carpet and curtains. The cream must have been the furniture – it was upholstered in cream satin with gold stripes. It's a big room . . .'

'Oh, hush . . . I want to hear what happened, not where it happened,' Bella said. 'Who was there beside you and Mr Warburton? Oh, apart from Flo and her parents, of course.'

The party had been a discreet dinner for no more than twenty-four people held by the Oxenhams to allow Flo, who was having a very large eighteenth birthday dance the following month, to get used to social events. Adeline started counting up on her fingers.

'Well, there was Flo's aunt, Mrs Fowler, and her husband of course. And Flo's cousins, Amelia and Suzanne. Then there was some sort of great-uncle, I think, I didn't catch his name, and his wife, a very old lady but very smart and . . .'

'The young ones, not the old fogeys,' Bella put in. 'Just tell me about the young ones . . . what they wore and said and how they looked . . . *you* know, Addy!'

Adeline, who knew perfectly well what her friend wanted to hear and had been merely playing for time, nodded and smiled.

'Yes, I know. Well there were only eight of us really. There was me, in my white . . . you know . . . and your brother Arnold and Flo herself, of course. She wore pale green silk, nothing special; she's saving the special dress for her party next month. Her cousins Amelia and Suzanne were very modish, though. Amelia had a very elegant gown in dark red velvet, just a bodice and a beautifully cut skirt with a ruched train. And Suzanne wore topaz silk with a brown velvet ribbon round her throat and she carried a brown velvet bag with gold threadwork and strings. Her hair was the same colour as her gown. I heard Mr Lyndhurst say it transformed her. And I must say I agreed,' Adeline added candidly, 'for I've always thought her a bit plump and spotty before.'

'She could do with a bit of transformation,' Bella concurred unkindly. 'Go on, that's only five; who were the other three?'

'Well, gentlemen obviously. Except I said eight and that counted me, so I'm one of the three,' Adeline said rather confusedly. 'The others were Mr Gerald Bailey and Mr Alfred Shown.'

'I say . . . I've always rather liked Gerald Bailey. Did you dance with him?'

'Yes, I did. He was very pleasant. I danced with everyone, in fact, and someone . . .' Adeline had suddenly realized that in mystery itself she could release some of her pent-up feelings to her friend '. . . and someone said he admired me and wanted to see me again!'

Bella's eyes nearly popped out of her head.

'At your very first dinner party? Good gracious, Addy! Who was it? It must have been one of those four . . . not Arnold, obviously, nor Mr

18

Lyndhurst because he's rather keen on Flo, or so she says. That just leaves Gerald or Alfred. Which one?'

'Neither,' said Adeline hastily but truthfully, and began to wriggle out of the trap into which she had very nearly fallen. 'At the end of the evening some other people came, just for the dancing.'

'Oh Addy, how thrilling,' Bella said, hugging herself. 'Who came afterwards?'

'I can't tell you. No, it's no use pleading and carrying on because he wants it kept secret . . . for a while, at any rate. He says I'm too young, and he thinks my father wouldn't approve . . . so we're keeping it quiet for a bit.' Excitement and the glamour of it got the better of her. 'Oh, Bella, we're even meeting secretly, every single day! He's . . . he's very splendid and I admire him very much!'

'Secret meetings?' gasped Bella, her eyes like saucers. 'Oh, I can't bear not to know! I'm your dearest friend; surely you could tell me, I wouldn't breathe a word to a soul.'

'*I* know I can trust you, but my . . . *he* . . . doesn't know that at all, you see,' Adeline explained, with far more truth than Bella could possibly have guessed, since Arnold had told her that his sister could no more keep a secret than she could sing in tune. This cruel though apt simile had forced a smile out of Adeline, who had perfect pitch and was often driven to put her fingers in her ears when her friend insisted on performing.

'Oh, well, I suppose you must keep your secret, then,' Bella said. 'But you can tell me the rest, can't you? Not his name, but everything else?'

'Oh, yes, of course. He's very handsome and tall; that goes without saying, I suppose. He's . . .'

'Dark or fair?'

'Dark. Do stop asking me questions, Bella, or I'll lose the thread. Where was I? Oh yes, he's handsome, of course, and tall, and he thinks I'm really rather pretty, and he wants us to meet every day so that we get to know one another properly and are sure of our feelings before we speak of them to others.'

'That's the most romantic thing I ever heard,' sighed Bella. 'How many times did you dance with him?'

'Twice.' Even as the words left her lips Adeline wondered if she had said too much, but then remembered, with relief, that she had also danced twice with Flo's cousin George, who had come along for the dancing, being engaged with friends earlier. She did not like George and had no intention whatsoever of pretending she did, but he was tall and fairly dark and he was, she supposed, quite eligible.

'Hmm. I've no doubt I could find out, if I put my mind to it, but I won't because I love you too well, Addy, to risk putting a spoke in your wheel. Tell me about Arnold, since he *is* my brother. Did he seem fonder of any one lady than another? He's a great one for parties is my big brother, and he always talks as though every young lady present had eyes for no one but him, but I don't suppose it's true.'

'He is very handsome,' Adeline said rather stiffly. 'I danced with him, of course. He dances very well. I could see that Amelia and Suzanne both admired him, and Flo told me that she likes dark men because they can easily look sinister!'

'Well, I hope he doesn't decide to marry Flo. She's very nice, but her hair is so red and she's the bossiest person I know.'

'Oh, I shouldn't worry; I don't think he took any more notice of Flo than he did of the rest of us,' Adeline said airily. 'Now I've told you everything, Bella, so shall we walk into the village whilst the sun is still shining? I could do with some elastic and Miss Palling wants a reel of white cotton.'

'Oh, all right,' Bella conceded, getting to her feet. 'When we come home, though, Mama's got some magazines you really must see – there's the prettiest way of doing your hair . . . and a pattern for a new type of jacket . . . and several stories which made me cry buckets . . .' She and Adeline were descending the stairs by now, arms linked once more. 'I dare say it's cold out, isn't it? I wonder, should I ask if we can use the carriage?'

But this was not Adeline's idea of a walk at all and she said so in forthright tones, so Bella agreed to set out on foot despite the cold.

'I sometimes think you should have been a boy, Addy,' she said crossly, as they set off. 'It's not feminine to want to be outdoors all the time, and to enjoy walking and riding and things like that.'

Adeline returned some peaceable answer, but inside she was laughing. So she was unfeminine, was she? Well, Arnold didn't think so!

# CHAPTER TWO

'Adeline, my dear, don't rush off, I'd like a word with you.'

It was breakfast time and Adeline and her father had just drunk their coffee together, as they did every morning. The small, panelled room was bright with June sunshine and even the faded curtains and chair seats, which Adeline had been meaning to replace for months, looked brighter, newer on such a morning. Adeline, who had indeed been about to leave the room, returned to the table. She took her seat once more and shook her head chidingly at her companion.

'Well, Father? Why didn't you talk before, instead of reading your paper? I'm going over to the Hall to see Bella; not that it'll matter if I'm a bit late, knowing her rising habits!'

'That just shows, miss, how much you notice, for I laid aside the paper quite a quarter of an hour ago. I've been reading my post, and that's why I want a word with you. Now have some more coffee or another piece of toast, and listen for once, instead of chattering.'

Adeline smiled affectionately at her father and poured herself a fresh cup of coffee. She would be eighteen in five months and was beginning to interest herself in the running of the Manor; one day in the not-too-distant future she hoped she would marry and have a home of her own to run. Now, she glanced critically at the liquid in her cup. It was only luke-warm; they should have either a smaller pot which could be refilled when it ran out, or a spirit-stove for the coffee as well as for the food on the sideboard. She must suggest it to Mrs Gilmour, the housekeeper.

'Go on then, Papa, don't keep me in suspense. Have you had the bills for my summer dresses? I'm shivering in my shoes!'

Sidney Warburton shook his head and wagged an admonitory finger; he never questioned her expenditure, as she knew very well.

'Now, Addy, I'm serious. You have known for many years that when I die this house and the land will be yours. You have also known, because it's family history, that many years ago Saintley Manor belonged to another branch of our family but came to my father as a result of a bitter quarrel.'

'Yes, I know, Papa. You once said that a cousin of yours probably had a greater moral right to the property . . . but you didn't care for him, as I recall.'

'That's true. But recently that cousin died, leaving a son, Geoffrey, who has a son nearly ten years older than you. Geoffrey has written, expressing the hope that he and I might bury old grievances, and telling me that his son John would like to come over and see us, and the home that his ancestors built up.'

'Oh? Well, as long as no one's going to dispute your right to the Manor, or my right to inherit it, I suppose it doesn't matter, if you want to invite him.' Adeline half rose. 'Is that all, Papa? I'll be happy to meet this young man if you ask him here.'

'Very well. His father suggests he arrive in three weeks. He sounds a very proper young fellow. He's a qualified doctor of medicine, and his father speaks of his going abroad to practise, so I thought we'd get him to come fairly soon, whilst his plans are not too settled.'

'All right. If you ask him to wire the time of the train he'll be arriving on and the exact date, we can meet him at the station.' Adeline jumped to her feet. 'Is that all, Papa? Can I go now?'

'Of course you can, love. Have a good day.'

Adeline left the room. She and Bella were going to drive into Langforth to do some shopping, have a light luncheon there, and come home in the carriage with Arnold and his father. Arnold would walk her home as a duty . . . the very thought excited her.

She had a new hat, pale straw with cherries bobbing on the brim, and a new light jacket to go with it. Arnold had seen neither of these garments and she trusted that he would be dazzled by such finery.

She popped her head round her father's study door as she was about to set off, for she never left the house without telling him where she was bound.

'I'm off, Papa,' she said gaily, touching her hat. 'Do you like the cherries? We're going into Langforth, Bella and I.'

'Very nice, dear. Will the carriage bring you home?'

'If not, someone will walk back with me. I'll be in plenty of time for dinner.' She waved her new, straw-coloured linen gloves at him. 'I am very smart aren't I? Goodbye, Papa!'

Sidney watched his daughter as she tripped past his study windows, and then turned back to his work with a sigh.

It had cost him a lot to say nothing when he realized that Adeline was meeting young Arnold Haslington in secret and obviously building a lot on the clandestine relationship. Young puppy, he thought wrathfully now, he wasn't the man for Adeline, with his handsome looks and half-hearted attendance at the pot-bank. The boy had never done an honest day's work in his life. He spent all his spare time strutting round the village looking at his reflection in shop windows and buying pomade for his hair . . . he probably polished his nails!

The mischief was that Sidney was not supposed to know that the two young people had the slightest interest in one another, so he could scarcely criticize her choice. And it annoyed him that Arnold was insisting on secrecy, for Sidney knew his daughter too well to believe for one moment that it was her idea. Adeline was transparently honest, which was how he had come to realize she was meeting Arnold secretly. She simply did not know how to lie, and her flushed cheeks, downcast eyes and obvious embarrassment when her father mentioned her sudden passion for early morning walks had been enough to make Sidney follow her on one occasion just to see that she was not getting into any sort of trouble.

Five months ago, he had thought it would all blow over – and so it would have done, he told himself wrathfully now, had Arnold not insisted on secrecy. It made a mundane affair with a mundane fellow into high romance, and whilst Adeline continued to think of the young man as her secret lover she was most unlikely to pay attention to anyone else.

So the letter from Geoffrey about his boy John had been a blessing. Geoffrey had said, not seriously perhaps, that it would be rather nice if their children fell in love, so that the Manor would be shared by the two families who both had claims to it, and Sidney had been enchanted by the idea. If only this John Sawyer was a decent young man, then surely the very fact that her father liked him would be enough to make Adeline think again about her liaison with Arnold? At least he would put the idea to the test. He would ask John to stay, and see that the two young people spent a good deal of time with each other. Even if Adeline could not fall in love with John, at least a close relationship with a worthy young man might make her see the glaring faults in Arnold which were so obvious to her father.

Sidney pulled a piece of paper towards him and dipped his pen in the ink. He would write to Geoffrey this very day and arrange for John to come to the Manor. And he would make it clear to Adeline, gently but definitely, that he felt they had a duty to get to know this unknown cousin, to appreciate his good points, and to try to right, in some small way, the wrong that had been done to his branch of the family. He would never force his girl into a distasteful marriage, but he was sure that if she and Arnold wed deep unhappiness would follow. It was his duty to try to avoid such an event.

Despite the girls' plans, which had been for a day's shopping with just the two of them going round the town, Arnold met them at three and insisted on treating them to tea at a very smart pastry shop. Bella was delighted by such brotherly behaviour but Adeline felt, guiltily, that she had taken Arnold from his work too early, for she had been brought up to consider that a man's work was paramount and play came a good way behind it. Not that her father was a joyless man, quite the opposite, but he valued his land and believed that he owed it to his tenants to work as hard as they did.

However, she salved her conscience by telling herself that Arnold must know his own business best, and when they arrived back at the Hall and he said he would walk her home she accepted at once. They set out into the meadows, golden with sunset, which led down to the river, making for a quiet spot on the bank where they could sit and talk.

'Alone at last!' Arnold said dramatically. He gave his sweetheart a chaste kiss on the side of her mouth. Adeline turned and kissed him back equally gently.

'Yes, isn't it nice? Though it was a lovely day out. Arnold, when are you going to London?'

The trip had been planned for some time. Mr Haslington had agreed to send Arnold to the capital so that he could see for himself what sort of sale of fine china was possible.

'If you get 'em to buy, then you can go ahead and mek more,' Albert Haslington had said jovially to his son, so Arnold had reported. 'If the buyers aren't interested, then neither am I.' But Arnold was sure they would be interested when they saw the samples and designs he had to show.

'How did you guess, my love? I've a definite date at last. I go in three weeks. I'm to stay with my cousin Thomas in his new hotel near Covent Garden, and I'm sure I'll soon prove to everyone that quality is wanted.'

'Three weeks,' Adeline said thoughtfully. 'Well, that's quite a good time, because Papa had a letter from his cousin Geoffrey today . . .'

She explained at length about the original quarrel and the subsequent invitation to young Mr Sawyer, but instead of being interested Arnold looked startled and annoyed.

'Can't you see why your father wants to entertain this man?' he said in an aggrieved voice. 'He hopes you'll marry the fellow so that the Manor will belong to both sides of the family once more.'

'That's silly,' Adeline said, taking his hand. 'As if I would! No, you're wrong; Papa isn't like that. If you'd only agree to tell him about us, Arnold, then you'd soon stop worrying.'

'I'm not worried,' Arnold said stiffly. 'You love me, don't you? Well, I certainly love you!'

'Of course I love you,' Adeline said at once. 'So . . . why can't you speak to my father, Arny?'

'I will, in a few months' time . . . when I've made lots of money from my sales of fine china,' Arnold said, inspired. 'Then he'll see I'm good enough for his daughter!'

'That could be ages. I think you ought to speak to him right away,' Adeline said, but Arnold could not agree.

'If I spoke to him now he'd think I was afraid to let you meet this cousin of yours . . . or he might think it was odd that I turned straight round and went off to London,' Arnold said. 'Look, when I get back and your cousin's gone we'll discuss it again.'

For the first time, Adeline was aware of some constraint between them as they walked along the river bank towards the Manor. But Arnold seemed unconscious of it and chatted comfortably about his triumphs to come and how proud she would be of him.

They parted at the fringe of the woods and Adeline went on to the Manor alone. She felt rather cross with her lover.

Walking home, Arnold scuffed his feet in the dust of the path and thought about marriage. The reason he held out against an immediate appeal to Mr Warburton was not nearly so simple as he had led Adeline to believe. He was twenty-one years old, totally inexperienced with women, and very anxious to learn a lot before he committed himself to marriage with anyone, even the delicious Adeline Warburton. And he was uneasily aware that, despite his father's money, Mr Warburton might very likely want something more for his only child than the rather idle elder son of his industrialist neighbour. What Arnold knew or indeed wanted to know about running a large estate could have been printed in large type on a halfpenny stamp, and he had no desire to increase his knowledge. Farming bored him.

However, he was extremely anxious to increase his knowledge of women, and was hoping that the London trip would help him do just that. His cousin Thomas was a bit of a black sheep, though since having been cast off by his father he had done very well for himself. But a black sheep, Arnold thought hopefully, would be the very person to introduce a young cousin from the unfashionable north to a bit of high life. A flighty woman or two would surely not object to teaching a fellow like him a few tricks.

Of course he could scarcely say any of this to Adeline, but he knew very well that a fellow needed a Past. It was what he offered the pure young girl in modern romances; a Past he would willingly give up for her sake. Matrimony and making pots would be very nice, if only he could get himself a Past to give up first!

Sometimes Arnold wondered whether Bella suspected, but as a rule he was sure his exciting secret was a secret still. His mother, a large and domineering woman who adored her sons and bullied her daughters, gave him knowing looks from time to time, and had even hinted that she knew he had a girlfriend tucked away. But she could not have guessed that the girlfriend in question was none other than the heiress next door. He and Adeline never let their masks fall for a moment in public; they were very much Miss Warburton and Mr Haslington. But his mother was a knowing one; he would have to keep his eye on her.

Arnold reached the house, let himself in, and changed his outdoor shoes for slippers before going straight to his room to change for dinner. He examined himself in the mirror; what a dark and dangerous face he had. He was one devil of a fellow really, suave and knowing. It was about time he became as wicked as he could look. He was really looking forward to his trip to London, though he intended to miss Adeline and think of her several times each day. Cousin Thomas was no end of a fellow. He had been chucked out of two really first-rate public schools, whilst Arnold had only attended the local grammar, and had been a by-word for idleness and wicked ways until he had gone into the hotel business, when even his parents' gloom had lifted on seeing his talent for the catering trade.

London will be my last fling, Arnold told himself, drawing his razor carefully across his chin, for he was sufficiently dark to feel a twice-daily shave a necessity. I'll do my best to live it up whilst I'm there, meet lots of women, learn a thing or two. After all, I'm doing it for my dear Adeline's sake!

'Good to see you, old fellow.'

Cousin Thomas was in fine fettle, handsome as ever though a little thinner and paler than he had been when Arnold saw him last. But it suits him, Arnold told himself loyally, pumping Thomas's hand and exclaiming how well he looked. Even the slightly thinning hair, slicked down with strong-smelling pomade, even his suit, which fitted rather too well at the waist and not quite well enough at the leg, were signs of fashionableness, and his smile had not changed at all; neither had the twinkle in his toffee-brown eyes.

'You've got a grand place here, Thomas,' Arnold exclaimed, glancing around him. The reception hall gleamed with cream-coloured paint and gold leaf, the carpet was a dark red Turkey one and a great chandelier twinkled above their heads.

'Aye. Not bad. We're all electric, as you can see, from the basement to the attics. Everything of the best's been my motto.' He winked at his cousin. 'Then you can charge 'em well and no bother.'

'So I see,' Arnold said appreciatively. He glanced over towards the reception desk behind which sat a highly coloured young lady wearing a very low-cut black dress, with very upswept, very yellow, hair. 'It's all most impressive.'

'Wait till you see my quarters – and the bar, I'm proud of the bar. But you'll want to get settled after your journey.' He whistled and a boy of about twelve in a maroon and gold uniform appeared and grabbed Arnold's cases. 'Take them up to my suite, Willy. Has the cabin trunk gone up already?'

'Yessir,' the boy said, making for the stairs. 'Be up in a brace of shakes sir.'

'I – I hope they were careful with the trunk,' Arnold said in a slightly apprehensive voice. 'I've got my china samples in there.'

'Oh aye, they'd treat it like glass,' cousin Thomas assured him. 'Let's get you settled in, and then we can have a drink or three.' He chuckled at his own wit. 'I've got what you might call the penthouse suite. Up we go!'

The stairs led on to a landing from which another staircase ascended to the heights. They went up the next set of stairs and the next and the next, and Arnold was just beginning to wonder whether they would presently reach the roof and still continue to climb when they stopped on a small, bare landing right at the top of the building. Thomas took out a key and unlocked the door on the left of the stairs, which had a proper little brass knocker and a bell-pull, just like an ordinary front door. He was not breathless at all, but Arnold could feel his heart hammering somewhat faster than usual and was ashamed that he was in such bad condition. Thomas, however, appeared to have noticed nothing.

'Here we are, home sweet home,' he said.

They stood in a tiny inner hall, carpeted wall to wall, with flowers in a huge vase to the right, and a silk upholstered chair, a small table, and a wall telephone on the left. In front of them were two doors, one of which Thomas flung open.

'Here we have the living-room or parlour; what do you think?'

The room was large and airy, with two sizeable windows curtained in gold velvet. It was overcrowded with furniture, knick-knacks, occasional tables, two chiffoniers and any amount of ornamentation. The carpet was a rich wine colour, the sofas and easy chairs upholstered either in wine or

26

in gold plush. Arnold supposed, blinking a bit, that it was all very modern. Feebly, he said, 'I say, it's a dream!' whilst secretly thinking that it was more like a nightmare, but Thomas seemed pleased.

'Had it all done on the cheap when the hotel was refurbished,' he said. 'Wait till you see my room!'

Thomas's room was a boudoir in shades of pink and vermilion. Arnold blinked. Thomas in that bed must look like an earwig in a rose.

'Very tasteful,' Arnold said, however. 'It must have cost a packet.'

'It would have, but I got it done at the same time as the parlour,' Thomas told him proudly. Arnold wondered what the decorators had in mind when they put his cousin to sleep in a vividly coloured bower, but he just murmured that it must have been a real bargain and moved on to the guest-room.

The guest-room was different. It had a brown carpet, luxurious to the feet but quiet on the eyes, and the bed, though a four-poster, was hung with brown and cream-coloured curtains. There was not much furniture but what there was Arnold considered to be in good taste: a couple of comfortable chairs, a settee, a little writing desk under the window, a large chest of drawers and a dressing table. A door in one corner led into what Thomas said with a certain regret was a shared bathroom and lavatory.

'No room up here for one each,' he said sadly. 'Still, we'll make do, I dare say.'

'The room's nice; did you . . .?'

'No, not this one. I bought a job lot when an old lady died. My father didn't like the way I'd done this place up, you see; said it wasn't suitable for him and m'mother when they came to stay. So I bowed to convention, as they say, and did it more in their style. I'm sorry, old chap, but you can go and sit in the parlour whenever you're at home.'

'Thanks. I'd better unpack now, though.'

Arnold approached his case and Thomas went to the door.

'Right, you get unpacked and tidy yourself up, and then come down and meet me in the bar for a drink, say in half an hour? Just ask the receptionist; she'll tell you where to find me.'

Thomas disappeared, leaving Arnold to unpack and take a wash, wondering wildly as he did so whether he dared ask his cousin just why his bedroom resembled an exotic love-nest when he was supposed to be a single man. In the end he decided a straight question between cousins could not be misinterpreted as criticism, and sought Thomas out in the bar.

Directed by the friendly and well-upholstered receptionist, Arnold found the bar easily enough, and there was Thomas telling the barman how to pour double brandies for two fat old men with white moustaches and prominent paunches. When he saw Arnold, however, he left the barman to finish the drinks and went behind the bar himself, grinning at his cousin.

'Your health, Arnold! What's your tipple?'

'Oh . . . beer, please.'

'Coming up! One light ale, one whisky and soda.'

Presently, with the drinks in front of them, Arnold put his question. Far from resenting it, Thomas greeted it with a knowing wink.

'Well, Arny, London's a lonely place, right?'

'I'd never thought of it, but I suppose it may be, if you say so, Thomas.'

'I do say so. But no one's got to be lonely, not in London, and especially not if they've got a nice little love-nest like mine. Get my meaning?'

'Oh . . . well, yes, of course.' Arnold glared at his beer, trying to work it all out. Did Thomas mean he had a *wife*, and it was she who had furnished the love-nest? But his cousin's next words cleared away that misconception.

'The pater keeps suggesting I cast round for a nice girl and get myself married, but I don't need marriage to hold me back. It's variety I need, and many a pretty little girl from the back row of the chorus agrees with me. Why, half the cast of the opera house have applied their street make-up in that very mirror – the one in my room with the pink satin seat in front of it – and I'm only too happy to oblige them with a night's free lodging!'

'Half the cast . . .' Arnold began, feeling out of his depth, but his cousin quickly interrupted.

'The female half, of course . . . ha ha ha! And now that you're here, old fellow, I'd be happy to introduce you to one or two little girls who'll see that you aren't lonely during your stay either. In fact we'll go along to Covent Garden tonight and ask a couple of the chorus to join us for supper after the show. Would that suit you?'

'Oh yes, very much,' Arnold assured him, relieved to know just what Thomas was talking about. If it was girls . . . well, he had done just as Arnold had hoped he would!

'Right. We'll have a snack now, and then you can go up and change for dinner. We can't eat before the show because there won't be time, but afterwards we'll take some girls out for supper and see how we all get along. You might click or you might not; can't ever tell till you try. Look, I've got to go – dinners to organize and so on – but you finish your beer and have a sandwich – I'll send it through – and then go and get into your evening clothes. We'll meet in the parlour upstairs at eight o'clock. Right?'

Arnold agreed with this exciting plan, drank up his beer, munched his way through a plateful of beef sandwiches generously daubed with mustard, and then went up the hundreds of stairs to his own room.

Once there, he took careful stock. The large bed was comfortable – he lay on it to make sure – and the view from the window fascinating. He was so high up that the people on the street below looked like ants, but even so he could see nursemaids wheeling their charges back from the park, postmen delivering parcels, girls, arms linked, giggling along the pavement. Businessmen were everywhere, dark-suited, dark-hatted, walking briskly, hailing hansoms, leaping aboard trams. Arnold thought he could have stood and watched all day, but he must remember his cousin's remarks. They were meeting at eight, so he had best get a move on.

He went into the bathroom. It was clean and well fitted, with a cork-matted floor and a deep and narrow bath of white porcelain embellished with blue roses and lilies. The lavatory matched save that its seat was dark red mahogany and its chain ended in a china knob which looked like a cluster of grapes. Arnold sat on the cork-topped bath stool and viewed his domain with appreciation. A chap wouldn't be short of much here – electric light even in this little room, and running hot water virtually in your bedroom! Arnold considered that he lived comfortably, but nevertheless he shared a bathroom with three sisters and the governess and in order to reach it he had a lengthy walk along a cold corridor. And even when you reached the bathroom you still had to wrestle with the vagaries of the geyser . . . here it seemed you merely turned a tap!

Having merely turned the tap, Arnold went back to his bedroom and sorted through his clothes. His evening things laid out ready on the bed, he tested the little settee for comfort, and then he began to comb his hair into different styles, pulling faces in the dressing-table mirror and seeing himself not only full-face, but in profile as well when he moved the side mirrors around. He was trying to get a back view, by using one of his hairbrush backs as a reflector, when he remembered the bath.

He reached it just as the water was about to cascade on to the floor, and had to run out a good six inches before he could get in without causing a flood. This had a chastening effect on his high spirits; to flood a cousin's hotel and ruin his bathroom was not a good start for a visit. But then, as he vigorously scrubbed his back with Thomas's long back-brush, it occurred to him that no one would ever know what a narrow squeak he'd had, and this cheered him up in no time so that very soon the bathroom was resounding to his rendering of 'The Flowers that Bloom in the Spring', sung with verve and many tra-las.

If the penthouse flat had impressed Arnold, he was positively bowled over by the theatre. Thomas had bought the best seats, he impressively informed his cousin, and the two young men made their way through the lush splendour of the foyer and down to the front stalls. Very soon it became apparent to Arnold that he and Thomas, both tall, both dark, both handsome, were the focus of a lot of interest. However, they had barely taken their seats before the orchestra started tuning up, and then the curtain gave a jerk, rose, and Arnold was watching his very first opera.

He was dazzled by it. He had heard Adeline sing and she had a pretty, true little voice, and naturally he had formed part of an appreciative audience when other young women entertained, but he had never heard singing like this. The opera was *La Bohème*, and from the moment Mimi appeared, even before she had opened her mouth, Arnold felt attracted to her. She was, for a start, the only slim young woman with a major part in the production, and though Thomas was constantly pointing out – and naming with the confidence of one who really knows – various members of the chorus with many a nudge and wink, Arnold could only nod, pretend to listen, and watch for Mimi to reappear.

She sang, her voice swooping and falling with a little quaver which was oddly attractive to Arnold, though several people, in nearby seats, did not seem to think it intentional at all. One stout matron said, 'She's nervous, poor thing,' and Arnold glared at her and thought her the most insensitive of women.

Another attraction, though Arnold would have denied it, was the fact that Mimi was not quite big enough for her costume, so that when she moved a little more of her than was perhaps intentional appeared in the square neckline of her large gown. Arnold goggled. Actresses were really daring! When she flung herself down on her bed in the last act, Arnold actually leaned forward, the better to see. Most of her, he was certain, was out of her dress and lying on the blue coverlet – lucky coverlet! When the curtain fell at last after repeated curtain calls, and he and Thomas were making their way out – or rather trying to do so, for there was little forward movement as yet, people merely standing in the aisles waiting patiently for their turn to go – he cut across Thomas's eulogy on one Hester, who was as generous as she was beautiful, with the brusque question, 'Do you know Mimi?'

'Mimi? I don't think I do . . . oh, you mean the lass that played the part, do you, on stage? No doubt we've met, but . . .'

'I want to meet her, Thomas. Can we go backstage and invite her to supper? You did say . . .'

'My dear old chap, she's a *principal*. Principals don't hang around backstage waiting for johnnies to invite them to supper, they have rich protectors who drink champagne out of their slippers and keep them in luxury, or so I understand. Why, she's got better things to do than wait for the likes of us! Don't worry though, Arny. You and I, we'll do all right, we'll . . .'

'What's her real name? D'you know, Thomas, she kept looking at me . . . at *me*, not at anyone else in the audience. I've got to meet her, I've got to!'

They argued all the way out of the theatre and round to the stage door. Arnold had completely forgotten Adeline in the sheer glamour of the girl who had sung her way into his heart and died on stage with such conviction that his eyes still felt hot with the tears he had blinked away. He must meet her!

'She's not for us, not a principal,' Thomas was still insisting as they tipped the stage doorkeeper and slipped inside, into the dim lighting and the smell of greasepaint, sweat and perfume that has captured many a young man's heart. 'Look old boy, I'll have a word with Hester and she can take a message, but . . .'

He tapped on a door and it was opened, after a moment, by a young woman Arnold recognized as being the member of the chorus whom Thomas had ogled most frequently. Hester.

'Tommy, love!' Hester hugged his cousin, leaving smears of powder on his evening suit, then dragged him into the room, smiling at Arnold over her shoulder as she did so. The smile was less effective than it might have been due to the fact that she had one false eyelash on and one off, but it was still a very friendly, forthcoming smile. Arnold, however, was peering past her. Sitting with her back to him, in front of a huge mirror, was the slim straight back and the glory of chestnut-coloured locks which he recognized at once as belonging to Mimi. He pushed past Hester, rather rudely ignoring her playful demand to be told his name, and stood at the shoulder of the girl before the mirror.

'You were wonderful,' he told her as she raised startled eyes to his in the glass. 'I – I'll come and see you every night, if I can get a ticket.'

The girl turned. Even near to, like this, she was pretty, with a clear colour in her cheeks and eyes of light, warm blue.

'You won't see me another night, duckie – or not as Mimi, at any rate,' she said regretfully. Her voice had a touch of the north in it; Arnold warmed to her even more. 'I was only understudying for the principal, Rachel Dubois. She'll be back tomorrow, worse luck.'

She smiled on the words. Her mouth was a tilted V when she smiled and a dimple appeared in one cheek. Arnold swallowed.

'Oh! Then if you don't usually play Mimi, who do you play?'

'She's chorus, like me,' Hester said. She had taken a seat alongside the other girl in front of the long mirror and was now peeling off her second false eyelash. 'She was dead lucky to get a chance of going on stage as Mimi, though – dead lucky. But the costume fitted more or less, and so did her face. Rodolfo wanted a chance to get her on to a bed, and the play was the nearest he's likely to get, eh, Lily?'

The girl who played Mimi giggled.

'Fred's awful,' she assured Arnold. 'Fifty-five if he's a day and forever pinching and pawing. Still, he got me a break, so I shouldn't grumble. But that's it, until someone else has to go and have a tooth pulled.'

'I thought you sang beautifully,' Arnold said stoutly. But Lily shook her head.

'No, I didn't. It was a real effort to reach the high notes. I'm out of practice, I suppose. But at least I've kept my figure; not many singers do that.'

'So've I,' Hester protested with understandable indignation. 'You have to be fairly trim in the chorus; we all are.'

31

'That's true. But then you could never play Mimi, dear. Don't think I'm being spiteful – you know it's true, don't you, my love?'

'Oh, I don't have the range,' Hester said readily. 'I thought you went after them high notes like a real trouper, Lil, honest I did.'

'You're a good girl, you are,' the girl who played Mimi said. She swivelled her chair round and held out a hand to Arnold. 'I don't know your name, but I'm Lily Rivell. How d'you do?'

'Oh . . . I'm Arnold Haslington. How d'you do, Miss Rivell?' Arnold held on to her hand, reluctant to let the moment fade. 'Will you have supper with me tonight? Supper with . . . with oysters and champagne, just to celebrate you playing Mimi? And . . . and I'm sure you'll be a principal yourself, one day,' he ended in a rush.

'Go out to supper? I don't mind if I do. Hester will come too, of course, and your friend.'

'That I will, especially if it's oysters and champagne,' Hester said. She and Lily had taken off their elaborate stage costumes and were in faded and unglamorous dressing-gowns, but now she reached for a paper screen and stood behind it to change into her street clothes. She slung her dressing-gown across the screen and Arnold, drop-mouthed at such sophistication, stared as though the very heat of his gaze could turn the paper transparent. He even forgot Lily for a moment . . . but then she joined her friend behind the screen and her dressing-gown landed on top of Hester's. Every now and then a head appeared, struggling into or out of some mysterious undergarment, and Arnold felt that he had reached heights of sinful experience never before attained by one of his name. Who at home would believe him if he said he'd stood in a chorus girls' dressing-room and watched them changing out of their costumes and into street clothes? Even Herbert Maxwell, who boasted that he had slept with his mother's parlour maid and a weaver from Leeds, would be envious and disbelieving if Arnold were to tell him about this evening!

'Here we are then,' Hester said presently. She and Lily folded the screen against the wall once more and emerged, two butterflies from one chrysalis. Hester wore a black and red walking dress with long sleeves and a flared skirt. Arnold thought she looked a little too bright for evening, but neatish, nevertheless. She had a good figure if you liked a woman to be buxom, and her skin was lovely – roses and cream; good enough to eat – but otherwise she did not hold a candle to his Lily. Lily herself wore a light green ruffled skirt with a little jacket over it which buttoned tightly to her form. The lapels were large and the collar stood up so that her neck reared out of it like the flower she was named for. She looked like an angel, Arnold told himself.

'Well, girls, shall we go back to my place?' Thomas said hopefully. But Hester, though she laughed and took his hand, still shook her head. 'Not for champers, me lad. Let's go to Smithsons!'

Arnold saw Thomas give a little jump, like one who has felt a needle

32

enter his unsuspecting thigh, but he himself had no qualms. So Smithsons was expensive, was it? Well, he was quite willing to lavish any amount of money on this delightful young lady who was gliding towards the door and smiling at him so enchantingly over her shoulder. And if he had to treat Hester and Thomas as well, for that matter, what did he care? To please Miss Rivell would be worth every single penny!

'Well, my dear fellow, how did your first day go?'

The enchanted evening was over and so, now, was the day which had followed it, in the course of which Arnold had visited a great many shops and warehouses and showed his samples and patterns to a great many people. He had been, by and large, successful, although his customers seemed to come mostly from the smaller shops in the less salubrious parts of the city. But as his father was fond of saying, it was better to sell a hundred saucers for a penny apiece than two teacups for fourpence.

The cousins had met in the foyer of the hotel, and now Arnold raised a hand in salute before heading for the stairs.

'It went well, thanks, Thomas. It's early to say yet, of course, but I look like taking a good few orders home with me, for the new coloured ware which is a cut above the mass-produced stuff we sell in the main. I'm very pleased. And you?'

Thomas accompanied him up the stairs.

'Fine, thanks. Had a big party in for luncheon; said they were very satisfied so they've booked in for dinner tonight. I've a good staff on, but nevertheless I'll eat in tonight, keep an eye on things. You'll join me, of course?'

'Oh . . . I thought we might go to the opera again,' Arnold said hopefully. 'It was capital last night.'

Thomas, however, was shaking his head.

'Not tonight, Arny; I must see to my customers. But go alone by all means, if you want to. I'll find something to amuse me here, never doubt it.'

'Oh no, I wouldn't dream . . . what shall we do then?'

'We'll eat here, and then we'll go for a stroll up west. We might take a look at a theatre – just the last act you know. This time you might fall for someone a bit more accommodating.'

Lily had not endeared herself to Thomas by her steadfast refusal to return to his rooms above the hotel for a nightcap, but Arnold thought this enchantingly pure of her. What was more, she had promised him, if he returned to the opera house tonight, that she would show him round the stage and introduce him to anyone who was still about. To Arnold, abruptly stage-struck, this seemed the nicest way possible to spend an evening. His more sophisticated cousin, who could think of at least a hundred better things to do, could be seen almost physically curbing his tongue, and Arnold had been ashamed of his own persistence. So now he

33

decided, if they went to a theatre, that he would pretend enjoyment. After all, he could go to the opera again the following night.

But he had reckoned without Hester's attractions.

'And then, when we've watched the play and had a word with the girls backstage, we'll make our way to Covent Garden,' his cousin said, grinning at him. 'We can stand the girls supper again – but at my place this time, and no champagne or oysters, if you please!'

'You are the best of friends, Thomas,' Arnold exclaimed.

'Well, I want you to enjoy your stay. We'll change into evening clothes right away and then we won't have to come up here again. We insist on dinner jackets at the hotel, of course.'

The two young men went to their own rooms, having agreed to meet in the dining room at eight thirty. Arnold was there on time and was much impressed by the sombre splendour of his surroundings, by the starched white tablecloths and by the waiters who seemed to skim the carpet on noiseless feet, coming and going at great speed but with no sound whatsoever.

It was a varied and exciting menu, as well. When Arnold first sat down Thomas was busy seating his party and directing the staff, but presently he dashed over to his cousin to tell him that he might order anything he liked on the menu.

Arnold, after due consideration, was about to order fresh green pea soup followed by roast chicken when Thomas appeared like a genie at his elbow, hissed, 'Not the chicken,' and disappeared again.

Arnold revised his choice. He would have a prime sirloin steak with mushrooms and asparagus spears. He had barely raised his hand to beckon a waiter over, however, before Thomas was there once more.

'Not the pea soup, old fellow,' he implored in a breathy whisper. 'Those old buggers have ordered the soup to a man; I'm afraid you'll have to make do with whitebait, or melon in port wine.'

'I don't mind what I have. It all looks absolutely delicious,' Arnold said, throwing in the sponge. 'Just you order for both of us, old fellow, and I for one will be completely satisfied.'

He was, too. The meal was delicious and well cooked, the helpings generous. By the time they had finished off with coffee and cheese he felt slow and sated, and would have agreed quite happily to call the entertainment off and go straight to bed.

But it was not to be. Thomas jumped to his feet, straightening his tie, and they set off for the outside world at a smart pace.

'We'll walk to Charing Cross Road; it'll do us good,' he announced. 'We've got to shake this meal down so we've got room for supper with the girls . . . and take a tip from me, old chap; don't call yours "Miss Rivell"! That's drawing-room talk. She's just your little darling, your own little Lily . . . got it?'

'Yes, but . . . what difference does it make?'

'It makes the difference between saying goodnight to her in the foyer and saying it in the penthouse,' Thomas assured him. 'Just wait and see. She'll unbend a bit tonight.'

Arnold, meekly following his brisk pace along the busy pavements, could only hope that his experienced cousin was right.

The two young men, by dint of fast walking, managed to get into the comedy of Thomas's choice just after the first act had finished. They had good seats, the young ladies on stage were pretty, polished and saucy, the gentlemen amusing, but Arnold's attention could not remain wholly on the action. He glanced continually at his pocket watch, laughed and clapped in the appropriate places, but never really allowed the play to capture him. Indeed, as soon as the curtain fell on the last act Arnold was on his feet and making his way to the exit.

'What a fine evening,' he said, as they emerged into the dusky night. 'This breeze is really balmy . . . shall we get a cab? It's quite a walk from here.'

Although Thomas thought a cab was unnecessary and said the girls would wait, their reception, when they arrived, was everything either young man could desire. Hester was full of enthusiasm for an evening at the hotel and had clearly managed to persuade Lily that it would be perfectly respectable.

'No monkey business, my love,' she assured the other girl. 'I've been many a time with Tommy, haven't I old son? We have a real good meal in the dining-room, a few drinks in the bar, and then we go up to the penthouse for coffee before we leave for home. Right Tommy?'

'Right, Hes,' Thomas said solemnly. And if there was a twinkle in his eye and a smile lurking about his mouth, that was nothing to do with Arnold or Lily, sitting crushed together in the cab with Arnold's hand resting, ever so lightly, on Lily's knee.

'Well, I'll come for the meal and the drink in the bar, though I only take soft drinks,' Lily said, making big eyes at Arnold. 'Then will you see me home, Arny?'

'Of course,' Arnold said resolutely. Perhaps she would repent of her hastiness when he showed her how a true gentleman behaved. He moved his hand off her knee. 'I'll take you all the way to your lodgings, and then I'll take myself back home. You shan't have anything to worry about, I promise you.'

Under these circumstances Lily agreed to accompany them, and nothing could have been more charming than her enjoyment of the supper, nor her hesitant agreement to go up to the penthouse flat for a hot drink before being taken home.

Once there she was pressed to drink a glass of red wine, and then she sat very close to Arnold on the opulent red plush sofa whilst Hester, far more daring, sat on Thomas's knee and made no demur when Thomas turned the main lights out, leaving only one very subdued wall-light to illumine the room.

Arnold held Lily's hand, kissed her soft cheek, and then slid his arm round her small waist. Presently, Thomas and Hester lurched off the chair they had been occupying and made their way out of the room. Arnold feared they had gone to Thomas's boudoir and waited for Lily to ask difficult questions, but she did no such thing. Instead, she curled up close to him, very innocent and confiding, and Arnold actually felt her small fingers brush against him in a place where no one had ever touched him before.

He stiffened. Involuntarily. She had meant nothing by it, she was an innocent child . . . she pressed herself against him, warm and confiding, and put her face up to his. Presently, she took the lobe of his ear in her warm mouth, between her little white teeth, and first nipped and then licked it.

Something exploded in Arnold's brain. His hands, of their own accord, undid things. He waited for Lily to scream, and she did, but it was such a tiny, breathless, excited scream that it did not seem worth stopping what he was doing if she only minded that much. All the while he was fumbling with buttons and fastenings, Lily was doing very nice things. She pushed her soft breasts against him, she tugged at the front of her gown so that the aforementioned breasts spilled out of it, she hooked something – he presumed it was a leg – over him, and hitched up her skirt and wriggled and tugged at his trousers.

And in the middle of all this disgraceful behaviour she said, 'Oh, Arny, let's go to your room!' and Arnold astonished himself by not even answering but simply lifting her up and carrying her through into the bedroom.

There, for some reason, things were simpler. Lily undressed with neatness and speed and Arnold did the same. Then they fell upon the bed and upon each other, and Arnold discovered what it was he had been missing and how to do it and why one did it, and he enjoyed all these revelations very much and thought what a jolly girl Lily was, and even whilst vigorously clutching her it crossed his mind how nice it would be to teach Adeline all the wonders of making love when they got married.

When at last they lay quiet, Lily fell asleep. Arnold propped himself up on one elbow and considered her. She looked weary, a little smug, not as young as she had done, but he supposed it was the weariness which follows extreme exertion and thought no more of it. He realized, of course, that she was not quite as innocent as he had thought her, but it did not cross his mind that she might have seduced him. No, he was the bold seducer, although he had enjoyed it far too much to feel ashamed.

Presently, because she was asleep, Arnold also lay down and pulled the covers up over his shoulders. When she awoke, even if it was in the early hours, he would be true to his word and take her home by cab, but until then they might as well both get some rest.

# CHAPTER THREE

Adeline, lonely for Arnold despite her cousin's presence, wondered wistfully a dozen times a day how he was getting on, but she was well reared and far too kind to let her feelings show in her dealings with John Sawyer. Besides, she liked him. He was older than either her or Arnold, a man of twenty-seven, a doctor who had practised in a Manchester hospital and was about to take his skills to China, where he intended to work as a medical missionary. He was intelligent and strong-minded, with a marked streak of humour which saved him from ever appearing dull, and Adeline soon thought him the kindest of men. He was a notable raconteur, too, and kept her amused by the hour together with tales of his experiences at medical school and the hospital.

Her father, she knew, had wanted to like John but had feared to find him a prig and a bore. Instead, he quickly decided that John was the best of good fellows. He was a first-rate horseman and an excellent shot, and his deep interest in the running and upkeep of an estate was genuine, though he made it clear that he had no personal interest in the Manor.

'I may never be fortunate enough to own a place like this,' he said as the three of them went round the home farm. 'But even as a medical missionary I dare say I'll need to rear beasts for my own use and plant such acres as I acquire. I've always enjoyed helping my father to run our small estate.'

He might not have lived on a place like the Manor but he was quick to learn, picking up the essentials of farming as fast as he was picking up Cantonese, which he would need in his far-off mission. After a few days, seeing that Adeline was often at a loss for something to do, he offered to teach her Chinese – so that he himself would grasp it better, he said. Amused, Adeline sat with him in the schoolroom for a couple of hours each day, whenever it was too wet to go out, and together they worked on his language primers.

Despite the fact that he was going to be a missionary he was happy to attend the dances and parties to which he was invited, and because of his looks and charm such invitations soon multiplied. Adeline saw a good many young ladies eyeing her cousin with undisguised interest, and was always proud to be with him. He was tall, taller than Arnold, with an athlete's fine figure. His light brown hair was rain straight and fell softly across his eyes – for he did not favour pomade – and his eyes were grey and steady and always, Adeline thought, interested in what they lighted on. John had the gift of genuinely listening, really concentrating when one spoke, making the speaker feel that what he or she said was truly important.

He was a good teacher, too. Adeline spoke French adequately but had never become fluent despite her many Mademoiselles. After only ten days, she had a working grasp of Cantonese, a much more difficult tongue. John said she had a natural talent, but Adeline knew better. He was fascinated by his subject and managed to pass the fascination on, so that she wanted to learn herself.

But of course he was not Arnold, not the beloved. He and Adeline both liked walking and they covered a great deal of ground, but whenever she fell silent it was because she and Arnold had walked here, weeks before, and she could not help wondering what he was doing now. He had written once, a loving letter full of information, and she had replied to it immediately, but since then she had heard nothing. Of course he was busy . . . but he could, surely, have dropped her a line?

One fine morning about a fortnight after John's arrival the two of them set out to walk to a village ten miles away where John had heard a retired missionary who had once been active in southern China now lived. A letter had elicited a courteous invitation to visit, so John and Adeline had decided they would enliven the journey by having luncheon at an inn on the way, visit the old gentleman for tea as he had suggested, and then walk home again if they felt like it or catch the 'bus if not.

As usual, Adeline was comfortable in John's company. Their way led them first along the river bank, and Adeline enjoyed pointing out to her companion the meadows which belonged to the Warburtons, the Haslingtons and other neighbours.

'Do you fish, Adeline?' John asked presently, as they skirted a deep pool overhung by beeches, their leaves already hanging a little limp from high summer. 'I've done a bit, but it isn't my favourite sport by any means. Too much sitting still and waiting.'

'Like cricket,' Adeline said, laughing. 'No, I don't fish, though at one time I used to watch the anglers who came down to the river. I say, John, will you fish when you go to China?'

John glanced sideways at her, then smiled. Adeline smiled too, content that he should see through her transparent attempt to change the subject to one she found fascinating.

'Ah, China. Did you not notice, little cousin, that I had a letter this morning? I'm sure I must have frowned over it for quite ten minutes though neither you nor your father mentioned it.'

'Yes, I noticed, of course. I said nothing because I thought it was none of my business. You have a life of which I know nothing. I only know you here, looking forward to China.'

'That's true, I suppose. Well, the letter was from the missionary service I've applied to join. They will be happy to have me as one of their number, but the particular job I applied for must go to a married man. They have other jobs, of course, but none so suited to my particular talents, if I can call them that.'

'Oh, John, how unfortunate! But does that mean you'll be in England for a bit longer? If so, I'm sure we'd love to see more of you . . . it's been really fine having you here. I've never seen Father more energetic and interested. You're good for him, you know.'

'I don't think I'll stay in England long, anyway,' John said rather apologetically. 'It isn't that I'm not happy here – you and your father have made me very welcome – but I think I ought to take some post in China just so that I'm on the spot and learning the language and so on. Unless, of course, I marry myself a wife and take the better job.'

They were strolling rather than walking now, absorbed in their conversation. The path was narrow, and Adeline tucked her arm in John's so that they might continue to walk side by side, looking up into his face as she did so.

'*Is* there a young lady, John? You've talked of the nurses at your hospital, and there must have been girls in your home village . . . even other medical students perhaps, if they have girl medical students? Surely one of them . . .'

'There is a young lady, but I hadn't intended to marry yet. I meant to go to China and make a suitable home for my wife, and then come home in a year, say, and take her back with me.' John looked down at his cousin, his eyes enquiring. 'Adeline, my dear, you have shown the liveliest interest in China, but how would you feel about actually going out to that country and living there?'

'If I were your young lady, you mean?' Adeline considered, her eyes on her sandals as they trod confidently along the towpath. 'Why, I think I'd love it! Adventure, excitement, strange places and even stranger people . . . and then one day your wife will come back to England and be mistress of her own home.' She laughed, looking up at her cousin. 'What young lady could resist all that, John? You must pop the question as soon as you leave here!'

'That sounds promising. But suppose my young lady was very fond of her parents, and her home. What then?'

'You mean she's *rooted*, like me,' Adeline said, frowning. 'Well, if she truly loves you she'll go like a shot, and if she doesn't truly love you she'll say no. And as I said, she'd be coming back one day to England, wouldn't she?'

'Oh, yes, one day. But is that good enough, do you think?'

Adeline thought of Arnold. If he told her that he was going to work in

London, and still wanted to marry her, what would she say? Yes, yes, a thousand times yes! She looked up at John once more.

'Yes, I'm sure it's good enough. If one's a Christian, it has to be people who matter, and not places. A man's work may take him to good or bad places, and a woman follows her husband, surely?'

'You're right. But as well as practising medicine I'm going to do the Lord's work, and one does not expect such work to be easy or pleasant. My wife, if she agreed to marry me, would have to understand that.'

'I'm sure she would. And you'd have a family, wouldn't you? Well, your children would come home to be educated, I suppose? And you and your wife would come back to see them every couple of years, so neither of you would be stuck in China for ever.'

'That doesn't follow, actually; there are very good schools in China. Do you think it would hurt my children if their mother and myself dealt with their British education and allowed a local school to do the rest? After all, they'll probably speak better Chinese than either I or my wife will ever manage.'

This was fascinating, and made Adeline feel very grown-up and sensible. John was twenty-seven years old and he was not too proud to ask her advice! She wished she could know his wife, but that would be impossible, situated as they were. She frowned, bending her mind to how a woman would feel, living in a foreign land and having her children educated by foreigners. And of course to have the children speak the local dialect better than one did oneself . . . that would be a facer. She began to see herself in such a situation, not able to go home to England, perhaps for years. But she was young and foolish. John's fancy had probably alighted on someone nearer his own age, a sensible, intelligent woman who would live her life for the good of her husband and family and put her own desires far behind theirs.

'So what you're saying, John, is that your wife may find herself in China for years at a time, rather than months? Well, so long as she has you, and a full life, won't that suffice?'

'Would that be true for you, Adeline? Is that what you most want, the man of your choice and a full life? Come to that, what is your idea of a full life?'

Once more, Adeline hesitated. To tell John, whom she admired very much, that her idea of a full life was to stay right where she was and marry the boy next door sounded pathetic, feeble. Besides, if Arnold did decide to go off somewhere she would gladly go with him, relish the adventure, the change of scene. Only she would always know she could go back home whenever she wanted.

She said as much, though without mentioning Arnold.

'I suppose I've always wanted to play some sort of role in life,' she concluded. 'Have you ever seen my sketchbook, John? I'm thought to be quite good. My watercolours are admired and I've done some portraits, in oils, which are actually hung on people's walls! I'm not saying that I want to paint a masterpiece or die in an attic, but I'd like to take my painting further – accept commissions, perhaps. Become known for my landscapes around here.'

'That's very natural. You must show me your sketchbook when we get home. I've often wished I could paint, but I'm afraid I'm quite useless. Tell me, have you ever painted the Manor?'

Adeline laughed. 'A thousand times! I've done sketches, watercolours, even a few small oils, showing it at various times of year. It's a beautiful house. I'll show you some sketches later, and if you like one or two you can take them away with you. Then, even in China, you won't be able to forget us completely!'

'As if I could forget you . . .' John was beginning, when a great grey heron, which must have been fishing on the far side of a reedbed, took to the air and flapped slowly away above their heads. The sight of the bird made John think of the white cranes of China, and then he told Adeline about the panda bears which lived in the north and were so rare that they were almost never seen by Europeans. They struck away from the river at that point and walked by meadows and woods and along little, deep-sunk lanes. In this way the time passed pleasantly until they stopped for luncheon, and when they had eaten a simple repast and set off once more John started talking about the tropical diseases he was studying, and about his father's practice in their quiet country village, which his father hoped one of his sons would some day take over from him, for out of the three Sawyer boys one – John himself – was already practising medicine, one, Paul, was in his third year at medical school and the last, Ned, would begin his studies the following month.

They reached the missionary's home and were welcomed by the old man and his younger wife. She was a charming, intelligent woman who pressed a magnificent tea upon them and showed them photographs of their children, one of whom was still in China running a mission in the north, and the country that they had, for twenty years, called home.

'It's a good life,' she told Adeline now, with a reminiscent smile curling her lips. 'You'll enjoy every minute of it, my dear, once you get over being homesick. Oh, dear, at first I thought I'd die with longing for my own land and people . . . but gradually, so gradually, I began to make a better life for myself out there. And when we came home for good, so contrary is human nature, I wept for a week!'

Adeline did not like to tell the friendly Mrs Capper that she was not going out to China, but looked at all the photographs, admired the souvenirs, and ate a good tea. On the way home, however, she confided in John that she had felt the most awful cheat.

'Letting her tell me all about China under the misapprehension that I was going out myself,' she said remorsefully. 'But I couldn't disillusion her; it would have been very unkind. And weren't they the nicest people

41

you could wish to meet? Not a bit smug or holier-than-thou. I really took to them.'

'I hope I'm neither smug nor holier-than-thou myself,' John said, looking amused. 'A calling like mine doesn't necessarily mean that the person involved is a prig and a bore, you know.'

'I know now I've met you, but before, I based my opinion on curates and a few vicars, and . . . well, I was wrong,' Adeline admitted handsomely. 'You are a good man, John, but you don't keep trying to prove you're good.'

John put back his head and roared, causing several heifers to come at a gallop towards them, tails raised high, curiosity in every line of their young bodies.

'Oh, Adeline, you'll be the death of me,' he gasped when he'd stopped laughing. 'Let's step out now. Your father said he'd ordered a saddle of mutton for dinner and I'm hungry despite that tea!'

At home again, changing for dinner, Adeline got her small photograph of Arnold out of its hiding place and stood it on her dressing table.

'John is a worthy man, my dear,' she told the photograph. 'Far worthier than you or me – but no one, surely, falls in love with a man for his worth!' This made it sound as though Arnold himself were not worthy, so she added hastily, 'In your way, though, you have all that John has – integrity, honesty, loyalty – only you have the extra spice of being the man I love.' She kissed the photograph and slid it back amongst her underwear. Poor Arnold. If he was here to speak for himself she was sure he would make a better job of it. She had made him sound as though his only merit was that she loved him!

Her evening dress was primrose organza; she wore a string of pearls in the low neckline and as she fastened them round her throat it occurred to her that for all the time she had known Arnold, all the talking they had done, she really did not know him at all. She said he had honesty and integrity, but on what did she base the assumption? He was not being honest in hiding their love from everyone, for example. She had said he was loyal, but he had been away now for over three weeks and had only written to her once. As for integrity – the word meant perfect, unbroken, entire; she had looked it up in the dictionary. Arnold was not perfect.

The pearls slipped out of her fingers and disappeared down her cleavage. Adeline fished them out and scolded herself. Words were only words, after all. She loved Arnold and accepted him for what he was. She fastened the pearls again, then heard the gong and hurried from the room.

All this introspection meant only one thing: because of knowing John she had been forced to take a long, hard look at Arnold. But even after that long, hard look, her determination was unshaken. She loved Arnold and would marry him, whatever his faults.

She went in to dinner on the thought.

\* \* \*

42

Later that night, as he made ready for bed, John Sawyer wondered about his cousin. Had she understood what he meant when he said that there was a young lady? On reflection, he doubted it. She was an innocent, was his Adeline – he was amused to realize that even in his mind she belonged to him – and without guile. She liked him, enjoyed his company, but had never for one moment considered marrying him. He was ten years her senior and bound for an unglamorous job on the other side of the world where he could offer her little but hard work, so why should marriage enter her head? But her father had assured John that his daughter had no tendre for another, only a half-formed calf-love for a young man who had gone off to London, so the coast was clear. John had come to the Manor without the slightest expectation of finding Adeline anything but a pleasant companion, and had tumbled head over heels in love with her from the first moment they had met. He had told her the truth when he said that he had meant to go out to China, make a home there, and then return to England for his bride. He had not added that it was she to whom he referred. How could he, when she was so patently unready, a child not yet eighteen, for an ordinary straightforward marriage to an Englishman who intended to stay in Britain, far less a man who meant to leave the country within weeks?

The letter had come as a shock; he could see the mission's point, of course, although they had chosen to wrap it up and had not come straight out with it. A married man brought a free pair of hands to do the work of the Lord, no matter how little his wife might relish the idea. Probably a medical missionary needed a wife more than most, for an able assistant was a necessity in a hospital situation.

There were other problems with an unmarried man, as well. He would have to examine Chinese women without the presence of a nurse, until he could train one. And he might marry a Chinese which, no matter how the missions might deny it, meant trouble from all sorts of angles. A wife who was placed in a position of authority over her fellow countrymen was likely to find the situation difficult. A man could marry himself such a one and then discover that her whole outlook was fundamentally different from his own.

The maddening thing was that he had no time to wait around and court the girl and try to get her to see that he was right for her. And though he had only known Adeline for three weeks, he was sure he would never love another the way he loved her. It was not her looks, either, pretty though she was. It was her keen mind, her good sense, her love of the outdoors and perhaps most of all her lively sense of humour, which complemented his own. John had no use for a grim, joyless approach to God. To him, God was the fount of all goodness and happiness, so it followed that God wanted His creations to enjoy His world, to go about their business with a bright face and a ready laugh. In his training John had been fortunate in having a tutor who had spent many years in China and had impressed upon his students that the Chinese were a poor, hard-pressed people who needed hope and joy more than most. Our way is the right way, the way they should tread, he told them. But because of their natures you must show it as it is – a happy path, a joyous journey. Their present religion, Buddhism, gives hope for the life to come, but the people want hope *now*, happiness within their grasp, not something remote and somehow sterile, which can only be gained through death. So John had studied the Buddhist religion in his spare time and had seen exactly what his tutor meant. He intended to bring joy to his congregation in China.

And for this task, he could think of no better helpmate that Adeline. Joy came naturally to her, shone out of her eyes, gleamed in her smile. She sympathized with one, her expression clouded with your sadness, cleared with your pleasure. She was sunshine on a dull day, a ray of light in the darkness.

Her father, moreover, was extremely keen to see them marry. Obviously, he wanted Adeline to be provided for after his death, and he wanted Adeline's children to inherit the Manor when he and she were both gone; that was only natural. But it was more than that. He knew John would be taking his daughter far away for a number of years, but even that did not deter him. He thought the marriage was right, would be happy, and his child's happiness meant everything to him.

Night-shirted and ready for bed, John got between the covers and lay in the dark, listening to the night-sounds around him. The breeze stirred the leaves of the oak tree near his window, ruffled the foliage and fruit on the apple trees in the orchard. A sleepy owl gave a half-shriek and birds stirred in the creeper, adding to the rustle of the wind. Somewhere a dog-fox barked at the stars, the sound barely reaching John's ears. She would lose all this for a time, but what riches John could offer her! The beauty and strangeness of China, a new life, a new people. She was not particularly devout, but she attended church regularly, visited her father's tenants when they were sick and taught Sunday-school. She would be a wonderful missionary's wife!

I'll put it to the test; I'll ask her tomorrow, John told himself just before he fell asleep.

Arnold had had a good day. He had visited a very large store indeed and had come away with an impressively large order. It must be something to do with the time I arrived, he thought as he walked along the street, lopsidedly because he was carrying his samples case and it was a fair weight. Or perhaps it was because I saw someone really important and not just some tinpot little clerk who enjoyed telling me that it was all 'quaite naice' but not the sort of thing they were looking for today, thank you.

Whatever the reason, though, the outcome was plain. He had no need to remain in the capital another day. He had done enough business, now, to justify producing the new biscuitware in large quantities. And when other firms in the rest of the country are told that it's being sold in London, I dare say they'll be keen to buy as well, Arnold thought, hailing a cab. He climbed aboard, lugging his heavy case, whilst the cabby admonished his horse and assured Arnold that he knew the Hotel Rycliffe very well indeed.

But now it was on the cards that he was finished here, there was another problem. Arnold sat in the cab, head in hands, and worried about it.

Lily. Such a little charmer! But she had done a very foolish thing. She had gone and got herself chucked out of the opera company, and now she was suggesting that Arnold might take her home with him, find her a little job in the factory or one of his father's other businesses, anything just so long as he didn't abandon her in London.

To be fair, she had not got herself chucked out on purpose, and it was partly his fault that she had been so dismissed. The thing was, after their night of love it had seemed downright foolish, as well as wasteful, for Lily to continue paying out for lodgings when she could live with him, in the penthouse flat, rent-free. So she had cancelled her room and moved in with him.

Arnold had enjoyed it at first. Make-up all over his dressing table, stockings hanging to dry over the bath, and a pretty woman to kiss him goodbye – amongst other things – when he went off to work each morning. The trouble was it turned out, when it was too late to do anything about it, that young ladies who worked for the opera company were supposed to be chaste. The company, it appeared, found their lodgings for them and expected them to remain where they were put.

So someone in the lodgings had squealed – probably the landlady, foiled of her rent, Arnold thought bitterly – and one of the chaperons had followed Lily back to the hotel after a performance and had, or so she claimed, hung about all night waiting to see Lily leave her lover.

Lily, all unsuspecting, had gone off to work at her usual time but had come home very much earlier, and in floods of tears.

'They've given me the sack,' she had wailed, red-eyed and flushed. 'Oh, what'll I do? I don't have any money, and no one else will take me on now I've been sacked . . . I'm ruined.'

He had felt sorry for her, it's true, had cuddled her and promised to see her all right. It was only when she began to make sprightly plans to accompany him home that he realized that what he meant by 'all right' and what Lily meant were poles apart. She thought he would set her up as his mistress in some nice little flat – in Langforth, mark you, that narrow-minded, censorious, nosy town – and come and see her two or three times a week whilst paying her expenses and helping her to find a genteel little part-time job. For his part, Arnold's meaning had been somewhat vague. Money, certainly, to tide her over. A visit, even, a couple of times a year. The odd new dress or jacket, possibly even a hamper from time to time. But not . . . not *mistresshood*, if there was such a word. Not in Langforth!

And then, of all things, she had told him she might be expecting a baby. Not, thank God, that she knew she was, but that she easily might be. 'I should've taken precautions,' she had moaned, to Arnold's mystification. 'But I never thought . . . it was all so sudden, and you never said you weren't serious.'

Arnold could have replied that he had never said he was, either, but it was the sort of remark that comes to one long after the event. Instead, he had turned a bit sulky and defensive, and said he was very sorry but . . .

'It's all right; I can always gas meself,' Lily said. Then she had rumpled his hair and kissed the side of his face and told him they'd find a way round it, they would indeed.

So now, sitting, head in hands, in the cab, Arnold bent all his powers of concentration on the problem of what to do with Lily. Should he borrow a large sum from his father, set her up somewhere far away from Langforth and hope she would make out all right? Or dared he do as she suggested? Take me back home with you, like a proper guest in your old man's house, she had said, and introduce me to one or two business people, and the chances are I'll be in a job before the week's out.

Arnold did not like it. Disgraceful though it might seem, he had no desire whatsoever to see Lily become someone else's mistress, and it did rather look as though that was what she wanted. When he had reminded her of her career she said quite perfunctorily that they might as well both forget it. 'I'm not good enough,' she explained. 'Not to get principal parts. And they won't take me on in the chorus, not once they hear why I was kicked out of the last lot.'

'Why should they hear?' Arnold had asked. 'Who's going to tell them?'

Lily had laughed. 'Why, it's like one huge family,' she declared. 'They gossip and tell tales when they meet like a load of old women; management's as bad as the company itself. It'll be all over the country that they picked a bad 'un in me.'

Arnold groaned at the recollection, yet she was a good-natured girl and, in his way, he was fond of her. He knew she would never try to force his hand; if he said he'd done all he could and she must go her way whilst he went his she would shrug, wipe her eyes and go. There was a sort of gallantry in her loneliness, too, which appealed to him. She had never made friends, real friends, with her fellow chorus girls, but that was because she was a good bit older than them. Arnold had been shattered to discover that she was twenty-eight, eight years his senior, but she had not hidden the fact as many a girl would have done; she told him straight.

'That's another reason why I won't make it on the stage,' she had said. 'I started late. Most of 'em's started before they're twenty. I was twenty-seven before I even tried out my voice in public.'

She had been a milliner's assistant, doing dressmaking on the side, and stage-struck as can be. Then someone had heard her singing and had advised her to audition for a part in the company. She had done so, they had taken her on, and a mere eighteen months later here she was, out of work.

Now it occurred to Arnold that he might very well set Lily up in Langforth in a small hat shop. Why not? Provided he was not directly implicated no one need know they were anything but acquaintances. He would go home and buy a place for her, a little shop with a flat over. Cheered by this thought, he decided to put it to Thomas that evening and see what his cousin thought of the scheme. Thomas had strongly advised him to 'ditch' Lily, when he had first heard, but then Thomas was not a very honourable young man, a fact which had only gradually penetrated Arnold's skull. When it did he was disappointed but not heartbroken. After all, Thomas was a black sheep; one does not simply get given such a title, one earns it, and Thomas was clearly in some respects every bit as black as he was painted.

The cab stopped with a jerk and Arnold peered through the window, saw the hotel frontage, and began to lug his sample case out on to the pavement. Then he paid the cabby, tipped him, and whistled for the commissionaire. He sang a little tune beneath his breath as he climbed the stairs behind the pageboy who was heaving the case, gritting his teeth, from step to step. Things were not so bad after all! He would have a word with Thomas, another with Lily, and if they were all agreed he would write a note to his parents with some jolly convincing reason why he was bringing home with him for a few days a young woman who was down on her luck . . . but nothing whatsoever to do with him!

# CHAPTER FOUR

'My dear, if you don't feel you love him of course you must refuse. I understand that. After all, though I found him extremely likeable I'm not a young woman with a young woman's views. But . . . are you sure you're not making a mistake? Because I've watched you both, and I thought you really liked him very much – as indeed he likes you. He's one in a hundred, Adeline.'

'Yes . . . and I do like him, very much, Papa. But it's all too soon, too sudden . . . and I'm sure I could never be the sort of wife he wants. I'm not ready; I want to stay here with you, not go away for thousands of miles.'

Adeline shifted uncomfortably against the carved wooden back of her father's visitor's chair. They were in his study, whither she had been summoned to tell him why she had refused John's offer of marriage. Adeline, who associated visits to the study with requests to amend her behaviour or enquiries as to why she had not practised the piano for five evenings, found herself feeling uncomfortable almost before her father had opened his mouth. Poor Papa – it was clear he was grievously disappointed in her, but far too kind to admit it.

'Well, dear, it's flattering to hear you say so, but you must leave me some day, you know, if you're to get married, and I hope you may. As to the time – you said it was too soon – I'm sure John would happily wait a few weeks if, by so doing, your answer could be different.'

'No, Papa, I've said I won't marry him and I mean it. I do like him . . . oh, how muddling this is . . . but I won't marry him. I'm sorry if you don't understand; I can't put it any more clearly. Perhaps I don't quite understand it myself.'

Her father was immediately remorseful; he came round from behind the desk and gave her a hug.

'Yes, of course, you're perfectly right. If you don't have that certain feeling for him then it would be a great mistake to marry him, a very great mistake. I won't tease you any more, Addy my dear. It's just that I've grown very fond of John and felt I could give my greatest treasure into his care without a qualm. I could not say as much for many young men.'

'Papa!' Adeline squiggled in his arms and returned his hug. 'You are so good to me! I wish I could oblige you in this, indeed I do!'

'Nonsense, nonsense,' Sidney Warburton protested, going pink right up to the balding crown of his head. 'Well, so I shan't be losing you after all, eh? When does John leave us?'

'Not for several days . . . and we shall remain friends, so you won't find yourself sharing a table at mealtimes with two people who can't meet each other's eyes.'

'I'm glad to hear it. What are your plans for today, my dear?'

'Well, I'm spending the morning with Bella, because I've not seen her for weeks, except fleetingly, and John has some letters to write. And after luncheon John and I are taking the horses out on the moors, to shake the fidgets out of their legs. Why? Do you want to come with us?'

'I'm not only too busy, minx, I am well aware that you and John are both neck or nothing riders compared to me. No, I'll exercise my old Sultan with a quiet trot down to the village and back. Off with you now, and let me get on with my monthly figures.'

Adeline left the room and hurried to the cloakroom to fetch her jacket. She opened the side door, glanced up at the grey clouds and at the way the poplar tree on the bank bent in the wind and returned for an umbrella.

Better safe than sorry, she told herself, skipping out of the door and hurrying through the orchard, across the meadow and on to the towpath. For she did have quite a lot to tell Bella, though she would not be so mean as to reveal that John had proposed and she had refused. She could tell her friend, however, that she and John had got on so famously that they were to exchange letters once he left England. That alone would be an interesting topic, for Bella had admired John from afar but had rarely spoken to him, being still shy with any young man over twenty-one.

Reaching the stile, Adeline climbed it and dropped down the other side, thinking how astonished she had been when John proposed, though rather touched, as well. But despite her secret feeling that John had paid her a great compliment, she had not hesitated to refuse very firmly. Liking, even great liking, was not love, and only Arnold wore, for her, that halo of specialness which was first-love. She had been tempted to tell John about Arnold, if only because he had suggested that she might reconsider his proposal at a later date, when he returned from China . . . say in a year? he had asked hopefully. He had also suggested that he might delay his departure for a while, if, by so doing, he could take her out with him. If she had told him about Arnold then he would obviously have ceased to hope, but she knew that her feeling for Arnold was not her secret alone. When he returned from London she would tell him that they must either agree to part or admit their love, but until then she would say nothing, not even to John, for she knew that John would be the first to tell her she must never betray a confidence.

When Arnold comes back . . . it had become a litany, a good-luck charm. Everything would be all right when Arnold came back; her father would agree to their marriage, Bella would suddenly see how glamorous her brother really was and would envy Adeline's choice, and of course Arnold himself would sweep away all doubts, all fears.

If only he had written! Or if he had telephoned, wired, got in touch somehow! But he had not, so it was no use repining. And when he came back she would hear his explanation and understand his apparent neglect completely.

The sight of Bella, skipping down the path towards her, put an end to such thoughts. Adeline waved and began to hurry. Bella waved back, called something inaudible, and then put all her energy into reaching her friend, running seriously, her high-piled hair bouncing on her head. When they were only a couple of yards apart she began to speak.

'Oh, Addy, you'll never guess, the most *extraordinary* thing! Arnold's coming home this very evening, and he's bringing a young lady with him! It's ever such a romantic story . . . she's an opera singer, awfully good he says, but she lost her job when a cruel woman in the opera company made up lies about her and there she was, this young lady, with no job, no roof over her head, nothing. So of course Arnold wouldn't stand for that, and he got her a room in the hotel our cousin Thomas keeps and he's bringing her back here. He says she's very ladylike and quite charming, but she has to earn her bread, and she's got some money put aside and he's going to help her . . . she's going to set up a little hat shop, what about that? Her name's Miss Rivell . . . she's poor but proud, he says . . . Addy, isn't it the most exciting thing you ever heard?'

'Y-yes,' stammered Adeline. 'Does he mean to . . . to *marry* this young lady or is he really just going to help her to buy the shop?'

'Well, I don't know, but it sounds likely, doesn't it? I mean you don't go bringing milliners back from London to live in your parents' house for a few days unless you like them rather a lot, do you? I'm glad, because Arnold's never been much of a one for the ladies, has he? I mean he's polite, and he dances with you and one or two others . . . in fact I believe he rather likes you, for he talks to you more than most, but nevertheless, he's never shown proper interest in anyone that I can recall.'

'No, he doesn't . . . isn't . . . did he write to you Bella? It must have been a l-long letter.'

'Oh no, not to me, but to Mother and Father. It was the longest letter; it must have taken him hours and hours and *pints* of ink, I should think. To tell you the truth, Mother isn't pleased though Father didn't seem at all put out. You can see Mother thinks an opera singer, even a fearfully good one, is a real let-down for her eldest son. But it's up to Arnold, really, wouldn't you say?'

'Oh . . . yes. Yes, indeed. He's coming back this evening, you say?'

'That's right. On the five-ten from Euston station. I wanted to ask you to come over tomorrow morning. Will you, Addy? You'd like to see this opera singer . . . Miss Rivell . . . wouldn't you? It will be a great lark. I'll tease Arnold unmercifully, the dark old horse!'

'Well, not tomorrow, it's a bit soon. Bella, I'm awfully sorry, but I really only came over to tell you I can't spend the morning with you. My cousin John has only a few days left before he leaves us, and I want to spend as much time as possible with him.'

'Oh, Addy, I thought you said you were riding with him this afternoon,' Bella said, greatly dismayed. 'You said . . . you said . . .'

'Yes, I know.' The ache in Adeline's heart was hurting so much that she simply had to get away, yet to rush off too quickly would only make Bella wonder what she had said and she must never know . . . no one must ever know . . . what the foolish, unsophisticated Adeline felt . . . had once felt . . . for Arnold Haslington. 'Look, Bella, not a word to anyone, do you swear it if I tell?'

'Not a word,' breathed Bella, wide-eyed. 'On the Bible, Addy, I won't say a word!'

'Well then, my cousin John . . . only he isn't my cousin at all really, as you know . . . cousin John has asked me to marry him. I haven't said yes but I didn't say no, either. We both need time, I feel, to sort our feelings out. So . . . so we're going for a long walk this morning to have a private talk about things.'

'Addy, why ever didn't you say so the moment we met? How lucky you are – not even eighteen yet and you've had your first proposal! Will you say yes, do you think? He's awfully handsome, though he's quite old, and he's awfully nice, too; everyone seems to like him. My goodness, Addy, you'll be a doctor's wife.'

'If I agreed I would. And a missionary's.' The two girls laughed together over this reminder.

'Well, I know. But your father says he doesn't shove his religion down one's throat and Mother – my mother – says he's awfully nice and natural. Oh, but you'll go to China; how shall I bear it, Addy?'

'I expect you'll manage,' Adeline said heartlessly. She had turned back towards the manor but Bella had fallen into step beside her; plainly the news was too intriguing a subject to be dropped until Bella had extracted the last spot of information. 'But John is ten years older than me – don't you think that's too big an age gap?'

Bella, who had just denounced John as 'quite old', promptly changed her tack.

'Ten years? No, indeed, ten years is just right,' she declared. 'It would be awfully dull to marry a very *young* man; younger men are boring . . . does John have any friends who might do for me?'

'I don't know. I keep telling you I don't know him very well,' Adeline said mendaciously. 'Marriage is an awfully big step – it's for life, Bella.'

'That's true, of course. Gracious, only think, you and Arnold may be getting married!'

Adeline's heart gave a great bound followed by a deep swoop. It had been exciting and delicious to hear her name and Arnold's linked like that, although she realized it was merely Bella's phrasing and not her assessment of the situation which was at fault. She must have changed colour, however, for Bella grabbed her arm.

'Are you all right, Addy? You've gone ever so pale. It's the thought of being married, I dare say. Are you still riding this afternoon, with John, if you're walking with him this morning? You are? Oh well, you can meet me tomorrow and tell me what you've decided. Though I don't see why you won't come over in the morning to see Arnold and his lady-friend.'

'It would look rude and curious,' Adeline said, at her most damping. 'Look, you come over to the Manor tomorrow, at about three. I expect John's got packing and things to do, so we can have a good talk. Can you manage that?'

'Oh, Addy, of course I can. I wish I was nearly engaged, but no one's that serious yet, not even Lionel Goulding, though he's always coming to call.' She turned disconsolately back as the two girls reached the stile. 'I'd better go in. Mother thinks you're coming back with me, and I don't want to worry her particularly as she's still awfully cross about Arnold's friend. See you tomorrow, then.'

'Yes, at about three. Goodbye, Bella,' Adeline said, climbing the stile and walking quickly in the direction of her own home. But once Bella was out of sight she turned left and walked through the trees to the river bank.

Beneath the friendly, concealing boughs of a big willow tree she sat down and gazed unseeingly at the river whilst huge tears rolled down her cheeks and her mouth pulled itself into ugly shapes.

Arnold had a lady-friend – he had played her false! He was going to marry her; there could be no other explanation for his bringing her home to stay with his parents. And she had so longed for his return . . . she had planned an early walk again the moment he was back so that the two of them could meet before the rest of the world was up and doing and exchange news.

Presently, sitting was no longer the right position to express her grief. She lay on her front and wept until she had no more tears. Then she sat up, drily hiccupping, dipped her handkerchief in the water and mopped her hot eyes and dirty cheeks. Finally she tidied her hair with her fingers and got slowly to her feet. She had said she would be spending the morning with Bella, so she would not be missed. She would walk along the bank as slowly as she could and think bright thoughts to recover her composure and complexion, and then she would go back to the Manor and straight to her room, where she could easily skulk until it was time for luncheon.

She had never been so unhappy in her life.

The ride with John went well. Desperate that her cousin should notice nothing amiss Adeline was at her gayest and best. She even managed to mention that Bella's big brother was returning that evening after a visit to London, though she kept her head carefully turned away as she did so.

At dinner, however, knowing that Arnold – and That Woman – would probably even now be sitting down to their own meal at the Hall, Adeline's precarious calm crumbled and after answering at random, staring at her plate without touching the food on it and knocking over a full glass of wine, Adeline pleaded a severe headache and went to her room.

Her father, of course, knew that Adeline and headaches were, happily, strangers to one another, but he would put it down to what he termed 'feminine troubles', and would probably share this opinion with John.

Adeline pulled her curtains to shut out the cheerful glow of the sunset, undressed and donned her nightgown. Then she read for a little, but found it very hard indeed to concentrate on the page before her. Finally she tried to sleep but very soon realized that she was so tense that her eyelids would not stay closed but kept popping open so that she lay there, stiff as a board, staring into the dark. Crossly she got up again, drew the curtains back, pulled up a chair and sat on it, brooding out into the dark. Far away there were tiny, twinkling lights. It would be the Hall, of course, and the lights were on to illumine Arnold and That Woman.

*Had* he played her false? Fallen in love with someone else? It certainly sounded like it, but Adeline decided she would not jump to conclusions. For all she knew Arnold might have meant every word he said – he might have met the woman, felt sorry for her and brought her back here so that he could set her up in a little shop in Langforth. All at once she knew just what she must do. She would go to the tower the next morning and if he was there she would ask him what this woman meant to him. If Arnold had fallen in love, she supposed it was scarcely his fault, because men were different from women and, she knew, could fall in and out of love a great deal more easily. If it was all gossip and false rumour, then they would have a beautiful reconciliation scene, during which she would cry and vow eternal love and Arnold would reproach her for her disbelief in him.

This was much better! But suppose he did not come? That, Adeline knew, could only mean that their love was a thing of the past, for his last words to her had been, 'Bella will tell you when I'm expected home – see you at the usual place, early, on my first morning back!' She had agreed. Nothing could be firmer than that. But he would be there, of course he would, if only to tell her that he loved another. Arnold was a gentleman and kept his appointments.

Adeline watched the tiny pinpoint of light for a long time, but at last even that was extinguished, and she made her way to bed.

'She's going to be *married*? Oh come on, Bella, the girl's only seventeen. Besides, Mr Warburton's so careful of his precious daughter that he wouldn't let her marry without knowing the johnnie awfully well.'

Arnold stared at his sister across the landing as if she had gone out of her mind, and Bella, who had only told him in the hope of surprising a like announcement from him – oh, is she, I'm getting married too! – scowled up at her elder brother and wondered why she bothered with him.

'She'll be eighteen in a month or two,' she said. 'Eighteen isn't so young after all. And anyway, it's that chap who's staying with them. You know, a distant cousin, John Sawyer. He's ever so nice, Arny, really he is. Handsome and friendly and such a good rider . . . he shoots, too, but only targets at this time of year, and rabbits I suppose. Mr Warburton thinks he's a grand fellow, I heard him saying so to Father, so their marrying isn't at all unlikely, whatever you may think.'

'Well, I think she's being a fool,' Arnold said through lips that trembled unaccountably. 'She can hardly know the fellow. I've been gone a month and he didn't arrive until after I left.'

'Then you hardly know Miss Rivell,' Bella said triumphantly. 'Are you coming down to the billiard room or are you just going to stand there, staring?'

Since Lily, tired from her journey and overawed by the size and magnificence of the Hall, had elected to go to bed straight after dinner, Arnold had suggested that Bella might like to give him a game of billiards. He had hoped to get her talking about Adeline – now, he wanted nothing better than for her to stop! He was heartsick and dismayed at her words; could not, would not, believe them. If Adeline was going to marry this

John fellow, then some pressure must have been put on her – but he would not believe it, not until he heard the words from her own lips.

'Oh . . . come on, then, I'll give you a game,' Arnold said bleakly. Halfway down the stairs he added, 'What made you say that about my scarcely knowing Miss Rivell? The circumstances are quite different.'

'Oh? Aren't you . . . well, interested in her? In a nice sort of way, I mean?'

'Miss Rivell and I are mere acquaintances,' Arnold began, then hesitated, his innate sense of honesty reminding him, dourly, that he was being a regular Judas. He had been happy enough to share Miss Rivell's bed, but now he was home again he was downgrading her from mistress to mere acquaintance in the most ruthless way imaginable. 'Well, perhaps acquaintance isn't quite right,' he said grudgingly. 'She's a good friend.'

'There you are then,' Bella said brightly, as though she had scored a point. They continued down the stairs, across the hall and into the billiard room. Bella began to poke the balls out of the pockets and arrange them on the table whilst Arnold selected a couple of cues and chalked the tips. 'Anyway, I met Addy this morning and told her you were coming home this evening. I asked her to come over tomorrow but she said she wouldn't, it was nosy. So I'm meeting her at three at the Manor, and then I'll find out a bit more.'

'You'll find out she was teasing you,' Arnold warned her. 'And as for being nosy, you put everyone in the shade. All you think about is "finding out"!'

'That isn't true, and Adeline *is* getting married,' Bella stated firmly. 'You'll hear it for yourself soon enough.'

'Gossip!' Arnold sneered unkindly. 'Tattle, tale-bearer!'

He waited until Bella had slammed out of the room, crashing the door behind her, and then, with clenched teeth, he whacked the balls around the table so hard that the dust flew and the noise brought a servant running to see who was making such a din. Probably, Arnold thought ruefully, he suspected young Bertie; certainly he showed a good deal of surprise when he clapped eyes on Arnold.

'Oh . . . sorry, Higgins, a mis-shot,' Arnold said, glib but red-faced. He picked up the balls, which were all over the floor, and returned them to the pockets, then took himself off to bed.

He would jolly well go to the tower first thing, as they had arranged, and demand an explanation. He was sure it would be a satisfactory one – she loved him, she had said so often enough! He had meant to write and had failed to do so, but surely that was not a sufficiently heinous crime to turn a girl against a fellow so completely?

Comforted by this thought, he slept at last.

Bright and early next morning, before anyone else was stirring, Arnold got up, dressed in his most inconspicuous tweeds and set off for the tower.

54

After what Bella had said he did not intend to hang around close to the folly, for what an ass he would look if Adeline turned up with her beau in attendance, or with his ring on her finger, glittering away for all to see. So he lurked in the thick undergrowth for well over two hours, staring all the time at the path down which she would come.

At the end of that time he made his way quietly back to the Hall, for people were up and stirring. His heart ached, but he intended to put a good face on it, let Adeline see that he was not heartbroken despite her jilting him.

He went upstairs two at a time; perhaps she had been taken ill, perhaps that John-fellow was an early riser and had prevented her from keeping her appointment. But the chances were she preferred another to himself and he had best accept it.

He banged on Lily's door and went in without waiting for her to call. He meant to tell her to get up and come down to breakfast right away so that she could come into Langforth with him to look for her shop whilst he was working at the pottery.

Lily was still in bed. She was very pale; she had been sick, she said, and did not fancy breakfast. She accompanied him downstairs, however, at his insistence, and sat at the table with him and his father, and presently colour came back into her cheeks and she decided that toast and marmalade and some coffee would not come amiss.

Arnold watched her eat. After weeks of sharing a bed with her he had missed her sorely the previous night. Well, last night he had still believed Adeline to be true to him and would not have contemplated going to visit Lily. But now that Adeline had failed him there could be no harm in seeing more of Lily. It would help, he told himself morosely, to mend his broken heart.

Adeline was up and out before sunrise, sure that Arnold would come. But she did not intend to hang around too near the tower in case he brought That Woman with him. What was more, she would feel a fool being there first after he hadn't even bothered to write to her more than once. So she made herself a nice little nest in the undergrowth and settled down to wait.

Adeline watched the sun come up, ride high in the heavens, heard people begin to call and trudge to and fro in the Hall gardens. Only then did she give up and go home, her misery too dull and cold for tears.

Breakfast was long over but John was still in the breakfast parlour, with an enormous map of China spread out on the big table.

'Hello there!' he said cheerfully as she came into the room. 'How's the head?'

'The head . . . oh, much better, thanks,' Adeline said dully. 'I'm not quite myself yet, though.'

'Poor old thing. Would you like to come into Langforth with me? I'm going to buy some of the things I need for China and have them packed and sent up to Scarborough by train.'

Adeline was about to refuse when pride came to her aid. If she stayed here moping, it would certainly reach Bella's ears and from Bella to Arnold was a very short step indeed.

'Yes, I'd enjoy that,' she said, unable to sound delighted but at least managing to infuse a little pleasure into her voice. 'Have you ordered the carriage?'

'Yes, for nine o'clock. And I want to have that little picture you gave me framed.'

'My picture?'

'Yes, your picture. Don't you remember giving me the little oil painting of the Manor?'

'Oh . . . that. Yes, of course. How nice that you're framing it.'

'You're an artist of some talent,' John said. 'I shall treasure the picture and boast about my clever little cousin when I'm far from here.'

A small voice spoke, a voice which Adeline scarcely recognized as her own.

'John . . . may I change my mind?'

If she had doubted his sincerity she could have done so no longer. As she spoke her eyes were on his face and such brilliant excitement transformed it that she could not have misinterpreted it. He came round the table in two bounds and in a moment she was in his arms, his mouth searching for hers. And in that position she felt for a moment so warm, so safe, that she could easily have believed herself in love. Had it not been for Arnold's treacherous courtship, she realized, she would have married John without hesitation. And as he caressed her, kissed her, she could tell herself that she was doing the right thing, for she was very fond of John. So she hid her face in his chest and hugged him and let his love work for both of them.

Only afterwards did she consider that her words had been somewhat ambiguous. *May I change my mind* could have referred to John's proposed trip to Langforth, though in fact she had meant just what John had taken her to mean. She wondered, a little uneasily, whether her words, spoken on impulse, ought to be retracted, but John was being very fair. He said he would stay another month and if, at the end of that time, she still wanted to marry him, then they would tie the knot. She was at liberty, he assured her, to change her mind back again without a word of reproach from him at any time.

They did not intend to make their engagement public, but a maid had come into the breakfast room to clear the sideboard and had seen Miss Adeline in Mr John's arms. She backed out quietly, raced down to the kitchen, and told everyone in sight. By lunchtime it was common knowledge at the Hall that Miss Warburton was to marry her cousin John.

Arnold heard it from his father's elderly valet and from the butler but finally, dreadfully, believed it when his mother told him.

By the following day it was equally public knowledge that young Mr Haslington was to marry the young woman from London. He had taken her round the pottery and had then kissed her long and hard in the stableyard at the Hall. He had kissed her again in the drawing-room whilst waiting for the dinner gong to sound and had stared straight into his mother's angry eyes and told her that the following day he was going shopping for an engagement ring for Lily.

'He's been a slow starter, but he'll be wed before many weeks are out,' the Warburtons' housekeeper announced. 'First our Miss Addy starts a-kissing people, then it's Mr Arnold. It'll be two autumn weddings, I reckon.'

Bella was in her element. It did not worry her that Adeline came rarely to the Hall, for Adeline was engaged to be married and she and her betrothed were getting ready to leave the country, so they had a great deal to do. But she visited the Manor whenever she could and never thought it strange that her friend was hungry for news of Arnold, for he and Lily were to be married quite soon and it was only natural that one bride should be interested in another.

The two young ladies did not meet, however, for Adeline was building her relationship with John with all the care and tenderness she would have lavished on building a card-house, and she wanted no sight of Arnold or his betrothed to metaphorically jog her elbow. Instead, she threw herself into the task of preparing for the long voyage to China, and she and John spent a lot of money on what he termed 'indispensables', though time alone would prove just how indispensable they were. Mr Warburton, though grieved to think of Adeline's going so far away, comforted himself with the delight of knowing she was marrying a good man and with John's repeated promises of a return within a year or two, certainly when their first child was able to travel.

Mr Warburton offered the young couple the dower house for their leaves and John and Adeline went over it and said it would be ideal. Neighbours came with gifts and advice, friends came to meet John and envy her.

Without ever having to put it into words, the die was cast long before the end of that trial month. It was clear to John that Adeline would be accompanying him to China, and if, in the dark hours of the night, she wept, she never told a soul and always came down next morning with a bright smile and a host of suggestions for their future life.

'How happy and busy you are!' Bella cried when she came visiting, and no one, least of all Adeline, contradicted her.

Arnold and Lily, safely engaged to be married, were walking round the rose garden admiring the last blooms when Lily broke the news that she believed herself to be pregnant. Arnold stopped short, a hand still outstretched to a rose, and stared at her.

'Pregnant? But you said . . . you said you didn't think you were, you just might be. And now you are? Oh, my God!'

'Well, it isn't so awful,' Lily said apologetically. She had changed in all sorts of ways, mostly for the better. She was an actress, of course, and ever since she had been at the Hall she had spoken only in the most ladylike and refined accents, but Arnold sometimes wondered if it fooled his mother. 'We are already engaged, remember, dear.'

'Well yes, but . . . oh well, we'd better get married quite soon, then.'

His tone was so lugubrious that Lily's round, scared eyes dwelt uncomfortably on his dark face. Did he mean it? It was what she had hoped for from the very first moment they'd met. She had enjoyed her work at the opera house until she had had a taste of being Arnold's mistress, when she realized that she much preferred the latter. Singing, even in the chorus, was awfully hard work; late nights and lots of rehearsals and when one was understudying the main parts one had to learn them too. She had taken a fearful chance, though, in handing in her notice when she could see that Arnold was just about ready to leave the city. But it had paid off and she was all right, and would be all righter, if there was such a phrase, when he had married her. Then she would have no need to worry ever again. She would spend the rest of her life in the lap of luxury, eating when she felt hungry, sleeping when she felt tired, and making love to Arnold every night.

It wasn't just the material things, either, she reminded herself now. She had found herself growing genuinely fond of Arnold, so fond that at times she had hated deceiving him, had wished she could come straight out with it and say, 'I'm planning to marry you, so you'd better come to terms with it,' but in the end it hadn't been necessary. She'd missed her monthlies twice now; a baby was most certainly on the way.

She decided, as they walked slowly back through the rose garden, that she was going to like being a mother. She was beautiful, she knew, so the baby would be a nice-looking little thing. Arnold, of course, was wildly handsome, so if it was a boy presumably it would look just like him. But she was fairly sure it was a girl . . . she felt like having a girl, not a boy. A pretty little girl with curly hair and big blue eyes who would wear tiny replicas of Lily's grown-up dresses and sing pretty songs when her mama taught her to do so.

But the time had come to test Arnold's love for her. She stopped short and stopped him too, turning so that they were face to face and holding his forearms firmly with her small hands.

'Dearest, this engagement does not have to end in marriage, you know. We can give it out that I've changed my mind, moved away. I'll go wherever you like to send me and I won't embarrass you, so long as you'll keep me and the child in some little place somewhere.'

She read the hesitation, the first wild hope, in his eyes before the look changed to true tenderness. He put his arms round her waist and drew her gently to him, then spoke strongly, firmly, in her ear.

'Goose! We meant to get married – this will just mean we'll marry a bit sooner. I'll make you happy, Lily, love. You'll enjoy being my wife, I'll see to that!'

Lily felt tears rise to her eyes, tears of relief and joy. She stammered that she would be the happiest girl on earth to marry him and that she would work hard to be the right wife for him. She meant it, too. Mrs Haslington didn't like her, didn't think she was good enough for her son, but Lily would prove her wrong. If it took the rest of her life she'd prove to everyone that Arnold had done the right thing by marrying her. I'll make him happier than some little chit with no experience, still wet behind the ears, she told herself. Just wait and see!

In the end, the wedding race, as Bella called it, was won by Arnold and Lily, but only by three days. Neither couple attended the other's wedding but both had perfect, watertight excuses. When Arnold was married Adeline was visiting John's parents and younger brothers in the small village of Scalby, near Scarborough. When Adeline was married Arnold and Lily were on their honeymoon in the South of France.

When the invitation came, Adeline looked at it and knew a moment of total, black despair. Then she told herself that seeing something in black and white – or rather silver and grey – did not make it any more real than it had been yesterday, and explained, in her best copperplate, that she would be away in Yorkshire upon the occasion of Arnold Henry's marriage to Lily Elizabeth.

'We shall be visiting my fiancé's parents,' she wrote in a covering letter, because she was still very fond of Mr and Mrs Haslington and wanted to hurt no feelings save those of Arnold. Not that she would succeed in hurting his feelings, for he had none. 'We will spend two weeks in Yorkshire, and the wedding comes towards the end of the second week, I could not ask John to leave his parents sooner, when he is going so far away.'

Arnold's rejection of the Warburton invitation was, of course, even more understandable.

'My wife and I will be honeymooning in France for a month,' he wrote. 'But we wish you and your husband every happiness in your new life together.'

Adeline read it and sniffed; easy for him to talk about happiness when he had blighted her life in order to gratify his taste for cheap actresses. For tales had come to the Manor via one of the parlourmaids that lovely though Miss Lily undoubtedly was she was not quite out of the top drawer. In times of stress her pretty accent slipped just a trifle, and she spoke as one who understood more than a young lady of twenty commonly did. Which was scarcely surprising, had they but known.

Not that the servants did not make shrewd guesses about the bride-to-be's age, past and future prospects.

'Done well for herself, for she's not the little innocent she pretends to be,' was the general opinion. Her own maid, a young country girl called Betty, knew very well that Lily was pregnant, but she liked her new mistress so kept the information to herself.

And if the weddings did one thing for the people most concerned, it was to take their minds off everything else. Arnold, who in normal circumstances would have left most of the arrangements to his bride's parents, had to work day and night to see that everything was done properly and had, furthermore, to placate his mother. She had, she revealed, harboured hopes for him in quite another quarter, but these hopes had been dashed by his foolish betrothal to Lily.

'She'll make me a good wife and she'll be a good mother to our child,' Arnold insisted, his voice lacking conviction because he had not dreamed that his mother had somehow managed to sniff out his attachment to Adeline. He would very much rather no one knew, but at least she was unlikely to talk about it. 'And anyway, I *like* Lily. She's good fun, she's lively, and she knows how to make a fellow feel ten foot tall.'

He did not add the obvious rider – that his mother's constant criticism made him feel about two inches tall – but at least it checked her overt antagonism to the idea of the wedding.

Bella was to be flower-girl at both weddings, a fact which thrilled her almost speechless. On Lily's great day she helped her future sister-in-law to don the white gown, not making a single rude remark when they had to fasten the waist with safety pins. Radiant in pink tulle, she held the train up beautifully as Lily swanned down the aisle, looking as lovely and pure as the flower after which she had been named, and then followed Lily up the aisle again, a married woman at last, Mrs Lily Haslington, or Mrs Haslington junior, or Mrs Arnold, as the villagers would call her.

Adeline worked hard for her wedding as well, harder than Arnold, for she had no mother to do the work for her. She planned the wedding breakfast, chose and arranged the flowers, accompanied Bella to fittings for her pale blue voile gown and went by herself for her own fittings. John worked hard too, but he was so happy that hard work seemed nothing. His parents loved Adeline, thought her a charming, gentle, beautiful girl, and congratulated him on winning her.

The second wedding day, as indeed had the first, dawned bright and sunny. Adeline walked down the aisle in her beautiful dress with her heart high and her hand resting lightly on her father's arm. If she got an attack of panic in the vestry when she was signing the register no one knew of it, least of all John, and by dint of biting her lips and squeezing her nails in to the palms of her hands it passed off.

The reception was held at the Manor and was lavishly catered by their own servants and those of friends who could spare them for the day. The carriage which took them to a big hotel to spend their wedding night was decked with blue and white ribbons and had silver horseshoes pinned all over it. They could not go far since Mr Warburton intended to accompany them down to Southampton the following day, to see them off aboard their ship.

John was wonderfully kind and gentle when they reached their hotel. They had a long journey before them, he told Adeline, so it would be best if they did not consummate their marriage until they were settled in China. True to his word, he kissed her fondly and then allowed her to sleep undisturbed for the rest of the night and Adeline appreciated his generosity, for she was worn out and far too nervous to enjoy the strangeness of a man in her bed.

Next day was a scramble to get into the train, change at various stops en route, and finally transfer from the train to the docks and from the docks to the ship. Mr Warburton held his daughter very tight and shook hands with John very vigorously. There were tears on his cheeks. Then John and Adeline were alone, leaning over the rail and waving to the tiny figure of Sidney Warburton far below them.

It was only then, when she felt the deck heave beneath her feet and the strong salt air buffet her face, that Adeline fully realized what she had done. And how she regretted it! She was adrift in a strange ship on a strange ocean, heading for a strange shore, with a stranger beside her. She was too frightened – and very soon too seasick – to do anything but hide in her cabin and pray for death.

# CHAPTER FIVE

'Are you nearly ready, John? If so, do you want me to start the clinic, with Lin Shen, whilst you see the new patients? Most of them just want dressings done and so on, nothing too difficult. Though we'll leave it until you've completed surgery, if you'd rather.'

Adeline and John were at breakfast. They sat on opposite sides of a small table made of polished cherry-wood and ate milky porridge followed by boiled eggs and bread and butter. They had tea to drink, made with milk in a thoroughly British fashion. It was the one meal of the day which owed nothing to the Orient and they both enjoyed it, though they were happy enough to allow the servants to make their luncheon and dinner in the Chinese way to which they were accustomed.

'Yes, I'm nearly ready, and I'd be most grateful if you and Lin would start without me,' John said. He smiled affectionately at his wife, who was snugly clad, Chinese fashion, in a quilted jacket and trousers, though she was wearing her own sensible boots on her feet. 'You're a good girl Adeline, and the most tremendous help. But don't forget your rest . . . off you go to lie down as soon as I come and take over from you.'

'I'm so much better now,' Adeline protested, as John finished his last piece of bread and butter and drained his tea-cup. 'I don't really need to rest. In fact it probably does me more good, in this cold, to keep active.'

March had only just come in and the weather was still very cold indeed. A fortnight previously the snow had been thick on the ground, but it had gradually dwindled until the previous day a shower of rain had seen off the last of it. Not even in the hills to the west of them did the snow linger, though when she awoke this morning Adeline had been forced to conclude that the rain had not heralded spring, for it was once more bitterly cold.

'Don't forget I'm your doctor as well as your husband,' John remarked, standing up and crossing the room to begin assembling the things he would want for surgery – a notebook, pencils, his thermometer in its battered little metal case, his stethoscope. 'I don't know if you realize it, young woman, but there were moments, down south, when I thought I was going to lose you. I'm making extra-sure that I never have such a fright again.'

Adeline sniffed. It was true that, on their arrival in Shanghai, she had been very ill, for her constant seasickness had weakened her and so she had had very little resistance to the illness she had almost immediately contracted. A fever had raged within her for days, and she still remembered the pains in her joints, the constant thumping in her head, her raging thirst and continual vomiting. But on the good side, it had gained John – and consequently herself – a far pleasanter position than they might otherwise have been allotted.

'She's far too ill to go to Nanking,' the head of the missionary house had said, standing by her bed talking to John and obviously assuming that she was incapable of hearing a word he said. 'I believe she'd die there, in that appalling heat. But fortunately we do have another post. Abraham Instadt and his wife were at Ayiteng, just outside Peking, in the north. He's retiring – he's over seventy – and wants to move out as soon as possible. They've built themselves a very pleasant bungalow in the hills and they're taking several of their staff with them, but they'll be leaving three reliable people. Mrs Sawyer would be better there – the climate's far more equable.'

'But you said I was needed in Nanking,' John said doubtfully. 'Is there another man who could go there? If it wasn't for the fact that she was so seasick, I believe I'd have sent my wife home . . . how could I guess she would be so ill?'

'Of course you could not. And if the voyage weakened her, to send her home would be out of the question.' Adeline had sensed the older man patting her husband's shoulder. 'Don't fret yourself. She'll be fine once you get her up-country.'

So John had agreed and she, too weak in any event to argue, had been put aboard a coastal vessel – her horror at the thought of further sea-voyaging tempered by pleasure in the light sea-breeze – and taken north.

Down in Shanghai she had hated and loathed China, the Chinese, and poor John for bringing her to such a place. But once settled in Ayiteng, she had quietly begun to appreciate not only her surroundings but the man she had married.

Her new home, in its compound, seemed strange at first, but its beauty and the friendliness of the people compensated for its unfamiliarity. It was built on Chinese lines, with each room facing out into a courtyard, but unlike Chinese homes she and John could go from room to room without venturing outdoors, and there was glass in the windows instead of the paper or reed blinds used by the locals.

It was like a small village really, Adeline thought when she first got to know it. The surgery and the clinic were built on to the house itself, the servant's quarters and the stables and outhouses were also a part of the compound, and the whole property was surrounded by a very tall, very substantial wall with big wooden double doors to keep out wandering vagrants and soldiers of fortune by night, though such doors were usually kept open during daylight hours. The wall, made of russet brick, was topped with slanting golden tiles and their house was made of the same pleasant and colourful materials. There was a big brass bell on a tower by the gates which could be rung if she and John wanted to get people within the walls during times of trouble, and a good many trees. A walnut tree grew quite close to the entrance doors and overhung the wall so that passing children vied for the nuts in autumn, and just now a cherry and several almond trees were budding breathlessly towards the moment when they could show her, for the first time, the beauty of their blossom.

The courtyards were beautiful, too. One had a pool, a tiny waterfall and goldfish, with a willow weeping over the water. Others had cobbles, and round barrels filled with spring bulbs which were just pushing glistening green noses out of the earth and little, grave trees, kept small by root pruning, John told her.

Adeline was fond of John's church, as well, which was also within the shelter of their wall. It must have started out as an attempt to look like a conventional church . . . grey stone walls, stained glass windows, a small square tower . . . but that was not really practical and now it had patchwork green and gold tiles on the roof, the paint which had turned the russet bricks into a semblance of grey stone had flaked and dried and dropped off, and the stained glass, which had been made by the Instadts using some sort of transparent coloured paper stuck to plain glass, had long ago succumbed to the curiosity of small Chinese fingers and the weather.

As for John, she had known he was a good man when she married him, but she had not realized the extent of his goodness. He had waited to make her his until they were settled in and she was better, but their union, when it came, had simply swept her off her feet because his passion had been gentle always, and she had been aware that he was thinking of her own pleasure and comfort even in the wildest and most abandoned moments of their lovemaking.

He was a first-rate doctor, too. He seemed to get on well with everyone. He teased the shy young women who tottered painfully in on their tiny, crippled feet, he played with the babies until they stopped howling because his features were strange to them and began to laugh, he spoke seriously to the old men who wanted seriousness and frankly to the young men who needed frankness. And because they trusted him, they trusted his medicine, too. They took the pills, they took the advice, they even thought twice about exposing unwanted girl babies on the hills so that they might die without their deaths being on their parents' consciences. And of course there was Yenala, the living, breathing sign of John's commonsense and goodness.

Yenala had been a bond-maiden, a child who had been sold by her parents soon after her birth because they could not afford to rear her. Most such children go to good homes where they are bound to serve until they are eighteen years old, when they are found husbands and married to them and are free henceforth.

But in China, as in the rest of the world, there are bad employers, bad owners. Yenala was sold to a wicked, cruel woman and a weak, lustful man. When she was twelve years old her mistress caught her husband with the girl . . . the terrified child, in pain and humiliated, was fiercely beaten, beaten almost to death, and when she recovered was given to understand that it was as a consequence of her own wickedness that she had been raped. From that moment on the mistress, who had only overworked and underfed her before, began to torture and torment the child. Yenala, bewildered, terrified and sick at heart for the crime she had never committed, crept into John's surgery late one afternoon and asked for poison. She told him that her life was insupportable and she wanted to end it. She blamed no one but herself, said she was a bad girl and that she could bear no more.

John saw the burns on her skinny arms, the starved little body, the weals across the backs of her legs, and went straight round to her mistress's house. What he said there Adeline never knew, but when he came back he took Yenala on his knee and told her that she was his little girl now, his and Missie Adeline's.

'First of all you will eat well and sleep a lot and grow strong and fat,' he told her. 'And then you can be a friend and a helper to Missie. You can

64

learn to read and write and you can teach Missie your local dialect, and you can help us both with our work, for Missie works with me in the clinic, you know. And when we have a little baby, you can nurse it for us, and sing it to sleep at nights and teach it to talk your language, as we shall teach it ours.'

Adeline had been awkward with Yenala at first. The child was so spiky and thin, her hair sparse, her skin covered in sores and burns. She had found it difficult to think of Yenala as a person and not an animal, for the child had attacked her food with starving ferocity, had scarcely spoken, had flinched and cowered away every time Adeline moved.

But that had been weeks ago. Now Yenala was well fleshed, her hair thick and shiny, her eyes bright. She was intelligent, learned eagerly and quickly and had a most delightful, purring giggle which rang out whenever she was amused. She was beginning to speak quite good English and had taught Adeline to understand the local dialect almost as well as John did. She was a treasure, Adeline told herself now as the child entered the room, with a big smile and a swift greeting, to clear their breakfast things away.

John, his hands full, went towards the door, having greeted Yenala, then stopped and turned back.

'Now remember what I said, Adeline, my dear. Work until you're tired, or until I can take over if you feel up to it, and then go and rest. Yenala, you keep an eye on Missie Adeline for me, won't you? She thinks she's so clever, but she really doesn't know best all the time.'

'How unfair . . . I don't see . . .'

'Darling, you are having a baby, and women who are going to have babies *do* rest for an hour or so in the middle of the day. Trust me!'

'I'm not even sure about the baby,' Adeline grumbled. 'I want to go into the village . . . there's the prettiest rug in one of the shops, and I thought I'd go and ask the price, see if I can afford it. We do need another rug in our bedroom, and . . .'

'*I'm* sure about the baby and I'm . . .'

'A doctor,' Adeline and Yenala chorused, both laughing. 'All right, John,' Adeline went on, 'I'll rest when I'm tired, but surely that won't stop me from going out this afternoon?'

'No, of course it won't. Not if you rest earlier.' John shook his head at her, smiling. 'Independent! I knew how it would be when I married you, I knew you wouldn't let me get away with anything, I knew you'd question my every action, so I shouldn't grumble when you do it, I suppose.'

'I'll rest, I'll rest,' Adeline said quickly. 'Can Yenala help in the clinic too? She's awfully useful, really she is – she can change a dressing as well as Lin or me, and she's even getting to know about the pills.'

'Yes, she can help, though I think you and Lin must do the pills,' John said. The local people, if given tablets to take, would either eat the lot at one go or would hand them round amongst friends and family, so now, at the daily clinic, pills were handed out in tiny quantities, a day's supply at a time. A patient who had to take three tablets a day was told to come back at midday and when the sun was setting and either John himself, Adeline or one of the servants would solemnly watch the pill being swallowed. Adeline's present difficulty was that, with the best will in the world, she could not fit faces to names, so Lin had formed the habit of whispering to her as the patients reached the head of the queue: 'This one Li, this one Shena,' and then Adeline would consult John's written list, match the name up with the tablets required, and carefully hand out the correct dose.

'Don't worry, we'll see to it,' Adeline said now. 'Yenala, my dear, can you go and fetch Lin? I expect the clinic's filling up already, so we might as well get started.'

Yenala hurried happily out and Adeline went across the courtyard, under the arch, and into the main compound. As she had anticipated, the area before the clinic was already crowded, but as soon as she unlocked the doors and let the first few people inside, Lin came hurrying over to her. He was a small, skinny Chinese with greying hair and a head which always looked a bit too big for his body, but he was an old hand at clinics, having been the Instadts' chief boy for about thirty years. Adeline had been surprised that he had not chosen to go with his master and mistress, but he had explained that his entire family lived in Ayiteng, and since he could scarcely take them all with him to the retirement bungalow he had chosen to stay and serve the next incumbent.

'Morning, Missie,' he greeted her. 'Morning, Yenala.' It always amused Adeline that he spoke English with a Scottish accent, for the Instadts, despite their name, had been Scots. 'Would you like me to take the first few dressings off?'

'Yes, please. Yenala, can you fetch the clean ones for me? Is there warm water?'

There was. For half an hour they worked quietly, joking with the patients, in Adeline's case in her somewhat limited dialect, getting down pills and medicine, filling in the treatment book. Only Adeline could do this since she was the only one present who could write English and the treatment book had to be kept in that language, but, she reflected, the three of them were quite evenly matched otherwise with regard to the work.

A woman with an arm and shoulder a mass of bandages came to the head of the queue and was quickly unwound by Lin with little regard for her equilibrium, for he just seized the end of the bandage and twizzled her briskly round, but when the wound was revealed Adeline gasped and had to look away for a moment.

It was a stinking, suppurating mess, and amidst the yellow and creamy colour of the sepsis small maggots writhed. Adeline forced herself to examine the wound, and saw that it was possibly a little better that it had been in the previous week. John had heard that surgeons in the Crimea

66

had used maggots to eat away septicaemia and had decided to have a try himself, so this ghastly practice was really modern medicine.

'Mr John put the maggots on, did he, Lin?'

'That's right, Missie Adeline. He tried other things first, but . . .' He bent forward and looked at the mess. 'It's cleaner, it smells better,' he announced. 'Shall we put the dressing back, or shall the woman wait and see Mr John when surgery's over?'

'I think she'd better wait,' Adeline decided. She told the patient what she should do and watched as the woman, with a bandage now loosely holding the dressing in place, went out into the courtyard once more, squatted uncomplainingly on the roots of the walnut tree, and taking something out of her clothing, popped it into her mouth and began to chew, her eyes fixed on nothing, her mouth in constant motion.

As she started on the next patient, Adeline thought that poor John was in for another full day – no wonder he complained that he had no time to write exciting sermons in the language he was still busily trying to master. He worked solidly from about seven in the morning until three in the afternoon, when he would clean up, do some chores, prepare for the next surgery and probably see more people for an hour or so in the evening. When the two of them finished their work for the day and went into their own room they were usually too tired to do more than pen a short letter home, or in Adeline's case painfully sew along the seam of a small pillowcase, or knit another few rows of a tiny matinée jacket.

On top of all this John had his church services, for Mr Instadt had been a good missionary as well as a competent doctor, and his converts thronged the church twice a day on Sundays and for a brief service on weekdays as well.

'Some people run a mission school, but thank goodness we don't have to do that,' John often said. 'I approve of Sunday school teaching, but as to straightforward education, the Chinese teach their own people far better than we could, and they are beginning to do so now, whenever the opportunity occurs.'

It grieved John though, Adeline knew, that the people came to him more for medical than spiritual advice. She told him that it was bound to change when he spoke the local dialect with more ease, but privately she doubted it. Nor did she think it particularly important. When he gave a man ease from pain that man often came to church, sometimes even converted to Christianity, from gratitude. What did it matter whether the initial cause of the conversion had been physical or spiritual, so long as the end was the same?

Now, working on the endless stream of patients, tipping pills into thin, shaking hands, spooning medicine, changing dressings, Adeline was aware of her own gentle satisfaction. She had never expected to enjoy working in the clinic, but that was exactly how she now viewed it – as something done to please John which had, inexplicably, gradually grown dear to her. She liked the people she treated, enjoyed the comradeship which had grown up between herself, Lin Shen and Yenala, and found that actually being of use brought its own reward.

At home in England she had often been bored and had had no very high opinion of herself save as her father's daughter. Here, she knew she was valued for the knowledge that she was painfully acquiring and the expertise she was beginning to show in the clinic. She was Mr John's wife and would have received respect for that reason alone, but how much better to earn that respect in your own right!

'This is Mr Wang, Missiè Adeline; he says it was pills, but if I remember correctly it was medicine. Can you check for us?'

Lin's elegant Highland accent often caused people to stare, but as she went through the list and got out the prescribed drug Adeline reflected that it was a sign, more than anything, of what a good man Abraham Instadt had been. He despised Pidgin, which was what most of the English-speaking Chinese used, saying that it made a fool of a man, robbed him of dignity. Consequently, all of his own staff spoke good English – or good Scots – and even his converts, when they needed to speak English, steered clear of the graceless baby-talk that was Pidgin.

I'd like to carry on that tradition, Adeline thought now, pouring red medicine into a spoon and feeding it to an enthusiastic baby with a horrible rash. She renewed the ointment in the woman's small jar, hoping that it had been used on the rash and not either eaten or handed to a friend, and reflected on the impossibility of changing a woman's language once she had become Pidgin-speaking. Yenala spoke beautifully, in good English, though she had not learned enough to be at ease in the language yet, but Amatei, the cook's wife, who cleaned and helped in the house, had been speaking Pidgin for years and got very offended if Adeline corrected her, no matter how tactfully.

'You won't give the baby any more fermented fruit, will you?' Adeline said to the mother, who smiled and held the fat baby still for the medicine. 'He's a very fine boy but the fruit does not agree with him.'

'No, no more,' the woman said softly, in her gentle, pretty voice. 'He loves it, but it is not for such small ones.'

Adeline nodded, handed over the ointment and moved on to the next patient. Looking sideways, she could see that the line was diminishing at last, with fewer than a dozen people still to see. Good! Much though she enjoyed her work, it was still pleasant to realize that soon she would be able to sit down and relax for an hour or so. It was tiring to be on your feet for hours, especially when you were carrying a little more weight than was your wont. She glanced down at her waist, which was still so flat that no one, save herself, could have known it was already slowing her down a little. A baby! She had not known at first whether to be dismayed or delighted, but after a few weeks delight had won. The babies in the clinic, fat, cuddly, skinny, sweet, enchanted her, so why should a baby of her own be any different? It would, she decided, be even nicer than the Chinese babies with their dark eyes and golden-brown skin.

Her baby might have golden-blonde hair or rich, light brown locks, or even a shining black mane like Adeline's own. She and John both had blue eyes, so the baby would almost certainly follow them there . . . but she had very pale skin and John was tanned . . . Dreamily, Adeline stared before her, seeing babies of every shape and hue, whilst beside her Lin tidied up and put things away.

The door swinging open brought Adeline back to the present. It was Yenala. She usually helped with the clinic but this morning she had been learning how to make chicken soup with dumplings and then how to make the paste from which noodles would eventually be manufactured. John was determined not to rob Yenala of her cultural heritage so that when she was eighteen and wanted to marry she would have everything a Chinese girl needed to take care of her man. Amatei thought this was an extremely sensible view and volunteered to teach Yenala everything she could, whilst her husband, Yo Liu, taught the girl more intricate cookery skills and even P'an, the gardener, insisted on giving her instruction in the making of a garden and the rearing of plants. As a result, Yenala could do most things about the house, could cook a meal, weed a garden bed and trim a young fruit tree, to say nothing of the tasks she did with Adeline.

But now she smiled at her mistress, bobbed a curtsy, and said: 'It's time you rested, Missie Adeline. Mr John says if you go and sleep now, for an hour, he'll bring you your luncheon and you can eat together.'

'Well, we have finished here,' Adeline agreed, as Lin swung the door of the dispensary shut and locked it with the key at his waist. 'How did the cooking go?'

'Quite well. But you can judge for yourself presently; my chicken soup will be served for luncheon and tomorrow my noodles will accompany whatever Yo Liu prepares for dinner.'

'Lovely,' Adeline said, returning with Yenala across the courtyard, under the arch and back into her own quarters. 'Come and tell me how you got on whilst I undress.'

It was a cold day, but her bedroom was warmed by a small fire of charcoal which was lit beneath the brick bed-platform. Like the fairly well-to-do Chinese, they had bed-platforms throughout the house with quilts piled up on top and a small charcoal fire burning beneath. In the other rooms the fire was allowed to die out during the day, but because of Adeline's condition her fire was kept alight. Consequently, when she and Yenala came briskly in from the cold, the warmth met them comfortingly.

'Into bed with you,' the child said, helping Adeline off with her quilted jacket and trousers. Adeline, even in good linen camisole and drawers, was happy enough to leap into the warmed quilts and burrow herself down until she could feel the benefit of the charcoal burner. When only her face was showing she began to relax, and smiled drowsily at Yenala.

'I don't really need a sleep,' she said, feeling guilty because she felt that at twelve Yenala probably needed rest more than a young woman who had passed her eighteenth birthday. 'Do you want to read to me, show me how far you've got in that book?'

Yenala was reading to Adeline in Mandarin, but at the same time translating into the local dialect. It was good for both of them – but now Adeline was truly grateful when Yenala said no, she thought it would be better if she went over to the surgery and helped Mr John to finish up there.

'And then I'm going to dish up, with Amatei,' she confided. 'She is going to teach me to use two long spoons to help guests with.'

Adeline barely managed a mumble before she could feel her lids sliding down over her unresisting eyes. It was gloriously warm in the nest of quilts; she had not realized how cold she had got in the clinic.

Being in bed, though, reminded her of being in bed with John, and that made her think about Arnold. The fact of marriage had not really struck her until she and John had made love, but ever since she had been haunted by the unworthy suspicion that, if John was so very good at a pastime he clearly considered should not be indulged in too often, how much better Arnold might be, who no doubt indulged himself in that same pastime continually. John was abstemious by nature, never grabbing. He had kissed her rarely during their courtship, had been married to her for two whole months . . . possibly even more, now she thought about it . . . before he had made love to her. Arnold had been forever kissing, touching, even though he had never gone too far or embarrassed her. But still, she did not believe she could have shared a bed with Arnold and remained pure, so her curiosity was aroused. She could not imagine getting more pleasure than she did with John, but she supposed that this was simply her lack of experience. It never crossed her mind that a man who abstains from indulging the flesh might, for that very reason, be better at making love than one who grabs every opportunity for surfeit.

The bed was warming up beautifully and Adeline with it. Drowsily, she let her thoughts slide away from China and her home there and back to England, to the Manor, where by the end of February the snowdrops would be showing beneath the copper beech and the flowering currants and the forsythia would be in bud, just waiting for a mild day to show their bravery to the winter weather. Here, the bulbs were above the ground already – just – but at the Manor they would be six or eight inches tall and the crocuses would be making the borders under the library windows a blaze of purple and gold. Indeed, if it had been a mild February there would be daffodils in bud, possibly even beginning to shake out their yellow skirts in the wood, where they were sheltered from all but the most violent weather.

70

Adeline's fingers touched her stomach, feeling for the bulge that she half longed for, half dreaded. She had told John she was not sure about the child yet, but this was not really true. It just seemed tempting fate to talk about it as though it were a settled thing when she was not showing at all. But nevertheless she believed herself to be about twelve weeks pregnant and John thought she was right. Still, she had not told her father yet, because he would get so very excited and would be so very pleased. Better to wait a few months, until she stuck out like the bows of a ship, and then tell Father to get the dower house cleaned up because they would be coming home just as soon as the baby could manage the journey.

In the little brazier beneath the brick platform the charcoal settled with a tiny creaking sound. Adeline allowed herself to indulge in a fantasy which, for all she knew, might easily come true. She would fall asleep and John would come quietly in to wake her, with their luncheons set out nicely on a tray. He would come under the quilts with her because it was foolish for him to sit outside in the cold, and they would eat their food and talk, and drink tiny cups of delicious green tea and then . . . well, very probably they would walk into the village together to buy that rug, or they might get her some drawing paper and pencils . . . but you never knew, today might be a day when John would wriggle down into the quilt nest, and pull her into his arms, and . . .

Adeline slept at last on a glorious wave of anticipation.

When she awoke John was leaning over her with the tray. The rich smell of chicken soup tantalized her nostrils and she saw that it was not just the soup today, but a bowl of mixed greenstuff with a clear, piquant sauce poured over it. She struggled upright, pushed her hair behind her ears and held out her hands.

'Oh, John, it does look so nice! I didn't mean to sleep, you know, but I just couldn't help it. Come into the warm, do, and then we can eat together.'

John slid into the quilts and they both propped their backs against cushions and began to eat. The soup and dumplings were very good, the vegetables cooked so that they were still crunchy. Even if she had not been hungry, Adeline thought, the food was so delicious that she would have eaten it all up. As it was, she finished before John and then drank three cups of green tea in quick succession, finishing the last cup just as Yenala knocked and came in with plum puffs, a favourite delicacy.

'Amatei let me help make them,' she announced importantly, putting the small dishes before John and Adeline and whisking the tray with its used crockery away. 'P'an says he will teach me to ride the pony if you don't want me for anything else this afternoon.'

'You go with P'an, and enjoy yourself,' Adeline said. 'Mr John and I will probably walk into the village later. I'll speak to Amatei, see if she needs anything.'

71

Their compound was no more than a quarter of a mile away from the village but nevertheless Adeline liked to do at least some of the marketing for herself. It forced her to speak to local shopkeepers, and though she was sure she was usually cheated she appreciated that it was one of the better ways for her to learn all about the currency and the local produce.

'I'll tell her you'll be round,' Yenala said. She bobbed her little curtsy and whisked away, shutting the door softly behind her.

'She's a good girl,' John said lazily. 'She looks much better, too, don't you think?' He gathered the used crockery into a pile, leaned over and stood it down on the floor. Then he turned and took Adeline in his arms. 'Two good girls,' he remarked. 'How nice to know you take me seriously and sleep just as you ought.'

Adeline laughed against his neck and felt his fingers busily unbuttoning her camisole; dreams were about to come true, it seemed!

'Wake up, Lily, you shouldn't be asleep at this time! Mother suggests you might like to go down to the drawing-room for tea later – she's got some friends coming and she'd like them to meet you.'

Arnold had been at the pottery all morning and had returned home for luncheon, although it was not normally his habit to do so. But Lily was nearing her time and it worried him that she spent so much of her day in bed. The doctor had said it was not good for her and Arnold's mother was always on at him to stir Lily a little, to make her move herself, to think instead of always choosing the silliest books, the sweetest food.

'That child will be born fat as a pig and slow as porridge,' she said crossly two or three times a day. 'My grandson should have had a mother with a bit of life in her.'

Of course she said this partly to annoy Arnold, who had vowed that his Lily was full of life, but she believed it and it worried her. Arnold, who appreciated his mother's good points whilst deprecating her bad ones, knew from the doctor that her worries were genuine. Lily never exercised, never put herself out, seldom even walked downstairs. How could she expect to have a normal birth and furthermore to bear a normal child, if she was not prepared to exert herself even a little?

Lily gave a little jump, then slowly opened her big blue eyes. She looked very lovely, rosy from sleep, warm and snug, and even though Arnold was cross with her he was conscious, through his annoyance, of desire stirring. With the covers tucked beneath her arms so that he could see her smooth creamy skin but the heavily pregnant body was hidden, she was a charming sight.

'Oh, Arny, you woke me from a lovely dream! Come and give your girl a cuddle, to show there's no ill-feeling.'

Arnold sighed but approached the bed. Pregnancy suited her; her breasts were full, her face was a little more rounded, her skin, which had always been good, fairly glowed with health. Going solely by the look of her, Arnold reflected, you could not say that her life-style was doing her much harm – quite the opposite!

'You're a bad girl . . . here, up with you!' He slid his hands beneath her and heaved; she sat up reluctantly and he heaved again, then gave up, bent his head and blew in to the side of her neck, making her giggle and wriggle in his grasp.

'Stop it! That isn't fair . . . you musn't make me laugh . . . oh, how nice you are!' She threw her arms around his neck and began to kiss his chin. 'Don't go off back to that horrible pottery – get in beside me!'

Well, it's one way of getting her to exercise, Arnold told himself, getting in to bed with alacrity and then getting out again to remove his city suit. A little cuddle wouldn't hurt, and when she was soft and pliant and sweet to him he would remind her that she must go and have afternoon tea with his mother, and she would be too affectionate to resist.

'If I didn't go into the pottery you'd have no pretty things, no nice food . . .' Arnold was beginning, when he discovered that his wife, to all appearances fully dressed, was in fact wearing almost nothing. 'I say, old girl, you haven't got your armour on!' He squeezed her uncorseted body close to him, and began to run his fingers up and down her bare back in what he hoped was a seductive and suggestive fashion.

'Oh, Arny, do give over! You wouldn't wear those things either if you were as fat as me. Come to that you wouldn't go to tea-parties if you were me either. You should see all the old pussies, doing sums on their fingers and staring at my waist and then nodding their heads, nod nod nod, like a set of Chinese mandarins.'

'Well, what does it matter?' Arnold wrenched at his shirt; buttons popped. 'They can't tell for sure, and anyway, it's no crime. We're married, aren't we?'

'It does matter – they'll say I trapped you, didn't catch you fair and square, and that makes me look a fool . . . which does not displease your mama, Arny! So I'll just stay up here, if you please.'

'I don't please,' Arnold said. He rolled her, none too gently, on to her back and began to heave and pull her around like an outsize doll. 'Goodness, you're a fair old weight.'

'So would you be . . .' Lily gave a small shriek as Arnold lowered himself on to her. 'Oh, Arny, that hurts . . . don't . . . ow! You're kneeling on my leg!'

'Are you all right?' Arnold said, trying to sound solicitous instead of merely lustful. 'You'll be all right, I'll be careful.'

'No, I'm not all right. It's impossible like this; we're just too . . . I'm not the right . . .'

Arnold climbed off her and they rearranged themselves. He put his arms round Lily just above waist-level and took a big breast in either hand. Curled together, like two spoons, they lay comfortably for a few moments, until Arnold judged that Lily's annoyance at his behaviour had cooled. Then, very gently, he began to make love to her. Mrs Haslington senior's tea-party no longer seemed important to either of them. And presently, as Lily began to move too, as she clutched and moaned, Arnold decided it was no very bad thing to come home and find an uncorseted wife lying in bed. It was very convenient, in fact. Presently, when he had her at his mercy, so to speak, he would tell her in no uncertain terms that she must go downstairs this afternoon and mix with his mother's friends. But just now he was enjoying himself too much to worry about such things.

Going back to work later, with a feeling of gloom and failure hanging over him, Arnold wished he had never come home at all. What good had he done after all? In his excitement he had forgotten to extract a promise from Lily to visit his mother, and when the excitement was over and Lily was sitting up and tidying herself it was far too late. When he mentioned his mother's tea-party again she laughed and told him to go himself but not to expect her to appear.

'Your mother talks about me as if I weren't there,' she said resentfully. 'And her friends aren't much better. They stare at me as if I were a raree show and then they turn back to each other and talk about people I've never met. I think they're rude and they think I'm boring, and we're probably all right.'

This, Arnold was sure, was just Lily being over-sensitive and silly. His parents welcomed her, and even Bella had said they would like to see more of his wife. Of course his mother had been a bit disappointed that Lily was not some rich heiress, that was only natural, and his father didn't care about much apart from his meals and the money which came in from his businesses, but they had made Lily welcome, he had seen it with his own eyes. They were thrilled to think they were about to become grandparents, and his mother had said that with his father none too keen on society and with a heart condition as well, they would be grateful for a pretty young daughter-in-law to take Bella and Dorothea to parties, once the child was born. What they were afraid of now was some sort of scandal, with Lily perhaps continuing to lead her separate life on the first floor, keeping the baby away from them, becoming a legend rather than part of the family. It was true that hardly anyone had met his wife since the wedding, and there were always going to be those who thought Lily too superior to come down and mix with her in-laws; whilst others would hint at madness, or physical disability, if this attitude of his wife's continued.

The carriage bowled along over the muddy road, for winter had broken in showers of rain and the daffodils which grew in many gardens hung their yellow heads and grew increasingly battered as wild day succeeded wild day. One good thing had happened, however – Arnold had had a word with Bella.

74

'I went up and tried to get her to come down to luncheon,' she had told Arnold in a low voice when they met in the hall. 'She said she would, then made some excuse. The thing is Arny, that Mother was a bit unkind to her at first and that's put her off all of us. Oh, Mother didn't mean it, she just kept talking about Lily's parents and so on, and saying how big Lily looked for six months. But I do believe her when she says she'll feel better about coming downstairs once she's had the baby and isn't such an awkward shape. She's due quite soon, isn't she, so perhaps she'll be happier with us then.'

This was more or less what Lily had said, but when he was not enslaved by her sensual charms Arnold sometimes wondered whether she would become easier, or whether she intended to split the household asunder.

It was a worrying thought for a young father-to-be and Arnold pushed it out of his mind and concentrated on glaring out at the rain and wishing for a decent day for a change. Next time, he told himself firmly, next time I'll take her downstairs myself and insist that she stops hiding away like this! Next time I'll do it, not just talk about it.

Lily waited until Arnold had clattered away downstairs and then fished her box of chocolates out from under the bed, opened the lid and selected a large violet cream. She popped it into her mouth and lay back on the bed again, but somehow the chocolate had lost its appeal and when she had finished it she did not return to the box. Instead, for the first time for days, she climbed clumsily off the bed and went over to the window.

She was miserable. She had always thought it would be wonderful to have lots of money and all her favourite food, but she had reckoned without in-laws. They expected her to show herself when her figure had gone and her face was fat, to say nothing of her bosom, which she thought hideously huge. She did not look at her stomach any more, kept her eyes averted even in the bath, because she had looked about three weeks ago and seen what she had taken to be snail-tracks all over her lovely smooth skin. Her shriek had brought Arnold running and after a word with the doctor she had been assured that the snail-tracks were perfectly natural and were, in fact, stretch marks. Stretch marks! What had Arnold and his great fat child done to her, she had demanded at the top of her voice. Her skin, her actual own skin, had been stretched out of shape, thinned down, by the abominable baby, and it would never go back to the smooth and supple state of her before-marriage self.

The doctor had not known what he was saying of course, since she had had no scruples about telling him she was twenty-one years old.

'Well then, Mrs Haslington, you won't have those marks long,' he had said cheerfully. 'At twenty-five or twenty-six I couldn't be so sanguine, but you're young; your skin will simply go back to its usual shape, like a new piece of elastic when you stretch it and let it go again.'

Being pregnant was horrid enough without being told that you were like

75

a piece of old elastic, past the stage of returning to your original shape. Being pregnant was far worse than she had been led to believe. First she had been sick, then she had developed the most amazing appetite and had got grossly fat, and now she kept having little, digging pains and awful indigestion, and something dire had happened to her bladder since she wanted to wee all the time, and indeed, frequently did wee in the most unnatural places. Once in the pantry, on to the quarry tiles, when she had sneaked down in the middle of the night for a bacon sandwich, once smack bang in the middle of the black and white tiled hall when she had been startled by the unexpected sound of a servant coming through at three in the afternoon when she thought everyone was safely out of the way. Several times in the park . . . she had nearly told Arnold when he had been nagging at her to go out more . . . and once in bed, when she had been deeply asleep and dreaming one of those embarrassing dreams where you have no clothes on and need, desperately, to use the water closet!

So one way and another, pregnancy left a lot to be desired, and Lily was pretty sure that bearing the child would prove even less of a pleasure. The midwife had called four or five times but her brisk references to bearing down, swaddling, heaving on ropes and biting a piece of blanket had so terrified Lily that she had let her eyes unfocus until the scene before her was nothing but a blur and had made herself sing, inside her head, the longest operatic aria she could imagine. When she heard the midwife making departure noises she had come back again, to find that stout person looking at her as though she feared for her sanity. Well, let her think what she likes, Lily thought now, gazing out at the rain-soaked garden beneath her window. She'll know soon enough that I don't like a lot of pain when I start shrieking and hitting out.

The thought of landing a fist squarely – as if accidentally – upon the midwife's little pug nose did cheer Lily up for a few moments, but then she thought about biting a blanket and heaving on a rope and bearing down and decided she had better not lay the midwife out no matter how objectionable she was; Lily might need her.

When I've had the baby, I wonder whether Arnold will let us have a home of our own, Lily thought, tapping her fingers on the window frame. It wouldn't be so bad being married if she didn't have her mother-in-law a stone's throw away, forever asking spiteful questions and having little digs at her because Lily did not always understand the things she ought – or the things Mrs Haslington thought she ought, anyway. The girls, Bella and Dorothea, were rather nice, and old Mr Haslington, short of breath and thin of hair, with food stains all over his waistcoat, was an old rip and had enjoyed many a joke with her, but that mother of Arnold's . . . well, it was too bad Arnold could not see through her.

For Lily had tried, whatever the Haslingtons might think. For the first two months she had gone downstairs to most meals and had done her very best to be good company and to mix. But now that she was so huge she could not bear Mrs Haslington jabbing at her, and it was probably a lot worse for the baby than being shut away in their own rooms, upstairs.

Sighing, Lily waddled back to the bed and cast herself down on it. It was all that girl's fault, of course, that girl Arnold had been going to marry. Oh, he thought she didn't know, and to be fair to him he'd never reproached her or let her suspect that he didn't love her better than anyone in the world, but she knew. She'd overheard Mrs Haslington talking about it to one of her friends one afternoon when they'd thought that she, Lily, was safely tucked away upstairs having her rest.

'He was wild about her, and she was wild about him,' Mrs Haslington had said. 'Poor Arny! She was a real little lady, just the sort of girl I'd dreamed of his marrying, but her father's a bit of a stickler and the other feller had money and prospects . . .'

'And so does your Arnold, my dear,' the elderly friend said. 'A handsome young man he is too . . . and richer than most, with marvellous prospects.'

'Ah, yes. But my son won't inherit a stately home . . .'

'A stately home!'

'Yes, indeed. And possibly even a title. So you see he didn't stand a chance and nor did his poor little sweetheart. They were parted, and then Arnold went to London and met the lady who's now his wife.'

'Well! Well, I never did! Not that young Mrs Arnold isn't a real charmer . . . she is, indeed she is . . . but a title!'

'What might have been, you could say,' Mrs Haslington said. 'But there, what's done is done. Don't ever speak of it, Mrs Gibbons, I beg of you. Arnold's done his best to put a brave face on it but his heart is still not mended. His wife will just have to learn to live with it.'

As the wife in question, Lily very much doubted that Arnold was bearing a broken heart in his bosom, but of course she could scarcely say so, since she was hidden behind a potted palm in the hall, eavesdropping as hard as she could. This did not lessen her resentment, however. She knew that Arnold was happy and fulfilled, she doubted if he ever thought of his lost love, but she was very sure that Mrs Haslington probably thought of her daily and made Lily's life as miserable as she possibly could just to prove to herself, if no one else, that her son had married beneath him and could have had a title, or if not a title, a woman who had been deemed a worthy consort for a title.

Thinking of the other girl, Lily wondered just how much truth there had been in Mrs Haslington's remarks. Very little, she decided. There had been another girl, but she was sure she had snatched Arnold from her, rather than picking him up after the other had cast him down. He had been ebullient, almost aggressively cheerful, when she had first met him, not suffering in any way from unrequited love.

Still, whatever the story, she was going to have to speak to Arnold. Oh, not about the other girl, but about his mother. Either he takes me away from here, to a house of our own, or he must speak to his mother and tell her to treat me different, Lily decided, quite enjoying a common think after months of speaking with care. I'd like a nice little house with a few devoted servants and a very good cook . . . some garden . . . yes, some garden would be nice, for the summer, and a gardener of course, and someone to chat to me as I lie on the garden seat, eating strawberries dipped in sugar and drinking iced lemonade.

Lily was lying on her front, which was extremely uncomfortable, so she rolled over on to her back, which was not much better. Finally she got up again and returned to the window. The trees dripped dolefully and the earth was dark with moisture; far away on the horizon she could see a lake which was not a lake at all but floods. Arnold had told her that as he drove into Langforth now he could see nothing but water at one particular point along the road, where the river had burst its banks.

For the first time for weeks, Lily felt restless; not at all like returning to her bed to eat more chocolates whilst she read something light and cheerful. She knew the baby was due any time, but of course no one else did because they were going to announce it as a seven-month child or she was much mistaken. She did not care, they could call it what they liked; the point was that it would be her very own child and it would tie Arnold to her for ever. But suppose she had the baby tomorrow, for instance. Then she would be lying-in for weeks, the doctor had told her, simply not allowed to leave her bed because it was not good for her. In that case, perhaps it was not as foolish of Arnold as she had thought to keep suggesting that she get out of their rooms for a bit. Perhaps he was being quite sensible.

Lily wandered over to the wardrobe and began selecting clothes. A big, loose smock dress was comfortable, for she did not intend to put any underwear on, apart from a few petticoats to keep the cold at bay and some stockings, woollen ones, with garters to hold them up. The garters hurt – her legs must have got fatter – but she donned them nevertheless, put on her boots and a cloak which swirled round her in a very satisfactory and disguising way, and set off for the door.

It was late afternoon and no one was about. A walk would do her good, she decided, slipping out through the side door. One of the things which Mrs Haslington had kept nagging her about was riding. Lily had never ridden in her life and had no intention of starting – horses had been equipped with big teeth and huge feet for a purpose, and since she did not enjoy being bitten, kicked or trodden on, Lily saw no good reason for getting within striking distance – but she did think, momentarily, that it might be nice to be *able* to ride. The idea of riding was glamorous, even if being bumped up and down on a saddle was not. She pictured herself stealing out through the side door, round to the stable, and mounting a snow-white horse to gallop dashingly away to Langforth and her dear Arnold.

However . . . she gave the stableyard a wide berth and made, instead, for the meadows which led down to the river. She and Arnold had walked there once or twice, and it was a pleasant place to be when it wasn't raining. The rain having ceased, if only momentarily, she decided that she would walk by the river again. If it was flooding she would have to turn back, but Arnold had said it never flooded this high up because the banks were steep and the water fast-running.

As she walked, Lily wondered what they would say if they knew she had escaped. She had a maid, Meg, a nice little thing, but it had not occurred to her to ring for the girl any more than it had occurred to her to suggest Bella accompanied her. She wanted to be alone, she wanted to walk, and she wanted to take a good look at this countryside that Arnold was so fond of that he refused to move away from it to a new little home with her.

The grass in the meadows was short but extremely wet. Before she had gone ten yards Lily's skirt was soaked to the knee and her cloak was draggly, but she cared not one whit. She was out, striding along, her eyes busy with every detail of her surroundings. It was March, so there was not a lot to see at first, but then she gained the woodland which lay between the Hall and the river and saw her first aconites, a sparkling carpet of gold and green, and bent over them, astonished that they should be growing wild when they were so beautiful and colourful.

Presently she saw some tiny white flowers and picked a couple to add to the bouquet of aconites she held. She thought they must be wild strawberries, never having heard of *Potentilla sterilis*, and congratulated herself on having made a rare discovery; then picked an alpine cinquefoil, admiring its bright yellow petals and orange spots, and telling herself that there was something in the country after all – fancy so many flowers being in blossom this early in the year! There was quite a mild breeze now, and Lily forgot her soaked skirt and the weight of the wet cloak. She was enjoying this walk!

It was probably the blackthorn which was her undoing. She saw the great bush of it, starred all over with white, and made up her mind at once that she would take some for her bouquet. But it was some way off the ground that the first blossoms appeared, and even by standing on tiptoe Lily could not quite reach.

A bank seemed the obvious answer. One side of the blackthorn was on higher ground than the other so Lily stood on that side, stretched, still just in vain, then gathered herself and leapt wildly upward, scattering aconites as she did so.

But she reached the blackthorn blossom and dragged it down to her level, conscious of a tiny nagging tugging pain in her back as she did so but ignoring it in the thrill of conquest. She had got it! She broke the branch off and added it to her other finds, then bent and picked up all the fallen aconites. She admired the bouquet for a moment, then wandered back to the path again. She continued along it, with the river clucking and gurgling on her left, until she reached the stile. Here, she hesitated. She had never come this far before; really, she should go back.

She looked over the stile, and was lost. Where the path crossed a flat and grassy space there were a number of gorse bushes, several of which were massed with their bright yellow flowers. Gorse was very prickly, Lily remembered, but she could surely twist off a piece? Just enough to show Arnold how many flowering plants she had found in her little walk.

She climbed the stile, thumping heavily down on the other side, aware for the first time that she was a bit breathless. Not used to exercise, you bad girl, you, she chided herself, heading for the gorse. Never mind, this walk will do you lots of good!

It took a bit longer to twist a piece of gorse free than she had anticipated and by the time she had added an unmangled piece to her bouquet she became uneasily aware, for the first time, that it was getting dusky. Still . . . she abandoned the gorse bushes and went back to the river path. A mist was rising, ghostlike, from the water, fascinating Lily's city soul. How beautiful it was, not menacing at all, simply curling and swirling above the current, now hiding the water and now revealing it, now becoming entangled in a tree which bent over the water, now rising higher, so that you could see under it as though it were as solid as cotton wool.

But still, it was getting dusk, and she had better turn back. Lily headed for the stile once more and received a most unpleasant surprise. On the other side of the stile the trees gathered close. And beneath them the dark tunnel down which she would have to walk to gain the Hall again was most uninviting. It was far too dark for her to be able to see roots or tussocks of grass . . . and, even as she watched, the mist, which had swirled over the river, began to invade the trees, curling round trunks, scarving bushes, hiding and revealing all in a moment as though it knowingly played a game.

As Lily hesitated, a friendly smell assailed her nostrils. It was wood-smoke and, unexpectedly, tears pricked her eyes. It made her remember chestnuts roasting on a charcoal brazier beside a wooden barrow, an old man standing beside the fire sliding a big shovel full of the nuts across the heat . . . herself, a small girl, mittened and muffed, waiting with watering mouth whilst her mother fished pennies out of her purse to pay the old man for the stout brown paper bag with its sizzling contents . . . the shrieks when she burnt her fingers, the laughter she and her mother shared . . . the delicious taste of the roast nuts.

It was her only memory of her mother, who must have died shortly afterwards, and Lily was glad it was a happy one. Certainly the rest of her childhood had not lived up to that marvellous moment. Indifferent relatives who treated an orphan as a skivvy did not deserve a moment's recollection and she never let them darken her mind.

Standing reliving her past with the scent of woodsmoke in the air, however, did not send the mist away or bring light to the darkness. But it brought her attention to the fact that where there was woodsmoke there was usually a house, and that meant there was an alternative to plunging back over the stile and into that dark and now mist-enshrouded wood. As she had turned her head towards the smell of the smoke she had seen the house through the trees, seen its lights twinkling through the bare branches. All she need do was to beg the occupants to send a servant to the Hall and someone would bring a carriage for her. She turned aside from the towpath on the thought; she believed that Mr Warburton, her father-in-law's friend, lived at this place. He would help her, would probably send her home in his own carriage.

She pushed her way through the trees and emerged on to a meadow which she immediately began to cross. But the ground near the gateway was deep in mud and poached by cows' feet. She sank, gasped, floundered, slipped. In a moment she was on her knees, then she was up, a hand to her side . . . down again, dragging herself upright by means of the gatepost, fumbling for the gate-catch, failing to find it, slithering and slipping and falling to the other end of the gate when she realized she was at the wrong end . . . another crashing fall as the gate began to swing . . . another slithering skid as she hauled her considerable weight to her feet.

By the time she managed to get through the gate and away from the mud, which must be a foot deep, she was totally exhausted, her head swimming, her heart banging away in her breast like a steam-hammer. She tried to stand still for a moment to get her bearings, but there was a pain, now, which she could no longer ignore. It clawed at her back, making her whimper, and one of her legs would scarcely swing forward at all, so that she was going short, dot and carry one, dragging herself painfully up the slope which led, eventually, to the lighted windows above her.

Halfway there she doubted that she would make it. She was going as fast as she could but the pain was getting stronger, so strong that she felt like giving in, just lying down and letting herself drown in it. She was in a garden or an orchard now, she did not know which, and the house lights were nearer, but she could not make it, she could not, she must lie down!

She swayed to a halt and then a terrifying thing happened. From out of the blackness hurtled a malignant ghost, small, shrieking. It flew straight at her, dodged at the last minute and then, with another fearful wail, came round at her again.

Terror lent her wings; Lily hurled herself forward, her foot found a flight of stone steps, she stumbled up them and fell across the white painted garden seat at the top. She was on a terrace of some sort, she managed to register, and then the pain came again and she thought it was the ghost, clawing into her oblivion. She screamed, her voice sounding pathetically thin to her ears, and then knew no more.

Sidney Warburton was sitting behind his desk working out last month's figures for the home farm when he heard what sounded at first like a screech owl, closely followed by another scream. Both noises appeared to emanate from just outside his library window. He waited for a moment, then heard a low anguished moan and hurriedly dragged the curtains back. What on earth was happening out there?

At first he could see nothing, for the french windows only gave back a reflection of the scene in the room behind him, so Mr Warburton threw them open, then looked again. The sounds were coming from what appeared to be a bundle of rags thrown down on his white-painted garden seat – then the rags stirred convulsively and Warburton could see that it was a woman, her dark clothing rain-soaked, lying half on and half off the seat.

'Just a minute, my dear,' Mr Warburton called. He fetched a candle in its stick from the mantel and stepped out on to the terrace. His candle illumined her, sheet-white and with her mouth opening now to release a long, terrified moan. Mr Warburton spoke quickly, trying to let her see that he was a friend. These gypsy women were strange creatures, either so bold that they spat and scratched at a friendly hand or so wild and terrified that they fled.

'It's all right, my dear. I'll fetch help at once. Are you ill?'

The woman groaned again and made a pathetic attempt to sit up, but her rescuer pushed her gently down.

'It's all right, stay there . . . I shan't be a moment.'

He hurried back into the library, pulled the bell, then returned to the terrace. She was still making jerky, abortive attempts to regain her feet and even as he pressed her gently back on to the seat he realized she was pregnant. He rushed towards the house, nearly knocking over Frank, his butler, as he reached the french windows.

'Ah, Frank . . . and here's Mrs Gilmour – thank God! A woman's collapsed on the terrace. I think she's having a baby . . . she's a gypsy, I think, but I want a hand to get her into the house.'

'A gypsy? In the house?' That was Mrs Gilmour, the kindest of women in normal circumstances. She came out and put a hand on the woman's forehead, then turned decisively to the two men. 'You're right, sir, she's going to give birth. Come on, Frank, help the master to carry her indoors.'

'I wonder how she came here?' Mr Warburton mused as they got the woman through the french windows and put her down, none too gently for she was heavy, on the chaise-longue in the corner. 'The mist's rising quite fast, though. Perhaps she lost her way, and when she felt the child begin, simply made for the nearest lights.'

'I dare say,' Mrs Gilmour said. 'She's no gypsy, though, sir. That's quality stuff she's wearing; cost a pretty penny. And look at her! She's a lady – see her face, her hair.'

'Probably she's a lady's maid,' Frank volunteered. 'Ran off when she realized she was in an unfortunate condition and didn't have anywhere to go.'

'She's wearing a wedding ring,' Mrs Gilmour remarked. 'Sir, I'll send one of the men for the doctor and the midwife, and I'll boil some water and get a clean sheet or two. In the meantime, do you suppose you and Frank could get that cloak off her? No doubt we'll discover who she is quickly enough, once she's warm and knows she's safe. I'll send Mary in to mend the fire.'

At this point Lily opened her blue eyes and looked straight up into Mr Warburton's face. With her long, golden hair flowing about her and the look of suffering on her face she looked nothing like the radiant bride Sidney Warburton had seen several months before, but suddenly something clicked in his brain. Of course, the Haslington heir's wife was pregnant; this must be she!

'It's all right, Mrs Haslington,' he said soothingly. 'You're safe now; we're fetching the doctor, he'll be here before you can say Jack Robinson. Now just try to relax.'

Lily started to smile and then her expression changed to a grimace of pain. She groaned, then clutched blindly at the air, so Mr Warburton took her fingers in his. He patted her hand gently and Lily, eyes still tightly shut, said: 'Help me! Oh, please, please help me!'

'Of course we'll help you. Just lie quiet; you're doing very well.'

The words had the desired effect. Lily let out her breath in a long sigh and relaxed, but she did not let go of Mr Warburton's hand.

That was how Mrs Gilmour found them when she returned presently, with various bowls, potions and preparations all balanced on the tea-trolley which she trundled into the library with a very determined air.

'I've brought some laudanum, sir, in case she needs it for the pain,' she whispered. 'And some hot tea . . . I wonder if she'd like some?'

'I'd like a whisky,' Mr Warburton hissed back in heartfelt tones. 'But perhaps I'll need a clear head, so tea will have to do. Pour me out a cup, please, Mrs Gilmour, and another for yourself and for Frank.'

'Frank, you pour the tea,' Mrs Gilmour said. She whisked a big, thick tartan rug off her trolley and spread it over Lily's lower half, then began to undo Lily's cloak and wrestle with the fastenings of her blouse and skirt.

'We don't want these dreadful muddy clothes on her,' she said, when her master questioned her behaviour. 'She'll want to be clean and sweet when her baby's born.'

'Oh, but Mrs Gilmour, she can't have a baby here,' Mr Warburton said, shocked. 'We'd best take her up to a bed if you think the birth's imminent.'

'We can't move her,' Mrs Gilmour pointed out. 'It wouldn't do for her to have the child halfway up the stairs, sir. Frank, unbutton the lady's boots.'

'The master says it's young Mrs Haslington,' Frank said breathily as he obeyed. 'Gracious, where the devil's she been? Through marsh and mire, seemingly.'

'Marsh and mire and cow-dung,' Mr Warburton contributed, taking the rain-sodden cloak from his housekeeper. 'I wonder how long the doctor will be?'

Mrs Gilmour had just discovered that Lily was not wearing drawers; she piled the heavy petticoats on to the floor, though, and turned to see Mr Warburton looking a little pale about the gills for such a ruddy-cheeked country gentleman.

'I wonder, sir, could you fetch me a nice clean sheet or two, and a pillow for the lady's head?' she enquired tactfully. 'And then if you go and keep an eye out for the doctor, I think Frank and I can manage here.'

'Of course, of course,' Mr Warburton said, thankfully making his escape. 'Ring if you need me – shall I send Mary back, in case you need another pair of hands?'

'Yes sir, if you would.'

Mrs Gilmour had managed to undress her patient without once causing Frank to blush. Now she bade him build up the fire and herself began to hoist Lily into a sitting position.

'Come on, my dear, up with you, and then when the pains change you'll be able to help yourself,' she said cheerfully. 'There's some jobs as a man only hinders and birth's one of 'em, so you take yourself off, Frank, and Mrs Haslington and I will get on with the job in hand!'

Lily saw the doctor in the light of the candle whilst she was still on the terrace and relief flooded out pain for a moment. So he had come, he had somehow managed to find her! He carried her indoors and laid her on a bed and then the midwife arrived, but not the frightening, tight-lipped woman who had so distressed Lily before. This one was plump and friendly and practical, and she sent the doctor away and made Lily sit up and held her hand and chattered away until Lily found she wanted to have the baby quietly and easily so that this woman would think her a sensible soul.

Presently, though, the pains got closer and closer, so that it was hard to think straight at all. Sweat ran continually down her face, stinging her eyes, salty on her lips, and the midwife took both Lily's hands in her own and said, 'Shove, my dear, shove with all your might and main. Hold on to my hands and concentrate . . . close your eyes and just shove as hard as you know how.'

Lily had been frightened to be told to bear down, bite blankets and pull rope, but this was natural, this woman was helping her, supporting her in a way which no one had done for a long time. She clung to the friendly, slippery hands and shoved as she was told and in between shoves she let the woman wipe the sweat from her face, sipped the hot tea she was offered and smiled and smiled and tried to say thank you to her new friend.

'You're doing well – the head's showing,' the woman said at one point. 'Bless me, your littl'un will be born before you know it.'

Heartened by this and similar comments, Lily worked hard. Scarlet-faced, she strove and the midwife strove and in between shoves the midwife told her she was a really good gal, a right brave lass, and all of a sudden, when she had begun to believe that she would shove for ever and never give birth, there was a sudden blinding, splitting pain followed immediately by a great easement, a slithering relief, and the woman shouted, then let go Lily's hands.

'You've done it, my gal, you've done it!' she crowed. 'My, you've had a right handsome little lad!'

Lily felt blankets lap her round, allowed herself to sink back on to the pillows, and heard, from what seemed far away, a fractious but determined howling.

'Now isn't that a thing?' demanded a voice above her head. 'A fine lad, Dr Maddison, delivered by meself and the young lady with not a doctor nor a midwife nearer than a mile. Come along in now, Mr Warburton, for it's all over, and Mrs Haslington's got her little lad.'

The man Lily had thought was the doctor came forward, a hand held out, but he changed his mind when he saw her exhausted face and patted her shoulder very kindly instead.

'How do you do, my dear? I'm your neighbour, Sidney Warburton, and this is Dr Maddison who was to have attended you. The midwife isn't here yet, but never fear, we'll clean you up as soon as the doctor's seen to the little lad.'

'I don't think . . . Dr Maddison? I was to have been attended by Dr Paulet.'

The man with her baby in his arm smiled, looking at her over the top of a pair of gold-rimmed half-glasses.

'That's right, my partner. I'm afraid he was out when Mr Warburton's man called, so I came instead. I'll just see to this young man, Mrs Haslington, and then I think we'll get you upstairs to a proper bed. Do you know what time it is?'

'Er . . . I suppose it must be quite ten o'clock,' Lily said. 'I was walking in the grounds at four o'clock, I remember that much.'

'Ten o'clock? No, my dear, it's three in the morning! I dare say your husband's out of his mind with worry, so we've sent a man round to the Hall with the news of your whereabouts and I don't doubt he'll be here by the time you're tucked up in that bed I mentioned.' He transferred his attention to the child in his arm. 'We'll get this chap into a warm bath first, then Mrs Gilmour can wrap him up warmly and put him in a drawer lined with blanket . . .'

'We've a perfectly good cradle,' Mr Warburton said, smiling at Lily.

'My daughter screamed very lustily in it when she was first born and I've kept it so that her child can be rocked to sleep in it one day. Your little lad is welcome to it, whilst he's under my roof.'

'Is your daughter having a baby too?' Lily asked, as she was carefully lifted on to the kitchen door, removed from its hinges for the purpose of acting as a stretcher to get her up the stairs.

'Not that I know of, but my daughter's far away, in China, with her young husband,' Mr Warburton said. 'So I shall claim the honour of carrying young Master Haslington upstairs to your new abode. What will you name him?'

Lily turned to smile at Mrs Gilmour, still hovering.

'I think that's up to the lady who helped him get born. What would you like to call him Mrs . . . er . . .'

'I'm Josie Gilmour, Ma'am,' the housekeeper said. 'Dear me – I'm to have the naming of him? Well, what do you think of the name Philip? That's the name I'd have given my son, if I'd had one, but I only had daughters.'

'Philip Haslington. Yes, that's lovely,' Lily said languidly. She was quiet as they carried her up the stairs, and rolled into the clean sheets in a pretty, candlelit room without speaking again, for she was so tired even a word was an effort. She had actually fallen asleep when Arnold was ushered in.

'Lily! Darling! You've had us all in the most fearful flap – we've had search-parties out, we sent a man into town to inform the police, we almost started to drag the river – Mother's been in tears, the girls were distraught . . . but all's well that ends well!' He bent and kissed her, stroking her cheek with fingers that shook a little. 'What happened?'

'Go and look at your son,' Lily ordered, and smiled as Arnold's cursory glance became an intent and rather gratified stare. 'What do you think of him?'

'He's nice,' Arnold said. 'What a fat, puffy little face he has, but I like it. What's his name?'

'Philip. Do you like it?'

'Yes, of course I do, if you do. Actually, it's rather a good name. I don't remember you suggesting it before, though. I thought you rather favoured Edmund.'

'Yes, but this baby is Philip,' Lily said, defeating any argument before it began. 'Why did you want to search the river?'

'Well, Mother thought . . . she said she hadn't always been as kind as she should have been . . . I told her it was all nonsense, but the girls reproached her with the way she's behaved . . . she was so sorry, she cried like anything . . . when she heard you'd been found she kept saying, *Thank you, God, oh, thank you, I'll never behave like that again,* which I dare say you understand better than I.'

86

'Yes, I do,' Lily said drowsily. 'Perhaps now you'll agree to us having our own house.'

'We'll see,' Arnold said. 'Just you go to sleep now, my love. Mr Warburton says I can stay here with you and keep you safe until you wake tomorrow.'

'Oh, Arny,' Lily was beginning, when there was the sound of footsteps clattering up the stairs and then a maid burst into the room without knocking.

'Oh, Mr Arnold, it's your father,' she said without preamble. 'A man's come running from the Hall in such a state . . . he's been taken ill. Your mother says will you come at once, please, as fast as you can.'

'I won't be long, my love,' Arnold said, getting to his feet. He bent and kissed Lily's brow. 'Go to sleep, and I'll be back before you know it.'

But he was gone all night and when he finally returned, as dawn was paling the sky to the east, it was to tell Lily that her father-in-law had died an hour earlier.

# CHAPTER SIX

It was a warm day in early June. Adeline had taken her small folding stool, her sketch book and pencils into the village and had set the stool up in front of the temple. The scene before her was so irresistible that she had felt impelled to have a go at immortalizing it on paper; and despite her initial doubts, what was gradually growing beneath her pencil pleased her.

It was an attractive temple, gold tiled and gaily bannered in scarlet and blue, but as far as Adeline was concerned it was merely a backdrop for the courtyard with its red-trunked pine trees, the thicket of bamboo which rustled every time the wind stirred, and the children playing in the dust. They were attracted by the pool, of course, with its fishy denizens moving in the depths and the surface half grown over with beautiful lotuses. Adeline did quick sketches of the people – a round-faced girl child with a severe fringe and a centre parting, a little boy, still in girl's clothing so that the vengeful spirits did not realize he was his parents' heir, the old grandmother keeping her eye on them, thin and bent and grey-haired, but with a shrill voice to call the children to attention and an unnervingly fast scuttle when a charge strayed too near the fascinating lotus pool.

The background did not move, however, so that could be drawn in properly, at her leisure, and this was what Adeline was doing now, having sketched the children in a dozen different poses. She had a paintbox and some water, too, and now she was putting in, delicately, the suspicion of colour which she would later build up with long, firm strokes into the finished product.

The big sketches she kept in her folder but she usually made smaller ones, quick drawings, briefly coloured, which could be sent home to show friends and family where she was, what she was doing. She finished the background on the easel and pinned a piece of paper over it. She would do a small sketch now to accompany her latest letter to Bella. She always took great care over such work because you never knew, Arnold might pick it up and give her a momentary thought in the midst of his busy, happy life.

It was not easy to put her memories of Arnold behind her, to forget him altogether, though it should have been a simple matter enough. He had been her first love, she supposed, and even now, very much in love with John and without the sight of Arnold and his wife to distress her, she still thought of him surprisingly often. Whenever she enjoyed something with John she found herself wondering what it would have been like with Arnold. What would Arnold have thought . . . felt . . . said . . . went through her mind a dozen times a day. And now, of course, he was a father – and she was shortly to become a mother! It gives us a link, Adeline told herself, deftly pencilling in the group of pines and the small figures playing in their shade.

Arnold had a son, Philip. The news had taken weeks to reach China, but Bella had been full of it in her last letter and so, oddly enough, had Adeline's father. Fancy that girl having the baby in my father's library, and fancy the baby sleeping in my very own cradle, where I once slept and where my child will one day lie, Adeline thought, awed by the way that even fate seemed determined not to let her forget Arnold. Her father's letter, written a day or so later than Bella's, had described Mr Haslington's funeral, his own sense of loss. Bella had been stunned by the suddenness of it, had confided to her friend that she did not, in her heart, believe he was gone.

'I wait for him at mealtimes,' she wrote, 'and seem to hear his tread on the stair, but of course we will all adjust, with time. And it will make a difference when Mother and I move out, because I think we shall have to; Lily wants the house to herself, big though it is, and I suppose it's for the best, for she and Mother don't get on and Arnold says she'll never learn to keep house if she isn't given the opportunity to be mistress here. So we'll move into a house which Arnold is buying for us in Langforth and come out to the Hall on high days and holidays, or when Arnold and Lily invite us. It will be strange, and seems very hard on the younger ones, but

Mother is very subdued since the night Lily ran away to have her baby by herself, and just agrees with whatever is suggested.'

Reading the letter Adeline had wondered, not for the first time, if this Lily was perhaps not a very nice person. Fancy turning her husband's mother and his sisters and brother out of the home they had been born in, just because she fancied keeping house without a mother-in-law to advise and interfere! But her father had been most impressed with young Mrs Arnold.

'A delightful young woman, just the type of girl who would make you a good friend one of these days,' he had written. 'She's brave and very pretty indeed and sensible . . . she'll make Arnold a fine wife when she's found her feet a little more, and of course she'll make our Philip a fine mother!'

*Our* Philip, Adeline noted, and felt a little shaft of sourness, a taste of jealousy, on her tongue. But this was petty, mean behaviour. Her father wanted a grandchild and heaven knew he was too far away to see a lot of the child she would bear in a couple of months' time, so it was nice for him to become attached to Arnold's little son.

As for she and Lily becoming friends – who knew, perhaps they might be as close as she and Bella had once been, when she and John returned from China to live at home. After all, Arnold liked me and then decided he liked her better, Adeline argued when her baser self announced that it had nothing whatsoever in common with the young Mrs Haslington. It stands to reason, surely, that two women, both beloved of Arnold, would find they had many mutual interests?

But she had finished her sketches, so she packed them all into the big folder and strolled to the archway to see where P'an was. He had carried down her things for her and would be waiting somewhere, but no doubt he had found someone to talk to during the hour or so she had spent drawing.

He was not in sight and the stool was cumbersome, so Adeline went and sat on the low stone bench in the courtyard, facing the archway on to the road. Here, some five minutes later, she was surprised by her friend Joanna Wang, who came into the courtyard in a rickshaw and jumped down, hailing Adeline loudly.

'Here you are! I've done a heap of shopping . . . dear Wang let me down at your place and Mr Sawyer said you'd gone into the village, so I thought I might meet you at the market. Your P'an was there and he said he thought you'd still be drawing at the temple, so I got the boy to bring me straight here.'

The latest in a long line of husbands, for Joanna, was a Chinese merchant and haulier, a very rich man who did not appear to mind that Joanna's feet were unbound, her hair crinkly and mouse-brown or her eyes grey, for she was his chief wife.

'His only wife,' Joanna was apt to remark, 'for all the rest are concubines.'

Adeline did not know whether this was true or merely wishful thinking, but she did know that Joanna had become a Buddhist and was the most interesting person, so far, to visit her in Ayiteng. She had come to Shanghai originally, she said, as wife to a sailor and upon his death had married another seaman and on *his* death, a diplomat. This made even the trusting Adeline blink, for Joanna was warm, strident and jolly and painted her face without even trying to imitate naturalness. What diplomat would put up with that? But perhaps when she was married to the diplomat she had not painted, perhaps that had come in later years, like the Buddhism.

When asked about her conversion to that faith, Joanna was typically blunt.

'I don't see much to heaven, and harps,' she said. 'It wouldn't suit me – I wouldn't enjoy it at all. Now the Buddhists say if you're good you come back as a higher form of life – so I might be a princess, or wife to a lord – and if you're bad you come back as something lower, say a bond-maiden, or a Persian cat. Now I'm no saint, but I'm better than a good few people I know. Got a kind heart, I have, and I'm generous to a fault, always have been. So I thought it all out and decided I'd rather put all my money on one horse and go for a lord's wife next time round.'

Adeline knew it was vain to try to persuade Joanna that a belief was a belief and not a certainty and that backing the Buddhist horse did not necessarily mean she would therefore become a part of the Wheel of Life, to return to earth again in some different form. Instead, she had turned the conversation to babies, and though Joanna thought it very nice that her new friend was pregnant, she assured her that having children had never been one of her own ambitions.

'Good thing, too,' she said. 'It's bad enough getting a new husband when one of 'em snuffs it, but imagine trying to persuade each feller that they wanted someone else's sprogs! No, dear, I'm better on me tod.'

Now, however. Adeline got to her feet and waved P'an over to collect her belongings.

'Nice to see you, Joanna,' she said cheerfully, arranging her long gown so that it fell in disguising folds across her stomach. 'Will you come back to my place for some tea, or shall we go to a tea-house?'

'We'll go to your place,' Joanna said. 'I've got something to tell you, and I don't want a lot of Chinks overhearing.'

Adeline winced; she could not help herself. Joanna was married to a Chinese; did this not make her feel guilty at using words like 'Chink'? But apparently it did not.

'Wang's gone on to Peking, to see the Old Buddha – or her ministers, rather – about a shipment,' Joanna said, heaving herself back into her rickshaw and then leaning confidingly nearer to Adeline so that the vehicle sagged alarmingly over to one side. 'He left me here because of the troubles . . . said it would be easier to sell his stuff if he didn't have a foreign devil alongside him.' She giggled. 'Imagine me, a foreign devil, and married to him for seven years next October.'

'Yes, John said something about the secret societies becoming dangerous in the north,' Adeline admitted. She was walking quite fast to keep up with the rickshaw and Joanna, noticing this, shrieked something to her coolie which caused him to grin and glance over his shoulder at her even as he slowed. 'What's your husband selling, do you know?'

'Yes . . . look, you save your breath for walking. We'll talk when we reach your place,' Joanna said. 'Here, P'an, want to dump that stuff across me legs? Make life a bit easier.'

There was no doubt about it, Joanna was an enigma in some ways, Adeline thought as they passed out through the village gates and began to make their way back to the mission. She was often very rude about the Chinese and used a rickshaw when Adeline felt so sorry for the coolies pulling them that she almost always walked, yet she had offered to take the painting things and the stool across her knees when she was already hot and would become hotter under the extra burden.

It was clear that she was hot because her paint was running, her face gleaming with sweat and colours. Joanna noticed Adeline looking and dabbed at her face with a handkerchief, then examined the now colourful piece of linen.

'Hmm! Always happens in the heat, but what's a girl to do once she's past her first flush? Never mind, better a warm day here than the oven that's Shanghai. And better either, I dare say, than London on a rainy day. Ah, here we are . . . what's Amatei got cooking?'

There was a fair to-do in the courtyard whilst Joanna got herself and all her shopping untangled from the rickshaw, paid the man off, handed over Adeline's stuff and then headed for the big courtyard where tea would be served on a terrace surrounded by shade trees and cool with the tinkling of a tiny stream. Presently the two women found themselves seated in comfortable chairs with a small table between them, and before they had had a chance to exchange more than the most commonplace of remarks Amatei and Yenala were approaching them from the kitchen with trays of delicacies and of course with the inevitable tea-making paraphernalia.

'Afternoon, Amatei; hello, Yenala, my dear,' Joanna said briskly. 'You'll see to the tea, will you Yenala? Good, for I think you should hear what I'm going to tell your mistress.'

In vain to try to explain to Joanna that she was not exactly Yenala's mistress . . . and vainer to try to explain the same thing to Yenala, who considered herself very much Adeline's slave. So Adeline let the remark stand and handed round rice cakes and tiny sandwiches whilst Yenala boiled the kettle on the spirit stove, put the dried leaves into the pot, combined the two and finally poured the tea into three beautiful lily-leaf cups.

'These sandwiches are delicious,' Joanna declared, her mouth full of thinly sliced cucumber. 'Now are you listening?'

'Of course. And after all this mystery it had better be worth listening to,' Adeline replied with spirit. 'Not bazaar gossip, I hope, Joanna?'

Joanna did not rise to this promising bait, however. 'No, not bazaar gossip, though that comes into it,' she said. 'Adeline, my dear, do you know what type of goods the Old Buddha has been buying from Wang and other traders?'

'Marble carriages, to go with her marble ship?' Adeline asked flippantly, for the spending of state money on a large marble ship to embellish her lake had long been held against the Empress Dowager. 'Or could it be more concubines for the Lord of Ten Thousand Years?'

'How do you know they call the Emperor that?' asked Joanna, momentarily distracted. 'Poor fellow, he has no say in anything, you know; the Empress Dowager treats him like the weakling he is. But she isn't buying ships or slave girls, she's buying guns.'

'Guns? Well I suppose her troops need them.'

'Also siege guns.'

'Siege guns? Is she afraid that someone is liable to lay siege to Peking?'

'No one knows. Has John talked to you about the secret society called *I Ho Chuan*? Literally translated it means the Fists of Righteous Harmony.'

'Oh, you mean the Boxers,' Adeline said at once. 'He's said they're a bad lot. There was gossip in the bazaar . . .' both women giggled over the familiar phrase '. . . but John said it was just superstitious mumbo-jumbo and if there was real trouble the Old Buddha would soon put a stop to it. I say, is that why she's buying guns, do you think?'

'That's what I thought when Wang first mentioned it. But when Wang said he'd do better in Peking without me I began to wonder. You know the Chinese have genuine grievances against us, I dare say?'

Adeline nodded vigorously. 'Yes, I do. Real grievances as well as imagined ones. I mean they say we offend against the *feng-shui*, but how could we not? The Chinese bury their dead in a very random fashion and then don't even mark the graves, so of course when the railway was built it probably did cross unmarked burial grounds. And then there's the business about making the Chinese trade whether they want to or not, and pushing our badly made goods on them. But on the other hand in the clinic the other day a woman was thanking me for saving her baby's life and saying I was different from other *yang kuei-tzu* because everyone knew that when a foreign devil built a house or a pig-sty he buried live Chinese babies in the foundations to placate the gods! That sort of talk just makes me so furious!'

'Yes, I've heard that,' Joanna nodded. 'Well, let me get on or Wang will be calling for me before I've finished! So the Chinese have grievances which are real enough, not just the *feng-shui* being offended and so on but the way we all behave – coming into their country and calmly annexing bits of it, forcing them to sign treaties which are to our advantage and their disadvantage, making them buy goods from us which they would far rather manufacture themselves . . . oh, the list is endless, but right at the top of the list, I dare say, they would put our desire to change their nice, comfortable religious beliefs for our own.'

'Oh, dear, don't let John hear you say that! I try to tell myself that Jesus wants everyone to believe in Him, but . . . go on, what else?'

'Well, the Boxers are killing Rice-Christians and genuine converts whenever they get the chance. They say they'll make the country Chinese again and that must mean they'll attack Westerners. I wonder if the Old Buddha is buying guns to secretly arm the Boxers.'

'My goodness, Joanna, this is frightening. John's going into Peking tomorrow and I was wondering whether to go with him, but perhaps I ought not? I'd be a heavy burden on him if he had to fight off these men . . . and I'll tell him to make sure to take a gun and several of our people with him. What else ought I to do?'

'I can't tell you, my dear, but hopefully you're sufficiently out of the way here to escape trouble. Ayiteng is a tiny village, and your mission is mainly the clinic and the surgery. Even your converts – forgive me – are few in number compared with some missions which run schools or orphanages. Does John have to go to Peking tomorrow?'

Adeline sighed.

'Yes, indeed he does, for we're rapidly running out of medicines, and quite a lot of things like dressings, bandages . . . yes he must go tomorrow, we can't leave it much longer. But I'll tell him what you've said and beg him to take care.'

'Good,' Joanna said, rising. 'I had best gather my parcels together for Wang will call for me before sunset. I hope I haven't worried you for no reason, dear Adeline, but I've lived in China long enough to know that frightened people who believe everything they're told can do desperate and wicked things.' She turned to Yenala, who had been listening, wide-eyed, to every word. 'Take care of your mistress,' she said. 'And of yourself, little one! Incidentally, does John possess a gun?'

'Well, yes, he does,' Adeline said rather guiltily. A gun for shooting ducks and things. At home he was a keen marksman but he hasn't had very much chance to shoot over here.'

'Then I'll only leave you with two pistols, one for yourself and one for Yenala,' Joanna said, putting two parcels down on the table amidst the ruin of the tea. 'No, on second thoughts I'll leave the three anyway. Lin might need one.'

Whilst the two girls were still staring at her, however, there was a shout from the outer courtyard and one of the servants came running in.

'Missie Wang, husband here,' he said breathlessly. 'You come now?'

In the fluster and bustle of departure, Adeline only had time to thank her for the pistols and to assure her that she very much hoped they would never be used.

'For I'm sure neither Yenala nor I could aim the things, let alone fire them,' she admitted. 'However, perhaps they will be a deterrent.'

'I hope you won't need them at all,' Joanna assured her. 'But remember, love, if all else fails and you fall into hands which . . . which mean you harm . . .' She looked at Adeline, started to speak again, and then shook her head ruefully. 'No, I can't put it into words. Take care!'

After she had gone Adeline and Yenala cleared away the tea things and fed the fish in the pool, casting the food gleefully on the clear water and watching the eager mouths gulping, the fat sides gleaming. Then they went to Adeline's room so that she could get ready for the main meal of the day, with John.

'Missie . . . what did Mrs Wang mean, when she said if you fell into hands which meant you harm . . .' Yenala asked presently, brushing out Adeline's long fall of hair.

'Umm . . . I think she meant . . . well, that I could use the gun on myself,' Adeline said awkwardly. 'But I dare say she was being a bit over-dramatic. I hope she was!'

Yenala continued brushing for a moment, and Adeline, looking at her face reflected in the mirror before her, remembered that not so very long ago Yenala had seriously tried to poison herself because life had been unbearable.

'Don't worry, my love,' Adeline said softly. 'I'm sure it won't come to that. Mrs Wang was just trying to prove to me that she was serious.'

But Yenala, brushing away, continued to look sombre.

'Mrs Wang was right,' she said at last. 'Missie Adeline, I've not said anything, but they're saying in the market that . . . that a missionary has been killed in Shantung province. A white missionary and his white wife.'

Because of Joanna's visit, John put off his trip to Peking for a week, but at the end of that time, since nothing had happened and the Boxers appeared to have got no nearer Peking, he put it to Adeline that he really should go.

'But how are you, love? Are you fit to be left?' he asked her anxiously, on the evening prior to his proposed departure. 'There's no danger here, I'm sure of it, otherwise I'd take you with me. If there is danger, it'll be in the city . . . no, not in it, because the Imperial troops are quartered in Peking, but near it . . . on the outskirts, perhaps.'

'I'm very well,' Adeline assured him. 'Can I give you my shopping list? There are just a few things for me, most of it's for the clinic. I can always buy sweets for the children in the market, but I want some cotton stockings now that the weather's better, and some mosquito netting to keep the flies off the patients who stay overnight.'

94

'I'll see to it; just give me your list,' John told her. He put an arm round her shoulder and steered her towards the door. 'Let's go over to the dispensary now, and then through to the clinic, and check that I've got a note of everything we need.'

'You'll take Lin?' Adeline asked anxiously. 'He can ride my mare – she's faster than the mule.'

'Of course I'm taking him. And Pao and Chu. The four of us will be more than a match for any Boxer lurking around the city. I'll leave you a pistol, of course, but I'll take Yenala's because I'm sure you won't need either of them.'

They did the rounds of the dispensary shelves, checked the clinic, and then returned to their living-room to eat pork and rice with spring greens followed by a dish of wild strawberries lightly dusted with sugar which Adeline gobbled with such gusto that John told her she must be expecting triplets at least.

'I hope not!' Adeline said, horrified at the thought. 'One baby at a time is plenty, thank you!'

After their meal they sat for a while chatting and writing letters home, and then they made their way to bed.

'I won't wake you when I leave in the morning,' John said, kissing her on the tip of her nose as she snuggled into the quilts. 'And don't expect me back until the evening of the following day or perhaps even the day after that. It's a forty-mile ride to the city, and then we've got to order all our stuff and wait for it, and the journey home will be a hard one, encumbered as we shall be with our goods. Now take care of yourself, and look after Yenala, if she'll let you!'

'I'll take great care,' Adeline murmured sleepily. 'I thought we . . . that is Yenala and me . . . might take a picnic up by the lake either tomorrow or the day after. It's getting very hot in the compound now, and it's so cool and lovely in the mountains.'

'Yes, do that,' agreed John, shrugging the covers up over his shoulders. 'There's a beautiful valley up in the mountains, all green and gold, and the wildlife's special, so they tell me. Not bears or anything frightening but very beautiful birds and small mammals.'

'Hmm. Any snakes?'

'Oh, I shouldn't think so. Yenala will know, she's none too fond of snakes herself. Now don't forget, I may not manage to get home the day after tomorrow, but I'll definitely make it the day after that. Now go to sleep, and I'll try to get up very quietly so that you may have a good rest.'

Despite John's care, however, Adeline awoke when he was stealing about the room getting dressed. At first she merely sat up, leaning on one elbow, and watched, but as he pulled on his riding boots she jumped heavily out of the quilts, scrambled into a dressing-gown and slippers, and sallied forth beside him out to the stable yard, her bedtime pigtail swinging over one shoulder.

John mounted his horse, a big black gelding with a white star on its forehead and three white socks. He had named the horse Thunderer and loved it devotedly. Lin Shen was riding Adeline's chestnut mare, Bridget, and the two Chinese menservants rode the square, strong little local ponies, Pao on a dusty roan, Chu on a sturdy bay with a hog-cut black mane.

Adeline waved them off as the sky was lightening and saw that they were all armed, though inconspicuously, and that they were clearly in holiday mood. John loved riding and was looking forward to visiting the head of his mission in the city; Lin Shen had relatives in Peking; and Pao and Chu were young enough to simply look forward to seeing the big city for the first time. Once they had gone out through the big wooden doors the old doorkeeper swung them closed once again and Adeline went back to her bedroom, feeling rather flat and empty. She looked at the pile of quilts but the thought of trying to sleep alone, without John's comforting warmth at her back, was not appealing. Instead, she poured water into the bowl and began to wash. She might as well get dressed now that she was so thoroughly awake, she supposed. Dawn was turning the courtyards into charcoal pictures but soon the sun would edge over the horizon and she could start her daily tasks.

Breakfast would not be arriving for a while yet, however, so Adeline took a packet of charcoal and some grey paper and sat on the little terrace, reducing the scene before her, with stark and simple lines, into a thing of extraordinary beauty despite its total colourlessness.

She finished the first sketch, cast it on the ground, and reached for the next piece of paper. Far away in the dark blue of the sky above her there was a fine nail-paring which was the moon, making its way down the brightening sky. Seen through the branches of the tall pine which grew in the stable yard . . . its top showing over the crenellated and tiled wall which stood between . . . Adeline's charcoal swooped and smudged, never faltering. Soon the slender moon, the dark sky and the pine were committed to paper and Adeline was picking up yet another sheet.

By the time the sun came up and Yenala called that breakfast was ready Adeline was surrounded by sketches. She gathered up her work, smiled at the younger girl, and glanced at the sketches as she made her way to the breakfast table. They were good. More than that, they were very good. She had somehow managed to catch the very essence of that oriental dawn simply by drawing lines, and what was more, if you looked at the sketches in sequence, as they had been drawn, you could see the dawn coming, giving way to the sunrise, in a way which Adeline would have thought impossible without using colour, had she not seen it with her own eyes.

Pleased with her early work, Adeline sat down and began to eat her porridge. Presently, Yenala joined her, for she usually shared her breakfast with Adeline and John though she preferred to eat her luncheon in the kitchen with the rest of the staff.

'Yo Liu wants to know whether you'd like bacon-egg today,' she said, with a twinkle in her eyes, for every morning Yo asked the same question and every morning – or very nearly every morning – Adeline said that she would prefer a soft-boiled egg and some bread and butter.

'Other Europeans eat bacon-egg,' Yo grumbled over his sizzling pans. 'These ones have to be different, oh yes, different so Yo can never show them how good he make bacon-egg.'

Having ordered her soft-boiled egg, which arrived with an alacrity which showed that Yo had already cooked it in anticipation of her request, Adeline ate it whilst Yenala made bread and butter fingers and poked them seriously into her own runny yolk, the two of them chattering comfortably as they had their meal.

'This morning we'll do some shopping,' Adeline decided as Amatei began to clear the table. 'Is there anything you want in the kitchen?'

Amatei paused, a laden tray on her hip.

'Yes . . . mushrooms, Missie, and egg . . . many egg . . . the chickens aren't laying much. We've plenty rice . . . my man kill chicken who don' lay, so plenty chicken. You get us pork-meat maybe? And cinnamon for little cake.'

'Right. Yenala, would you write those things down, please? And in English, if you can. I'll tell you what the words are if you've forgotten.'

Presently, the two of them, the little girl and the young woman, made their way out of the compound and into the village, a basket on Adeline's arm and another swinging from Yenala's hand. The market was all set up by the time they arrived, the stallholders trading briskly, though as Adeline and Yenala began to move along the colourful rows it struck Adeline that there was less talk and chatter than usual. Quietness follows me like the wake of a ship, she thought, awed. The Chinese are a friendly, noisy people; it's not natural for them to let a stranger pass unchallenged, not to ask as many intimate questions as they can fit into the time you are within range. Yet today . . .

'What's the matter with everyone, old man?' Yenala asked gaily when they reached the sweetmeat stall. The sweetmeat seller liked Adeline. It was from him that she bought all the sweets which she gave away to good children at the clinic, and because she was an excellent customer and a cheerful, friendly soul the sweetmeat seller saved little gifts for her and gossiped away to her as though she and he were friends of long standing.

'Ho . . . troubles in the land,' the sweetmeat seller said evasively. 'Gangs of ruffians, roving bands of evil men . . . there are always rumours.'

'Do you mean the . . .' The look in the old man's eyes cut the words off short. He was genuinely frightened, Adeline saw. She cleared her throat.

'Do you live here in the village, my friend? If not, would you care to come in to the mission compound and stay for a few days, until rumour says the ruffians have moved on?'

'I shall do very well; I'm old and I earn my rice,' the old man said. 'And your compound is no shelter for such as I.'

Adeline frowned down at her sandalled feet.

'Is it true, then, what they say? That those who wear the white and scarlet hate the Christians? So you feel you are safer here, in the village?'

She had spoken in a low voice and the old man leaned forward, cupping a hand round his ear as if to hear her better, but instead of listening, he spoke.

'Go back to your compound, Missie, and keep your gates shut and tell your gatekeeper to open to no one unless he knows them well. Bring water and set guards.' This he had hissed beneath his breath but now he spoke out loud. 'The ginger sweets are hot for the mouths of the small ones; take the red, sticky ones, for they are delicious, flavoured with mint and apple, and cheap, Missie, very cheap . . .'

Considerably shaken, Adeline and Yenala went back home to the compound, clutching their purchases. It was a clear, bright day and Adeline made her way into the kitchen to consult Yo Liu and his wife about what the sweetmeat seller had said.

'If there is going to be trouble it will be today,' Yo said heavily, after some thought. 'It is ever thus . . . market day, you see, Missie. If evil men come, then they want rich pickings. But I don't think anyone will come to a little place like this. They'll go to a decent-sized village, or a town, even.'

'Then what should we do? Must we close the gates?'

'It wouldn't hurt,' Yo said. And have P'an get some of the boys to keep a look-out. You can see people from a good way off coming across the paddy fields. Tell him the Boxers wear red and white . . . though I dare say he already knows.'

Accordingly, Yenala ran to tell the gatekeeper to let people in for the clinic only if they were old patients. A cheerful young man called Lao Kuang, in whom John reposed much confidence, who was changing dressings and administering pills to the chosen few, finished with his patients and locked the clinic doors, then went to join the look-outs. They perched in trees or on the walls of the compound – for the walls were very high and tiled steeply – and called out to each other, cracked dried melon seeds and spat the shells on to the ground. At Adeline's suggestion P'an cut back the branches of such trees as actually overhung the wall, then everyone waited.

In vain. The day passed peacefully. As the sun set they could hear the traders from the market wending their way home, calling to one another, laughing and joking. If they fell silent for a little as they passed the mission, it was not to be wondered at, for though Adeline was sure it was all nonsense the sweetmeat seller had clearly believed that Christians were less safe than villagers.

'Shall we leave watchers on the walls all night?' Adeline asked P'an as dusk crept across the compound. 'It seems a bit far-fetched now.'

'They could see nothing anyway, and our gates are stout,' P'an said. He was a young and cheerful Chinese, pockmarked but always happy, and a great favourite with the young women. He wore his blue summer cotton with an air and was always smartly turned out considering he worked hard in all the courtyards in the compound. Adeline got on well with him and frequently set him knotty horticultural problems, all of which he managed to solve. She had actually acquired a very fine wisteria to remind her of home, and P'an had planted it in an auspicious spot and was already predicting great things for it.

By bedtime, Adeline was feeling a good deal more relaxed, but this feeling was speedily put to rout by Yenala, who came into her room dragging her quilts behind her.

'Missie Adeline, I'm going to sleep in here, on your floor,' she announced firmly. 'Amatei just told me that the Boxers are only soldiers of the War-Lords, and everyone knows that War-Lords attack at night. So they've locked and bolted the gates and some of the younger men are up in the trees, listening and watching, and they'll keep watch until dawn.'

'You aren't sleeping on the floor. You can share my quilts; it'll be very cosy,' Adeline told the child firmly. 'It will be nice for me to have you to keep my back warm!'

After this, she thought she would not be able to sleep at all, and indeed she and Yenala lay awake for an hour, discussing in low tones what Mr John was doing and how glad they would be when the endless night was over. But without either realizing it they must have been growing sleepier and sleepier, for both abruptly fell asleep soon after midnight and slept soundly and apparently dreamlessly until the first cock started to crow.

# CHAPTER SEVEN

In the bright light of a sunny morning, the fears of the previous day seemed foolish in the extreme. Adeline sang as she dressed and Yenala sang too, her pretty little girl's voice rising in a trembling treble as Adeline switched from English songs to Chinese ones and back again.

Everyone was cheerful and breakfast was eaten in excellent spirits, with

Adeline showing Yenala how, as a child, she had made her porridge into a marsh riddled with paths by scooping out lines across it and then filling in the lines with milk.

'No news from the watchers?' she asked, as they finished their breakfast and prepared to leave the table. 'I saw P'an go by just now, whistling. He was pushing the wheelbarrow and didn't look at all warlike!'

'The danger's over; market day is over for another week and there will be no more fear of an attack until then,' Amatei said wisely, piling crockery on to her tray. 'Will you go out today, Missie? You said yesterday you might take Yenala to the mountains.'

'I think we shall,' Adeline said slowly. 'We can't stay in the compound for ever, and I shouldn't think brigands would attack two females and a little donkey, would you?'

'Not unless they could see you carried riches of some sort,' Amatei agreed. 'You have your outing; take P'an with you if you like . . . and you will take your gun, won't you?'

'Yes, I'll take it,' Adeline said. John had loaded the pistol, put the safety catch on and spent an afternoon teaching her how to shoot it. She supposed, doubtfully, that she could pull the trigger in earnest if she had to; she just hoped it would not be necessary.

'Well, then! Shall I pack you a basket of food?'

'No, Yenala can do it, then she can include all her favourite things,' Adeline said, smiling at the child. 'Go and get our picnic now, dear, and I'll put my sketching things into a folder. What would you like to take?'

'My fishing basket,' Yenala said promptly. Adeline laughed and shook her head at the child; the Chinese were a practical people. Yenala would enjoy a day out but it would grieve her to be up by the beautiful lake watching all the fish and unable to even try to catch some of them for a meal.

'All right, you little huntress! It's very hot already . . . I shall bathe in my camisole and drawers, so we'll take a towel, shall we? Or shall we just dry in the sun?'

'We'll dry in the sun, I should think,' Yenala said, giving her delightful, purring giggle. 'What a sight we shall be, Missie Adeline, both of us bare in the sun! Shall I put in the primus stove so we can make tea and cook the fish I catch?'

'Most certainly, although I don't think we'll rely on your fish making us a meal; we'll take plenty of food. But I'd like to be back well before sunset, just in case Mr John manages to get home today. What's more, if they shut the gates we don't want to be benighted out in the fields, do we?'

'Definitely not; though we wouldn't freeze,' Yenala said. 'I wish I could draw pictures, Missie Adeline! But at least I can fish.'

'I'll teach you to swim if you like,' Adeline offered. 'Just like a little frog.'

100

'Or a little boy. Do girls swim in your country? In China, girls aren't taught ever, I don't think.'

'Oh, I'm sure some girls are. Actually, Yenala, in my country most girls don't swim, which is very foolish of them. But we lived by a big, deep river and my father insisted that I learn to swim and row a boat just like a boy. He was afraid that I'd fall in and drown you see.'

'A big river? As big as the Yangtse?'

'What do you know about the Yangtse, young lady? No, not quite as big as that, but big for England. Go on, off with you and get our picnic or it will be luncheon time before we even leave!'

'I wouldn't mind two luncheons, one before we leave and one as soon as we arrive,' Yenala called over her shoulder as she flew across the courtyard. 'Will you tell P'an to get the donkey ready, Missie Adeline? I'm really excited!'

But when Adeline and Yenala, heavily laden, reached the stableyard they found that P'an had saddled not the donkey but the mule, a big, strong animal, though not fast.

'The mule can carry both,' P'an explained. 'He stronger; you be better with the mule.'

Because she often wore local dress, Adeline found it almost as easy to ride astride as sidesaddle, so she raised no objection to taking the mule. Indeed, it would have been next to impossible to have ridden sidesaddle on the tiny donkey which the servants used, so she was quite glad of the exchange. She had envisaged the donkey as a means of carrying their baggage, but the mule, with its great, muscular rump and shoulders, would make light work of both herself and Yenala as well as their belongings.

However, when at last they set out it was on foot, herself holding on to the mule's bridle on the left side and Yenala clinging on the other so that when they conversed they did so by leaning forward and talking across the mule's long brown nose.

'It is going to be a very hot day,' Adeline remarked after half an hour's solid trudging. 'I wish there was more of a breeze. It's stiflingly hot whenever the path goes between a tall crop, though at least it means there's shade on one side of the track.'

'It'll be cooler when we reach the mountains,' Yenala said hopefully. 'Did you know that Europeans from the cities often spend the summers in the mountains, where their children are safe from heat-fevers? Rich Chinese are beginning to follow suit.'

'In these mountains?' Adeline thought it might be rather nice to meet other Europeans. So far she had only met people like Joanna, who were passing through, and the odd missionary who was bound for the city and went out of his way to meet a fellow religionist.

'I don't think so, or not as far in as we're going,' Yenala admitted. 'They go high, high up, where the air is really cool and healthy. It would take us a very long time to go that far!'

'Well, never mind. But we'll reach the lake if it takes us all day; I'm just longing to paddle in cool water and feel able to bathe if we wish. What's more, everyone's told me how beautiful it is and I want to draw it.'

'And I want to fish it!' Yenala leaned over and checked, by touch, that her fishing basket was still hanging by the mule's side. It looked a bit like a wastepaper basket with no bottom and Yenala fished by staring down into the water until she saw a likely creature and then plopping the reed cylinder firmly down over her prey. She then plunged her hand and arm into the trap, seized her catch and flipped it up on to the bank. Though they had never visited the lake before, Adeline had watched the child fishing in the river and the irrigation dykes, and admired the skill and speed with which she sent the cylinder hurtling into the water.

'I wonder if we ought to ride for a bit, whilst we're still on the flat?' Adeline said presently. 'Once the track starts to climb it would be unfair to the mule, but now it ought to be able to carry us without too much bother. It isn't as though we want it to hurry, after all.'

They climbed on to the creature's patient, broad back, Adeline sitting in the saddle and Yenala clinging, monkeylike, round her waist whilst she perched on the broad rump. The mule lengthened its stride and after another half an hour or so Adeline saw that they were in the foothills.

'Do we just follow the track?' she asked Yenala. 'Or do we have to strike off presently?'

But Yenala assured her that the track led to the lake, so the two girls – for Adeline was little more – continued on their way, talking, telling each other stories, and learning each other's language in the best and least painful way.

Whilst they were on the plain the view had been restricted by crops, by the banks of the sunken lanes they had traversed, and by clumps of shade trees grown near the track, but as they began to climb the foothills they could see more. Looking behind them they could even see Ayiteng, the temple roof gleaming as though it really was tiled with gold, the other rooftops a pleasant jumble of assorted colour and the trees which were grown for their beauty as well as their shade towering over the high, reddish wall which completely surrounded every small village and town in northern China.

'The compound looks like a toy fort,' Adeline said as they paused for a moment to look back. 'Bright and clean and new . . . there's the big pine which P'an climbed last night, and the cherry tree whose branch was lopped off because it overhung the wall. I hope John isn't cross when he sees it . . . and that must be my walnut tree. Lin says it has wonderful crops and I love walnuts.'

'Let's keep moving, Missie Adeline,' Yenala said, ever practical. 'Or we won't arrive by the lake in time to eat our luncheon.'

They climbed on. Presently, Adeline remarked on the dearth of people and houses, for if she had learned one thing about China it was that the huge country was as densely populated even in these remote northern parts as some cities in her own land. She had travelled from the coast to the nearest station to Peking on the railway when she and John had first reached the country, and had been astounded to see from the window that every inch of the rich plain was cultivated and that you could not travel half a mile without seeing small dwellings, animal shelters and, always, people.

Open country, it seemed, was unheard of, but now the foothills were showing her another side of China, for though there were huts and cottages, they were already farther apart and less overcrowded. Yenala had the answer.

'The ground is not rich, not good for cultivation,' she told her companion. 'As we go higher you'll see fewer and fewer farms, fewer and fewer people. Herdsmen go high with their flocks, but because the grass is precious each great herd moves on continually during the summer, so though we may see goats or sheep the herdsman might be a mile away with the rest of the flock.'

'I'm glad,' Adeline said as they breasted a rise. 'To have so many people surrounding you can make you long to be alone for a while.'

Yenala was silent; she could not imagine anyone wanting to be alone, obviously. Adeline leaned forward and rumpled the child's hair.

'Families like being together in China, don't they? A man's sons work on his farm and continue to live in his house until they have sons of their own – and sons of their sons! All they do is build on another courtyard.'

'That's right. It's good too, until the crops fail and famine strikes. Then men leave home, go to the cities.'

They had been climbing as they talked and presently the landscape began to change again. There were trees now, not trees deliberately grown for shade but trees which had seeded themselves so that they stood amidst the rocks in family groups, rather like the Chinese themselves, Adeline thought. A group of pines, a group of maples, a group of willows, each one having found its niche and cast its seed to form its own gentle courtyard of trees, restricted only by the rocks which surrounded them.

There was grass here too, whenever the earth had managed to get a grip on the rock, thin grass dotted with wild flowers. As they climbed they saw trees and great bushes which Adeline associated with cultivated parks at home. Lilac, blooming sweetly, came to them first as a scent on the breeze before they saw its purple, and rhododendrons too, their brilliantly coloured blossoms mostly fallen now, but colourful still.

"Just a little further,' panted Yenala presently. 'See those tall trees? We go past them and then the path begins to wind down, towards the lake.'

Adeline doubted privately whether one clump of pines could possibly be used as a landmark, but her fears were shortlived. They reached the pines, the path began to curve downwards and there, below them, shining like a sapphire, was the lake.

'Oh!' gasped Adeline. 'Oh, it's so beautiful!' She might have sat down there and then and produced her sketching materials, but Yenala urged her on and the mule was already taking the first careful, dainty steps down the steep and rocky track.

'It is more beautiful down by the water,' Yenala said. 'Come on, Missie Adeline!'

Sooner than she had believed possible, Adeline found that they had reached the margin of the lake. A sandy shore was backed by pines and rocks and the water lapped, warm and inviting, as they sat themselves down beside it.

'Shall we bathe first?' Adeline said hopefully. Rather to her surprise the lake was deserted; no one fished on it, no one swam in it, no one picnicked by it.

'I'm hungry!' Yenala objected. 'Couldn't we eat first? Then we can bathe and I can fish and we'll eat my catch for our supper!'

As she spoke she began to open the picnic basket and Adeline discovered that she was hungry too. Behind them the mule, hobbled to prevent its wandering too far, cropped the short grass.

'Oh, all right, we'll eat right away then.' Adeline knelt beside the basket and watched as Yenala extracted the contents. 'Goodness, my dear, there's enough food there for an army! What shall we have first?'

'I'll light the primus and boil the kettle,' Yenala said, going down to the lake to dip out water. 'Let's have some bean curd first, to fill us up a bit. After that there's hard-boiled eggs with red peppers and then some sesame seed turnovers. Lovely!'

'That's fine,' Adeline said, nodding. 'Off we go, then!'

The two girls spread their picnic out on a convenient flat-topped rock and for a short while there was no sound save that of munching. But quite quickly the bowls were emptied, the turnovers eaten and the scented tea savoured and drunk. Yenala took their bowls down to the lake and swished them clean in the water whilst Adeline did the same for the lily-bloom cups, her favourites, as Amatei well knew. Then, replete, they lay in the sun until the heat forced them back into the shade, and there they slept.

Adeline woke to find the sun still high in the sky, but a good deal of the breathless heat seemed to have gone and a breeze lifted tendrils of her hair away from her head as she sat up. She looked round; no one about. Good!

In her drawers and camisole top she went into the water, and splashed the still sleeping Yenala until her companion shouted and sat up. Then the two of them paddled and Adeline gave Yenala her first swimming lesson before she decided she was getting tired and went and sat on a rock to dry off whilst Yenala fished.

It was always absorbing to watch Yenala fishing. How still she stood, how fierce the gaze that she bent on the water round her pale legs, how swiftly her trap entered the water, with scarcely a splash, when the inquisitive fish came over to see what two legs were doing, standing so still in their lake! Adeline watched for a bit, then reached for her sketch book. It was hard to immortalize Yenala fishing, but within Adeline's capabilities.

By the time Yenala tired of her task four good-sized lake trout had been flipped out on to the bank where Adeline cracked them dead with a rock sooner than see them suffer out of their natural element. Yenala came slowly out of the water, both sleeves, which had fallen down, soaked to the shoulder. She had taken off her socks, shoes and trousers but had retained the tunic, for modesty's sake, she said. Adeline smiled fondly at her. The younger girl's clothing was crumpled, her hair hung in wet rat-tails where she had splashed it when plunging the trap in and snatching the fish out, and she had dried water-droplets on her cheeks. But she radiated happiness and the pride of success.

'Well, Missie Adeline, what about that? Two big fishes each . . . never have I caught so many. I must be getting quicker as I grow bigger.'

'You gut them, then, and I'll light the primus,' Adeline said. She watched Yenala as the girl dealt with the fish; never had a child changed so much, she thought. A few months ago, when Yenala had first come to them, she had been totally incapable of laughing, shouting, or even of crying; fear had sealed in all her emotions. But trust, love and a full stomach had given her the confidence to enjoy almost everything she did. Adeline had heard the shrieks she gave as her hand encountered the trout, the triumphant yell as she flipped it to the bank, the breathless hoot when a fish managed to escape her trap. Even her silences are happy now, she told herself, remembering the quietness in which Yenala stood in the water, eyes steady on her feet, concentrating completely and gladly on the task in hand.

If there's a judgement, then I'm sure John and I will get more credit for letting Yenala become a natural, happy child again than for all the converts in China, she reflected. Not that their tally of converts was in any way remarkable, because it was not. By and large, the Chinese rather preferred their own religion and their own ways, but those who converted from conviction rather than hunger had proved to be loyal and zealous. Yenala was a convert, perhaps less from conviction than from a desire to please those who had done so much for her, but one day, John was convinced, she would realize that in Christ was salvation and for the time being he was happy to see her in church and to know that she strained every nerve to believe and to make sense of the faith that her beloved master and mistress embraced.

Cleaned and gutted, the trout fought for room in the pan and very soon Adeline and Yenala were eating freshly fried trout with fat bread rolls and butter to go with them and tea to wash them down. By the time they finished their meal, however, the sun was low in the sky, and Yenala bundled everything back into the basket and tied it into position on top of the mule's saddle bags whilst Adeline removed all traces of their picnic, buried the rubbish and smoothed the sand neatly once more.

'There! Always clear up after yourself and leave a place nice,' she instructed Yenala as they led the mule back up the steep mountain path. 'That way, everyone who comes here can enjoy the beauty, and it won't be spoiled for them by traces of another's meal.'

'I'll be glad when we reach the top and we can ride the mule again,' Yenala said breathlessly, as they scrambled upwards. 'I had a lovely time, but somehow I'm most awfully tired now.'

'Me too; but it'll be much quicker going home than it was reaching here,' Adeline comforted her. 'And as you say, we'll ride the mule once we're over the worst. It's still got your fish trap and my sketching things to carry, but we've eaten at least half the food, and it'll be going downhill all the way, pretty well.'

'What time will Mr John be home, if he gets back today?' Yenala asked presently. It was already quite dark beneath the trees and Adeline could see the whites of Yenala's eyes as she turned them from side to side. Realizing that the child wanted to talk so that she did not think about the loneliness of the encroaching dusk, Adeline immediately began to chatter.

'Well, it'll be late, probaby after dark, and possibly not even until tomorrow, so he said we weren't to worry. Now, my love, tell me how you come to know the lake so well!'

'I was born here,' Yenala said at once. 'I was not sold into bondage until I was almost five – my old mistress would not have bought a younger child; she would have had to feed such a one for many years before it was any use to her – so you see I once knew the foothills very well indeed.'

'And it never occurred to you to run home, back to your own family, when the woman began to mistreat you?'

'No, for a year after they sold me my whole family was wiped out in a cholera epidemic,' Yenala explained matter-of-factly. 'I did not find out for another year after that, of course, and when I knew I was only seven and still quite popular with . . . with . . .'

'I see.' The mule emerged from the trees which clung to the scant-soiled slope and they were at the summit once more. Gleefully, Adeline hoisted first Yenala and then herself back on to the animal's back. 'Well, at least we can ride for a good while now, provided the downward slope doesn't get dangerously steep.'

'We shan't be able to ride if it gets very dark, or poor Mule will put his foot in a hole and we'll all tumble,' Yenala remarked. But once they got through the forested part of the ride they realized that though the sun was sinking behind the mountains there was still plenty of light left in the sky. When they reached a convenient vantage point Adeline pulled the mule to a halt and slid off his back in order to take a good look, from this height, at the village and the mission compound.

From here it was little more, at first, than a conglomeration of roofs, walls and courtyards; they were still too far off to be able to see whether there were extra horses in the stableyard.

'We'll walk for this last bit,' Adeline decided, 'and mount again when we're on the flat. Step out now, Mule, and we'll be home before you know it.'

At the top of the next ridge she would not have bothered to stop again, but Yenala tugged on her side of the reins, bringing the beast to a lopsided halt.

'What a lot of cooking fires,' she said uncertainly. 'There's quite a haze over the compound, and I can smell smoke from here.'

'Dear me, I hope dinner's not been ruined,' Adeline said with rather forced cheerfulness. She jerked at the mule's head-collar. 'Come on, old thing, put your best feet forward!'

The animal hesitated, then moved on, but at the next ridge Adeline needed no encouragement to stop and the mule came to a dead halt, its big ears pricked. Against her fingers, Adeline could feel the beast trembling.

'What's the matter with the mule?' Adeline asked Yenala. 'I can feel . . .'

She stopped short. Now that they were nearer she could see that whatever had happened in the compound, it was not a natural occurrence such as several cooking fires. There had been a conflagration down there! The mission wall still stood but the gates were down and inside the wall were gaps she was certain had not been there when they had stood here and looked back earlier in the day.

'There's something wrong,' Yenala said. 'I can't quite . . . oh, Missie . . . the trees!'

She was right. The great pine tree, the walnut by the wall, the cherry tree whose branch had been lopped off, they were all missing. Not even the bell-tower, which could be seen from a great distance, reared against the pale grey sky of evening.

'They've had a fire . . .' Adeline was beginning, but Yenala cut across the words.

'No! It's the *I Ho Chuan*, Missie, the Boxers! They've come, and they've laid waste . . . what are you doing? You mustn't go down there!'

'We must, we must! We must try to help them, see if Mr John is back . . . come on, Yenala . . . let's hurry!'

But the mule was as reluctant as Yenala. He pulled back against his bridle, snorting with fright, and showed every sign of breaking free and galloping back into the hills if they tried to get him to return to the plain.

'Look, Missie Adeline,' Yenala said after a few minutes of unavailing struggle. 'We're not going to get the mule to go willingly, not yet. If we wait until it's dark we can hobble the mule up here, or tie it to a tree, and make our way down very quietly. If we see lights we'll be cautious, but at the moment it would be madness to go down.'

'If we see lights we'll know someone's all right,' Adeline said, but Yenala shook her head.

'No. We mustn't take chances. Now let's have something to eat whilst we wait. We can make some tea . . . I filled the kettle with water before we left the lake in case we got thirsty before we reached home.'

And in the end that was what they did, largely, it was true, because it was clear that the mule would not accompany them quietly. It was an anxious wait until it got dark but Yenala would not hear of their leaving until then, and shook her head vigorously when Adeline suggested going to a farmhouse for help.

'No. Not until we know we need help, and why,' she said. 'We'll take a quiet look round first.'

As darkness fell it became obvious that there would be no lights lit in the compound, though a quarter of a mile away the village was showing the odd illuminated window.

'But not nearly so many as usual,' Yenala said unhappily, and Adeline, after a long and searching scrutiny, agreed that it was so.

'Can we go down soon?' she asked hopefully. It occurred to her then that their roles had somehow been reversed, but she was willing to do as Yenala said because it was plain that as the situation now stood Yenala was more experienced than she.

'Presently,' Yenala told her. 'We'll wait a bit longer, just in case someone's hiding near the compound expecting people to venture back as it gets dark.'

But the longest day must end, and when the darkness was full and complete, save for the faint shine from the thin young moon, Adeline and Yenala tied the mule to a tree, piled its saddle, saddlebags and bridle under a bush and made their way, slowly and fumblingly, down on to the plain. There they stole along the sunken lanes and through the crops and all was silent in the little houses and shacks they passed, no one came out to challenge them, there was no sound of the people within. As they approached the compound Yenala became so nervous that they abandoned the dusty road and took to the fields, where they made the acquaintance of deep and muddy ditches and were soon scratched and tripped by brambles and tall thickets of bamboo. But at last they reached the outer wall.

The gates, as Adeline had seen from afar, no longer barred the way into the mission. They had been burned, and Adeline knew it had been no accident, for the gates were solid old hardwood and would not have caught light easily.

They reached the gateway and kept close to the wall, trying to peer in. There was something cast down near the stump which had once been the bell-tower; they had no option but to go forward. They crept past the burned gates, holding hands, dreading what they might find.

There were bodies everywhere. Even the faint moonlight could not disguise the horror of it. Some were burnt, some were dead in pools of their own black blood, others had been horribly mutilated. Adeline recognized no one. Please God let mine be all right, she was muttering soundlessly as she and Yenala rounded the bell-tower and made for the servants' quarters. Please God let mine be alive!

The servants' courtyard was a charnel house. The aggressors had fired the buildings, Adeline thought, and then waited for the inhabitants to run out. Some had emerged already too badly burned to survive; they were probably the lucky ones. As the two girls crossed the courtyard, shuddering, Adeline saw Amatei's head. The woman's eyes were staring, her face pulled into an expression of dread and fear. And Yo Liu . . . Adeline tried to make her eyes shut, to keep out the nightmare, but they would not close. She saw Yo Liu; he had not died easily. He had been cruelly mutilated. P'an too.

Adeline looked wildly round, her hand flying to her mouth. This was worse than her worst imaginings! This was total horror, total outrage! Sickness churned in her stomach, slithering weakness gripped her bowels. She dared not move . . . but she must! She tugged feebly at Yenala's hand, because Yenala, her face like stone, was trying to persuade her to go through into the inner courtyard, where the servants' dependants lived. Babies, old parents . . . my God, they could not have done this to the babies? Adeline almost ran through into the inner courtyard.

It was worse. Small children, innocent little ones . . . her stomach gave a great convulsive heave and then, in the deep shadow by the burned-out building, something moved.

Terror lent them wings, then. They flew out of the courtyards, across the compound, and did not stop running until they fell down, out in the fields with the smell of blood and fire still in their nostrils and the sickness of despair acrid in their mouths.

It was long minutes before Adeline felt the earth beneath her and smelt the freshness of crushed vegetation and clean dust. She tried to sit up, gagged, and began to vomit, her hands clawing at her stomach, then at her throat. Beside her she could hear Yenala being sick too, but she could not so much as stretch out a hand to comfort the child.

They reached the mule long before dawn but though they lay down together, their backs against a convenient rock, and cuddled close for comfort more than warmth, they could not sleep. The horrors they had seen haunted them, and although Yenala had looked back and seen that the movement had been caused by a great, raw-boned dog, Adeline felt deeply guilty that they had not stayed to see if there was anyone still left alive, anyone they could help.

'I hope that if anyone lived the villagers would have taken them in,' Yenala said. But Adeline did not think that was likely. Chinese peasants, indeed the Chinese people as a whole, did not waste time or energy in helping people who were not either family or friends. That is why so many children became beggars or outcasts; they had no family, therefore they were not. A Chinese would not take in a child or see that it was fed merely from pity. He would have to know its parents or guardians, feel some responsibility for its well-being.

'When it's light, we'd better go back,' Adeline said at last. 'Someone must be alive . . . well, we both saw lights in the village earlier. Surely the villagers will go to the mission today, bury the dead?'

'The lights may belong to the Boxers,' Yenala pointed out. 'We aren't going back there by daylight, Missie Adeline, because it's too dangerous. If you feel you must, then we'll go back tomorrow night, but I don't see why you want to. We can't bury the dead, we couldn't possibly do so, and there's no one there alive.'

'But suppose . . . oh, my God, suppose Mr John had arrived back? Yenala, I must know! If he was there . . . I must go back!'

'Very well, but after dark,' Yenala said. 'No good can come of it, Missie Adeline. I'm sure Mr John wasn't there . . . we didn't see Lin, or Pao, or Chu. And Mr John had his gun and the other men had revolvers; you don't think they would have let every single Boxer get away, do you? They would have killed some.'

It was this, finally, which convinced Adeline. Undoubtedly the slaughter was the work of the *I Ho Chuan*, and if they were active in the province it might well have taken John far longer than he expected to get to Peking and home again. No doubt he would arrive next day.

'Then shall we go to the village after dark?' Adeline said. 'They will help us, surely?'

But Yenala shook her head once more.

'No, Missie Adeline. Even if the Boxers have left Ayiteng there is no certainty that the villagers would not betray us. Oh, I know they've lived side by side with us for months, been glad of the medicines and treatment they've had from the clinic, but the Boxers are said to have magical powers. If the villagers know the *I Ho Chuan* are coming back they won't dare *not* betray us.'

'So we'll stay here today, then,' Adeline said at last. 'And go down again tonight . . . but only briefly into the compound, I promise you, Yenala. Then we'll hide somewhere where we can watch the gateway, because John should come home tonight . . . he must!'

The day dragged. Sunshine had deserted them and a light rain fell. They let the mule graze on the thin grass higher up in the mountains, hobbling his feet so he could not go far. And waited. They tried talking in low voices, tucked away as they were in a narrow ravine with trees all around, but soon fell silent, their thoughts too active and frightening to be pushed aside by light conversation.

They ate sparingly but drank several cups of increasingly weak tea. Small, chilly streams abounded in the upper reaches of the mountain and it gave them something to do to climb up, fill the kettle and come quietly down again.

Now and again they heard a farmer or one of his sons or daughters passing by, going up to their herds, perhaps, or simply visiting a neighbour. But they never came far enough up the mountain to see either the two girls or the hobbled mule, and then, at last, the rainy, miserable day began to give way to dusk, then to dark.

'We'll leave the mule again,' Adeline decided. 'We'll go down to the compound first, Yenala, and just make sure J-John isn't there. Then we'll come out again and hide. You don't suppose the villagers will have gone in and buried the dead?'

'We'll see,' Yenala said. 'Quietly, now.'

They were quiet. Fear and despair dogged them as they made their way once more over the plain and up to the gates. One glance was enough to confirm that no one had done anything within the compound. This time the clouds overhead made it easier to see and yet less terrifying, for features were not thrown into sharp relief by the light and shadows cast by the moon. The dead were just shapes, grey on grey.

They went straight to Adeline's own courtyards. A dead child, who must have escaped the carnage in the servants' quarters only to be run down here. A woman, or at least her trunk. Something dark in the pool was probably . . . Adeline left the courtyard. There was no sign of John here.

She searched the rest of the compound, but he was not amongst the pitiful dead. A good many of them had not even been living here, Adeline realized, but must have come to seek help from the clinic or the doctor. And they had been foully murdered – the Boxers, it was clear, did not care, when it came down to it, whether a peasant was a convert to Christianity or a good Buddhist with a medical problem. If you were in the mission compound you were fair game.

'It's all right, Missie Adeline,' Yenala whispered when they had gone through every courtyard in the place and poked their heads into every burned building. 'Mr John isn't here. Can we go now?'

'Of course,' Adeline said. 'We'll hide in the maize growing down in the dip outside the gates. 'When Mr John does come we'll see him even before he realizes what's happened. We can warn him to go no further.'

Accordingly, they made their way towards the gateway, went through it . . . and heard voices, men's voices, coming along the road from Peking.

'It's John!' Adeline exclaimed, her voice lifting, her step immediately lighter. 'Oh, thank God, it's John!'

There were three or four men, she could not quite make out which, and some animals – that would be the horses. She set off at a run with Yenala some way behind, was actually calling out 'John! John, over here . . . we've come . . .' when she realized her mistake. The men were peasants, or possibly soldiers, but they were certainly not the men who had set off to Peking two days before. They had pulled their beasts to a halt and were staring in her direction.

Flight! She was half-turned when she realized the futility of it; they were only yards away. But Yenala was further off. She shrieked, 'Get out, dearest . . . get out!' and then turned back towards the men, who were heading for her with all speed. She ran, but not after Yenala, towards the compound. She was struggling to get the pistol out of her pocket, trying to slip the safety catch . . . a young man seemed to be ignoring her, heading after the child . . . she brought the pistol up to shoulder level and fired wildly after him. He staggered and fell . . . she could see Yenala for a moment, just a shadow amongst other shadows, before she disappeared. Triumphantly, Adeline swung the gun round to her pursuers and fired once more before harsh hands clutched at her and she heard her tunic tear.

She took two more steps and felt her knees give. She crashed into the dust and rolled on to her back. A man was bending over her, his hands held out. With the memory of the atrocities she had witnessed in the compound vivid still in her mind, Adeline waited for the blow that would end her short life.

# CHAPTER EIGHT

John's trip to Peking had begun well, with a ride into the brightening morning and the big horse moving easily between his knees. The air was fresh at this hour, though it would seem less so once the heat began to bite, and the beauty of the landscape, what John thought of as the *differentness*, was more noticeable than ever in the long, slanting light of sunrise.

He and Lin rode together, with Pao and Chu behind, because he and Lin spoke English most of the time and Pao and Chu the local dialect. John and Lin, in the seven months or so they had worked together, had grown easy with one another. Lin was a convert but by no means a rice Christian; he had chosen his religion with the same care and thought with which he had determined to stay with the new missionary instead of retiring to the mountains with the old one. He had weighed Buddhism and Christianity in the balance and selected the one he felt was better for him, John knew. He did not know why Christianity had come out on top, unless it was because old Instadt would not have liked having a head-boy who was not of his religion, so he took this opportunity of asking Lin for an explanation.

'I listened for many months before I decided to become a Christian,' Lin said now, as they rode along a deep-banked, rutted lane. 'I heard all the arguments and tried to put myself into each pair of shoes, if you understand me. But finally I chose Christianity because, much though I revere the monks and priests of Buddha, it is quite easy to see that to these men we, the ordinary people, are grains of sand. They cannot tell one from another and care not at all for our differences. It is a bit like our law – often a man will carelessly offend a great one, and lose his head not for his offence but because the great one was given a hard-boiled egg for his breakfast when he wanted fish and rice, or because the great one's wife was sharp with him before the servants. Do you read my meaning, Mr John? Mr Instadt taught us that Jesus cares for each of us, and this one can only hope is true, but Mr Instadt cared for each of us, and he is the representative of Jesus on earth. So I became a convert.'

'And have you ever regretted it?'

'No,' said Lin, adding with great honesty, 'for don't I have the best of both worlds? I take part in all the festivities of the Christian church and also of the Buddha. I make prayer flags and sing and dance at times of rejoicing and fly my kite when everyone else does and go to weddings and funerals for my Buddhist friends and relatives. But inside me there is Christian quiet and Christian peace and a well of belief which grows with each day that passes.'

'That's wonderful, Lin,' John said sincerely. 'You understand that I don't usually ask, but you and I have grown close and I must admit I've wondered.'

For a while they rode on in silence whilst behind them Pao and Chu, neither of whom had converted, argued amicably over which of them Kuein Sing preferred.

They stopped for a meal at midday at a pleasant little village where they bought lily root stew and hot rolls, fresh strawberries and a light and sparkling local wine. The villagers were friendly, gathering round and chatting, and John obligingly took a look at the chief man's son, who had an injured arm, and a little girl with weeping and swollen eyes.

Neither was difficult to treat. The arm was cleaned, disinfected and bandaged and John promised to stop on his way back to Ayiteng the next day or the day after that and renew the dressings. Lin asked whether the villagers had been troubled by bands of roving soldiers or the *I Ho Chuan* and was told rather reproachfully that the Boxers would not interfere with law-abiding peasants, but rather with the rich and . . . eyes slanted sideways at John and slanted away again . . . and the wicked.

'They have magic powers,' a fat-faced, garrulous peasant told them as they sat on the wall by the fountain in the square and ate their food. 'You can't kill one of their members – they will simply lie there for a few hours

113

and then get up, put their heads back on their shoulders and walk away! Ay-yi, that's a thing to see! And if you fire a bullet at them they put up a hand and turn the bullet and it speeds back and kills the firer. What about that?'

'The local peasants sneak out and bury the dead, and then say, when they're asked, that the bodies disappear,' Lin muttered, *sotto voce*. 'It's like their cures for poisoned wells – naturally they work and the water is sweet, because the foreign devils don't poison wells! It is all a trick to make the *I Ho Chuan* appear immortal, magical. Why, even the Old Buddha . . .'

The fat-faced one overheard the last few words and nodded approval.

'Aye, that's right, friend, even the Old Buddha, heaven bless her, sees that the *I Ho Chuan* are a wonderful thing for China, a very wonderful thing! Under their sway our country will recover her lost greatness and the Old Buddha will reign over a land which obeys only her and not a motley collection of provinces where foreign devils . . . saving your presence . . .' he added to John, 'where foreign devils lay down the law and take upon themselves the honours due only to mandarins and high officials.'

'That's a dig at the Catholics,' Lin told John, as the fat-faced one, having spoken his mind, wandered off about his business again. 'I dare say you've heard about the Roman Catholic bishops?'

'No . . . I'm very much a new boy to all this, Lin. When I joined the mission I was told where I was needed, what my duties were to be, and how I must tailor my preaching to suit local people. Of other denominations I've been told almost nothing . . . well, if I'm honest, nothing whatsoever.'

'Ah! Well, the Roman Catholics have made themselves extremely unpopular by insisting that their bishops – and, indeed, others of their church – shall be granted the rights and privileges which are normally only shown to higher officials in China. It has annoyed everyone, not just the court and the Boxers. Indeed, Mr Instadt was really worried and upset when the news first broke, just over a year ago. He said it could easily be the end of us all . . . but no doubt, with so many other things to worry about, the court and all its officials have put Roman Catholic privileges to the back of their minds.'

'It doesn't sound as though the peasants have,' John said thoughtfully. He stood up, dusting crumbs from his riding breeches. 'Well, if we've all finished we'd best be moving on if we're to arrive in Peking in time to start our business.'

But the peasant's words kept niggling away in John's mind. The man had actually said that the Dowager Empress was in favour of the Boxers. John had assumed that the Empress, who had a short way with people who annoyed her, would presently set the Imperial Army on the Boxers and wipe them out of existence. But if the fat-faced one was to be believed, the Old Buddha approved of the sect.

114

'Lin . . . does the Dowager Empress really believe in the Boxer movement? She must know, of course, that their claims are false . . .'

'*If cut with axe or chopped with axe, there will be no trace. Cannon cannot injure, water cannot drown,*' Lin quoted, with a smile. 'That's one of their boasts and they've been going round the country giving demonstrations of their invulnerability. All tricks, of course, but clever enough to convince most of their audience. As for knowing that their claims are false, perhaps she believes because she wants to believe. You've not heard about the most recent Edict?'

'No. I appear to be singularly ill-informed,' John said heavily. 'When I was last in Peking I talked to the ministers at the British Legation and they laughed at the Boxer threat, said they were nothing but a group of ill-armed, ill-disciplined peasants and it would soon be past history. You don't agree, do you?'

'No, not any more. Not since I heard about the Edict. The Dowager Empress sent it out to all her officials. It said that the secret societies were, for the most part, composed of men who were law-abiding and merely wanted to protect themselves and their families. She made it plain that anyone acting against such societies would have her to deal with, and no official who wants to keep his head on his shoulders is going to ignore that warning!'

'My God! And the missionaries have not been warned? But this is criminal!'

'I agree. However, wiser heads may yet prevail; she may see that she's going to run into terrible trouble and retract. But, Mr John, I think you should call at the Legation again today. See what they're saying now; they may well have changed their tune.'

They rode in silence for the last mile, with Peking's great walls and towers coming ever closer. Presently Pao and Chu joined them and the four of them rode in through the big gates and prepared to go about their business.

The next day John was up betimes, but even so it was soon clear that he would have to spend another night in Peking, for he was not halfway through his shopping list.

'We'll go to the mission-house and get a good night's sleep, and start again first thing in the morning,' John told Pao and Chu. 'Lin has relatives he wants to see, but you can come with me.'

The two men, however, preferred to visit friends in the city, so John went off to the mission-house alone. He explained his position and was offered a bed, but before he could get into it another missionary came in, and then another, and very soon an impromptu meeting was being held.

'The Boxers are roaming this province now, burning, murdering and looting,' one earnest, bespectacled man said. 'I've left my village and

115

brought my flock here for safety. There are only ten of us, and I dare not stay in such a remote spot.'

'I'm holding out for a few days yet; we run an orphanage and it would mean moving eighty small children,' another man said, but he looked worried. 'I've left my wife and my assistant there with strict orders to keep the gates shut and locked and to have buckets of water at strategic spots. Unless they attack in force we should be all right, but I'm very worried. I'm going to the British Legation in the morning.'

'Me, too,' John put in. 'I've left my wife . . . I didn't know how bad things were. I've only been here seven months. Should I go back at once, do you suppose?'

'Not until you've spoken to the authorities,' another man advised. 'I don't know where you are but they'll know how great your danger is, and whether you should simply lie low or come in. The trouble is, once you move your people out the rest will simply steal everything that isn't nailed down and blame the Boxers even if they never came within shouting distance of your place. One has to weigh up the problems before coming to a decision.'

'My wife's expecting a baby in a couple of months,' John said, and surprised a look of shock and pity on the nearest face before the owner made it carefully blank once more.

'Well, if I were you I'd bring her in,' another man chimed in. 'And your converts, of course . . . how many are there? They've killed hundreds in Peking already, mind you. Converts, I mean, not Europeans; they won't dare go that far, but your wife could be horribly upset and scared.'

'They killed Brooks,' someone muttered. 'He was as English as you or me. I wouldn't take any chances.'

John, who had flung himself back on his bed, sat up.

'I really should . . . oh, no, I can't just leave now, even if the gates are open, which they won't be. I've three men with me, staying with relatives in the city. But first thing tomorrow . . .'

He lay down again and soon the murmur of voices faded and snores took their place. But John had to exert all his willpower before he could make himself sleep.

Next day, John was up early. He did most of his shopping and then went straight to the British Legation, for he had promised Adeline that he would return by evening and he had no intention of letting her down and worrying her. And the minister who spoke to him at the Legation, a medium-sized man with an enormous grey moustache, almost no hair and worried, light blue eyes, assured him that if he and his wife were to take refuge in the Legation they would be very welcome.

'No one knows the extent of the trouble that's brewing, but we've got some members of the forces here and they'll do their best to see we're safe,' he said. 'Probably it'll all come to nothing – the Imperial Army is strong in the city, and although they've done nothing to prevent the Boxers from killing as many Chinese converts as they could lay hands on, if they start on the ordinary people no doubt the Imperial troops will soon set them by the ears. But out in the country our writ doesn't run . . . you bring your people in.'

John agreed to do this, gathered his small group together, and tried to find someone in Peking with a quantity of laudanum, which he desperately needed for his dispensary.

'The whole city's run out of the stuff,' he was told by a fellow-seeker. 'It's coming up from the coast by rail – couldn't you wait until tomorrow?'

'No, I'm due home later today,' John said. 'What a nuisance. It's the only thing I've not managed to get.'

'Where do you come from?' the other asked. 'The train stops at Machiapu, or you might find it easier to ride to Fengtai if you leave fairly soon. There will be at least one Englishman on the train taking care of the drugs; tell him you're a doctor and want a supply of laudanum and I'm sure he'll oblige you.'

'I'll do that,' John said, relieved. 'Thanks very much, old chap.'

So he and his small band rode out of the city in mid-morning and made for the railway station. They stopped first at Machiapu, but John was told by a wrinkled old Chinese that the train was not due for another hour. If he rode on to Fengtai, however, he would undoubtedly find it just about to pull in. It was a fairly long halt at Fengtai, for the driver changed there and they took on water and coal.

It was a miserable day, overcast and gloomy, yet with the sun strong behind the cloud so that the horses were plagued by flies and the riders had to keep wiping the perspiration out of their eyes in order to see the track ahead. When the rain began John was almost glad – anything was better than the humid heat – and he and his companions rode along to Fengtai in a good deal more comfort despite the rain which soaked steadily into their shoulders and knees.

It was easier to ride alongside the railway in one way and more difficult in another. The railway was up on a high embankment, so they got some shelter from the rain by pressing close to it, but the track was narrow and they could only ride in single file. Also, after a time, John began to feel oppressed by his inability to see out across the countryside. He was relieved when at last he saw, ahead of him, the engine sheds and cluster of European and Chinese houses which denoted a sizeable stopping place.

He was concentrating on his horse and thinking that he had best spend all his remaining money on laudanum in case it was some time before he had the opportunity again when, from behind him, Pao said, 'What's that?' There was a tenseness in his tone which made John look up sharply.

Ahead of them, one of the engine sheds was suddenly enveloped in a pall of black smoke. As they watched, another shed seemed to burst into flames, then another.

117

'Trouble!' John said tersely. 'We'd better go and see if we can help. Get that pistol out, Lin.'

His own rifle was down by his stirrup. He pulled it out of its holder and kicked Thunderer into a canter, but as they neared the smoke he allowed the animal to slow.

Little figures were dancing round the flames, figures which, even at this distance, were clearly not trying to douse the fire. And more sheds were belching smoke now. He saw houses suddenly beginning to smoulder, heard screams.

A horse shouldered up against his. It was Lin, his face grim.

'We'd better get out of it, Mr John. It's the Boxers right enough; they'll kill us as easily as you'd swat a mosquito . . . no sense in playing into their hands. Think of Miss Adeline.'

'But Lin, we're armed. We can't just let people *die*!'

'We've got a dozen shots between us, Mr John, before we have to break off to reload. What chance have we of helping anyone? Before we'd even got close enough they'd be all over us.'

John knew the man was right, but it went against the grain to simply turn and flee. In the event, the choice was not his. He slowed his horse . . . and heard a bloodthirsty shriek from ahead of them. They had been seen! A man on a horse pointed, shouted, more men joined him, and they set their horses along the railway, to the very track which John and his band had followed so faithfully.

'They outnumber us three to one,' Lin said desperately. 'Mr John, think of Missie Adeline!'

But John knew a vain hope when he saw one. The men ahead of them, dressed in white with red ribbons round their heads, wrists and ankles, were riding fast and one of them at least was armed with a rifle. Even as John and Lin turned their horses in the confined space a shot whistled over their heads . . . adding urgency, if nothing else, to their manoeuvre. As they managed to get the horses round John slewed in the saddle and took a pot-shot at the pursuers; he doubted if he hit anyone, but felt that at least it proved they were armed and might discourage the followers from getting too close. After that, he simply bent over Thunderer's neck and concentrated on willing the horse forward.

Thunderer, Lin's chestnut mare and the mules ridden by Pao and Chu put everything they'd got into their flight, and John found time to be glad that clearly Pao and Chu had turned some moments before he and Lin had done so, for they were well in advance of the others, their sturdy mules galloping, rumps swaying, several hundred yards ahead.

Once or twice he looked over his shoulder. Thunderer was last, his nose almost resting on the mare's neat hindquarters. The gelding was terrified, as much by the screams from the rear as by the bullets, which were all aimed far too high. 'Sha, sha, sha!' shrieked the Boxers, and John turned again and fired, a quick snap shot with only one hand, almost impossible to aim correctly.

But it discouraged the pursuers; they fell back, though they did not actually give up. Still, it meant that the horses could gallop on without bullets reaching them, and it gave John a chance to snipe once or twice more, though he had small hope of actually hitting anyone at this range.

The horses tired, but happily no sooner than the pursuers. They were within hailing distance of the walls of Peking when the Boxers decided to call it a day and turned back towards Fengtai.

'We'll have to ride into the city,' John said breathlessly to Lin Sheng, now riding knee to knee with him. 'Thunderer needs a rest or he'll founder, and we must warn the mission and the Legation what's happened at Fengtai.'

'You're right. But we could set out again, once it's dark, for the village,' Lin said, between gasps. 'We'll have to travel more discreetly, though, if we're to escape detection. I think we ought to abandon the horses and use donkeys. They're less likely to attract unwanted attention.'

But this, however, John was loth to do.

'If we'd been on donkeys we wouldn't be alive now to tell the tale,' he said grimly as they rode in through the city gate. 'It may well mean a slight delay, but we'll sleep tonight and ride out again when the horses are fit to carry us. Well, I never thought I'd see Peking again so soon,' he added. 'I think you'd all better come with me this time to the mission.'

But first they went to the Legation, to pass on their grim tidings.

They left the following evening, at dusk, and rode hard, avoiding villages as best they could. They had agreed with the mission head that they would go back to Ayiteng and then turn straight round and accompany their converts and John's wife to the comparative safety of the Legation at Peking. They saw no sign of Boxers or other insurgents, but then, as Lin pointed out when John remarked on it, they had avoided the only places they were likely to meet up with the *I Ho Chuan*: villages, and particularly villages with Christian communities.

Dawn was greying the sky when they drew near Ayiteng and the mission. 'No one's working in the fields,' Pao remarked uneasily.

'They wouldn't be out yet,' Chu scoffed. 'But . . . there are no cooking fires either.'

'Why would anyone light a cooking fire at dawn?' John asked, and Lin told him that at the height of summer, when the days were very hot, field workers liked to start out at dawn to get the best of the cooler hours.

'The gates are open,' John remarked, as they drew nearer.

'Where's the pine tree?' Pao's voice was sharp with fear.

After that no one spoke. They saved their breath to urge their mounts onward.

\* \* \*

119

'Are they *all* dead?'

John spoke in a low voice, looking at his companions. They had gone unbelievingly from courtyard to courtyard, seeing the sights that had shattered Adeline and Yenala two days before. 'All dead?' he repeated.

'Missie Adeline isn't here,' Lin said. Tears had run down his face and soaked into his thin cotton tunic. 'But Amatei . . . Yo Liu, P'an . . . everyone else is dead.'

'My pretty Kuein,' Pao said beneath his breath. 'Oh, my poor, pretty one!'

'The babies, even,' John mourned. 'This is a terrible thing. As soon as it's light we must go to the village, see what happened.'

'No. Not you, nor I,' Lin said with unexpected firmness. 'Pao and Chu will go. They are neither of them Christians – they can go as if they were merely returning after a trip away. They'll find out as much as they can. And you'd better bring some men back with you,' he added to the two young men. 'We'll need to get these buried before predators start on them.'

'Your father, Lin . . .? He wasn't a Christian,' John muttered. 'Is he here?'

'Yes, for he lived in the compound and would be dealt with as though he were Christian,' Lin said soberly. 'But I have aunts and cousins in plenty in the village. I'll get word of them later. For now we must bury our dead.'

The villagers came to help. They had been afraid to come before, but now that someone else had been, and assured them that only the dead occupied the compound, they were quite willing to assist with the grisly task. After all, they had no wish to be haunted by the unquiet spirits of men who had died violently and been denied the peace of the grave.

They were shocked by what they saw, and angry too, for many of the dead, as John had immediately seen, were not converts at all but patients waiting to see the doctor. But the Chinese are a race of fatalists; shoulders were shrugged, tears wiped away, and the work of burying the dead was carried on with a will.

At first, questions were greeted with shrugs and mumbles, but presently people began to emerge from their fear and disgust and many remembered that John and Adeline had been good to them. The old fellow who kept the village gate remembered seeing Adeline and Yenala setting off for their picnic. Yes, it was early on the morning of the massacre, which was how they had come to miss it. Surely, he supposed, they must have come back . . . had anyone seen them?

No one had, until a small boy came in from his father's fields and volunteered the information that he had heard a commotion one night when he had been accidentally locked out and had curled up in a field of maize, determined to sleep there until sun-up.

'Two of 'em, there were,' he said. 'They came out of the compound . . . the mission compound, I mean . . . and there were some men . . . they ran towards them, the biggest woman calling out, a name, something, I couldn't catch it. And then the big one gave a yell, and the little one ran away, and there was a shot . . . bang, *bang* . . . and the big one turned and ran as well, only they caught her. And they all went off together.'

'All? How many were there? And did the little one join them?'

'No,' the boy said crossly. 'I told you, the little one ran *away*. I don't know how many there were, four or five. Or six, perhaps.'

'And did they . . . the brigands . . . kill anyone in the village?' John asked, as he had longed to ask earlier. No one, he noticed, had used the word Boxer.

'In the village? Where we are all humble peasants? Why should they do that, when they are fighting for China?' the boy said aggressively. 'Well, they killed old Tung when he tried to make them pay for what they took from his shop, and the old woman he has there too, and a girl and a boy, I think. But no one else, or not that I've heard.'

John walked away. No one of any importance, because the whole Tung family was wiped out so that there was no one to mourn them, no one to call the killings wicked, unnecessary. I will never understand the Chinese character if I live here for a hundred years, he told himself vehemently. And the way I feel right now, I shan't even want to.

When all the bodies had been buried, John turned to Lin, Chu and Pao.

'I'm going up into the hills, to search for my wife and Yenala. It sounds as though they may well have escaped. But I think the three of you should return to Peking. If you ask me, the people in the village might easily turn on you, give you away to the Boxers, if they return. I know you aren't converts, Chu and Pao, but that may not save you; look at the Tungs.'

'I'll search with you,' Lin said at once. 'What use is Peking to me, who am without my father, my two sisters and their husbands and my nieces and nephews? I'll stay with you.'

'And I,' Pao said without explanation or preamble. 'Wrong things have been done; I shall do my best to right them.'

'And I,' agreed Chu. 'With four of us, we can cover more ground, question more people. We'll find Missie Adeline and little Yenala, don't you fear, Mr John!'

The four men stayed for three days in the vicinity of Ayiteng, then moved purposefully up into the mountains, but they were driven from there by two things. Rumours of the Boxers' being in the vicinity were quite enough to close the most helpful peasant mouth, and they came across a missionary's assistant, an earnest young man with a stammer and a very tiny donkey, trying to lead thirty panic-stricken children to safety in Peking.

'Mr Redvers was killed, with his wife and son,' the man told John, his voice trembling. 'It was sudden . . . terrible. They killed all our orphans, too, but for these thirty here. I had taken them out into the countryside on an expedition – Mr Redvers and I have been teaching them how to find edible roots, how to light a fire with two sticks, you know the kind of thing . . . and we got back rather late. It – it happened whilst we were gone, you see. There was blood . . . blood everywhere. Heads . . . limbs . . .' He shuddered, his face greying at the recollection. 'We didn't linger; I dared not. The peasants in the village were horrified that we could not bury the dead but I gave them money and they promised to do it for us. Then we left. We've been walking ever since, but I fear the plain. They say there are bands of Boxers everywhere . . . how can we escape when we are so many?'

John looked at the thin, earnest countenance, the myopic eyes, the rounded shoulders of a man rather academic than built for action. There was only one course open to him, for he had searched and not found.

'We'll go with you, the four of us,' he said gently. 'Lin Sheng and myself are both armed and we've got four mounts, two horses and two mules. We'll get through, don't you worry.'

But it took them much longer to cross the forty-odd miles to Peking with thirty children and a weary and footsore young man. It was 18 June before they arrived once more before the gates and made their way to the British Legation.

'If she's alive – and I'm sure you're right, my boy, and she is – they'll bring her to Peking. If she escapes, where else should she come? You could roam the countryside searching and never get within a mile of her, but if you stay here, sooner or later she'll come in.'

John sighed and turned to look out of the window. He was in the British Legation, talking to one of the junior diplomats in a small first-floor room which overlooked the street. The Legation was crowded, stuffed to the roof-tiles with refugees. Fortunately it was still hot, and the Chinese converts inhabited the gardens, while the missionaries and their wives and children had been put in various outbuildings or in small dormitories with straw mattresses carpeting the floor. There was talk of all Europeans being evacuated down to the coast, but it was evidently unlikely to happen; it was far too dangerous, though there were those who still maintained that the Imperial troops would be true to their trust and get them through safely.

'You're probably right, Sir Alfred. And if she comes here she'll be well received. If she's out there somewhere, alone, frightened, then I might get word . . . you never know.'

He was looking out of the window as he spoke and saw a man strolling by, down the centre of the road. He was clad in white, with scarlet ribbons at his wrists and ankles, and a scarlet bandanna round his head. He was a dull, stupid-looking fellow with a flat, heavy-browed face and broken teeth, but he also had a great double-edged sword hanging by his side and an axe tucked into his scarlet sash. He did not even glance towards the Legation windows, but John was suddenly sure that the Boxer was aware of his presence and would, if the opportunity offered, take great pleasure in killing him.

'Look at that chap!' Sir Alfred said suddenly; he had moved over to the window whilst John had been engrossed in the sudden appearance of the Boxer. 'My dear fellah, you wouldn't last two minutes alone, and you couldn't expect your men to go with you now, not as things stand. Think of your little wife and the child she's expecting. They'd rather a live man than a dead hero, what?'

'Yes, I see the sense, but . . .'

'And we need every able-bodied man we can get here, or we shall do,' Sir Alfred added. 'You're a medical man, too . . . we may need doctors before we're through. They tell me you came armed? That right?'

'Yes, I brought my rifle and some ammunition. I bought more yesterday in the city; several boxes. And ammunition for my boy's pistol as well. I thought I might need it when searching for my wife.'

'You'll need it here, waiting for her,' Sir Alfred said positively. 'I'm not offering you safety, you know, old boy – wish I could! All I'm offering is a chance to help us to defend this place and all the innocents within who would be butchered otherwise, and the hope that your wife will join us here before many days are out.'

'I'll stay for a few days, then, but if she doesn't come in . . . I'll reserve the right to think again. Is that fair?'

'Very fair. You've got a bed?'

'Yes, in the outbuildings. There are eight of us in it, all good chaps; the Marines are bedded down near at hand.'

'Good, good. Then we'll consider it settled . . . for the time being, at any rate.'

John left the Legation building and went to find Lin Shen and the others. They seemed to have settled in a good deal better than he had, he thought ruefully, but perhaps that was again the difference between an Oriental and a European outlook: fatalism told the Oriental to accept what came and make the best of it, while a European defied fate, railed against it, changed it if he could.

Crossing the garden, John saw his erstwhile companions. They were filling sandbags with soil from the flower beds. Odd sandbags. John went over to have a closer look. Lin turned as he reached them.

'You are staying, Mr John?' He nodded as though he had expected nothing else. 'Do you admire the sandbags? Lady French is making them from the chintz chair-covers in her living-room. Colourful, perhaps, but strong.'

'It doesn't look as though Lady French has much hope of a peaceful settlement then,' John observed. Lin looked quizzical.

'After Von Ketteler's murder? Or haven't you heard about that? He

123

went to the Yamen for a meeting and was shot dead, deliberately, by a member of the Imperial Guard.'

'It happened the day we arrived, I suppose,' John said wearily. 'There was some talk . . . I've been so preoccupied and there have been so many deaths. Who was he?'

'The German Minister. A man of some importance, Mr John, and engaged on a diplomatic mission. So you see . . .'

'I do indeed,' John said slowly. 'I do indeed.'

'And the ultimatum expires at four this afternoon.' Lin anticipated John's next question and adroitly continued to speak. 'The Europeans must leave the security of the Legations and set out for Tientsin by then or they will be at war with the Imperial troops and the Dowager Empress.'

'And no moves are being made to leave, which means . . .'

'We will be at war and under siege in about three hours.'

'I see.'

So it was leave in the next three hours or not at all, John told himself, as he made his way back into the Legation to see where he could be of most use. But a European force was on its way to Peking from the coast; the siege would not be of long duration once the troops arrived!

Yenala lay low in the maize crop for about fifteen nervewracking minutes, then sat up. The men who had taken her mistress were just moving away from the compound, going towards the village. Were they villagers? If so, surely she had nothing to fear. Perhaps they would simply take her to some safe house and hold her there until morning.

But the village gates were closed and barred, and in any case the men stole past without even a hail or a cry. Two men were mounted, the rest were on foot. Yenala rose from her hiding-place and began to follow. She would not let Adeline out of her sight. It had been bad enough to run and hide, but now she would make up for that. Adeline and John had saved her life once; now she would save Adeline's.

Following them, however, was not going to be a simple matter, for they were taking a track which would lead them quite soon into the mountains. They were clearly not Boxers, though, to Yenala's inexpressible relief. Boxers would scarcely head up into the mountains, where there were few people. They would stick to the richer towns and villages of the plains where the railroad ran.

So if they were not Boxers, what were they? A wandering band of soldiers who owed allegiance to some War Lord with a stronghold in the mountains? Or perhaps just brigands, outlaws who found robbing peasants easier work than tilling the fields. It scarcely mattered. Whoever they were Adeline must be detached from them as quickly as possible, before they either sold her into slavery or gave her to ill-wishers . . . stronger words than that Yenala dared not contemplate.

As the path grew more rugged Yenala's tiredness nearly overcame her.

She was exhausted and longed to sleep, but if she did she would lose Adeline and the men and that she must not do.

At last, however, dawn began to lighten the sky in the east, and to Yenala's great joy the men seemed to decide that they must take shelter, perhaps eat a meal. They chose a leafy dell high off the track, so that they looked down on the path. It was an ideal spot for an ambush, but Yenala thought they did not have an ambush in mind so much as the idea of not being surprised themselves.

Now what I must do is go round them, and ahead, Yenala told herself. They are going to stick to the track for a while at any rate, so they'll have to pass me, and then I can pick up their trail again. But first I'll sleep, because they'll have to sleep as well.

She acted on this plan, moving slowly and cautiously above the men, taking great care not to disturb stones or twigs, for the slope up here was honeycombed with tiny caves and covered in shale. Below her, she saw the light from a fire and heard the low murmur of voices, but she went on, determined not to be distracted though her head was buzzing with tiredness and every moment she feared that she might simply fall asleep on her feet, like a donkey.

At last, after about an hour, she decided it was safe to stop – indeed, to go on was extremely perilous for, although the light was strengthening with every minute, she was growing careless. One more slip and I'll be lying in the bottom of a gorge with a broken neck, she scolded herself, and looked around her for the perfect place to rest.

She found it. A fold between two crumbling brown rocks, a tree clinging precariously to what little soil there was which would give shade when the sun came up, and a bird's-eye view of the track, empty now but down which, presently, Adeline and her captors would come.

Yenala settled into the crack and was asleep before she had time to wonder how long it would take her to drop off.

She slept soundly; too soundly. She did not wake until the sun was making its way down the sky again, and by then the brigands – and her mistress – must have been long gone. Angry with herself and hoping against hope, she returned to the spot where the men had camped. Nothing. No warmth in the stones which had held their fire, no sign of them at all.

Yenala stood and stared at the camping place for a long time, tears gathering in her eyes and slowly rolling down her cheeks. She had failed at the very beginning, and now her mistress might be anywhere!

She followed the track forward for a bit, but then it divided, not just into two but into three, and she did not have the skill necessary to follow any trail they might have left in the dry ground. But what to do?

I'll go back and fetch the mule, and then I'll go into the village and beg them to help me to find Missie Adeline, Yenala decided. Who knows, perhaps Mr John will have arrived home . . . yes, that's what I must do!

She set off briskly along the track which would lead eventually back to the compound.

# CHAPTER NINE

At first, Adeline had been too terrified, bruised and breathless to think much about her captors, save that they seemed rather frightened of her than otherwise. They spoke very little, roped her ankles lightly so that she could walk but not run and her wrists quite tightly, and then they simply walked, with the two chief men riding ahead.

By the time they stopped she was very tired indeed, but still awake enough to appreciate the spot they had chosen. A little dell with several huge boulders against which they could lean when they rested, above the path so that they could look down on it, and with a slope of shale and small caves rising behind so that they would hear anyone trying to pass above them. They sat her down by a boulder and then lit a fire, squatting round it as the dawn gradually broke. They were cooking something and presently one of the men brought her a bowl of meat and noodles and a cup of some sort of sweet, heady wine. The man was young, brown-skinned, clearly nervous. He did not hand her the food but put it down within her grasp and then backed away, his eyes on her. It occurred to Adeline that she was probably the first white woman he had ever seen, so she gave him a small smile. If she could only gain his confidence . . . but he showed the whites of his eyes at that and backed hastily away further still before sitting down with the others.

It was difficult to eat from the bowl with her hands roped, but Adeline managed. The food revived her somewhat and the desire for sleep, which had seemed overwhelming, began to recede, to be replaced by a stale and febrile alertness which, she knew, would presently disappear again as exhaustion took its toll.

Her captors, it soon appeared, were not nearly as tired as she; they must have slept all the previous day, she supposed, and marched in the cool of the night. Presently, as the wine sank in the bottle, they began to talk freely amongst themselves and Adeline listened. At first their thick accents defeated her but then she began to pick out a word or two and finally she found she was understanding about three-quarters of what they said.

'I thought she was a *huliching* when she first ran up to us,' one of the younger men confided. 'But who ever heard of a *white* evil spirit? And anyway, a *huliching* would have used her magic to get away. She wouldn't have let us rope her hands and feet.'

'A *huliching* wouldn't bother with you, Chien,' another man said, laughing. 'What have you to offer, after all? She'd want a man of experience, like myself.'

'I don't see the use of her,' the young fellow who had brought Adeline's food over said sulkily. 'She's just another mouth to feed and she'll slow us down if we need to hurry.'

'If we need to hurry and she slows us down we can cut her throat,' one of the riders said with unimpaired cheerfulness. 'But she could be very useful. If we get involved with the *I Ho Chuan* we can hand her over and whilst they deal with her we can get away. If the law or the Europeans chase us – and this Boxer business is going to mean the land will be swarming with foreign devils soon – then we can use her as a hostage for our own freedom. If none of these things happen then General Ho has a wish for a white concubine. He'll pay good money.'

'But is she young? He won't want an old one,' someone pointed out. The first speaker laughed.

'What a fool you are. Did you not note her black hair and unwrinkled skin? I know it's difficult to tell with them, but hair and skin are good signs. They go grey much sooner than our women, and wrinkle more quickly, too. She's young enough.'

Adeline was still listening, but not with as much concentration as before. She had discovered that the rock to which she was tied had a spur sharp as a knife and she was rubbing her roped wrists against it with tiny, secret movements. Nevertheless, she could feel the strands parting.

'I'd like to be alone with one of the *I Ho Chuan* for a moment,' the other horse-rider remarked. 'The damage they're doing to our peace and quiet! They're stirring up the military as a boy with a stick stirs up a wasps' nest and in the end someone will get badly stung – us, very likely.'

'That is exactly why we're going right through the mountains and back to General Ho,' the other horse-rider said with barely restrained impatience. 'We've done well this time – we've got plenty to take home with us, and we're safe enough there whereas here we could well take the blame for activities which are none of our doing. Look at that mission we visited – not a soul left alive and the evidence everywhere. There's no sense in it.'

'Good job too,' the youngster who had brought Adeline's meal remarked, scowling. Adeline was free now, except for her ankles. She moved her position so that she could reach the knot and found it had already worked half loose with the motion of walking. Would the men sleep presently? But it did not look as though they planned a rest; they were damping down the fire, packing things away. I'll have to make a move, Adeline thought desperately, and turned to survey the terrain. Above her was impossible; they would soon catch her up on that tricky

127

shale even supposing she didn't simply slide down again into their midst. But if she went back . . . not on . . . she remembered they had been passing caves for some time. Perhaps she could reach those caves and find one deep enough to hide her? It was a pretty thin chance, but then she was desperate.

The men had packed their belongings but were settling down again, apparently for a smoke. They had a pipe, water, some little saucers of stuff . . . it was opium. Let them get going on that and she had a plan which might actually work!

She waited until the pipe had gone round the circle once, then scrabbled out a round, smooth pebble from the ground on which she sat. She tossed it sideways, towards the path.

It made the slightest of slight rustles as it fell through the trees, a little more noise as it hit the path; not much, but it got everyone's attention. Every head turned towards the path, but apart from that one involuntary movement no one stirred. You could almost see their ears prick, Adeline thought, like eager dogs when they scent prey.

'Listen!'

Adeline obligingly threw another pebble. It made a bit more noise as she had thrown it sideways rather than straight this time. The men looked at one another, grinning. It was clear they thought they were about to surprise a band of unsuspecting travellers. Hands sought knives, men crouched, looking to the leaders. You could feel the tension humming in the air. Adeline was almost sorry for the non-existent travellers on the path below, so clearly could she imagine them just from looking at the expressions on her captors' faces. She wondered whether to throw again, then sat very still. They were stealing down the slope, absolutely noise-lessly, leaving no one, no one at all, in charge of her! What was more, in seconds they were out of sight and she knew that they would be getting as near as they dared to the path before hiding in ambush.

She stood up. She was stiff and sore but ignored the physical discomfort. She must get herself hidden away somewhere before the men returned!

She climbed quickly up the mountainside, then turned back the way they had come. Quite soon she found a cave amongst a hundred such which was large enough to take her. She was devoutly glad that she was not yet big with the child or it might not have been so simple, but as it was she wriggled into the cave of her choice, face-first so that there would be no pale skin showing to give her away, and made herself ignore the myriad discomforts which immediately attacked her. She would stay here for a couple of hours, that was all, then get out – if she could; she fitted into the cave like a cork into a bottle – and make her way back to the village where Yenala would be and, by now, John.

It was hot in the cave. Sweat trickled down her face and she could not wipe it off, for it was impossible to move without risking giving her hiding-place away. She heard the exclamation of surprise and shock when the men discovered she was gone, even heard the young man, as he searched, repeating that he had known all along she was a *huliching* – had he not told them as much? Why should they search for a woman who had probably, by now, either turned herself into a tree or a pigeon or simply flapped her arms and flown back to that haunted compound.

'There were unburied bodies . . . not all converts, either,' one of the other men said uneasily. 'Perhaps we were the first by there . . . the youngster could be right.'

'Oh, nonsense.' It was one of the horse-riders, but even in her cramped little space, Adeline could hear the uneasiness in his voice. 'Still, she's gone; we might as well go too.'

And go they did. Adeline heard their voices growing fainter and fainter until there was silence once more, but even then she was afraid, at first, to move. Suppose it was just a trick – suppose they were hiding, waiting for her to emerge from her bolt-hole? She had never been afraid of confined spaces but now she began to suffer from claustrophobia. She was a part of the earth, jammed in here like this, as good as fossilized. If she did not move soon she would be found here, in the future, entombed in rock, her bones cramped up into a tiny cave-shaped mass.

The thought galvanized her into action and, at first, action frightened her more than anything, for it really seemed as though she was stuck in all truth and would never escape. It was terrifying. She fought against the constricting walls, scraping elbows and knees, cracking her head, taking the skin off her knuckles. But then she reminded herself that she had got in and must therefore be able to get out, and slowed all her movements down. In under a minute she was free, sitting outside the cave and taking great gulps of the fresh air. She was sore and bruised and her scalp was thick with rock-dust, but at least she was free. She stood up, shaky and uncertain still, and realized she was simply too weak to set off right away. She would have to rest; but where?

Finally she chose a good-sized cave and dragged a branch of a tree across the opening, which at least gave her a feeling of security even if it would have been little use in reality. Then she curled down in the sand on the floor of the cave and, thankfully, slept.

Adeline awoke as the sun was setting. She was stiff and cross and her mouth tasted horrible, but she was still alive and felt better for the long sleep. She glanced around her and saw no one. Well, she would set off now, sleep when she needed rest, and try to get back to her home.

She walked steadily half the night, then rested and even slept a little. When she set off again she could see even by the tricky moonlight that the country was beginning to be familiar to her – she had been lurking here for several days and nights now and could not fail to recognize certain landmarks. Indeed, if she climbed a ridge and looked out over the plain, she could see the village, even the outline of the compound. Nearly there, she told herself, nearly there; don't give up now, Adeline!

The sky began to pale. The mule is round here somewhere unless Yenala came and fetched it, Adeline remembered. She climbed up, dropped into a small ravine, climbed out of it. Yes, she recognized the place well. The mule was just around the next big boulder.

She had meant to be so careful but the climb was hard work and sweat ran into her eyes, blurring her vision. She had a stitch and hurried now, desperate to see if the beast was still there. She came round the boulder fast, holding her side, and there was the mule . . . and a figure, heading away from her.

She should have withdrawn at once round the boulder again but she was so surprised to see a living person that she gasped.

The figure stopped moving, the head turned . . .

It was Yenala.


It was a glorious reunion. Kissings and huggings went on for quite a while before Adeline finally stepped back and surveyed the mule and the saddlebags.

'Yenala, I'm ashamed to admit it, but I'm starving. Is there any food left?'

'There's an apple and a bread roll. I nearly ate them both – I'm glad I didn't, now!'

'We'll share them, half each,' Adeline said. 'You should have the bigger bit, being a growing girl, but I'm eating for two as everyone keeps telling me.' She split the roll and the apple and then bit a large piece out of her share of the fruit and gave it to the mule. 'Oh, Yenala, my dear, I'm *so* pleased to see you! Tell me where you've been and what you've done and then I'll tell my story.'

Yenala's story was quickly told, for she had arrived back with the mule barely an hour before her mistress had turned up.

'I lay down by the tree and slept for a bit,' she confessed. 'I was terribly tired, though I feel quite fresh now. And then you came . . . how on earth did you escape?'

Adeline told her and the two girls laughed together over how she had fooled her captors.

'Then you'd already gone when they passed below me,' Yenala said. 'Oh well, then it wasn't so awful me falling asleep. And you're here now, safe and sound . . . you're a bit battered, though. Worse than me.'

'That was the cave,' Adeline said and made Yenala laugh with the description of her frantic fight to emerge. 'Look, we could go back to the village but I'm not sure I fancy it. Why didn't the villagers at least bury the bodies, if they couldn't help the converts and the patients to fight the *I Ho Chuan*? What I think we ought to do is throw ourselves on the mercy of a friendly farmer. Oh, not here, that would be far too dangerous, but a bit further along. I thought, Yenala, that if the mountain won't go to Muhammad then Muhammad should go to the mountain. In other words, we must try to get to Peking. Clearly if John's come back he'll have gone again, believing us to be dead or captured, and China's too big a country to wander through hoping to meet someone. Do you agree?'

'Yes, I think it would be best,' Yenala agreed. 'But do let us find a farmer fairly soon. In fact if we do find one and he refuses to help us I might easily bite a lump out of him, I'm so hungry.'

'Then in that case, we'll try a mountain farmer,' Adeline said at once. 'It must be days since we had a proper meal, and the mountain people are less likely to come into contact with the *I Ho Chuan*. Also, we shan't have to go so far to reach a farm. Come on then, step out!'

Human nature being what it is, though, they hung around on the ridge which gave them the clearest view of the village and the compound for the best part of the day, until in fact they were both quite certain that no one was searching for them or endeavouring to mend and tidy the compound. 'For John would do both if he was there,' Adeline said sadly. 'I hope he's all right, Yenala.'

'So do I,' Yenala said earnestly. 'Now let's find this farmer and ask him for shelter.'

They reached a likely little mud-brick cottage before darkness fell. They went openly to the door, leading the mule, and greeted the farmer with a confidence they were far from feeling. We were driven from the compound by the *I Ho Chuan* and would appreciate being allowed to buy a meal, Adeline said. Her captors had been too much in awe of her to search her, so the small amount of money she had on her person was with her still.

A certain caution crossed the farmer's face at the mention of the Boxers but he opened the door and bade them enter, promising them a poor meal which might not so much fill as touch their bellies, and a night's sleep on the straw which all the family shared. As soon as Adeline got inside she realized why the farmer had let them in at all. There sat his wife, and on her knee the fat baby who had been cured of a nasty attack of croup by John's medicine and her own quickness.

'Ah, hello! And how is your son?' Adeline said at once and the woman looked gratified and said he was well, very well, and would they like a cup of tea whilst dinner cooked?

The tea tasted like nectar to the girls, and when they came the rice and vegetables were sublime. Adeline ate sparingly, however, conscious that the farmer had his work cut out to feed himself, his wife and the fat baby, who stared round-eyed at Adeline throughout the meal whilst he himself was attached, limpet-like, to his mother's breast.

'What will you do tomorrow, when you've eaten and rested?' the farmer asked courteously at the conclusion of the meal. 'We are poor people; our home is not fit for ladies such as yourselves.'

131

Adeline knew what he meant. He could neither afford to feed them nor risk sheltering them.

'We hope to make our way to Peking,' she said slowly. 'We cannot go back to the compound, because it has been burnt down and we feel the villagers would not welcome us.'

'Men have asked for you,' the wife put in, smiling, eager. 'Your men from the compound, Missie Adeline. They went away after; I think they've gone to Peking.'

'Really? Was my husband with them?'

'I don't know, but I can find out, or rather Chang could.' She nudged her husband. 'Go round the neighbours, ask about. Some went into the compound for the burying, they'd know if the *yang kuei-tzu* . . .' She put her hand over her mouth and giggled. 'I mean, if the white man was with them.'

'I'll go first thing in the morning,' her husband said. He was plainly anxious to see the last of his uninvited guests. 'How will you reach Peking? They say the railway's been burned and the track pulled up.'

'We'll walk,' Adeline said, coming to a quick decision. 'I think we'll be less conspicuous on foot. We – we would like to make you a present of the mule. You've been very kind.'

'The mule? You would give us the mule?' the farmer gasped. 'Why, Missie Adeline, you've no idea how wonderful it would be to us to own a mule. Now, I am the mule. I carry the ripe crops up from my little field down on the plain, I carry down the seed, I heave and wrench the plough through the heavy soil in autumn . . . I am a mule, you see! Such a gift! A mule is something we have only dreamed of owning!'

'Well, it's yours,' Adeline said firmly. 'If . . . if we can stay for one more night and one more day, so that we are fit for the journey.'

The wife broke in, her face expressing even more joy than her husband's.

'You stay and welcome,' she said. 'And no matter who it is that asks we'll say we've seen no one, no one at all. Unless it is your man, of course.'

'Then the mule's yours,' Adeline reiterated. 'It's a good animal, strong and obedient. Be good to it and it will serve you well.'

Her host and hostess assured her that they would be souls of kindness to the mule, and Adeline and Yenala, with grateful smiles, curled up on the straw for their first night under a roof for days.

In the Legation quarter, the siege commenced on the dot of the hour appointed with cannon fire from the east of the city, and from that moment on there was no time to be bored, though John fretted because he could not get out to search for Adeline.

Hard work, though, was a panacea against too much thought. With others he dug fortifications, carted sandbags and leapt in and out of barricades as they tried to see from where they could best defend their position. Along with another missionary of about his own age, Adam Carruthers, John volunteered to keep watch, and from the first day they took their turn on the Tartar wall and other danger points. At first John was not required to fire his rifle but merely to stay behind the hastily erected barricades and make sure the enemy was kept at bay. The Tartar wall was a massive structure, wide enough on top for four carriages to race abreast along its length, and of course the Chinese soon raised their own barricades further along it so that they were able to answer the Europeans' fire from an equal height.

On that first day, the Dutch and Belgian Legations were abandoned by the Allies and burnt by the enemy.

'They'll try fire on us too, I dare say,' Adam told John. 'The Boxers always fire a village to start with and then massacre those who run from the flames.'

'They've got to get near enough first,' John said grimly. They were on the Tartar wall and he cocked his rifle suggestively. 'I never thought I'd fire this on another human being, Adam, but I find I'm quite as willing to defend my own as any soldier.'

'And I,' Adam agreed. 'But it may not come to that.'

'It may not. But if it does I'll aim straight, Adam. Not above their heads.'

The other man turned the subject, and soon they were relieved from their watch and could make their way to their quarters in the British Legation.

'There's a fire in the jewellers' quarter of the city,' someone remarked as they were all getting ready for bed. 'Hope the wind doesn't change; it could be unpleasantly close if the flames blow this way.'

'John and I were talking about the possibility of fire earlier,' Adam said. 'Well, we're safe enough here, at any rate. The only building abutting on to the Legation is the Hanlin Yuan, and they aren't likely to see all their history go up in smoke even to get rid of us!'

John, settling down on his squeaky straw mattress, reflected that this was some comfort. The Hanlin Yuan was probably the oldest library in the world, containing books and artefacts from the very start of the ancient Chinese civilization.

It was a small comfort, but better than none, and John fell asleep on it.

'There's a fire! Grab anything that'll hold water and come at once.'

John had been on night watch by the tunnel that he and others had burrowed under the Legation wall earlier in the day. Mr Gamewell, the engineer in charge, had deemed it wise to have this bolt-hole in case of trouble, but surely even that sensitive and intelligent man had not dreamed that the Chinese really would fire the Hanlin Yuan?

There were seven men in the dormitory. They all stumbled out of their beds and grabbed chamber pots, water jugs and anything they could lay their hands on before following John in a rush out of the building, across the lawn and down to the tunnel.

The garden was a scene of wild activity. Over the wall they could see the smoke, billowing up all white and grey and studded with glowing fragments of wood. Occasional tongues of flame were licking up to the very top of the building, and as the men made their way from the well to the tunnel with their receptacles filled there was a roar and a brilliant light and one of the big old trees in the Hanlin courtyard went up with a rush, its brittle branches flaring like fireworks as the flames climbed higher.

'They've formed a human chain,' John shouted to his companions above the roar of the fire. 'I'm going down the tunnel . . . Come with me, Adam.'

'What's under here?' Adam asked rather apprehensively as he bent to crawl through the tunnel. 'I don't want to be decapitated by a fire-raiser as I get into the Hanlin courtyard.'

'You mean the enemy? My dear chap, the Chinese aren't exactly lion-hearted, you know! They fired the place, going from building to building with torches, and then they made off as fast as they could, leaving the fire, they hoped, to do their work for them. It's odd, isn't it, that they don't even give us credit for self-preservation, or they'd have left a strong guard to try to stop us dousing the flames.'

The tunnel was low and difficult of access but fortunately it was also short. The two men emerged filthy and breathless but otherwise unharmed and were immediately seized upon by the man in charge, a captain of Marines.

'Two more . . . well done! As the water comes through take it over there . . .' he pointed '. . . to your right. Our only chance, apart from prayer, is to get the flames down at that particular point.'

'Right,' John said. 'I'll pray as well.'

The marine shot a quick glance at him, raised an eyebrow, then grinned.

'You do that. Pray for the wind to change, just as the English prayed in 1588.' He saw John's face begin to frown and added kindly, 'Drake, old boy . . . the Armada . . . the wind changed for them.'

'Of course. They used fireships too – the British, I mean. Well, at least I'll know what to pray for!'

But in fact he had very little time for more than a steady background hope, for the fire raged on and despite their efforts it seemed as though nothing they could do would save the Legation. For hours the men ran, walked, and finally staggered between the end of the tunnel and the inferno, throwing their pathetic little pots of water on to the blaze. Then someone thought of bass brooms and these, well soaked in water, seemed at last to be making some impression.

John and Adam met once or twice, smoke-blackened and exhausted, to compare notes. It was clear to both of them that only a miracle would save the Legation, for despite their best efforts the wind was still carrying the flames ever closer to their walls.

But God, John thought exultantly, was on their side. Like Drake facing the Spanish Armada, they were saved by a sudden and inexplicable change of wind direction. One moment it was blowing on the left side of his face, the next it was his right cheek which felt the hot and fierce wind against it. John stopped feverishly wielding his bass broom and watched almost unbelievingly as the flames faltered, checked, and then went back on themselves so that they were devouring not the great trees which lay between the fire and the Legation but the already charred wood of the Hanlin itself.

It was only then that the order to leave was given and John, Adam and the others crawled back through the tunnel. Fresh men took their place, however, for no one would sleep sound in his bed until the danger to the Legation was completely over.

The siege dragged on. Soon John had no time to count the days and scarcely noticed what was going on outside, for he was too busy in the hospital. It was in the chancery of the British Legation and was over-crowded and hot, the windows sandbagged to prevent stray bullets entering, and flies, thick as currants in a Christmas cake, swarming on every available surface including the bodies of the wounded.

Days passed and the relief force did not come. Neither did Adeline. John worried, but his immediate preoccupation was with his patients and with the Chinese converts in the gardens of the Prince's palace who were so short of food that their children were starving to death. Despite the shortage of ammunition the soldiers shot crows and other birds for the converts whenever the opportunity offered, but even so, they died each day, each night.

After a hard night on duty, John and Adam went for a walk as dawn was breaking, strolling beside the still waters of the canal and talking quietly.

'It's a good thing the Chinese don't care for straight fighting or hand-to-hand encounters,' Adam observed, as they passed the wall behind which Colonel Shiba defended the garden of the Fu from the enemy. He nodded towards it. 'Have you been in there lately? Shiba has a handful of men, the Chinese are numbered in thousands, yet the Chinks spend more time scrambling out of reach of his fire than they do replying to it.'

'It's fairly typical of an untrained mob, which is what the army largely consists of,' John pointed out. 'The officers lead from the rear, as the saying goes. They aren't a warlike people.'

'Quite. They enjoyed chopping the converts into little bits before the siege started, and firing missions and burning people alive, or killing defenceless missionaries and their wives and children, but firing at some-one who fires back is a very different matter.'

135

For a moment John quite literally could not answer. In his mind the dreadful scenes in Ayiteng reappeared, vivid and disgusting. He had known the smell would haunt his nightmares, but now whenever he went near the outer defences it came to his attention once more, for the Chinese did not bury their dead, neither did they move them. They left the bodies where they lay to rot or be devoured by rats, pigs or dogs, all of which scurried out after dark and partook of the grisly feast.

'What's up?' Adam said, then saw John's set, white face. He gripped John's shoulder with a big, tanned hand. 'What a fool I am . . . look, old boy, your wife will be all right! The Tsungli Yamen have offered a reward for white women. They're paying forty taels for each white woman brought in alive, and twenty-five taels for each Christian convert. So no one will kill your wife, or the lass with her, whilst they can get money like that for them.'

'Is that true?' John said, the colour returning to his face. 'You wouldn't lie to me, Adam? But . . . what do they pay for a dead white woman?'

'Nothing, I dare say,' Adam said airily. 'Don't worry, old fellow, you must have realized by now that the Chinese love money. They won't harm a hair of her head whilst they stand to gain by her.'

'I hope you're right . . . I'm almost certain you are. I'd best get back to my bed now, though, Adam, to have an hour or so's rest. Where are you bound?'

Adam pulled a face.

'To the wall, for my sins. Keep your pecker up, old lad!'

After he had left John, Adam went on his way to the wall. He scrounged a handful of melon seeds from the kitchen, then took his place behind the barricades. I'm a crass idiot to have spoken to poor old John like that, he scolded himself as he settled into position in front of his loop-hole, but at least I undid some of the harm by telling him about the rewards. And I didn't go and blab about the other reward – I didn't say that the Imperial Council will pay thirty taels for a dead white woman.


# CHAPTER TEN


After their two days of rest and food, Adeline and Yenala left the foothills. Because of the gift of the mule the farmer and his wife did their best to help. Adeline was dressed in peasant-like garb anyway, the tunic and trousers of a well-to-do Chinese, perhaps, but the farmer's wife went into Ayiteng with Adeline's silky clothing and came back with genuine rough peasant cotton and, even better, with a large straw coolie hat for each girl. Not only was the hat a wonderful shield against the sun, it was also a good disguise. After Yenala had worked on Adeline's face with a stick of charcoal, elongating her eyelids and dusting her skin with a mixture of flour and saffron, it was not easy to see that a foreign devil lurked beneath the hat.

Adeline's last little store of money was spent on a few eggs, which their hostess hard-boiled, some rice and some bread. Just as they were about to depart, moreover, the farmer's wife, with a shy smile, produced a large honey cake and some dry and wrinkled apples which she besought them to take as a reminder of her humble self.

So at last the two girls set off, if not with confidence, at least with determination and high hopes. They would get to Peking and find John somehow and they wouldn't let themselves be captured in between their farmer's home and the capital.

But at the very first village they reached their determination to go to Peking received a knock.

'Peking?' the village baker said incredulously. 'Haven't you heard? China is at war with the foreign devils at long last. They've got them bottled up in the Imperial City and will kill them all at their leisure. But life there is impossible. A good many Pekingese have left, for the guns thunder night and day and there is great danger from the desperate bullets of the doomed. Why, my uncle and aunt, who have spent the last twenty years in the city, have come to throw themselves on our hospitality until the troubles are over. No, no, my dear child, you and your sister must not go to Peking; you will be killed for sure.'

Yenala soothed the baker by assuring him that they did not mean to go into Peking itself but only to a village three or four miles away. Nevertheless when she and Adeline had left the baker's and walked on through the street and out at the further gate, they only went a few paces before stopping to gaze at each other with dismay.

'They're at war! Then that's why John didn't return to us. You heard what the man said – the Europeans are imprisoned inside the Imperial City. But that means we won't be able to reach them even if we manage to get as far as the outer walls. What's more, with the Boxers in the city and the Imperial troops obviously helping them, we'd be in greater danger there than in almost any other part of the country. Yenala, what on earth should we do for the best?'

Yenala considered the matter. Like Adeline she had her wide straw coolie hat on her head; now she tilted it forward so that she could only look down at her bare feet, slap-slapping along the track, for they had begun to move forward again since standing still might arouse suspicions. She and Adeline were both barefoot and Adeline was glad of it in the torrid heat.

'You're right, we can't go to Peking,' she said at last, her young voice grave. 'But *where* can we go and be safe? Oh, Missie Adeline, if only you'd been in the country long enough to have made *safe* Chinese friends!'

'And we dare not turn back now, or the villagers will wonder,' Adeline said distractedly. 'Dear God, in a country this immense you would think there must be a safe harbour somewhere for two desperate females, yet I can think of none.'

'I know!' Yenala said suddenly. 'What about Missie Joanna Wang? Does she live around here.'

'Not really,' Adeline said gloomily. 'She uses a bungalow in the Western Hills sometimes . . . now why did the Western Hills give me a jolt . . . Western Hills . . . Ah! Got it!'

'Got what, Missie Adeline?'

Adeline had been frowning and clicking her fingers in a fury of almost-remembering, but now she turned to her companion, beaming.

'Why, can't you guess? Before we came to the mission there was another missionary there – we took over his house and everything. He's retired now, but he didn't want to leave the country so he built a beautiful bungalow in the Western Hills. I've never set eyes on Mrs Instadt but I've met the husband a couple of times and he's a grand old chap. What's more, he told me how to get to his place . . . it's remote, but there will be people who can tell us how to reach it once we get near. The bungalow's called Distant Lightning, and of course the Instadts have a memorable name – though knowing how the Chinese like nicknames, he's probably called the ancient foreign devil, or little Mr Big-Nose, or something like that.'

'If you know his name, the name of his home, and a few more details like that, we'll find him,' Yenala said confidently. 'Right. As soon as it's dark we'll turn back and make for the mountains once more.'

It was unfortunate that they had been ten miles on their way before they heard that China was at war with Europeans, for it was ten additional miles they could well have done without, but they curled up in a bamboo thicket until it grew dusk and then walked through the night, arriving in the foothills just as dawn was breaking.

'This baby will think human beings are meant to spend their lives walking,' Adeline said, patting her stomach as they sank down on to a convenient rock from which they could watch the sun come up, yet which was hidden from passers-by by thick undergrowth. 'I'm not even tired the way I once was. I say, Yenala, do you suppose we've enough food to get us to the Instadts' place?'

'We'll certainly manage with a bit of help from the country,' Yenala said. 'After all, we were making for Peking. Shall we sleep for a couple of hours, Missie Adeline, and then walk on, or do you need more sleep still?'

'An hour will be fine,' Adeline said. 'By the way, Yenala my dear, you must stop calling me "Missie Adeline". Just plain Adeline will do. When my baby's born you will be his big sister, and he'll call you Yenala and you will call him . . . by his name, whatever it is. After this adventure, besides, I shall never let you go off and be someone else's girl. You'll still be my dear Yenala even when you're married to a man of your own. So you shall be my adopted daughter and my baby's adopted big sister, and you must call John and me by our first names.'

Yenala stared, incredulous.

'Be the baby's big sister? Oh, M . . . I mean Adeline, that would be wonderful!'

'Yes, for when the baby's about a year old John and I will take him back to England to see my own dear father and John's parents, and we shall want you to come as well. How will you like that? A sea voyage and a strange country.'

'Oh, M . . . Adeline,' Yenala said rapturously. 'I would like that!'

'Good. But now we must sleep.' Adeline was becoming expert in falling asleep whenever the opportunity occurred and she had noticed that Yenala, too, could drop off in almost any circumstances. Now, she put her arm round the younger girl, let her head fall on to Yenala's shoulder, and very soon slept.

They travelled all that day, and by evening were high in the remote mountain country where few farms or cottages were to be seen and the only people they met were animal herders. They slept by a little mountain brook which chuckled and bubbled merrily all night and gave Adeline delightful dreams of Saintley Manor and home.

'We should reach Distant Lightning by afternoon, or before the sun sets, anyway,' Adeline said hopefully, as they set off next morning. 'Won't it be wonderful to have a bath? And sit at a table to eat a meal?'

Yenala agreed that it would be nice, particularly the bath, and several hard, uphill miles were beguiled by listing the food the girls would find most welcome and the niceties of civilization they had missed the most.

Presently, however, they found that they were in what Yenala gleefully called 'the real mountains'. Here, the peaks were too high for vegetation to flourish and the rocks flung back the sun's heat, making it seem even hotter than it really was, though as Adeline said at least it was a dry heat. But of course it slowed them down and when their way sloped gently down into the trees once more they were glad.

It was here that they met the charcoal burners: two men and a young boy. They had been directed some hours before by a girl with a herd of goats, but now, as they stumbled through a forest of deciduous trees, they saw the charcoal burners' huts and made hopefully for them.

Yenala asked directions, and though the two men were taciturn, mumbling that the lad would know, the directions, when they came, were clear and precise. It appeared that they were only an hour away from their destination.

'He says we'll see it clearly in an hour, just a short way away, but it may take another hour to reach it,' Yenala reported, making her way back to where Adeline stood out of sight amidst the trees. 'I don't understand how that can be, but we'll make the best speed we can. He says it's high, up in the peaks, so we don't want to get there when they've closed the gates. It's bad country for sleeping out in.'

They followed the lad's directions and sure enough in an hour or so they found themselves on a ridge, looking across a narrow, rocky gorge to a bare mountain peak. And built into the rock itself, with its courtyards steeply sloping, was an unmistakably European bungalow, though it had the usual Chinese wall round it on three sides to keep it from attack by wandering groups of soldiers or bandits.

The fourth side, of course, was the side which faced across the ravine, which meant, as the girls could clearly see, that they had a good climb in front of them still. They could not possibly descend the ravine nor scale the other side, so they would have to go round.

'Oh dear, I would have liked a rest,' Yenala said, but Adeline, infected by her companion's fear of having to spend the night on the inhospitable mountainside, was firm.

'It may take hours to get round there, and most of it's climbing,' she pointed out. 'I don't think we ought to linger. These very bare hillsides make me nervous.'

'I hate them,' Yenala said. 'And they hate us; don't you feel that, Adeline?'

Adeline liked the lonely splendour of the hills, but she knew all too well what the younger girl meant. There was almost no cover in the peaks, and although she knew it was foolish she felt that hidden eyes watched her as they crossed the loneliest, barest stretches.

'Well, they certainly don't hold out much hope of a comfortable night,' she said. 'We must get to the bungalow before it gets dark and the sun's sinking already. Off we go again!'

'Phew! Well, we've made it. Thank heaven the sun hasn't gone down yet, so they won't have closed the gates.'

Adeline was almost too breathless to speak, and her words came out in short spasms, for the climb and the trek had both been longer and harder than they had anticipated. But now, below them, they could see their destination, only a few hundred yards away. No wonder the Instadts had felt safe here! It was an incredibly steep and stony track which led to their gates, and few would bother to struggle up and down it unless they actually intended to visit the missionary and his wife. No wonder the old man rode a donkey, Adeline thought. No horse could have negotiated that track!

'It has been too much for you,' Yenala said, looking anxiously at her companion. 'Are you sure you're all right?'

'Well, I wouldn't have got this far it hadn't been for you, and the baby's

140

showing me he objects by kicking like anything, but I'm all right, thanks to your strong right arm,' Adeline told her. 'Oh, how I long for that relaxing hot bath!'

They hurried forward. The gates were open, the porter nowhere in sight. They went into the compound and checked the man's niche, but it was empty. However, they could hear someone singing somewhere, so obviously the Instadts and their servants were home.

Yenala found the bell and rang it vigorously. As she did so she looked through the arched entrance into the first courtyard. Despite the slope on which it was built it was a pleasant place, with shade trees grouped around a pool and rhododendron bushes hiding the wall. A big Chinese woman was crossing the courtyard, carrying something carefully in both hands. She came to a mound of clothing lying on the ground and stepped over it, then turned to see who had rung the bell.

'Is Mr Instadt available?' Adeline called. 'Could you tell him that Mrs Sawyer and Yenala have come to see him?'

The woman smiled and turned. She called and a man came out of the house; a large Chinese. And then Adeline saw the pile of clothes and something clicked in her mind. She seized Yenala by the shoulder and pushed her violently towards the gateway.

'Run, Yenala! It's a trap! Run!'

She turned, knowing she was too tired and too heavy with the child to escape herself, hoping to gain time for the younger girl. And Yenala nearly made it. Young and fleet, she rushed out of the gateway and on to the cliff path, then hesitated, looking back. Other men had appeared when the woman called and they pushed past Adeline, knocking her to the ground. Adeline shrieked again, commanding Yenala to go, to leave her, and it looked as though the girl would obey for she took two scrambling steps upward, then paused again.

She had lost her chance. A man grabbed for her shoulder and swung the blade in his other hand. The coolie hat fell to the ground and toppled slowly down the path until it was only yards from Adeline's horrified eyes.

The coolie hat was bleeding; Yenala's eyes stared back at Adeline even as the blood seeped from her severed neck.

Adeline came slowly back to consciousness. It was pitch dark and she was lying down. She could remember nothing of what had gone before save that it had been terrible, with a residue of fear and disgust which still dried her mouth.

Cautiously, she moved, meaning to sit up, but her limbs were so heavy that she felt as if she was nailed to the ground on which she lay. She fell back again. Her heart was beating sluggishly and there was a low pain in her back. She moved her right hand and the left one moved too. She was tied up!

Immediately her heart began to hammer, a staccato beat. She and

Yenala had arrived at the Instadts' bungalow, someone had come out to greet them . . . and Adeline saw again Yenala's head, bloodstained in the dust with the coolie hat still in place, and above, on the path, her little trunk, sinking down into the dust. They had killed her friend, the faithful child who had saved her life many times, who had been dearer to her, in the end, than the child she carried within her.

Sick and shaking, she tried to move her feet. They were not tied, but when she moved again she realized why. Her wrists were bound together and roped to something, probably to a piece of furniture. Not that it mattered, she told herself dully. What was the point in trying to escape? They had killed the Instadts and their servants, they had killed her child Yenala and John was far away. She was alone and would soon be killed. They could not let her live, she knew too much. She just hoped they had not kept her alive in order to torture her to death, as they had tortured the servants in the Ayiteng mission compound. Let me die, dear Lord, she pleaded. Let me die now, here, in the dark, cleanly and with dignity, don't let them do what they did to the others . . . let me die now!

The pain in her back was worse. It must be the way she was lying. She tried to move, to ease it, but it became more and more severe until, without knowing it, she began to moan aloud as great spasms racked her. Soon she no longer thought about release or escape. She just tried to bear the pain, drawing up her legs and then, in a moment of terrifying lucidity, struggling out of her peasant trousers because she knew, now, what was happening to her.

As dawn came through the cracks in the shutters, Adeline gave painful birth to a baby who neither cried nor stirred. When it was all over, when the pulsing mound of her stomach was still, the door opened and a woman came in. She threw back the shutters and then exclaimed sharply. She came over to where her prisoner lay. Adeline's eyes were closed but she knew the woman was there, could feel her presence without having to lift her lids.

'She's given birth,' the woman called to someone outside the room. 'It's dead.' Adeline's eyes opened a slit, enough to see without being seen. She saw the woman scoop up the thing which had emerged from Adeline's pain-racked body and leave the room again. She shut the door behind her.

Adeline rolled on to her side and curled her knees up close to her chest and tried to will death to take her. But in the end, it was sleep which complied. A deep, exhausted sleep, like a little death.

Hours later she woke again, raging with thirst and filled, now, with the pain of loss and emptiness. She gathered her strength and courage and shouted feebly, hoping that someone would hear her and come in and simply smite off her head. It would end the pain and the heartache quickly, at least. Instead, the woman came with a big jug of water. She sat Adeline up and poured water ruthlessly into her mouth so that it soaked her as

142

well as slaking her thirst. Then the woman threw what was left in the jug over Adeline's bloodstained hips and thighs and left again, all without speaking a word.

The next time she woke it was high noon and the room buzzed with heat. She was lightheaded and knew she needed food, but inertia made it impossible for her to call out again. Instead, she just lay where she was and presently heard voices. She listened for want of something better to do.

'If we take her to the Viceroy, Yu Hsien will kill her and keep the bounty money for himself,' one man said. 'On the other hand I'm not walking all the way to Peking with a dead body . . . the Old Buddha's a strange one. Last week she wanted 'em dead, next week she'll probably have the head off your shoulders for a wrong word to one of the *yang kuei-tzu*. There's no saying what she'll do.'

'She's annoyed with the *I Ho Chuan* anyway, because our men died when the foreign bullets flew,' another, deeper voice said dispassionately. 'The silly old fool. As if anyone with a grain of sense could believe we were invincible. It was all right to tell the peasants no gun could kill and no axe could break but we shouldn't have tried the same thing with the Old Buddha. She soon proved it was a lie, anyway; had old Wang's head off him in a second, just because he waved his sword whilst she was talking.'

'If we took her to Yu Hsien, I mean her body, he wouldn't punish us, he'd be pleased,' the first voice said pensively. 'But he wouldn't pay us the reward; you have to get that in Peking.'

'No one but Peking will pay us forty taels for her, that's sure.' It was the woman's voice, harsh but unmistakably female. 'If we can get her there alive, the Yamen will pay up, and if the laws have changed they'll pay the dead rate of thirty taels. And consider, brothers, how useful it could be to have a live white woman if the *yang kuei-tzu* win! They would undoubtedly pay the highest ransom of all.'

'She's right,' the deep voice said. 'It's the safest thing to do. Suppose we turn up with a body and the Old Buddha suddenly decides it's a crime to kill a white woman?' He made a sound which Adeline recognized shrinkingly as an imitation of a throat being cut. 'We don't want that, do we?'

'True.' A new voice, lighter than any of the others. 'If we take her to Peking alive we can't lose. Kalli is right – women so often are! But does anyone suppose the *yang kuei-tzu* might win? I thought it was simply not possible, not with every hand against them.'

There was a long silence. Adeline, interested despite herself, thought that the leader – if the deep-voiced one was the leader – was weighing truth and diplomacy in the balance. Finally, he spoke.

'This time, yes, I believe they will win,' he said. 'But in the years to come we'll win. We always win in the end. Look at the Manchus. They

143

came down into our country and conquered us but they were eaten up by China in the end. Now we keep them in Peking because it suits us to do so, not because it is their will.'

Adeline listened as they dispersed once more about the house, the deep-voiced one having announced that before they left they must make the place safe for their return.

'It's a real fortress,' he said. 'A pity the old people had taken themselves and most of their servants off to Peking or we might have had two more hostages to sell. And I wouldn't trust the Edict that promises money for live converts – a man would forswear his own mother, let alone a foreign God, when his life was at stake. As for dead ones . . .' He made a derisive noise. 'I can't see anyone passing over good money for a dead peasant on the grounds that you *say* he's a Christian.'

Adeline, who had sat up the better to hear, lay down on the floor once again. So it sounded as though they did not intend to kill her, not yet at any rate. And the Instadts were alive, which was good news. But I would like to die please, God, Adeline prayed, because I have nothing left to live for. John was far away and remote from her troubles, and she could not believe she would ever see him again.

But God clearly did not see why she should simply die for want of a little spirit, for presently the woman entered the room. She cut the ropes that bound the prisoner and then wrapped her in a quilt, effectively imprisoning her once more, though her feet were left free. Not that I could struggle, Adeline told herself dully, as she was led out of the bare little room and into another, a pleasantly furnished living-room, and sat down on a small settee. I'm still far too weak.

Once she was seated the woman crossed the room and picked up a bowl from a hatch which must lead, Adeline supposed, to the kitchen. She began to feed her prisoner, and though Adeline might wish to die the will to live was stronger. The stuff in the bowl was rice made into a sort of porridge with milk and honey and, the spoon rapidly travelling between bowl and mouth, Adeline finished it up in no time, drank the tea which was held to her lips, and then submitted to being pushed flat on the settee whilst the woman secured the quilt with two lengths of string.

Once the woman had left the room again, Adeline tried to get out of the quilt which, she thought, should be a simple matter. It proved quite otherwise, however. She could roll from side to side and had she managed to stand up would probably have been able to hop about, but she could not get her hands or feet free.

Presently, with the food warm inside her and the quilt warm without, she fell asleep.

After several weeks of the siege the Chinese, for no logical reason that John could imagine, announced a truce. They sent food and fruit to the besieged, allowed the exchange of letters once more, and even let a certain amount of fraternization take place between the troops. But it did not last, and though John pleaded with Sir Alfred and others to allow him to go into the main part of the city to search for Adeline, it was deemed far too dangerous.

'We need you,' Captain Todd, who commanded the section of the Tartar wall on which John now frequently served, told him. 'You're one of our best snipers, quite apart from your medical abilities. We can't risk you getting yourself killed.'

John had to admit that this was true, and all too soon he and Adam found themselves making their way up the long rampart to the Tartar wall once more, the attackers' shell-fire ringing in their ears.

'It was nice whilst it lasted,' John observed, settling down behind the barricade.

'True.' Adam touched his shoulder lightly, then moved to his own position. John saw, out of the corner of his eye, Adam peering out at the enemy before settling down, satisfied that no one was about to lead a sortie from the Chinese barricades.

John had been active on the wall now for some time, and was uneasy about it still. At first he had been unable to accept the necessity of killing, but then he had gone round the Fu, where hundreds of Chinese converts eked out their miserable existence. He saw once more the dying babies, the frail women who shared their tiny rations with their children. This was China, he told himself, just as much as those murderers outside were China. Here, skinny, exhausted Chinese did the physical work of building the defences, fought as best they could for those less able to defend themselves, proved that their Christianity – and their humanity – were not only skin-deep. When he fired at the enemy, when a sniper toppled, then he was making a conscious effort to keep those converts alive, he told himself sternly, and had no further pangs of conscience over manning the defences.

But he had realized there was a dark side to his nature which he had never previously acknowledged. Side by side with his doctor's desire to heal and his missionary's desire to save souls was another desire – to shoot down the man who threatened him and his. There was a dark triumph in the shot that picked out a sniper and sent him tumbling from the wall, a stab of glee when a man threw a blazing torch at a wooden building which sheltered innocent children and was brought low himself by a single bullet. He would not let himself worry about this – he knew he must remain single-minded whilst the crisis lasted – but one day he would have to bring it out, look at it, and see if he could come to terms with it. Perhaps his vocation had not been strong enough, for there were missionaries in plenty amongst the besieged who had not lifted a finger to help in any way, not even volunteering for hospital duties. They preached, but they would not raise a hand against their fellow men, they said.

Perhaps John should have admired such people, but he did not. He was proud to be doing everything in his power to beat back the men who were trying to kill Christ's children. If I just stood back and let another fire for me, where would be the credit to my soul for not killing? he asked himself, and knew the answer lay in his own hands.

Slowly, he raised the rifle, cuddled it to his cheek and pushed the barrel through the loop-hole.

# CHAPTER ELEVEN

Sergeant Hagworthy had decided he did not like China ten years earlier, when he had first come to the country. Now he decided all over again that it was the worst terrain he had ever come across for a forced march. What was more, the Chinese peasants were all the same . . . hateful was his favourite way of describing them. They lied as they breathed, without reason or necessity, simply because they preferred it to speaking the truth. They also exaggerated all their good points – not that Sergeant Hagworthy could have been prevailed upon to admit they had any good points – and denied all their bad ones. He had soldiered in India, he had soldiered in Africa, but nowhere were the natives as bad as these Chinks. Cowards to a man, which made it worse. A Chinese army fights with umbrellas, they said, but didn't they talk big! All piss and wind, Sergeant Hagworthy told himself, marching grimly across a beastly paddy-field with rice ready for harvesting pricking his legs above his puttees. He smashed the crop down as he went and was glad. There isn't one of 'em I'd let clean my boots, he told himself, and tried to concentrate on how hateful were the Chinks so that he wouldn't have to remember the sights he had seen in the compound of the chief man of these parts.

It wouldn't have been so bad if we'd caught some of the swine what did it, Sergeant Hagworthy told himself as his boots created vengeful havoc with the crop. If we'd got just one . . . the chief feller, the one who'd ordered it done, that would have been best. His stomach crawled as he remembered those piled bodies, the little children, the things which had been done to them. For a moment he literally saw red and against that redness an Oriental face, wicked, grinning. In his mind his fist smashed into the face, withdrew, smashed again and again. Teeth showered out of the grinning mouth, the nose turned to bloody pulp, but still the sergeant's fist continued its pleasurable retaliatory work. If only they'd caught one of 'em!

However, he must not get carried away and forget his responsibilities to his men. They were young men for the most part, a contingent of Welsh Guards told off to try to reach a mission where some nuns ran a convent school for orphan girls. Too late. All dead. Little Chinese girls along with the Europeans. It was odd; he had been as savagely, hotly outraged by the little dead Chinese girls as he had been by the small white children who belonged to the missionaries themselves, attached to the convent. And the nuns. In a way almost more outraged because those swine had killed their own . . . it was cannibalism, that was, Sergeant Hagworthy told himself rather confusedly. But then he expected nothing else from the Chinks. No wonder they grew up bad, though, when that sort of thing went on. A child learns what he's taught, copies what he sees . . . no wonder the peasants lied and cheated and sold their babies and stuck little girls on mountain tops for the wolves to eat! They needed good examples, that was the trouble.

Sergeant Hagworthy glanced back at his men. He had been in the army long enough to be able to read the faces of young soldiers and this lot were marching in a daze . . . but not a daze of exhaustion, a daze of outraged fury. They could not see the crop they trampled flat, because like him they were still seeing the massacre in the compound.

They had thought, naturally, that the outrage had only just happened, even though the flies had risen like a great black lace curtain at their approach. Because what sort of man lets bodies just lie on the ground in a tropical country? Especially when . . . Sergeant Hagworthy jerked his mind back as he would have jerked the reins of a recalcitrant horse. They had quickly realized their mistake, known the futility of searching for those responsible. The massacre had taken place two or three days earlier and those who had wielded the axes, swords and other implements had gone, leaving no trace of themselves behind.

There had been no one in the mission or the convent, of course. A damn big place it had been, too, with perhaps thirty of those little courtyards leading one to the other and all sorts still lying around to show what it had once been. School books, hospital equipment, bits of kitchen stuff, stable items, though nothing valuable had been left by the aggressors. A broken slate, some chalk, a board duster, little things which were no use to anyone now. But little things which spoke clearly enough of what the place had once been . . . busy, happy, useful.

The sun beat down on Sergeant Hagworthy and to take his mind off what he had seen he glanced about him. Over to his right he saw a peasant's wattle and daub cottage. He wondered what the occupants thought, seeing white men, soldiers, trampling their crop. Not that he cared . . . they were murderers too in their way. They hadn't gone to the rescue of the people in the mission compound, had they? They had just shrugged and turned the other way – unless they had gone to watch the *yang kuei-tzu* and the little girl-children dying.

'Get some chickens or a pig, two of you,' Sergeant Hagworthy ordered as they drew level with the cottage. 'If you see anyone, give us a shout.'

Two of the men detached themselves from the column and approached the cottage, but before they could do more than seize a wildly shrieking and struggling cockerel, someone opened the cottage door and stood leaning against the door-jamb, looking out. He was a big, heavily built man dressed in ragged blue cotton, but something about him made the sergeant doubt if he was the owner of the dwelling. He did not so much as glance at the cockerel but stared, long and hard, at the column of men and then at the sergeant himself.

Finally, having apparently made up his mind about them, he crossed the intervening space until he stood no more than six yards from Sergeant Hagworthy.

'You in charge, mistah? You head-man this soldiers?'

'That's right,' Sergeant Hagworthy said cautiously. A closer inspection confirmed his suspicion that this man was no peasant; he was truculent, muscular, evidently well fed. From behind him he heard a murmur and turned to shoot the men a blazing look. Shut up or there'll be trouble, the look said. He did not want to scare this fellow off; he might learn something from him.

'You have money? Much money?'

'That's my business,' the sergeant snapped. He expected some sort of reaction from the man before him but there was none. The calculating eyes merely remained fixed on his face. 'Well? Have you anything else to say for yourself?'

'What you pay for white woman?'

Sergeant Hagworthy felt rage rise in his chest like a balloon, threatening to choke him. This ruffian was trying to sell him a white woman! He could not be such a fool as to try to sell a body, so someone must have escaped from the massacre back at the convent.

'Pay? What do you mean?'

Of course it was typical of a Chinese peasant to demand money. Any other nationality, the sergeant told himself, would have said, 'I've saved her life . . . is there a reward for helping her?' But not a Chink! Money was their god, no doubt about it, the sergeant thought grimly. A good job, probably, or heaven knew what would have happened to the white woman.

'I mean pay taels, not just dollar. Peking pay fifty taels for a live white woman, thirty for dead one. This woman mean fifty taels to me in Peking.'

'Let me see her!'

The man hesitated and then, with a shrug, turned towards the cottage and shouted something in his heathen tongue. They waited, then a slight figure lurched into the doorway.

She was a white woman, all right; the sergeant could see that even across the distance that separated them. Her wrists were tied, he thought, but she was standing on her own feet. But only just. She looked ghastly,

148

near death. The sergeant, having seen her, could quite understand why the man was trying to sell her now rather than wait until he reached Peking – if she was worth fifty taels by the time they got her there he would be very surprised.

'We don't pay for white women,' Sergeant Hagworthy said. 'Bring her over here.'

The man shouted and the woman was immediately dragged back into the cottage, out of sight. Sergeant Hagworthy's blood ran cold. Behind him, he heard a growl; it came, he knew, from the throats of seventeen outraged young Welshmen all dying to get their hands round a Chinese throat. Hastily, he turned and glared at them again. The man had the upper hand; if they refused to pay or rushed the house he would kill the woman, that was clear as crystal.

'Many men in house,' the Chinese said, his voice flat. 'Many guns too. We kill woman first, then soldier if you no pay.'

Sergeant Hagworthy tried to stop his fists clenching and unclenching in what he knew to be an international language. He made himself speak reasonably.

'Very well. Fifty taels, you said? Send the woman out first and then I'll give you the money.'

He had money to buy food. He could, at a pinch, buy the white woman's life and simply commandeer food. Once they had her safe, this creature before him should see what Welshmen were made of, how they treated murdering swine. He must have been at that compound, the sergeant thought, whilst the man obviously dredged up the pidgin he needed from the depths of his slow brain.

'No. Money now. Woman in house, you fetch. Money now.'

His voice was becoming harsher. The sergeant had no doubt that he would not hand the woman over until the money was in his hand, but if he didn't realize that the soldiers had seen the massacre he might believe they thought him merely an avaricious peasant and would simply pay up, take the woman and go.

'Very well.' He dug in his pocket for his money and hoped it would be something in the region of the sum demanded. Behind him, because the men knew what was happening, money clinked as it was dragged from pockets and handed along the line to add to the cash in his own hand. 'Where you find this woman?' he said conversationally, as he sorted out the change. He looked sideways, past the man's shoulder. The soldiers with the cockerel had disappeared. Good. They had seen the way the land lay and had gone round the back. Possibly they would be useful presently.

'Found her in house; all other dead. We soldier, not *I Ho Chuan*.'

Sergeant Hagworthy sniffed and held out their accumulated money. It was nothing like fifty taels, he was sure, but it would have to do.

'There you are; it's all we've got. Now get back and send out the woman and if you hurt a hair of her head . . .'

149

The man grabbed the money and headed for the cottage. In the doorway he turned.

'Count one hundled before you come or we kill,' he shouted. 'Now!'

He was safe enough, Sergeant Hagworthy thought, counting out loud so that the man could hear. The terrain was ideal for ambushes; he had been uneasily aware of it for miles. All the brigand and his men had to do was scatter into the crops of waist-high maize and they could shoot anyone searching for them and probably never be found. But of course they had forgotten the cockerel-catchers. Ned and Huw. They were good lads, both of them, intelligent and quick on their toes.

'Ninety-eight, ninety-nine, one hundred!' Sergeant Hagworthy announced. He had been standing like a statue, sure that unknown eyes were fixed on him, but now he began to run towards the cottage, bellowing as he ran.

'Round the back to the right, four men,' he shouted. 'Round the back to the left, four men. The rest . . . follow me!'

They all but outpaced him as they ran. He felt every one of his thirty-eight years as they bounded past him, then paused to let him lead. They burst open the door of the cottage, not bothering with the latch, and found themselves in a low-ceilinged, one-room hovel, with wooden steps leading up to the attic under the reed thatch. The woman, her wrists still roped, was lying in a corner. Dead? Oh, God, don't let her be dead, the sergeant pleaded as he rushed forward and knelt down by her. His men surged past, searching the place with a glance and then hurrying to the back door, their guns gripped purposefully before them.

She was lying face down, her matted black hair hiding her from view. He turned her over and wide, lacklustre eyes stared expressionlessly up at him. As he watched, she blinked. His hands checked her limbs; she was not wounded, just bruised and grazed and drugged by exhaustion. He cut the rope with his knife and chafed her wrists until they were pink, and then he lifted her to her feet and supported her as she stood, swaying, in one corner of the room.

'There, Miss, we've got you, you're safe now,' he heard himself crooning in the tones he would have used to those little dead girls, had any of them been alive to hear him. 'We'll soon have you out of this place . . . we'll get you a hot drink first, though, and something to eat . . . there there, my lovely girl, you'll be right as rain in an hour or so!'

It was as though she had not heard him. She just stood and swayed and presently he sat her down, very tenderly, and one of the men came in with a raw egg which he must have found somewhere, broke it into his tin cup and handed it to the sergeant. Sergeant Hagworthy fed it to the girl slowly, spoonful by spoonful, and she swallowed it down eagerly, but still said not a word.

'Light a fire; we'll bivouac here tonight,' the sergeant decided. 'Any sign of the Chinks?'

150

'No, sir. They lit out faster than you'd think,' one lad said. 'But there's no sign of Huw, neither. Nor Ned.'

'Right. Get some straw down from the loft, one of you, and we'll start a fire with that.'

The boy who went up came down again, white-faced.

'There's people up there . . . all dead,' he said. 'A man and two women, one very old one. And . . . and kids, sarge. Two little kids.'

Sergeant Hagworthy jerked his head at the girl, sitting on the floor now and staring at her bare feet.

'Yes, all right. Might've guessed. Knew he wasn't a peasant, and anyway he said he was a soldier, come to think. Get a couple of lads to dig a grave. Brought some straw?'

The young soldier went back for the straw and presently, to the sergeant's relief, Huw and Ned returned.

'There were only four of 'em,' Ned reported. 'And only one with a gun, so far as we could make out. Shot the feller that talked to you, sarge . . . bullet in the base of the spine, fell like an ox . . . and one other. The woman and the young chap got away.'

'That's bloody well done, Ned . . . and you, Huw. You got the second one, eh?'

'That's it, sarge,' Huw said. 'Never knew what 'it 'im.'

'I don't care if . . .' The sergeant stopped, aware of the small figure in the corner. 'Take a look in the loft if you've any qualms.' He picked up a thin cotton quilt from the pile of bedding in one corner of the room. 'Wrap 'em in this; we'll bury 'em decent as soon as the grave's deep enough.' He turned as the door opened and a young soldier bent under the lintel to enter. 'Got me something to cook? Ah, that's the spirit, a nice fat hen. Get it plucked, boyo, and put it in that pot, and we'll have chicken stew 'fore we sleep.'

The men worked hard and within the hour Sergeant Hagworthy woke the girl to have her meal. She sat on a chair when he suggested it, in front of the rickety wooden table, and never looked at any of them but just down at her thin, dirty fingers where they lay in her lap.

Sergeant Hagworthy looked at her. She had long, blue-black hair and dark blue eyes. She must have been pretty once, the sergeant decided, but now she was just skin and bone, dirty and barely human. But she would be better fed and watered, made a fuss of, told where she was going, reassured. He said as much to her . . . you're with us now, you'll get decently fed and we'll not let you out of our sight until we can hand you over to your own folks again.

She did not seem to hear, but later that evening, when she had been persuaded to feed herself with a spoon from a bowl of first-rate chicken stew, Sergeant Hagworthy chatted to her and teased her and actually pulled a stump of comb through her filthy, matted locks and then, when he thought she was listening a little, he asked her who she was.

151

Silence. She looked not at him but through him. Uncanny, really. So he asked her a few more questions . . . was she English, did she come from his part of the country, which did she like best, chicken stew or peaches? She said nothing at all until, quite by chance, Sergeant Hagworthy struck the right note.

'I'm not askin' questions because I'm nosy,' he said a trifle reproachfully. 'And anyway, I want to know what to call you! My name's Arnold Hagworthy. Don't you think it would be polite to tell me yours?'

She looked across at him – really looked, this time. There was a long pause. Her forehead wrinkled up and tears came into the big eyes, and then she moved her mouth, experimentally, as if she had not used it for speech for a long, long time.

'I . . . I'm Addy,' she said simply at last. Her voice was high, like a five-year-old child instead of the young woman she plainly was. 'I'm Addy.'

'Well done, Addy,' the sergeant said heartily. 'You're a good girl, you are. Now tell us where you live and we'll think about getting you home.'

There was a longer pause this time, the mouth tightening, opening, closing and tightening again before she spoke.

'I'm Addy,' she said. 'I'm Addy.'

'The only time you could say her eyes lit up was when I said something about Peking. She stared at me looking real bright, sarge, but then of course like a fool I said, "Do you know someone in Peking?" and she just said she was Addy and wouldn't say another word.'

Sergeant Hagworthy and Dai were sitting on a pile of railway sleepers eyeing the empty, mid-afternoon countryside and wondering what to do next. They had marched by easy stages to Yangtsun where the sergeant had hoped to receive help and advice from the staff at headquarters. They had reached their destination some ten minutes earlier to find no head-quarters, a torn-up permanent road, burned-out buildings and a number of Imperial troops who had first stared, then yelled, and finally turned and fled when the Welsh reached for their guns, disappearing into the landscape like rabbits into burrows.

'So you think she's connected with Peking, eh? Lives there, maybe? Or perhaps her husband's there.' The men had realized she was married by the gold ring she wore on her left hand; it was not a valuable ring and the thugs she was taken by had not bothered to steal it. 'Well, that's possible. But I dare not set out for Peking until I get some orders from somewhere. We'll march to Tientsin. That way we're going in the right direction for the coast; we can always get her on board ship until the fuss dies down. So far as we know the trouble's mainly in northern China.'

'Right, sarge,' Dai said. 'Get the others together, shall I? Who's carrying the litter?'

They had rigged up a comfortable litter from webbing, puttees and any other piece of material they could lay their hands on and the girl had travelled many miles in it, sleeping sometimes, looking at the passing countryside, sometimes simply staring up into the hot blue sky overhead. Addy, as she called herself, was undoubtedly growing stronger. Sergeant Hagworthy had washed her hair himself with his own piece of hoarded soap and had rejoiced to see the great mass of it gleam in the sun as it dried. Her clothing, however, could not be renewed, so she still wore the stained and filthy tunic and trousers they had found her in.

Now, Sergeant Hagworthy stood up and stretched, then yawned hugely. Another move . . . he was beginning to feel like a chess piece whose board had suddenly extended to include the whole of China. 'Who's carrying the litter? I dunno . . . Bob and Euan, probably. She's a light enough weight, poor kid.'

The sergeant set off to where the men were making a cup of char round a fire which consisted largely of railway sleepers. He was a Welshman from conviction rather than birth and it still seemed a little odd to him to call his men by their first names. With a company half of whom were surnamed Evans and the other half Williams, however, it was the only way to avoid hopeless muddles. He reached the men and Addy, who was sitting primly on an upturned barrel sipping tea from the tin mug she shared with the sergeant himself.

'Right, lads, we'll move on in an hour, then. To Tientsin, nearer the coast.'

'Okay, sarge,' Ned said. 'What's up with Meirion, then?'

One of the men was coming towards them at the double, scarlet-faced and excited.

'Sarge! Hey, sarge!' he burst out. 'Come and take a look at what I've found!'

Sergeant Hagworthy strolled up the railway track beside him, expecting to find the other men grouped round a kitten, or some animal or insect which was strange to them. They were young, after all, and in a foreign land their curiosity was endless. But they were all looking down at a longish patch of mud. The sergeant stared, but he couldn't see anything in the mud at all, not even a weird beetle or frog. All he could see was churned up mud and footprints and . . .

'Boots, sarge,' Ned exploded. 'See 'em? Boots . . . 'undreds of 'em. Them's army boots too, our boots, not them narrer-toed things the Chinks wear.'

Sergeant Hagworthy looked more closely. Undoubtedly the lad was right. Soldiers, a good number of them, had passed this way. He looked harder. Fairly recently, possibly even within the last four or five hours. He stared a moment longer, then straightened.

'This changes things,' he announced. 'We'll follow them, get a move on, see if we can catch the fellers up. At least that way we'll get up-to-date news.' He turned to Dai, who had followed him up the track. 'Get the lads together and get young Addy on to her litter. We'll march at once, and keep marching till we catch up with them boots!'

There was only one dissenting voice amongst the lower ranks when the men were marshalled to leave.

'We aren't going towards the coast, then? What if them boots are Imperial Army boots? The northern Chinks are bigger than the southerners; you said so yourself only last week, sarge.'

'Don't worry, lad,' Sergeant Hagworthy boomed over his shoulder. 'British Army boots made them prints, with great big broad British feet in 'em. We don't issue good army boots to furriners, let alone to the enemy. Everyone ready? Then by the left . . . quick . . . march!'

They often sang on the march when they were in open country and stealth was not an object. Now some wag in the ranks set up a chorus.

> *'Boots boots boots boots,*
> *Chasing great big army boots,*
> *Broad boots fat boots,*
> *Boots for British feet;*
> *Boots boots boots boots,*
> *Chasing loverly army boots;*
> *See them all set out in rows,*
> Hextremely *clean and neat!'*

A ripple of laughter ran along the ranks. Even the girl called Addy, lying in her litter, allowed a faint smile to touch her lips.

And five hours later they were proved right. They caught up with the tail of a long column of British troops just on the point of bivouacking for the night. Sergeant Hagworthy went up the column until he found an officer, and explained the situation right down to what Addy was doing, marching with his company.

'She's underfed and scared out of her wits, but she's a good gal,' he told the young officer. 'She's not come to herself yet, but give her time, she just needs time. And we need news, sir, if you'd be so good.'

'Well, we're the relief force for Peking,' the officer explained. 'Did you know the Legations have been under siege for several weeks? Nearly two months, in fact. There's an international force marching to relieve them, and we're the British bit. You'd better tag along – we need all the men we can get. And if you think the young lady comes from there, what better destination could you have? I say, I wonder if she can ride a horse?'

He turned to Addy, who had been watching them silently, possibly listening to their talk but probably still in her own tiny, tight little world.

'We're going to take you to Peking,' the officer said chattily. 'Do you want to come to Peking? There will be lots of English people there; you may know some of them.'

Sergeant Hagworthy waited for the inevitable pause, followed by the words, 'I'm Addy.' Instead, she said, 'Peking?'

'That's right, Addy,' the sergeant said gently. 'Do you want to go to Peking?'

The girl nodded, looking from one to another. Then her lips formed the word 'Yes'.

'Then you *shall* go,' the officer said heartily. 'With Sergeant Hagworthy and his boys. Is that good?'

Addy looked at the sergeant and smiled. It was only a small, fleeting smile but it warmed the sergeant's heart.

'Arny,' she said. 'Thank you.'

The two men moved away from her then, to see to the bivouac, but Sergeant Hagworthy confided that he had just heard Addy say more words than in all the previous weeks they'd been together.

'God knows what sights she's seen or what happened to her, but I believe something's turned her brain,' he said. 'I hope we can turn it back again, that's all.'

'Yes, she appears to be in some kind of shock,' the officer agreed. 'But once she's found her people she'll probably make a complete recovery. Children are amazing, and she's only a child, after all.'

'She's a married woman,' the sergeant assured him. 'She wears a wedding ring. Why, when we first picked her up she could have been a woman of fifty, she was so sick and gaunt and old-looking. She's a princess now to what she was, I can tell you.'

'Well, she's making progress at any rate,' the officer said. 'Shall I send you down some rations for tonight or are you provided for?'

'We'll do very well tonight,' the sergeant said, conscious of a number of ducks, several dozen eggs and a great deal of rice, to say nothing of heads of maize and even some butter. 'We've been living on the country, of course. You've got supplies, I take it?'

'Yes, our stuff's coming up-river in junks. We took Yangtsun a few hours before you caught up with us . . . did you stop there?'

'We did. Couldn't make it out, rails all up and no one about except some Imperial troops who cut and run as soon as they took our measure. Then one of my chaps saw the boot-prints and we followed on as fast as we could.'

'Well, we could do with you,' the officer said frankly. 'We're marching at the rear of the international column because the Russians worry that we'll fraternize with the Japs and get into Peking first, so our commander put as much space between the two forces as possible. The Japs are in the van, of course. There are a lot of disadvantages, as you'll soon discover – marching in the dust of the men before you, reaching the wells when they've been drunk down to mud, being last in when we stop to rest so we're unable to grab some shade – but we manage. We manage. Your chaps will be hardened to conditions by now, I dare say, so you'll stand it better than some. The Yanks, poor chaps, are brave and dogged, but they find they have to drop out during the daytime marches and then catch up

155

in the night, when it's cooler. Now about the girl riding . . . we've some baggage ponies, good little beasts . . . would you care to let her have a try?'

'Yes, I think we should. And what's more, I wouldn't be at all surprised if she was quite good in the saddle. Plucky little lass she must be, to have gone through so much.'

And next day, try they did. The girl called Addy scrambled on to the pony's bare back and sat there, at first like a sack of potatoes and then with increasing confidence until by the time an hour had passed she was riding like an old hand. Sergeant Hagworthy, marching near by, heard her talking softly to her mount beneath her breath and felt that her cure had begun.

The forced march on the capital, however, despite the girl Addy's apparent pleasure in riding her pony, gave few others enjoyment. It was mid-August and everywhere crops stood tall, waiting for harvest. A particular bugbear for the troops was a kind of millet which reached a height of ten to a dozen feet. Marching across a field of the gigantic crop, or along a lane which led between two fields of it, was like walking naked into a lake which you knew might well be full of crocodiles. The simile was Dai's but Sergeant Hagworthy knew exactly what he meant. The millet could have hidden the entire Imperial Army, or so you began to believe when you had marched along beside it for miles, and at any moment you might hear a manic shriek of 'Sha! Sha!' from before or behind and feel the cold steel of a sword at your neck. It was also very hot, since the millet effectively shut off the breeze but was not sufficiently high to shut out the midday sun. The dust was stirred up mercilessly by the troops in front, and the Welsh Guards, right at the rear, marched doggedly on, calling out to each other, commiserating with foreigners who dropped out, and trying not to mind the sweat channelling down their dust-caked features or stinging their gritty eyes.

The most dangerous foe, however, was the heat. Twice the column was ambushed by small bands of the enemy who sniped and fled, but by a miracle – or the Chinese belief that one should shoot the spirit which danced above a man's head rather than the body beneath – no one was even wounded in either attack. But the heat did take its toll. Sergeant Hagworthy kept a fatherly eye on Addy and made sure she slept when she should and ate and drank whatever he could acquire for her. She was like an obedient child; if he spoke kindly but firmly she would do her best to please him, but in a very few days he could see that the heat was pulling her down again. Her pallor was startling, and once she fell off her mount during the midday march, more from sheer weakness than from a lack of attention. But she was game; she climbed straight back on to the pony, biting her lip and clutching the reins, clearly determined not to fall again.

He worried about her a lot when they took a town, but everyone was very good. Someone in the ranks would be told off to stay with her, though once the town was theirs it would have been too much to expect the soldier not to join in the looting and Sergeant Hagworthy usually returned then to keep an eye on her. Chinese towns, moreover, put up little resistance. Thus they captured Hosiwu on 9 August, Matou on 10 August and Changchiawan on the 11th. They ate well, too, when they had sacked a town, Addy with the rest of them, though she could never be persuaded to accompany them into the fallen strongholds, even after resistance had been utterly crushed. Indeed when, on 12 August, they took the walled town of Tungchow, the hardest obstacle between them and Peking, she curled up under her blanket and refused to move, worrying the company and the sergeant considerably. Only when the men returned from the fighting, which had been very half-hearted on the Chinese side since the garrison had fled at the first sign of the Allies, did she uncurl and sit up, to eat her share of the looted food.

'Soon be in Peking, love,' Sergeant Hagworthy said, peeling Addy an apple. He had fallen into the habit of speaking to her as though she was a small child and she rewarded him with a childlike devotion. Now, he patted her hand and she smiled at him, put her head on one side, considered the fruit, and tucked it back into his hand.

'Addy says . . . Arny have it,' she said triumphantly.

'Does she, now? No, love, you eat it up for Arny. There's one for me here.' He held out his own fruit and pressed the peeled apple back into her hand. She eyed it, then gave him her quick, shy smile and bit into it. When she had finished he said, 'A spot of shut-eye for us all now. Off you go, Addy,' and watched as she trotted off and rolled herself up in her blanket beneath the trees.

'She's coming along nicely,' Sergeant Hagworthy muttered to himself as he rolled up in his own blanket. 'Yes, she'll do.' He was secretly delighted because she had used his name, though she never addressed anyone else directly at all. It was another breakthrough.

'The gossip in Tungchow was that because we're getting through so well and winning wherever we go, the Chinese will steal a march on us and kill all the foreign devils in Peking,' young Dai observed the next morning, as he helped the sergeant to prepare breakfast from the mass of provisions they had 'liberated' from Tungchow the previous day. 'They say they'll do it to prevent loss of face.'

'Oh, rubbish,' Sergeant Hagworthy said roundly. 'Isn't that bloody typical? Boasting's all they're good for. Just how do you think they're going to kill the foreign devils when they've been trying to do just that for nearly two months without any success whatsoever? Why, they were still holding out merrily enough five days ago; they sent a despatch through to our commanding officer.'

'I don't suppose they will,' Dai said quickly. 'What'd be the point,

157

sarge? It'd only make us blazing mad and more likely to wrench their miserable little pointed 'eads from their bodies.'

'Well, it's true that it does happen – prisoners have been killed at the last minute to prevent them being saved – but as I say, if they've not been able to do it until now, why should they suddenly be successful? But I won't deny they'll try their best once they see us within rifle shot of the walls.'

'Well, we'll know soon enough,' Dai said. 'The cavalry came back a few moments ago and they say there's nothing between us and the city now. We march as soon as everyone's fed.'

'That's it, that's Peking . . . Gawd, listen to them guns!'

Sergeant Hagworthy heard his men exclaiming behind him and told himself that it always happened: the Chinese would make a lot of noise and fuss to try to prove to themselves and their leaders that they were doing their best to wipe out their enemy.

'You're right there – that's Peking and them is guns,' he said sharply over his shoulder to his flock. 'But we're hearing English guns too, and French, American, Russian . . . we're hearing guns replying, even though you can't pick 'em out.'

'Course, sarge,' someone said peaceably. 'We'll be in time, we know that.'

The sergeant grunted. Beside him, on a small bay pony, rode the girl Addy. She had jumped when she first heard the guns but probably they had little significance for her. The sky overhead was dark with cloud so she may have thought, as many of the raw recruits had, that it was thunder and not gunfire she heard. Sergeant Hagworthy saw the pony, startled by the din, cavort sideways and then buck, its sturdy hindquarters rearing up, but the girl on his back kept her seat. By God, but she's a good little horsewoman, Sergeant Hagworthy told himself. He felt as proud of her as though she were an urchin from the gutter suddenly revealing a talent for playing Chopin on a concert grand.

She brought the pony under control and leaned down to whisper in its ear; he did not know what she said but it calmed the animal. It was a pity they could not take her into Peking with them, but she would have to stay behind with the baggage and any wounded who were not capable of fighting. If resistance was slight, however, he would go back, fetch her. He hated the thought of leaving her but he had no choice. This was a battle in which he would need his entire force. This time he could not leave her with a friendly young Welshman, but he would see her all right before they marched away.

That night they bivouacked within a stone's throw of Peking. The massive gates were shut, of course, the walls heavily defended. Most of the troops were in action by dawn but the British did not make their move until

158

noon, when they advanced on the Hsia K'ou Men gate. It was hot, the rain which had fallen all night had ceased, and there was no sound whatsoever from the great ramparts above them. As they passed the tower over the Ha Ta Men they were fired on, but no one was injured; they were not even particularly shaken by the small and half-hearted attack. What really worried them was the silence. There was firing in the distance, to be sure, the thunder of cannon and yells and shouts, but nearer at hand, from the Legations, there came not a sound.

'They've wiped 'em out,' a young Guard said in a low voice. 'After all that time, the way they held out . . . we'll make 'em pay for that, and for the other things.'

He meant the massacre at the mission school, the sergeant realized, as they marched through the deserted streets of the Chinese city. In fact this part of the city was largely empty anyway because the houses had been knocked down and the place was cut about by trenches, barricades and redoubts, all of them deserted.

Good thing young Addy isn't here – no terrain for a pony, Sergeant Hagworthy was thinking, when he had cause to glance back at his men and there she was, sitting neatly on her mount, her face white and set. The sergeant almost lost the step, which was difficult to maintain anyway with so much rubble about the streets. He snapped, 'Come here, Addy!' and she obeyed at once, riding up close to him.

When she reached him he read her a lecture about stupidity and disobeying orders and she hung her head, but he could tell by the glint in her eyes that she did not care at all for his strictures and was glad she had come. And there was no reason for sending her back as things stood; besides, she was probably safer with him than wandering through the Chinese city alone.

They were picking their way across the rubble of a big house when someone said, 'Look up there!' Every eye turned to the summit of the Tartar wall. A signaller stood there, dwarfed by distance, his signalling flags hanging limp in the hot air, but when he saw he had their attention he began to use them.

'Come in by sewer,' someone read out, and Sergeant Hagworthy saw the man on the wall point directly below him.

Everyone surged forward and, as he followed, the sergeant saw a great tunnel, easily big enough to take the men and the girl Addy's pony. They pressed forward, wading through noisome water. A grille barred the way but men attacked it and it fell. The smell was appalling, the mud thick and black and clinging, but the way was clear; they could go forward.

As they saw light ahead the men broke into a run. Sergeant Hagworthy ran with a hand on the pony's bridle, for he had no desire to see an over-excited animal knock his men down. Once more youth and excitement had prevailed and he and Addy were in the middle of a stampeding mass. Together, they surged into the daylight. A street, lined with buildings, on

159

the right a high wall . . . They were in the Legation quarter at last!

John was on the tennis court with everyone else to welcome them. The troops were filthy and dying of thirst. Women in fancy hats and their best dresses offered them champagne, but the first British troops in were Indian regiments and the sepoys' religion would not let them touch alcohol. They asked for water, however, and pretty girls ran to fetch it in fancy jugs and long champagne glasses. All around there was cheering and shouting, even a little weeping.

John felt exalted and filled with pure relief. Now his own personal struggle could start: now he could leave this place with a clear conscience and find Adeline! He pushed across the tennis lawn, searching for someone from the outside world who might be able to give him news of his wife. A neat little bay pony with a Chinese youth on its back looked promising . . . no, it was a girl, not a youth . . . he was near enough, now, to see the waist-length midnight-black hair. He reached up and touched her arm. She turned.

Adeline.

He could only stare whilst tears overflowed his eyes and ran down his cheeks. She stared too, her eyes widening just a little. She did not cry, neither did she say a word. She looked . . . different.

'Adeline, my own dear love! Oh, I've been so worried, so desperately anxious! I came back, you know . . . darling, don't look so frightened, don't you know me? It's your own dear John!'

She looked away, like a shy child. Anxiety gripped his throat, turned his bowels to water. She was ill, terribly ill. She did not seem to know him!

A man shouldered between him and the pony. A decent brown-faced man of perhaps thirty-five. He wore the uniform of a sergeant in the Welsh Guards.

'Excuse me, sir. Well, Addy? We said we'd get you in and we have, haven't we? Seen your old man yet, or your ma or pa? Eh?'

John touched his arm.

'I – I'm her . . . er . . . her old man. She's my wife. Adeline Sawyer, my wife. Did you say you brought her here?'

'That's right. Found her up-country – oh, weeks ago. She'd had a bad time. Still won't say much, but she's all right.' He turned to Adeline. 'Going to say hello to your . . . to Mr Sawyer, are you? He'll take care of you now, Addy; you won't need us no more.' He turned back to John, reddening beneath the tan. 'Sorry about that, sir, but all she'd say for weeks was that . . . *I'm Addy*, she said, even if you asked her what day it was.' He saw John flinch and took him by the elbow, shaking it a little. 'She's had a bad time,' he repeated. 'She'll be all right, just give her time. Is there somewhere . . . .?'

At that moment firing broke out. Someone was hit; a woman fell to the ground and cried out. The entire group of people turned and sauntered for cover but John stayed out because Adeline did, and so did the sergeant. John held up his arms.

'Come on, love. Jump down and we'll go into the house. You'll be . . .'

The words dried in his throat. She ignored him as though he did not exist. Instead, she held out her arms to the sergeant, her eyes warm and bright on his face.

# CHAPTER TWELVE

They would never return to Ayiteng. Neither of them could have faced it. Instead, John took the advice of his mission and he and his wife caught a ship to Japan, to the island of Hokkaido, in the north. There was a mission there, just one, and the natives were grave, courteous, friendly people.

'It is a very lovely place, full of wildlife and quite different from the rest of Japan,' John was told. 'There are only two fairly large cities, and all the rest is beautiful, quiet, remote countryside with long glorious beaches . . . and it is cool, even in September, but not cold. Just right. Go there and get your wife well.'

John knew that Adeline had lost the baby because another doctor told him she had miscarried and in fact was still losing. He had not dared to examine her himself, so different and remote was she. When she parted from the sergeant and the Welsh guardsmen she almost came to life; she clung to the sergeant, saying, 'Arny, Arny,' in a coaxing, beseeching tone, but when John took her back into the Legation, where they were to live until transport could be arranged down to the coast, she scarcely wept at all.

John was terribly worried about her. He had to ask about Yenala and that provoked a storm of weeping but no verbal response. Only when he said he would go back to Ayiteng to look for the child did she answer him.

'Yenala's dead,' she said flatly. 'They cut her head off.'

'She'll recover completely, given time,' Dr Poole said comfortingly, after he had examined and talked to Adeline several times. 'Her mind has had a horrific shock from which it will take time to recover; you must not expect too much of her, but she's an extremely courageous woman. She'll pull round and you'll forget this nightmare, I promise you.'

But it was like living with a stranger, and one who was afraid of you, furthermore. John wondered whether he should have taken her home, but he was ashamed to show her to her father. As it was he had to write her letters home for her, pretending that because of her miscarriage and the way she had been treated she was unable, at the moment, to sit down and pen a few lines.

He knew that it was all his fault, that he had brought her to this barbarous country, exposed her to the thousand cruelties of a cruel race, and finally left her behind when he went to buy supplies when he should never have let her out of his sight. He had thought he was doing it for the best, but now he supposed that he had only left her because a pregnant woman was too much responsibility on a long horse-ride. Selfish wretch that I am, he thought, and let her sleep in a room of her own until he found that she had fearful nightmares most nights and woke up screaming and streaming sweat; only then did he move her into his room, though even then she slept, from choice, in a little truckle bed well away from his larger one.

He remembered her seasickness on the voyage from England and told Dr Poole that he was worried about making her even more ill on the ship to Hokkaido, but Dr Poole said he would give her something soothing. Whatever the reason, she was not ill on board. She ate sparingly but she did at least eat, and she spoke once or twice to the cabin staff and once or twice to John himself. But for the most part she stayed down in her cabin and drew jerky, many-legged cats and lizards with double crests and four eyes, and birds with horribly stunted wings and great, muscular legs. She hated the drawings, though, and tore them up as soon as she finished them with a kind of revulsion, as though her own imaginative creations disgusted her.

They went ashore at Hakodate and she seemed interested, in a vague, rather unfocused way. Then they hired a pony and cart and drove to their destination, a small timber-built house by a beach with a beautiful lake a short distance away and mountains as a backdrop to the scene.

On the very first day there, she walked on the beach with John and they heard the long rollers crash on the shore and she found an oyster shell with a mother-of-pearl lining and saw a great-eyed seal hauled out on the shingle to rest. She said, 'How pretty!' and John took her hand and she did not pull it away.

After a week she was actually laughing; John had thought she would never laugh again. After ten days, when they were stalking a rare kind of crane through the reeds by the lake, she suddenly said to John: 'I've been very unhappy, but I'm getting better, aren't I?' He assured her that she was very much better and she fell silent for a little, then said, quite naturally, 'I miss my little baby, you know. My stomach aches with emptiness.'

'You'll have another baby one day,' John said awkwardly, but she only put her hands flat on her stomach and sighed and looked out to sea.

A few days later still, she told him that the baby had been born, a proper baby, only dead, she supposed. The woman had said it was dead.

John listened and tried to sympathize without seeming to want to know what had happened and before either of them really knew what was happening Adeline was pouring the whole story out, spewing it up almost, telling him every ghastly, painful detail in a jerky, impassioned voice which broke now and then as she cried, gulped, wiped her eyes with the back of her hand and continued with her tale.

They were on the long beach, Adeline's favourite place, lying on the sand, side by side. When her voice gradually faltered to a stop John said nothing, just put his arms round her. And Adeline, instead of pulling away, clung to him and wept into his neck; he could feel her tears, hot and salty, trickling down his neck and on to his shoulder beneath the white shirt he wore and he held her fiercely and told her that she should weep it all out of her system, let it all flow out of her, so that she could be at peace once more.

'But . . . but John, I killed Yenala!' she muttered against his neck. 'I should be hanged . . . I killed her, indeed I did, though I didn't mean to do so. I told her to run . . . her running excited them, and they ran too, and caught her and the sword swung . . . I killed her, I tell you!'

'No. You might say I killed her, by leaving the two of you alone when I should never have let you out of my sight,' John said vehemently. 'My poor darling, how you've suffered, and it's all my fault, all mine!'

Adeline moved her tear-drenched face from his shoulder and looked up at him with a kind of wonder.

'You too?' she whispered. 'You think it's all your fault as well? Oh, John, that's the worst part, the really bad part, thinking it was all my fault. I tried to shut it away but it just got bigger and bigger until I couldn't talk or think or look at people because I knew I was a murderer.'

'I was the same,' John muttered. 'But it's not true, sweetheart, not true for either of us, and we mustn't ever think it again. Do you promise me?'

'And we really aren't to blame for Yenala's death? Really not?'

He held her tightly, pressing her painfully skinny body close to him.

'Really not. I'll promise if you will as well.'

She hesitated, then promised, and John followed suit.

As they made their way back to their funny little timber house close by the shore, John knew that this would be a new beginning for both of them. And that night he and Adeline shared a bed for the first time since Ayiteng.

'I've had a letter from Adeline, a proper letter, the first for months and months.' Sidney Warburton lifted his godson on to his knee and turned him in his arms so that Philip was astride one thigh. 'Here we go . . . this is the way the colonel rides . . .'

'That's wonderful,' Lily said. The three of them were sitting on the terrace at the manor with the sunshine glinting on the puddles left by yesterday's April showers. Lily felt perfectly at home here, and enjoyed being with Mr Warburton and with the friendly and helpful Mrs Gilmour far more than she enjoyed life at the Hall.

'Yes, and in fact it's more wonderful than you could guess. They're coming home!'

'Really?' Lily tried to infuse warmth and pleasure into her tone, to hide the immediate diving of her heart. This was Adeline's home, her place, and Lily had come to think of it, insensibly, as her own special refuge in times of doubt and trouble; even as a place where she could be herself, did not have to remember, all the time, that she was Mrs Arnold Haslington of the Hall.

'Yes, really. After all my poor girl's dreadful experiences, losing her baby and so on, John wants to come home to reconsider their lives.'

'Does that mean they may stay here?' Lily asked, her heart sinking another notch. Sidney Warburton bounced gaily on through the nursery rhyme and little Philip bounced too, holding on tight, his small face split by an enormous beam of pleasure.

'Stay here? Oh, for always, you mean. Alas, I doubt that very much, but it might mean they'll stay in England. I rather gather that John's having second thoughts about being a medical missionary in China, though I could be mistaken, of course – they were both very vague.'

'It would be awfully jolly for you if they came home for good,' Lily said, trying to show the sympathy she felt for him and to hide her dismay. She and Philip were prime favourites here at the Manor; she had not realized before how much she relied on Mr Warburton's friendly acceptance of her and her small son. 'I've never met your daughter, nor her husband.'

'Oh, you'll like 'em both,' Mr Warburton assured her. '*This* is the way the lady rides, trip-trap, trip-trap, trip-trap . . .'

'I'm sure I'll like them. When exactly are they expected?' Lily got up and made to take her son. 'He's too heavy for you, Mr Warburton – you'll be quite worn out at this rate. Play something quieter, you bad boy, you!'

Philip, in a language all his own – for at thirteen months one's command of one's native tongue is far from complete – gave his mother to understand that he was quite happy as he was and would be obliged if she would mind her own business. Lily laughed, but took the child as soon as the game paused again, for she could see that Mr Warburton's cheeks were growing much too rosy and he was breathing far too fast.

'That's enough, lad,' she said firmly to her struggling son. 'How about showing Ga-Ga how you can walk all over the place? You'd like that, would you?' She turned to her companion. 'Do you mind if we go back into the library, Mr W? His boots are quite up to keeping out the wet but unfortunately his knees and his napkins aren't.'

'Certainly; and I'll ring for Polly and get her to bring us up a nice tray of tea and some biscuits.' Mr Warburton got to his feet and reclaimed his godson, who clasped him fondly round the face and dribbled into his ear whilst telling him some long, involved and probably apocryphal story which contained the words goggie, puddy and piggy. 'Yes, quite, my hero! You like bickies, don't you? If we ask Mrs Gilmour ever so nicely she might bring you the sort with icing on top!'

He went in through the french doors and rang the library bell whilst Lily settled herself on the sofa where, over a year ago, she had given birth to her son. The son in question, released to try his feet, took four steps and sat down hard on his well-padded bottom.

'There we are, then.' Mr Warburton came back and watched Philip get to his feet and start, wobblingly, for the nearest bit of supportive furniture. 'Do you know, Lily, I've never yet seen the boy cry when he falls over – a real tiger, that's what you are, Philly my lad!'

Polly came in answer to the bell at this juncture and was despatched with an order for tea and biscuits plus a reminder that Master Philly would be delighted to see his godmother, if she could spare a minute.

That had been the first serious discord between Arnold and herself, Lily remembered now, as godfather and godson began to take each other for short tours of the room. When she had named Mr Warburton as a godfather Arny had been been rather pleased than otherwise, but when she had added that Mrs Gilmour was to be godmother he had been at first flabbergasted and then really annoyed.

'It won't do, Lily,' he had blustered. 'It'll cause talk . . . she's the man's housekeeper, damn it!'

'I don't care,' Lily had said, her cheeks warming with annoyance that Arnold, who had not even stayed with her after the baby was born because his mother was distraught over his father's death, could not appreciate her feelings. 'She's a very nice person and she'll make Philly a very good godmother. It's the least I can do, Arny . . . don't you see that?'

He had agreed in the end, of course, but grudgingly, and had never quite let Lily forget that she had done Philip no good by her insistence.

But now, Mrs Gilmour herself bustled into the room with the tray, Polly bringing up the rear with the hot water jug and the cups, saucers and plates.

'Morning, Mrs Arnold; hello, Master Philip,' she said very correctly, and then dumped the tray on the occasional table nearest Lily and knelt on the carpet, holding out her arms to the child who ran into them and kissed her noisily – and wetly – on one round, appleblossom cheek.

'Who's a good boy, then?' Mrs Gilmour demanded. 'Want a bickie with a moo-cow on, Master Philly? Or one with a shiny top?'

Philip opted for both, one in each hand, whilst his mother cried out rather unconvincingly at such shocking manners and everyone else cooed over him.

'Now, Mrs Arnold,' Mrs Gilmour said, when Philip was engrossed in his biscuits and occasionally taking a swig out of his mug of milk, with his godfather's eager assistance, 'how's it going at the Hall? Did you show Mrs Albert how to serve salmon trout?'

'I would have, but she said ladies had cooks to do such things for them and I'd do better to try to learn how to control my staff,' Lily said ruefully. 'Never mind, Mrs Gilmour, just let her wait. One of these days . . .'

Mrs Gilmour agreed that one of these days Mrs Arnold would show them all a thing or two, and the conversation moved on to cleaning silver, turning mattresses and the gentle art of pickling eggs. Then Lily looked at her little fob watch, gave a cry of alarm, and plucked Master Philly from the floor.

'We must go or we'll be late for luncheon, and recently Mr Arnold's been coming home to eat,' she said distractedly. 'Thank heaven I carried you, Philly, and didn't bring the perambulator! Now we can go back through the woods and by the river – it's so much quicker.'

With many goodbyes all round Lily hurried off, only remembering as she began to go through the wood that she had not actually found out when Adeline and John would be returning. But never mind; no sense in meeting trouble halfway. You never knew, that girl Adeline might turn out to be quite nice after all, and she might live somewhere far away so that Lily and her son could still be welcomed daily at the Manor.

But despite herself, as she got nearer the Hall, Lily's footsteps faltered and slowed. She dreaded going back there after a carefree morning at the Manor!

The trouble, she knew, had started with her insistence that her mother-in-law and the younger children should move out of the Hall and into a house in Langforth (or indeed anywhere else they liked to choose provided it was not too near the young Haslingtons). It had not pleased Arnold, who, she suspected, rather enjoyed the feeling of power that a house full of dependants gave him, and neither had it pleased Mrs Albert. She did not like the new house, it was too small, the garden was cramped, people were talking, hinting that she had been turned out of her own home by a chit of a girl.

But even then, it might have worked had it not been for Mrs Consett. Mrs Consett had been housekeeper at the Hall for as long as Arnold could remember and she had taken against Lily from the first. She made her life as difficult as she possibly could, therefore, constantly exceeding the housekeeping allowance and blaming Lily, turning out dreadful meals and saying she had only done as Mrs Arnold ordered, and even tricking Lily into making wrong decisions by suggestions which she afterwards flatly denied ever having made.

Then, one morning, Lily caught Mrs Consett out. She had ordered fish from the man who came round touting for business, and Mrs Consett had sniffed and warned her, in front of Cook and all the kitchen staff, that the man was a fly-by-night and not their usual supplier, so the fish was bound to be either poor quality or downright bad.

Lily pointed out with some asperity that the fish supplied by their own fishmonger the previous week had most definitely been bad, and Mrs

Consett, with a darkling look, said that she would, naturally, be pleasantly surprised if the fish turned out to be as fresh and delicious as the man had claimed.

By a piece of good luck, Lily was actually out in the garden with the baby when the fish was delivered, and being naturally interested she strolled over and examined it herself. It was freshly caught, bright-eyed and with a smell of the sea, just as it ought to be. That night, at dinner, Mrs Consett announced that she was unable to serve the fish since Miss . . . when she was being particularly offensive she frequently called Lily 'Miss' . . . had begun to use a new fishmonger, one in whom she herself had no faith whatsoever.

'It wasn't right, sir,' she said, addressing herself exclusively to Arnold, who had been looking forward to halibut in a shrimp and parsley sauce. 'Stale . . . smelt dreadful. More than Cook's job is worth to serve it, she said, and I agreed.'

Lily stood up.

'Show me,' she said briefly. 'Bring the fish up here.'

'Why, Mrs Arnold, I dare say Cook threw the stuff away an hour ago,' Mrs Consett said. 'But still, if you'd like to come down to the kitchen and go through the bin . . .'

'Yes, I would,' Lily said. Without more ado she marched from the dining-room to the kitchen with Mrs Consett trying to shame her out of it every inch of the way. And there were the kitchen staff, happily eating halibut!

Useless then for Mrs Consett to assure Lily that it was not the halibut she had seen delivered, but inferior stuff which she herself had ordered for the staff. A remorseless demand that Mrs Consett produce the bill produced instead a mixture of rage and tears.

Lily told Mrs Consett crisply that she refused to let anyone make a fool of her and then lie into the bargain, and sacked the woman with effect from the next day.

She told Arnold about it and he was horrified, apologetic, assured her that all would be well now.

Two days later her mother-in-law, Mrs Albert, turned up in the drawing-room like an avenging angel.

'Mrs Consett has worked for this family, and never a wrong word, for thirty years, Lily. I cannot have you dismiss her for her first mistake.'

'Mistake? To deliberately set out to make a fool of me by lying and cheating? I don't call that a mistake, Mother-in-law, I call that deliberate malice.'

'She's an old and trusted servant.' Mrs Albert appeared to unbend a little. 'My dear, I've told Arnold I'm moving back to the Hall . . .' She flapped a hand at Lily's obvious amazement. 'Oh, not permanently – I know that wouldn't be wise – but just until you know a little more of the ways of a big house, how to deal with servants and so on. You need someone to help you settle in, Arnold says, and I'm the obvious person. But don't worry; when I go, so shall Mrs Consett.'

That had been eight months ago; her mother-in-law and the detested Mrs Consett were there still. Mrs Albert had simply taken over the running of the house with never a word to Lily, and Arnold, who liked his comforts and maintained that having his mother in residence was far easier for his wife than trying to cope with such a barn of a place unaided, never backed Lily up in her efforts to dislodge either woman. Bella, of course, no longer lived at home, but Dorothea was actively antagonistic to Lily, blaming her for the two months she had spent in the small house in Langforth, and obviously determined never to see herself or her mother ousted again.

So Lily, despised by her own servants and set aside by her mother-in-law, took to going almost every day to the Manor, where Mr Warburton welcomed her and Mrs Gilmour did her utmost to teach her all she herself knew about running a large house.

But now all this was to change; Adeline was coming home and the place that Lily had so gladly taken would be needed for the real daughter of the house.

'I can't believe we'll actually see Father and the Manor and Mrs Gilmour and everyone else in a couple of months!' Adeline exclaimed as she and John said goodbye to their little timber house by the beach and boarded the ship which would take them back to China. 'I've longed for this moment . . . though of course I'd thought we'd be going back with a grandchild for Father.'

'We very well might be,' John reminded her. They were standing on deck, watching Japan grow smaller behind them. 'There's a good chance that by the time we get to England you'll know for certain . . .'

Adeline shook her head at him and put a gentle hand over his mouth.

'No! Don't tempt fate, dearest John! Let's talk of something else. What, for instance, do you mean to do in Shanghai?'

'I intend to take you, and myself of course, to Cheiping, to the mission we originally meant to take, only you were so ill from the voyage and the heat that they sent us to . . . to northern China instead. I think we should take a good look at it, and decide whether we could bear to live there first of all. Then I must talk to the head of the Chinese missions about my vocation. There are times, now, when I feel that I am the last person to preach of Christ's love and forgiveness, when I forgot both during the siege.'

'I bore the heat in Peking very well, didn't I?' Adeline said with a certain pride. 'I can't imagine it being much hotter in the south than it was in August riding with the relief force.'

'In the summer women and children go to the mountains so they don't suffer so much from the heat,' John assured her. 'The men go as well, for

168

a few weeks, but the women usually stay there from June to the end of August. It gives everyone a break and makes them better fitted to tackle the rest of the year.'

'I'll stay with you,' Adeline said with just a shade too much vehemence in her voice. John put his arm round her and bent to kiss the top of her head. It will always be a part of her now, the memories, the dread of being left, he reminded himself, as it will always be a part of me. Only I did not suffer as she did, so I can push the pictures out of my mind most of the time, and even my dreams are mostly trouble-free.

Aloud he said comfortingly, 'And so you shall . . . stay with me, I mean. It will give me an excellent excuse for spending the majority of the summer in the mountains. If we decide to go back to China, that is. When you've seen your home again and spent some time there, who knows? We may decide we can't bear to leave!'

'But John, it's your life,' Adeline pointed out. 'To save souls for Christ and bodies for themselves, you said.'

'We'll see, when I've talked to the head of my mission,' John told her. 'Now let's go below and get ready for dinner. We're on the captain's table, you know – very honoured!'

'Adeline, coming home?' Arnold, who had been eating his lunch far too fast for his mother's peace of mind, put down his knife and fork and stared across the table at his wife. 'Whatever next, I wonder? I thought she and John were to stay there for ten years, or some such story.'

'I dare say Lily's got it wrong,' Mrs Albert said, taking a sip of water from her glass and tapping the carafe with one carefully tended fingernail as a sign to the maid that it needed refilling. 'She's probably only been half-listening . . .' She gave what was no doubt meant to be a playful laugh, but it turned sour halfway through and sounded, to Lily at any rate, merely spiteful. 'You know what these young women are like!'

Arnold turned a dark glance on his mother. I wish he looked at her like that every day, Lily thought wistfully. She wouldn't last long then!

'Oh, Mother, what nonsense you do talk. Of course Lily was listening. She's on excellent terms with Mr Warburton and she wouldn't be so high in his good books if she only "half-listened" when he spoke. Now tell me, my dear, just what did the old boy say?'

'He said he'd had a letter from his daughter, and she's coming home. Probably not for good, but for a nice long stay.' Lily put a forkful of cold chicken into her mouth and chewed industriously, until she was sure that Mrs Albert was not going to try again to discredit her remarks. 'She's been very ill.'

Immediately the words were out of her mouth she wished them unsaid. She had been so careful, never telling either Arnold or his mother anything about life at the Manor, for fear it would somehow be turned against her.

169

And now she sensed a tension, a tautness, from one or other of them, which might easily bode ill for her in some way.

'Adeline? Really? I've heard nothing of this!'

That was Mrs Albert, fork suspended whilst she no doubt speculated on her gossip-machine's unexpected breakdown. Mrs Albert was a great one for knowing everything that happened to everyone, though she would have killed anyone who even hinted that she was a real tattlemonger.

'Oh, weren't they involved in the siege?' That was Arnold, easy, relaxed. 'Only I thought Adeline was safe in her home and poor John was stuck in Peking and couldn't get out again.'

He had addressed his remarks to his wife, and Lily answered him readily enough.

'Letters take ages to get through, so that's probably why the news isn't general knowledge. But Adeline was very ill whilst John was away from her, in Peking. She's fine now, her father says, and longing to see England and her home again.'

She could have told him a lot more, but instinct forbade it. Mr Warburton had been desperately worried, knowing that his daughter was expecting a child. He had confided in Lily, and Mrs Gilmour knew, but absolutely no one else, and Lily intended to keep it that way. And even I don't know all the details, Lily reminded herself. Only that John had been in Peking when poor Adeline was captured by bandits and lost the baby.

'So she's all right now?' Arnold scraped a piece of bread round his plate and Lily winced. If she had done a thing like that she would have been roundly scolded by Mrs Albert, but Arnold, being a man and her mother-in-law's eldest son, could get away with murder.

'Yes, she's a lot better. I suppose that's why they're coming home, because she's well enough to travel.'

'Hm. Well, it'll be good to see young Adeline again.' Arnold took a drink of water, then leaned over and rang the handbell in the middle of the table. One of the maids, who had been waiting outside the door with the dessert trolley, came in and pushed her vehicle round to Mrs Albert's side of the table. Arnold glanced, said, 'Cheese, please, Mary,' and then addressed his wife. 'You never met her, of course, but no doubt you will.'

'I hope so.'

The tension was still there, but Lily could not tell from whom it emanated. She only knew that it existed and that it worried her.

Arnold, going off back to the pot-bank that afternoon, let the thought of seeing Adeline again wash round in his mind, a bit like champagne, heightening his awareness, making him tingle.

He had fallen out of love with Lily very soon after their son's birth, he told himself, but his feeling for Adeline had remained true, and even the thought of seeing her again excited him. Oh, she was married to someone else, but she was still the woman he had intended to marry. But for a quirk of fate it would have been she sitting opposite him at the luncheon table just now, she fencing with his beloved but domineering mother. Not that she would have needed to fence, because he was well aware that his mother would never have behaved to Adeline as she behaved to Lily.

For a moment he felt a pang of shame over his own behaviour, but he stifled it quickly. So he did not always stand up for his wife – well, she was old enough to stand up for herself, and anyway she had more or less tricked him into marrying her so she did not deserve to be protected from a natural hazard like a mother-in-law. If she'd been a different sort of woman she would have dealt with his mother pleasantly but firmly and he, Arnold, would not have to sit between them at mealtimes feeling, on occasion, very like a worm between two large and hungry thrushes.

But Adeline was coming home – and she would meet Lily. He had very soon realized that Lily, despite her beauty and her self-confidence in certain areas, was common. She even looked common sometimes: she wore her hair in too many curls, her dresses tended to frills, she showed too much ankle when she climbed into or out of the carriage and too much bosom when they were dining *en famille*. So what would Adeline make of his choice? Would she despise Lily, as he knew he often did, or would she dislike her? Perhaps she might befriend her for her father's sake . . . but he had never seen Adeline act against her own conscience, so that was unlikely.

Adeline would also see Philip, of course. Arnold liked Philip. He thought he was a grand little lad and could often be found playing with his small son in the nursery. But he did not approve of Lily spending so much time with the child. His mother often remarked that it was not right for a lady to be so taken up with a boy. She thought Nurse should have more of a say in Philip's upbringing, even intimated that she herself knew a great deal about children – was Philip not the image of Arnold, at that age, and had she not done an excellent job of rearing her own son?

But on this point at least Lily was firm. Philip was her child, the apple of her eye, and no one else was going to interfere between her and her little boy. On one occasion she had actually ordered her mother-in-law out of the nursery, and Arnold had it on good authority that his mother had stared, boggled a bit, and then turned and left Lily in possession of the field.

But it did not make for a quiet life, and Arnold, like most men, liked his home to be peaceful and well run. And there was no doubt about it: whilst his mother had lived in Langforth the house had not been well run. The servants had defied his wife, ignored his wishes and run amok with the housekeeping allowance. With his mother's return, however, everything had gone back to normal. He had his meals on time, his linen changed daily, his shoes polished until they shone like glass. All his favourite dishes, which had mysteriously disappeared off the menu when his mother left, had returned to grace his table once more. Wine tasted good and rich, not thin and a trifle sour. Meat was lean and undercooked, not stringy and fat. Even the fruit in the big dishes on the sideboard was ripe and well polished, not green and tasteless.

Lily had once cried passionately that the whole period of his mother's absence had been a trick created by Mrs Consett for her own undoing, and though Arnold had told her she was being absurd, in retrospect it did seem odd that things had gone so very wrong in his mother's absence and so very right the moment she was back in the saddle. But perhaps his mother was right and it was Lily's sheer inadequacy and lack of firm discipline which had wrought the damage. Anyway, he did not intend to risk another fiasco by sending his mother away again. Lily must just learn to live with the older woman, and profit by her help and advice.

The carriage was in Langforth now, wending its way through the narrow streets, heading for the pot-bank. Arnold stirred and sighed. It was exciting to think about seeing Adeline again, but it would not change things. He was married to Lily, with all her inadequacies, and he would just have to make the best of it.


'I'll never like Shanghai if I live to be a hundred,' Adeline remarked as their ship moved sedately up-river, carrying them to what might well be their new home. 'But the shops are rather fun.'

'You must buy presents to take home when we get back,' John said, remembering his duty. 'Something for my parents and brothers and something for your father and Mrs Gilmour. And something extra-special for Bella – or should I call her Mrs Patrick Phillimore now?'

'Yes, she's married, of course,' Adeline sighed. 'I wish we could have gone home for the wedding. Never mind, though. We'll undoubtedly meet her Patrick and see her new home. Won't we?'

'Of course. In a way, you know, we were lucky to start our lives in Peking – have you ever seen anything flatter or vaster than that plain?'

'Or duller,' Adeline agreed. 'What a horrid colour, yellowy-grey. I hope the Yangtse crosses more exciting country than this before we reach your ancient city.'

'Cheiping isn't *my* ancient city,' John pointed out. 'And of course the mission won't be right in the city, but outside it.' He closed his eyes, quoting from the letter they had received describing the spot. 'A green and fertile valley set amidst gentle hills, with the mountain known to the locals as the Mother of Dragons brooding in the background.'

'Very poetic,' Adeline said drily. 'As you say, dearest, it's better not to take anyone's word for it but to see for ourselves.' They were passing a river port now and the quiet which had prevailed when they were in midstream was changing as the sounds from the town were wafted towards them. Children shouting, a cacophony of the traffic sounds of beasts and men pulling carts, a mother calling to her little boy, the little boy answering in a stream of high-pitched, liquid sounds.

172

A young girl was walking along the top of the Bund; she walked with grace for her feet had not been bound and she had a long plait with a bit of red ribbon on the end. Before she could stop herself Adeline had grabbed John's arm.

'Look, it's Yenala!'

She knew, as soon as the words were out of her mouth, that it was not, could not possibly be. She had seen Yenala die with her own eyes, had told John about it, her voice choking with tears, and yet . . . and yet . . .

John slid an arm round her waist.

'Steady, old girl. Do you know, I still do that . . . think I see someone when I know perfectly well that they're not here to be seen. It happens all the time, but it'll ease. It's probably a good sign, that you can forget the horror of her passing for whole hours together, but I know how it hurts. I know, believe me.'

Adeline said nothing until the pain had subsided, the tears had been blinked back to whence they came, and then she turned easily to the scene on the Bund.

'Goodness, look at that old woman. She must have a dozen cats all around her. What a picture she'd make!'

'You'll have to draw her, when you've got a moment free,' John said. Adeline smiled at him but said nothing. She had not picked up a pencil to draw from life since the day she had sketched Yenala fishing, and what had happened to those sketches she could not imagine. Neither did she care, except that perhaps one day she would wish she had a picture of the beloved younger girl. But now she's in my mind so clearly, Adeline told herself, that if I could draw now, I could draw every detail of her face, every strand of hair, every line of her neat, graceful, young girl's body.

She had drawn monsters when John first found her because there were monsters in her mind, because she felt herself to be as wrong as the creatures she had created on paper. But now, with a tired but peaceful mind, she had no wish to draw at all, so ignored the pencils and paper which John left lying around. One day, perhaps. But until that day dawned she would concentrate all her energies on simply being alive and in her right mind.

She was looking forward to going home to England, but even that was less anticipation than a sort of gentle acceptance. If John had come to her and told her the trip was off she would have said all the conventional things, but real, harsh sorrow and disappointment were strong emotions and strong emotions were, at the moment, more than she was prepared either to feel or to acknowledge.

John had told her that she would learn to live fully once more, that the invisible screen of ice she had erected around herself would melt of its own accord, but she was in no hurry for that moment. Being involved hurt too much, and for the time being Adeline had had her fill of being hurt. She watched life flow by contentedly enough but had absolutely no urge to participate. When John had suggested adopting another young girl to be a companion to her she had vetoed the idea with unexpected firmness. She could not understand why John did not see how painful it would be to see someone just like Yenala moving around their home, day after day. A constant reminder of what might have been, a girl by whom she would measure Yenala's lost years. She would see the girl bend over a pool to pick lotus buds and she would think, Yenala would be that tall now, she would bend like that, her hands full of buds, her mouth curved in just such a smile. Oh no, that might melt her ice, but the pain of it was beyond contemplation.

# CHAPTER THIRTEEN

They arrived home in early May, when the shadows in the woods were pools of bluebells and the leaves still held their fresh, greeny-yellow spring tint.

It seemed to Adeline and John that it was a magical spring, staged especially for their benefit. In the manor garden the lilacs hung heavy purple heads and the great laburnum in the stableyard dripped blossom on to the cobbles so that when Adeline went out to visit the horses she trod on a carpet of gold. Around her window the birds chuckled and rustled in the wisteria, and the scent of those blossoms alone was enough to bring a lump to her throat with its power to bring her childhood back into her mind at a bound.

On the second morning, the dawn chorus woke her, though John slumbered on, undisturbed. Adeline tiptoed out of bed and went to the window, drawing the curtains back a little to let in the grey dawn light. A thousand birds, it seemed, were shouting their heads off in the orchard, yet in this dim, other-worldly light she could not see so much as a sparrow. It was cool standing there, a light breeze stirring the tendrils of hair round her face, though her heavy bedtime plait did not move – indeed it would have taken a hurricane to move it, Adeline thought with an inward smile, for her hair had always been thick and heavy, a silken curtain, and now, in the soft air of England, it would gleam as it once had, feel healthy and springy, lose the dead weight it had taken on after her ordeal.

She glanced back towards the bed; John was sleeping easily, on his back, one arm flung up, the other lying on the coverlet. It would hurt no one if she went out into this beautiful English dawn, just for half an hour.

She did not bother to dress but slipped sandals on her feet and put a

174

cloak around her shoulders. Then she left the room and pattered softly down the stairs, feeling almost young again, almost happy. It would be just like old times to be in the gardens alone, before anyone else was up.

Outside, she wandered around the garden for a while, dazed with pleasure at its complete and gentle Englishness. Flowers hung their heads, waiting for the sun to rise so that they could give forth their perfume. Adeline could see tulips, pansies, carnations and wallflowers, and she could smell lilies of the valley, though for the life of her she could not run the tiny flowers to earth.

In the orchard, the apple blossom was over and the trees were starred with their pale, greeny-grey leaves. Without thinking where she was going, Adeline went down through the orchard and into the meadow beyond.

The grass was long enough to soak her cloak and the nightgown she wore beneath it, but the morning was so warm and pleasant that she never thought twice about it but walked on, the grass swishing against her legs. The sky was blue now and, looking up, Adeline saw a dove, its white turned to gold by the sun she could not yet see. She stopped in her tracks as she reached the trees which grew between her and the river . . . this was foolish. What on earth was she doing so far from the manor, still in her nightgown? But it was so wonderful to be safe, to know she was in her own place where no evil lurked. She walked on through the woods and emerged on to the river bank.

She watched the sun come up then, blood-red in the east, as she had watched it often before, standing still and breathless as it edged over the low line of the distant hills. Only when it had flooded the land with colour did she step out again, walking along the towpath by the river, staring at everything – the sheep on the further bank, the bright yellow buds on the flag irises, the fast-expanding circle on the water as a fish rose to a fly.

She reached the stile and hesitated, a hand on the topmost bar. Should she climb over? Oh, but her nightgown . . . though it was still far too early for anyone to be about and it might be her only chance to visit the tower . . . a sentimental journey, for it had been months since she had thought about Arnold.

Threading her way between the trees, it struck Adeline that she was a completely different person from the girl who had come this way to meet her lover only a little over two years before. She could still understand the attraction that the illicit meetings had held for that girl, but she knew that for her as she was now, such a timid, lacklustre little romance would seem a complete waste of time. No doubt Arnold, also happily married, would feel just the same. Still, for old times' sake, she would walk as far as the tower before retracing her steps.

She saw the tower through the trees and at the same time heard someone moving in the wood. Immediately she stopped short, feeling extremely foolish. Then she glanced down at herself; the cloak was a good long one and covered all but the hem of her nightgown. Fortunately it was a primrose-yellow nightgown, what was more; if someone did happen to see her they would only think she had slipped the cloak on over a summer dress. And she *wanted* to see the tower now, having come this far.

Adeline walked resolutely – but quietly – on through the trees and came out in the clearing at exactly the same moment as a man emerged from the trees on the opposite side.

It was Arnold.

'Hello! Good God, Addy, you look a child again – I've not seen you with your hair in a plait for years . . . it seems like centuries!'

Arnold had not changed at all, Adeline thought, staring at him with pleasure. The same dark hair with a bit of a wave to it, the same blue-grey eyes with the dark lashes which were unfairly long and would have looked wonderful on a woman. The same cleft chin, the same slightly petulant mouth . . . and his expression, too, was the same. He was looking at her with admiration and . . . she supposed . . . affection.

'Hello, Arnold,' she said, admirably calm. 'This *is* a strange place to meet! I'm so excited to be back in England that I came out early for a quiet walk, but I never expected to meet a soul, let alone you!'

'I hoped you'd come,' Arnold said. He moved towards her, his hands held out. 'Addy, Addy, it's been a long time.'

Adeline smiled but kept her own hands severely clasping each other. She saw no point in an emotional reunion, particularly with someone who had let her down heavily the last time they were supposed to meet.

'Why?' she asked bluntly. 'Why should I have come here? Last time you didn't bother to turn up.'

'I did! I waited two hours, damn it!'

'Really? How strange, for I waited three . . . I sat amongst the trees in the bracken and you never came near nor by, Arnold.'

'I did! I watched the clearing . . .'

'So did I!'

There was a moment of appalled silence before Adeline broke the tension with a little giggle.

'My goodness . . . what a pair of fools we were! So you did come! But it doesn't matter . . . are you and Lily as happy as John and me, Arnold?'

'How can I tell?' Arnold growled. 'Are you happy with your missionary chappie, Addy?'

'Yes, very,' Adeline said firmly. 'And you?'

'No, I'm not,' Arnold said frankly. 'I made a terrible mistake . . . though I wouldn't have, if only you'd waited, instead of going and throwing yourself at that chap's head.'

'I didn't throw myself at anyone's head,' Adeline said crossly. 'If you hadn't gone and brought that . . . brought Lily back to the Hall, I'd probably have made the biggest mistake of my life and waited for you. Though from the way you carried on, that wouldn't have meant marriage, by a long chalk. You just enjoyed having a secret, Arnold Haslington; that's all I ever was to you!'

'That's not true,' Arnold assured her, his face reddening. 'I loved you, Addy . . . I love you still, only you're as tied as I am. It's all been a mess, a horrid mess.'

'No, it hasn't. John is the best man in the world and I'm extremely lucky to be married to him,' Adeline said hotly. 'When I think of the two of you . . .'

'Oh, come off it! He took you hundreds and hundreds of miles away, got you mixed up in all that trouble in Peking, made you ill . . . and you try to tell me . . .'

'Goodbye, Arnold,' Adeline said firmly, turning her shoulder on him. 'I must be getting back to the Manor.'

Arnold crossed the clearing in a couple of strides and Adeline felt his hand on her arm. She tried to pull herself free, stumbled, and the next moment she was in Arnold's arms. He hugged her tightly for a moment and then began kissing her, though Adeline not only gave him no encouragement but kicked out at his shins with her sandalled feet and thumped him as hard as she could with her fists.

'Stop it!' she squeaked breathlessly. 'Stop it at once, Arnold!'

Arnold groaned but let her go.

'Why deny your heart . . .' he began, but Adeline waited for no more.

'Theatrics will only disgust me,' she said forcibly, heading for the trees. 'Go back to your actress, Arnold, and don't you dare ever bother me again!'

Arnold walked home aflame. He had never held her like that in their previous timid courtship, never kissed her lips with such force and abandon. She had repulsed him, but he was sure she had only done so because she was a married woman now and he was a married man. He could still feel the small bones of her in his arms, smell her flowery scent. Even her voice when she berated him was sweet to his ears.

I loved her then and I love her now, he told himself, striding up through the sunny garden to the Hall where by now the servants would probably be up and doing. She's beautiful, quite beautiful, and my intended wife! I should never have allowed Lily to part us; I've ruined things for both of us.

If Adeline had been able to read his thoughts she would have been even more annoyed than she was, but fortunately for Arnold's peace of mind he had no conception that Adeline had outgrown him. All he could think of was how he could change things, bring her triumphantly home to the Hall as his wife.

'Did you have a good walk, my love? You look so pretty when your cheeks are flushed with exercise . . . but your cloak and nightgown are

177

soaked through. You must be more careful. Don't forget you have to think of the baby now, as well as yourself.'

Adeline, impatiently casting off the wet cloak, stood on tiptoe and kissed the line of John's jaw as he shaved himself with long, careful strokes in front of their dressing-table mirror.

'Am I flushed? Well, I've been hurrying. As for the baby . . .' She touched her stomach protectively and a smile crossed her face. 'I think of him all the time, you know. All the time.'

'Have you told your father yet, my dear? After all, you must be four months pregnant, I imagine.'

'I'll tell him today,' Adeline promised. 'Are we going out later? If so, and if Papa's coming with us, I'll find a quiet moment to tell him then.'

John finished shaving whilst Adeline was still having her bath and took himself off downstairs to breakfast. As he walked down the stairs he thought, with considerable satisfaction, that he had been absolutely right to bring Adeline back here. The flush on her cheeks as she entered the room just now, he told himself, was not the only good sign. She had said very little, but what she had said had been spoken with animation and her manner had been sprightly, cheerful. She was beginning to recapture all her old spirit, and very soon, he was sure, they would be able to put the terrible past behind them. He had hoped the birth of the baby would bring recovery in its wake, but it looked as though she would be better long before the child was due to be born.

'I never thought, when Papa first came into my room and said, "Come down, my dear, there's someone I want you to meet," that you and I would be friends.' Adeline smiled. 'But it's almost as if I've known you all my life, as I once knew Bella. It's made an enormous difference to me having you so near, Lily.'

The two young women were taking Philip for a walk in his perambulator, pushing it, turn and turn about, along the upward-sloping lane which wound between the trees for nearly two miles before it finally reached their destination, the village.

'I didn't, either,' Lily confessed. 'I was jealous of you, because I really do love your papa and I thought you'd push me out and I'd be all alone, instead of being able to visit whenever I liked. And poor Philly would have been lost without his Ga-ga.'

'Push you out! As if I could! Papa's so fond of his godson – he talks about him all the time, you know, boasting about how Philly does this, that and the other twice as quickly as most boys of his age. And it isn't only the boy – Papa's extremely fond of you, as well.'

'Really?' Lily's gratification showed. 'He's been ever so kind, Addy, and so's Mrs Gilmour. They've done their best to make me feel at home – which is more than Mother-in-law up at the Hall has done.'

'Father told me she'd been difficult,' Adeline said sympathetically. 'It's a problem I've never had to face, being so many miles away from home, but I can imagine that sharing a house with another woman must be very hard. I never did understand why she and the children came back, though, after Bella wrote that she'd moved into Langforth with Dorothea and the rest.'

'She moved back because . . . oh, it's a long story . . . I don't want to bore you.'

'You won't,' Adeline assured her. 'You know, Lily, after all the terrible things which happened in China, just to hear people talking about nice little things like family quarrels and a late frost is bliss, absolute bliss.'

'Well, it's to be hoped you won't go back there,' Lily said decidedly. 'It wouldn't be the same here without you. Has John got a permanent job in Langforth?'

'No, just a temporary one. You see, we don't have any real income apart from John's salary, so he's taken a junior post with a medical practice in the town just for the few months we'll be home. If we do decide not to go back then he'll have to find himself something a bit more permanent, and a bit better paid as well.'

'I see. And you still haven't made up your mind about staying?'

Adeline shook her head.

'No, not yet. I feel it's John's decision, really, because I'm very much better now, quite healthy and well, and if he wants to go back at least I know it isn't for ever, just for a couple of years before we come home again. Anyway, when we married I knew John wanted to go to China. Just because I had a bad few months there shouldn't affect the whole of John's life. Being a medical missionary's a vocation, you know, not just a job. But here I am, boring on about my troubles, when you had started to tell me what's wrong with things between Mrs Albert Haslington and yourself.'

When Lily's explanation came to an end, Adeline whistled.

'Phew! I never would have dreamed she could be so awkward, though Bella did sometimes say that her mother ruled her father with a rod of iron and would do the same to any child who didn't stand up to her. That's what you must do, Lily, stand up to her. Can't you get Arnold to see things your way?'

'No. That's the really awful part, Addy. Arnold . . . well, he doesn't even seem to like me much any more, let alone love me. He's always telling me off and taking his mother's side if we argue even a little bit, and he'd like to see me hand Philly over to a nurse, only I just won't – I love him far too well.'

'I'm sure Arnold loves you very much, really,' Adeline said hastily. 'But he's easy-going, I believe, as his father used to be. He'll take the smooth path always, if there's a choice to make. You're so very pretty, Lily, that you should be able to wind Arnold round your little finger.'

'Well, I can, of course, in bed,' Lily said with blush-making frankness. 'But that doesn't last . . . does it? I mean, he'd sweet-talk me all night if need be, and then in the dining-room or the drawing-room find fault with every blessed thing I do – particularly if his mother or Mrs Consett is around.'

'That Consett woman!' Adeline said with unusual vehemence. 'She's the root of the trouble. If only you could get rid of her . . .'

'I know. As I've told you, I tried. But it's no use. Arnold would never hear of it, and so long as she's there, and Arnold's mother, I'll never get a chance to prove I can run a house.'

'Then they'll have to be persuaded to move out again, I think. You can't simply put up with Dorothea and the dreadful Bertie until they marry and leave home . . . you'll be old by then, if not dead from despair.'

'They never will,' Lily mourned. 'I sometimes think I'll be the one to go, and I'm not even certain Arnold wouldn't give a secret cheer if I did.'

'*You* go! Why, of all the . . . but hold on a moment . . . that's it, Lily! You go . . . you and Arnold and Philip here. You move into Langforth. Do you have the courage to stand up to them all? You can say Mrs Albert is right and you can't run a great big house but you could run a smaller one. You'll have to convince Arnold, of course . . . have you ever seen our dower house? Father offered it to John and me when we have a family, but quite honestly so long as we're away we'll come back to the Manor for our leaves. Why don't you try it? Arnold can only say no, after all.'

'But . . . but your dower house isn't in Langforth,' Lily said, grasping at straws whilst her mind wrestled with this new suggestion. 'I thought you said I should move to Langforth.'

'I did, but really I just meant move away. Look, Lily, it seems a sensible solution to me. It wouldn't be for long, of course, just until Arnold could be persuaded that you really can run a house. Once he knew how comfortable you could make him, he'd probably join you in insisting that his mother and the whole crew of them move out. Isn't there a dower house attached to the Hall? Well, there jolly well should be, then Mrs Albert wouldn't feel she was being completely ousted – Langforth's a dozen or more miles away, so of course she was a good way from her friends and her son. Will you try it? I'll speak to Papa, but I'm sure he'll be very willing to help you out.'

'I'll try it,' Lily vowed, a smile spreading across her face. 'And if it works . . . my, how happy I should be!'

John stood up, remembering to keep his head bent, for the roof in the cottage bedroom was low. The woman in the bed smiled a thank you as he went out of the room, and then John made his way down the steep little staircase to the kitchen where the daughter waited.

'Your mam will be fine,' he said reassuringly. 'She's just doing a bit too much . . . . she's to stay in bed for another two or three days and then try taking it a bit easier until the child's born.'

'Awright; I'll tell me dad,' the girl said. She was a cheerful, plump child in her mid-teens who had stayed away from work today to let the doctor in. 'She's working at the pot-bank. It's none too hard there, but because of the baby she's been doing overtime, see? But she'll lay off, now you've said. Thanks, doctor.'

'That's all right. And make sure she eats a bit of meat when she can, and drinks milk.'

The girl agreed, sunnily, to do what she could, and John left and hurried out to where he had left his horse. Real doctors, he knew, drove neat little traps, but it simply was not worth his while acquiring a vehicle, not for the length of time he would be in England.

For John had made up his mind what he wanted, and it was not a country practice in his own land. He wanted China, the size of it, the challenge, the difficulties, even. He would stay here for another month or two for Adeline's sake, but settling down here, becoming just another harassed doctor treating people who spent their lives fearing his bills . . . no, he could not stand it. He had mentioned it to Adeline, asked her whether she did not find it somehow constricting, inhibiting, all the little fields and hedged roads, all the smug women who called a doctor in for an ache in their little finger, all the men who despised his calling and showed it.

Adeline, he remembered, had smiled gently and told him that she would be quite happy to return whenever he felt they should. She, too, was missing China.

He did not know whether he completely believed this, for her pleasure in the English countryside had far exceeded his, but it was what he wanted to believe. She adored her father, of course, and enjoyed seeing her friends again after her absence. But here she had no real work, no useful place. He believed that she would miss that very much, once the child was born and she had time on her hands and the energy to work once more. He remembered her in the clinic, quick, matter-of-fact, incredibly useful as an assistant and a nurse. All that would be wasted if they stayed in England, where a doctor did not expect his wife to do anything more than keep his consulting room and waiting room tidy and answer the door if he was out on his calls.

In Cheiping, what was more, she would have a proper social life, for there were a number of Europeans in residence there, and cultured Chinese families as well, with whom they would, he hoped, exchange visits. Ayiteng had been too remote, he realized in retrospect, though at the time it had seemed ideal. Now, he could scarcely wait to get back to Cheiping, to start his life there.

The horse was a bright brown, leggy gelding which belonged to Mr Warburton; its name was Peter, an absurd name for a horse, John thought, but it was an obliging, well-mannered animal and showed no sign of unease when it found itself tied up to a strange gate every ten or fifteen minutes. But you aren't Thunderer, John told it as he mounted and clicked it back on to the carriageway. He had not sold his horse but had put him in a good livery stable used by the British minister when he was visiting Cheiping. John had every hope that Thunderer would be greeting him with pleasure some time in the next couple of months, so did not repine over the animal, but he could not regard poor Peter with anything but comfortable indifference.

Dr Maddison's surgery was in Langforth but on this occasion John had been doing visits nearer home, in the village, so he turned Peter's head towards the Manor once more with considerable satisfaction. Another day's work over . . . and that meant he was a day nearer to going back to China.

It occurred to him, as he rode up the short drive and passed the Manor, that one day he would have to come back here, when he was the owner of what Mr Warburton was apt to call 'the prettiest manor house in England'. But that was a long way off. His father-in-law was the picture of health, but even if something did happen before he and Adeline were ready to return there were always bailiffs, responsible people who would look after an estate with care and affection in its owner's absence.

So John, whistling beneath his breath as he unsaddled Peter, put the future firmly into perspective. For the time being, China. Later could take care of itself.


'It's been a wonderful visit, Papa,' Adeline sighed, linking her arm through her father's. They were strolling, in the warm September afternoon, around the orchard, pointing out to each other the best crops on first this tree and then that. 'But all good things come to an end and John is desperately needed in China. Here you have many good doctors, but over there medicine is still in its early stages. The Chinese are beginning to train their own physicians, but they'll need help for a good while yet.'

'I always knew you'd go back, I suppose,' Mr Warburton told her. 'Only . . . I thought you'd stay until the child was born, and perhaps even a few months longer. Why don't *you* stay, love? And let John go back to this Cheiping place, get it ready for you? Then the lad . . . or the girl, of course . . . could be born here, in the home he'll inherit one day.'

'To be honest, because I couldn't face the journey by myself, and because I'd miss John so dreadfully,' Adeline sighed. 'I would have liked the baby to be born here, but I can see what John means; he says it's either go back now or miss the mission at Cheiping, and he's set his heart on living there. And if I can't . . . well, if I can't live in England for a few years yet, I'd rather Cheiping than anywhere else, I think. So you see, Papa, we must both be brave and say goodbye, for the next year or so at least.'

'And . . . you can tell me the truth, Addy my love, for I won't say a word to anyone . . . you really want to go back? You can be happy there, after all that happened?'

'Yes, I think so. Anyway, Papa, I married John knowing he wanted to work in China. And once I'm there, working, I'll be very happy. I was before, truly.'

'Then that's all I need to make me happy too,' Mr Warburton said. 'I'll write every week, as always, and tell you what's going on here.'

'Lovely. And Lily says she'll write as well, which will be a new departure. Fancy, she's going to be living so near to you, Papa, that you'll be able to wave to each other through the windows!'

'If Arnold agrees.'

'I'm sure he will; after all, he keeps saying he wants Lily to learn to manage a big house. What better way is there than by starting with a small one and working up?'

'Well, love, I don't know so much . . . about Arnold, I mean. It'll be a bit of a blow to his mother and she's a woman who doesn't take kindly to being taken down a peg. So there's that, and the fact that at the moment Arnold's master of a very large house indeed, whereas if he moves into the dower house he'll not even be master of it, he'll be my tenant.'

'Well, let's hope it works out,' Adeline said. 'Now, Papa, if you're really going to put a bit of that pasture down to apple trees, I suggest . . .'

She rattled on merrily, but privately she was worried about Arnold and Lily. Twice since that memorable early morning meeting she had come across Arnold, and both times he had vowed undying love for her in a manner she found extremely annoying. He was not giving his marriage with Lily a chance, and she could not help being glad, for Lily's sake, that she herself would soon be out of sight and, she hoped, out of mind. What had become, for Adeline, a girlish infatuation had, it seemed, loomed larger in Arnold's mind. He was, for reasons best known to himself, trying to build that tenuous, fragile relationship into a Grand Romance . . . he had even had the gall to send her two poems through the post, which had caused her extreme embarrassment. Fortunately John was not the sort of husband to demand to read her letters, and had he done so he would probably merely have thought the poet was comical rather than serious, for Arnold was not a gifted writer and his idea of rhyme seemed to be that if two words had a number of letters in common it would do; but even so, the poems had annoyed her.

Telling Arnold this, forbidding him ever to address her by letter again, had merely made him sulky and defiant. He would jolly well do what he pleased, and anyway – belatedly – how did she know the poems came from him? They had not been signed.

Adeline was a kind girl, or she might have told him honestly that she knew of no one else who would write so badly and address her so confidently. Instead, she said tartly that they had his stamp all over them and she would have given them back, only unfortunately she had thrown them straight on the fire.

'Do have a little more dignity, Arnold,' she advised him, and then turned on her heel and walked over to join another group – they were at a garden party at a house in the village – without another glance.

Her friendship with Lily, furthermore, had made it plain that even if Arnold was no longer in love, Lily still thought Arnold wonderful. Oh, his attitude to her hurt and annoyed, she thought him cruel and selfish. But she loved him, though not uncritically, and longed for their marriage to be a success.

It would break Lily's heart to know that Arnold had actually chased after another woman, Adeline realized, and though Lily had come to terms with the fact that Arnold's love for her had lapsed she still hoped that if the two of them and the child had their own home she might rekindle Arnold's love.

She was probably right too, Adeline considered. Arnold might be a stupid boy who had never grown up, but he was not deliberately cruel, and Adeline was certain that his affections had not left Lily completely, but only cooled in the face of his mother's constant presence and obvious disapproval. Mrs Albert obviously did not want her son to break his marriage vows, she plainly adored her grandson, but she wanted to be the most important person in Arnold's life, and if this meant breaking up the marriage, then Adeline was quite sure she would cheerfully do so.

'Move into the Warburtons' dower house? Most certainly not!'

That had been Arnold's unvarying reply to Lily's suggestions, pleas, and, finally, tears. But at least her request had made some impression on him, for he came in one day, a little sheepishly, with a sheaf of prospectuses in his hand.

'Town houses,' he said briefly. 'I was talking to one of the fellows at a business meeting and he was saying that in London everyone of consequence has a town house and a country place. I said we were thinking of doing the same . . . I popped into the agent's office this morning and dropped a word in his ear, and he came up with these. See what you think.'

Lily was enraptured by them all. It would have been nice to have lived a stone's throw from the Manor, but, failing that, living a long way away from Mrs Albert was the next best thing. Possibly it would suit her even better, for Arnold told her that the better families now lived in their town houses through autumn, winter and most of the spring, merely spending the summer in the country.

'A town house?' Mrs Albert said, when she was told that the young couple were going to view two or three properties. 'With all the room you've got here? Rather unnecessary, surely? And the cost, dear . . . you'll need a big place, of course, until the children leave home.'

Lily, who was present at the time since she and Arnold had met her mother-in-law on their way to the stables, held her breath. Would Arnold let her get away with it? But it appeared that Arnold could be devious when the occasion demanded.

'We're only looking,' he said. 'When we see something we like . . .'

'I hope you'll tell me well before you make up your mind,' Mrs Albert said in a minatory manner. 'I don't intend to move into a house I don't like, Arnold!'

Lily held her breath again. Would he tell her now?

'No, of course you don't, Mother. I wouldn't expect you to,' Arnold said soothingly. 'Now if you'll excuse us, we have an appointment.'

'An appointment? I'm not busy, and if you could wait just a moment . . .'

'An appointment, Mother, precludes waiting even half a moment,' Arnold said briskly. 'We must be off.'

In the carriage, Lily looked at the prospectuses and wondered if she dared express a preference for the smallest house on offer, or if Arnold would immediately guess why she wanted it. It seemed safest, on the whole, to wait and see.

After a whole four hours scouring Langforth for a suitable house, Lily was nervous in case Arnold decided not to move after all, for she had to admit that the home they were looking for had not so far put in an appearance despite the lyrical prose on the prospectuses. But after they had lunched well and Arnold had drunk the best part of a bottle of an excellent claret, he suggested one more house before they gave up for the day.

'Lime Tree Road,' he said, studying the long sheet of paper. 'Well, it *sounds* all right.'

'They all sounded nice,' Lily pointed out. 'Is this the one with ten bathrooms and an acre of billiard room, because if so . . .'

'No, we saw that last but one. This one sounds quite simple, so I expect it's hopeless; probably hasn't been lived in for a hundred years and is falling down and a prey to rats and woodworm,' Arnold said with the gloom natural to one who has been up and down stairs, round and round gardens, and burrowing in basements for the best part of the day. 'The description is suspiciously brief . . . five bedrooms, two bathrooms, a morning room, a drawing-room . . .'

'Don't tell me; my head's spinning already.' Lily leaned out of the window as the carriage slowed. 'I say, this is an awfully pretty road; what delightful trees!'

'Limes,' Arnold said professionally, and then laughed at Lily when she expressed surprise at his knowledge of dendrology. 'Can you see the house? I bet it's that one . . . there . . . with the dead-looking curtains and the green mould growing on the window frames.'

They got out of the carriage, Johnson began to walk the horses and Arnold, with Lily on his arm, examined the nearest houses.

'It's called "Silver Birches", but I don't suppose . . .' Arnold began, but stopped at a squeak from his wife.

'Arny! Can it be *that* one?'

'That one' was an elegant residence with two silver birches growing by the gateposts, a short, gravelled drive and a fine sweep of well-tended lawn.

'It can't be.' Arnold, after only four hours of house-viewing, was already a pessimist. 'Isn't it jolly, though? I wouldn't mind living there!'

'It is! It is! Look, on the gatepost!'

Arnold looked and read the words 'Silver Birches'.

'There are clean, bright-red curtains,' Lily said as they began to walk up the drive. 'Oh Arnold, and window-boxes . . . I've always wanted window-boxes.'

'And a nice range of stabling, by the looks,' Arnold said exultantly. 'And two greenhouses . . . I think. Can we take a look at the back?'

'No, don't be awful, we must ring.' Lily tugged at the bell-pull and then stood back the better to examine the yellow rose which grew beside the front door. 'Isn't that a delightful colour? And the scent, Arny! Oh, I *do* like this house.'

'It's probably in a terrible . . .' Arnold was beginning, when the front door opened and he hastily changed his remark to a cough.

A maid stood there, capped and aproned.

'Yes, sir? Who shall I say?'

Behind her, Lily could see a small but pleasant hall with polished oak boarding on the floor and a gently curving staircase leading to the upper regions of the house.

'Mr and Mrs Haslington; we've come to view the house,' she said before Arnold could open his mouth. 'Is it still for sale?'

If Arnold thought this a peculiarly stupid remark he did not say so; indeed, he had caught a little of his wife's anxiety, for this house was the only one they had so far seen in which he could imagine himself living.

'Oh, yes, ma'am, it's still for sale,' the maid said seriously. 'If you'll step inside I'll call Miss Engells.'

Arnold and Lily stepped inside and were led to a pleasant, panelled reception room with an enormous mahogany table in the centre and an equally enormous mahogany sideboard laden with cheerful blue and white china, a big glass vase full of full-blown pink roses, and a silver container of peacocks' feathers.

'It's a nice room,' Lily whispered. Arnold, examining a collection of sporting trophies on a shelf, nodded absently. This fellow was quite a sportsman; quite a shot, as well.

They were an hour in 'Silver Birches' and came out a trifle shattered but still determined that they must buy.

'Two *ladies*, though!' Lily remarked several times as they drove back to Langforth. 'How unusual, Arny! That Miss Engells was so like a man . . . well, I nearly made the most awful fool of myself. But the house is lovely – just what I've always wanted.'

'I'll put in an offer at once,' Arnold said eagerly. 'That conservatory is prime. Have you ever seen a better display of rare blooms? And the big greenhouse . . . you don't see many vines that laden with grapes.'

'And they say country houses are bought for their gardens,' Lily agreed. 'This house has the most delicious garden . . . and they do most of it themselves! Thank goodness Miss Pratt wants to retire to the seaside, or I'm sure they never would have sold.'

'Thank heaven,' agreed Arnold. Then his face grew gloomy. 'I'm not looking forward to telling Mother that we've decided to buy without consulting her, though.'

'But she isn't going to live there; there isn't room, apart from the fact that she insisted she must live at the Hall,' Lily pointed out. 'So really it's no one's business but ours.'

'Yes. So why don't you tell her? She's bound to be annoyed, and if you tell at least one of us will be in her good books.'

'I don't mind,' Lily said, with a boldness she was far from feeling. 'She can't eat me, after all!'

In mid-September, whilst they were still at sea, Adeline was so ill that she thought she would die. Seasickness, that mysterious complaint, which had spared her throughout the voyage towards England, nearly turned her inside out on the way back. It must have been the reason why, after two weeks of violent retching, she once more found herself going into premature labour.

John was the only doctor on board and he did everything in his power to help her, but it was useless. A storm had raged for a couple of days and made things even more difficult. After hours of pain and unbelievable distress, Adeline gave birth to the child, which died within a few minutes of its arrival.

Looking back, John thought he would never forget that dreadful night. The wild rocking of the lamp suspended above the bunk on which Adeline, white-faced, her eyes like burning black pits, her hair a tangled mass, strained to expel the child. The way her fingers clung to his own, digging in, the nails biting blood from his palms. The roaring of the storm was such that it was to all intents and purposes a silent scene, a sort of demonic magic lantern show in which the characters suffered in silence under the enormous, swingeing blows fate dealt them.

Afterwards, when the pathetic little bundle, wrapped in sailcoth, had been launched on its last journey into the raging sea, came tears. John wept and clung to Adeline, sobbing out his gratitude that she had survived, telling her of his love, his enormous, welling pity. She had gone through this before and alone, save for her enemies. She had wept alone, suffered alone and not until this moment had he realized the depth of that suffering.

But now she was the calmer of the two. She held him, rocked him gently in her arms, and then spoke, her voice low, assured.

'It's all right, John. The Lord did not even give, He simply took away. It wasn't meant to be; I'm not going to have a child. I'm sad too, but perhaps it's for the best. I didn't look after Yenala when she was in my care, and God forbid that I should lose my own child as I lost her.'

'You mustn't talk like that,' John told her, struggling to regain his own self-possession. 'Don't you remember our promise?'

'Oh, that. Yes, I remember. Then why did I lose our baby, John? If God isn't angry with me, why did I lose this one, too?'

'Because you'd been so seasick, my love, my darling,' John whispered, holding her. 'Because I'm a wicked fool . . . I should have insisted that you stayed in England until the child was big enough to travel. I should never have let you take the risk. I wouldn't have, only going in the other direction you were marvellous – you weren't ill at all, even when we had that awful gale, remember? I thought you'd got over it – I never dreamed you'd be ill again.'

'Going home to England I was looking forward to arriving,' Adeline said in a small voice. 'Leaving it I was homesick, just a little, for my own place. But it's happened and no good can come of going over and over what's done and finished. We must put it behind us, John my dearest, and start planning the rest of our lives.'

The remainder of the voyage was uneventful. Adeline lay on deck when it was fine and stayed in her cabin when it was not. John paced the deck and tried to tell himself that everything would be all right, that soon they would be ashore and could start their lives anew. He wrote a dozen letters to Sidney Warburton and tore them all up, deciding in the end that it would be best to wait until they were settled in at Cheiping before giving the older man the bad news.

By the time the ship docked Adeline was looking a little better, eating better, and had some colour in her cheeks. They went ashore in Shanghai and spent a night at the Rudolfo Hotel before catching the river-boat.

Once more they watched the plains pass and the mountains come up on the horizon. They stopped at the river ports and bought fresh fruit: oranges red as blood, rosy apples, paw-paws and mangoes and purple grapes. Adeline chattered away and laughed at his jokes, but her eyes ached with emptiness and now and then John saw her hand go unbelievingly to the flatness of her waist.

They reached Cheiping and took a rickshaw for Adeline and the luggage. John walked alongside, and they went to their modern, Western-style bungalow in its beautiful compound, set as they had been promised in a green, tree-filled valley, with the mountain called the Mother of Dragons crouching, purple and enormous, behind the gentler hills. There were new servants to meet, for Lin Shen would not come south to them and the other young men, Pao and Chu, had families in the north.

Adeline was exhausted and went straight to bed, but John strolled out on to the verandah as night came creeping down over the purple mountain and breathed in the sweet, autumn-scented air and thought that this time he had brought Adeline to a good place, the sort of place where she might thrive, and was glad to be home at last.

He knew he would have to be gentle and careful with her, but he saw no reason why, when she had recovered her strength, they should not try for another baby, nor why, this time, their efforts should not be crowned with success. Adeline was young; still barely twenty. Once she had a baby to look after she would love China as much as he did, and be as reluctant to leave.

The town house was bought, Mrs Albert was, if not placated, at least made to see that she must appear to view the new acquisition with complaisance, and Mr and Mrs Arnold Haslington and Master Philip moved in, along with the servants necessary for the running of the establishment, a nurse for Master Philip and a lady's maid, the reliable Ellen, to see that Lily was well turned out.

Lily, bustling round setting the house to rights, ordering the meals, entertaining one or two friends, was in her element, and thought that at last all her troubles were over. In fact, they had barely begun.

# CHAPTER FOURTEEN

Philip stood quite still in the middle of the nursery floor, gazing down at the scarlet, swollen palm of his small hand where even as he watched a blister was forming. It hurt! It hurt worse than he could ever have imagined a hurt . . . but that must be why, he saw now, he had been told never to go near the nursery fire. Nor would he have dreamed of doing so, had Grandmother not burned his cuddy.

She had been in a temper since lunch, though Philip did not know quite why. It was winter, and in the winter he and Mama and Papa lived in the house called 'Silver Birches', though in the summer they all moved out into the countryside and lived here, at Haslington Hall. Which meant that

Grandmother had invited them to spend a weekend at the Hall, presumably because she wanted them. So why had she been so cross and cruel? She had insisted that he ate with the grown-ups instead of in the nursery, but instead of being nice to him, spoiling him as a grandmother should, she had found fault with his manners, told him to sit up straight, and finally, as he was going back to the nursery, had snatched his cuddy from him.

'A big boy of five doesn't suck on a dirty piece of blanket,' she said crossly. She grabbed his hand, nearly jerking his shoulder out of its joint, and marched him back to the nursery. His own dear Nanny wasn't there, of course, she was in Lime Tree Road, 'seeing to things', as she liked to phrase it. Instead, Maud, the nursery maid, was waiting.

'He doesn't need this,' Grandmother said to Maud, and she had thrown poor cuddy straight on to the fire. But then she had told Maud to come outside with her for a minute as she wanted a word with her and the two women had disappeared, leaving Philip alone.

He had done what any boy of spirit would have done. He had heaved and heaved at the heavy brass fireguard until there was a gap against the wall big enough for a skinny boy to slide through, and then he had crawled into the wicked area twixt fire and guard. Kneeling on the rug he had seized the poker, intent on rescuing what was left of poor cuddy from the flames, and had been most cruelly punished. Pain, searing, terrible, had burnt through his hand and for one dreadful second his attempt to drop the poker had been foiled as the metal clung grimly to his sore, wincing flesh. He had succeeded in throwing it down, however, leaving a strip of skin adhering to the almost red-hot iron, and then he had crawled back into the room, whimpering over the pain in his hand, urgent to escape from his crime, for cuddy was consumed by now, only an evil smell of burning wool remaining of his old favourite.

Philip had gone at once to the window, rubbing his palm on his knickerbockers, thinking to ease the agony, only to find that the pain intensified with touch. Tears fell, grey and dreary, on to the front of his clean blue smock and he held his hand close to the cold glass, gaining a moment's ease as he did so.

It was then, with his tearstained cheek close to the window and the pain seeming a little easier, that he heard the music. Or perhaps became aware of it would be more accurate, for it was so faint, so far away, that he sensed rather than heard it at first. It made him think of Mama, who often played the piano in her little sitting-room at 'Silver Birches', and sang to him there. If there was music, he told himself, then Mama must be near and she was his dear love, his champion. She would take away his hurt and bring cuddy back if anyone could. If he could but find the source of the music he would very soon find Mama!

At lunchtime there had only been Grandmother, Aunt Dorothea, Great Aunt Regina, who moved in to the Hall during the winter months to keep

Grandmother company, and Papa at the luncheon table. Mama must have gone back to the house in Lime Tree Road, Philip had supposed. The grown-ups had talked, in hushed voices, and every now and then someone had said, 'Remember the boy!' and there had followed an awkward silence, soon broken as someone forgot he was there again.

Now, Philip listened, standing in the middle of the nursery floor with his hurt hand palm uppermost. Grandmother had not returned and nor had Maud. There was no sound at all – they must have gone downstairs, for they were not even out on the landing. Very well, so Grandmother thought he was a baby, did she? She would soon learn better! He would go out and find Mama, and that would teach them all!

He was not allowed outside the nursery alone but, for all that Grandmother had said, Philip knew himself to be a brave boy, so he ran across the room, reached up and tugged the door open, and began to tiptoe along the landing towards the stairs.

It was mid-afternoon on a chilly February day and the stairs and landing were dark and cold, even frightening when you were not used to being on them alone, but Philip ignored the dark shadows. His stout little boots carried him as silently as they knew how down the wide, shallow steps and across the great dim hall with its mysterious closed doors. He had instinctively headed for the front stairs rather than the back ones, since it would be up the back stairs that Maud and possibly Grandmother herself would return when Grandmother had finished lecturing, but now he hesitated, for when Maud took him walking in the summer they emerged not through the big front door which faced him at this moment but through a small side door which they reached from the kitchen side of the baize door rather than the master's side, as Maud called it.

But a moment's reflection brought memory flooding back. Usually, they came out of the baize door and turned . . . *that* way . . . into a little lobby. Philip crossed the hall on tiptoe and found the lobby just where it should have been. Although he had only been at the Hall a day his winter coat hung on a peg far above his head in the lobby, and his rubber boots stood sentinel below. Philip could not possibly have reached his coat, and although it would have been sensible to have changed his indoor boots for the rubber ones it would have involved a lot of unbuttoning, and Philip knew his limitations. Instead, he reached up to the big round knob of the side door, turned it . . . and the door creaked open, swinging towards him with the slow steadiness of a door that is frequently in use and thus has well-oiled hinges.

As the door opened cold air rushed in. Philip looked longingly up at his coat, hesitating. He would get into the most awful trouble if Grandmother found him out in the cold without it! Although she had been perfectly beastly to him, Philip knew that she loved him very much really, and would wallop his small bottom not because she wanted to hurt him but because being out in the cold without a coat was dangerous. Nevertheless, he would have to risk it. He poked his head out through the doorway and immediately he heard the music again, sweeter, closer! He hesitated no longer but slid out into the garden, letting the side door close behind him without a qualm. If he could undo it from one side he could undo it from the other, and besides, he was going to find his Mama. She would see that he got safely back indoors.

Outside it was a horribly chilly day and there was a ground mist so that Philip could see his hands a good deal better than he could see his feet; also it was growing greyer by the minute, but Philip had set his heart on finding Mama. He set off at once, briskly, towards the sound, his burnt hand liking the cool mistiness of the air, feeling much nicer out here than it had felt in the fuggy nursery. He hurried along the little gravel path which led to the wide sweep of the carriage drive, but when he reached it and looked back to the house he decided at once to keep close in under the trees. The house seemed to be watching him, disapproving of his escape, probably hoping to get into Grandmother's good books by telling on him so that he could be dragged back indoors without ever having seen what made the music, let alone finding Mama.

He knew, the way children do know, that Grandmother and Mama did not like one another. He knew that a good deal of the talk at luncheon had been concerned with Mama, had heard the note in his grandmother's voice which always entered it when Mama was the subject of conversation, but further than that he could not go. He loved Mama, he was moderately fond of Grandmother, he was slightly in awe of Papa. A child did not question the rights and wrongs of his feelings, but simply felt them, so Philip did not wonder why he loved Mama terribly and only liked Grandmother, nor why Grandmother did not really like Mama at all. He simply accepted the status quo.

Now, however, he was concentrating on the music and it was quite definitely coming from the road which was only a short run away. Philip broke into a trot and rounded the corner to come face to face, not with the road as he expected, but with the big wrought-iron gates. They were firmly and unequivocally shut; clearly they intended to stay that way. And the grounds were walled with brick, topped, at the point where the wall ran alongside the road, with broken glass.

But the music was loud and the hope of finding Mama too strong to allow Philip to hesitate. He ran at the gate like a little goat, head down, body briskly determined, and thrust first his head and then most of his body through the bars. In fact, he was almost on the further side when the music stopped. Just stopped, as though the entire band had suddenly been struck dumb or dead.

Philip hesitated, staring up the road towards where the sound of the music had been seconds before, and even as he stared, he realized abruptly how very dark it was getting. And how cold it was. How cold *he* was, indeed, and how the burnt palm of his hand was aching. There was no music, no sign of Mama, and if he hurried and was very lucky he might just get back into the nursery before Maud returned and gave the news of his flight to the rest of the household.

His decision reached, Philip began to wriggle back the way he had come, and made a most unwelcome discovery. His head, which had slid through the bars of the gate with such ease only seconds earlier, seemed suddenly to have grown a good deal larger, for it resolutely refused to slide back. His body obeyed him at once and was on the home side of the gate at a stride, but his head was still out in the road and, despite his tuggings, it stayed there.

It was almost dark now and Philip began to be really frightened. Grandmother and Maud would find him gone and be terribly angry. A malevolent person would see his plight and steal his boots, possibly all his clothes, for Nanny was always telling him how thankful the poor would be for his nice sailor suits, his warm woollen stockings and his reefer coat with its round wooden buttons. Or suppose someone came along determined to get him back on his rightful side of the gate and pulled off his ears – he knew it was ears which were causing his dilemma – in order to facilitate his return, in one piece though earless, to the nursery once more? He gave a desperate heave and his ears seemed to enlarge immediately; they also hurt as much as though an indignant adult had already boxed them a dozen times over. His burnt hand hurt too. Philip's eyes swam with tears despite his stern resolve not to cry twice in one day. He could only look to the left because of the angle at which he was wedged and look now he desperately did, torn between a longing for rescue and a fear of bringing something dreadful down on himself, trapped as he was in the gate, like a small bird half in and half out of a cage.

No one was approaching. Darkness hid the bend in the road and all of a sudden Philip was sure he was alone in the world, quite abandoned. He would be here all night, ghosts would come and eat him up, beggars would cut his throat, smugglers would smuggle him . . . and if there was anything left by morning, Grandmother and Papa would finish it off.

But there was Mama. Could he *wish* her here, conjure her up by the strength of his longing? Once he had done so. He remembered it well; he had been ill, hot, helpless, lying in bed with a big hammer beating out a rhythm in his poor head and his hands swollen up like puff-balls floating above the bed. He had cried inside his head for his mama and, behold, she had arrived! Bending over him to kiss him, smiling at him, cooling his face with a lovely soft handkerchief soaked in lavender water and then singing to him until he fell asleep. When he was better, next day, she had still been by his bed, smoothing his brow, reading to him when he wanted amusing, simply being there when he fell quiet. Although he had seen her with her glorious hair piled up on her head and decorated with sparkly stones, had admired the cream-coloured silk evening dress, he had not realized until Nanny had pointed it out that she had been off to a party when she came to his room and had remained by his bedside all night and all the following day, not leaving him until she was quite certain he was well again.

Philip stopped fighting against the iron bars. He closed his eyes and concentrated. *Mama, come to me, come to me, your Philly needs you awful bad!*

After a moment he heard a sound and opened his eyes. A faint whistle, coming from his left. A person? It might be a boy; boys whistled – he sometimes heard them as they made their way down Lime Tree Road. He could hear footsteps, too. They were firm, marching footsteps. Too heavy for a boy. A soldier, perhaps? Then he caught sight of a figure approaching. It was a man, a tall man, jauntily walking along and whistling as he came, with a stick in one hand and something, a pair of gloves perhaps, in the other. He came steadily on, eyes ahead. Then he stopped whistling and Philip could see he was smiling, ignoring the gates with their small captive, going past with never a glance.

Philip took a deep breath, ready to shout to the man. He was a gentleman, Philip could tell, unlikely to steal boots, unlikely to tear ears from heads. But then, all of a sudden, Philip held his breath and said not a word, because he could feel his mama's presence though he could neither see nor hear her. But he was sure she was near, he could smell the sweet, flowery perfume of her, and he felt safe suddenly because of it, no longer alone.

The man drew level with the gate and his footsteps stopped, as indeed did he. He held out both hands with a welcoming smile, then began to move again, just out of Philip's range of vision. He was greeting someone . . . it had to be Mama!

'Mama? It's Philly, Mama. Do come and help me, I'm stuck!'

She always called him Philly and now her son waited confidently, sure of help at hand. Mama never failed.

There was a gasp, a soft cry, and then Mama was before him. She was wearing a soft blue dress with a dark coat open over it. She bent over him, her fingers brushing his cheek.

'Philly, darling, whatever are you doing there? Oh, my dearest, your little hands are like ice!' She touched his fingers and Philip, wincing, drew back the burnt hand automatically, the breath hissing between his teeth as he did so.

'What's the matter, darling? Are you hurt?'

'Yes . . . Mama, I'm stuck. I can't get back.'

Mama laughed softly and said something so quietly over her shoulder that Philip did not catch even the meaning of the words, and then she said, 'Come to me, little man,' and gave him the gentlest of tugs . . . and he was standing on the road beside her, on the wrong side of the gates, to be sure, but that scarcely mattered now he had Mama to take him home.

'My silly son!' Mama said. She picked him up, kissed his tear-wet cheeks and rumpled his hair, and then set him down to lift the heavy latch and swing the gate inwards, slipping through the gap and bringing Philip through with her. 'Now we'll go quietly along to the side door and have you back in the nursery before anyone knows you've been out.'

Hand in hand they walked up the drive. After a moment or two Mama said, 'Philly, darling, what on earth were you doing down by the gate, so late in the afternoon? Did you run away from Maud? I thought you liked her!'

'I do,' Philip said hastily. 'She's nice, Maud is. But it was Grandmother; she burnt my cuddy . . . I saw poor cuddy on the fire and tried to get him out and then I burnt me, on the poker. So I wanted you, and I heard music and you like music, Mama, so I thought you'd be there and I ran down the stairs and out of the side door and down the drive . . . and then the gates were shut, so I squiggled through, all but my ears . . . and you found me!'

'So it was Grandmother, was it?' Mama said, in a tone which boded ill for Grandmother. 'How dared she . . . but it's typical, absolutely typical! And where was Papa?'

'He was home at luncheon, but she burnt cuddy after that. She said . . .' Philip's sense of grievance rose to the surface again, having been slightly damped by his horrid experience '. . . she said I was too old to suck a dirty piece of blanket . . . as if I suck cuddy, Mama!'

'No, of course you don't. But Philly, darling, you must never go near the fire, it's dreadfully dangerous. Your poor little hand . . . it could have been your smock, though, and then all of my own Philly. You could have been burnt to death.' Mama stopped short and knelt on the gravel drive so that she could look very seriously into her son's face. 'Darling, you must promise me never to do such a thing again.'

'I won't. It hurts me dreadful still. What will Grandmother and Maud say to me?'

'Nothing, for I'll have a word with both of them first. And we won't go back to the nursery after all, but straight to my sitting-room, and I'll leave you there with Ellen whilst I speak to Grandmother and Maud. And what's more, Ellen had better clean you up before you go back to the nursery. You really look in the wars, little man!'

Philip glanced down at himself. His smock was crushed and dirty, his knickerbockers and boots were splashed with mud and his stockings were wrinkled like concertinas.

'It was running, and the gate,' he said. 'Mama, who was that man?'

A stillness ran from Mama's hand down his arm, and a tension, too. But when she spoke it was in her usual gentle tones.

'Man? What man, Philly?'

'The man who whistled; the one with a stick and a twirly moustache. He smiled at you and started to speak . . . *that* man.'

'I didn't really notice, my love, but now you mention it I believe someone did pass me just as I saw you. I'd been visiting Mrs Colman, who used to work at the Hall until she was taken poorly – her husband still works in the garden; the one with the white straggly moustache and the spade-shaped beard. And we'll see if we can find you another cuddy. In fact I'm sure I can, because I still have the blanket he was cut out from. Here's the side door. Let's go in quietly, and we may be able to convince Maud that we've been warming our toes by the fire for an hour or more!'

Philip followed his mother gleefully up the stairs and into her small sitting-room, though once there he tried to explain to her that he did not want another cuddy. It was no use saying that cuddy had been cut out of a particular blanket. To Philip there was cuddy and there were bits of blanket, and never the twain would meet; nor did he wish them to.

'I really don't need anything to cuddle me to sleep now,' he said when he was being cleaned up by Mama and the faithful Ellen. 'I am a big boy, you know.'

Later, Mama went and 'bearded the dragon in her den', by which she meant, Philip knew, that she was going to talk to Grandmother. She came back humming beneath her breath, so her foray had obviously been successful. 'I told her you'd come to me, but not that we'd been out, so I think, my love, you'd better say the same to Maud,' Mama said, getting out her tin of special biscuits and letting Philip choose himself a nice fat handful. 'Now eat these and drink your milk and then you'd better make your way back to the nursery. And don't forget, darling, no more solitary jaunts.'

Philip returned, therefore, to the nursery, to be met by a cross Maud who plainly felt that, by skipping off, her charge had somehow been expressing a lack of confidence in herself.

'Where did you get to, Master Philip?' Maud said as soon as Ellen had left them alone. 'Oh, your gran was in a taking when she found you'd disappeared.'

'I went to Mama's sitting-room,' Philip said promptly, not at all averse to telling Maud a fib in a good cause. 'We had milk and biscuits and I picked a hot coal off her best carpet and burned my hand, so she's tied a clean white hanky over it. It still hurts – there's a huge blister, Maud!'

'Well, aren't you a blighter, then?' Maud said rather admiringly. 'For your gran went to your mama's room as soon as we realized you weren't here and neither you nor your mama did she see.'

'We hid from her,' Philip said at once. 'Grandmother was horrible, she burned my cuddy, so we hid from her, Mama and me.'

'Ha! I'll wager your mama didn't tell your gran that, no matter what story she came up with. You shouldn't tell fibs, Master Philip, or the devil will come in the night and sew your mouth up so you can't tell no more.'

Philip snorted.

'Jesus wouldn't let him; Jesus loves little children.'

Maud, faced by a statement both irrefutable and extremely irritating, cast wildly about for a riposte. Failing to find one she remarked that that was all very fine but wasn't it time Master Philip changed his boots for slippers and got himself ready for nursery tea?

Philip, sensing a truce, went over to Maud to have his boots unbuttoned, whereupon Maud got her revenge.

'What, help a big boy like you to unbutton his boots? You ask for a bit of help from on high . . . after all, Jesus loves you.'

'Yes, but loving me won't undo my boots,' Philip pointed out reasonably. 'People don't get miracles for *boots*, Maud.'

Maud was not a spiteful girl and moreover she was fond of her charge. So she laughed, shook her head at him, and bent to the task of boot removal.

'All right, Master Philip, I'll undo the right one and we'll work on the left one together. That way, you'll learn to do them in no time at all.'

Philip was eager to agree, having a vested interest in learning to unbutton and button his own boots. Mama had promised to take him to the theatre just as soon as he could master the task. So he and Maud bent to their work with a will and by the time Grandmother paid her usual visit to the nursery Philip was in his slippers, a pinafore hiding his smock and knickerbockers, about to tackle nursery tea.

Maud, pouring milk from the earthenware jug into Philip's blue mug, stiffened apprehensively; Mrs Albert could have a short way with her when she felt she had been crossed. But whatever Philip's mama had said to her, it was clearly not going to be shared. Grandmother said she was glad to see Philip eating up his egg, found fault with the thickness of the bread and butter Maud had prepared, criticized the presence, on the table, of a chocolate shape which would undoubtedly cause Master Philip to scamp the rest of the meal in anticipation of such a delicacy, and finally remarked almost as an afterthought that she hoped, in future, that Philip would not take advantage of the temporary absence of the nursery maid to run away and hide for half the afternoon.

Philip was rapidly learning all about diplomacy.

'No, Grandmother,' he said, dipping a soldier boy into his egg, which was runny inside and firm out, just as he liked it.

'I'm glad to hear it,' Grandmother said, then unbent to smile at him. 'You aren't a bad boy at all, really. In fact, by and large, I couldn't ask for a better grandson.'

The unpleasantness which had caused cuddy to be devoured on a funeral pyre had clearly vanished. Philip smiled sedately at his grandmother and continued to eat his egg.

'She brought us all here for the weekend, Ellen, to try to tell Mr Arnold that I was playing around,' Lily told her maid as the two of them prepared her for the evening. 'Can you imagine, the spiteful old biddy! And instead, what does she find? That it's Arnold who's been playing around, and what's more I've got proof, not merely an unconfirmed suspicion. Not that she was taken aback, not really. She just said that it's different for men, because a man needs more than one woman can provide. Of all the stuff and nonsense I've listened to in my life, she comes out with the worst! Not that she got away with that, mind you. I recited the marriage service, I reminded her that it was me and not Arnold who nearly died eighteen months ago when I miscarried of another child . . . in the end she was glad to change the subject.'

'I can imagine, ma'am,' Ellen said. She was putting her mistress's hair up and allowed herself to pat Lily's shoulder comfortingly as she did so. 'What had she heard, ma'am, if I may ask?'

'A lot of rubbish. Well, she'd heard that I'd joined the choral society and she was trying to make something of that . . . said it was well known locally that one man in particular was always very keen to accompany me upon the piano when I sang . . . that he often drove me home, visited me in Lime Tree Road when my husband was at work . . . when I asked, she couldn't even supply me with a name, let alone one single occasion on which I'd behaved unwisely. And of course she didn't pursue it because I began to tell her about Arnold and Mrs Edith Wragge . . . how he'd taken to dogging her footsteps, singing her praises, inviting her to go round the pot-bank, and generally making a great fool of himself if you ask me.'

'Yes, ma'am. By the by, where did you find Master Philip this afternoon? Because Mrs Albert and Maud popped in here at various times and asked for you. I told them you were visiting old Mrs Colman, but of course I didn't mention young Master Philly.'

'I told them I met Master Philly on my way down, very distressed. So of course Maud got defensive since she should never have gone off with Mrs Albert and left Philly to his own devices, and Mrs Albert got equally defensive because she had no right to take her temper out on my son. Indeed, if Mrs Albert hadn't been so unpleasant in the morning, I'd never have fled the way I did.'

'So, ma'am?' Ellen curled a big sausage ringlet round her finger and pinned it in place. 'That doesn't explain where you *did* meet Master Philly.'

'Nor it does.' Through the mirror, Lily gave her maid a quizzical glance, then batted her lashes. 'If you must know, I found him down by the gate, crying bitterly, with his head stuck in the bars.'

'Poor little lad,' Ellen said perfunctorily. 'And . . . was you alone, ma'am?'

Lily chuckled.

'Ah, now we've come to the nub of the matter! Yes, as it happens I was, more or less. It was most awfully lucky, actually, because Captain Harcourt-Jones was just hurrying up the road towards me when I spotted Philly, so no harm was done. Not that I care, after the way Mr Arnold has behaved. It would serve him right if I . . . but I don't suppose I shall!'

'No, ma'am,' Ellen murmured comfortingly. 'Will you wear the gauze scarf and the spray of orchids, or will you leave your shoulders bare?'

'Bare, in that barn of a dining-room? No, I'll wear the scarf, please, Ellen. And the orchids . . .' she reached for the spray and held it in her cleavage '. . . so. Or . . .' she moved the spray along so that it lay on the boning of her bodice '. . . perhaps *so*.'

Presently, beautifully gowned, her hair dressed to perfection, a tiny smear of colour on lips and eyelids, Lily set forth to meet her mother-in-law, her husband and various other members of the family around the dinner table. Ellen, left alone, cleared away all the make-up, the dusting powder, the pins, the spilt water from the orchid spray and the discarded garments which her mistress had tried and found wanting.

Poor lady, she thought, as she worked. She's been a good wife to that Mr Arnold. She's learned to run the house, to entertain his guests – she's behaved just as she ought, and what does he do when she's down and ill after losing the baby he gave her? He goes and takes up with a skinny black-haired creature who's no better than she ought to be, if you ask me. Some think Mrs Edith Wragge's a fashion plate, and others say she's elegant. Why, even Mr Warburton, such a sensible, kind man, made a fuss of Mrs Wragge at one time because he said she reminded him of his girl what's out in China, but my Mrs Arnold's worth half a dozen Edith Wragges. She's prettier, rosier, and she's got a beautiful hour-glass figure, has my Mrs Arnold. That Wragge, she's nobbut a clothes-peg!

What was more, Mrs Wragge's husband, Richard, had an eye to the ladies all right. He was always escorting this one and that one to parties, dances, picnics and balls, but rarely on hand to take his own wife about. And servants, who know everything, said amongst themselves that Mr Wragge escorted some ladies right up to their bedrooms, and stayed there too long for decency. So if Mr Arnold wanted to get involved with a woman married to a man like that, well, one could scarcely blame Mrs Arnold for deciding to live it up a bit!

'Now you're to take care, this time. Don't try to do too much, and when Kei wants to help you, let her, do you hear me? Dearest Addy, you know I never meant . . .'

Adeline put her hand over John's mouth. They were sitting on a swingseat in the shade of a clump of maple trees with the hot summer sun burning down on them. It was five years since Adeline had travelled out from England and lost her baby on the voyage, and in those five years she had never quickened with child again because John had been determined that she should not take the risk until he was sure she could stand it.

For it had affected her health, there could be no doubt about that. The superbly balanced, fit young woman had gone, perhaps never to return. Adeline now was fine-drawn, prone to catch any infection that was about, and John guarded her constantly, terrified of losing her. Indeed, that was why he had walked in one day with Kei. He knew that Adeline would never stop trying to do all the housework which the servants were not able to manage for one cause or another, that she insisted on doing as much as possible for herself. She worked each day in his clinic, taught in his Sunday school, put herself out to help mothers with sick babies and old people who had no children to see to them. She needed, he decided, an assistant.

Kei had been chosen because she was as different as could possibly be from Yenala, for John was quite sensitive enough to realize that Yenala herself was irreplaceable. Kei was all southern Chinese, dark-skinned, small, almost square in her sturdy fashion. She would never be graceful or beautiful, but she was loyal and hardworking and she adored Adeline.

She had come, of course, from the nuns' orphanage. Three years ago she had been twelve and judged fit to take a job with the friendly medical missionary and his beautiful, hardworking wife, and so John had brought her home one day to meet Adeline, in fear and trembling, if the truth be told, in case Adeline should tell him to take her away again.

But she had not; she had taken one look at the twelve-year-old girl, plump and friendly as a puppy, and had found in her heart quite a different love from that she had showered on Yenala. She had not managed to teach Kei very much English, but her own dialect was, by then, too good to let that be a bar to having a local girl to assist her.

Now, however, sitting in the garden they had made together, Adeline shook her head chidingly at her husband.

'As if I blamed you for my condition! I've longed and longed to be well enough to try for a baby again and this time you know I'm as fit as I'll ever be. And what's more I've felt better, these past seven months or so, than I've felt since I was a young girl. This time everything will go well, just wait and see. For a start, I'm not going to the mountains without you, you're coming with me, and for another thing we shan't undertake any long voyages or troublesome journeys. This baby . . .' she patted her stomach '. . . will be perfect. I can tell. I have quite a different feel about this child.'

'Yes, I know all that, I'm just trying to point out to you that whilst we're in the mountains you mustn't let the pleasant mountain breezes and the cool waters go to your head. You must still rest, walk slowly, eat well. I'll be with you, of course, but it is Kei who spends most time in your company and you must let her do the little things which involve lifting, carrying, bending down too much and so on. Otherwise you'll be ill and I'll feel so guilty . . . so you'll let Kei help you?'

'Of course! What a monster you make me sound! But . . . John, do you think we'll still be in the mountains when I have my baby? Because I should very much rather be down here, in our own beloved home.'

'You'll be home, unless the baby arrives betimes,' John said, smiling down at her, but in his heart he worried over this very point. It was a long trek up the mountains where he and Adeline had built a holiday home for the worst of the heat, and the thought of his wife giving birth en route after her previous experiences could not but worry him dreadfully. However, she had another eight weeks to go and they would either stay for a full three months, thus ensuring that the child was born in the mountains, or make it a mere six weeks, so that the child put in its first appearance in the valley. John wanted to stay in the mountains – at this time of year it was a good deal healthier for both mother and child – but everything depended on whether the mission authorities could find a replacement for him for the last two months. However, he was hopeful, for he had explained the situation and his superiors were aware of Adeline's worth both as his wife and his hardest worker for the good of his patients and congregation.

He knew, of course, that Adeline's protestations that she would rather be in the valley when the baby arrived stemmed, quite simply, from her conscience. She was afraid the mission would not manage to get a replacement and she was far too conscientious to view with approval the idea of Cheiping's being without staff for two months because of her condition.

'Oh, well.' Adeline leaned her head on John's shoulder, then sighed blissfully. 'The mountains tomorrow! Friends all around, the lake to bathe in, delicious salads from our own garden . . . I can hardly wait!'

John's substitute came through and so it was in the mountains, when her pregnancy had gone full term, that Adeline started once more to give birth.

But this time, how different! She was in her own room, overlooking the blue lake far below, with friends near at hand and John and a competent Kei, now fifteen and very sensible, to help her.

She was only in labour for five hours and at the end of that time she gave birth to a beautiful baby girl. The child lay in her arms, black-haired, blue-eyed, white skinned, and Adeline counted every tiny finger and toe, every minute nail before she handed the baby back to Kei.

'Her name will be Yenala,' she told John, when he asked her what she wanted to call her little daughter. 'After our first girl.'

'She shall be Yenala Adeline, then,' John said. 'A mixture of East and West. Isn't she a lovely child?'

'Lovely,' Adeline said but her voice was very faint. John knew she was terribly tired.

'You must sleep now, and grow strong,' he said, pulling the blankets over her shoulders, for here in the mountains it was cool as evening drew on and quite cold at night. 'Sleep, now, dearest Addy.' He turned to the baby, snug in its stout oak cradle. 'Sleep sound, Nala.'

For five days Adeline and her child were as close as though Nala was still actually inside her mother, but then Adeline's milk began to fail and the baby grew fractious and cried too soon after her feeds.

'We'll have to get a wet-nurse,' John told his wife. 'Don't mind about it, my darling. It will be just another reason to say our daughter's a mixture of East and West.'

'I don't mind,' Adeline said, but it was clear that she did. 'Just another failure,' she remarked conversationally to her small daughter when the two of them were alone once more, John having gone off to find a wet-nurse. The baby lay in her arms, milky, content, having drunk its fill for the moment, and Adeline lay quiet too, looking into the tiny creature's face, gazing deep into the dark blue eyes so very like her own.

Presently John came back, having found a suitable woman.

'Her baby died at birth,' he told Adeline. 'She's only a peasant woman but big and strong. The baby should have lived, but these things happen, and she'll take good care of our little one.'

'As long as you're sure,' Adeline said. Her cheeks were flushed, for she was running a slight fever.

John took her temperature but he was able to assure her that it was nothing much and that many women suffered as she was doing within a few days of giving birth.

'I'll get you into a cool bath presently, then Kei shall squeeze oranges to make you a refreshing drink and you'll be better by morning,' he promised her.

He kept the wet-nurse away from his wife, though. She was, as he had said, a strong, comely peasant, but he thought it would be better if Adeline did not, at this stage, actually see another woman suckling her child. And Nala undoubtedly thrived on the extra milk, for Adeline still fed her as much as she could and the child grew fatter and stronger with each passing day.

The fever abated and John rejoiced to see Adeline growing bright-eyed and confident once more. One afternoon he went off to the lake to see if he could catch a trout for Adeline's supper, and she and Kei sat in the garden with the baby in her cradle and enjoyed the pleasant breeze and the sunshine.

Just before Adeline gave the baby her feed, however, she remembered that she was supposed to drink plenty of milk herself, so Kei trotted into the bungalow to fetch her a glass just as the wet-nurse arrived. Kei gestured to the terrace, where Adeline and the baby lay beneath the shade of a fine maple tree.

Adeline stared curiously at the woman at whose breast her child had nestled. She had seen her before! Once, long ago . . . she saw the woman's face in her mind's eye, this time across a bowl of food . . . the woman had been feeding her, staring impassively before her, and she, Adeline, had been wrapped in a quilt and tied!

It was Kalli, who had set her companions on Yenala!

Adeline screamed. She should have been able to make a lot of noise,

202

for all her terror and disgust, all her pain, came out in that sound, yet it was not nearly loud enough for no Kei came running from the house, no John came galloping up from the lake. And the woman Kalli looked back at Adeline and recognized her too, and Adeline saw realization dawn in the flat, slitted black eyes. Kalli knew that Adeline recognized her as a female Boxer, a murderess, and she knew too that Adeline would betray her.

The woman raised huge hands and lifted Adeline out of her chair like a little puppet. She tried to carry her over to the wall at the back of the bungalow where there was a good drop to the river below, but Adeline fought like a tigress because she suddenly knew that if Kalli got rid of her, she would get rid of Nala next.

Adeline screamed again . . . thinly . . . and abruptly Kalli dumped her back on her chair.

The woman grabbed the baby from the cradle, quick as a striking snake.

'If you tell, you'll never see her alive again. If you tell, I'll strangle her,' she said.

'I won't tell.' Adeline's whisper was smaller than her scream.

'Do you swear on your holiest things?'

'I sw . . .'

Out of the bungalow, carrying cod liver oil, came Kei; and froze. She must have read the desperation in Adeline's face and body, the threat in the Chinese woman's stance. Adeline did not look at her but she prayed that Kei would just save the baby – that was all. She must save the baby!

'I swear that I won't tell anyone you are a murderess who killed men and women during the Rebellion,' Adeline said clearly. 'Nor that you have threatened my life and that of my child. If only you'll just go away, now.'

But the woman must have sensed it was a trick; she moved forward, her eyes on Adeline but her attention on the baby, and Adeline knew that she would take Nala as a hostage for her own safety.

'Kei!'

She and Kei leapt simultaneously on the woman, their combined weight and the unexpectedness of Kei's attack bearing her to the ground. She struggled and fought and Adeline felt herself shaken as a rat is shaken by a terrier but she managed to grit her teeth and keep hold of the woman's arm and Nala rolled free, squalling lustily.

'Get Nala!' Adeline screamed. 'Kei, get Nala!'

And then someone was picking up the baby, someone with a deathly white face who had scattered a string of trout across the grass as he came and Adeline felt a very strange, fierce pain, and then an ebbing, sinking feeling, and the world turned black.

She regained consciousness, much later, in her own room. John was sitting on the bed. He had been crying.

She tried to speak, to ask about the baby, the woman Kalli, their own young Kei, but she found she still did not have the strength for words. Her eyes, however, must have asked her questions for her.

'It's all right . . . the baby's fine, she's in her cradle right by you. Kei's fine too . . . and the woman's . . . gone. Kei told us what you said, what she'd threatened. But don't try to talk or move, my love, you're very weak.'

She closed her eyes and slept. In the night the baby cried and John must have stopped her crying somehow. Sometimes when she opened her eyes there was a candle burning, at other times the shutters were back, but even then the light that filled the room was dim, grey, uncertain.

Once she woke and asked John what had happened to her. He had been on his knees by the bed, praying, but he stood up slowly, his limbs obviously stiff from being in one position for so long, and came and sat on the bed.

'You haemorrhaged badly,' he said. He looked older; grey and exhausted. 'You've . . . you've been very ill. You mustn't tire yourself with questions.'

She had tried to sit up, but could not. It took her all her strength and minutes of patient trying to move her hand about six inches. Speech was an effort which was almost beyond her, but she had to speak.

'Can I . . . see . . . Nala?'

The baby was sleeping. She seemed to have grown a good deal since Adeline had last seen her. John put her down, very gently, so that Adeline could look into the small, peaceful face, the mouth working a little as though she tasted a good meal long past.

Adeline put out her hand and it flopped on to the covers close to the baby. John picked her fingers up as though he knew what she wanted and put the baby's tiny hand into them. Nala's small fingers closed round Adeline's thumb. Frail happiness in a touch!

'I wish . . . I could have . . . been with her . . . longer.'

'Yes, but when she wakes she cries,' John said. 'You're very weak; she'd upset you if she cried.'

'Mm. I'd have . . . liked to see . . . her . . . grow up.'

He knew, then. She watched his face and saw it change, the lines themselves seeming to deepen.

'Never . . . mind. She's beautiful.'

'Yes, she's beautiful,' John said unsteadily. 'Like her mother.' He held her hand.

Soon, because she could not help herself, for what was the point in sleeping for one who was about to sleep for ever, she slept.

Waking grew slower, more reluctant. The weakness pulled her down into the dark, the struggle up to the light was harder with each effort. Always

John was there and usually Nala. Sometimes Kei too, only she wept and could not be comforted.

Once, she said, 'Was . . . I born for . . . this?' and John tried to comfort her, but she had not really been complaining, only voicing her puzzlement over a life which had started so well, with such high hopes, only to end at the point where she should have been most useful.

Once she said, 'Will I . . . go on, John . . . as some believe?' and John, that devout Christian, said that she would indeed go on, for was not the baby made in her image?

'You'll love her.' Adeline's thin voice stated a fact, did not ask a question, and John said steadily that he would love her because she was his dear love's child, as well as for her own small sake.

She could not hold the baby in her arms, she was too weak, but she kissed her, once. And then John held her very tenderly in his arms and his love carried her over the dark threshold.

# Part II

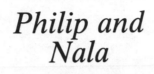

*Philip and
Nala*

# CHAPTER FIFTEEN
## 1916

It was a big funeral. Philip should have been in school, but he was sent for and came home willingly enough, still in the black arm-band and black tie that he had been wearing since Uncle Bertie's death.

Grandmother's death did not impress the fellows at school quite as much as Uncle Bertie's death had done, but that of course was because Uncle Bertie had been killed in action which was the way, if you'd got to die, that most of the chaps at school would have preferred.

Philip was standing next to his father, because that was the form at family funerals; he wished he was standing with the chaps in uniform over there, those friends of Uncle Bertie's who had known Grandmother and had managed to get a spot of furlough to pay their respects. But still . . . another two years before he himself would be eligible to join the army. He just hoped the whole thing wouldn't have finished by then, though it was beginning to get a bit depressing reading the casualty lists. Perhaps it would be best if it finished . . . but two years is a long time.

Beside him, Rose fidgeted, fiddling with her black gloves, pulling the fingers off and folding her hand up tight in the palm, then having a struggle to get her fingers back again. When she'd done that half a dozen times she began to dig in the rain-beaded turf with the toe of her black strap shoes. Of course she was only ten but she should know better – she had been fond of Grandmother, in her way, though being Father's favourite had meant that she had not needed Grandmother despite their own mother having died . . . oh, years ago.

The vicar was droning on now, reminding everyone that Mrs Haslington had never really recovered from her son's death . . . now they were together at last . . . old Mr Albert Haslington . . . hum hum mumble mumble . . . whilst Philip tried to stand still and look suitably grief-stricken. His father looked thoughtful and a little cross. He was in uniform too, though so far he had not been sent to France; he was in London, at the War Office. He had been fond of his mother, Philip supposed, had been fonder, perhaps, of his reckless, feckless young brother. To lose them both within three months of each other must be, surely, a severe blow? Yet Arnold's expression did not convey grief or the pain of loss. Petulance was what showed most, as though his mother, in dying, had removed from Arnold's life something not of value but rather of convenience.

209

Philip was rather pleased with the simile, possibly because he had suffered from his father's critical indifference, if there was such an expression. Arnold, who doted on Rose, had always been hard on his son, and Philip was not the only one to think so; his godfather, Sidney Warburton, had told him it was not unusual to find a father doting on a daughter but very much more critical of a son.

'My old friend Frederick Sands spoilt young Therese until she was nigh on unbearable,' the old man said reminiscently. 'But his son Archibald could never do right. The thing is, old man, a father expects nothing but pretty looks and sweetness from a daughter; he looks on her as a charming extravagance, if you like. But a son has to do better than the father, make more money, succeed in a much more substantial way. The father loves the son as much as the daughter, maybe even more, but he knows he's got to be hard on the son to get results. A spoilt boy is ruined for life, whereas a spoilt daughter soon pulls herself together once she's married.'

Now, Philip looked across at Uncle Sidney, standing with the other people from the Manor. He looked pale and exhausted, his usual ruddy colour quite gone. It had rained within the last couple of hours although the sun was now fighting its watery way through the clouds, and the long grass in the churchyard was drenched. Uncle Sidney's coat hem was draggled with water and with grass-seeds. He must have come across the older part of the churchyard this morning; no one else was as wet. But he had put an *In Memoriam* plaque up to his daughter Adeline in his family plot and, by turning his head slightly, Philip could just see it. Good detective work, he told himself; the plaque held a container of sweet peas, fresh as the morning, the colours shading exquisitely from fuchsia to palest rose. Uncle Sidney always chose the flowers that Adeline had liked best, Philip knew, and he changed them whenever they began to look weary. Undoubtedly he had visited the plot this morning, before the service.

Once, Philip had asked Uncle Sidney where his own mother was buried; he was careful with his godfather, though, because the older man had lost so much – his wife, his beloved daughter, and Philip's own mother, Lily, who had been a great favourite. But Uncle Sidney had looked very uncomfortable at the question.

'Ask your father,' he had said. 'I can't tell you.'

Philip had not asked his father; they were not on those terms. He could, of course, have prevailed upon Rose to ask him, but Rose had been only months old when her mother had died. She had no recollection of Lily and no interest in the other woman. Vaguely, Philip supposed that his mother had been taken home to be buried. As Adeline Warburton – he never thought of her by her married name, doubted if he had even heard it – would have been brought back to this quiet churchyard had such a thing been possible.

The vicar was droning on again now; Aunt Dorothea was snuffling into a little lace handkerchief and Aunt Bella was trying not to hit her small boy, who was behaving abominably, even by the usual Phillimore standards. Philip rather liked Aunt Bella, who was a sport, and the young Phillimore – Toby, Philip thought – though a brat, was an engaging child. Just now, with his collar half up and half down, his jacket open and his shirt crooked, he was merely an irritant to his poor mother, but normally he was a happy kid with plenty of pluck.

'. . . whosoever liveth and believeth in him shall not die eternally . . .'

It must be nearly the end, Philip thought. Handbags were being surreptitiously checked, gloves were being straightened, and the men present were standing that little bit taller, as though they were expecting that there would presently be a stampede for the car park and wanted to be amongst the first out.

'. . . with us all evermore. Amen.'

The slight rustlings became a tempest of movement as people began to move away from the new grave back towards the church. There would be a huge meal presently, at the Hall, with all the relatives and friends present. Uncle Sidney would come for numerous reasons but perhaps the strongest of them would be his affection for Philip himself. Accordingly, Philip made his way over to his godfather. The church was only a mile or so from the Hall and thus only another half mile from the Manor, but most people, Philip knew, would have brought their cars. He reached his godfather and put a hand on his arm.

'Are you coming back with us, Unk? I'm sure we could squeeze you in . . . or if you've got the Rover I could come with you, if you liked?'

Uncle Sidney laughed, squeezing Philip's arm.

'You're on, my lad. I have got the Rover and since only Mrs Gilmour and myself will be coming back to the Hall you're welcome to join us. Come on!'

'I'll just tell Father,' Philip said hastily. He had no desire to find himself in Arnold's black books since he rather hoped to be able to extend this brief period away from school into something considerably longer, like a fortnight's stay. School was fine, of course, but it would be nice to be unexpectedly at home for a bit.

Arnold, however, was quite glad of his son's absence from the crowded family vehicles.

'Fine, fine,' he said. 'Come along, Aunt Regina; there's room for a small one in the corner.'

'If you aren't going back to school until the end of the week it would be useful if you were to come down to the pot-bank with me,' Arnold said next morning, over breakfast. 'My God, the life you lead in schools these days. When I was your age it was the grammar school, work like a demon, then into the factory at fourteen. You're sixteen and still don't know what hard work is!'

'I don't mind work,' Philip muttered. No matter how hard he tried he

211

seemed to get the rough edge of Arnold's tongue; a simple question like 'When am I going back to school?' was met not with a straightforward answer but with a grumble at modern youth. Anyway, Arnold wasn't yet forty; old, of course, but not as old as most chaps' paters.

'How can you say you mind it or don't mind it when you've never done any?' Arnold was reading the paper, or at least he had it in the air between himself and his son, but now he lowered it the better to glare at Philip over the top. 'I'll be back at the War Office in ten days so I want to take a look at the pot-bank whilst I'm here. You might as well come down with me. Who knows, you might be able to make yourself useful for once.'

'I work hard at school,' Philip said, determined on this one occasion to have the last word. 'You want me to get to university, don't you?'

'Pass the coffee.' Arnold sat back and considered the last remark as Philip stood up and fetched black coffee and hot milk in their respective jugs from the sideboard. 'Want you to go to university? Well, that depends on how you use all this expensive education you keep demanding. Any ideas?'

'Oh, I don't know. It depends how well I do in the exams . . . but I did wonder about either medicine or the sciences in some shape or form.'

'Oh, you did, did you?' Arnold's glare, which had died down, became positively basilisk. 'No son of mine's going to be a country doctor, nor a medical missionary if that's what you've got in mind!'

'It wasn't, actually.' Philip took a deep breath, trying to control a foolish desire to speak simply to annoy the old man, which wouldn't take much doing. 'Research . . . drugs . . . that sort of thing, I thought.'

'Hmm. Well, you come down to the pot-bank with me today, see if there's anything there that might need all this education. If not, seeing as how you're going to have to take the place over when I retire, then I'd advise you to think twice about a university career.' He poured his coffee and then blew on it. 'I've never taken you down there before – didn't want you to develop a distaste for it – but you never know, it might be your cup of tea. It might have been mine, once, if I'd been allowed to produce what I thought was right, but your grandfather wanted to make thick stoneware to sell to scullery maids and not fine china to sell to duchesses.' He sighed, then for once grinned at his son. 'I'm lazy, or I was as a young man, and I take the easy way out. When I took over, full of big ideas, I found I didn't really know enough about the production side of it, though I had a good grasp of marketing. And then I bought the house in Lime Tree Road, had one or two other biggish expenses, and found I didn't have money or time to spare on new ideas. So the fine china got pushed to the back of my mind and it's never materialized. But I don't suppose that interests you . . . and now I can't say I'm particularly interested in the pot-bank at all, though the money it brings in is . . . useful. But my interest, as you know, lies in the Haslington Saddlery.'

Philip nodded. He remembered being told when he was quite a small boy how his grandfather had bought a little saddlery and his father had nursed it and tended it until now he had four wonderful shops, one in Chester, one in Manchester, one in Nantwich and the original one in Langforth, all extremely large and all acknowledged experts on leather goods from saddles and bridles to soft ladies' gloves and long driving coats.

'Yes; even now, with the motor car pushing horses off the roads, my shops are crowded from early morning until closing time,' Arnold mused. 'The motor accessories bring the motorists, the saddlery brings the riders. And I know enough about it to know what I'm doing, whereas in the pot-bank it's the workers who know what's what.'

'It's remarkable, Father,' Philip said. 'But I don't see myself becoming fascinated by pots, no matter how . . .'

But Arnold's brief spell of actually talking to his son like a human being was over, it seemed.

'If you want to inherit one day, you'll do as you're told,' he said brusquely. 'Pass me the marmalade.'

Progress, Arnold considered, was what business was all about, and progress decreed that he now had a motor car and a uniformed chauffeur to drive him to work – or rather had had. The War had changed all that. His chauffeur had been called up and he himself was mostly in London. But there was a car in the garage still and Arnold could drive in a manner of speaking. Now, he called for assistance in the shape of one of the staff, Evans, who could start the motor for him whilst he got his books and papers together, and then he set off for the stableyard where Lily's boy awaited him.

It was too bad to think of Philip as Lily's boy, but she had doted on her son. Rose, on the other hand, had received scant attention, or so Arnold considered. But she had only been seven months old when Lily had departed this life, so perhaps he should not altogether blame his wife.

He had been hurt by Philip's attitude, of course, when he was still nursing his own shock and pain at Lily's departure. Philip had been not quite six and inconsolable. He had wept night after night in his little bed in the nursery, had sulked when Arnold had tried to comfort him, had kept demanding his mother in a tone which brooked no argument.

Arnold had tried, at first, to persuade Edith Wragge to leave her husband and marry him instead. But Edith, although she vowed eternal love, had not been at all keen to take such a drastic step. After two or three years, Arnold was glad she had not fallen in with his plan, and after five or six downright delighted.

Edith had not worn well. She had reminded him sharply and quite painfully of Adeline when he had first met her, and he had told himself that their liaison had started solely to comfort him for Adeline's loss. But with the years Edith's features had grown sharper and thinner, like her temper, and her figure had waxed stout. He had not been sorry when she and he had finally fallen out . . . and he was much better off now! A pretty little painter at the factory had caught his eye . . . Bess Thwaite, her name was. He had waited for her, on the quiet, and had walked her home, chatting idly all the way. Next day he had suggested picking her up after her shift; we could take a picnic out into the hills, he had said.

Bess had agreed with considerable alacrity. Off they went that first day and he had really enjoyed himself. They had made love in a gully full of heather and bracken, with the scent of the stuff all round them and the sound of a seagull circling high above coming faintly on the summer breeze.

It had set the seal on their relationship, Arnold thought. He had asked Bess, with some trepidation, if she would not rather have a nice little flat in a house in Langforth than live with her mam two miles away from her place of work. She dimpled at him and said who was to pay, then?

I'll pay, Arnold had said, emboldened by her smile, and she had agreed quite sunnily to become his mistress, only insisting that she remain at the factory, 'for the look of the thing' at first and 'for a bit of me own cash' next.

He could have married her, of course, but he had learned one thing at least from the disastrous marriage with Lily; you did not marry a girl from the chorus or from the factory floor and expect them to be able to behave like the lady of the manor all at once. He realized, in retrospect, that he had been hard on Lily, had not helped her as he should have. And when she had learned on her own, what had he done? He had imagined himself in love with Edith Wragge, because she was a little like Adeline, and had gone chasing after her instead of appreciating the woman he had married and who had given him a son.

He had bought Lily a fine house and put her in it, and then left her alone for days at a time whilst he chased round after Edith. Then he had blamed Lily for the bills which were not really her fault at all, for she had become a good little housekeeper. The fault lay with his indifference to the pot-bank and the fact that he was running a huge old barracks of a place like Haslington Hall, paying all the bills for his brother and sisters and for his mother, as well as the house in Lime Tree Road. And not to put too fine a point on it, Edith had pretty well bled any spare cash out of him with her demands.

His interest in the production of fine china had not survived his father's death, however. His father had known all there was to know about the pot-bank; all Arnold had known was how to do the paperwork and how to sell. So he had begun to pour more and more of his energy into the leather business and into the running of the Haslington estate, and to let the pot-bank limp along under the management of folk like Roger Trewin and Marcus Bates, reliable men enough but without the spur of personal interest and imagination to carry them on. They saw to it that the crocks which were made were well made, that the materials were reliable, that the heats in the bottle ovens were correct, and that was about their limit. And of late, Arnold had noticed when checking the books that the big white chamberpots and mugs and bedroom sets were not selling as they had once done. Everyone put it down to the War, but Arnold thought that was just a convenient peg to hang dwindling sales on. He thought people's expectations were getting a bit higher. They wanted something with a bit of class, were prepared to save up for it and spend a bit more. What they didn't want was more of the same.

But he could not start at the beginning in the pottery, follow the work through, see what became of a new line, a modern idea. That was for someone else, someone younger, keener. He enjoyed his work at the War Office and kept persistently putting his name forward to go to the Front, but he knew very well that when the War was over he would not dive gratefully back into making pots again. Not him! The saddleries would be all the thing then, he hoped. He would work at what he liked best, and if the lad wasn't interested then the pot-bank could go to the devil for all he cared. Well, he amended, he could scarcely wish it at the devil since the money was useful. What he really hated was having the management of it round his neck. Now if the boy was really interested, that would put a different complexion on it.

'Are you ready, Father?'

That was Lily's boy, all spruced up in his best suit with his golden-brown hair slicked down and his face newly washed. He was so like Lily! Useless to say the lad couldn't help it, useless to try to do away with the resentment the mere sight of his son created. He had to learn to live with it and do his best to hide it.

The worst of it is I know damned well why I resent him, and it's because I feel so confoundedly guilty over my treatment of his mother, Arnold reminded himself. It would have been easier by far if he could have blamed Lily for her defection and his own subsequent loneliness, but he knew very well it was all his fault. So, lacking a wifely whipping boy, he blamed his son for looking like her.

'Philip, this is my manager, Mr Trewin. Trewin, my son, Philip. If you show the lad round, Trewin, you can bring him back to me in my office in about an hour.' Arnold turned to his son. 'Take in as much as you can,' he said pleasantly. 'I dare say it's pretty interesting, it's just that I've known it all my life and don't much care for the modern procedures. See you in an hour, then.'

Which left Mr Trewin and Philip in the middle of the yard eyeing one another cautiously.

Roger Trewin was in his late fifties, balding, overweight, with wire-rimmed spectacles and a large, squashy nose. He looked rather shyly at his young charge as he began to speak.

215

'Eh, sorry I'm not too good at talking, Mr Philip, but I'll do me best. Now, back of us is the bottle kilns – we use them for firing the pots – to our right's the offices, to our left the painting sheds and straight in front of us is the main factory. We'll go round more or less as a pot does, so we'll start where the clay's mixed with water to become a slip. Then . . . but showing's better than telling, I always say. Follow me, sir.'

They crossed the yard and went in through a small side door, across a large, empty space and into another room with whitewashed walls, a good deal of machinery thumping away, and an open gully, like a small, enclosed stream, running through the centre. There were several young women in overalls with their hair tied up in mob-caps and a couple of elderly men standing about. Mr Trewin nodded to them but did not attempt to introduce them.

'This is where the powdered clay, what we buy in, is mixed with water to form a slip . . . that's what the stuff there is called . . .' he waved an explanatory hand at the stuff gurgling and churning in the gully '. . . and then it's dried and pugmilled . . .' he led Philip out of the first room and into a second where there was yet more machinery '. . . and comes out here . . . see? Looks like long clay sausages, don't it?'

'Yes, I see what you mean,' Philip shouted above the clamour. 'Is it fit to be made into pots now?'

'Good Lord, no,' Mr Trewin said cheerfully. 'Now it'll be wedged and kneaded, to remove any air bubbles, you know, and then it'll go through into the throwing room. Or some of it. A good deal of it will go through as slip, to be cast.'

'Cast? I thought all pots were thrown.'

Mr Trewin smiled, but a trifle sadly, Philip thought.

'Dear me, it's easy to see your father doesn't talk about his work much – now years ago, when Mr Arnold was full of ideas to get *his* father to change his ways, it was nothing but throwing different pots from morning till night. No, Mr Phil, most of the stuff here's cast in plaster moulds, dried, biscuited, glazed, then fired. Some wares are fired up to five times, enamels and so on. But to make a mould you have to make a pot, so we'll go round that way, eh? Show you right from the start, Mr Arnold said.'

They went into the throwing room, where an extremely ancient man sat at a potter's wheel, making what looked like a large, full-bottomed vase, until he put a pouring lip on to it with a clever finger and turned it over to his assistant, who added a handle in a very professional way.

'A water jug!' Philip said, pleased with his own perspicacity. His mentor nodded.

'Aye, that's right. Now come through into casting.'

In casting, Philip watched whilst slip of the right consistency was poured into the plaster moulds and sent off to dry, and then he went into the turners' room where a number of girls and old men took the ware out of the moulds and finished them off.

'They're jiggering and jollying,' Mr Trewin said enigmatically. 'Moulded ware needs more handling and fettling than a properly thrown pot, of course, but it's a lot cheaper and quicker to produce. These days no one can survive on hand-thrown pots alone.'

'Everyone's quite young or quite old,' Philip remarked presently. Mr Trewin nodded.

'Aye. Didn't used to be so. It's conscription, you see, takes the young men, leaves us the old and the boys. Mind, there's some likely lasses in the factory now, good as lads any day.'

'I'm sure,' Philip said politely. 'What happens next?'

'Next is in here.' They went through into yet another room. There were a number of curious objects piled ceiling-high which looked, to the untutored eye, rather like different-sized hat-boxes.

'Them's saggars,' Mr Trewin said. 'When you fire a pot, each pot goes into a saggar which saves 'em from being heat marked or fired uneven, like. Then the saggars are piled on a trolley and taken out to the kiln . . . here, follow me.' The two of them solemnly marched out across the yard and up to the nearest bottle kiln. 'On a firing day the saggars would all be inside, piled high, and then they'd light up – coal-fired, all our kilns are – and you'd be away. You keep a check on the heat and when they've been fired for long enough to harden them but not too long because you need 'em to be water absorbent still, you get them out, cool 'em first of course, and then through to the painting shed they go . . . follow me!'

The painting shed was full of girls, mostly young, all pretty to Philip's untutored eye. He went round with Mr Trewin, admiring the work, for some of the girls were skilful and all of them were efficient.

'When the ware's painted then it's glazed and fired again,' Mr Trewin told him. 'Of course we don't hand-paint everything by a long chalk. Most of the stuff's done by transfers and printing . . . these girls do that as well.'

'It's very impressive,' Philip said politely, as they left the painting sheds behind and began to mount some stairs. 'Is this the offices, now?'

'Well no, not exactly. I'd like you to meet my lad – not that he's my son, but he's my nephew . . . Frank Hawthorne. You and he, being young, might have something in common. He's . . . but I'll let him tell you for himself.'

At the top of the stairs was a short corridor with doors leading to the rooms beyond. Mr Trewin indicated them.

'All unused now, except for Frank's little place,' he said. 'A pity . . . but these things happen, times change. Here's Frank.'

He opened a door and ushered Philip inside.

Frank Hawthorne was a thin, bespectacled young man with dust-coloured hair, large hands and feet and an anxious expression. He came towards them, looking diffident.

'Hello, Uncle Rog! Good morning, Mr . . . er . . .'

'This is Mr Philip, Mr Arnold's son,' Mr Trewin said. 'I've been showing him round, and I thought perhaps the two of you ought to meet. Mr Philip will own the pot-bank one of these days, d'you see?'

There was one of those little silences which are so difficult to bridge, then Philip plunged in.

'What do you do up here, Frank?'

'Well . . . I'm trying to come up with some new formulae for glazes and colours, Mr Philip. Not that Mr Arnold wants to reproduce the effects they used to use years ago, in China and in Greece, only he said I could use this room . . . I'm not a paid member of staff, you understand . . . to do some experiments in.'

Philip looked round, light dawning. The small room had a table, a cupboard and a Bunsen burner on a bench, and in one corner, a small, iron-clad stove. The cupboard had no door so he could see the rows and rows of chemicals set out with an attempt at neatness therein.

'I say . . . chemistry! It's what I'm keenest on at school, what I'd like to do at university – if I'm allowed that is. But when your uncle was taking me round the place just now he didn't say much about the glazes, nor the colours.'

'That's because I don't rightly understand,' Mr Trewin confessed. 'Frank's very keen, Mr Philip, and knows no end about it. He didn't go to university but he did chemistry up to the highest level at school and worked for a year in the big chemical research place . . . Widgett's place. Only he weren't qualified and there weren't much future in it for him, so he came home and started to take evening classes and Mr Arnold let him have this room to do small experiments in.'

'And you're trying to discover something new,' Philip said. 'Or something different . . . what precisely was it that you said?'

'Old glazes and colours, the ones the ancient Chinese used but which have somehow got lost over the centuries,' Frank mumbled. 'I need to know much more about heat . . . the properties of chemicals . . . I get some help at night school, but never enough. We thought, Uncle and I, that if you were interested . . .'

'I'm interested in almost any form of chemical experimentation,' Philip said with a new eagerness. 'Look, talk me through what you're doing there . . . only don't forget I've only got about twenty minutes to spare . . .'

Two hours later Philip was practically dragged from the small room by Mr Trewin and as he left he shouted over his shoulder at Frank to keep up the good work because he, Philip, intended to go to university to do chemistry just as he had planned, and to come back every summer, rich with knowledge, to help in the work.

'You'd best have a chat to your father,' Mr Trewin advised him, as they retraced their footsteps through the factory and up yet another flight of stairs. 'He's int' first door ont' left. And I don't like to put meself forward, lad . . .' he had now dropped the *sir*, to Philip's satisfaction '. . . but just remember, will you, that our Frank won't be there next time you come unless you can persuade the guv'nor to pay him a bit for his work. Mind, he'd not like to 'ear me say it, Frank wouldn't, but it's the truth.'

'I'll talk to him,' Philip promised. He put a hand out to the door, then turned to the older man. 'Thanks very much for showing me round, Mr Trewin; it's been quite an education!'

'I'm back, sir.'

Arnold was writing when Philip entered the room and merely grunted at his son's greeting, but presently he closed the book, laid down his pen and looked up.

'Well?'

'It was far more interesting than I expected, Father, particularly one part of it. Sir, do you know what Frank Hawthorne's doing?'

Arnold frowned, then his brow cleared.

'Ah, Trewin's lad . . . the nephew who lives with Trewin and his missus. Now let me see . . . so far as I can recall he's doing a course of some sort at night school and comes here during the day, on and off, to muck around with heat . . . I said he could use a little oven and an old Bunsen burner. Is that right?'

'Only partly,' Philip said patiently. 'He's got almost no real equipment and very few chemicals but he's managed to do some really exciting experiments. He's experimenting into colours . . . glazes . . . all things that could make a world of difference to the stuff you produce at the pot-bank, Father! But the thing is he hasn't had the training or the experience . . . yet even so, there's a feather effect he found quite by chance which could revolutionize the art of potting, if only he knew how he'd got it.'

'That's helpful; if only he knew how he'd got it! Well, well, if it interests you . . . what do you think about going into the pot-bank when you leave school, then?'

'I want to . . . but first, Father, I want to go to university to study chemistry. I know it'll take me two or three years but at the end of it I'll have a degree and the expertise to use Frank's experiments with a view to producing something not just beautiful but saleable, too.'

'And you think a degree in chemistry's important?' Arnold queried without much hope. 'I'd thought you'd want to go in as soon as school was finished for you.'

'I'll be down here for all my vacations,' Philip said eagerly. 'You see, sir, it isn't just the colours and the glazes, fascinating though they are. It's the ware itself, the shapes . . . Mr Trewin showed me a classic tea-bowl shape from Japan . . . it wasn't anything special, as he said the glaze was only fair and the colour was just natural, you know, reddy-brown, but the shape . . . for village pottery it was so light, so delicate . . .'

'You sound like your Uncle Bertie,' Arnold said, 'only more sensible.

Bertie was keen on the look of the pots, kept nagging me to do away with some of the casting in favour of hand-thrown stuff. Well, if you're sure that's the way you want to do it, and if the War doesn't interfere anyway . . .'

'Then I can do it? Go to university first, then come into the pot-bank?'

'You can.' Arnold said. He stood up and lifted a pile of books from the desk. 'Come on, time we were making for home. I'll finish these figures tonight and you can give me a hand with checking them. If you're coming into the works eventually it's high time you learned a bit more about the place, and this is one way to see it all working.'

'I'd be glad to,' Philip said, clattering down the stairs ahead of his father. 'Anything, sir . . . I want to get to know the place and the people as well as I possibly can.'

In bed that night, Philip thought over the events of the day and was satisfied with what he had attained. He knew very well that, had he simply asked his father if he might go to university to study for a degree in chemistry, then his father would have refused. More than once Philip had heard Arnold telling all and sundry that university was a waste of a young man's time and his father's money. But because it would mean that Philip would enter the family business, it put a different complexion on the whole matter. Arnold, obviously, desperate to cut his own connection with the pot-bank, was willing to accept a graduate son if, by so doing, he could see that son settled in his own erstwhile place.

'The end justifies the means,' Philip murmured to himself as he turned out the light and composed himself for sleep. He wanted to go to university very much and it had not, in any case, been a deception he had practised on his father, for from the moment of sharing Frank's first experiment he had known that this was what he wanted to do. Even more surprising, he had been intensely interested in the entire business of making a beautiful object out of a lump of clay. He felt smug; not many lads of his age were lucky enough to know just what they wanted to do with their lives, and neither, he realized, did they have the means of gratifying such a desire at their fingertips. It was not until he was very nearly asleep, in fact, that it occurred to Philip that he was not the only one to be murmuring *the end justifies the means* over today's outcome. His father had agreed without demur to employ Frank and had consented with positive equanimity to send Philip to university with never a reproach about the cost, despite his avowed hope that Philip might decide to leave school here and now and dive into the pot-bank without a second thought.

Oh well, what mattered really was that two people – three, if you counted Frank – would be happy in their chosen occupations.

Philip stopped thinking and began dreaming, instead.

\* \* \*

220

That evening, Arnold strode out into the autumn chill, a pipe gripped between his teeth, to walk over to the Manor. He was feeling at peace with the world. So things had not worked out exactly as he had planned, but even so they had worked out well. He would have to give Lily's boy the rest of his time in school and a few years at a university, but from the way the lad talked it might even pay him to do so, if he was right about these wonderful colours and glazes; lost arts, the lad said they were, which he and young Frank Hawthorne meant to rediscover.

For himself, the work at the War Office was satisfying and interesting and when the War ended and he came back home he would simply keep an eye on the pot-bank, knowing that Philip would be there in his vacations. No one could blame him for that – indeed, people might think he was being very generous, moving over to let the younger man take his place.

Arnold did not go to the front door of the Manor, but did as many other Haslingtons had done before him – he went round to the terrace outside Sidney's library and tapped on the french window. Sidney shouted at him to come on in and he opened the pane and stepped through into the friendly warmth of the room he had come to prefer to his own home. A warm friendship had grown up between the two men since they had both been on their own and Arnold walked over to the Manor most nights.

'Well, I took the boy down to the pot-bank earlier, as I said I would,' Arnold said as the two of them settled down on opposite sides of the fire and began packing their pipes. 'You'll never guess what his reaction was!'

'Hated it; suggested you send him to university instead,' Sidney said, looking smug. Arnold remembered that his son was his friend's godson and smirked. So he had been right: Philip had wanted university badly and had discussed his chances of being able to go there with his godfather.

'Wrong! Well, mostly wrong. He's agreed to go into the pot-bank – he was extemely keen, in fact. However, I think he should go to university to take a degree in chemistry first. You see, he saw the experimentation that's being carried out in our little laboratory on glazes and colours and so on and was extremely interested; in fact he wants to head our effort in that line. And of course, I'm delighted. It'll mean the boy gets the pottery and I'm free to do what pleases me most.'

Sidney Warburton, Arnold was glad to see, could not hide his surprise. His eyebrows rose almost to hairline level.

'Experimentation? At the pot-bank? Well, Arnold, you have surprised me; I thought you'd lost all interest.'

'No, not *all* interest; haven't I mentioned our experiments before?' Arnold said airily, metaphorically crossing his fingers for the lies he was about to tell. 'We've got a young chap doing nothing but research and he's good, too. The trouble is he isn't a trained scientist and doesn't have the know-how necessary for commercial success, so Philip thought it would help if he himself went to university and did chemistry. As you know, he's always excelled at science, so it does seem like a good idea.'

'It does indeed. I've often thought, Arnold, that if you'd had an eye for beauty you could really have made a tremendous success of things, but you're a practical man and no one can be what he isn't – not successfully, anyway.'

'If you're meaning Lily,' Arnold said defensively, 'I've admitted to you though not to another living soul that I'm ashamed of the way I treated her and would give a good deal to get her back. But it's too late. Ten years is a long time . . .'

'I wasn't meaning Lily, so don't leap to conclusions, my friend. However, since you brought the subject up, don't you think it's about time you told Philip the truth? I know you think everyone believes she's dead, but once he's working in Langforth he could easily meet someone who knows that old rumour was just a rumour. And believe me, Arnold, if that happened you'd lose your son.'

'I never lied to him,' Arnold said at once. 'I told him his mother had gone away and then later I told him he wouldn't be seeing her again. It was Nanny who said she was dead; I just went along with it.'

'You let them believe, my dear fellow, which is just as bad. You have a difficult relationship with the boy, I know that, but you're fond of him, aren't you?'

There was too long a pause whilst Arnold fought with his conscience. Sidney shook his head gently.

'Yes!' Arnold got out at last, but even to him it sounded defiant. 'It's just that he's so like Lily! Every time I see him I think of his mother . . . the way I behaved . . . he adored his mother, you know. I'd *like* to be fond of the boy but he makes me feel too uncomfortable.'

'You're letting guilt over behaviour ten years old ruin a loving father and son relationship,' Sidney said sadly. 'You've got to stop seeing him as Lily, old fellow, and start seeing him as a son to be proud of. Work at it!'

'I will,' Arnold promised. 'He's got more to him than I thought; perhaps it was a mistake to send him to that school, too. He doesn't realize it but there are times when I feel he despises me.'

'Nonsense,' Sidney said at once. 'He admires you, admires the drive which made the pot-bank a success and got the leather works from one run-down little shop to what it is today. Just cling on to that . . . and think about telling him the truth regarding Lily.'

'I'll think about it.' Arnold got to his feet. 'Better be making tracks now. I've got quite a lot of work to do now I know what Philip wants out of life.'

Walking home through the dark, with a few bold bats flittering and soundlessly squeaking between the trees, Arnold wondered about his wife. Where was she? Where had she fled that long-ago night, when she had discovered the diamond necklace he had bought for Edith Wragge? He could still remember the look on her face, the tears that had stood in her big blue eyes as she had turned to face him, the little box in one hand and the note in the other.

What on earth had possessed him, he thought now, trudging along the river path, to leave the necklace in its blue velvet box on the dressing-table in his wife's room? What evil quirk of fate had caused him to take it through there to compare the length with a string of pretty crystals his wife owned? And then, when he saw her pick up the box, give a cry of delight, why had he not blustered, pretended it was a surprise present for later, not to be opened now? Instead, when she exclaimed, 'What on earth is this? How pretty!' he had simply thought crossly that she would now claim the necklace as of right and he would have to find the money for another one for Edie.

He had forgotten the note, or rather, had forgotten the wording.

'A present to enhance your night-dark locks, my love, from your devoted Arnold.' He had written it, thinking himself a rather poetic sort of chap, and had nearly destroyed it with the recollection that a necklace was not worn in the hair . . . but Edith would know what he meant, he had reflected, and left the note where it was.

There had been no scene. She had simply put the necklace down, very slowly, in the middle of the dressing-table once more, and walked out of the room. He had shouted at her, calling down the hall that, for God's sake, she should hear his explanation before condemning him . . . it was not his necklace, he had merely bought it for a friend to give to his wife . . .

He had never seen her again. She had walked out of the room, the house and his life. She had left without any luggage, without any destination so far as he knew, and certainly without either of her children. Indeed, he supposed that she could scarcely have taken Philip and Rose no matter how she might have longed to do so, since she had no means of supporting herself, let alone others.

But for a long time, her leaving the children had been his justification for his own behaviour. No wonder he had not behaved well towards her, had not been faithful! She had been a poor sort of wife and mother to walk out on a husband and two children, the little girl only a few months old. He had not considered what it must have cost her to do such a thing until long afterwards, when he had given it out that she had gone to a friend's for a holiday . . . had had a breakdown there . . . was very ill . . . had died.

It had seemed simpler, then, to pretend she was dead, but now, ten years later, he really did wonder if he had spoken no more than the truth. She had never reappeared, and though he had meant to question Ellen as to her mistress's whereabouts he had not had the opportunity so to do, for Ellen had left almost as rapidly as Lily.

His own mother had tried to persuade Arnold that Lily had run off with a Captain Anthony Harcourt-Jones, who lived a couple of miles away, but discreet enquiries soon gave the lie to that; the gallant captain was to be seen in all his usual haunts, he was informed. Arnold supposed that Lily must have fled to old theatrical friends in London, for no one locally looked at him askance or spread whispers that Lily was very much alive.

Arnold reached the stile and climbed over it. It was foolish to consider saying anything to Philip, let alone dear little Rose. Time enough to admit the deception if Lily ever turned up again. And in the meantime he would be off to London again quite soon, leaving Trewin to keep the factory running, that Frank fellow to continue his experiments, and Philip to return to school where he would waste no time, he had assured his father, in beginning to study like mad for the university entrance examinations. And Rose, of course, would be well taken care of by the adoring servants at the Hall.

Leaving the Manor and approaching the Hall as he was, Arnold's thoughts turned naturally to another man doing his best to bring up a ten-year-old daughter; John Sawyer, far away in Japan . . . or was it China? Sidney seldom talked much about his granddaughter or son-in-law now that Adeline was dead.

One day, he knew, John would bring his daughter home to the Manor and they would be neighbours – and friends, he hoped, for they had a good deal in common. Not that John would have taken a mistress to comfort him in his loss as Arnold had. Missionaries did not do things like that, Arnold was sure. But still, it would be nice for the two small girls to play together. They might even share their lessons, as Adeline and Bella had done long ago.

Heading up through the woods now towards the distant gleam of the Hall lights, Arnold remembered the unusual affect Adeline's death had had on him. It was very strange, because he had first taken up with Edith Wragge precisely because of her similarity to Adeline. But with the news of his old love's death he had suddenly realized how much Edith had changed since they had first become lovers, how she had coarsened and become demanding. Very soon, he began to find Edith's company repellent, her very voice an irritant.

If only it had occurred before Lily had left! But that was not the way things happened. He had known it was wrong of him to have an affair with Edith whilst he was still married to Lily, but it had been wickedly exciting and thrilling. When it was too late, when Lily had gone and Adeline had died, he could see Edith in her true light: not as someone who reminded him of his lost love but as a calculating, greedy and immoral woman whose once-pretty face had begun to show the strain of too much paint and too liberal an appetite, and whose generosity with her favours was offset by her insistence on frequent and valuable presents.

His liaison with Bess, on the other hand, was a steadier affair altogether.

224

She asked for nothing, made him laugh, was clearly fond of him and never even considered marriage. Which was just as well in the circumstances, he thought ruefully, now.

He was crunching across the gravel, heading for the side door. He opened it, turned to bolt it across, and, turning back, nearly stopped breathing. A small, ghostlike figure was flitting across the hall!

'What the . . .'

'Father! Oh, Papa, I was searching for you, I . . . I've had the most awful dream . . . give your Rosie a big hug, dearest Papa!'

Rosie cast herself into his arms and Arnold obliged, picking her up as he hugged her.

'Now, Rosy-Posy, what on earth are you doing down here? Yes, I know you say you had a bad dream, but what's Nurse for, eh, if not to settle you when you wake?'

Rose, adorable in her long, full white nightgown with her golden curls tumbling around her rosy little face, pouted deliciously, looking up at her father through her dusky lashes.

'Poor Nurse, she's so tired today, she's been asleep for ages. I didn't want to wake her, so I thought I'd come down and find you. You always tuck me in nicely and read to me kindly, and then I can go to sleep again without any trouble.'

'Naughty puss,' Arnold said. 'Very well, I'll tuck you in nicely and read to you kindly, but don't make a habit of it, young lady.'

'Course not, Papa! I'll have *Alice Through The Looking Glass* tonight, please. And could I have some milk and biscuits? If I have milk and biscuits I sleep much quicker, actually.'

'Oh, all right, just this once,' Arnold said. He stood her down. 'Walk up the stairs, puss; you're a bit too heavy to carry up.'

Accordingly father and daughter made their way to the night nursery and Arnold read the chapter requested, fetched biscuits from the nursery cupboard and reached down a chocolate from the box kept on the top shelf, since it was too late, he told Rose, to ferret around in the ice-box for milk and heat it up on the oil stove. Then he tucked his daughter in, kissed her, and made his way downstairs once more.

It was not until he had regained the hall that it occurred to him that wherever Rose had been going it had not been to his study. Not heading in that direction.

Little minx, Arnold chuckled to himself, making for the library where he would find a tray of drinks set out ready for him. She was probably going to sneak into the kitchen and bag herself something to eat. Still, what did it matter? Dear little soul, full of fun and capable of any sort of harmless mischief. And pretty as well . . . folk said she was very like Lily, but he couldn't see it, himself.

# CHAPTER SIXTEEN

Ever since Nala had arrived at Amitri's work-place the sun had been trying to edge up over the tops of the distant mountains and now at last it succeeded, pouring brilliance over the land, gilding the reeds which grew by the lake, turning a glade of bamboo into a miracle of green and gold.

Beyond the lake the mountains reared, blue-grey against the morning-flushed sky. Nala could have drawn the shape of the mountains in her sleep, she knew them so well, and now she watched appreciatively as a white heron, outlined against the mountains, flapped lazily across the lake, selected a good spot near the margin, and slid into the water with scarcely a ripple, composing itself, one leg tucked up, eyes like gimlets, for fishing.

Having watched the heron until even the water around it stilled, Nala turned her attention back to Amitri and not a moment too soon, either. The potter had selected his ball of clay, placed it in the centre of his wheel and was splashing water on to it. His foot, narrow and prehensile, gripped the kickwheel, waiting for the propitious moment to start the movement. The wheel started, at first slow and jerky, then speeding up to smoothness, the clay still wet from the constant splashing whilst Amitri's fingers hovered above it, waiting until the motion was both smooth and fast enough for him to start shaping the clay.

Nala knelt in the dust and watched, almost without breathing. Amitri sat cross-legged on his tatami, the mat made of pressed rice-straw which was the common floor-covering in all Japanese houses, from the greatest to the least, though here of course they were in the open. Nala would have liked to have sat cross-legged too, but her father had a theory that the Japanese were frequently bow-legged because of their diet and also because of the way they sat. Had her father been present, Nala knew he would have told her to sit on a rock to watch instead of kneeling in the dust, so it was as well that John Sawyer was probably only just getting out of bed back at the mission. Nala could not have borne to be kept back from the fascination of the potter's art; she had to be close, to be able to watch every movement, every flick of the clay, every turn of the wheel.

Presently, Amitri leaned forward and his right hand plunged into the ball of clay, though his left countinued monotonously splashing the water. Nala leaned forward too, her curtain of long, gleaming black hair swinging concealingly across her face. With her hair thus, all she could see – or wished to see – were the potter's hands. She drew in a deep, happy breath.

This was the moment she had waited for, crouching patiently nearby whilst Amitri selected his clay, set up his wheel, shook out his mat and generally made ready for the day ahead. To watch the magic of the pot emerging from the seemingly unresponsive lump of reddish clay was one of the high points of her day, an experience of which she never tired. What would the clay become this time? Amitri would never tell her in advance because he said the shape waited in the clay for his fingers to discover it, but Nala could make a rough guess from the volume of clay selected. This piece was not very big; a little jug, perhaps, or a vase, the sort that would hold only one spray of almond blossom, or a round seed-pot, or a bowl?

Soon enough, the pot began to emerge. A round shape first of all, then a stiffened thumb straightened it, moved again and the pot was suddenly on a pedestal base. Fingers straightened, curved, the water fell continuously, and suddenly Nala could see that the clay was a bowl for use in the tea-ceremony, a ceremony which was both important and significant, though Nala was not at all sure why. The wheel slowed, stopped. The tea-bowl stood there, waiting for Amitri to cut it free from the base clay at its foot. It had a spare, severe beauty and was just, Nala knew, as Amitri wanted it to be. He was a master-potter, an artist, famed throughout Japan, and he was looking at the bowl with affection. She sighed and relaxed.

'Will it be painted, Amitri? Glazed? Or coloured, perhaps?'

Amitri shrugged. His thin yellow face was turned to her, the dark and narrow eyes fixed on her own round, dark blue orbs.

'A design, I believe. I shall make three more such.'

Nala studied the tea-bowl closely for a silent moment, then nodded.

'Yes. Bamboos. Two clumps, one thick and quite high, the other smaller and thin.'

Amitri smiled, satisfied, then turned to cut the pot from the clay whilst Nala scrambled to her feet, dusted the earth off her pointed knees and pulled her kimono into respectability. When the sun came over the mountains it meant it was almost breakfast time; she should leave Amitri now, though she might return later, perhaps. With no more than one long, wistful glance at the pile of waiting clay she set off, but being easily distracted she hurried, to give her time for all the small, inconsequential things she liked to do on such a fine morning.

Amitri lived on the other side of the village in which her father had his mission, his cottage a little way away from the others. Nala had to trot along beside some paddy fields, with deep drainage ditches intersecting them. She glanced quickly up at the sun's position in the heavens, then slid down the bank and into the ditch. Her splashy entry had, naturally, scared the wildlife for miles around but Nala, wading as silently as she could, knew that this would not last. Very soon now, she might see something.

She did. A tiny frog, small and bright as an enamelled brooch, sat on a fat lotus leaf and croaked at her a good deal more loudly than one would have believed possible for a creature so small.

Nala knelt and got as close to the frog as she dared, holding her kimono well above the somewhat muddy water of the draining ditch. She liked the shape of the frog compared with the clean line of the reeds behind him and the round fatness of the lotus leaf. Nala picked up a twig and began to make a drawing in the mud. When it was finished it was just a few lines, and possibly it did not look much like a frog or a leaf, but to Nala it had a satisfying shape. Her father, looking at her early drawings, had remarked rather doubtfully that she drew like a Japanese and had then added, hastily, that he meant the remark as a compliment, but Nala did not mind at all. Already, at the age of ten, she realized that the Japanese did everything a good deal better than Europeans. Her friends and teachers at school politely did not stress the point, but it was always there. Her amah, Kei, thought that China was the most wonderful country in the world and filled with the most gifted people, but that was because she was Chinese. Nala, born in China of English parents but brought up in Japan, had few doubts on the superiority score. Amitri was a great and famous potter; people came from all over Japan to buy his work, and Japanese art, so sparse and civilized, was head and shoulders above all other art forms. Nala's own taste denounced European paintings, several examples of which hung on the wattle and daub walls of her father's mission. Sad-eyed Christs, a whey-faced woman with a bandage round her eyes and scales in her hand, an over-dressed female with a horrid little boy at her knee, all curls and vast, unbelievably large eyes . . . such things were not art but cheap frivolity. Art, for Nala, was a line, a colour wash, a shape.

The frog gave another croak, if anything louder than the croak which had preceded it, then leapt. There was a tiny plop! as it hit the water, widening circles, then silence. Nala stood up and rubbed mud off her unfortunate knees, though perfunctorily, then looked around her hopefully for some other form of amusement. Terrapins were lovely . . . but it would not do to be late for breakfast. Her father liked punctuality and since she adored John she tried her very best never to displease him unnecessarily. If it had been necessary, if Amitri had been engaged on a project which had taken longer than the tea-bowl, it must be admitted that Nala would probably have risked John's displeasure, but as it was she set off once again, this time at a brisk trot. As she went, she considered her breakfast with a healthy anticipation.

It would be a good breakfast, because John was a great believer in starting the day off with a well-lined stomach. They had a Japanese cook, a dear woman called Yesko, and if she had had her way Nala would have broken her fast, each morning, with green tea to drink and rice and raw fish to eat, but John did not approve. Sometimes he cooked the breakfast himself, sometimes Kei did it, but it was always good. First there was a sort of porridge made with ground rice and hot goat's milk flavoured with honey. Then there was a boiled egg each, sometimes two, and bread spread with butter and either jam or marmalade. Then there was usually fruit – oranges or persimmons, apples sometimes, or delicious, sharp-sweet greengages. And lastly rich water-buffalo milk for Nala and tea for John.

Nala, hurrying up the dusty track, hoped that John would have made the breakfast this morning and not Kei, because her father had the knack of producing a boiled egg with runny yolk and firm white. But on the other hand if Kei had made the breakfast it would be because John was off to some meeting or other, and that meant he would not have time for the long and elaborate grace-saying which sometimes held up the actual eating of their meal until the porridge was distinctly chilly.

Arriving outside her home, Nala shed her shoes and entered on tiptoe, sliding in through the door to the kitchen where the family usually ate as quietly as she could. The house was nice; thatched with reeds, the walls made of wattle and daub and whitewashed, it had small windows and was divided into four rooms by sliding bamboo and paper screens. The screen between the main part of the house and the kitchen quarters was pushed half back this morning and Nala could see her father just coming through from the main room, with a book in one hand and a cup of tea in the other. He looked up as she moved and smiled.

John Sawyer was beautiful in his daughter's eyes. Tall and tanned, with his dark hair thickly streaked with white, his face had a gravity and a solemnity about it which disappeared when his eyes fell on his only child. Nala tried to draw his face sometimes, and always destroyed her efforts, but one day, when she was older and cleverer, she would manage to get whatever it was he had, some trick of expression, which was compassion and goodness personified.

'Good morning, Nala. No need to ask where you've been . . . look at your knees, you little ragamuffin!'

'Oh . . . I'll wash,' Nala said hastily. She crossed to the bowl and jug set up on a low table and splashed water into the bowl. It did not take long to wash her face, screwing her eyes up against the water, then she dabbed at her knees with the flannel and last of all washed her hands, this time using the big bar of yellow, waxy soap which was always kept here, in the kitchen.

Kei was standing outside the house; Nala could see her through the open back door. She had a basket over her arm.

'We're a bit late this morning,' John said conversationally to his daughter as he moved over to the stove. 'The porridge is made but Kei's just fetching the eggs . . . dear me, and I'm even hungrier than usual! The truth is I'm off to the city as soon as you and I have breakfasted, so I've been getting my papers together, marshalling my ideas, and I forgot to collect the eggs, let alone cook 'em.'

'Oh . . . Father, Amitri's making a set of bowls for the tea-ceremony.

Can I go and decorate them for him? He'll let me try . . . not perhaps on the pots themselves at first, but on a bit of paper. If he likes the design he'll show me how it should go and perhaps even let me do one very small cup.'

John laughed.

'I thought all the cups were supposed to be the same size? And they're bowls, my child, not cups.'

'I know,' Nala said impatiently. 'But can I, Father? Can I go and help him?'

'See what Kei says,' John advised. 'Now come along, make yourself useful . . . go and dish up the porridge, would you?'

Nala loved dishing up and jumped to her feet with alacrity. She went over to the stove where the pan of porridge simmered and set out the three bowls, for Kei would eat with them presently. Then she spooned porridge carefully into each and carried them, one by one, over to the table.

'Here we are, Father,' she said, handing him his. 'Kei's still in the garden. Shall I call her?'

But even as she spoke Kei appeared, her basket now swinging, workmanlike, from one hand.

'Only one egg each today,' Kei remarked as she entered the room. She went straight to the stove, picked up a pan, slopped water into it from the big jug and then added three eggs. She put the pan on the stove, turned the flame up, for it had been turned down to keep the porridge hot, and took her place at the table. 'Have you been a good girl, Nala? Your father is going to the city today, so when you've finished your lessons I thought you and I might walk round to the Mariyama home. You could play with little Yenka whilst I chat to Toko.'

'Oh . . . but Kei, I want to work with Amitri! You go to the Mariyamas' place: I'm quite happy to stay in the village by myself.'

'Eat your breakfast, and don't argue with Kei, there's a good girl,' John advised his daughter. 'I'll be back for the evening meal, so perhaps you could go and see Amitri then.'

'It'll be too late; he needs the light for his work,' Nala moaned, close to tears. 'Dearest Kei . . .'

'That's enough, Nala,' John said mildly, but Nala was not deceived and fell silent at once. Her beloved father was almost never cross with her, and she did not want to make him so over something as unimportant as a visit to the Mariyamas. But she did want to see Amitri's tea-bowls!

'You can come out to the stable and see me off,' John said presently, when the meal was over. 'Yesko and Kei will clear away and wash up, and you and I will ride to school this morning, you before me on the saddle, to save Kei from having to take you down. I pass the school, after all, on my way to the city.'

'Oh, good,' Nala said, cheering up. She had been rather silent through-out the rest of her breakfast. 'Are you riding the grey or good old Pronto?'

Pronto was an elderly, sturdy horse, a bay with a hogged mane and an impassive and reliable nature, the grey a spirited young gelding with a rolling eye and a tendency to spook at the slightest thing. John laughed and took his daughter's hand.

'The grey, because he needs plenty of exercise to tire him out and it's a long way to the city. Poor Pronto is past his best for lengthy journeys.' The two of them had reached the stableyard by now and John hailed the groom, Loika, who came running at once. 'Saddle the grey, please,' John said and then added, to Nala, 'And you and I must have a chat, young lady.'

'What do you want to chat about?' Nala said presently, perched comfortably in front of her father as he rode the tall grey horse out from under the arched stable gateway. 'Are you cross with me still?'

'Cross with you? When am I ever cross with you? No, but, my love, you mustn't grow selfish in your desire to help Amitri, you know. Poor Kei is a long way from her own home, and has been for eight years. She's twenty-five years old and would have been married long since, had we been in China, but she wouldn't stay there without us, for we are all the family she has, you know. Now she wants to go and visit the Mariyama family for one reason and one reason only. She wants to see . . .'

'Toko,' his daughter interrupted. 'Toko likes our Kei, doesn't he, Father? But surely she wouldn't marry him, would she? He's so small and squat . . . he even makes me look tall!'

'I don't know. Sometimes I feel very guilty for having brought her here . . . for you and me it was the best thing at the time, it was a good idea to get right away . . . my dear girl, I've told you before how unhappy I was after your mother died, living in the home she had helped me to make. When the opportunity arose to leave China and come to Japan I seized it with both hands, convinced I could do more good away from the place where . . . where Addy and I had been happy. But now, after so many years, I'm beginning to have my doubts. So today I'm riding into the city for talks with various eminent people connected with my mission, and we shall see.'

'But . . . you wouldn't leave, would you, Papa? You wouldn't leave our home? I can't think of anywhere but Umo as home, and I'm sure I never shall! We're so happy here!'

'Yes, we've been happy; but my dear child, the school is tiny and your education is being sadly neglected. If the mission offers me a move to a large city where you can go to an English school then perhaps that would suffice; but, Nala, I'm hungry to see China again. It was to China that the Spirit led me all those years ago, when I first came to the east.'

'Oh . . . but you do good here, Papa! How would they manage without you?'

231

'Spiritually, very well indeed, and even medically not too badly. It's difficult to explain even to you, Nala, but my call was to China, not Japan. I've worked out the worst of my grief here and now I feel I should return to the land where my ministry began.'

'Perhaps they'll offer you a mission in the city,' Nala muttered, but with faint hope, for to a child reared in the quiet and peacefulness of Umo a move to one of the big, bustling modern Japanese cities was almost as bad as moving to another country. 'I'll tell Seimo she's to pray for you to stay in Japan and I'll pray as well; perhaps that will do the trick.'

John laughed, hugged her and slowed the pace of the horse as they arrived outside the tiny village school.

'Little heathen,' he said, sliding her down from the saddle. 'You should pray that I am given what is best for us all and not what you want yourself! Be a good girl now, and I'll see you this evening.'

John watched his daughter run up to her friend, Seimo, held the horse until he had seen the two little girls saunter into the playground, and dug his heels into the grey's smooth, round sides. The gelding, glad to be given leave to move, tried to seize the bit and take off, but John held him to a collected trot until the village was left behind and only then let his stride lengthen and become a canter.

As he rode, John went over, for what seemed like the hundredth time, his reasons for suggesting a move to his superiors. One reason of course had to be Nala's education. The little school was run by two very elderly Japanese with fixed ideas and only the most rudimentary knowledge of book learning. At five, it had seemed a good place for his daughter to go, for she needed to be able to read and write Japanese, and although John spoke the language by then with a degree of fluency he could only just manage to read certain words and phrases and did not even profess to have all the 700-odd characters by heart.

When he and Adeline had talked of education, they had taken it for granted that there would be two of them to teach their child how to write and read in English and then to carry on with sums, grammar, history and geography. They had also assumed they would be in China, where there were good English schools and many missionaries with similar problems to John's own.

Japan was quite different. It was a richer land with, by and large, a more intelligent and aggressive people, but most of all it was a land where everyone's sense of patriotism was uppermost. The Chinese were divided by the very size of their country, the Japanese united by the smallness of theirs. And the Chinese needed all the help they could get when famine or drought struck their immense land. Japan, on the other hand, although it suffered constantly from the typhoons and earthquakes which seemed to shake the land every few months, could feed its own. The Japanese tended to watch you and copy what you did . . . already they were training doctors up to the highest of western standards. The Chinese still distrusted anything which did not originate in China and had no real desire to copy anyone. What they would have liked, John knew, was to be left alone to scratch a living a hundred years behind the rest of the world, but they had to be dragged, by the scruff of their necks if necessary, into the twentieth century. He believed that God had sent him to do just that, and he had reneged and gone to Japan. Now that he had got his confidence back, surely he should think seriously about returning to China, possibly even to Cheiping, his daughter's birthplace?

Despite having lived here for eight years, he had no real love for the country and he found the people's attitude difficult. So many strangenesses! The reverence for a man who showed no emotion sickened him; man was made to laugh and weep and should do both in their season. The attitude to beauty – that nothing could be beautiful unless it was sparse, spare and severe – he could not identify with at all. To John a magnificent sunset could never be gaudy, nor could he consider a tree which grew as the wind took it to be an eyesore because it was not perfectly symmetrical.

The class system, too. Eta meant lowest of the low, the untouchables, and the Eta lived in slums, like animals. They were not allowed into the schools, they took no part in religious services. Had an Eta tried to become a Christian, John knew he would probably have lost all of the present members of his admittedly tiny flock.

It was no use preaching that his flock should love their brothers or even their neighbours, for the Japanese simply could not – or would not – consider the Eta as fellow human beings, let alone brothers or neighbours.

A train, rattling by on the railway line, brought the grey up on its hind legs, nostrils flared, eyes rolling with pretended terror. John let the animal dance, then gentled it into quietness and began to trot along the road once more. Here the road was lined with small houses, for the city was not far off. These were not peasants but city workers who lived out here rather than in the densely-peopled city streets.

Paper houses, John thought ruefully, eyeing the flimsy structures. But at least if and when they fell down they could easily be erected again.

Earthquakes were a way of life here. They killed people, of course, as did the typhoons whose vicious tails swung inland, scattering ruin in their wake, but the Japanese had a resigned attitude to them. Natural disasters were inflicted by gods too fickle and quick-tempered to placate, though they tried, through shinto, to gain a measure of immunity. And built their houses of paper.

Although John had told his daughter he was going to the city to discuss his future, that was not entirely true. In fact, he had been sent for. His superiors were not happy that his daughter was still in a local school. A year or two ago they had suggested Nala be sent back to England to complete her education and John had smiled and kept the child with him. Now, he rather thought, he would be told that he should either send her home or move nearer a proper school – and it was true, he acknowledged it. Nala was learning very little now that she had mastered reading and writing in Japanese . . . her grasp of English was fairly good but she could neither read nor write in that language. Yet where, in Japan, would he find a suitable English school for her? And indeed, why should he, when he and Kei both wanted to go back to China so badly?

They were getting closer. The road was becoming a street, lined with pine trees, beneath the shade of which clustered various booths. The grey slowed without being ordered to do so and stretched out a long nose towards a seller of watercresses. John forced the animal out into the centre of the road once more, just in time, for a counter spread with yellow rice cakes was next and the grey had a notoriously sweet tooth.

John, looking sideways, saw a man training a maple tree, as he would have trained it every day since he had first planted it and would continue to train it whilst it was within his power to do so. He stood by it, bending and guiding and pressing against the two lowest branches, coaxing it to some plan of beauty as yet only imagined. The rest of his garden, John saw, was equally planned. A large grey stone at a certain point in some celestial compass, a solitary, immaculate rhododendron, cream-coloured shingle in a neatly boxed path and a pool with lotuses on the water. If that was my garden, John thought with unusual viciousness, I'd run through it, kicking to right and left, until it was used-looking, human-looking, more natural. What that man is doing isn't gardening, it's feeding an obsession, and obsessions shouldn't be fed, they should be starved.

John kicked the grey into a trot again as the booths by the roadside grew more and more tempting. Shellfish caused the grey to wrinkle his nose but shining piles of fruit and nuts had him tugging towards them and sweetmeats and cakes threw him into an ecstasy of longing, almost stationary, ears pricked, nostrils flared, snuffling the sweet smells with great appreciation.

There was a skinny female beggar shuffling along the rows of stalls, being cuffed away from each in turn. Put that treatment along with the behaviour of the obsessive gardener and I can begin to rationalize my dislike of the strong national traits, John told himself. They will all spend hours training a tree or appreciating one blossom in a small vase but they would not give the time of day to an unfortunate like the beggar, far less empathize with her as John could. Passing by on the other side was the natural thing for a Japanese to do, unless the oppressed were a close friend.

I've lived here now for eight years, his thoughts continued, and I can say without too much shame that I have still not grown close to any of my people. Amitri loves my daughter and is polite and civilized towards me, but he would not claim to be a friend. Others in the village have cause to be grateful to me – a cross-birth successfully dealt with, a fever cured, an operation performed – yet this has made none of the people my friends.

My servants are loyal enough, but that's about all you can say. I am not needed here, therefore I should leave.

The city streets were all about him now, the pavements thick with pushing, impatient humanity and the roads thronged with traffic. I am going to ask for a posting to China, John thought, and knew that it had been what he wanted all along. All his agonizing had been window-dressing for the fact; he was going home to the country of his child's birth, to the place where his heart was.

'Wait for me!'

'Oh . . . if you hurry, then!'

Nala and Seimo, the inseparables as John had once called them, wrangled their way across the playground and out of the school gates. Their lessons had been boring, but the two girls were perfectly content with such education as came their way; indeed, Nala had spent most of the day drawing silently in her mind. Now, let off the hook, they would tussle and tease their way to Seimo's home where Seimo's mother would give them chestnuts, lotus roots, sweets and green tea. After perhaps half an hour Kei would come for Nala, and the two of them would either make their way to Amitri's kiln, or the Mariyama household.

They were tolerated there, Nala knew, because Kei was interested in Toko and he, presumably, in her, but by and large foreigners were not well liked, though Nala, who had been bred, if not born, in Japan was in most cases an honourable exception. Her friends at school accepted her and so their parents had come to do so too. She acknowledged that Japan was the most important country in the world and the Japanese the best people. She was ashamed of her own English looks, though thank goodness she had black hair, a point in her favour, and wished her skin was gold and her eyes black slits, like Seimo's. As for her father, with his big feet, popping eyes and awful intrusive smell, dearly though she loved him she wished him different. Smaller, yellower, more Japanese. Her friends often told her, kindly, that she could not help having a strange-looking father, but children are sensitive to such things. If her friends knew, though, that Papa wanted to take her across the sea to China, how horrified they would be! The Chinese – except for Kei, of course – were a gross and terrible people whom it was Japan's dire task to educate and change. To go and live amongst them voluntarily would be a sure sign of mental weakness . . . but on reflection Nala supposed that her father could not mean it. He knew how happy she was, that this was her home. Doubtless they would move to some other part of Japan; that would be perfectly respectable. Missing her friends and her home would be sad for her, but not as shaming as having to admit to leaving the Land of the Rising Sun . . . the only country in the whole world, according to her friends, worth living in.

'Here we are, home again!' Seimo said breezily, as they went in through the sliding door, taking their shoes off and placing them, side by side, on the tatami mat nearest the courtyard. 'I wonder what my mother has prepared for us today? Will we have time to play at Vega and Altair?'

'I wanted to go and see Amitri getting his tea-bowls out of the kiln,' Nala muttered. 'But it's too far for you, I suppose?'

Seimo's mother could not understand why a girl should want to go and watch a potter at work, and though Seimo herself thought it quite fun she much preferred to play at long, involved 'pretend' games with her best friend, or to sit cross-legged on the tatami matting whilst her mother fed her titbits and told her stories of the boy born of a peach, or the Tom Thumb hero, Issun-boshi, or terrifying tales of *tengu* demons and *o-bake* ghosts.

'Here, Mother has sent us some toffeed grapes and some wheat cakes,' Seimo said presently, coming into the room with a laden tray. 'Let's play at geishas.'

'All right, until Kei comes,' Nala agreed.

The two small girls arranged themselves neatly on the matting; they wore sensible kimonos in dark cotton, with red *obis* around their middles and the little white cotton socks with the divided big toe known as *tabios*. Their wooden clogs reposed outside the room.

'Now! I shall serve you with tea and grapes, and you can do the bowing and hissing bit,' Seimo said, graciously bowing as she spoke. 'What a pity you're leaving early this evening; we could have done our faces with flour . . . Mother's been baking.'

'Never mind . . .' Nala slipped into the part she was to play. 'I'm a big fat Japanese from Tokyo. You must entertain me well, geisha!' She made her voice deep and fat, scowling wonderfully. 'Give me toffeed grapes, geisha girl,' she boomed. 'And many cups of *sake* so that I may grow merry and fat as a rich man should!'

Walking home with Kei, Nala first told her all about school, then described her game with Seimo, and finally spoke of the matter nearest her heart.

'Kei, does Papa mean to take us to China? He was saying he might, when he took me to school this morning.'

'I wish he would,' Kei said at once. 'Oh, my dearest child, you would so love the land of your birth! It is very beautiful, far more beautiful than this little land with its little people. China is great and glorious, the moutains touch the sky, the lakes are so deep whole cities have been lost in them. Even the sea . . . ah, the sea is so blue, so clean and clear!'

'Well, so is the sea around the island of Hokkaido,' Nala pointed out. Each summer, she, Kei and her father went to Hokkaido, the northern-most island in the Japanese group, for six glorious weeks. They either camped out or lived in a farmhouse and they spent the time swimming, playing on the long beaches and exploring the empty and altogether delightful island.

236

'Ah yes, but . . . China is a marvel, a wonder! And the people . . . why, you would fall in love with the people at once. They are so warm, so friendly . . .'

'So are the Japanese,' Nala assured the older girl. 'Kei, I don't know anywhere but here, and I want to be where I know! And I am growing useful to Amitri, really I am. He is going to let me make a pot for myself, and decorate it and do the glaze . . . everything. And then he will let me give it to Papa for New Year . . . or perhaps for Christmas.'

'Yes, for Christmas,' Kei said quickly. 'New Year is a pagan festival. We Christians exchange gifts at Christmastide, when we celebrate the birth of baby Jesus.'

'Yes . . . except that Papa lets me celebrate New Year as well . . . and *tanabata*, and *shichi-go-san*,' Nala said, mentioning two other colourful Japanese festivals. 'Oh, Kei, if we go to China, how shall I bear it?'

'I've borne Japan for eight years,' Kei said slowly. 'Wouldn't it be fair, little Nala, if you came to China with me for a few years, now? Because once you're there, you'll never want to leave!'

'Hmm,' Nala said doubtfully. 'Where are we going, Kei? I thought Papa said you wanted to go to the Mariyama place.'

'Oh well, you want to see the tea-bowls come out of the kiln, you said. We'll go to Amitri this evening.'

But even as Nala squeaked with pleasure and ran ahead, it struck her that Kei was being suddenly generous for no good reason. Unless she knew that, very soon, Nala's hopes were going to be dashed? Unless she was certain that the pot her protégée hoped to make from clay dug by her very own self was never going to be finished?

Then Nala threw off the worry, for ahead of her she could see the pale smoke rising from Amitri's wood-burning fire-box and knew that within a matter of minutes she would be hurrying up to him and watching as he removed the first brick, let the oven begin to cool, and then slowly and carefully withdrew the glowing, perfect contents.

Kei, coming slowly along behind, thought a little sadly that she would be sorry to upset her charge with the journey over the sea to her own country, but regardless of how she herself felt, she could tell that Mr John had made up his mind. She had wondered for a long while now why her master did not return to China, for it was clear to her, if not to him, that he was fretting here in Japan. Many of the Japanese had been kind to the little family in their midst, and Kei herself had been accepted once her knowledge of the language was sufficiently good for the Japanese themselves not to be able to pick her out as a foreigner immediately, but for Mr John it had been a sterile friendship. They used his medical knowledge, but few converted to Christianity and even those who came to his clinics showed little gratitude for his help. It was as though acknowledging his superiority in the matter of medicine would make them lesser people, and

237

accordingly they simply did not acknowledge it. Instead, they came quietly, took advantage of his expertise and the drugs he used, and went quietly too, not admitting to friends and relatives that they had been cured by the foreign doctor.

Kei had known he cared, wanted desperately to be accepted at least as a healer if not for his spiritual powers. She had also known how bitterly he missed his wife. He was half a man without her, Kei thought compassionately, only half a man. The humour and deep, sincere contentment had somehow dried up, so that though he was as good a man as ever he seemed to perform his duties almost joylessly when you compared him with the man he had been during Adeline's lifetime.

But more and more, lately, Kei had been convinced that if he could get back to China all the old power would return and the happiness, which had somehow drained away when Adeline died, would begin to reappear, if not with its old, bubbling ebullience, at least with a quieter, steadier pleasure.

She was sorry for little Nala, who adored her friends and loved this strange, typhoon-torn land so passionately, but Nala was a child, and children forgot; everyone knew that. Indeed, Kei was young enough to remember her own haunted, disrupted childhood, at times with horrid distinctness. Her life had divided into three – before the Convent school, then in the Convent school, and then with Adeline and John. The first part was grim and quickly to be pushed to the back of her mind once more. The second part was boring, new, strange and delightful. But the third part had been unalloyed joy, with the love which had poured over her from John and Adeline making up, with its richness, for the lean years that had gone before.

And now? Now she must follow John and take care of Nala as Adeline had wanted her to do. She had come to Japan uncomplainingly and had stayed here for eight long years far from her own country and people. She had even begun to believe she might be here for ever and had considered marrying a local man, because she wanted a home of her own and a husband one day. But if it was the will of God that she return to China and take care of Nala amongst her own people, how much more willingly would she do her duty!

So Kei watched the potter at his work and saw her charge's keen attention on the tea-bowls as each one came forth from the kiln, and told herself that Nala would love China as it deserved to be loved, and would forget Japan in a week. Why not, indeed, when you considered that she was a native of neither land?

238

# CHAPTER SEVENTEEN

'Are you all right, my dear?'

Nala was curled up in a corner seat, watching the countryside as it rushed past the train window. At her father's anxious enquiry, however, she turned from the view and smiled at him. She felt very protective towards him now, for he was pale and thin from a recent attack of fever and needed all her loving care.

'Yes indeed, Father, I'm fine. Just taking a last look at Japan.'

It had taken them two whole years to actually get to the point they had reached now, Nala realized, as her father returned to his book, satisfied of her well-being. Two whole years! First, John had insisted on remaining at Umo whilst the mission people found a suitable replacement for him, then he had stayed because the Whitakers knew no Japanese and needed help with the language, and finally their journey had been delayed whilst the packing, crating and sending-ahead of most of their furniture was carried out.

But here they were, on a golden September morning, making their way through the peaceful Japanese landscape, whilst in the rest of the world, Nala knew dimly, a war raged.

Japan had entered the war a couple of years earlier and her fighting men had gone to aid the Allies, but Nala had only the vaguest picture of what it was all about and at twelve cared very little. She was more concerned with her own affairs, and the affairs of those she had left behind her.

The Whitakers, who had moved into the Sawyer house, were undoubtedly devout, but that was about all she could say for them. Paul Whitaker had once worked as a medical orderly in a hospital and his wife was an experienced nurse, but obviously they could not replace John so far as medical expertise went. However, the mission could not afford to use the services of a trained doctor in a small place like Umo, and the Whitakers were the best they could offer. Perhaps they'll settle in, Nala thought without much real hope. Father did his best to make them see; he warned them that if they laughed at Japanese superstition they would lose the converts he had so painfully gained, for by many of the native villagers superstitions were in fact more deeply held than religion, but Nala thought he was speaking to deaf ears. The Whitakers knew themselves to be right, and superior to their converts, and whilst they continued to think in that manner they were unlikely to make friends or indeed converts amongst the villagers.

Outside in the slanting rays of the sun they were harvesting the rice. Behind the paddy fields a great purple mountain reared up against the sky. Peasants, made tiny by distance, bent, cut, straightened. It was a beautiful scene, given an added warmth by familiarity. Nala sighed and looked towards Kei, who was reading a magazine with strained attention. She was so excited, dear Kei, to be going back to her own country after an absence of over ten years.

Kei felt Nala's eyes on her and looked up, smiling.

'Still teasing yourself about the Whitakers, Nala?' she asked. 'They'll manage, or they'll leave. You must look forward now, not back.'

'I didn't like them very much,' Nala owned. She lowered her voice in deference to her father's concentration. 'I know you say it shouldn't matter that she had hair like string and sticky-out ʼteeth, but she had no humility either, Kei.'

'Outward appearances should mean nothing,' Kei said without much conviction. 'It is the soul and the heart which matter, Nala. As for humility . . . you aren't overburdened with humility yourself, Nala-san!'

'I don't think I'm always right, though. I know I've got an awful lot to learn.'

Kei nodded and began to read again. Nala let her eyes roam over the scene outside whilst she thought of what Amitri had said to her the day before she left. She had put off telling him of her departure, sure he would be as dismayed as she was herself, for she had grown useful to him over the years, decorating pots and even helping with the throwing on a few notable occasions. She had broken the news to him in his little workroom when the two of them had been sitting cross-legged on the floor, putting the final decorative touches to a set of dinner-plates for a rich neighbour.

'So you are going at last,' Amitri said, peering at her over his battered little spectacles. 'It is good for a potter to see other countries and other methods of using clay. We Japanese are never too proud to take ideas from other nations and adapt them for our own use. Almost all Japanese pottery came, in the beginning, from Korea, and a good deal came from China. Whilst you are in China you must try to go to places where they have the ancient ware, made three, four, five hundred years or more ago. You will find it is good, sometimes better than we make today.' He had patted her arm kindly with a scrawny but immensely strong hand. 'Use what life offers you; clutch it, drain it. An artist must be selfish and suck beauty out of whatever is offered. You won't feed your talent by staying in one spot and looking only outward.'

'What about you, Amitri?' Nala had objected. 'You've lived in Umo all your life – you told me you had.'

'And how much greater, how much more of a genius, I might have been

240

had I been forced out into the world more,' murmured Amitri unanswerably. 'One day you will come back and we shall see who was right . . . you, to seize the opportunities offered, or I, who denied them.'

Now, in the train, as it clicketed on towards the capital city, Nala thought perhaps Amitri had been even more right than he knew. Because of her deep and abiding interest in pottery her father had bought her a couple of volumes on the art of the Chinese potters, and she had begun to realize that, good though she believed Amitri to be, he was not the greatest artist the world had ever known. Indeed, there were times when her own drawing on a pot was better than his, as he freely ackowledged.

'I am a potter first, for I love the shapes and the glaze and the feel of a pot more than its decoration,' he was wont to remark. But Nala thought that a first-rate potter must be artist enough to know which pattern went with which shape. Amitri could be obtuse over things like that on occasion.

'Hungry yet, my dear?'

John had roused himself from his book and was opening up the straw basket of food which Kei had prepared for them. Immediately Nala realized that she was starving, and leaned forward eagerly as the crab meat patties, the rice cakes and the soused fish were brought out. As she began to eat she was pleased to see her father tucking in as well. He had not yet fully recovered from his last bout of fever, she knew, but perhaps the sea breezes would restore his health. She hoped so, for she and Kei had both worried about John lately. The fever seemed to have sapped his enthusiasm and even his normal good humour had been affected. Not that he was cross or unreasonable, she reminded herself hastily; but he no longer joked and chatted to her in English, to keep her knowledge of the language green, neither did he discuss things with her as he once had. He was quieter, more serious, less involved with her life.

'Soon be there, Nala,' Kei said, taking a ripe pear from the basket and cutting in into juicy quarters with her small silver knife. 'Then we'll be in the flat John has borrowed for us until the ship actually sails . . . and then . . . ah, how good it will be to see China's shores coming closer!'

'How very good,' John echoed. But Nala thought his eyes looked tormented. Did Adeline, her mother, haunt him still? Was he half afraid of going back to China, where he and she had known such happiness? Yet he had insisted on the return, though that might easily have been his conscience. He was disappointed, to put it no stronger, over his lack of success in Japan. Perhaps that had made him determined to go back to the country where, once, he had been both happy and much loved.

'Would you like a persimmon now, Nala?' John's silver knife was also busy, halving the fruit. He grimaced as juice ran down on to his trousers, then flicked half the persimmon into his daughter's lap and laughed at her wail of protest as the juice sank into her silk kimono.

'Never mind, once we're on the ship we'll change into Chinese clothing. It would never do to arrive looking like little Japanese! Kei will go

241

shopping with you and buy you the right things . . . you'll enjoy that, won't you, you little peacock?'

Nala agreed that she would love it and the small party continued with their picnic. Her father was definitely recovering at last, Nala thought happily as the fruit was devoured.

'Is he well enough to travel, Kei? If not, we must delay yet again!'

Nala and Kei were in the kitchen of the little flat they had borrowed, talking in lowered tones, for John, lying on his *futon* in the next room, had been very ill.

On the very day they had got off the train in Tokyo, John had been told by a fellow missionary of an epidemic of some sort of typhus-like fever which was sweeping the poorer section of the city, and he had gone at once to the hospital. He had worked night and day for a week, until their ship was due to sail. On the very morning they should have left, John's temperature had soared, he had not known either of them and they had been forced to call a doctor.

Now, however, Kei nodded reassuringly.

'Yes, it's all right, Nala, the doctor came very early this morning, before you were up. The fever has broken, John is no longer in danger, and the doctor says he may leave in seven days, when the ship sails. He even said the sea breezes would do him good, whereas because of the unseasonable warmth here, and the fact that we are stuck in this . . . this tenement, he is not recovering as quickly as he should.'

Nala looked round the cramped little room and was heartily grateful that they were soon to leave it. They had been here a month and it was a month too long so far as she was concerned. But it had taught her a valuable lesson; it was not the entire country of Japan she loved but Umo. Had her father been given a mission in a big city she would have been every bit as miserable as she had at one time expected to be in China. And in China at least they knew they would be going to a mission set in the countryside and not in a big city. Nala, who had once dreaded leaving Japan, was now only too anxious to shake the dust of that country from the soles of her clogs!

What was more, ever since they had been in Tokyo they had been plagued by earth tremors; houses creaked and leaned, people ran out on to the pavements, animals stood stock still, ears back, eyes rolling. Nala had grown accustomed to earthquakes and knew what to do, but Umo had not been as bad as this; furthermore, an earth tremor in a village was not nearly as terrifying, or as dangerous, as one in a big city where a good number of the buildings were not suitably flimsy and could cause many deaths if they fell.

'Then we'll tell the ship's captain that we'll definitely be on board with him in a week. And we'll tell Father, too. I'm sure that simply knowing we're about to leave will give him a new lease of life.'

\* \* \*

The sea was smooth, the sky above blue. A couple of tiny, oddly shaped white clouds scudding across the heavens was the only sign that there was any wind in the whole world, so calm and pleasant was it.

John, Kei and Nala were sitting on deck, enjoying the sunshine and watching three missionary children playing a complicated game with chalk, sugar cubes and the top of a round cocoa tin. The children were all younger than Nala but nevertheless she had played with them quite a lot . . . it was good to feel young again, to be relieved of the fearful weight of having to take care of a sick man.

For John was recovering fast, not only his physical health but his mental vigour as well. He was still thin, pale and a bit shaky, but Nala did not doubt his fitness when she heard him laugh, saw his hand reach out quickly to help an elderly lady up and down the companionway.

'He feels he's going back to find something of my mother, I'm sure he does,' Nala had told Kei. 'See how he plays with those children and teases you and me about getting fat with all the good food we've been eating; it's as though he was coming out of darkness into light.'

'That's how I feel, too,' Kei confessed. 'And how you'll feel, Nala-san, when you reach China and grow to love it as John and I do.'

'Anna and Elsa like China,' Nala admitted. 'Their parents are at a mission far in the north but they're very happy. They liked Japan as well, but they were only there for a few days – a sort of staging post between their home country and China.'

Anna and Elsa were the missionary's daughters; his son, Karl, was too young, at three, to have many opinions. They were Germans, but because the children had been born and bred in China they spoke that language better, probably, than their own. Kei had given Nala a good few lessons in Cantonese already, so the children had been able to talk to one another.

But now, sitting on the deck watching the game being played, it occurred to Nala that she would like to join in, if her father and Kei did not need her. She looked across at John, eyes closed, nose pointing straight up to the sky. And Kei was embroidering a long piece of linen – no doubt part of her trousseau, for though she was not about to be married, indeed knew no one suitable, she was always making things in anticipation of that happy day when she would pledge her loyalty and obedience to some man, somewhere.

'Can I play with the others?' Nala whispered to Kei, therefore. 'I don't want to wake Father . . .'

A deep, amused voice came from the still figure by her side.

'I should hope not. As if you could wake me, Miss Nonsense, when I'm not even slightly asleep! Run off and play by all means, but play quietly just in case I should fall into a snooze.'

As Nala crossed the deck she felt a breeze on her cheek. Good, she thought, a cool breeze is nice for Father.

She reached the children and squatted down beside them. As she did so she noticed that all the pieces of sugar had slid to one side of the deck and fetched up in the scuppers against the rail – and that little, plump Karl was following suit. The child was simply sliding down the deck, giggling.

Nala half stood to go and fetch him back . . . and the breeze which had touched her cheek was suddenly like a wall of wind, forcing her unwillingly back. The deck continued to slope, steeper and steeper, until it was like the side of a house. Below her, the sea was no longer smooth and blue; it was black, the waves, white-crowned, rearing up like mountains and the noise battering at her eardrums.

Nala tried to glance behind her, to call to Kei and John for help, but she could not turn her head, being too busy trying to keep a scrabbling hold on the deck. The wind tore at her eyelids, her hair lashed across her face like a whip, she heard screaming, voices . . . and then she managed to grab hold of something and it was Anna, and Anna was holding on to Elsa, and Kei was gripping Nala by the neck as a mother cat grips her kitten and trying to tow all three of them back from the terrible sea, up the wall of the deck and into shelter.

Three of them. Where was Karl? Kei had got them into the top of the companionway and, once in its shelter, she could look out at the scene of madness which was the deck of the ship.

The waves were breaking over the rail now, crashing on to the decking, and there, pressed flat against the rail by the wind, was her father, with Karl in his arms. The little boy had his face against John's shoulder and John, bent double, was taking the brunt of the water against his own back whilst trying desperately to claw his way back up the sloping deck to the comparative safety of the companionway.

'What is it?' Nala heard one of the small girls say, in Chinese, to Kei. In the wild storm the words were lost, whipped out of Kei's mouth even as they were uttered, and just as Nala, bending double and clinging with all her strength on to the frame round the companionway, began to edge her way out to take the child from her father, she heard one word, shrieked even above the scream of the wind and the thunder and roar of the sea.

'Typhoon!'

But she was launched on her mad career now, unable, even if she had wanted to, to stop. She slithered down the deck and her hand reached out for her father's . . . perhaps, together, they might regain the shelter of the companionway, keeping the child safe between them.

The deck was slanting in the opposite direction suddenly, the waves which had broken over John receding a little. Now John was coming downhill towards her and it was Nala who was struggling up a long slope.

They met, their hands touched . . . and with the abruptness of a door slamming the deck tilted once more and a huge comber, black and green-grey, curled up high over their heads. Nala grabbed for John and felt hands clutch . . . then the great sea was descending, as fast as a steam-train, on top of them.

244

It hit her with the force of a hammer, driving her down on to the planks of the deck, tons of water tearing at her, suffocating her, making her slither despite herself along the wood. She felt her skin tear, her bones grind and crunch, but she still clung to the hands which had caught at hers. She was losing consciousness, the water was all about her, she could not breathe . . .

And then the water drained away and she saw the companionway only a few feet away, with the round-eyed, terrified faces of the children framed in it and Kei, on all fours, crawling towards her.

Nala uncurled herself stiffly, and Karl was clutched to her breast. He was not breathing and his face had a greyish whiteness which was terrifying.

'Kei . . . he's drowned!' Nala towed the child's body and Kei reached her and helped. They got themselves and Karl into the shelter of the companionway and Kei put the small body on the top stair and began desperately pumping his chest in and out, moving his arms, with his head hanging down over the top step. And suddenly there was water gushing out of his mouth like a small fountain, and then he gave a gasp and a little choke and began to cry, a faint mew little more than a kitten's first sound.

'He's alive!' Nala said. She looked around her, began to smile . . . and then the smile froze. 'Where's my father?'

The round eyes looked past her, over her shoulder. Nala whipped round. The deck still heaved, the sea still threatened, but there was no living soul out there to see.

She could not believe it at first. Even when the typhoon abated and they could – and did – search the ship from stem to stern she could not believe it. Only when Kei sat her down and made her listen could she begin to accept what had happened.

'Nala, listen to me. Your father died saving Karl . . . if it had not been for him Karl would have been drowned. It was a good way to die, darling; he would have wanted to die like that rather than of a fever in a foreign land! You must grieve, of course you must, but you must grieve with pride, for John was the bravest and the best. Now do you want me to tell you what happened?'

She had refused to listen at first, in her frantic search, her frantic hope, but now, three hours later, she nodded dully. Nothing could be worse than this, nothing.

'He passed the child to you . . . you were further up the deck than he was, nearer to safety, you see. And then the wave caught you both, but it caught him off-balance, still standing. You were on your knees, so you just remained flattened to the deck. John was lifted up by the mass of water and taken right over the side. Oh, dearest, he didn't suffer; it was too quick, too final. He must have died before he even hit the sea. His only thought was for Karl, you see, not a whisper of worry for himself. If

245

he had curled round the child he might have saved himself . . . but he must have known it was far likelier that the child would die under the weight of water. Oh, Nala, it's cruelly hard, but John would be happy to know you understood what he did!'

'I do understand,' Nala said. 'The Behmanns understand. Mrs Behmann keeps saying he was a saint. But Kei, understanding isn't enough! I want him here, I want him for me!'

'Of course you do . . . oh, of course you do. But perhaps it's Adeline's turn now, my dearest heart. Do you think that perhaps Adeline has been without her John long enough? As I pined for China, so Adeline must have pined for her John. For twelve years they've been kept apart, my littlest love, but now they're together. Can't you let that comfort you just a bit?'

'It should,' Nala said. She was weeping. Big tears slid down her cheeks and ran down her neck and wetted the collar of her blue cotton tunic. 'Father would say . . . he'd gone to his . . . reward . . . but it doesn't seem like that, not to me. It seems as if he's been punished for being brave and kind.'

'No, no,' Kei mourned, kneeling in front of the younger girl, her eyes steady on Nala's face though they were brimming over with tears. 'If you felt that it was *us* who had been punished . . . but even that is not for us to say. God wills, my dearest love, God wills.'

On the day the ship docked the sky was blue again, the treacherous sea rippling like a length of watered silk. Kei and Nala had made their plans, for it had very soon occurred to Kei that without John they had no place, and no one would want them in the little mission that John had been allocated.

'If we declare ourselves, go to the mission and say what's happened, they'll send you away from me, back to England, to the old man in the old house that John talked about sometimes,' Kei told her charge. 'If we go quietly away by ourselves, though, Nala, we can at least be together.'

'I'm not going to be sent away from you,' Nala said between gritted teeth. 'I've lost everything else; I won't lose you. But Kei, how shall we live?'

'I've thought that all out,' Kei said. Nala looked at her friend's face and saw by her shadowed eyes and pale skin that she had probably spent nights lying awake and making plans. 'I am an experienced *amah* and also an experienced housekeeper. I can cook, in both the English and the Chinese style, and I can clean . . . I can even garden. So I shall get work in a rich man's compound as a servant and you, as my little sister, will live under his roof too and go to school with the other children until you are old enough to work for yourself.'

'Could we do that?' Nala asked. 'I won't deceive my mother's father, nor John's father either – I'll let them know I'm safe; but I won't be sent back there, I won't! We'll stay together, Kei, just you and me. It's what my father and my mother would have wanted.

In truth, Kei was infinitely dear to Nala now, dearer than she had ever been. She could not bear the thought of travelling further over the sea to go to a man she had never met whose very language would be strange to her, for she had all but forgotten her English. Furthermore, she had somehow got hold of the idea that all her relatives, even the old man in the old house, were missionaries, and dearly though she had loved her father she was not a devout child, nor did she much admire the missionaries she had known in Japan. The Behmanns were kind enough, their children delightful, but she would not have chosen the family as friends in ordinary circumstances. She disliked the way they tried to force their own beliefs on the sailors and officers on the boat, and guessed that it was such a natural thing for them to do that they could no more stop it than stop breathing. But Nala, brought up by John, had a good deal of respect for the religions of others, and though she had never considered either Shinto or Buddhism as an alternative to Christianity, she knew from what her father had taught her that all religions had their good points and that none should simply be dismissed out of hand or ridiculed by an unbeliever.

'Then when the ship docks we will go on together,' Kei said with simple satisfaction. 'We have each other now, Nala . . . just two orphaned sisters in Jesus.'

Nala's eyebrows rose.

'You don't want us to be *nuns*, do you, Kei?'

Kei laughed.

'Nuns? Indeed I don't; I want to get married and have children one of these days! No, but anyone can see we aren't sisters by blood; we are sisters by faith and adoption, I suppose I meant.'

'That is what Father would want, to know we were together,' Nala said. 'We won't be able to take much luggage, though, and none of our lovely furniture and books and things.'

'They'll be kept for you for when you need them,' Kei said with simple faith in the honesty of missions. 'The ship docks in a few hours, Nala. Do you want to leave a message or a letter with the Behmanns so that they can pass it on to your relatives?'

'That's a very good idea,' Nala said. Accordingly she went to the small cabin she and Kei shared and wrote a brief letter saying that she was going with Kei to friends and would be quite all right. Then she gave the note to Elsa to give to her parents 'after we've landed, please, Elsa', and prepared to pack her belongings.

'What a huge, muddling place Shanghai is,' Kei said as the two girls left the ship with their cases and made their way across the docks. 'This isn't like China, Nala, this place has many, many nationalities . . . there was a black man directing traffic, did you see?'

'Yes, I saw,' Nala said, clutching Kei's hand nervously. 'Where shall we go tonight? To an inn somewhere? Oh, the noise of the traffic!'

'We're going to go straight to the railway station to catch a train which will take us far from here,' Kei said firmly. 'We'll get a ticket to somewhere small and quiet where we can rest for a few days and think.'

'I wish I could speak better Chinese,' Nala said presently, as they wove their way through the crowds. 'I keep hearing tantalizing little snatches of conversation, understanding a bit and then losing the meaning again. I should have tried harder when you were teaching me, Kei.'

'You're doing very well,' Kei assured her charge. 'Ah, there's the railway station . . . how huge it is! We will have a meal at this eating-house and then catch our train. Come along, we've got enough money to do ourselves quite well.'

Nala, who had been eating a conglomeration of English, Japanese and Chinese food all her short life, very much enjoyed the meal and delighted Kei by saying so several times. When it was finished she stood up, dusting crumbs off her lap.

'Well, Elsa will have delivered my note by now, so it's probably time we were off. Will people chase us, Kei? After all, we're not hurting anyone.'

'No, they won't chase us, they'll understand. Straight to the station now, I think. You wait with the luggage whilst I buy the tickets.'

The two of them, still holding hands, still carrying their small suitcases, disappeared into the throngs on the station as a teardrop disappears into a lake.

And at the dock Elsa, wildly excited by arriving in China once more, suddenly remembered the note she had been given and plunged a small and sticky hand into her pocket.

The note had gone. Elsa glanced round her, then decided to say nothing. It could not have been important, after all, she told herself, for no one would give anything important to a little girl like her!

John had been drowned in September but it was past Christmas before Sidney Warburton gave up the search for his granddaughter. He had been told of his son-in-law's death and had immediately cabled to the mission in Shanghai, asking them to put Miss Sawyer and her companion, if the other girl agreed, on the first ship bound for England. A series of confusing messages had resulted, so Sidney had hurried up to London to talk to the people in the mission office there. The result had been a long letter from a Mrs Behmann who, it transpired, had travelled on the same ship as the Sawyers and whose small son had been saved from drowning by John just before he died.

Mrs Behmann wrote in German, and the letter had to be translated by one of the missionaries, but the story seemed clear enough. After John's death the Behmanns had done their best to comfort the child but she had clung to her *amah* and the two girls had nursed their grief alone. When the ship docked they had left together, everyone had assumed to head for the mission where John was to have taken up his place. They had never arrived there. Mrs Behmann, out of gratitude for her son's life, had gone to great lengths to try to trace his daughter, but without success. She had managed to find people who had seen the couple making their way through Shanghai, she had even interviewed a waiter at an eating house just outside the station and several rickshaw coolies who had noticed the two girls enter the railway terminal. After that they had simply disappeared into the seething millions of China.

Sidney Warburton had offered rewards, sent a clerk from his solicitor over as his envoy, all expenses paid, had put advertisements in the papers, but in vain. Before Philip returned to school after Christmas he visited his godfather to hear the latest on the disappearance of the little girl whom Sidney wanted to love as he had loved Adeline, to find his godfather almost in tears over his complete lack of success.

'When summer comes, you and I will go ourselves, eh, Philip?' the older man said. 'I won't give up like this. Surely no harm could come to a lass of twelve in a country with missionaries scattered over every mile of it? I dare say she and the *amah* are in a decent house, waiting for me to arrive, eh? Well, I'm a stranger to her; you can't expect her to trust me yet. Poor little soul . . . poor little Adeline.'

Philip sympathized, and assured his godfather in cheerful tones that he would be happy to go with him to China when summer came. But although he kept his feelings to himself, he felt terribly sorry for Sidney Warburton.

Look at it how he might, he could not believe they would ever see Addy's girl alive.

# CHAPTER EIGHTEEN

In the night the snow had fallen thickly, the first snow of winter. When Nala awoke and struggled out of her quilts to pad to the window, she scarcely recognized the courtyard. It was perhaps a foot deep in snow, the willows hung with icicles, the pine trees bearing a deep burden of white on each branch, every needle spread to hold the weight.

'Kei! It's been snowing!'

She and Kei shared a sleeping platform and a pile of quilts because it was warmer for the two of them to curl up together. But because Kei was a servant here and herself just a dependant, they shared the small room with others as well. Loa Kang, P'ei Shan and Falia Kang were all fellow-servants, all unmarried, and the three of them curled up under quilts on the sleeping platform with Kei and Nala.

'Kei? Did you hear me?'

A mutter from one of the other servants indicated that she very much wished Nala would shut up so that everyone could get some sleep. Nala had quickly learned to speak the language; it was not after all so very different from Japanese, and in any case Kei had often spoken to her and John in Chinese. It was English which had got rarer and rarer as her father grew more fluent in Japanese himself. Now, Nala turned from the fascinating scene at the window and shivered, then gave a huge jump, landing back amidst the quilts once more. Kei, a portion of whom had been hidden in the quilts on which Nala had landed, squeaked a protest and jerked herself crossly away, then opened one dark, liquid eye and sighed deeply.

'Am I to have no peace, little wicked one? The other children sleep until they're woken – why can't you do the same? Presently I have to get up and cook for the family whilst you go off to school. We should rest whilst we have the chance.'

All this was said in a breathy whisper, but nevertheless, from the groans and the elaborate way in which the other sleepers clutched the quilts around their ears, it was keeping the girls awake when they would much sooner have continued to sleep. Nala burrowed back into the quilts and poor Kei squeaked again when her charge's icy feet collided accidentally with her nice warm ones.

'*Must* you wriggle so? What's so exciting about snow, anyway? It will probably snow for weeks now. You'll soon get sick of it.'

'I shan't,' Nala muttered, curling up with her arms round her knees. 'It's the most beautiful, the most beautiful . . .'

'Silence,' moaned Loa, the eldest of the servants in the room. 'The most beautiful thing is silence, right now. Quiet, little chatterer, or I shall personally make sure that you have no breakfast.'

'Your wish is my command,' Nala said cheekily, but it was warm in the quilts and the snow, as Kei had indicated, would not go away for several weeks yet. Soon, she slept.

Later she woke to find herself alone. The others had taken pity on her and gone quietly about the work of dressing and getting ready for the day. Nala jumped up, scattering quilts, and reached for her clothes, which were kept on the sleeping platform so that they would be warmed. The little charcoal brazier beneath the platform would burn for another hour at the most, so she had better get herself washed and dressed quickly. The servants shared a bathhouse with the big jars in which one immersed oneself by crouching up to the neck in hot water, but that was not possible at this busy hour of the morning, when the family needed the servants to carry hot water for their own baths. All Nala would get by way of a wash, therefore, would be a quick, cold, strip-down sluice, standing in the little brick-paved bathhouse. Not wanting to waste time, Nala crammed on her clothes before going through to the bathhouse, keeping a weather eye on her surroundings in case someone saw her skipping out unwashed, or rather dressed before washed, and told Kei, but there was no one about. Nala donned clogs, glad that the distance to be covered was short, and sprinted, but even so the snow soaked her thin socks and the hem of her trousers. Gaining the bathhouse, she had the briefest possible wash, pushed her hair out of her eyes with her fingers, and then dashed back to their sleeping quarters. Back in the warm, she relaxed a little. A hand-carved wooden comb soon tidied her hair and after that all she had to do was to arrange the quilts in four neat piles, scatter the charcoal in the brazier so that it dulled and died, and make her way through to the kitchen where the servants' breakfast would presently be served.

It was rather exciting, wading across the courtyard through the thick snow with the cold air tingling in her nostrils and the kitchen, transformed by the thick snow on the roof and the dangling icicles, looking a bit like the gingerbread house in 'Hansel and Gretel'. But once inside, it was the same as usual, a big room crowded with people, the smell of food enticing, and Cook doling out green tea, fry-cakes, sliced belly pork and bean sprouts.

We were lucky to get to this house, Nala thought, taking her plate from the cook and going across to the big wooden table to sit down and eat. This was the family compound of the Te Ku family. They were big landowners and important people, and their family by now must have numbered a hundred or so souls. There were the old people, the great-grandparents of the children of Nala's own age who thronged the court-yards; the grandparents who ruled, though they always deferred to their own parents, then the children's parents, all with their own apartments and courtyards yet all within the compound. Then there were the unmar-ried aunts and uncles, those widowed and alone, and finally the children themselves. A hundred souls, Nala reflected, was probably a conservative estimate of the family's numbers.

The Te Ku family lived in a small, walled village close by a mighty river, in country as wild as it was beautiful. The mountains were no more than a day's walk away, untilled save for tiny farmsteads whose owners scraped a living from the thin soil.

'There are tigers in the mountains,' the beautiful, spoilt elder son of the old man's favourite concubine told Nala. His name was Ouyang, and he was just a year older than Nala and the handsomest boy she thought she had ever seen. His skin was pale, but burnt brown from the sun in summer, his hair was thick and black, capping his head and so shiny that it made one blink, and his eyes were the true almond shape. He was tall, athletic, with a ready laugh . . . Nala adored him and sympathized with the village girls who clamoured to sit next to him in class and brought him little presents – a tiny tortoise-child, no bigger than a hen's egg, with a shell still a pale, goldy brown, a handful of walnuts saved from the autumn crop, a shiny propelling pencil bought in the big city. But he took no particular notice of any of them, saving his friendship for the foreign devil who spoke such excellent Chinese that people often mistook her for a native.

'I don't believe it,' Nala said at once, for her knowledge of tigers was slim; there were none in Japan.

'Well, it's true. Tigers and the hairy man of the mountains, too. He stands taller than a man, with a big, broad chest which he beats to terrify his enemies. He has almost no nose, little bright eyes, and fangs like the tusks of the wild boar. Oh, and there are bears, as well, which look very pretty with their black and white coats and their smiling faces. But they have long, curved claws and will rip you to death as soon as look at you.'

'I don't believe *any* of it,' Nala said grandly. 'You make it all up, Ouyang, to terrify me.'

'Wait until the summer, when we go to the mountains for picnics and parties; then you'll see I speak the truth,' Ouyang said, laughing at her, but Nala had the last laugh.

'If it's true, why go to the mountains?' she challenged him. 'Not even the mighty Ouyang Te Ku can enjoy being eaten, clawed to death and beaten into the ground by the Man of the Mountains.'

'You're a clever one, Nala Chang,' Ouyang said, not at all ruffled by her success but apparently rather enjoying it. 'One of these days you'll be wandering in the mountains and a tiger will gobble you up and you'll think *Ouyang was right* as he takes you down all in one swallow.'

Nala had taken Kei's name as being easier to explain than if she were to admit to Sawyer. And indeed, living constantly amongst the Chinese in the compound, going to school with them, thinking all the time in their language, she had almost forgotten that her name was not, in fact, Chang.

But all this was going to change. On this very day, this snowy first day of real winter, she was to go out of the village and across to another one, even smaller than theirs, where a retired missionary and his wife lived, giving lessons to make their pension go further.

'Mr and Mrs Hamish Ellis will teach you English for a few *cash*,' Kei had explained the day before, returning triumphant from a visit to the missionaries. 'They are very nice people and they quite see the advantage, for I told them you once spoke English a lot.'

'I don't mind,' Nala had said. 'But what *is* the advantage, Kei? I don't suppose I'm ever likely to need English now, do you?'

'Yes, of course you will one day, when you decide to go back to your own kind,' Kei said briskly. 'But I told them that the Te Ku family wish you to teach English to their children, and of course this way the mistress will only pay for one child to be taught. The rest will be taught free, by you.'

'I shan't teach them for nothing,' Nala said firmly. 'I must be paid, Kei, so that I can help you when you need something.'

'Yes, that's true. The old mistress said she would pay you, but not as much as she would have to pay the Ellises. And in addition, Nala, you will be here, on the spot, to do your teaching. As each child is old enough you will start; that's how the old mistress plans it. I must say I think it's a very good idea. In the big cities a lot of English is spoken, and most of the traders expect a businessman to know English.'

'I'll do it because I want to help you,' Nala said. 'But when I'm old enough I'm going to be a potter.'

'Yes, my little one . . . but girls aren't potters, not in China, nor in Japan. A girl is a wife, you see. Even I, even poor Kei, will be a wife one day.'

'Soon,' Nala said firmly, knowing how Kei longed to be married. 'As soon as we have saved a bride-price.'

'Yes. There is a fine upstanding young man who comes to the market to sell his vegetables . . . he looks at me and I look at him, and perhaps we wish we could get to know one another . . . I think he could do with a strong wife to help him till his acres, and a good little sister to teach English and play *amah* to the babies when they come.'

'Soon,' Nala reiterated, smiling affectionately at the older girl. 'It will all happen just as you say, dearest Kei.'

And today I'm going to learn English from two old missionaries, Nala told herself, putting her chopsticks down on her well-polished plate, for the cook was good at his job. Today I shall go to their bungalow and try to remember the words I used with Papa . . . the words which are really my own language, though they don't seem at all like it. And once I start remembering, and I suppose I shall, then I shall be able to pay dearest Kei back for the kindness she has shown to me since Father died . . . no, long before then . . . from the time I was born she showed me kindness, for she stayed and looked after me and loved me when she would far rather have returned to her own land across the sea.

The cook turned in her direction. He grinned, showing the gaps between his strong white teeth. He was quite a young man, but too much of his own good cooking had wreaked havoc with his teeth, though because of the state of them he was now eschewing most of the sweetmeats at which he excelled.

'Did you like that, little Nala? Was it good?'

Nala called that it was excellent as always, Cooky-san, the best food she had ever tasted, and the cook went off into hoots of laughter both at the Japanese title and at her use of the English word 'Cooky'. He bowed and Nala bowed too; neat little bows, dozens of them, as she made her way out into the snow once more.

Outside, a wind had got up. It whisked the top of the snow towards her, causing a miniature snowfall again as it also brought the snow tumbling from the pines. But Nala gritted her teeth and ploughed across the courtyard, under the arch and into her sleeping quarters. She was already wearing the quilted jacket and thicker trousers which all Chinese peasants wore in winter, but now she added another layer: a bigger jacket and another pair of trousers, more socks, and finally a bright pair of local boots. She knew she must look like a football, absolutely shapeless and extremely unwieldy, but everyone looked the same so there was no shame in it. She searched the room for a stub of pencil and a notebook – the old mistress had sent both to her when she had announced she wanted Nala to learn English well enough to teach the children – and then, with her hair tucked into her collar to give added insulation, Nala set off.

She crossed the courtyard, went under an arch, and found herself in the entrance yard. There was a big gate and a porter who spent his working hours in a little booth to the right of the gate so that he could monitor all who went in or out. He was eating an apple and stopped to grin at Nala and to say cheerfully, 'Off to get an education, are you? No school for you today, then?'

'Not today . . . well, I suppose it's like school, really,' Nala told him. 'It's just for the morning – after noon I shall be back in school, I suppose. And we're doing sums, which I'm no good at, so I wouldn't mind if it snowed worse and I had to stay at the missionary bungalow for a week,' she added.

The old man laughed and spat an apple pip into the snow at his feet. It sank, leaving no trace.

'It will snow again,' he prophesied. 'But you won't do sums this afternoon, not with the new snow down. The teachers will take you out to enjoy the snow . . . did they not do so in Japan? Or don't they have snow over there, the yellow dwarves?'

It had taken Nala a little while to come to terms with the strong dislike, one might almost call it hatred, that the Chinese felt for the Japanese. But now she accepted that the two peoples disliked one another and tried not to take it personally. Indeed, she could understand it to an extent. The Chinese had been beaten in combat by the Japanese, and far from leaving when they had done their conquering the Japanese had retained an iron hold upon that part of China where they had fought. What red-blooded Chinese could possibly like a country who did that? When the Manchus had marched into China and beaten them in battle they had, in time, become Chinese themselves, but Japan was not like that. Japan took, she did not become a part of. She sent her little warriors to steal, not merely to conquer.

But now Nala answered the porter at the gate truthfully.

'Yes, they have snow in Japan,' she assured him. 'Deep snow, too, as deep as it lies out there; and in the island of Hokkaido, in the north, they have worse snow and much colder weather altogether. But I don't remember ever being taken out to enjoy the snow whilst I was in Japan.'

The porter shrugged.

'Well, that's our custom, as you'll discover for yourself this afternoon. Good learning, little one!'

Nala replied with quick little bows and took herself off over the snow in giant strides, soon growing weary of this, however, and using a more normal tread.

She knew where the other village was situated, having been taken there once or twice when Kei needed to buy something not available in their own village. The Ellises' bungalow had been built in a pretty little glade halfway up a gentle hill. A stream ran close by and the old man had enclosed a part of it, and he had built a bridge, as well, leading to the road which, in its turn, led to his gates.

Nala had never seen the bungalow, of course, since it was surrounded, as were all private houses, by high walls to discourage bandits and the soldiers of roving war lords, but she knew quite well how to reach it.

She found it harder going in the snow than she had anticipated, though. It was too early in the day for the narrow track to have had much traffic and most of the way Nala was blazing her own trail the hard way, pushing through virgin snow. She enjoyed it, though, her cheeks soon hot, her breath coming quickly and warmth tingling up from the soles of her feet to the top of her head.

Presently, to her vague annoyance, it began to snow again. The flakes fell like iced kisses on her cheeks and danced before her eyes, but it was not a storm, so she pressed on. Despite knowing the way she became a little worried, for the country looked so different covered in snow. A bamboo glade she always particularly admired seemed to have disappeared, until she saw it in quite a different position to how she remembered it. When at last she saw the high arch of the bridge with the beautiful carved handrails on either side she felt relieved. What a silly creature she would look to get lost just because of a little snow! But her face was saved, for the bridge was only yards away from her and the bungalow merely a short way beyond.

She reached the bridge and stood for a moment looking down into the water. It flowed swiftly here, though the edges of it were dulled by ice, creeping out from the banks. Nala frowned. Just for a moment she had a sense of *déjà vu*, of having been here before, seen ice encroaching on water just like this, but then it passed and she was looking hopefully towards the bungalow. She did hope Mr and Mrs Ellis would offer her a hot drink when she reached their dwelling; she was beginning to feel cold despite the healthy glow the exercise had given her.

The gatekeeper saw her and came out.

'Hurry along, little one, for the snow will soak you to the skin,' he called, so Nala ran over the bridge, down on to the road, and along to the gateway. She bowed several times to the gatekeeper, and stood waiting whilst he rang the big bell. A woman came to the door and smiled at her, beckoning her within. Nala ran, then did her little bows once she was in the shelter of the bungalow.

'Good day,' the woman said. 'I'm Mrs Ellis's servant. She said you would be along shortly. She's going to teach you, today, whilst she does some cooking. So come along to the kitchen, please, my dear.'

She was a friendly-looking Chinese of perhaps fifty, though Nala always found it difficult to guess at the age of anyone over fourteen. However, she ushered Nala into a big, warm kitchen with a wood-burning stove and a scrubbed wooden table, bowed a couple of times at the occupant and left them alone.

'Hello, Nala . . .' the woman began, then stopped short. She stared. So did Nala.

Mrs Ellis was a grey-haired little lady, very small indeed, even shorter than Nala. She had a round, cheerful, rosy little face with hazel eyes, a retroussé nose and a wide, comfortable smile. When she spoke Nala discovered that she had a deep voice for such a very small, very feminine little person, with a slight accent with was strange to the child.

'Nala, forgive my surprise, but no one told me you were a European! Where are your parents? I am sure the girl who came here said you were living with the Te Ku family, in their compound.'

'Yes, we are. Kei is my sister, the only relative I have left in the whole world,' Nala told her, airily killing off, by her words, the old man in the old house and her father's doctor-parents, let alone the uncles John had mentioned, and her cousins. 'Our father and mother died long ago.'

'I see. Then . . . as your name is Chang, your mother must have been European?'

'Yes. She was. But I don't remember her; she died soon after I was born. Kei looks after me.'

'And Kei is your half-sister?'

Nala looked blank. Mrs Ellis began to explain, then changed her mind.

'How rude of me, to shoot questions at you like that! Now, Nala, I am going to bake some bread and you may stand by me and ask any questions you like. Your . . . your sister told me that you speak some English, but not very much. What I thought I'd do at first is to address you in English and perhaps tell you what I'm doing in English and see how much you remember. All right?'

'That will be interesting,' Nala said politely. In English, she added, 'I love you, goodnight, my child, say your prayers now, give your old father a kiss . . .' and then stopped short, feeling foolish.

'Very good!' Mrs Ellis said, looking a little taken aback. 'Now, here we go!' She picked up a small shovel and began to scoop flour out of a big sack into a yellow mixing bowl. 'This is flour; do you know flour, Nala? Say flour, after me. This is flour.'

* * *

256

It was an interesting morning and Nala enjoyed every moment of it. When Mrs Ellis had made the dough for the bread, she and Nala had a cup of what the older woman described as 'real tea', a brew which Nala had never tasted before and which she at first thought very nasty. However, it was hot and it became sweet when she pulled a face and Mrs Ellis, laughing, added two spoonsful of sugar.

After they had drunk their tea they sampled what Mrs Ellis called 'scones', a kind of bready, caky thing with currants. They ate the scones with butter and jam, and Nala enjoyed them very much. Then they talked a bit more, but all in English, to Nala's initial disappointment. She was a garrulous child and wanted to know all sorts of things about the Ellises and the bungalow which, as yet, she was totally incapable of asking in English, but Mrs Ellis was a good enough teacher – and a good enough psychologist, too – to realize that by whetting her pupil's interest and curiosity she would provide a strong spur to learning.

In fact, Nala's progress astonished her. By the end of the baking session the child was dredging up from her memory whole chunks of English . . . words, sentences, phrases. Some she simply repeated parrot-fashion, but others she clearly understood, and as they talked she began to understand more and more of what Mrs Ellis said to her, though she had to scowl with concentration and keep asking for repeats, or an easier word.

'You are doing very well indeed, Nala,' Mrs Ellis said, when her husband popped his head round the kitchen door to remind her that he was hungry and her lesson must be over. 'If you come every morning I think by the end of a month you'll be speaking very fluently indeed.'

'That little girl . . . she's a European,' Mr Ellis remarked over a very English luncheon of oxtail soup, ham and mashed potatoes, followed by an apple pie. 'Whatever is she doing in the village, living in the Te Ku compound as a servant?'

'She's not entirely European,' Mrs Ellis said, looking worried. 'I think she's a little half-and-half, my dear. But she looks pure English, wouldn't you think?'

'Yes. In fact, I'd swear to it,' her husband told her. Unlike his wife he was a very tall man, straight as an arrow despite being over seventy, and it was his proud boast that he had all his hair still, though it's once-dark locks had faded to a pale mouse-brown. He had a gentle, scholarly face, thin but with high cheekbones, and dreamy brown eyes. He looked what he was: a good and contented man.

'Swear to it? To her being English, you mean? Oh, but Hamish . . .'

'My dear, that little face never owns to Chinese blood! If she thinks she's half-Chinese then let her keep her illusions, but she's not.'

'Don't you think so? But her name's Nala Chang, and her sister's all Chinese, not even half-and-half. She does have very black hair, love, and she speaks Chinese like a native.'

'No doubt; she's living in a Chinese house surrounded by the natives and probably hasn't spoken anything but Chinese for months and months. Well well, what a mystery! But I trust you to fathom it out before too long.'

His wife nodded. Her head was covered with tiny, silvery-grey curls which bobbed up and down, giving her more than ever the appearance of an elderly but angelic cherub.

'I'll fathom it out, if there's anything to fathom,' she agreed. 'But in fact, Hamish, since the child said her parents had both been dead for a long time, she may not know the truth herself. As for the elder sister . . . she couldn't be less like! She's short and squat and sturdy, dark-skinned, not at all beautiful, her hair's thick and coarse . . . really, they're quite different.'

'That'll be because they aren't sisters, of course,' her husband said, forking ham placidly into his mouth. 'I am not a natural cynic – in fact I would say I was rather a credulous man – but believe that child is a half-and-half I cannot! What is her English like?'

'Awfully good. I'm not teaching her the language so much as reminding her,' his wife told him. 'Dear me, Hamish, have we stumbled upon a mystery here? What an adventure! Well, I hope we may help the dear little creature, for I've taken a great fancy to her. I'd hate to think of her becoming a servant to the Te Ku family, pleasant though they may be. We must do our best to see that she goes back where she belongs . . . if she knows where she belongs, of course.'

'Quite. But we mustn't interfere, and we mustn't frighten her off,' Hamish Ellis said. 'Play her gently, my dear, play her gently.'

Nala, plodding home through the still-falling snow, was totally unaware that she was a mystery. Indeed, right now, with her fingers freezing cold and her toes quite numb, she felt very commonplace indeed, and positively longed for the warmth of the Te Ku kitchen and one of Cooky-san's meat dumplings, all hot from the soup.

She was not halfway home, however, when she saw someone toiling towards her across the snow. She peered through the dizzying flakes. Was it her dearest Kei? But as they got closer she saw that it was Ouyang, dressed in his best red quilted coat and tugging a sledge behind him.

'Hua, little Nala!' he shouted when he was near enough. 'Look, I've come to give you a ride home.'

'Oh, how glad I am to see you!' Nala exclaimed. 'Isn't it cold, Ouyang? I'm terribly tired in my legs, as well. I was just longing to sit down and rest.'

'You mustn't ever do that in the snow,' Ouyang told her, looking shocked. 'Didn't your mother tell you that if you lie down in the snow you'll fall asleep and never wake up? Now come on, hop on to the sledge and I'll get on behind you. Fortunately the ground slopes most of the way; we'll be home in no time.'

'Wonderful,' Nala said, taking her seat with her knees under her chin and her arms wrapped round them. 'Is it school this afternoon? The gatekeeper said we would enjoy the snow with our teacher, but I can't see that happening if the snow keeps falling like this.'

'You're right. We're not going to school this afternoon. We're all to go into great-grandmother's room, and she will tell us stories and we'll roast chestnuts on the stove. I expect they will be *improving* stories,' he added gloomily, 'But even an improving story will be better than those confounded sums.'

As he talked he was trying to climb aboard the sledge while stopping it from skidding into motion before he was settled, and after some grunts and exclamations of annoyance he thumped into position, grabbed Nala round the waist and said, 'Take the strings and steer . . . we're off!'

They were. Careering downhill, frequently missing the path beneath the snow altogether and shooting off over the frozen stubble, snowflakes pressed into their faces by the wind of their going, Nala and Ouyang bucketed over the uneven ground, whizzed round a tall pine tree and spilled off the sledge, giggling mightily, just outside the Te Ku compound.

'That was all right,' Ouyang said negligently, picking himself up and dusting off the snow as best he could. 'You all right, Nala? Shall we go down again, or shall we get some food first?'

'Food first,' Nala said; she was extremely hungry. 'Thank you for fetching me, Ouyang.'

'That's all right. How did you get on with the old foreign devils, by the way. Were they kind to you?'

'Yes indeed, very kind. I know quite a lot of English already, though as the lady said she didn't exactly teach me, she made me remember what I'd forgotten. Shall I say some to you? Then you will learn faster than the other children.'

'Not now. But if we come sledging again this afternoon you can say it to me then. I would like, particularly, to learn faster than Chien Te Ku.'

Chien was older than Ouyang and the son of their father's wife instead of a concubine, though this did not necessarily mean that he would get a better inheritance when their father died. Nevertheless Ouyang was always eager to prove himself the cleverer and braver of the two.

'You will learn faster anyway, because you have a better memory and a keener mind,' Nala pointed out as they towed the sledge under the arch into the central compound. 'Oh, what a marvellous smell; how hungry I am!'

'It is good,' agreed Ouyang, sniffing the air. 'Will you eat with us today?'

'No, with Kei. She'll want to know how I got on. It is to earn her a dowry that I'm learning to speak English again, don't forget, Ouyang.'

'I don't forget. See you later, little Nala.'
The two children hurried on their separate ways.

# CHAPTER NINETEEN

Philip lay on his back, a canteen of tea held between both hands, and gazed up through the leaves and the fruit growing overhead, deep into the brilliant blue of the sky.

They said it was all over bar the shouting, that the Turkish Army had surrendered. Certainly Philip knew for himself that Damascus had fallen, though to Colonel Lawrence and his Arabs rather than to the main British force.

'Last year, who would have dreamed that one day I'd lie in an orange grove and see the fruit ripe above my head,' Philip said dreamily, aloud. His companion, a stocky, shock-headed young man from the Black Country whose accent was so heavy that Philip had scarcely understood a word he had spoken for the first two or three weeks of their acquaintance, grunted.

'What about me, then? Scarce seen an apple on a tree, me, until now. Do you know it's November? The fellers say we'll be 'ome be Christmas.'

'They've been saying that for years, probably.' Philip hitched himself up on an elbow and sipped tea. 'Look out there,' he said, pointing. 'The Judaean Hills, and beyond them, Jerusalem. We're living in the Bible, Sockeye.'

'Aye, you're right there. The stuff they call bread . . .' The other young man pulled a face and the prominent eyes which had given him his nickname rolled expressively. 'Still, the fruit's all right.'

'And the weather.'

'Uhuh. And the women . . . what you can see of 'em.'

They both chuckled. Women swathed in long robes with their faces hidden were the norm here, though lustrous dark eyes would flash provocatively above the veils they wore round the lower part of their faces.

'When it's over . . . I wonder if we'll be given a chance to take a proper look at the country,' Philip said yearningly. 'It's so primitive . . . I saw some pottery in a village we went through a few days ago, when we were taking the Turkish stronghold at the Pass, which had been sun-dried, I reckon. It's very rough, but they've got a way of salt glazing . . .'

'It's what's in them pots I like,' growled Sockeye. He had finished his

260

own tea and turned the cup upside down on the ground. Now he produced a slice of unleavened bread and a chunk of crumbly goat's cheese. 'T'best you can say about this is it stops your belly rubbin' against your backbone.' He took a huge bite and spoke through his mouthful. 'I thought you was keen to get back and go to college? Now you're talkin' as if you want to go sightseeing!'

'No . . . I want to get back, but doesn't it seem a waste to turn tail and run home when you haven't seen the half of this country? Remember, Sock, I've never been abroad before and I don't suppose I ever will again.' He hesitated. 'Unless I go to China.'

'To China? I tell you, Phil, this is enough foreign parts to last me a lifetime. I'm for 'ome.'

'Yes, but I had another letter from my godfather a few days ago, and he's had no word from his granddaughter. She's only a kid . . . imagine it, Sockeye, a young girl of . . . well, thirteen or so . . . all alone in China! He worries, my godfather does, and I did say if he wanted to go to China to see for himself I'd go with him.'

'It's up to you, of course, but I don't reckon you could find anyone, not in a place that size. Look around you . . .' In his turn Sockeye gestured to the blue hills and the rolling countryside bright with orchards. 'What chance would you have here, where there are more goats than people? They tell me China's crowded, like.'

'Well, we'll see,' Philip said evasively. The truth was he wanted to get home and go to university, he wanted to start work in the pottery, and he wanted to go to China with his godfather. Now he also wanted to take a look at the land he had only glanced at in passing, so to speak, as he marched and fought with his regiment and chased the Turks out of the Holy Land and Arabia. He knew, of course, that he could not do all of these things, but he was anxious to cram as much experience as possible into the next year or two before he actually went into the pot-bank and settled down.

Sockeye grunted again and got to his feet, still chewing.

'Well, I'm going to see if there's any more char going. Coming?'

Philip also got to his feet.

'I might as well. Regardless of what I want I'll be told, won't I? And more char's always welcome.'

The two young men crossed the orange grove to where their section had set up a temporary cookhouse.

I'll write to Unk tonight, Philip told himself as Sidney Warburton's letter crackled in his pocket. Reassure him that I'm still alive and kicking and that I'll do whatever he wants once I get home. But it was still his privately held opinion that they would never find Addy's girl.

'The lad's coming home,' Sidney told Arnold jubilantly as the two of them, pipes gripped firmly in teeth, sat on either side of a blazing fire.

'He's said he'll come to China with me in the summer . . . I wouldn't ask it of him, Arnold, if I didn't think he'd enjoy the experience, but he's young enough to take in his stride what to me is a fearful chore. And he won't be at college then . . . he'll only need to leave the pot-bank for six or eight weeks . . . you never know!'

'I think you're mad,' Arnold said, but kindly. 'Still, if you think there's a chance you'll succeed where others have failed . . .'

'I don't know quite what I think, I just feel Adeline would expect it of me . . . John too,' Sidney said thoughtfully. 'John adored the child . . . she's all I've got.'

'Yes, and I respect your right to go searching,' Arnold assured the older man. 'But I don't think you ought to hope too much. All the missionaries and the people at the Legations and so on have told you the same thing – that it's a big country and if the child and her *amah* have decided they would prefer to remain hidden then there's very little chance of anyone finding them.'

'She's not dead,' Sidney said firmly. 'I'd know if she was dead. For some reason best known to herself she's decided to stay out of sight and remain in China.'

'It's all she knows,' Arnold reminded him gently. 'You told me John said she spoke almost no English and went to a Japanese school, mixed with the local people on equal terms. She must have been horrified at the thought of having to travel right across the world to a country she'd never even visited, to live with someone whose whole way of life would be an enigma to her. And then the *amah* – Kay, isn't it? – must have been dearer than any stranger could have been, no matter how closely connected by blood. I don't suppose she realized you'd have let her bring the Chinese woman with her.'

'You're right and she may even have done the right thing; but one day, Arnold, that child will inherit this house, these lands. I wanted her to at least see it before I die, so that I could feel I was doing the right thing by leaving it all to her. After all, her mother adored this place, so I should think she has a good chance of loving it too.'

'That's true,' Arnold said. 'But we were talking about Philip coming home . . .'

He turned the subject successfully, but later, making his way home in his Sunbeam Talbot – for the weather was too severe for walking by the river – he reflected that you could scarcely expect Addy's daughter to be very much like Addy. She had been brought up in a foreign land surrounded by people who had never seen Britain, let alone this particular small part of it. What had been bred in Addy – love for the land and for the Manor – could not possibly be present in her daughter; the circumstances were too disparate. He thought about Rose and an involuntary smile curled his lips even as he brought the car to the end of the drive and turned right into the country lane which linked the two houses. Dear little

Rose! At thirteen she was just budding into womanhood, as pretty and self-conscious a child as one could wish. She was not studious and she upset him a little by refusing to take part in any sort of sporting activity – she would not ride or skate on the river when it froze, nor did she take part in organized games at school unless she was actually forced to do so – but she already danced very well indeed, and could charm the birds out of the trees when she wished.

She went to a day-school in Langforth and sometimes brought friends home with her or visited their homes . . . she was extremely interested in clothes and the one thing at which she did excel was music. She played the piano better than most girls her age, and sang . . . like an angel, Arnold told himself now, and hooted the horn at an inoffensive mongrel dog, dawdling along the verge. Of course she got her musical ability from her mother, he supposed, and often told Rose quite proudly about her mother's stage career.

Odd, that Rose's resemblance to Lily charmed him rather than annoyed him, when you thought how angry it made him to see Lily in Philip. But then Philip had idolized his mother as a child and his very likeness to her, somehow, was a reproach.

But what he had started thinking about was how he would feel if it was Rose who was missing in a strange country, and how Rose would cope with such a happening. He could hardly bear to think of himself worrying about his child and it was simply impossible to imagine Rose having to put up with any sort of hardship. He knew she would have declared herself at once had she been in the Sawyer girl's position, because she was used to being protected and coddled and could not, he was sure, even begin to manage alone.

I'm glad she's like that, Arnold told himself, as he drove the car into the stableyard and got out to open the big garage doors. I wouldn't want her to be tough and independent. It's extremely unfeminine; unnatural even. He remembered Rose last week, wanting a particular party dress, winding round him like a cat, purring and pleasing, until he had capitulated and promised.

He got back into the car, drove it right into the garage and then climbed out again, locked up, closed the garage doors and returned to the house. The side door was unlocked as usual and he dealt with it, hung up his coat, and headed for his library and the drinks tray which would be set out ready. As he poured himself a whisky and added water he realized that he, too, would be ill-equipped to live entirely unsupported in a foreign land . . . and he was no young girl, either.

This is nonsense, he chided himself, taking a sip of the drink and feeling its warmth tingling down into his stomach. How absurd that I should compare myself with a little girl! But when he came to think about it, it was true that he had never had to stand on his own feet, not entirely. There had been the pot-bank and the money from it all his life. He had

263

tried to make, or rather cause to be made, a different type of ware at one time; he had gone to London and sold some of it to the big stores. But he had never pressed on with the venture, because it had seemed too much like hard work persuading his father to continue with the new lines, taking a chance, gambling that they would prove a financial success.

Even with the leatherworks, the money had been there, from the pot-bank, to finance the first small steps he had taken. And he had known nothing about any of it – he had merely paid men who did to do the work for him.

So . . . suppose he had been cast adrift on the world, as the Sawyer child appeared to have been? Would he have managed any better than his own small daughter? I can't throw a pot or cast one, he realized with a sense of considerable unease. I can't cure leather or stitch a saddle or dip a pot in glaze and fire it until it's hard. I can't even cook a meal or make a bed or speak a word of any language except English and a bit of schoolboy French!

Once Haslingtons had been a force to be reckoned with; his own father had started the pot-bank from scratch, after his grandfather had bought a bit of land to add to his coal mining empire and had found not coal but clay. Grandfather would have sold the rights at once but Albert, his father, would have none of it.

'Nay, Guv'nor,' he was reputed to have said. 'We'll use t'stuff; we'll mek pots!'

And make pots they had, for Albert himself had gone through the pottery with the men learning to throw a pot, to cast a pot, to fettle a pot . . . Albert had known more about glazes than most of the men doing the work now, Arnold thought with shame. He could talk about colours and finishes and shapes with the best of 'em, could my father. But what have the Haslingtons come to? Useless, that's what we are! Young Bertie might have done well, but he had been killed early on in the war, and Dorothea and Bella had married young, reared families of stolid, well-mannered children and looked all set to become grandmothers of stolid, well-mannered children in their turn. He himself had married and not even managed to keep his wife, and he had reared two children . . .

Philip! A warm glow quite unconnected with the whisky coursed through Arnold's veins at the thought of his son. Of course the Haslingtons weren't finished: there was Philip! Going to college, getting a degree, then going into the pot-bank not because it was the family business but because he wanted to do so! His rare letters from that God-forsaken part of the world . . . well, it might be the Holy Land but it was pretty wild and desolate according to popular report . . . were full of the colours he had seen, the glow of the oranges in their dark green foliage, and the pots the natives used, how they made them and baked them.

He's fought his first war, the first Haslington to do so, Arnold thought exultantly. He'll go to university, and be the first Haslington to do that, as well. And then he'll go into the pot-bank and produce something to be proud of, to give the name of Haslington an extra lustre. I'm sure of it! And he's coming home! In five or six weeks I'll be going to the station to meet him, bringing the conquering hero home!

Although Philip had no idea of it, thanks to the little Sawyer girl his welcome was now assured.

'So Kei is to marry at last,' Mrs Ellis said thoughtfully, as she and Nala made bread in the bungalow's warm and airy kitchen. 'When she goes to her new home, will you go with her?'

Despite the girls' best efforts, it had taken two years to save up the bride-price, with Nala teaching English to half the village and all the Te Ku clan and supplementing this income by working in the fields during harvest and planting times and in the house and compound when there was no agricultural work to be done. Now that her knowledge of English was complete, moreover, she worked for Mrs Ellis two or three times a week, cooking, cleaning and helping with the marketing. Now, Mrs Ellis eyed her young friend thoughtfully.

Nala had changed a lot from the twelve-year-old child who had first made her way into this kitchen two years earlier. At fourteen, she was beginning to show traces of the woman she would one day become. She was taller, with a willowy slenderness which made every movement graceful, and her figure was beginning to curve into breasts and hips from the straightness which had gone before. But her face was still that of a friendly child and her long hair, although she often plaited it now, was still a gleaming sheet of black silk.

'Go with Kei? She wants me to, but I don't think it would be a very good idea, do you? After all, Kei will want to live her own life, without me tagging behind her all the while, and she's marrying a good man. Do you know Lichou Chan, who will be her husband very soon? He has been married before so there are already three children, but Kei does not mind that at all and it means that Lichou Chan is able to provide her with a very nice home and . . . and lots of fields and so on.'

'Do you like this man?'

Nala considered carefully before she answered, for she was a truthful child.

'Like him? Yes, I suppose I like him very much. He's kind and generous and very fond of Kei. But . . . he isn't the sort of husband I'd imagined her having. He's older, you see. Kei has always talked about marrying a young man, but Lichou Chan is well past forty, maybe even fifty. The children are nice, fortunately, and will welcome Kei, but the eldest boy is twenty-three, and the next one is twenty. Only the girl is still a real child . . . Peipei is ten, younger than I am.'

'I see.' Mrs Ellis sprinkled flour on the wooden table and began to knead her big lump of dough. 'Look, Nala, I've been discussing this very matter with Hamish, and we would be happy to offer you a home with us. We can't support you properly – you know our pension is small – but we can continue to pay you for the tasks you carry out for us in food rather than in money, and we thought you could probably supplement your income as you have been doing, by working in the village. But not, my dear, in the fields, for indeed the work is too hard for one of your years. And anyway, now that Kei is to be married, you won't need the money for her bride-price.'

'That would be wonderful . . . but the Te Ku family have also said they would be glad to continue to keep me there,' Nala said rather hesitantly. 'The thing is, Mrs Ellis, I do have a reason for getting money together. I've never told you, but . . .'

'You do have relatives!' Mrs Ellis said before Nala could get another word out. 'Hamish was right – he's always said you weren't half Chinese, my dear, right from the beginning, but recently he's started saying he didn't believe you had no relatives. Is that what our little mystery visitor has been hiding for the past two years?'

Nala was so surprised that she dropped her dough. Then she laughed and began kneading it again, though the colour rose in her cheeks.

'I wasn't going to say that at all. What I was going to say was that back in Japan I had a great friend, an old potter called Amitri. I was very fond of him and he taught me a lot – not only how to make a pot and fire it, but also how best to decorate it. You've seen some of my drawings. Well, anyway, when I told him I was coming to China he told me that I should try to see the old pottery which was made here four or five hundred years ago, and then I might get ideas and try to create such works of art for myself. I never have gone into the city to museums or such places and of course I've never had the opportunity to make pots for myself. But I thought with Kei marrying, I might go to the city and see if I can get work helping a potter.'

'Really, Nala, what an impetuous little soul you are! It would be highly unsuitable – you must not even consider it. You would be at the mercy of all sorts and types of people . . . I am sure if you told the Te Ku family that you had any such intention they would speedily argue you out of it.'

'Then how am I ever going to learn?' Nala said piteously. 'Dear Mrs Ellis, when you were young, did you know you wanted to be a missionary?'

Mrs Ellis laughed. She began to press a piece of dough into a greased loaf tin.

'No indeed, for women rarely become missionaries; it was Hamish who always knew what his destiny was to be, not myself. I simply wanted to marry a good man who would take care of me and love me and give me a home and a family to bring up. Unfortunately we were not blessed with children, but otherwise, as you know, I have been happy.'

'Oh well, all right, then Mr Ellis knew right from the moment he was old enough to think about it that he wanted to be a missionary. And I, when I was big enough to think about it . . .'

'Mr Ellis wanted to be a train driver,' Mrs Ellis pointed out, waving a floury finger at Nala. 'Children rarely want what is good or right for them, Nala.'

'Oh dear, you are making it hard for me to explain! You see, from the time I started school in Japan, when I was perhaps four, I knew I wanted to draw and to make pots. I came to China when I was twelve, as you know, and for two whole years I haven't had my hands in clay and I haven't really drawn anything, except for a few little sketches when I've been with you. But inside me, like a bubble, the urge to make pots has been swelling and swelling, getting harder and harder to keep under, and now I feel I must do it or burst! So you see I thought I'd stay in the Te Ku compound until I'd saved enough money to support myself in the city or wherever I might find someone willing to teach me.'

'I see. Well, that's very laudable,' Mrs Ellis said approvingly. 'But as to your living alone in the city, that really must not happen. My dear child, there are war lords in the remote mountain areas who would buy a European girl for their harems . . . I dare not let you take such a shocking risk. Will you promise me not to try to run off until Hamish and I have talked things out?'

'Yes, of course. I've promised Kei I'll do nothing hasty,' Nala assured her. 'And if we can do it without hurting anyone's feelings, I should very much like to move in with you when Kei leaves. But I have a friend amongst the Te Ku – do you know Ouyang? – who is dear to me and must not be hurt by what he will see as my sudden defection. He believes his home is the best place in the world to be and will not easily accept I might be happier elsewhere.'

'Amongst your own kind,' nodded Mrs Ellis. 'For as I began to tell you earlier, Nala, neither Mr Ellis nor myself can believe that you had a Chinese father. My dear, don't you trust us? What is your real name?'

There was a long silence. Nala stared first at the dough beneath her hands, then at the floor, and only finally at the older woman. At last she sighed deeply.

'I'm not half-Chinese, but it's true my people are dead. I don't want to be taken back to England, to a family who might feel obliged to help me if they knew I existed. Believe me, Mrs Ellis, I'm better off here and a good deal happier. I was born in China and brought up in Japan . . . what would I do in England? And I'm awfully sorry, but if you try to find out any more about me I'll just go.'

'That seems fair enough, I suppose,' Mrs Ellis said ruefully. She picked up the full tins of dough and stood them near the wood stove to prove. 'Very well, then Nala, I'll speak to Hamish and we'll see what we can arrange with a local potter, if that's what you want. When you come next perhaps we'll have some news for you.'

\* \* \*

'My dear boy – my dear Philip!'

Philip came off the train with his kit-bag still slung over one shoulder even though he was in civvies, his uniform having been handed in some while previously. He did not recognize Arnold at first, then looked back and felt oddly disconcerted, oddly shy. He had last seen his father just over a year ago and yet . . . how the older man had shrunk! He had always been a big fellow to the young Philip, but now he's shorter than me, Philip saw, and his hair is white at the temples, his face lined. This can't have happened in a year – I must have stopped noticing what the old man looked like long before I joined the army.

'Hello, Dad.' Philip grabbed his father's hand and pumped it up and down, smiting him on the shoulder as he did so. Despite the smallness and the greyness, he found he was glad to see his father again – more than glad, delighted. And Arnold was one huge beam from ear to ear – he looked proud, Philip thought dazedly, or something very like it, at any rate.

'You look marvellous, old boy – life in His Majesty's Forces suits you, it seems! You've absolutely shot up – you must have grown a good six inches whilst you've been away – and your hair's bleached by the sun . . . you've a tan . . . I nearly walked straight past you!'

'Yes, I suppose I have grown a bit,' Philip said. 'Where's the car? Did you bring Rose or Unk with you?'

'No, I came by myself; I wanted to take a good look at you before I lost you under a sea of admiring relatives . . . just wait until Rosie sees you! She'll be absolutely bowled over by her big brother! She's been talking about you enough, goodness knows.'

'Is this the car? Very smart!' Philip got into the passenger seat of the big silver-grey Sunbeam. 'I can drive, you know, Dad – the army taught me, though I suppose the tracks in the Middle East aren't too similar to the streets of Langforth! Still, with a bit of practice . . . you're driving yourself, I see. No chauffeur?'

'Oh yes, we've still got old Bill, but I wanted you to myself,' Arnold said, climbing into the driver's seat. 'I've arranged a quiet dinner party at home tonight, just you, Rosie, myself and your godfather, but I'm afraid you're very much the conquering hero to half the neighourhood, and we've been besieged with invitations.'

'The Prodigal Son,' Philip murmured and then wished he hadn't, but Arnold clearly noticed nothing amiss with the remark.

'Yes, that's right, with a dozen or more fatted calves being prepared for your delectation,' he chuckled. 'And of course you'll need a few weeks at home, resting, catching up, before you go off to the laboratories of Cambridge.'

'No such thing; I'll be off after a week at the most,' Philip assured his father. 'I've lost a whole year because of the war – how does it feel to be at peace, Dad? – and now I can't mess about, I've got to start catching up.

In fact first thing in the morning I'll be down at the pot-bank, talking to Frank Hawthorne. How's he doing, can you tell me?'

'He isn't back full-time with us yet, as he's still working in the munitions factory,' Arnold said. 'But it's as well, lad, because he didn't have the knowledge to do more than mess around with the various ingredients and compounds. He kept coming down to my office all excited to say he'd discovered something new but when it came to the crunch he couldn't repeat the identical experiment because he hadn't monitored it closely enough. It seems, from what I gathered, that heat is a lot more important than he'd imagined. But there, you'll see him for yourself if you go down tomorrow, because he works in his little room on Wednesday evenings as a rule.'

'I'll spend all day there,' Philip decided. 'I say, sir, do you suppose I'll be the oldest student of chemistry in my year? Or will there be others who deferred their education because of the War?'

'Bound to be others; bound to be,' Arnold said. He was driving along roads which were as familiar to Philip as the back of his own hand; now he looked out, dreading changes yet compelled to search narrowly for them. Seeing none, he turned back to his father.

'It's April – any daffodils still in bloom? I missed the snowdrops under the Warburtons' copper beech, worse luck, but I'll be in time for that massed bed of lily of the valley . . . out in the Middle East you see some wonderful wild flowers, but for some reason there's something about your native plants that's special.'

'Aye, there would be. That's what makes a man fight for his own, I suppose.'

'Yes . . . there's the Collinses' cottage. I wonder how Jim's getting on? And the shop . . . crumbs, newly painted, what's got into Mrs Dickens?. . . Oh, and the blacksmith's got a petrol pump! Wonders will never cease. I'll have to walk down here later, catch up with everyone's news.'

'That's right,' Arnold said, rather glumly, Philip thought. 'If you want to visit the village before you've so much as had an hour's rest . . .'

'Oh no, I didn't mean *today*,' Philip said at once. 'I meant later in the week; plenty of time before I go to Cambridge.'

'Yes, plenty of time,' Arnold said, visibly cheering up. 'It's been a long year without you, lad.'

Philip, making some sort of reply, thought that things were really looking up if his father could say that and mean it. Clearly, all the old antagonism, the old impatience with his only son, were for the time at any rate being kept out of sight. I just hope it goes on for ever, Philip thought, watching for the first glimpse of the Hall as the car dived into the tunnel beneath the rhododendrons which lined the drive. Not long now and I really will be home!

\* \* \*

It was a mild evening and Philip and Rose were chatting, so Arnold walked his old friend home. Sidney Warburton was nearing seventy but he still strode out well and walked like the soldier he had once been.

'Pleased with the boy?' he asked presently, as the two of them, contentedly puffing their pipes, crossed the stile between their two properties. 'He's filled out . . . looks years older. You could take him for mid-twenties instead of just nineteen.'

'Very pleased,' Arnold said. 'Best thing Lily could have left me with, if she had to leave me – a son like Philip.'

'Change of heart?'

'Well . . . let's say the lad's changed, and for the better. He's a man any father could be proud of.'

'That's true.' Sidney bit back the words *he always was*; he had no wish to make things difficult for Philip, and indeed the boy had changed. He was taller and broader, his tan made his hair seem almost gold, and there was a quiet self-confidence in his bearing which had never been there before. I'm glad Arnold's come round to realizing Philip's true worth, but even if he hadn't it wouldn't affect Philip now, Sidney found himself thinking. Philip will be glad of his father's good opinion but it won't make any real difference to him. Once, he had needed that good opinion desperately but now it was just a pleasant feeling to have roused in the older man's breast. Now, Philip quite simply knew his own worth and was content with it. He did not need anyone's good opinion to bolster his self-confidence; he had earned his independence from them all and did not intend to accept anyone else's opinions in place of his own again.

'What does Rose think of him?' Sidney asked presently, as they turned up through the belt of trees which hid the Manor from the river. 'I'll be bound she was impressed.'

'Oh, she thinks he's marvellous . . . absolutely wonderful,' Arnold said. 'Pestered him a bit to bring friends home . . . natural that she should want to get to know his pals . . . but he told her she must make her own friends, for all his army pals will be too busy getting back into civilian life to think about exchanging social visits. A bit harsh of him, perhaps, but not said unkindly.'

No, and that little madam wouldn't be put off from her purpose by anything but a sledgehammer, Sidney found himself thinking. If Rose wanted to meet soldiers she would meet soldiers, and heaven help the poor lads who got into her thrall.

He was no admirer of Rose. Too old for her fourteen years, he thought her, and too conceited by half. She aped her elders, a trait he disliked in the young, and gave herself airs, another unpleasant feature in a girl of her age. He had noticed she kept one voice for those she wanted to impress and used quite different tones for people whose opinion she considered worthless. If Lily could see her now, he found himself thinking sometimes, how shocked and disappointed she would be. Lily might have

270

married Arnold for all the wrong reasons, she might herself have been quite shallow and thoughtless when they were first wed, but she had matured into a charming and sensible woman. Lily would be the first, he was sure, to condemn the manners and attitude of her spoilt and selfish younger child.

'And what do you and Philip intend to do tomorrow?' Sidney asked as the Manor came in sight. 'I've told the lad to enjoy his time home and to forget about my wild idea of visiting China in the summer, incidentally. He's nervous in case he's dropped far behind his contemporaries, thinks he'll have to work terribly hard in order to catch up. I don't agree, but I can quite understand that he won't want a trip to the Orient right in the middle of the best revision time he'll have – the summer vac.'

'If you want to go, Philip will go with you,' Arnold said. 'In fact, old boy, if Philip didn't go, I'd take his place.'

But Sidney, though he thanked his friend, still shook his head.

'No, you were all right and I was wrong; I wouldn't find her any more than better men than I have done. When . . . if . . . she decides she wants to declare herself to her old grandad she'll do so. Until then all I can do is wait and hope.'

The wedding was a grand one, given in the southward-facing hall of the Te Ku compound. Everyone wore their best clothes; the men were gowned in figured silk, the women in splendid satins and brocades. It was the first wedding Nala had ever attended and she was very impressed, though she would have liked to sit with Ouyang so that they could discuss everything. However, it was immediately apparent upon entering the hall that men and women sat separately, so Nala bobbed her way over to where P'ei Shan was sitting and took the chair next to her.

As a member of the family as well as a guest, she was sitting facing the red-draped table at which Lichou's family and the elder members of the Te Ku family were seated in place of Kei's parents. Behind the table was a magnificent curtain of scarlet silk embroidered all over with gold in a stylized pattern.

'Does that mean anything?' Nala asked P'ei, who nodded vigorously.

'Of course it does. Do you not recognize the two symbols which make up the pattern? They are the characters for happiness, and that means Kei and Lichou will have a good marriage. If you look at the candle-holders you will see that they are made in the same pattern . . . the *shuang-hsi*. See how the great candles burn and splutter! The bride and groom will use the candles to affix their seals to the nuptial bond. When I'm married, I hope I may have a wedding like this, with all the family here, and my husband's family sharing the honour.'

'I wonder how Kei feels?' Nala said in a hushed whisper. But before her friend could reply there was the murmur which always precedes a bride and then Kei and Lichou entered and made their way between their guests and up to the table, to stand facing the family elders. Lichou wore a long grey silk gown embroidered round the neck and hem with black and gold silks, and Kei was dressed traditionally, with the scarlet veil considered to bring happiness and good luck to the wearer. Nala thought she looked very happy, though she was pale from nerves and anticipation.

The ceremony was not a lengthy one. Neither bride nor groom said much, though they did a good deal of bowing and were admonished on their future lives together by the presiding elders. Then those who stood to Lichou and Kei in place of parents spoke at some length, after which seals were affixed, there was more bowing, and the presiding elder announced that the couple were married at last. The feast would take place in the courtyard, he added, so would the guests please leave the hall as soon as the bride and groom and the wedding party had done so.

Kei, looking radiant, smiled very sweetly at Nala as she passed her and soon they were all clustered round the long tables in the courtyard whilst food, which had been in preparation for days in advance, was brought through from the kitchen quarters by the servants who had been specially employed so that the Te Ku servants might join in the wedding feast.

At last the men and women began to mingle, though there was still a tendency, amongst the older people present, to stay in either a male or a female group. But the younger children converged on one end of a long table and Nala, by dint of pushing and shoving, managed to sit down triumphantly next to Ouyang.

'Didn't Kei look pretty?' she demanded and Ouyang, who was a kind boy, smiled and said that she did, though Nala could tell that he was being polite rather than factual.

'And now we have the best part,' Ouyang added, as the big tureens of steaming food were carried across the courtyard. 'Oh, Nala, I wish we had a wedding in our courtyard every day . . . look at the roast duck and the black bean sauce and the prawns with mushroom and the crispy white fish and the . . .'

'You are greedy, Ouyang,' Nala chided him. 'If you'd been helping to cook all these dishes you might not be so keen to talk about them.'

'I'm not keen to talk about them, I'm keen to eat them,' Ouyang pointed out virtuously. 'I never talk when I can use my mouth for eating, dear Nala! When will it be polite to start?'

'Everyone's filling their dishes,' the girl on the far side of him said, craning her neck. 'Children are supposed to start after their elders, of course, but . . .'

Spoons filled bowls, then chopsticks were taken in hand and very soon the grand work of eating their way through the biggest feast most of them had ever seen began. Nala ate with the best and joined in all the chaff and laughter. She had not yet told anyone, expect for Kei of course, that she would not be remaining in the Te Ku compound once the wedding was over, but would be going up to the Ellis bungalow. Nala did not suppose that the family would mind one way or the other. They had plenty of servants and were extremely good to all their dependants, but she knew Ouyang would be annoyed, and a good few of her friends amongst the numerous children who thronged the family home would be disappointed that she was no longer to live with them.

However, the Ellises had promised to see that she got the training she wanted in pottery, and not only that, but they had also told her that they would do their best to see that she had instruction from an artist, for Mr Ellis was very impressed with her drawings.

'She has a considerable flair for line,' he had told his wife whilst Nala listened, somewhat bemused but very flattered nevertheless. 'A gift like that is rare and must be nurtured. Do you remember Sven Han-ti? I think he'd be interested in her work.'

As she ate, it occurred to Nala that it might be a good idea to break it to Ouyang now, whilst he was enjoying a first-rate meal, that she was about to start a career in painting and pottery and would not continue to live with the Te Ku family. So she waited until her friend's mouth was blissfully crammed with wind-dried crispy duck and then spoke.

'Ouyang, when the feast is over, not today nor tomorrow but probably the day after that, I'm leaving the compound. I'm going to live with the Ellises in their bungalow and they're going to send me to study with Sven Han-ti, who is a great artist and potter and who will teach me how to use my abilities for the best.'

'Oh yes? I can't see *that* happening,' Ouyang said as soon as he was capable of speech. 'You're only fourteen, a year younger than me, and I'm still at school. Anyway, you're happy here. Just you forget all that nonsense. If you want to be a potter one day then my father will probably help you, but not until you're a grown woman, of course.'

'Your father couldn't help me to become a potter,' Nala said crossly. 'Why should he? I'm not a member of his family, I'm only a servant . . . not even a servant, a servant's sister!'

'Oh no you aren't,' Ouyang said calmly. 'No one was fooled for a moment into thinking you were Kei's sister; you're a little *yang kuei-tsu*. But of course we understand you wanted to be Chinese, so you pretended a little. And my father knows Englishwomen aren't like Chinese women, so he'd help you, I dare say, if that was what you wanted.'

'If you knew I was a foreign devil why didn't you say so, instead of pretending to believe Kei's story?' Nala said, much incensed. 'Really, Ouyang, I don't believe a word you say, sometimes. You just make things up.'

'I don't! The elders had a family conference when you and Kei first came and decided it was none of their business what the two of you said provided there was no skulduggery going on. So honourable great-grandmother took Kei aside and Kei explained that your parents had

273

adopted her because she was an orphan, and then they'd died. We did wonder about the name Chang, which is a good Chinese name, but great-grandmother said it was probably a good English name as well, and that satisfied everyone.'

'Then you didn't even think I was half-Chinese?' Nala cried, very put out to realize that her story had been seen through from the first.

'No, of course not. You're not at all Chinese-looking, you know. But you speak just like we do, and fortunately your hair is black so you don't stand out as being different. And now, after all our kindness to you, you're just going to run away. It's too bad of you, Nala, it really is.'

'I'm not running away; I'm going to live with the Ellises,' Nala said. 'I don't want to be a servant all my life, Ouyang, I want to be a potter!'

'I shouldn't think anyone will buy pots from a foreign devil who is also a woman,' Ouyang said, not unkindly but thoughtfully. 'Still, if you starve you can always come back and live here. Or I dare say Kei and her husband would have you at their farm, if you worked for your keep.'

'I'll work for my keep with the Ellises,' Nala assured him. 'I'm not a beggar, you know!'

'Oh well, if you're determined. You'll come back and see us from time to time, I suppose? On feast days and so on?'

'If I can,' Nala said. 'What is that you're drinking?'

'Plum wine; for boys only,' Ouyang said whilst the girls round the table cried out at this blatant fib. 'Oh well, because I'm fond of you I'll let you have a cup of it.'

He poured, Nala sipped, and her future was forgotten as the bride and groom approached the table to drink a ceremonial toast.

'A long life to you, Kei; a long life, Lichou! May you know eternal happiness and connubial bliss! May you have many sons, many sons, many sons . . .'

The cries echoed round the courtyard and Nala pressed Kei's hands in hers as Kei smiled and smiled and smiled.

Nala's apprenticeship to Sven Han-ti began very soon after Kei's wedding and was a very happy period in her life. She moved into the Ellises' bungalow and began work with Sven a few days later.

Work such as Sven demanded of her was hard, too. He told her that as his apprentice she should be able to handle a pot from the raw clay right down to the final glaze, and he threw himself with great enthusiasm into the task of teaching her not merely to do each part of the process but to do it properly and to the best of her ability.

Nala loved every hectic minute. She was astonished at how much she could absorb and very soon was doing all the things she had watched Amitri do with such skill so long ago. She took the prepared clay, worked it until it was sufficiently plastic to handle, and then kneaded it, cut it and threw it to get rid of air bubbles.

She became quite skilled at throwing a pot, using the wheel with a smoothness of touch unusual, Sven told her, in one of her years, and she learned the hard way, by ruining her first few pieces of work, how to judge the heat of the kiln.

Soon enough she was making a glaze, then painting a pot; and it was not long before she was carrying her first entirely self-made effort back to the Ellis bungalow, as proud as a dog with two tails.

She had expected her relationship with Ouyang to suffer as a result of all this busy-ness, but instead they grew even closer. She would go to the Te Ku compound at the weekend and Ouyang would come out with her and they would walk through the crops and up into the mountains with a picnic or a pile of books to study. There they would throw themselves down by a lake or under a tree whilst they put the world to rights.

Ouyang, who had been a handsome, boastful small boy, was turning into a serious and charming young man, but Nala doubted whether his proud family had any idea of his aims and beliefs. Indeed, when he first began to talk to her about the China that he hoped, one day, to help build, she was startled, and even a little worried.

'I agree with you when you say that China can no longer afford to cast aside her poor and see them die by the thousand-thousand every time the crops fail or the floods cover the land,' she told him. 'But when you say money must be shared, that your rich family must give to the peasants until all are equal, I think you must have gone mad! It isn't possible for such a thing to happen; men were not made to be *that* equal. You sound like a Communist.'

'Sometimes I think I am a Communist,' Ouyang said, heaving a deep sigh. 'What's wrong with being a Communist, Nala, my little one? It's better, surely, to be a Communist than a selfish pig of a landlord who wants only what he can grab for himself?'

'Well, I don't know,' Nala said doubtfully. 'The Communists in Russia talked about all being equal and then they killed anyone who had anything they wanted and took it for themselves. You say you want China for the Chinese and you want no more hunger, no more abandoning of girl-babies because their parents can't afford to feed them. You say that if each rich family gave a little of their land and a little of their gold then the poor could be fed . . . but by and large, from what the Ellises say, Communists take what they want and kill anyone who objects. You wouldn't want to be like that, would you, Ouyang?'

'No, of course not. But I've been reading the books about it and if you do it *right*, it's wonderful! There's a chance for everyone in Communism, not just the favoured few. But I dare say, if I go to university, I'll find out for myself what's the best thing to do for China.'

'It sounds good,' Nala agreed. 'And I expect as you grow older your views will change. Sven is always saying that to me.'

'Perhaps,' Ouyang conceded, and then the talk turned to other matters, to such things as a recent celebration in the village, the pleasure shown by Ouyang's mother at his school progress, and a certain method of producing blue glaze which Nala had found difficult to master. Even international trade was touched upon, since Ouyang was convinced that one way ahead for China was through producing goods which she could sell at sufficiently high prices to buy all the things a country needs for greatness.

'Like arms, I suppose, and cannon,' Nala said gloomily, but Ouyang laughed at her and said not exactly; he had had more mundane things in mind, such as rice and meat and flour.

'And modern methods,' he added. 'If we could get the peasants to use modern agricultural methods they could do a great deal better on the lands they own at present. I tell you, Nala, to be successful one has to look at the whole of one's life and the way one lives it, and change it accordingly.'

Nala shook her head sadly at him and returned to her dreams of the perfect pot. She thought Ouyang's ideas were wild and unworkable but she was sure that a few years at university would make him see sense.

That was, until she visited Shanghai.

It was their first visit to the enormous city. Sven was going to see about sales of his ware and he wanted to take Nala, so he suggested that she and Ouyang go along with him. Ouyang was examining universities and places of further education, so he was happy to be included on the trip, and his parents and the Old Mistress were glad to see the boy get the opportunity without having to be directly involved themselves.

The three of them set off one bright morning, travelling by train at first and then along the Yangtse, and it was here that Nala first began to sympathize with Ouyang's feelings.

'There are bodies in the water,' she said, as their ship approached the Bund where it would disembark them into the heart of the city. 'Look . . . I thought at first they were swimming but now I see they're dead! Isn't it horrible?'

The Chinese were not at all careful how they buried their dead at the best of times. Ouyang had taken her several times to the little graveyard where dead villagers were interred, and due to the fact that the graves were shallow, the graveyard was on a steep hill and the rains were heavy, most of the bodies had limbs or heads protruding from the soil after a very few years. But this sight – the swollen, waterlogged bodies floating out towards the sea – was something for which even the untidy village graveyard had not prepared Nala.

'Yes, it's pretty bad,' Ouyang said. 'But the people are too poor to bury their dead, so they cast them off from a funeral pier in coffins made of thin, useless wood which soon falls to bits in the water. Let's go ashore.'

Ashore, there were the beggars. Everyone in China is used to beggars: the professional ones who are not so much beggars as legalized robbers, for they hold threats over the heads of anyone who won't put money or goods into their begging bowls. Then there are the weak and the sick, the disabled, the mentally ill, all of whom carry their begging bowls around with them.

But here, in the great city, dreadful sights met the youngsters' eyes. Men horribly maimed by accident or illness, tiny children with ghastly diseases, blind, limbless, puffed up by starvation, their arms and legs like sticks whilst their bellies swelled with air or eating earth. The beggars swarmed the streets, and Ouyang and Nala saw them cuffed, ignored, beaten and screamed at, for even a sturdy rickshaw coolie would not hesitate to ill-treat anyone lower in the social scale than himself.

Sven, used to the place, tried to hurry them to his own particular destination, but he could not hide from them the facts that the city pushed under their noses every few paces.

'This is a terrible place,' Nala said quietly to Ouyang, when they had gained the shelter of the first workshop Sven wanted to visit. 'The smells and the poverty are beyond belief.'

'This is what I would see wiped off the face of China,' Ouyang said fiercely, waving a hand to encompass the beggars and the poverty, the ill-temper and the misery, which went side by side with the biggest, richest stores and hotels that either had seen. 'Isn't this wrong, Nala? Shouldn't someone put it right? That a man can live in a mansion and eat only the best whilst by his very door little children starve . . . you are a Christian and I am not, but I tell you I won't stand by and see this happen if I can help it.'

'When I can sell my pots I'll give money to the poor,' Nala said at once, but Ouyang put his fingers to her cheek and stroked it, whilst at the same time smiling and shaking his head.

'It's not the answer, little one,' he said sadly. 'There's a bigger answer which we're all too frightened to see. But I'll look it in the face and come to terms with it . . . and lead China the way she ought to go, too.'

And Nala looked into his stern face, at the eyes which no longer sparkled with fun but shone with serious purpose, and believed him. One day, Ouyang Te Ku would be a force to be reckoned with.

# CHAPTER TWENTY

It was dim and quiet on the upstairs landing. Rose had stolen up here now because in the middle of the afternoon, with the June sunshine making even the hardest-working servant eager to be out in the air, she could be reasonably sure of an undisturbed hour or so.

She made straight for the room that had been her mother's. Her father kept to his own room but for some reason that no one had ever bothered to explain Lily's room was more or less as its owner had left it. In fact the only time she could remember being shouted at by her father had been on the day, some twelve months earlier, when she had suggested she was old enough to move out of the bedroom next to Nurse's and down into her mother's old room.

'What rubbish!' Arnold had said crossly. 'If you want a room on the first floor, Rose, you may have the Indian room; you are most certainly not moving into your mother's place.'

'Oh, but Papa, that room is so big and airy, it has a lovely view, and there are all Mama's beautiful dresses in the wardrobes. I could use the material . . .'

He had shouted then and Rose, astonished, had immediately backed down, said she would not move at all, and had gone away to think things over. At the time, however, she had other things on her mind and it had gradually ceased to bother her. If Papa wanted to keep his dead wife's room as she had known it then let him. She, Rose, had better things to do than to live in the past.

Until today. Or rather until yesterday, because yesterday she had gone into Langforth with her friend Elizabeth to do some shopping and had been accosted, in one of the shops, by a wrinkled little woman with a face like a walnut and a great deal of wispy grey hair tucked inexpertly inside a mauve hat shaped like a coal-hod.

'Well, if it isn't Miss Lily!' the woman had declared. 'It's been many a long year since I've clapped eyes on you, my dear . . . how *are* you? And how's that nice Mr Anthony?'

'I'm not . . .' Rose had begun, to be cut short by her new acquaintance.

'I only saw you a couple of times after you left the Hall, and then of course Mr Arnold put it about that you'd died, but I knew it wasn't true, didn't I? I'd seen you, large as life and twice as pretty, with Mr Anthony in the stalls up in London; and my Celia, though there's them here who says she's no better than she ought to be, she kept in touch for years . . . she's living in style now, down in Dorset. Do you still write, you and Celia?'

Elizabeth was nudging and giggling, her face red, but Rose answered seriously, her curiosity thoroughly aroused.

'No, we haven't written lately. One loses touch . . . do you happen to have Celia's address on you?'

'Why, my dear, I know it by heart!' The old woman closed her eyes and chanted the address; you could see it gave her pleasure just to repeat the words. '17, Sycamore Court, Dorchester. And you won't have forgotten she's Mrs George Simpson now.' She nudged Rose. 'And you're a Captain's wife . . . no, I suppose he's dropped the old title. What's your married name then, Lil?'

'Oh . . . Smith,' Rose said quickly, unable to think of anything else on the spur of the moment. 'Well, it's been lovely meeting you, Mrs . . . er . . . but my friend and I have a lot of shopping to do. Goodbye for now.'

'Goodbye, my dear. Don't forget, if you get in touch with Celia, that it was me reminded you.' The old face crumpled. 'She's a good daughter, none better, but I don't see much of her.'

The two girls hurried away, Elizabeth clutching her side, in fits of laughter, though Rose was serious. At sixteen she was beginning to realize that life was not quite the wild, giggly business she had thought it a year earlier, but Elizabeth was six months her junior and knew no better.

'Let's go to the Coffee Pot and have some coffee and cakes,' she said presently, when Elizabeth had sobered up a trifle. 'Yes, I know you thought she was terribly funny because she mistook me for my mama, and because she wore a silly hat, but Liz, doesn't it strike you that she wasn't the only funny thing?'

'Do you mean you're funny?' Elizabeth giggled, making Rose long to clip her round the ear. 'Well, I'm sure she was funny enough for all three of us . . . hee hee!'

'That isn't what I meant at all . . . Look, Liz, are you my best friend or not?'

'I don't know; sometimes you don't seem to like me very much at all,' the incurably honest Elizabeth said, blowing her nose and wiping her eyes. 'Why? Are you going to tell me a secret?'

Rose sighed and turned into the small café.

'If you'd just use your brains, my dear girl, instead of simply assuming life's one long joke, perhaps you might realize that you've heard a secret, not more than two minutes ago. No, don't start asking me what. Sit down and I'll order, and then we'll talk.'

With coffee and cakes before them, seated in the bow-window table so that they could chat whilst watching the passers-by, Rose put her friend in the picture.

'So if that old woman's right, then my mother didn't die when I was a few months old, she ran off with another man,' she declared, when she'd gone over the elderly woman's words half a dozen times. 'Perhaps that's why my father keeps the room exactly as it was, because he hopes Mama will come back one day. Why, now I've got that Celia's address, I could go down there and find out where my mother is!'

'What, by yourself? All the way to Dorchester? You'd never dare,' gasped Elizabeth. She was a plump little person with dark curls and a rosy face, and though not over-endowed with intelligence had been friendly with Rose now for almost two years. Rose was not a patient person and her opinion of herself was high, but she did appreciate having a girlfriend to go about with and had no intention of letting Elizabeth see that she thought her extremely foolish, and would never have taken up with her at all had she been a blonde as well. Being dark, she was a good foil for Rose's golden prettiness, and being meek she put up with Rose's rather dictatorial ways. However, just now Rose did rather wish her friend could make a better contribution to the conversation than exclamations. After all, it isn't every day that a girl discovers her dead mother is alive, Rose told herself. It would be nice if Elizabeth was at least excited by the news.

'I wouldn't have to go alone; I've got Philip once he comes down for his summer vac.,' Rose told her friend. 'And I could trick Papa into taking me down there, too. Of course I couldn't tell him the real reason why I want to go but I could make something up. I'm good at that. I've always been able to wind Papa round my little finger . . . I expect it's the same with you.'

'No, but then I've got a mama,' Elizabeth said almost sadly. 'If you had one, Rose, you'd soon discover that they understand lots of things you'd rather they didn't, things that your papa simply accepts because you tell him it's so. If you're thinking of getting your mama back then you'd better think again . . . you might not enjoy sharing your papa when you've had him to yourself all these years.'

Taken aback by her friend's sudden rush of brains to the head – for such down-to-earth common sense was not at all in Elizabeth's usual style – Rose stared at her. Could it be true? If her mama did come back would life be harder for her? But then there was Philip. Elizabeth had no brothers, only sisters. Mama, if she did come back, would probably interfere more with her elder brother than with herself, and it would be rather nice to have a woman to advise and admire, instead of just old Nurse, who did more criticizing than anything else now that her charge was outgrowing her so rapidly.

'Yes, I see you've got a point,' she said slowly, still eyeing Elizabeth with respect. 'But I'm not really expecting her to come back, not if she's happy with the man she ran off with, and I suppose she must be or she'd have come back ages ago. No, what I want to do is find out where she is, take a look at her, and then see whether I want her back or not. And there are other things . . . does she really look like me. Is she nice?

What's her figure like, and her temper? I'd like to know her, without her knowing me back, at first. Then, if I like her, I'll tell her who I am.'

'And what about why she ran off?' Elizabeth said, once more amazing her friend with her perspicacity. 'Was it because your father wasn't very kind to her, or because you children, you and Philip, were such little pests? Or was the man she went off with rich and handsome and charming? You'll want to know all that, I dare say.'

'Yes, I shall. Do you realize, Liz, that there isn't one single photograph of her up at the Hall, not one? And the only place I've ever seen a picture is in Aunt Bella's wedding album and there she's wearing the most enormous hat . . . you can scarcely see anything except for her chin.'

'Your father must have destroyed the pictures,' Elizabeth said with ghoulish pleasure. 'You should be glad she's alive, Rose, or you might be thinking her dead and your papa a Bluebeard!' She looked all round her but there was no one within listening distance. 'I'm not one to gossip, but I've heard your papa has a young lady-friend who works at the pot-bank. Our cook's cousin works at the pot-bank too and she told the parlour maid who told the girl who looks after us older girls – Mary, her name is. Mary told me.'

'My *father*? A lady-friend? I don't believe it,' Rose said at once. How dared anyone intimate even in idle gossip that her father wanted anyone beside herself! 'Papa wouldn't. He just isn't like that.'

'Most men are, I believe,' Elizabeth said in world-weary tones. 'When it's raining and Mama sends me down to the kitchen to help clean the knives and forks in that pink powder stuff I listen like anything whilst they gossip, and men are really awful! Now that the war's over we have a boot-boy and a chauffeur and Papa's valet and the things the girls say about them would make your hair stand on end. Still, as you say, it probably isn't true.'

'I'm sure it isn't,' Rose said at once, rather spoiling the effect by adding, 'What's her name, this *lady-friend* of my papa's?'

'Can't remember. I'll find out.'

'Yes do. I'm in a finding out mood right now, so I might as well find out about everything whilst I'm at it.' Rose drank her coffee and picked up the last crumbs on her plate with a wetted forefinger. 'Shall we have another cake whilst we discuss our next move?'

'Our next move? What can I do?' Elizabeth asked in a frightened tone. She knew Rose quite well enough to guess who would do any dirty work if they were in it together. But Rose was reassuring.

'Nothing much, except listen a lot and try to steer the conversation round the way we want it to go. Can you go down to your kitchens and get them talking about my mother? See what's said, whether anyone suddenly goes quiet . . . that sort of thing.'

'They often suddenly go quiet when I'm down there,' Elizabeth observed. 'One of the fellows will say something, the younger ones will

281

giggle, and then there'll be this funny silence. Why, the other day the boot-boy said something which shut them all up . . . the gardener was boasting that he'd grown the biggest cucumber he'd ever seen and the boot-boy said his was bigger . . . you'd have thought he'd said the most shocking thing. You should have seen Cook's face!'

'Yes, well . . .' Rose murmured, a little more sophisticated than her friend. 'Just listen, that's all, Liz, and I'll do the same. And what's more, I'll take a look in Mama's room, see what I can find out. And we'll meet for coffee here at the same time the day after tomorrow. Can you manage that?'

'I'll ask,' Elizabeth said cautiously. The eldest daughter of seven girls, life was not always as easy for her as it was for her friend.

'You've got almost nothing to do,' Rose pointed out, as the waitress approached them. 'We'd like some more cakes, please.' She waited until the girl had gone and then turned back to her friend. 'I'll have to snoop in my mother's bedroom – even with my father being so sweet to me, I could get into awful trouble if I was found out!'

All that had led to this moment, as her hand closed round the white handle of the door which led to her mother's room. Truth to tell, with the house so quiet and the day so sunny, she felt as guilty as a burglar and half-wished she had never met the odd little woman in the street the previous day. But then she remembered that the stories were about *her* mother, and turned the handle, and slipped into the room.

She had seldom come through that door, and stayed for a few seconds just inside it, savouring the moment. The room was warm with sunshine and fresh-scented, as though it was never shut up at all but had only just been left by its occupant. The bed was made up, the sheets neatly folded over the gold counterpane, the pillows plump, enticing. It looked what it undoubtedly was, a comfortable bed ready for occupation. The carpet on the floor was cream-coloured with patterns in gold, and the curtains at the windows were gold as well, the colour echoed, now that Rose looked harder, in the brass candlesticks on the mantelpiece, the brass lamp in one window and even the coal scuttle and the fire irons.

The dressing-table was very large, with three immense mirrors; my mother was an actress once, and probably liked to have a theatrical mirror, Rose realized with a little stab of pride. An actress! She would have been a good one, of course – that went without saying. She had only left the stage to marry Arnold, her love being greater even than her desire for fame and fortune. Yes, that would be how the story would run, the next time she told it to someone.

There were three chairs and a stool in the room, all upholstered with cream and gold striped satin, all looking comfortable, used, without being in anyway worn. The room had two windows, a big one with a window-seat upholstered in cream and gold stripes and a smaller one which looked out not over the rose garden but down to the river. There were lots of wardrobes, taking up the whole of one wall, with sliding doors which were mirrored so that when Rose looked to her left she saw half a dozen Roses, all with an identical expression, half scared, half thrilled. She laughed involuntarily and so did the half a dozen reflections . . . and a seventh laughed too, in the mirror facing her.

It was tempting to stand for a moment as her mother must so often have stood between all the mirrors, watching her images gesture, pull faces, act out charm, humour, despair, but Rose had a task to perform. She went swiftly across to the dressing-table and pulled out the first drawer.

Gloves. Lots and lots of gloves. She riffled through them, pulled out a very elegant pair in pale grey suede and tried them on. To her annoyance they were a bit too tight . . . so her mother had smaller hands than hers! The next drawer held silk stockings in more shades than Rose had known existed; the third underwear, filmy, lacy, frothing with embroidery. The underwear of a woman who wanted to look beautiful from the skin up, Rose realized.

She moved round the room now, systematically searching. Such lovely clothes! In the wardrobes suits, skirts, dresses, gowns. For summer, winter, spring and autumn. Hats, coats, jackets, shoes. Walking shoes, court shoes, sandals, dancing pumps. She must be dead, Rose thought fearfully, and actually let drop the filmy scarf she had been teasing through her fingers. She *must* be dead; she wouldn't have left this lot behind!

She finished with the room at last and stood, a finger in her mouth, contemplating her next move. There was nothing here which she should not have seen, not so much as a letter or a note. Even the powder and paint her mother had used was still in its place, along with all the impedimenta of beauty which Rose hoped to own one day. Eyebrow tweezers, orange sticks for cleaning the nails and pushing down the cuticles, every available sort of hair ornament . . . even pins to keep the mass of her hair in place.

Rose dropped her hands; it was clearly all lies that the old woman had told her. If she knew one thing, it was that no woman on earth would walk out leaving such wonderful material possessions behind. No, her mother must indeed have died as her father had said.

She closed the lowest drawer of the dressing-table reluctantly, took one last glance over the assorted boxes and bottles on top of the side-wings, and saw the box she had missed. It was a long, blue velvet box, very beautiful.

It must have jewellery in, Rose thought, reverently taking the box up in her hands. I've found no jewellery – I thought Papa must have put it in a safe, but it must be in this box.

She opened it. A diamond necklace met her gaze and even Rose, who knew very little about precious stones, could see that it was a priceless thing. Every stone matched, they were beautifully set to show each gem to its best advantage, and they gleamed as though they had never been worn since the day the necklace was made.

It was too tempting. Rose picked the necklace out and held it to her throat. The dazzle was startling, reflected in her eyes and making her want to see the jewels properly placed. Gingerly, she undid the first three buttons of her high-necked white shirt and slid the stones round her neck. They looked good, but the shirt-collar obscured them from proper view; they would look best if she just undid the shirt a bit further and tucked it out of sight . . .

With a good bit of throat and shoulder and, regrettably, the top of her strong cotton chemise showing, the diamonds did begin to look considerably better. Rose was preening herself, admiring her reflection through half-closed eyes, and had put her hands up to her head to push the mass of her golden curls up on top to give her height and sophistication when she thought she heard a sound. She swung round and knocked the blue velvet case on to the floor, at the same moment letting go of the diamonds, which slithered straight down her front and plopped on to the carpet.

Rose stood still as a statue for a moment, listening, but whatever she had heard was not repeated and presently, with the thunder of her heart growing quieter and more even, she bent down to pick up both necklace and case.

In dropping the case, the bottom part of the velvet had come loose. Beneath it was a piece of paper with writing on.

'A present to enhance your night-dark locks, my love, from your devoted Arnold.'

What a lovely sentiment! Yet even this love-gift she had not taken. It was very strange . . . there was something else written on the slip of paper . . . Rose peered closer. Oh, no, it wasn't words, it was numbers. A date! Curiouser and curiouser, as Alice had remarked. The date must have been very close to the actual day on which her mother had left, for it was no secret that her mother had left to go to London to visit a dear friend, leaving her children with Nurse to look after them, and had been taken ill and died there. This necklace must have been given to her, by Arnold, scarcely more than days before she went away. Why on earth, then, had she not taken it with her? It was perfectly possible that she had owned so many clothes that she had not needed to take more than a few with her to her friend's home in London . . . but a diamond necklace of this rarity? Surely she would have taken it! And ladies did not usually go away without swansdown puffs and such niceties . . . even the tiny scrap of sponge her mother had used to apply cream with had been left on the dressing-table.

Rose scowled down at the necklace, still in her hands. She had forgotten that Mama had not died at home. She had gone away, so she would have taken things with her; it was just not possible that she would have left without them. Particularly the necklace.

Unless . . . Rose's scowl almost bisected her forehead, so hard was she thinking. Unless the old woman had spoken the truth – Mama had run away with a lover, taking nothing of her old life with her.

All the time, something had been niggling at Rose's subconscious. She looked again at the note, but it meant nothing save that her father had loved her mother to distraction. The date was not even a birthday or a wedding anniversary! I don't like to do it, but I'm going through to Father's dressing-room, Rose decided on impulse. Her mother's room had answered no questions; in fact it had raised new ones. Perhaps she would fare better in Papa's room.

There was a connecting door. Rose half-feared it might be locked but it opened easily under her touch. She slipped in and then realized she still had the diamond necklace in one hand. Rather than return it now, she fastened it about her neck and did up her shirt again so that it was invisible. I'll put it back as soon as I've taken a look round in here, she salved her conscience. Her father probably looked into the blue velvet case every time he entered her mother's room and she did not relish the idea of getting a servant dismissed for stealing by her carelessness, so back the diamonds must go, but not until her task was done.

The dressing-room was quite different from the bedroom. It was stark by comparison. The carpet on the floor was a rich blue and red Turkey one, the cupboards around the room were light oak, and the dressing-table was austere, just drawers with a large oval mirror on top.

Rose went straight to the drawers and began to rummage through them, and was immediately successful. A photograph was laid flat on the lining paper in the very first drawer, the one for gloves and silk scarves.

So this is my mother, Rose thought, astonished. How different she is from me, how totally different! The woman who smiled up at her from the silver frame was beautiful, perhaps, but not with the sort of beauty that Rose herself admired. The woman had night-dark hair, piled up on her head in the fashion of twenty years earlier. She had a pointy, elfin face with big dark eyes and eyebrows with a very beautiful natural arch, winged eyebrows, tapering to the merest thread of a line. Her mouth was half-smiling, and it was the sort of mouth which tilts upwards at the corner, producing a deep dimple in one cheek. A lopsided smile, some might call it, but Rose could see its attraction even though she herself admired a more conventional sort of beauty.

Having subjected the photograph to a close scrutiny, Rose laid it carefully back in the drawer once more. It was clearly her mother's picture, though why her father should keep it out of sight was more than she could understand. And only then, as she turned away from the dressing-table, did something click into place in Rose's mind.

*Your night-dark locks* . . . and the woman in the photograph had black hair . . . but . . . but my mother was a blonde, Rose thought triumphantly. Yes, she was a blonde! As fair as the lily she was named for . . . Arnold had said that of his wife on her wedding day once when he was telling his daughter about the happiest day of his life.

Rose returned to the dressing-table and produced the photograph once more, staring at it avidly. This was not her mother! Where was the magnificent white bosom, the piled-up gold of her hair, the brilliance of her light blue eyes? This was someone else, and therefore it followed that her father had been sending extremely valuable diamond necklaces to someone else . . . and her mother had found out! She had faced him with it and then fled, leaving her worldly goods behind, to go to the man who had not deceived her, not been unfaithful! Her mother really had run away from Arnold and Haslington Hall! Her mother, in fact, was still alive!

Rose and Elizabeth met as they had planned, but it was Rose who had the most success to report.

'I found out all about it,' she told Elizabeth, 'and I've quite made up my mind that I must seek out my mother. She did run away, I'm sure of it, and she went because my father was unfaithful, just like you said, Liz!'

'Oh, but I didn't,' Liz said, dismayed to find herself suddenly a scapegoat for whatever mischief her friend was planning. 'I didn't say he was unfaithful *then*, Rose, I said he had a lady-friend now, and there's no harm in that, with his poor wife dead these fifteen years and more.'

'He had one then, I'm sure of it,' Rose said. She had not dared to take away the photograph in the silver frame but she still had the necklace under her dress. She was now absolutely certain that her father had left the gems there because he was so ashamed he could no longer bear to look at them, let alone touch them. On the other hand the photograph, in its silver frame, was scarcely hidden at all, so he probably got that out every night and put it where he could watch it as he lay in bed.

'How do you know? Not . . . not old *letters*?' breathed Elizabeth. Rose was forced to shake her head but she still had her proof. She leaned forward across the table that separated them.

'Look!'

She pulled the neck of her dress down enough to show the sparkle of the diamonds, then pulled it into position again. Sure enough, Elizabeth was gaping.

'What's that? It looked like . . .'

'It's a priceless diamond necklace. I found it in their room, on the dressing-table, with a note in . . . to Someone Else! There's no doubt in my mind that Father could not bear to have anything to do with it after his wife left him, and he just pushed it back amongst all the powder and paint and tried to forget it existed. And there was a photograph of . . . Her . . . in his things; I saw it. She's quite lovely, though nowhere near as lovely as my mama. I can't think how he could be unfaithful to someone like Lily!'

286

'I told you, men are strange,' Elizabeth said with more than a touch of complacency. 'But I thought you said there were no photographs of your mother about the house.'

'Yes, well. I asked Aunt Bella and she said of course there were wedding photographs and got an old album out and showed me. My mother really was dazzlingly lovely and very like me, what's more. And then I asked her why Papa didn't keep some pictures of Lily around the house and she said she supposed it would be too painful for him. So of course I had to pretend to believe her . . . Aunt Bella looked *extremely* relieved when I stopped asking questions, I can tell you.'

'I can imagine,' Elizabeth said rather drily. 'But Rose, what are you going to do with that necklace? You can't keep it, that's stealing.'

And it was then that the Idea struck Rose with the force of a thunderbolt. In a few days Philip would be home for his summer vac., going to and from the pot-bank and spending hours, probably, in the study with Arnold talking about the future and about the plans he had for the pottery. She, as usual, would be left out. What was worse, this was the end of Philip's college life, for he had obtained his degree and would be starting work full-time at the pot-bank, making all sorts of discoveries and pushing Rose into the background yet further.

So why should she not simply go off in search of her mother? She could not tell Arnold where she was going, of course, or he would just forbid it. He would have been furiously angry at Lily's defection even if he had not been to blame for her abrupt departure, but because it had clearly all been his fault he would be more than angry, he would be adamant. She would never set eyes on her mother if Arnold had his way; he would find some means to circumvent any such efforts . . . once he knew she knew! But at the moment he was lulled into a false sense of security by ignorance, and she, for one, did not intend to enlighten him to the fact that she was mistress of his secrets. Her mother was not dead and he had driven her away because of his infatuation for the dark-haired woman in the photograph in his dressing-table. That was the information he had lied for years to uphold.

'I'm not going to steal the necklace,' Rose said now, in outraged tones. 'I'm going to take it to my mother. It is she who has suffered all these years, driven out by . . . by Him! Now she shall have the necklace and we shall be mother and daughter once more. Father can have Philip, if he wants anyone,' she added spitefully. 'Goodness knows the two of them do nothing but talk in Father's horrid study once the summer vac. starts.'

'I don't think you should do that,' Elizabeth said at once. 'For one thing your father will be out of his mind with worry – you know how fond of you he is – and for another, your mother could have taken the necklace when she left all those years ago. She can't want it, Rose!'

Rose was momentarily taken aback by this unemotional view of things, but then she remembered that her mother had fled in great unhappiness and also, presumably, on the spur of the moment.

'You've got it all wrong, Liz,' she said impatiently. 'She had to leave at once when she found the necklace; she didn't have time to pack or anything. And of course she couldn't take the diamonds with her, because they weren't hers, were they? They belonged to the dark-haired beauty, even if she shouldn't have had them.'

'She didn't get them, either,' Elizabeth pointed out. 'Your father must have gone off her very quickly . . . I mean, why buy them for a mistress and then not hand them over?'

'Oh, how can I tell?' Rose said crossly. 'You said yourself that men were very strange. Perhaps when he lost my mother he felt he never wanted to see the other lady again. Don't you think?'

'It's possible . . . but they look as if they're worth an awful lot of money, so why didn't he sell them?' Elizabeth asked.

'Sell them? My dear girl, they're an heirloom – I should have thought anyone would have realized that. You don't sell heirlooms; you keep them for your daughter.'

'Oh!'

'And I've got them, and I'm going to use them to find my mother,' Rose concluded triumphantly. 'And if she wants them, she shall have them. If she doesn't . . . well, they would be mine next, anyway.'

'I see. But listen, Rose, I thought you said your father bought those diamonds for his lady-friend? You don't buy heirlooms, surely?'

'Oh? And where do they come from? Out of the sky?' Rose enquired with awful sarcasm. 'Or are they found beneath gooseberry bushes, like babies?'

'No-oo, but they're handed down, they aren't bought!'

'You really are a stupid creature, Liz,' Rose said. 'The *first* one has to be bought, doesn't it? Well, this is the first one.'

Elizabeth, effectively silenced, could only nod. It was so obvious once Rose had explained it!

Walking back to the 'bus terminus later, arms affectionately entwined, they passed a group of young men walking along the opposite pavement.

'Do you know, Rose, there's something to be said for finding out your mother's not dead after all,' Elizabeth remarked, gazing after the young men. 'You haven't mentioned soldiers, or Paul Fazackerly, or your brother's friend Hugh Symonds, for days and days!'

'I've been too busy to think about boys . . . well, too busy to talk about them, at any rate,' Rose rejoined. 'Anyway, now that I'm to find my mother I dare say she'll know lots of young men and she'll probably encourage me to get to know them, unlike my dear papa.'

Rose's bitterness went unchallenged; Elizabeth thought Arnold Hasling-ton was downright lax with his daughter and allowed her far too much freedom, and she could not but remember her own mother's words on the subject of Rose and young men.

'If that young lady doesn't get herself into some sort of trouble in the next two or three years I'll be very much surprised,' Mrs Harlowe had said grimly after seeing the way Rose had flirted at a recent party. 'What she needs is a mother's hand . . . very probably applied, hard, in the appropriate spot.'

But Mrs Harlowe had been joking about the spanking, Elizabeth thought, for later she had repeated that there was little wrong with Rose that a mother couldn't cure.

'She's a handful,' Mr Harlowe had agreed. 'A real caution; spoiled rotten, of course, by a doting father. Pretty as a picture, too, which doesn't help. Someone will have to take her in hand . . . thank God it isn't either of us.'

Her parents had laughed, Elizabeth remembered, and then smiled fondly on their own daughters, grouped dutifully around the fire as their parents roasted chestnuts.

'Here comes the 'bus,' Elizabeth observed, as the big vehicle lumbered into view and pulled up beside the group of waiting passengers. 'Then you're serious? You really will go to find your mother? Will you tell Philip, or leave your father a letter?'

'No fear – Philip would probably stop me. He's too old to have fun now, old sobersides,' Rose assured her. 'But I'll probably leave a note. And Liz, do you swear on the Bible, cut your throat and hope to die, that you won't say a word to a soul, not even if they torture you?'

'I'm not swearing on anything,' Elizabeth said with rare firmness. 'But I won't tell, either, don't you fret.'

The two girls clambered on to the 'bus and made for the front seats. Elizabeth did not really believe that Rose would leave her comfortable home and her indulgent father and set off in search of a mother she could not remember. Even Rose had her doubts. But it was fun to talk and plan for an adventure of such magnitude. When the 'bus dropped the girls off in their home village they parted with promises to meet again soon to discuss ways and means. School had finished for the summer and they might otherwise grow bored.

'Well, old boy? Glad to be back?'

'Yes, sir. Very glad indeed.' Philip and his father faced one another across the medium-sized dining-table that Arnold had had installed at the Hall when he and Lily had taken over after the family had begun to marry and move away. Beside them, Rose glowered. 'You were serious, sir, weren't you, about my setting things going the way I needed them, now I'm at the pot-bank full time?'

'Nobody more so.' Arnold thought affectionately that Philip was a fine son, a very fine son by any standards. Tall, broad-shouldered, with the

289

hair that had been so fair on his return from Arabia darkened by three English winters and three even more English summers to the colour of a horse-chestnut, he dominated the table as he probably dominated the pot-bank.

Philip grinned.

'Then the first thing we'll want, sir, is a proper laboratory. I'm going to build one, but to save money what we'll do is knock those little upper rooms above the offices about a bit until they're all one long room. Then we'll put bigger windows in – you need a good light – and ventilation, and bring up some glost-ovens to start with to help out Frank's Bunsen burner . . .' He chuckled and Arnold chuckled too at the lack of equipment which even he had begun to think was rather a shame.

'It'll be grand.' Soup was being served by a maid from a big silver dish wheeled in on a trolley. Arnold sniffed. It smelt good, and it looked greeny-yellow and thick. 'Is it pea soup, May?'

'Yessir, fresh pea soup.'

'Lovely,' Philip said. He glanced at his sister. 'D'you like pea soup, Rose?'

Rose cast a discontented look at her plate, being filled by the maid over her right shoulder.

'It's all right. May, why don't we have something light to start with? My friends over in Appleton have things like salmon mousse sometimes, as a change from soup.'

'Your father likes soup, Miss Rose,' the maid murmured. 'But if you like to ask Cook . . .'

'It doesn't matter.' Rose began to spoon her soup, then cast the spoon down. 'It's too hot and thick,' she said pettishly. 'I'm not very hungry anyway.'

Ordinarily this remark would have cast Arnold into a state of anxiety, but today he was too interested in his son's plans for the pot-bank to take Rose's tantrums seriously.

'Oh dear,' he said perfunctorily to Rose, then turned back to Philip. 'And equipment? You'll want special equipment, of course.'

'Yes, we shall, but I'm going to have a good long talk with Frank about that. I know what equipment I'll want to do various experiments but he'll be able to tell me in more detail just what he'll need. We aim to work as a team, as you know, but he's bound to have more ideas in certain departments than me – I've been experimenting under orders, so to speak, without any chance of following up a particular piece of work. Frank's had a free hand for a year, ever since he got out of the munitions factory, so he's bound to have gone as far ahead as he's able and may well know better than I what we need to start off with.'

'Yes, but you'll know which standard chemicals . . .' Arnold started, but was interrupted.

'Oh, Papa, guess who I saw in Langforth this morning . . .'

With equal ruthlessness, Arnold cut Rose off short.

'That'll do for the moment, my dear. Philip and I have some business to discuss. As soon as we've sorted it out you may tell me all about your day.' He turned to his son. 'Now you'll know which standard chemicals you'll need for ordinary experiments, but I dare say the stuff Frank's been working with . . . glass, colour and so on . . . will need different chemicals altogether. And then you'll want containers, some ware to practise on, a supply of the standard frits we use to produce the glazes . . . were you hoping to find a different glaze? Frank told me that in the old days the Chinese used glazes which incorporated colour . . . very exciting it sounded.'

'I thought you weren't interested in the pots,' Philip said, half laughing. 'I can see you'll be doing the experiments instead of me at this rate.'

Arnold did laugh at this.

'No, no, it's just that because you were otherwise engaged I felt I had to show some sort of interest, but to tell the truth most of what young Hawthorne said to me went in one ear and out the other.' A hand bearing a dish of chops swimming in a rich brown gravy appeared over his shoulder. May scooped two chops and a good deal of gravy on to his clean plate and then moved on to serve Philip.

'I don't think I'll have any, thanks, May,' Rose said when her turn to be served came round. She felt she should have been served first anyway, as the only lady present, but to May she was still a child and came last in order of importance.

'Well then, you and Frank will want some time out, buying the things you need,' Arnold said, as he began to help himself from the tureen of vegetables. 'You drive, so you might as well take the Rover, go off to Manchester for a day's shopping.' He turned to Rose. 'Want to go with big brother, Rosie? You can take your friend if you like, make a day of it.'

'No thanks,' Rose said sulkily. 'Can I leave the table, Papa? I'm not hungry.'

'Certainly not. Just try a few vegetables, love, if you can't face the chops . . .' Arnold chewed and swallowed '. . . though they're excellent – tasty and tender,' he concluded.

'I'm not hungry,' Rose insisted.

Arnold turned and looked at her properly for the first time since the meal had started and drew the right conclusions. She's sulking, poor baby, because we aren't paying her any attention, and she's jealous of Philip, he decided. He had been worrying about Rose lately, and had been told by many friends and relatives, including his sister Bella, who knew a good deal about the young, and Sidney Warburton, a shrewd old boy, that Rose was so spoilt as to be rapidly becoming unbearable.

'You'll never marry her to a decent man whilst she's so wilful and selfish,' Bella had warned.

So now Arnold, the most easy-going of parents so far as his daughter was concerned, thought that perhaps, instead of giving in to Rosie and fussing over her, he ought to treat these sulks as precisely that. It would be better for the child in the long run.

'Not hungry? Well then, my dear, sit quiet whilst Philip and I have our meal. Perhaps you'll fancy the pudding,' he said.

Although he could not possibly have known it, he was adding fuel to Rose's newly formed opinion that he was a cruel man, from whom a wife had been quite right to run away years earlier, and who deserved no consideration from a daughter so undervalued. She would go – then they'd be sorry!

Even then, she might not actually have gone had not something most annoying happened. It concerned Lionel Brossard, a young man of nineteen or twenty, son of a local businessman, who had caused more fluttering in the Langforth dovecotes than any mere father could possibly have realized.

Lionel Brossard was tall and dark and willowy, with Byronesque waves of dark, over-long hair caressing the broadest and whitest of foreheads. He was rumoured to write poetry – certainly he was a most accomplished flirt, and one of the best dancers in the neighbourhood.

None of the young men liked him, Philip having gone so far as to say that Brossard was clearly a roaring pansy. Rose knew from his tone that the remark was derogatory; a visit to the kitchen and a casually thrown-out question revealed that Philip doubted Lionel's manhood. How absurd! It was jealousy, no doubt, for Philip never even recited poetry, let alone wrote it, and was far too involved with his wretched chemical experiments to notice girls, no matter how pretty.

However, Rose set out to entrap Lionel partly to annoy the males in her family, both of whom thought him of little account, partly because she thought he was terribly handsome, and finally because every girl in Langforth wanted to wear – figuratively, of course! – his scalp at her belt.

Since the war, not being actually 'out' was no longer quite such a barrier to a social life. At sixteen, Rose was going to any number of parties and dances and thus had any number of opportunities to interest the fascinating Lionel – and she used every one. The result was that when a party of young things decided to have a river picnic, with no more than half a dozen girls and the same number of young men, she felt quite entitled to suggest that Lionel should be invited to partner herself.

Elizabeth was one of the half-dozen, to be partnered by one of the other young men, and Rose was determined, on this particular occasion, to make it clear to everyone, Lionel Brossard included, that she was with him.

The day dawned bright and fair, and the young people set off in two cars, one driven by the Haslington chauffeur and the other by the

Harlowes' man. They were heading for a spot on the river renowned for its charms, the boats had already been hired, and from there they would row up-river to a quiet spot where they would picnic and then row back again later, to pick up the cars.

Everything went well, and Rose was in her element, full of fun and enthusiasm for the treat. The boats set off, two to each small craft, and Rose, of course, was to be rowed by Lionel whilst Elizabeth, looking extremely pretty in a rose pink voile dress, sat in the stern of another rowing boat with young James Hallisham at the oars.

Rose was also wearing pink, and felt that Elizabeth ought to have remembered that it was *her* colour before decking herself out in it. She would have been astonished and annoyed had anyone reminded her that on separate occasions in the past she had informed Elizabeth crossly that blue and gold were her colours as well. Her friend might even have felt that the deep pink she had chosen was the least likely to set Rose's back up, but she would have been wrong. Rose, in pale pink with her golden hair piled on top of her head in a pompadour, looked very pretty but perhaps just a trifle insipid. Elizabeth had recently had her strong, dark curls cut into a fashionable bob and in the deeper shade, with her bright colouring, she looked striking.

Before they climbed into their boats, Rose had all the annoyance of noticing that Lionel was being charming to Elizabeth, actually congratulating her on her new hairstyle and telling her that her dress suited her very well indeed. And when they drew the boats in under some willows which overhung the river for the purpose of a little quiet sparking, what was her chagrin to find that Lionel was manoeuvring their craft to lie alongside that containing James and Elizabeth so that they might all four of them chat together.

Rose came within a hair's-breadth of telling Lionel to move their boat because she had no wish to be close to Elizabeth, but fortunately for the future of her friendship swallowed the bitter words and put up with the foursome. And it was almost no consolation that James looked every bit as put out as she felt. Surely James was not going to pretend to be in love with Elizabeth? Clearly, Lionel was merely being rather over-polite, but James? He should have been delighted to be near Rose . . . instead he addressed nearly all his remarks to Elizabeth and as soon as he could decently do so he rowed off again, up-river, leaving the other two to follow when they wished.

What followed was far more satisfactory. Lionel turned all his attention to Rose and presently suggested that they should abandon the boat for a moment and sit on the bank. There he wasted little time in preliminaries but took Rose firmly round the shoulders and pushed her on to her back, proceeding to cover her with kisses and to maul her considerably, so that the strap of her new princess-slip, unused to such treatment, broke with a twang, leaving her having to get quite cross with Lionel just to remove him from on top of her.

'Why don't you have your hair bobbed?' Lionel remarked as they rowed up-river in the wake of the others, Rose at least feeling both hot and bothered and probably looking it. 'It might suit you very well – doesn't it suit Elizabeth, though? I was quite bowled over by her – I've always admired dark little things with curves.'

'Then you may clamber all over her when we reach the picnic spot,' Rose said sharply, not mincing matters. 'Really, Lionel, I'm sure my hair is a bird's nest!'

'It is a bit untidy,' the graceless youth remarked, having subjected her to a long scrutiny. 'That's the good thing about having a bob: it doesn't get in the way and it's easy to keep neat.'

They went the rest of the way to the picnic site in silence, but once there Rose was at her most charming. No one must be allowed to guess that they had quarrelled, or at least that she had quarrelled. She did not think that Lionel saw he was in disgrace in the least.

And yet it soon became clear that not all the charm in the world would re-attach Lionel to her side or even win her the unfortunate James. The two young men swarmed round Elizabeth like bees round a honeypot, so much so that the other young men, whilst not abandoning the girls they were with, also paid her a good deal of attention and Rose, literally grinding her teeth, was pushed into playing gooseberry for the first time in her life.

When they made to cast off again, the picnic eaten, the wine drunk, Lionel actually tried to get into the same boat as Elizabeth. James defied him . . . and then the two young idiots actually fell to fighting and jostling one another . . . over Elizabeth Harlowe, plain little Liz, whilst the beautiful Rose Haslington stood on the bank all by herself and longed to throw all three of them into the deepest part of the river and see them drown.

The trip back down-stream was accomplished, by Rose, in sulky silence. Lionel was polite to her but it would have been obvious to an idiot that he was smarting under the defeat he had suffered. Not only had James defied him but Elizabeth herself had said in her soft, easy-going little voice that she really thought they must go home as they had come.

The trip back in the cars was nothing less than a nightmare, for Rose at least. There sat Elizabeth with James one side of her and Lionel the other, chattering away as though she had known both boys all her life and making absolutely no effort to pretend that Lionel was really with Rose.

Rose had been polite, or fairly polite, all afternoon, but on arriving home she threw caution to the winds.

'I've had a horrid time,' she hissed to Elizabeth, quite loud enough for both young men to hear. 'And it's all been your fault, Lizzie Harlowe! Stealing my young man!'

Stamping up to her room, how bitterly she regretted those words, but how enjoyable they had been at the time! It would do her reputation no good, though, for everyone knew that Lionel was scarcely her young man or indeed anyone's. Spite towards a friend was not highly esteemed in the circles in which both girls moved and Rose knew, in her heart, that poor Elizabeth had never stolen anyone, nor tried to do so. She had simply enjoyed one successful afternoon when her prettiness had been as great as her good nature. Rose frankly could not imagine how Elizabeth had managed to appear pretty, but she admitted to herself that it was so.

At dinner-time, Rose appeared at the table and was, to her father's surprise, charming to her brother and to himself. She was silent on the subject of the picnic, dismissing it as 'Quite fun, but I had a headache', and for the rest of the meal she asked their opinions, agreed with much of what they said, and made no attempt to butt in when they talked business.

The following day she went round to Elizabeth's house to suggest that her friend might like to walk into the village with her. The maid went upstairs and came down again, looking embarrassed. Miss Harlowe, it appeared, was out.

In the village, two girls whom Rose had always despised as gossips and tattlemongers were cool towards her. A young man who had not been to the picnic asked her if she knew what all the fuss had been about, 'Because one of the fellows had been saying that one of the girls had been a real cat towards little Elizabeth Harlowe, and what did she think?'

'I don't know what you mean,' Rose snapped. 'I can't bear gossip, Tommy.'

Tommy, not unnaturally, was stricken dumb by this information from one whom he had considered to be as fond of gossip as the next, if not fonder. He reddened and the glance he cast at Rose was reproachful, but there was something else in it as well . . . could it be dislike?

Rose tossed her head and went on her way, deciding, on the spur of the moment, to call back at the Harlowe residence and see if Elizabeth would accompany her back to the Hall, where they could play croquet on the lawn which Arnold had fairly recently constructed.

This time, Elizabeth herself appeared, looking flushed but very determined.

'I don't want to play croquet with you, Rose,' she said. 'You think I stole your young man so I can't imagine why you want to go anywhere with me!'

'Oh . . . *that*!' Rose said with an air of great candour. 'I was only joking . . . I didn't mean it!'

'You weren't joking,' Elizabeth said definitely. 'No one says a thing like that in a joke. You were just being spiteful and horrid, Rose Haslington, because Lionel Brossard didn't fall at your feet the way you thought he should. And you can jolly well play croquet by yourself, for I shan't play with you!'

295

Rose was so surprised she actually fell back a pace. She turned to go, and was struck by the fact that although Elizabeth had lots of sisters and a good many friends she, Rose, was not in such a happy position. Philip was too old to play croquet with her and in any case she did not think he liked her very much, and as for school friends or friends in the village, she had none. She had only Elizabeth. She turned back.

'Liz . . . if I say I'm sorry . . .'

Elizabeth was a soft-hearted girl. Rose saw her hesitate, then someone from upstairs called, 'Liz! You know what I told you!'

It was Elizabeth's younger sister, a pert young creature with a long nose and a reddish complexion. Rose despised her, but Rachel seemed indifferent; she was clever, according to Elizabeth. Rose tossed her head.

'Oh, well Lizzie, if you're going to listen to Rachel . . .'

'What's wrong with my sister?'

Too late, Rose saw the trap she had just made and neatly fallen into. Criticizing any of the Harlowe girls had always been a dangerous pastime when Elizabeth was about.

'Nothing's *wrong* with her, only she's younger than us and anyway, what right has she got to interfere?'

Elizabeth turned dismissively towards the stairs.

'She's my sister. I'll see you in a day or two, perhaps, Rose.'

Rose slammed the front door as she left, slammed it with all her might. But the Harlowe house was old and solid and the door refused to make anything like the glorious bang which should have re-echoed round the hall. Instead it just shut.

Hell hath no fury like a woman scorned. Rose spent the walk home planning a series of vile fates for her erstwhile friend in which, as the Hall grew nearer, Lionel and Tommy and James Hallisham joined her. They were horrid . . . and cruel . . . and they'd be sorry when they heard Rose had gone!

# CHAPTER TWENTY-ONE

Philip was really pleased with the way things were going at the pot-bank. The laboratory was actually being built, doors and windows were being bricked up and opened out respectively, and he and Frank were choosing practical cupboard materials and equipment of every sort.

It was costing money, of course, but then everything cost money and we, Philip told himself about thirty times a day, are spending in order to make more money in the end.

But as yet, he had to admit, the spending was on a somewhat lavish scale. He had interviewed men for a job as your actual potter, and he did not want just any Tom, Dick or Harry either, but a man of experience and skill. In the end he had got one, too, not a particularly well-educated man but a chap whose father had owned an excellent little pot-bank not twenty miles away where a great deal of innovative work had been done before the war. The war, however, had ruined the business; no one wanted fancy stuff in wartime, all they wanted was practical, ugly pots, so Jim Tread-gold's father's had shrugged his shoulders and gone over to making what sold, but that didn't mean he'd stopped teaching Jim. And Jim had been an eager pupil with a natural aptitude for the art . . . or the craft if you preferred . . . of throwing a pot.

They had to pay him a master's wage, of course, or they wouldn't have got him. But he was young, intelligent and eager, and Philip had known right from the first moment of the interview, when Jim had looked him in the eye and told him he'd make good stuff but no rubbish, that this was the man for them.

Frank agreed, and Frank was proving himself to be no yes-man but a bloke of integrity and intelligence. He and Philip, unable as yet to start their experiments, had committed thousands of ideas and formulae to paper. One day soon they would begin to see what would work and what would not, but in the meantime they planned their way ahead day and . . . almost . . . night.

So now Philip was slogging away at pages of figures, trying to work out just how much they would need to sell in order to pay for all the equipment they had just bought. He did not want to pay for the stuff from the ordinary pot-bank profits; he wanted to pay for it with the money he would get for the better stuff. That way Arnold would not suffer, nor anyone else.

So when Rose popped her head round the study door it was difficult to look pleased. He worked hard at the pot-bank, he was polite and sociable – he hoped – at mealtimes. But he did like his evenings to himself. However, he gave Rose an absentminded smile and told her to sit down.

'I'm doing sums,' he said, as he saw her eyes fall on the masses of paper all over the desk in front of him. 'Father knows I'm having to spend money to get the place the way I want it, but I'm doing my best to keep expenses down.'

Rose sat down. Philip noticed that she was looking a bit red about the eyes and groaned inwardly. Not more tantrums, surely? She had been difficult for a couple of days, complaining that no one understood her, refusing to eat her meals and then annoying Cook by sneaking down into the kitchen when everyone was in bed and taking stuff from the pantry. But Philip had not suffered much from her moods – it had been the staff and his father whose lives had been made a misery. Now, apparently, it was his turn.

'Well, Rosy-posy? What can I do for you?'

Rose took a deep breath and Philip quailed.

'Well, it's like this, Philip. One day a while ago I met this old lady in the street when Elizabeth and I were shopping . . .'

The trouble was he only half-listened, because just as she began to talk he spotted a figure in amongst all the others which most certainly should not have been there. He pulled the page in question surreptitiously nearer, to get a better look at it. Rose's voice, which was inclined to be whiny and shrill by turns, was the sort of voice which was quite easy to turn off. He turned it off and tried to work out just what was wrong with those figures . . . he must have added instead of subtracted . . . or had he multiplied?

Opposite him, Rose stared and began another of her long, involved sentences. A great many had gone before but this one, his instinct told him, would involve a question so he had better listen.

'. . . So I took it, of course, because it was proof and besides, I think it really is hers – our mother's – so I thought she might like it back and I was going to take it to her, only then Elizabeth was absolutely horrible to me . . .'

It was clearly some story about that plump, giggly little friend of hers. Philip's attention strayed, only returning when his sister's voice rose towards the end of the sentence.

'So that's what I thought I'd do. But Philip, aren't you most awfully surprised? Shocked, even? You see, as I see it, it's most certainly our father's fault and we've all suffered for it – her most of all, perhaps.'

Her most of all? Who, Elizabeth? Mentally shrugging, Philip supposed that it must be. What a theatrical little creature this sister of his was, with her big blue eyes and wild, overdone gestures. But it was clear that some sort of a reply was expected of him. He shrugged, playing for time.

'Surprised? Yes, a little, I suppose. But not shocked. These things do happen.'

'Oh, yes . . . I know that men do take mistresses . . . but I didn't think Father was like that.'

The scales fell from before Philip's eyes . . . so that was what she had been running on about! Clearly she had discovered all about Bess Thwaite and was shocked. Well, perhaps she had the right attitude. Girls were sheltered from such things, but he did not think it would help if she thought that he, too, was astonished.

'No one ever connects such things with their own family,' he said. 'Now forget it, Rosy-posy; don't even think about it again. After all, it's none of our business, not really.'

'None of our business? Oh, but Philip, what about *her*? Don't you think she was ill-used? I do. And what about the necklace? No one shall say I stole it, for indeed I did not. Do you think I ought to give it back to her?'

298

'Definitely,' Philip said, glad to have a moral issue raised to which there was a clear answer. 'Oh yes, definitely. Wrap it up and explain it was all a mistake and give it back.'

'You . . . you wouldn't come with me? It's an awfully long way away – quite near Devon, I believe. I'm a bit scared of going all that way by myself.'

Philip really quite wished he had listened to the whole of Rose's story, but now was not the time to confess that his attention had been elsewhere. Women, he reflected, could be funny about such things. Instead, he blustered.

'Go yourself, all that way? Well, scarcely! Post it . . . Father will give you the money for stamps if you've no more of your allowance left. And now, Rose, I really must get on . . .'

She stared at him for a moment, then gave a strangled gulp and jumped to her feet. She stamped, like the spoilt child she was.

'You are too bad! Post it, indeed – as if I could! Well, you'll be sorry when I'm . . .'

The slam of the door cut the sentence in two and Philip, who had got to his feet as she did, sank back on the chair with great relief. No doubt she would rush to Arnold with a story of her woes and Arnold would pat her on the head and give her money for stamps . . . or perhaps, being Arnold, he would take her packet and put it on a train for Devon or wherever, and tell her that all would be well.

Philip pulled his sheet of figures towards him again and began to add up.

Rose was an impetuous girl, but she behaved quite sensibly in the circumstances. She had been wearing the diamond necklace ever since the day she had first abstracted it from its blue velvet case so she did not have to pack that, but she went straight to her room after her stormy interview with Philip and put a few things into a bag. Then she went down to her father's study and across to the safe. She knew the combination and opened it, took out what seemed like a small fortune in banknotes, and was about to close it again when it occurred to her that a servant might be blamed for the missing money.

There was a pink blotter on her father's desk full of fresh paper. She abstracted a sheet and printed on it, in blotchy capitals, IT WAS ME, and then put the sheet into the safe. On second thoughts she added her name to it . . . Rose H . . . and then tucked the money inside the top of her bodice and made for her room once more.

Her case was small, but it contained enough for a short stay. And she did not intend to stay away long – just long enough to find her mother and give her back the necklace. It would be quite an adventure, for one thing, and for another, she needed, right now, to get away from the place where she was derided and unappreciated.

It was a warm and sunny afternoon, so she took with her only a light jacket and wore her most comfortable walking shoes, though she had no intention of walking to Dorchester. That was not why she had stolen her father's money!

However, since she did not wish to be stopped before she had gone a yard, she did not ring for the car but walked out through the front door and down the drive for all the world as though she was merely going round to the Harlowes' house to play tennis, with her gear in the case. Indeed, that was probably what anyone seing her would have thought, for she and Elizabeth were always in and out of each other's houses . . . or had been, before their disagreement.

She reached the village and decided to catch the 'bus straight to Langforth station. She was in luck; she arrived at the station, glanced at the timetable, and saw that a train was leaving for London within the next ten minutes. To a girl from Langforth, London was the gateway to the world; certainly to Dorchester.

Ten minutes later, when the train steamed out of the station, Rose Haslington was seated in a first-class compartment, a magazine on her lap and a large box of chocolates on the seat beside her. She was going to enjoy her first solo rail trip!

'She's disappeared. No one has the foggiest notion where she's gone. I rang everyone I could think of who has a 'phone and visited all those who haven't and no one's seen her, no one's got the foggiest notion, Philip!'

Philip stared back at his father, his frown every bit as anxious as the older man's.

'Oh, lor',' he said slowly. 'She said something about sending a parcel to a friend . . .' not for the world would he have told his father, at this stage, that the parcel contained something which his sister had 'taken' and felt she ought to return '. . . she even mentioned taking it back herself. It was some friend in Devon,' he added, as though that clarified the matter.

'So far as I know, she doesn't have a friend in Devon,' Arnold said worriedly. 'The little minx . . . I've been half out of my mind!'

'Has she left a note?'

'No, not a word. I've been in touch with the police, of course, and they were very reassuring – said young girls do go off and usually turn up again quite soon. Said to speak to Rose's friends, not just their parents, but I'm at a loss . . . apart from young Elizabeth I don't know her friends!'

'Have you spoken to Elizabeth?' asked Philip. 'If not, I'll go round and have a word with her. But not until morning, Father. It's too late now to go rooting people out of bed.'

'I'll telephone her parents again,' Arnold said. 'I'll give Sidney a ring, as well. You go off to bed now, there's a good lad. No point in us both staying up and worrying.'

He left the room but was back in two minutes, waving a sheet of pink blotting paper.

'There was a note in the safe. She's taken some money . . . she must have gone by train or 'bus.'

'Not 'bus. Train. And first class, I'll be bound,' Philip said. 'She'll have gone to Devon.'

His father rushed out of the room and came back moments later, looking a little easier.

'She got a first class-ticket to London earlier in the afternoon; the station master saw her. She's not a fool and she's well provided with money, so she'll go to a decent hotel . . . we'll set a search going in the morning.'

'Liz, if you know where Rose has gone, I implore you to tell me,' Philip said earnestly. He and Elizabeth were closeted in her father's library at the Georgian house in the village street. It was a pleasant room lined with books and smelling slightly musty, as disused libraries often do, for Mr Harlowe was not a great reader. He smoked cigars, too, and the smell of them lingered, almost overpowering the scent of old volumes and added to by a whiff of dog . . . two fat speckled spaniels lay on the hearthrug before the empty fireplace.

'I don't know,' Elizabeth said unhappily. 'I knew she was thinking of going down to the south, but I've forgotten exactly where she was heading for or I'd tell at once, I promise you. It was some town . . . we met this woman . . . but she'll have told you that, I dare say? After all, it was your story too; she said as much to me a couple of days before we quarrelled.'

'She did say something,' Philip said, considerably embarrassed. 'But she was so mysterious . . . I didn't take much notice.'

'That's Rose all over,' Elizabeth said, and immediately looked conscience-stricken, as one who finds herself inadvertently speaking ill of the dead. 'I'm sorry . . . I shouldn't have said that.'

'If you don't mind, I think you'd better tell me whatever it was that Rose was trying to say,' Philip said tactfully. 'Don't feel you're giving away a confidence, because Rose truly did start to tell me just as I said. If only I'd listened more closely, but it sounded total rubbish and I was rather busy . . .'

'It will still sound like rubbish,' Elizabeth warned him. 'But here goes. It all started when Rose and I met this old lady in the street when we were shopping . . .'

She was quite a good story-teller and she certainly had an enthralling tale to tell. Philip listened, almost unable to credit what his ears were receiving. His mother was alive! Further, she had been driven from their home by his father's insensitive behaviour! And little Rose had actually found out what had happened all those years ago and had gone rushing off by herself to see if she could find her mother!

But even with Elizabeth at her most careful and lucid, Philip had difficulty in untangling the tale of the necklace. That, he soon realized, was because the girls were surmising and had no real idea as to what the necklace had been doing on his mother's dressing-table.

'But never mind,' Philip told Elizabeth, 'for Father is sure to know, and I feel certain that there is some perfectly respectable explanation for the whole thing. Now I must ask you, Liz, not to repeat what you've just told me to anyone else. As you can imagine it could make trouble for a great many people. Will you give me your word?'

Elizabeth thought Rose's big brother was wonderful and gave her word without a moment's hesitation. She even ran to the window to wave Philip off, and found she was hoping that he would find Rose before anything bad happened to her. After all, Rose had been a friend once, and would be a friend again, when she returned from her adventure. But Elizabeth still found herself extremely thankful that she had not been personally involved in the escapade. Mr Harlowe was not a particularly fierce father, but she could imagine his displeasure had he discovered that she had helped Rose to run away from home!

'A diamond necklace?'

Arnold repeated the words incredulously, then gave a gasp, clutched his throat, and subsided into a chair. Philip could see that his father, who had probably not given the necklace a thought for years, had indeed remembered where Rose might have found it.

'Yes, Father. Is it true, what Rose and her friend believe? That the necklace was meant for . . . for your mistress, and was found by Mother? And that she ran away because you were unfaithful to her?'

They were in the study. Arnold's colour was bad and Philip felt a twinge of remorse which he quickly stifled. He could still remember his lovely, laughing, beautiful mother . . . had his father really driven her away and then said she was dead so that her son would never search for her?

'Yes, of course I remember. It wasn't as bad as she . . . you . . . thought. Think. A stupid affair, a mere dalliance . . . I was very young when I met your mother, younger than she was by five or six years . . . I begged her to forgive me, but she ran out of the house and I never saw her again. I told you she was dead . . . that is to say, I never actually said she was dead, but I let you believe what Nurse told you . . .'

'So she's alive? Well, Father, Rose has gone to find her, if Elizabeth Harlowe is to be believed. So where do we start searching?'

He expected a quick response, but instead, Arnold shook his head in a hopeless fashion.

'I don't know! She never once got in touch with me. I tried to trace her, always without success. She left when you were five and you're past twenty-one now . . . Philip, I've believed her dead any time these past ten years and nothing has ever happened to change my mind.'

'Well, she's not dead,' Philip said positively. 'The old woman who thought Rose was our mother said she was still friendly with someone in Devon, or somewhere near Devon, and that's where Rose has flown off to. She actually got an address, not the address Mother would be at but the address of the woman's daughter, who would know where Mother was. I just wish I'd known . . . Rose tried to tell me, but I thought she was talking about Bess and tried to cover up for you.'

'You . . . you know about Bess?' Arnold quavered. He really did look ill, Philip saw. He went over to the drinks tray and poured his father a stiff whisky.

'Here, drink this,' he said briskly, and watched whilst Arnold downed it in one swallow. 'Better?'

Arnold sighed, wiped his mouth with the back of his hand, and nodded tremulously.

'Yes, better. It's been a shock, Philip, there's no denying it.'

'But you knew, didn't you? That Mother was still alive? So why on earth didn't you tell me, even if you felt Rose was a bit too young for such news?'

'I felt she wouldn't want you to be told,' Arnold said after a considerable pause. 'After all, it's been sixteen years! If she had wanted to do so she could have got in touch with either you or Rose or myself any time during those sixteen years. She could even have got in touch with Sidney Warburton – he and she were extremely friendly at one time – but she chose not to do so. Chose, Phil, she chose. So to tell you would, in a way, have been putting her in an invidious position.'

'But she must believe we know,' Philip said slowly. 'It wouldn't occur to her, surely, that you'd pretend she was dead? Look, sir, perhaps she's been wondering what sort of children we were, to ignore her, never try to get in touch.'

'My dear boy, whatever Lily's faults, her brain was as keen as the next woman's,' Arnold said briskly. 'For two or three years I left no stone unturned to find her and failed. What could a couple of youngsters do that I hadn't done? She didn't just walk out and take up a life somewhere else, she hid! It's my belief she changed her name and possibly she died and is buried somewhere under that name.'

'Well, Rose found a clue,' Philip pointed out. 'I know it was a bit of luck the woman walking slap-bang up to her in the street the way she did, but Rose had got a name now, and an address. I think she stands a good chance of finding Mother, really I do.'

He was watching his father's face closely as he said the words but was at a loss to interpret the expression thereon. Sadness, a trace of fear, excitement . . . they were all there, with something more.

'I'll re-advertise,' was all that Arnold actually said, however. 'I've not put an advertisement in the paper for years, but I'll do it now and at least we know which paper may do most good this time . . . I'll use the Devon ones.' He hesitated, looking a little shamefaced. 'If nothing transpires in the next couple of days, I'll go down there myself. But Philip, old boy . . .'

'Yes, Father?'

'Don't think too badly of me. And don't you go off, chasing after your mama, will you? We need you here. Me and the business.'

'I'm looking for a Mrs Celia Simpson.'

Rose stood at last on the doorstep of 17, Sycamore Court in the county town of Dorchester and addressed the maid who had answered the door. It was a pleasant, semi-detached house built of red brick under a slate roof and the garden was mature and well designed. It looked as though Celia Simpson had done quite well for herself . . . the maid was dressed in a black dress with a blue and white chequered overall on; plainly she had been engaged in cleaning the hall and had answered the doorbell in a hurry without first shedding the protective garment.

'Yes, Miss. Who shall I say?'

It would not do to hesitate.

'Lily . . . Lily Rivell.'

The maid gestured her into the hall.

'Would you like to wait there for a moment, Miss? I'll get Mrs Simpson through to you.'

Waiting in the hall, Rose hoped she had done the right thing. If the maid came back and said Mrs Simpson was out or not available she would have gambled with her mother's name in vain . . . what, then, would she do? To pass the time she glanced around her. A big hall for the size of the house, with a polished wood block floor and shallow bowls of summer flowers scenting the air. A staircase went into the upper regions, brass-treaded, the banister gleaming. Clearly the place was well tended and this, for some obscure reason, gave Rose a comfortable sort of feeling inside. She need fear neither rudeness nor indifference in a place so like her own home, she felt.

The maid had gone upstairs, so Rose moved over to stand near the foot of the staircase; perhaps she would hear what mistress was saying to maid. But instead she heard a rapid patter of footsteps and then a voice said: 'Lily! Well, who'd have thought it? My dear . . . you don't look a day older . . .'

Rose looked up; a handsome woman in her fifties was descending the stairs, smiling all over her face. It was an infectious smile; Rose returned it.

The woman stopped abruptly; her hand flew to her mouth. Then she took two more steps down the stairs.

'You aren't Lily! You're very like, I'll grant you that, but you most certainly aren't my old friend . . . you're young enough to be . . .'

'Her daughter,' Rose finished for her. 'That's right, I'm Rose Hasling-ton. I used my mother's maiden name because I thought she'd probably have reverted to it once she left us.'

Celia Simpson frowned, not angrily but thoughtfully. 'So she had a daughter . . . well, well, well. When did you last see her?'

'I believe I was six months old when she left,' Rose said truthfully. 'I've seen old wedding photographs but they aren't very helpful. I came to ask you whether you could give me her address; I would love to meet her, you see. It's a sad thing for a girl not to know her mother.'

'Ye-es . . . though there are times when most daughters wish their mothers in kingdom come,' Mrs Simpson said ruefully. 'Mine can be the most awful old rip. She drives poor George . . . but I mustn't keep you standing in the hall.' She turned to the stairs. 'Ruth, bring Miss Haslington and me coffee and fairy cakes, please, to the living-room. We'll see what it's like on the terrace.'

The maid, halfway down the stairs, murmured that she would do so at once and Mrs Simpson put a hand beneath Rose's elbow and ushered her through a cream-painted door into a pleasant reception room with wide french windows, one of which was open on to a rose terrace.

'We'll go outside,' Mrs Simpson decided, having crossed the room and peered out as though sunshine in the front of the house might easily presage a thunderstorm at the back. 'The chairs are only wicker, but very comfortable.'

She and Rose installed themselves in two bulging armchairs with generous floral cushions to protect the sitter from the garment-snagging properties of the wicker, and Mrs Simpson looked expectantly at her guest.

'Well? Do tell me what happened, my dear! The last I heard of Lily she was with the Jolyons, a very good little group, enjoying herself no end, acting her head off in all sorts of parts. I knew her marriage had broken up . . . Keith was a pompous ass if you ask me . . . but I didn't dream there were children . . . or are you the result of an earlier marriage?'

Keith? The Jolyons? Rose decided she had better make a clean breast of it.

'My mother married a Mr Arnold Haslington, my father, at the turn of the century, perhaps even before,' she said. 'She lived with him for five years . . . they were very happy, I believe. And then she left. He had behaved badly, you see.'

Mrs Simpson chuckled.

'Lily was no angel,' she said reminiscently. 'When I first met her she was singing with an opera company . . . it must have been in '98 . . . and having a gay old time. We lost touch then, for years, and didn't come across each other again until what, ten years ago, when she and Keith Butterworth got married and moved into a house not five minutes' walk away. Mind, they could have been married for years and years for all I knew, for it never occurred to me to ask, but they moved in further down the Court and naturally we fell on one another's necks, seeing as we'd

305

been friends, off and on, for so long. But as I said Keith was a bit of a pompous ass, and after three years Lily moved out.'

'She left him? Well, where is she now, then?'

'No, she didn't leave him, not exactly. He was a good deal older than her and retired . . . Lily wasn't cheap, you needed money to keep up with Lily Rivell . . . so she decided to go back to the theatre on a part-time basis. She joined a company in Dorchester, then moved to a bigger one in Bristol, I think it was. Came home now and then, only things like that don't last. Keith sold up and went off with someone else, I dare say, and when Lil came home there was no home to come to, if you get my meaning. So she spent a couple of nights here and told me there was a fellow wanting her to join a troupe . . . the Jolyons, I mentioned them earlier. She don't dance no more, not Lily, but she's what we call a good, middle of the road actress and the Jolyons put on all sorts – Pierrot shows, revues, you name it they'll have a go. So they needed Lily and she wanted to stay with 'em, Keith or no Keith. Last I heard of 'er, five years ago it must have been, she was on 'er tod . . . no man in sight . . . but enjoyin' every minute on stage and off.'

Her voice, which Rose had not been able to help noticing had grown less and less genteel as she told her story, abruptly reverted to very genteel indeed as the maid came on to the terrace, a laden tray held out before her.

'Ah, Ruth . . . our coffee at last! Pull the table over here, would you, Miss Haslington. Thank you very much . . . put it on there, Ruth! Now let me see, where was I?'

'You were telling me about the Jolyons; did you say they were working in Bristol?'

'They work everywhere, the Jolyons,' Mrs Simpson said. 'Mean to say you've not heard of 'em? Well, don't tell Lily that if you want to make a good impression. So you're her gel by her first marriage, are you? Do you know, Lily's a great talker – if she's fond of you she tells you everything, and I mean everything – but never a word did she breathe about you or your father.'

'She didn't mention my brother, Philip? She was very fond of Philip, I believe.'

Mrs Simpson shook her head.

'Not a word. You'd have thought Keith was her first husband, and when she talked about marriage it was always about Keith, if you see what I mean. She must have thought a lot of your father, never to say a word.'

'Or very little,' Rose ventured. Mrs Simpson thought about this, then shook her head again.

'No way. Lil was a talker, I tell you. If there was one thing she enjoyed it was talking about the old days, her old flames, what she'd got up to. But them five years of married life . . . well, as I've said, she never breathed a word, and that means it was too . . . too *special* to be bandied about, like.

That was Lil all over, tell you any amount of trivial rubbish, tell you all the high jinks she'd played, but never a word about anything serious, what meant something to the gal.' She had poured the coffee and pushed a cup across to her guest. 'Here, take a cake; Ruth's got 'er faults but she's a damned good pastry-cook.'

'Thank you,' Rose said prettily, taking a cake. She ate it like a starving wolf and accepted, without more ado, a second and a third, gobbling them whilst Mrs Simpson talked.

'. . . everyone in the business knows the Jolyons,' she was saying. 'Dorchester's a bit small, perhaps – our theatre, I mean – but if you can get yourself up to Bristol on the train and make for the Theatre Royal they'll tell you where the Jolyons are to be found this month . . . though I can't promise as Lil will still be with 'em, mind. Theatrics move around a lot from company to company – that's part of the thrill, always being somewhere new.'

'I don't mind; now that I've met you I'm sure I'll find her,' Rose said. Her hand reached out for the fourth cake, absently. With her mouth full she remarked: 'Shall I like her, do you suppose?'

Mrs Simpson considered.

'Like her? Well, I do – she's a great laugh is Lil. You're wonderful like her to look at, and all. Do you know, I don't know anyone who didn't take to Lil, come to think. Yes, you're bound to like her.' She smiled suddenly. 'Have another cake!'

'Oh . . . thank you. I'm awfully hungry, to tell you the truth,' Rose admitted. 'I was a bit scared in the London hotel so I didn't go down for breakfast and I got in so late last night that all I had was a ham roll, in the station buffet.'

'And you've come all this way without your dad knowing?' Mrs Simpson widened her eyes at Rose. 'Chip off the old block, that's what you are. Your mum ran away from home, you know, when she was about your age.'

'Tell me! Remember, I don't know anything; Father doesn't talk about Mother. We thought it was because she was dead so we didn't ask any questions – though mind you, I don't know how much Father actually knows himself.'

'If he lived with Lily for five years there won't be much he doesn't know,' Mrs Simpson said reminiscently. 'Look, Rose, you'd better stay here and have a bit of lunch, then I'll walk down to the station with you, see you on a train to Bristol. Don't forget she be might be known as Lily Rivell or Lily Butterworth, but if you ask for Lily Haslington no one'll know who you're on about. And the troupe's the Jolyons, with Granville Sinclair managing. Got that?'

'Yes, and I'd love to stay to lunch,' Rose said breathlessly. 'Tell me some more about my mother, please . . . and the stage, of course.'

Mrs Simpson took a deep, enjoyable breath and prepared to hold forth. Clearly, Lily was not the only theatrical who enjoyed talking.

Backstage, the Theatre Royal lacked the glamour of the frontage for most people, but not for Rose. She thought it was all terribly exciting, from the big posters out the front to the queue at the box office. But back here, with an old man grumpily saying she would have to come back the following morning, when the cast were rehearsing, rather than now, with a performance going on, she was still excited and impressed. There was the old man in his cubbyhole, a stretch of dark, rather dusty corridor, and then doors, noise, people . . . it was all so different from Haslington Hall and Langforth!

But . . . to wait until tomorrow? That would mean another night in a hotel and Rose disliked hotels thoroughly by now. The staff looked at her with such suspicion, one hotel manager even daring to insinuate that she had run away from boarding school, and she knew she was over-charged everywhere and given the least prepossessing accommodation on the grounds that she would never dare to complain.

'I could come back later,' she said timidly at last. 'I want to see Lily Rivell . . . is she acting here today?'

'No, she's not *playing* here today,' the old man said with mean emphasis. 'Can't say as I've 'eard of 'er . . . yet the name's got a familiar ring. Lily Rivell . . . now where've I heard that name before?'

'She's with the Jolyons,' Rose ventured, when no answer seemed forthcoming from the man's own subconscious. 'A friend told me they were here once . . . and someone might know where they were now.'

'Oh, the *Jolyons*,' the old man said at once, his brow clearing. 'Mr Sinclair's troupe; you should've said so at once. Yes, they're here . . . but you can't see Mr Sinclair right now, they're . . .'

Someone had approached the door unnoticed by either Rose or her elderly acquaintance. Someone whistling a catchy tune and twirling a stick. He stopped after two steps past the cubbyhole and turned to stare down at Rose.

'Hello! Want a job? Can you dance, though? Or sing?'

'Oh, good evening, Mr Sinclair,' the old man said. 'It's all right, sir, she's not after a job, she's come to find a Lily something-or-other, but I told her to come back later.'

'Lily? No one in the troupe of that name,' the man said at once. 'You sure you aren't looking for work, m'dear? I need someone like you . . . natural blonde, pretty, fresh-looking. We don't pay much . . .'

'I can sing,' Rose said. He was quite the handsomest man she had ever set eyes on with his thick black hair slicked down with hair-oil and a big black moustache which drooped appealingly on either side of his red mouth. He was wearing a striped blazer and flannels, which made her think he was probably quite young, a student in fact, though his face was that of a mature man perhaps in his mid to late thirties.

'There you are, Belman, she can sing,' Granville Sinclair remarked with satisfaction. 'Come along to the theatre tomorrow morning at about ten and I'll audition you. Got a place for the night?'

'N-no,' Rose admitted shyly, absolutely delighted to find someone willing to take an interest in her. 'I meant to book into an hotel but I haven't had time.'

'That's all right; I'll explain to my landlady. She's a good sort – she'll find you a room,' the man said easily. 'Got some money to be going on with.'

'Yes, but . . .'

'Then go and get yourself a meal and be back here by half past ten. Belman knows you now; he'll send you along to my dressing-room. Now don't forget, half past ten here, and here again at ten in the morning for an audition.' He made to continue walking down the corridor, then stopped. 'I should have said – are you a local girl? But if you were you wouldn't need lodgings, of course.'

'I'm from the north of England actually,' Rose said. 'I've come down to see if I can find Lily Rivell . . . or she may be using the name Butterworth, I'm told.'

That brought his head round all right. He stared, then smiled. 'Well I'm blessed! You're very like her, only of course a great deal younger and very much prettier. I never knew she had a daughter.'

'She didn't tell people, much,' Rose said a little stiffly. She was beginning to wish her mother had been a bit more forthcoming about her own existence. It must look as though Lily was ashamed of her! 'Is she here, then? Still with the Jolyons?'

'Bless you, no. She left two years ago at least. I'm not sure where she went but I can find out for you. See you later then, Miss Rivell . . .' He went to leave her and then turned back once again. 'What's your name, sweetheart? I'll have to give my dresser your name in case I'm still on stage when you turn up.'

'Rose.'

'That's nice; Lily and Rose. See you later then, Rose Rivell.'

He disappeared, the door swinging with the impetus of his going for several seconds whilst Rose stared after him, her heart in her eyes.

Rose Rivell! He had called her sweetheart and given her a wonderful stage name . . . he would audition her for a part on the stage, singing and dancing! It had never occurred to her to even think about it, but now she realized that she was indeed her mother's daughter. She would love, above everything, to sing and dance before several hundred people. They would adore her and she would be very good at it, a star in no time!

'Wait a minute . . . Miss, a word in your shell-like.'

It was the old man in the cubbyhole. Rose, in a dream, raised her eyebrows enquiringly and went a little nearer.

'Yes?'

'Umm . . . you say your mum's wiv the theatre?'

'Yes. She's Lily Rivell, the one I was telling you about.'

'And you reely do sing an' dance?'

'Yes. In a way. Why?'

'You look a bit young, even for Mr Sinclair . . . 'ow old are you, Miss, if you don't mind me asking?'

'I'm sixteen,' Rose said readily. It sounded a good age to her. The old man sucked his teeth, his expression doubtful.

'Sixteen, eh? Well, Miss, I wouldn't be doin' me dooty if I didn't warn you that Mr Sinclair's a terrible one for young ladies . . . jist you mek sure you've got a place wiv the company before you gives 'im *anyfing*; understand me?'

'Of course I do,' Rose said loftily, in complete ignorance of his meaning. She thought Mr Sinclair was wonderful, absolutely wonderful; had he not spotted her talent before even she was aware of it? But even so she had no intention of handing him the fast-dwindling sum of money she had stolen from her father!

'Well, vat's awright then,' the old man said, clearly feeling he had done his duty by her. 'Jest you come back 'ere when 'e said and I'll let you on through.'

'My dear Rose, nothing can exceed my embarrassment.' Mr Sinclair took both her hands in his and gazed deep into her eyes. 'When I promised you a room for the night I had no idea . . . no idea whatsoever . . . that Mrs Higgins would have let the room and then gone off to bed. But as you can see, my room is commodious enough for both of us. I'll just pull this screen across . . . here, you see . . . and then you can sleep on the little day-bed whilst I use the divan. If I were a shorter man and you a taller young lady we would reverse roles and I would have the day-bed, but as it is, we'll both be comfortable like this.'

Rose looked rather shyly round the room. It was quite large, as Granville had said, and there was indeed both a divan and a day-bed. She was far too well brought up to contemplate sharing a room with a man she scarcely knew, but he was old enough, she supposed, to be her father, and anyway she was in a very difficult position. Granville had taken her out to supper after the theatre, it was now well past midnight, and she knew she dared not contemplate waking a night porter in a strange hotel and demanding a bed.

'What do you say, Rose? Dare you trust me? What a cad I am to put it like that . . . you may trust me totally, I swear it on my mother's life.'

'Well, thank you very much,' Rose said. 'I'll get myself a room

310

tomorrow but in the meantime I'd be glad of somewhere to lay my head just for tonight.'

Granville Sinclair puffed out his cheeks in relief and patted her cheek.

'Well, that's settled, then. Now you just slip into your nightie and I'll get my pyjamas on and we can sleep sound all night.'

He erected the screen. Behind it, Rose merely shed her dress, jacket, shoes and stockings. Still in her camisole and envelope knickers, she felt better about curling up on the day-bed than she would have done more scantily clad in a nightdress. And indeed, when she remembered the nearness of Mr Granville Sinclair – and the redness of his mouth, the luxuriance of his moustache – she hastily kept her brassiere on, and would have put her stockings back, except that the discomfort of sleeping in them was self-evident.

'Shall I put the light out?' Mr Sinclair asked presently, too soon for Rose, who was just adding a chemise and a petticoat to her garments.

'Oh . . . yes, please,' Rose said however, scrambling into the last piece of underwear and taking a flying leap on to the day-bed, which creaked protestingly. 'I'm ready now.'

'Very well then; goodnight, my dear.'

'Goodnight, Granville. And thank you.'

Darkness descended.

Granville Sinclair got into bed not dissatisfied with his evening's work. She was a tempting little piece and she had fallen into his hand like a ripe plum, but he did not intend to spoil everything by acting too hastily. With an eye applied to a crack in the screen he had watched her undress . . . and dress again . . . with the interest of a connoisseur. Pretty undies, richly threaded with ribbon and lace . . . there had been money spent on the girl. He was an admirer of the new fashion for envelope knickers, too – the wide legs meant easy access and unlike cami-knickers they could be speedily pulled down; cami-knickers had to be taken off over the head. But she was very young, possibly even younger than the years she claimed, so it would not do to act hastily. Virgins, he remembered, could give a screech which would bring interference running if you so much as touched them where they didn't expect it. Better to wait until she was working at the theatre . . . there were always opportunities, a chance meeting in the wardrobe or the green room when the rest of the cast was otherwise engaged . . . he had sent his last woman packing only a month ago and Rose was the best replacement he had seen since.

So she was Lily's daughter, then? He remembered Lily with real affection. An older woman perhaps but excellent at her job, the sort of performer who would turn up in any circumstances, put in a first-rate performance and then tell you afterwards she'd got influenza or a broken wrist. She had shared his bed for several months and not only never a cross word but never a boring night, either. They had parted on the best of terms because she had found a company which paid more money and which also offered her the sort of parts she wanted. By then, in fact, Granville had begun to take an interest in their juvenile lead, and Lily must have realized it was only a matter of time before she was supplanted. She had taken it with her usual good humour, however, and had simply announced she was moving on.

Lying on his back in the dark, hands behind head, telling himself that it would be stupid to make any move towards Rose just yet, it occurred to Granville that when he and Rose became lovers, as he fully intended that they should, it would be in the nature of a 'first', since to the best of his knowledge he had not previously bedded a mother and daughter. It would be interesting to see just how alike they really were.

He knew the name of the company Lily had joined, and he could quite easily discover their various bookings, but he did not intend to share this knowledge with Rose until he wanted her to move on which, for obvious reasons, would not be quite yet. What was more, of course, if she was anything like Lily she really might be an asset, on stage as well as in his bed. In that event he would have to seriously consider whether to suppress the news of Lily's whereabouts for ever.

On this thought, sleep claimed him.

# CHAPTER TWENTY-TWO

'Right, Frank . . . lower it down . . . careful, careful!'

'Philip, Frank and their new recruit, Jim Treadgold, lowered the small but extremely heavy electric oven carefully into place on the plinth provided, then stood back, chests heaving, to examine it.

'It looks grand . . .' Frank was beginning, when a voice spoke from the doorway behind them.

'My goodness, what an improvement! This is beginning to look something like!'

Philip swung round, his face lighting up.

'Father! You're back! How did it go? Any luck?'

'She's not in Dorchester . . . neither of them are. But there was some news . . . you don't know, I suppose, that she's written to Elizabeth?'

'No! That's wonderful news. What did she say? Is she all right? Well. Where is she, anyway?'

'She's well and apparently very happy, too. We can stop worrying, because . . .' Arnold looked a little uncomfortably round the room. It was a proper laboratory now, with ovens, chemicals and all the things which Frank and Philip had wanted, but it also contained too many people for what Arnold needed to say. Frank, who had a good deal of tact as well as commonsense, looked at his watch.

'Come on, fellows, we'll take a break,' he announced firmly. 'We'll go down and visit the kitchen, see if Mrs Tasker can find us a cup of tea.'

Arnold waited until they had clattered away down the stairs and then came right into the laboratory and sat himself heavily down on a bentwood chair. Philip perched on the bench so that they faced each other.

'Well? They've gone now.'

'I went and saw Elizabeth as soon as her father telephoned me. She's a nice little girl; she handed me the letter right away.'

'And . . .?'

'Rose didn't say much. In fact, if I didn't know better I'd say she'd only written to gloat over her friend, but perhaps that was because she was excited. She said she'd done what she set out to do, which clearly means she's found her mother, and then went on to say that she'd joined the theatrical company herself, as a singer, and would let Elizabeth know when she made her debut on stage so that anyone interested could book seats.'

'As a *singer*? I didn't know Rose could sing,' Philip said, rather taken aback. 'And why should our mother encourage her to join a theatre company and leave home? She's only a child – she needs you, Father, and her friends.'

'Perhaps Lily's decided she should have a share of her daughter; after all, I had Rose for sixteen years,' Arnold said rather ruefully. 'But Rose is deliriously happy, that's clear. She tells Elizabeth she won't give her an address or even tell her which city she's in, because she doesn't want anyone interfering or taking her chance of fame and fortune from her.'

'That sounds like Rose, selfish little minx,' Philip said. 'She doesn't think of how worried you must be, just of what she wants.'

'Come now, Philip, that's rather unfair. I'm not worried, not any more. She's with her mother; that's good enough for me, and if she wants to go on the stage perhaps it's a desire she'll grow out of, though goodness knows why I should say that, considering I met Lily when she was singing in London. There are worse careers for a girl . . . not that Rose needs to earn money, for we've plenty for us all.'

'Well, if you're satisfied that she's safe and well I suppose I shouldn't grumble over her selfishness,' Philip said. 'It wouldn't occur to her that I'd like to see Mama after all these years, but then I suppose if Mama wished she could write to me herself.'

'I suppose so. And Philip, Rose added a postscript to the letter; she said that Elizabeth might tell me that she, Rose I mean, will write when she's got a minute. Which means we might hear from her any day.'

He sounded so delighted that Philip bit back more harsh remarks, but that did not mean he was not thinking them. What a nasty girl his sister was – she had run off to find her mother, had succeeded in her quest, and had not even bothered to add a word about her mother's state of health so that they could satisfy themselves that Lily was fit and well. Not that Rose would bother with Mother if she was a sick woman, Philip reminded himself bitterly. Rose would only cleave to someone who could be useful to her and an ill mother would be a dead loss. She had not even mentioned the diamond necklace, so far as he could make out; perhaps she had pawned it to help her with the expenses of living away from home!

'Well, now you know as much as I do,' Arnold said, getting up. 'I'll leave you to get on in here. I dare say the letter will give us a clue, by the way, when it comes. The little minx wouldn't think about postmarks.'

'Oh . . . any luck with the letter she sent to Elizabeth?'

Arnold, halfway through the door, shook his head.

'No . . . well, since Elizabeth threw the envelope away before it occurred to anyone to tell her to keep it, it wouldn't be much use. But never mind . . . our letter will arrive any day now.'

He went out, rubbing his hands, happier than Philip had seen him for many a long day.

Philip went over to the new oven and twiddled the controls thoughtfully. So Rose had found Mama . . . and neither of them apparently intended to give him a thought. Well, good luck to them! He was going to be far too busy making his own name with his experiments to worry about two foolish, stagestruck women!

'Who's that?'

Rose's voice was sharp but the chuckle which followed her words was reassuring. Nevertheless she glared into the shadows at the back of the stage and gathered her dressing-gown defensively close to her throat.

'Granville, don't be foolish! I thought I was alone . . . what on earth are you doing back there?'

It was Granville and not some wretched ghost or mischievous call-boy, Rose saw with a surge of relief as the shadow came forward on to the stage itself. Granville, in shirt and trousers, with a tape-measure round his neck, looked reassuringly normal. He smiled at her and slid an arm round her shoulders.

'Pretty wench! Still rehearsing those steps?'

Rose nodded grudgingly. It had come as a nasty shock to her to be told unequivocally that she must either practise more or put the hope of dancing in the chorus right out of her mind . . . and the chorus girls who danced had very much nicer costumes than those who merely sang.

'Well, let's see what sort of improvement all this industry has to offer.'

'We-ell . . . wouldn't you rather wait? I'd finished, and I'm quite tired. I thought I'd go back to my lodgings for a couple of hours, until this evening.'

She had lodgings now, in the same house as Granville, to be sure, but all perfectly respectable. There were other members of the troupe in the same lodgings but she had not grown close to any of them, mainly because she was Granville's chosen companion and as such was left pretty much to herself by the rest of the cast. Sometimes the girls looked at her as though they were sorry for her, but Rose guessed this must be jealousy, for she knew she had a brilliant future before her. It behoved her to be nice to Granville, of course, because without his championship she would never get out of the chorus and into a solo role, but sometimes he embarrassed her. He would stand on stage talking to the dancers with an arm round her waist . . . when he thought no one was watching that hand would slide lower, the fingers fondling the curve of her bottom. Or he would abruptly strain her to him, so that for a moment she could feel, pressed against the softness of her flat young stomach, something hard and somehow aggressive which seemed to live in his trousers. In front of everyone he would do it! Rose's face would slowly turn very hot indeed . . . but she could scarcely push him away also in front of everyone or her chances of stardom would recede into the middle distance.

There were other instances: a cheek pinched a moment too long, the fingers lingering. A hand held loosely enough, whilst against her small palm his forefinger would trace circles . . . a hand which brushed accidentally – only she knew it was no accident – against the curve of her breast.

She disliked these gestures but was growing accustomed. Still, at least when they were alone he always behaved like the perfect gentleman, which was a great relief. She supposed, vaguely, that touching her in public was some sort of showing off, or possibly a sign to the other men in the company that she was Granville's find and therefore, in a way, belonged to him.

But now he was nodding agreement . . . what on earth had she said? She racked her brains but could think of nothing.

'You're right, we'll go back to the lodgings. A quiet rest on the bed and you'll be fine for tonight. Just let me see those steps before we go.'

This was a Granville she knew and liked, the practical, managerial one. Obediently, Rose hitched her dressing-gown up so that he could see her feet in their ballet slippers. She began to dance, gaining confidence as she saw his head nod several times. She was good, she knew she was, and she was going to make Granville admit it as well.

'All right,' he called after a moment. 'Go and change; we'll get back to the house, otherwise it'll be straight back on stage without any sort of a rest. How's the song?'

'I know all the words,' Rose said. 'Am I going to do it tonight, Granville?'

But Granville just said he was not yet sure and Rose had to be content with that.

* * *

315

Back at their lodgings, Granville suggested that Rose might like to have the first bath since this was a big night for her. Rose agreed, but cautiously. It was their first performance in the city of Bath, to be sure, but she had sung with the chorus for a whole fortnight in Bristol. Did this mean that Granville was about to give way and let her dance? And sing her solo number?

She was soon to learn. She had her bath and went to her room to lie down on the bed for an hour or so. After a few minutes there was a tap on her door. She padded over and opened it and it was Granville.

'Just a few words before tonight,' he said, slipping inside the room before it had occurred to her that he might try to do so. 'Come here, Rose.'

Rose frowned, not sure what he meant; and Granville stepped close to her, took her in his arms, and somehow managed to get her on to the bed.

'Stop it, Granville,' Rose said crossly. 'I'm supposed to be resting for tonight.'

'Ah, tonight. You want to sing your song and do your dance, I dare say?'

He was lying almost on top of her, pressing her down into the feather mattress; it was uncomfortable and also embarrassing; the creature which lived in Granville's trousers was very intrusive at this moment – she could not only feel it, it was positively prodding against her . . . thoroughly nasty! Wondering why, Rose glanced down . . . and gasped. It had got free! It was . . . it was . . . Rose could not take her eyes off it, dreadful though it undoubtedly was to find oneself lying on a bed with a man beside you, his enormous Thing looking as embarrassed as Rose felt, standing rigidly to attention.

'Oh, Granville . . .' Rose gave him a push. 'Do get off. Do go away!' She wondered whether she should point out that his Thing had got free, then decided against it. She suspected that he knew and was not in the least abashed by it.

'Dear little Rose.' He hitched himself up so that he was supported above her on his elbows. Then he bent his face closer to hers. He began to kiss.

It was not the sort of kiss that Rose had imagined, from her brief kisses with boys back at home. It was frightening, with a good deal of teeth clashing and her mouth being forced open, hard though she tried to keep it shut, so that his tongue might lick at her . . . Rose contemplated a hard bite . . . but then all of a sudden she discovered that it was exciting in a horrible sort of way, and anyway she was quite intelligent enough to realize that if she refused to let Granville lick her she was unlikely to be allowed to dance on stage that night.

Rose took a deep breath and let her mouth relax, though her lips trembled and her chin shook. And it was not *so* bad, it was just that as soon as he had got her mouth open his hands became extremely active. Rose's breasts were his first goal. Kissing hard, with her mouth stopped

316

by his, she could not say much when he wrenched down her camisole to waist level, though it was a painful business, and the straps cut horribly into her shoulders and upper arms before giving up their valiant attempts to keep her respectable and descending to a mere huddle of material around her hips.

Then, still kissing, she realized he was struggling with her knickers. This was a bit much and she made smothered sounds against his mouth, whereupon he nearly choked her, he pushed his tongue so hard against hers. Rose tried to kick, but that meant she had to move her hips which, apparently, was just what Granville wanted since her knickers promptly slithered down to her knees, leaving areas of Rose which had seldom seen the light of day save briefly, in the bath, open to the air.

Granville's mouth left hers and began to trace a path across her throat, her upper breast, and then down to her nipple. He seized this in his mouth and for one horrid moment Rose thought he had taken it hostage . . . try to stop me and I'll bit it off. But then . . . then he began to play with the nipple, his tongue describing circles round it, and his other hand took the other breast, squeezing, rubbing, until Rose began to forget how she hated it, and what a beast he was, and trembled into response.

'Pretty Rose, good little Rose,' he murmured presently. He was kneeling between her thighs, his hands lifting her, coaxing her, she knew not why. But she was no longer resisting, and to her surprise her body seemed to know very well what was happening to her and to be enjoying most of it a good deal more than she had expected it to. Strong, experienced fingers moved down between her legs . . . she jumped six inches, but the fingers caused her no pain; they caressed, titillated, suggested, until Rose herself was breathless, giving little cries of pleasure, pushing herself against Granville, as eager now for him to continue as she had been reluctant earlier.

And then something pushed against a part of her as though it expected admittance . . . but there was no door, as Rose very well knew. She gave a little squeak of pain and tried to escape, but Granville had tight hold of her and he continued to push, forcing her knees apart in a way which made Rose think apprehensively of wishbones. 'Don't . . . it hurts!' she cried, but Granville – or the Thing – took no notice, and continued to push frantically against solid Rose.

'Lie still, lie still,' Granville soothed as she wriggled and writhed and tried to escape. 'Aaaah!'

'Eeeeek!' Rose shrieked as Granville's Thing, not to be thwarted, made its own doorway into her shrinking and suddenly reluctant body. But Granville took no notice. He was behaving very oddly; having gone to such lengths to get *in*, he now proceeded to pull out. And then go in again. And out. And in. And out. And suddenly there was a rhythm to it, and Rose's body stopped shrinking and shrieking and began to move too, as though it had always wanted to dance this particular dance.

Granville quickened the pace; Rose went faster as well. A glorious excitement filled her. She clutched Granville to her breast and her legs locked round his and she galloped and galloped away until suddenly they soared up into a heavenly, confused moment of fulfilment with cries of triumph, tears and kisses.

And as they sank to earth once more, wonderfully released and fulfilled, Rose found the strength to whisper in his ear.

'May I dance on the stage tonight, please?'

She saw Granville's face; he looked startled, a little annoyed, even. But then all his emotions seemed to smooth out and he bent his head and kissed her mouth. This time gently, with tenderness and a meaning which Rose could interpret. He was thanking her.

'Of course you may, if you can,' he said.

By the end of the summer, the first experiments had started. By that time both Frank and Philip had a good idea of what it was they wanted to find. They were experimenting with frits, the largest ingredient used when making a glaze. A frit itself is made by judiciously mixing silica and alkaline salts, finely ground; chemical additives to change the colour and consistency are introduced at a later stage. Philip and Frank wanted a basic frit for their colour and texture experiments, so this had to be produced before they began on more exciting work.

'We need one which will form a colour-glaze and hold the colour in the heat,' Philip said. 'What's more, it must be really resilient, so we can do different things with it. We've had some luck with the ordinary frits but now we must go for an extraordinary one.'

They worked for weeks, fining down their ideas, perfecting the amounts of each ingredient needed, until they had got a frit which was almost perfect.

'We'll use this standard mix,' Philip said on a bright autumn day when the grass outside the windows was touched with frost and every cobweb was a fantasy of crystal, glittering in the pale sun. 'Then we'll add some copper, I think, to see if we can get a greeny-blue glaze out of it.' He was measuring quantities into a flint-lined saggar as he spoke. 'We'll heat it to the usual extent, and see what we produce. Is the oven all right?'

'It's fine, fire ahead.' Jim, standing nearby, watched with interest as the saggar was insinuated carefully into the glost oven. He admired the work that Frank and Philip were doing but did not pretend to understand it. Instead, he worked doggedly away, producing shapes which had even the practical Frank whistling his admiration. But until they could give him the colours and the glazes – or try to find an artist who could design pictures for the pots – he and they felt his work was largely wasted.

'Is that safely in?' Frank looked at his wristwatch. 'Then shall we take a break, gentlemen? Anyone bring butties? Everyone? Good. Then we might as well take our food outside; it's a beautiful day, and there won't be many more chances before winter sets in. Come on, we'll talk about the artist once we're settled.'

The three young men made their way out of the pot-bank and past the rows of factory girls eating their sandwiches whilst perched on the low brick wall which divided the factory from the wild land at the back. The young men climbed over the wall and made for the long, rough grass whilst behind them the girls buzzed and chattered. Passing them was running the gauntlet for Philip, interested in girls but not yet sufficiently bold to ask anyone to go out with him. Having reached their objective, however, Jim, Frank and Philip sat down on the grass and produced their food. Philip made his own lunch each day because if he asked Mrs Parton she would be horrified that he should eat so humbly and would embarrass him by filling the bread with pâté de foie gras or by slipping in a lobster or a chantilly cream amongst the plebeian butties. At least, he imagined she would so never took the risk. Besides, he liked sandwiches made with great uneven chunks of bread, lavishly buttered and piled with cheese and delicious, strong-smelling onion rings.

'What you got?' Frank said as they settled themselves.

'Usual,' Philip said with his mouth full. 'Cheese 'n onion and a hunk of pickled cucumber, fruit cake for afters. How about you?'

'Chicken today,' Frank said, peering into his first sandwich. 'With Mother's home-made chutney. What've you got, Jim?'

'Meat loaf and ketchup, but I've got a piece of chocolate sponge for pudding.'

'Hmm. No swops?'

Frank was very good about swopping since he usually had the most interesting sandwiches, but today there were no takers so he sank his teeth into chicken and pickle and thought, as usual, about frits and why they never seemed to turn out quite as you hoped they would.

'Well?' Jim asked when their first ravenous hunger had been slaked. What about this artist, then?'

'You can draw pretty well,' Philip pointed out. 'Why not have a go yourself?'

Frank shook his head and swallowed, his adam's apple bobbing as he did so.

'No use, pinch-penny; he's good but nowhere near good enough. We want someone who's a bit special . . . why not advertise?'

'I could . . . but money's a bit tight and wages don't half run away with the shekels. I don't mind getting someone in but I feel we ought to make a success of the new frit first, not later. Then we could afford the best.'

'Why not get a woman? They aren't as pricey as men and you might get one who'd be happy to work part-time . . . come to that she could paint flowers on the chamberpots most of the time for a perfectly ordinary wage and work on Jim's ware when she was needed. Wouldn't that be the answer?'

Philip stared at Frank, his mouth ajar.

'A *woman*? Heaven help me, the bloke can't be serious! We don't want a woman up in the lab, stopping us from holding a decent conversation, meaning we dare not swear when something goes wrong! Oh no, I'm not going to employ a woman!'

'Everyone else works with women,' Jim broke in. 'I like women in a shop – they keep the tone up, somehow. Oh, I know we're very happy just the three of us, working away up there, but a woman wouldn't spoil all that because for one thing she'd only be called in on certain occasions. And you can't get away from it, Philip, most of the really good painters are women.'

'Have some fruit cake; you've taken my appetite clean away,' Philip said gloomily. 'I hardly have anything to do with women – the girls sitting on the wall scare me stiff – and I don't see why I should actually choose to work with one. But . . . well, the cost is important, I suppose. Are women really cheaper to employ than men?'

'And he's the boss,' sighed Frank. 'Don't you ever do the wages, Philip?'

Philip shook his head and started munching fruit cake. It was a rich and crumby one and made him thirsty.

'Nope. Leave that to the wages clerks, though I do check the figures from time to time, of course. Well, I'll take your word for it that women are cheaper.' He stood up, scattering crumbs. 'I'm dying for a pint; anyone coming over to the Carpenters' Arms?'

'Might as well.'

The three young men made their way out of the pot-bank and across the road to the pub where they bought their beer and dallied over it, sitting outside on a rustic wooden bench and watching the shift workers from another pot-bank streaming past.

'Well, that was nice,' Philip said at length. 'Better get moving, though. Now look, about this girl . . . she'd want to tidy us up, keep us out of the pub, make us have a proper meal at lunchtime instead of sandwiches and a beer . . .'

'Not necessarily; you've got a bloody funny idea of women, old man,' Frank said. Being Philip's senior by five years meant that he was easier with the younger man than Jim, who was Philip's age, could bring himself to be. 'What you want is a chemistry student who's got a flair for art . . . a sixth former would be ideal. Then she's young enough to train to our ways and yet old enough not to get giggly . . . old enough to be useful, see? I don't think you'd regret it, Philip, and face facts, you've got to do something! If we can't come up with a new colour or a startling glaze for Jim's ware then we'll have to use an artist.'

They had reached the stairs by now and Philip was just starting to agree, reluctantly, that Frank was making sense when Philip suddenly jerked back his head and began to race up the stairs two at a time.

'Jesus . . . that frit! It should have been out half an hour ago!'

The three of them jostled and fought their way up the stairs, scattering sandwich bags as they went, and burst into the laboratory. Philip, with his longer legs, reached the glost oven first and turned it off, staring up at the wall clock as he did so.

'Oh lor', it's been on the best part of an hour too long, and that means the heat'll have been greater too, probably as much as ten degrees. I bet we've ruined our chances. Still, won't know until it's cooled down, so no use worrying. We'll take a look in twenty-four hours' time.'

The next day saw the cautious opening of the small electric oven and the careful removal, with the aid of tongs and a thick cloth, of the saggar containing the latest frit. There it lay in its slate-lined container, smooth and transparent, without even a hint of the longed-for blue-green colouring. Philip sighed and lifted the saggar carefully across to the nearest workbench whilst Frank and Jim watched.

'No harm done, but no good either. It's just . . .'

'Hang on a mo, Phil. Jim . . . look at this!'

Frank was staring at the other side of the saggar and Jim had moved round to look as well. Philip walked round so that he, too, could see it. Plainly, they had left the frit for far too long; it had boiled over and run in a glorious swoop down the outside of the saggar. Philip bent over to look more closely.

'Frank! I *say!*'

'Well, what d'you know!'

'Cripes, fellows!'

The three exclamations burst simultaneously from three throats. For the frit had coated the outside of the sagger in a sheet of molten glass, and as it cooled the colour and texture were almost imperceptibly changing. As the three young men watched they saw a beautiful, delicately veined, opalescent glaze appear. It was quite different from anything they – or indeed anyone else to their knowledge – had produced before.

'It's beautiful,' Philip murmured. 'But can we do it again? Will it work when we want it to, or is it just one of those odd accidents?'

'We'll have to see. When it's cold we'll get it under a microscope and see just why it's done that and how. It'll be fascinating, but my bet is we've made a valuable discovery. It's . . . it's so very different!'

'You're lucky buggers,' Jim said as the two scientists began to peer at their inadvertent masterpiece. 'If I forget the time I clock in late and get a wigging. You forget the time and invent an entirely new frit!'

Later, they discovered quite a lot about their new baby. It appeared that the copper had separated out in the form of more or less spherical globules located chiefly in the lower part of the frit – an amazing result, for Philip had been convinced that the copper would blend with the other ingredients to give the required greeny tinge. Frits were made, then ground down

321

finely and applied as a glaze, and this particular frit responded as had no other when colouring agents were added. Indeed, using the frit as a starting point, the experiments the two young men performed brought astonishing results. With one oxide the resulting glaze was full of sparkling crystals, with another they achieved a full range of soft, variegated opalescent colours, with another a wonderful bluey-green which Philip swore he had only ever seen previously on ancient Chinese ware in the British Museum.

Ever since his father had first taken him into the pottery more than five years previously, Philip had made it his business to learn all about the works of the masters. The ancient Chinese, Korean and Japanese had all come under his scrutiny, though he thought the Japanese pieces, by and large, too obviously copies to have much intrinsic value as works of art.

'Now that we've got this frit, it just remains for Jim to come up with something new in the way of a piece of ware which we can begin to market and I reckon we're made,' Philip said to Frank after a few weeks of experiments had proved to their own satisfaction that they could reproduce all the various aspects of their frit at will. 'I want to stun people . . . in fact, perhaps we ought to go to one of those big exhibitions and show our stuff . . . they hold one each year, you know, in a capital city somewhere in Europe.'

'It's perfectly possible,' Frank said slowly. 'We're excited, but just wait until others see what we've got. I think you're right, we should exhibit.'

'Then we're agreed. But we'll say nothing for a bit, until nearer the time of the exhibition,' Philip said. 'Just imagine, Frank, what would happen if we could produce an iridescent lustre. Imagine the amazement!'

Frank had studied the ancient masters too, however, and he raised a brow at that.

'Iridescent lustre? Potters have been trying to make it for centuries with absolutely no success, so I don't hold out much hope of our finding the secret.'

'Yes, you think I'm mad . . . but we found our special frit, Frank. We just might, if we keep experimenting. We've been lucky once, but this time it'll be just sheer hard slog. And remember, we've got a most unusual frit which could be the key which unlocks the door of iridescent lustre.'

'I'm game to have a go, provided you don't expect me to spend my entire life trying,' Frank said. 'It'll be something to strive for, and you never know, it might lead us to another weird frit. But I wouldn't hold out much hope of iridescent lustre, old man.'

'Oh no? We thought we couldn't find a frit which would give opalescence, either,' Philip reminded his friend. 'You'll eat those words one of these days, Frank Hawthorne!'

Rose was blooming, as Granville, who was fond of a pun, remarked about five times a week. But it was true that she was looking lovelier than ever, and her singing was bringing audiences in from all over Somerset.

She and Granville spent a lot of their spare time making love, and Rose enjoyed that almost as much as she enjoyed performing her songs to a packed audience, but she never became carried away by it and most certainly not by Granville.

He had wanted her, she had used him. That was how Rose saw it. The fact that she now enjoyed as much as he the physical side of their relationship was neither here nor there. If someone came along who could do her more good than Granville, then there was no saying that she would not go off with him tomorrow – and Granville knew it, even, in an odd sort of way, admired her for it.

'You're a real little trouper, Rose,' he was apt to remark. 'Just like your mother!'

Rose no longer bothered to ask where her mother was, though she was sure Granville knew. It was not because he would not have told her, either. She simply did not care, not any more. Once it had been her desire to run Lily to earth but now, so far as she was concerned, if Lily wanted to see her then she could come and visit Rose Rivell. Theatrical people are all gossips and it would not be long, Rose was sure, before news of a very young girl named Rose Rivell who was blonde, blue-eyed and pretty, reached her mother. Then it was up to her.

The letter to her father had been written in a quiet moment backstage. It had been brief to the point of indifference, not because Rose did not love Arnold but because for her out of sight was out of mind. She was busy and happy, she had what you might call a father-substitute in Granville, even though he was her lover and not her parent, and she was rapidly clawing her way up the theatrical ladder to the top.

Clawing, furthermore, was a good description of her upward journey. Rose had her elbows akimbo as she climbed and heaven help anyone who got in her way, for Rose would certainly push them down or tread on them in order to continue to move upward.

'Winter's coming; we do panto at Christmas,' Granville remarked one chilly day when the east wind seemed intent on cutting the stage and all the cast in two. 'What'll you do at Christmas, Rosie?'

'Oh . . . act in the panto, I suppose,' Rose said, but though Granville laughed, he also shook his head.

'No, pretty Rose, not panto. You haven't had the experience. Singing's one thing, dancing's another, but panto's a third, and quite different from either. Unless you can be content with the chorus?'

Rose gave him a long glance from her suddenly glacial eyes. She did not intend to give up her starring role, not she!

'Show me a script,' she said briskly. 'I'll see if there's anything which might do for me.'

There was, of course.

'Principal boy,' Rose said, smiling. 'I'd like that.'

'No use. Got one. Peggy Ames.'

'Peggy? But she's *old*,' Rose wailed. 'She isn't even pretty . . . not like me.'

'She's got a first-rate figure, she's got lovely thighs in tights and she's got what you lack, my dear child, a sense of bawdiness, a sophistication. You wouldn't understand half the jokes she tells; you could no more slap your thigh and wink and flirt than fly to the moon. Tell you what, though. You can be Puss.'

Rose took instant and violent exception to that. Puss had to be small, and do a lot of gesturing and miaowing. That was not how Rose saw herself at all.

'I want to sing . . . I'm a good singer, the best you've got,' she reminded her lover peevishly. 'I'm *not* going to strut round in a catskin for anyone, not even you, Granville.'

'Well, I'll see if I can fit you into the action somehow,' Granville said, relenting. 'I thought you'd like to go home for Christmas, my dear; some of us do, you know.'

'Go home?' Rose looked amazed, and annoyed, too. 'This is my home now. I wouldn't go back to the north of England, not unless it was to play one of the theatres up there.'

The trouble was, the cast as a whole was getting a trifle tired of Rose. She looked a dear little thing, some of the time she acted like a dear little thing as well, but as everyone found out in turn, she was as hard as nails and as singleminded as a cat in pursuit of a mouse when the chips were down. In turn, she up-staged everyone. In turn, she denigrated them to each other. She was only a child, a pretty spoilt child, and it was time, Peggy Ames announced, that someone did to Rose what should always be done to spoilt children: time someone turned her arse-up over their knee and spanked some sense into her.

The trouble was, Granville was besotted by her, and Granville was the boss. They knew, none better, that the day would come when Granville too would decide he'd had enough of Rose and her ways, but that day had not yet come and in the meantime she was ruining the ease and friendship which had made the company such a pleasant place to be, as well as threatening everyone's job with her determination to be a Star.

'You haven't got the titties to be Principal Boy,' one of the chorus told Rose when she was reiterating her desire to play Dick Whittington.

'Nor the bum,' someone else chipped in.

'Nor the legs,' a third offered.

Rose scowled and wrote them down in her little black memory book to be got back at one of these days.

But she had to give way gracefully on this one, and Granville wrote into the pantomime a singing slave, which really pleased her and made her nice to everyone for a whole day. As the singing slave in the giant's palace she would wear an extremely transparent costume with big baggy trousers and a little jewelled top. Because of the nasty remark about her breasts, she

324

tried shoving bunched-up handkerchiefs down the jewelled top, but they looked ridiculous and in any case wouldn't stay put. Granville laughed when he saw her scattering hankies and that made her crosser than ever – and more determined not to be pleasant.

Then, at the first dress-rehearsal, she was sick.

It was a bit of luck, she considered, that she managed to throw up well clear of the jewelled top and the baggy transparent trousers, though the dame, a foul-mouthed comedian who had joined the company just for the panto season, did not share her relief. He was the recipient of the lion's share and he was wearing a very elaborate costume which cost the earth, he moaned, to have dry-cleaned, and he was not going to wear it until it had been dry-cleaned, not with that little slut's vomit all over it.

Granville added insult to injury by telling her to clean up after herself and by informing the entire cast, or all who were present, that she'd made a pig of herself that lunchtime with doughnuts and strawberry ice cream. Rose, who knew her enormous capacity for doughnuts and strawberry ice cream, assumed she must have eaten something which disagreed with her, and very soon felt better. She waltzed through the rest of the rehearsal . . . and was sick the following morning shortly after she got out of bed.

After that, things fell into a routine of sorts, if you could count feeling deathly ill for half an hour, being sick, and then feeling fine as routine. Because she was well aware that Granville could ruin her career if he chose, Rose kept her sickness dark, and indeed by the time the panto had been running a fortnight it looked as though her temporary malady was over. She was bright and cheerful in the mornings, efficient and cheerful at matinées, and positively brilliant at the main evening performances.

Small boys wrote her notes telling her they loved her; smaller girls sent sticky packets of sweets round to her dressing-room. Once or twice she had what the other girls called 'stage-door johnnies' asking her for dates, or simply sending in flowers, but Granville dealt with them and Rose was happy for him to do so. She had no urge for men-friends; all she wanted was Success.

By March, with the pantomime over and the dead season into its ghastly swing, she and Granville were living in lodgings and quarrelling quite a lot. The company had small bookings, a week here, a week there, but until Easter things would not be too bright for any of them. Money was scarce, the depression was beginning to bite at theatrical entertainment as at everything else, and Rose actually cast a thought, once or twice, at the prospect of going home for a few weeks' rest.

And then Arnold found her.

He had hunted, on and off, without any success whatsoever, and then by a stroke of luck he was talking one day to a business colleague who asked him whatever had happened to that damned pretty wife of his.

'What makes me ask is I was down in Bath a week or so back, selling to one of the big houses there, when I saw a theatre poster . . . the name struck me at once . . . Rivell. I remembered you once telling me your wife had been on the stage as Lily Rivell and I thought, well, bless me, here's a coincidence. *Rose Rivell sings you songs which will bring a tear to your eye* . . . that's what it said, more or less. Of course, your wife was Lily and this was Rose, but it was strange, what?'

'Yes, very strange,' Arnold said automatically, but as soon as the other had left he rushed home, packed a case and warned Philip that he might be away several days.

'Got a clue about Rose,' he said breathlessly, standing in the laboratory with his coat open and his hat perched on the back of his head and looking more like a bookie than a respectable industrialist. 'I'll let you know what happens. Take care of yourself, my boy.'

He left Philip staring and drove all the way down to Bath, though he was not actually driving himself; his chauffeur, Briggs, had been warned that he would be away for a few days and was quite looking forward to a bit more driving than the daily task of taking Philip to the pot-bank and Arnold to the leatherworks.

Bath proved both beautiful and hospitable. Arnold put up at a decent small hotel and paid for dinner, then found himself unable to eat it. He deserted if halfway through the main course and made his way to the theatre. It was easy to buy a ticket and slip into the auditorium halfway through the evening.

Rose came on, glittering with greasepaint, her features so familiar that his heart turned over, but she looked different, nevertheless. Taller, even a bit fatter.

When the show was over he went backstage, to be refused, with a quick, cold glance from the old man in the cubbyhole, even a word with Miss Rivell.

'What about Miss Lily Rivell then?' Arnold said, greatly daring, only to be told, crushingly, that the doorman knew of no such person.

'Take a message, then,' Arnold said commandingly. And because of his years – too old to harm the kid – and his gentlemanly bearing, old Belman took the note which Arnold hastily scribbled. A couple of minutes later the old boy came back.

'She says you can come in if you want,' the doorman said grudgingly. 'Foller me.'

Arnold followed, and was led into a small, rather scruffy dressing-room. Rose was sitting in front of a big mirror, cleaning off her paint. She did not smile at him because she was pulling a mouth, to get off the lipstick, but he thought her eyes warmed a little.

'Rose! My dear child . . .'

He bent over her and kissed her cheek, still sticky with cold cream.

'Hello, Papa. Did you see me? Were you out front?'

'Yes. I saw you. You were very good . . . awfully good. But my love, I thought you were with your mama. I was never so shocked to find you

326

here alone. You must come home with me now, you know. You're too young for all this.'

His gesture included the room, the theatre, the whole way of life to which she had been subjected. Rose, however, had other ideas.

'Oh no, I think not, Papa. These are the dead months, but very soon we shall be raking in the money and getting big audiences again. I'll stay for that . . . and then I dare say my fame will start to spread and I'll be really famous. You wouldn't want to spoil it all for me?'

She stood up. The dressing-gown she was wearing fell open and Arnold stared, a frown creeping across his face.

Rose? My dear child, you've grown very stout! I suppose you could say that . . .'

'Yes, I'm putting on weight,' Rose admitted. 'All round the waist, too, dreadfully difficult in costume. Something that fits me one day is too tight the next, and . . .'

'I think you're having a baby, Rose,' a quiet voice from the other side of the room said matter-of-factly. It was Peggy Ames. She had been changing behind a screen and Arnold had not even seen her. 'I think you'd better go home with your papa.'

Arnold watched as Rose's face turned slowly scarlet, but Rose was not finished yet. Eyes flashing, she turned on Peggy.

'Me, pregnant? That's just nastiness because you're jealous of me, Peggy Ames. I'm not pregnant; it's just that I've been overeating . . . I couldn't possibly be pregnant . . . and I don't want a baby anyway. I hate babies!'

Arnold turned to Peggy and read the sympathy in her eyes. He began to stutter that she could not be right, she must be mistaken, but Peggy shook her head at him.

'No. She's having a baby and she's little more than a baby herself,' she said. 'Take her home, Mr Rivell.'

'I've had the most extraordinary letter from Father,' Philip said one morning, as he and Frank mixed their mixes and planned their plans for the day ahead. 'He says he's taken a fancy to go down to Devonshire to live and is buying a little farm. It's a flower farm, whatever that may mean, and he's going to run it himself for a few months. I can't imagine what he's up to, but he says he's handing the pot-bank and the house over to my care until he comes back – and then, in a postscript, he says he may decide to stay there, in which case I'm at liberty to sell the Hall if I think it's too large for me, or I can hold on to it if I want to do that. It really is a most peculiar letter.'

'What about your sister? Did he find her?'

'Apparently not; he says it was a wild goose chase but he hopes to be able to catch up with her in six or seven months, when she'll be starting up on her stagework once more. It's a mystery, it really is. I wonder whether I ought to rush down to this place in Devon and make sure he's all right?'

'He says it's just for a few months, so I'd leave it, if I were you. Or you could get in touch with that girl of his, what's her name, Bess Thwaite, and see what he's told her.'

'I could. Can you get the oven open, please, Frank, and I'll start this frit off cooking. Did you see the extraordinary glow and the crystals in the last one? Good, wasn't it? Yes, you're right, you always are. I'll go down and see Bess Thwaite this evening. She's bound to know something.'

'He sent me some money, sir, to tide me over, he said.' Bess Thwaite asked Philip in, sat him down on a small, red-velveteen couch, and unburdened herself. 'Very hurt I am, sir, for our friendship's been above money . . . it's his company I'll miss. But there, I'm young, I suppose I should be grateful for that, and Jeff Harkness has been a-pestering me for months past to go out with him now and then, mek something of me life. So now I shall.'

'I'm glad . . . but my father said he was coming back in a few months,' Philip said. 'Didn't he . . . didn't he tell you the same?'

'Oh, he *told* me, all right,' Bess said rather scornfully. 'But readin' between the lines, he'll not come back. Why should he buy a farm for a few months – it don't mek sense. I think he's havin' one of his fits for something. You haven't known him as long as I have sir, beggin' your pardon for speaking frank, but he's always been the same. First it was the pots, before I knew him of course, but they say he was crazy to make good pots. Then it was banking, he dabbled in banking for a while, bought shares and all sorts. Then it was leatherworks, and you heard nothing but leather and all about his shops. Then he dropped that, or near as anything, and it was all your experiments and how you was going to do marvellous thing . . . and now it's farming.'

'Perhaps you have a point,' Philip admitted. 'I'm awfully sorry if you feel he's let you down though, Bess – if there's anything I can do to help just let me know.'

'I'll be fine sir, thanking you kindly,' Bess assured him. 'You go and get on with them experiments. Perhaps that'll bring him back.'

'So I don't know what to make of it, Unk,' Philip said earnestly that evening, as he and Sidney Warburton shared a meal at the Manor. 'He almost said he'd left me the Hall . . . as if I'd want that great barn of a place . . . and scarcely a word about Rose . . .' He fished the letter out of his pocket. 'Read it and you'll be no wiser.'

Sidney took the letter and read it slowly and carefully, then put it down on the table once more.

'He's had some news about Rose and it's pushed him into taking the farm and keeping away from here,' he said after a few moments. 'Didn't

328

you notice? He said he'd heard nothing about Rose, then told you he'd bought the farm, then said he hoped to have news of her in six or seven months. Does it occur to you that she might be with him in Devon?'

'No. Unk, why should he lie to me? I'm his son!'

'And Rose is his daughter. I'm just guessing, but don't you think it's possible that she's agreed to stay with your father but refused to come home? The disgrace, you know. Leaving in a temper to make one's fortune is one thing, creeping back with your tail between your legs having made nothing but a fool of yourself quite another.'

'Yes, that sounds more like Rose. He said nothing about Mama, either, though.'

'I always did doubt that Rose had found her mother,' Sidney said. 'No child, no matter how selfish, would fail to boast about a mission accomplished. Rose said nothing because there was nothing to say. She hadn't found her mama, she had simply decided to stay away. There's nothing particularly complex about your sister, my dear boy; she's rather more straightforward than most, indeed. She's just incredibly singleminded.'

'Then you think Father's found her?'

'I do.' Sidney sighed. 'I wish I had been as fortunate, but China's an awfully big country.'

# CHAPTER TWENTY-THREE

'That is good . . . very good, Nala. You have a talent many men would envy. I could not do better myself. It's a peasant, winnowing rice, isn't it? Yet you've managed to make it look like a design at first and even second glance. Possibly the less acute eye would merely enjoy the shapes without realizing their significance as a human figure.'

Nala and Sven Han-ti were in his workshop, bending over an exquisite little vase which Nala had just fired for the second time with her design boldly outlined in black upon the pale greenish glaze. Nala touched the lines, then smiled up at Sven.

'I'm pleased with it; I think people like shapes which remind them of a person rather than an actual drawing of a peasant winnowing rice. Do you remember how well the mother and child design sold? But few of the buyers realized it was a mother and child until they had owned it for some while; they only saw that the lines seemed to flow just right.'

'That was something I never taught you,' Sven admitted. 'My art is straightforward in that I draw what I see; you draw the spirit.'

329

'Well, I try.' Nala glanced around the workroom; at the rows of pots, the pages of designs and drawings, the comfortable clutter. Outside, Sven's climbing kiln, built to use the natural slope of the hill, would be quietly firing his pots at different temperature levels with old Han-ti, Sven's elderly uncle, keeping a weather eye on the proceedings.

'Now how about the tiles, Nala? Have you a suitable design for them? It is a big thing for us, this Paris exhibition, and I want to show our best, impress buyers. Indeed, I know very well that I should move the workroom nearer to Shanghai so that our ware can be exported more easily.' He smiled at the girl. 'I have a family to feed; we mustn't forget them.'

Sven's family was well known to everyone in the village since he had sons and daughters in their twenties and a baby of not quite eight months. Add to that his adopted children . . . seven girls and two boys . . . and the fact that his most recent wife had come to him as a widow with three little ones of her own, and you could understand his importance in the community. Half Swedish, tall and handsome even in his late fifties, he was a considerable power in the land, and though a craftsman of no mean order he was also as interested in money and success as any man Nala had ever met.

'If you don't want to succeed, if you don't crave at least a measure of fame, then you're no use to me,' he had said bluntly to Nala on that first visit more than three years ago. 'I'm a craftsman, one of the best, and I've done well in China, but I'm aiming, now, for a wider market. The war held me back but the war's over and I'm doing all sorts now to get my work seen – I travel, I spend time abroad, and I'll continue to do so until you can find Han-ti china and tiles in all the best homes in Europe.'

'I want to succeed, and I want to be famous,' the young Nala had said, pushing her hair out of her eyes and leaning forward to stare at the ware he had brought out to show her. 'That's beautiful . . .' she pointed '. . . and that . . . and that. But that one's bottom-heavy and the design's too light for the clay.'

It had been the right thing to say, though for a moment Nala had almost stopped breathing in case he took offence and decided not to have her working with him after all. But Sven had raised a brow, stared at the pot in question, and then barked with laughter before picking the pot up and crashing it to smithereens against the opposite wall.

'Only a wide-eyed beginner, yet she put her finger straight on the problem,' he had said to the startled Ellises. 'She'll do. Send her in first thing tomorrow morning and we'll see what we can make of her. I shan't pay her a penny piece until I see what she's worth.'

It had not been easy, at first. Pentai was a long way from Sven's village and Nala had to ride a dim-witted but obstinate donkey for miles along narrow tracks. But after a couple of years Sven had got his young wife to go along to the Ellises and offer to have Nala to stay with them six days a week, so that she could go home on a Sunday.

Sven was so big, so hearty, and so obviously fond of women that Mrs Ellis had been doubtful about trusting her young charge to him, but her husband saw it differently.

'Sven's a good fellow. He marries the women he wants, he doesn't seduce them,' he said bluntly. 'Nala will come to no harm with Sven; the villagers are more than half afraid of him, and they certainly admire his way of life. They wouldn't raise a finger against anyone in Sven's employ.'

It was true; in all the time she had lived in the Han-ti compound Nala had been shown respect by those villagers with whom she came in contact and affection from the Han-ti family themselves. At almost seventeen she was very like the young Adeline, but her face had more character and confidence than her mother's, Kei told her.

'Adeline was not always quite well,' Kei had said. 'She was by nature very pale, her skin was white; yours has a creamy, peachy tint.'

'Sunburn,' Nala had muttered and seen Kei laugh.

'Her hair was like yours, though; true black. But it was not as wavy nor as thick.'

'It's a pest,' Nala said. 'I wish it was beautifully straight and smooth, like your little Paiti's.'

'Oh, Nala, don't wish yourself different; one day you'll be glad you are as you are, when you meet more English people.'

But now, in the workshop with Sven, Nala concentrated on his question.

'A design for the tiles? Sven, I have so many beautiful ones, it's hard to choose which is the most suitable. But I thought we'd use typical Chinese designs because I doubt that many other Chinese workshops will be represented in Paris, and I've settled on two, with the possibility of a third if you agree. I've done one which I think could be used for kitchens and another for bathrooms. I'll show you.'

She drew the designs out from under the workbench and Sven took them from her and frowned over them, whistling soundlessly beneath his breath.

'The willow tree over the lake with the children bathing in the shallows, that's to be the bathroom one? Hmm, yes. A bluey-green colour, I think. And the kitchen one I like . . . a string of onions, a fish, a pile of cherries . . . yes, they'll both do very well. And the third?'

'Apple blossom,' Nala said, handing him the last design. 'Just a spray. But it's the way it lies . . . the number of blossoms on each twig . . . I think it feels right.'

'Yes . . . have you done them on the clay yet, though?'

'Not yet; I was waiting to see if you approve. Shall I start them today?'

'I think so. And later in the week we'll take ourselves off to the city and talk to someone about our exhibition. We'll go to Paris, of course.'

'We?'

'Yes, we, Nala. You and me. I think you'll find that your designs are very popular and if this is so then you must be there because when orders come in it is no use my saying "Yes she can do that," if you could not possibly manage it in the time available. Do you see?'

'Yes, but . . . Sven, what will it cost, such a trip? You have a family, as you're always telling me. I can't take money from their mouths and I certainly couldn't afford to pay for myself.'

'Don't worry about it; it will be an investment,' Sven assured her. 'Just get to work on those tiles and try not to break too many in the firing.'

So she was to go to Paris! Nala could hardly bear to wait for the weekend, when she could go back to the village and tell Ouyang. Of course the dear Ellises would be thrilled as well, but for her childhood friend the news would be even more exciting, for true to his early promise Ouyang had had no difficulty in getting into a university. He was doing a degree in languages because he wanted to be able to represent his country out in the world, he said.

It would have been simple enough to have written him a letter, Nala supposed, but since she knew that Ouyang would be returning to Pentai this weekend to see his family, she decided to save the news up until she could tell him in person. He had overcome the repulsion he felt for big cities and was in Nanking, studying at the university there. He told Nala happily that at last he had found many people with his own feelings exactly towards China; militant Communists, many of them, who took Ouyang to Party meetings and helped him to understand the complexities of the regime. Yet despite all this modern thinking he was still a very good son of his family, travelling home at least three times a term to pay his respects and assure his elders that he was going to make them all proud of him.

So Nala travelled home to Pentai and banged on the windows of the 'bus when it passed friends she had come to love and hopped off near the Te Ku compound, her heart beating harder at the thought of the adventure of going to Paris and how Ouyang would rejoice for her. He must have guessed which 'bus she would be on, indeed, for as she alighted she saw him strolling out of the gate to meet her. She raised a hand and he broke into a trot. He was smiling.

'Well, Nala? And how are you after a week of toiling over your clay?'

'Ouyang, I'm going to Paris!'

'You are? To show off your ware at this exhibition they're holding in France? Well, aren't you a clever little one, then! And do you know, I'm off as well? Oh, not to France, but to America. I am going for a year to study economics and agriculture and all sorts of similar things.' He saw her crestfallen expression and pulled her close, giving her a hug. 'Come along now, you knew I'd probably go abroad for a year or two! Don't let me see a long face – rejoice for me, as I'm rejoicing for you. You must write to me often and I'll write back, I promise you. A year will soon pass!'

After that they talked at very great length about his trip and hers, and about how he hoped to learn from the Americans how to grow all sorts of crops that the Chinese had never tried to cultivate. But under the chat and the banter, under their jokes and laughter, Nala was horribly aware of a well of loneliness, growing deeper and deeper. She was on good terms with the Han-ti family; she was dearly loved by the Ellises; even the Te Ku clan seemed fond of her. But her relationship with Ouyang had always been special and very sweet and she sensed that now they would begin to grow apart and go their separate ways.

It took some of the excitement out of the Paris trip and, she guessed, glancing sideways at him when he was not looking at her, it must slightly dim the thrill of a visit to the United States as well.

As if he could read her thoughts, Ouyang squeezed her fingers hard.

'I'll walk you home,' he said, tucking his hand into the crook of her elbow. 'And we'll stay good friends no matter what – you see if we don't.'

'It's perfection!' Philip breathed as the saggar was opened, to reveal the tall, slender jar with its narrow neck and swelling belly. 'Have you ever seen a colour like it? Frank, this will have to go to Paris!'

The jar was glazed in a deep, dramatic golden-orange, the colour of a flaming sunset, the colour of a glowing ember of charcoal, fanned to life by one's breath. There was, for once, complete silence in the workroom. Not a man present but was awed, this time, by their achievement.

'It's incredible; what will you call it?'

Philip smiled and sketched a shrug. 'What about sunburst orange?'

'It doesn't matter what we call it,' Jim remarked. 'A colour like that will name itself; the press will go wild. If you ask me, you've invented a brand-new colour!'

'It's beautiful,' a young lad who had been bringing the saggars out of the kiln said softly. 'That's t'best colour I've ever clapped eyes on.'

Philip turned to smile at him.

'Ay, you're right there, Ken . . . but wait till you see the jug . . . it's the most wonderful deep violet colour . . . and there will be more now that we've got the glaze right.'

'It's a nice pot, an' all,' Ken remarked. 'Good for that particular colour – strong, and yet shapely.'

'There's a bouquet for you, Jim,' Frank said. 'Wait till we get to Paris . . . I tell you, they'll go wild. But we've got to keep it dark till then so not a word outside this place, none of you.'

The men nodded and murmured. Just as it had affected everyone, the depression had hit the potteries. With the men back from the trenches there were just not enough jobs to go round. Anything that brought work to their pot-bank was welcome, and a secret which would bring orders flooding in was well worth keeping.

'Back to the lab then, fellows,' Philip said presently, when the saggars had yielded up their burden of brilliance. 'These pots are specially made for the exhibition, and we want to add to them before we start mass production. Not that these particular colours will ever mass produce – they'd be too expensive, for a start. But we can use them in the designs.'

Back in the familiar surroundings, Philip took off his tie and hung it on the peg by the door. Ties were a nuisance in the laboratory even if you wore your overall; they were too liable to break loose and end up in a boiling hot frit. Frank followed suit but Jim had not returned with them; now that the Paris exhibition was weeks rather than months away he was too busy downstairs, throwing new shapes, to be able to spend much time in the laboratory.

'We never did get that girl in to do some new designs,' Frank remarked presently as he mixed chemicals, weighing them with meticulous care before tipping them into the saggar. 'Still, we're getting awfully near iridescent lustreware, and in a way we don't need designs, not yet. First we want to sock 'em with the colours, right?'

'Yes, quite true.' Philip was stirring a tiny amount of material in a test tube over a Bunsen burner; he was using a thin glass rod and scowling down at his work. 'At the moment artwork would detract from the colours and the different glazes . . . that orange-peel effect is pretty startling. But later, perhaps . . .'

'Yes, later,' Frank agreed. 'I'm going to try to recreate the blister effect which you had on that jade green pot last week. It wasn't particularly pretty or anything, but it was weird. I predict that whilst we're popular for our colours almost anything we produce which is out of the ordinary will be in demand.'

'You're probably right,' Philip agreed. 'Ah . . . it's beginning to meld.'

A silence followed as the young men worked away at their separate yet allied tasks.

'You ready, Uncle?'

Frank usually went home with Roger Trewin when the day's work was over and today was no exception. They would walk along the light, early summer streets chatting and thinking about their work and the exhibition. Everyong in the pot-bank was excited over the exhibition, for great hopes hung on the outcome of it. But this evening Frank had other things on his mind.

'Uncle Roger, you know I said I was going to try to get young Philip to employ a girl in the laboratory to do artwork? Well, it didn't come off. That doesn't matter at all at the moment, since we don't really need artwork now that we've got the colours to show. But what does matter is Philip's attitude to girls.'

'He's about as useful as you are, Frankie, when there's females around,' his uncle said. 'Neither one of you'll say boo, that's the trouble. But you're young, same as Mr Philip; plenty time for sparking yet.'

'Yes . . . but I've got Martha,' Frank pointed out. 'I'm shy with girls, that's true, but not with Martha. Philip, now, he's not even got a sister any more, and in Paris he'll maybe see girls he'd like to chat with or take out and he's just about incapable of even approaching them.'

'He's no' much like Mr Arnold, then,' Roger Trewin said. 'A bugger for the lasses, was Mr Arnold. Even when his wife were alive he couldn't leave the girls alone. Known for it, he was.'

'Aye, I know. That's what makes it so odd that Philip's different. You know I'm going with him to Paris?'

'Aye. Like a pair of Siamese twins, the two of you. But it's a grand opportunity for you, lad, grand. Mek the most of it.'

'I will. But I thought before then we'd maybe better get to know a couple of girls . . . I wondered if I could ask Martha to come out with me and Philip and bring a friend along.'

'Oh, no, I wouldn't do that, lad,' Trewin said, taking instant fright. 'Mr Arnold might not like it. He wouldn't want his lad mixing with girls from t'pot-bank, I dare say. Better leave well alone.'

Martha was a flower painter in the china department, and Frank had known her now for nearly five years. He and she would marry one day, no doubt, but they wanted to be financially sound before they took such a big step and financial soundness was some way off.

'That's all very well, Uncle, but what's worrying me is Paris. He's a bit of an innocent, is young Philip; suppose he decides to toss his cap over the windmill in Paris and get himself a girl? I don't speak French . . . he doesn't speak much, but more than I do . . . and I don't fancy interfering between him and his first woman. But she could be a real gold-digger, Uncle, intent on parting the lad from his money . . . remember, Mr Arnold went off to London to buy china – 'twas his first time away – and came back with a wife. I remember you laughing over it when I was a bit of a lad. And her no better than she ought to be, you said . . . Philip was on the way before they tied the knot, you said.'

'Aye, you've a point there, for no Haslington can bear to be driven, though they can sometimes be led,' his uncle admitted uneasily. 'Perhaps you're right, lad, perhaps you'd best get Martha to bring a friend along. But tell t'lass to mek sure she brings a decent young woman what won't tek advantage of the lad. All right?'

'I'll tell her,' Frank assured his uncle earnestly. 'I wouldn't want to involve Philip with the wrong kind of girl.'

'I think we ought to relax, Philip, take ourselves out for an evening, so I've booked a table at the Star & Garter restaurant – it's a good place – and afterwards we could go to the flickers, or take a walk into the country, whichever you'd prefer.' Frank braced himself, forcing himself to speak casually. 'I've asked my Martha to come along and bring a friend . . . it'll do us good.'

'A girl? Oh, lor',' Philip groaned. 'I'm no use with girls, Frank, you know that. One glance from those little chicks perched on the factory wall and I just want to melt. Look, we've got a lot on our plate right now, we're doing awfully well with our experiments, let's be content with that, shall we?'

'All work and no play makes Jack a dull boy,' Frank quoted wearisomely. 'Come on, Phil, be a sport. It'll do you good . . . besides, I've arranged it now.'

'Oh . . . all right, if you've arranged it.'

Philip continued to work but he was surprised, really, at how much more cheerful even the prospect of an outing made him feel, though the inclusion of Martha and a friend took the shine off it. Too young for much interest in girls before he joined the army, he had had no opportunities to further his acquaintance with the female sex in the deserts of Arabia and the Far East, and in college he was too keen to catch up and keep up with others in his classes to have time to spare for women.

Home once more, his acquaintance with Rose and her friend Elizabeth had not been much of an introduction to the joys of pretty women; Rose he thought typical of her sex and Elizabeth was a silly little thing. So one way and another, what with shyness and being brought up in an all male school and then a male dominated household, Philip had managed very well without any women in his life at all.

And one evening out with Frank and his Martha won't change that, he reminded himself now, turning the latest vase for the exhibition this way and that to admire the strength and evenness of the glaze. A beautiful vase like this is a lot more use than the most charming of women. Women only let you down when it comes to the crunch – look at Mama. She ran off without a thought for Rose or me, and even now, when we're grown up and would simply like to know her, she keeps away. Well, let her! We don't need her.

The evening out with the girls arrived. Philip, to please Frank, dressed in a navy blue blazer with monogrammed gold buttons and his best light grey trousers. He slicked his hair down with water rather than Brylcreem, though, and decided to treat Martha's friend just as he would another fellow.

Frank and Philip, duly forewarned, waited well clear of the factory gates for the young ladies. Martha's friend, apparently, felt no pride in being taken out by the boss.

'He's queer about girls,' she was reported to have told Frank's girl. 'He never speaks to us on t'factory floor if he can avoid it.'

So now, both young men waited with a certain amount of trepidation.

But they need not have worried. Martha was twenty-five, only a couple of years younger than Frank, and a practical, kindly young woman. Her friend Freda was twenty-three and not only pretty but charming, too. Put her face to face with a feller and she'd be nice to him because she couldn't be otherwise, Martha told herself, and so it proved. Freda had dark auburn hair cut attractively short, a turned-up nose, a flashing smile and a fashionable figure, which meant flat-chested and long-legged. She came tripping up to Philip with a big smile on her face and a good deal of make-up enhancing her countenance.

'Hello!' she cried as gaily as though she and Philip had been friends for years. 'How are you keeping?'

Philip said that he was very well thank you, and how was she?

'Eh, I'm doing fine,' Freda said. She tucked her hand into the crook of his arm. 'Going to have some fun, are we? Eh, I do like a meal out somewhere posh, don't you? And a penn'orth of dark later.'

'A penn'orth of dark?'

She shot a glance pregnant with mischief up at him as they walked along the pavement towards the Star and Garter.

'Aye . . . you've not heard th'expression before, then? It means we're going t'flickers, see?' She squeezed his arm with her small, gloved hand. 'Eh, you learn a thing or two in t'back row, lad!'

Philip looked at Frank with new respect; this was clearly a modern young woman who thought nothing of teaching him a thing or two in the back row of the one-and-nines! It occurred to him that this girl was not frightening nor overpowering, just good fun, and he should take advantage of knowing her. Metaphorically, he squared his shoulders.

'I'll be happy to learn anything from you, Freda,' he said, and patted the little hand nestling in the crook of his arm. 'We'll have a grand time, I'm sure of it.'

They had a grand time, all four of them, though Frank was a little worried when he saw how Freda clutched Philip in the back row of the stalls and how she insisted that she be run all the way home in Philip's car, though she could very well have walked.

'I just hope she doesn't corrupt him,' Frank said anxiously to Martha. Martha laughed but pinched his hand reprovingly.

'Corrupt him? There's not an ounce of vice in Freda,' she said. 'She'll enjoy a good time and see he has one too, that's all.'

It certainly seemed as though Philip enjoyed her company, for he began to see more of her and became a little easier with the girls in the factory, though not to the extent of addressing a word to any of them which was not strictly necessary. Frank very soon realized that Philip did not see himself as either attractive or eligible, though he was clearly both. But still, at least he's capable of addressing a few words to a woman now without going bright red and stammering, Frank told himself. And one comfort is that no bad girl is going to get her claws into him in Paris or anywhere else, not whilst he's so desperately uncomfortable in female company!

They had booked into a quiet hotel for the whole week, though the exhibition was only on for four days. But Philip thought they really should take advantage of being in Paris to see the sights, and had talked of staying on for a further week himself, though Frank insisted that one week was quite sufficient for him, and that he would go back at the end of it regardless.

They packed days beforehand, of course, since the best ware was crated weeks earlier and would, in fact, be in Paris long before them, but they were adding to it all the time.

'If you come across an artist whilst you're there, remember we'll be needing someone good soon,' Jim called out to them on their last visit to the factory before their departure. 'Good luck with sales!'

'Good luck! Best of luck! Wish you every success!' The words rang round the pot-bank and Philip felt, not for the first time, the weight of their need resting on his shoulders. He was responsible for them in a way which, had he realized it would happen, would have completely floored him a year earlier. But he had taken on the responsibility bit by bit so that he had grown to meet the weight as it grew heavier and had never had to bear the full burden before he was ready for it.

'The sunburst orange is packed, and the violet, the ultramarine, the soft jade, the brilliant red,' Philip murmured as he got in the car and began to rev the engine preparatory to leaving the factory yard. 'Yes, it all seems to be going according to plan. Perhaps I'll pop round and see Freda later this evening.'

He had grown very fond of Freda. She was a delightful and generous companion and had, as she had promised, taught him quite a lot. But he had no illusions about her. She was not the sort of girl that, one day, he wanted to marry and he was not the young man to make her happy. She wanted someone much more extrovert, much less serious. But for both of them their liaison had been a happy time and one which they would look back on, one day, with a certain wistful pleasure.

Back home at the Hall, with the servants rattling round, or so it seemed to Philip, in the vast house, he wondered again what Arnold was doing and why he had not been more forthcoming. He had not written, save notes, since the first time and Philip himself had been far too busy getting his ware ready for the exhibition to think of going off down to Devonshire.

I'll have dinner, then go and see Freda, then come home and go to bed, I suppose, Philip thought rather dismally, greeting Mrs Parton with all the good cheer he could conjure up. A week in Paris, after this barn of a place, would be a real treat; seeing Frank's face opposite his own at the table would be friendly. Philip was lonely. He even missed Rose, for selfish and thoughtless as she was, she was at least another human being in the house. He scarcely saw the servants, though he knew enough about fending for himself to be grateful that they were there. Still, he had a new fellow-feeling for Unk, who had been alone in the Manor for so long. How he stuck it . . . but then I'm sticking it, Philip reminded himself. And I'll go on sticking it until Father comes back. But then I really think I'll

338

get myself a little place in Langforth, or even in the village, so that the running of this house isn't such a drain on our resources.

The thought pulled him up short, amazed at his own stupidity. As if he would need to move out . . . once his father came back there would be a good reason for the money which was being poured out on the upkeep of the Hall.

But in his heart, he realized, he did not think that Arnold would come back, not to stay. Why should he? He had bought this flower farm, whatever that might be, and he was, presumably, with Rose, his adored daughter. Why come back here, up to the frozen north (it was a chilly evening), when he could remain with his favourite child in what was, presumably, an idyllic situation?

Philip stumped into the dining-room and ate his dinner grimly. He looked round the room, at the panelled walls, the dark oil paintings of other people's ancestors (the Haslingtons had been in trade long enough to buy ancestors but not long enough to possess respectable ones of their own) and at the long, velvet-draped windows. It had scared him as a kid, he remembered, and over-awed him as a teenager. Now it simply bored and disgusted him . . . he thought of the Manor, and Sidney Warburton's easy-going, friendly servants, none of whom would have thought twice about having a chat with their master. I'll go over and say cheerio to Unk, and then I'll go and see Freda, he decided. And then . . . I've a good mind to ask Freda if I can spend the night on her couch. At least it would mean I didn't have to come back here.

Arnold, meanwhile, was in his element, though he did think about Philip and the experimental ware quite often.

But he was so happy! The flower farm was delightful, a small white-washed farmhouse perched on heather-clad cliffs, with the blue sea thundering below on the rocks and the smooth sand of the perfect beaches. He had Rose's undivided attention and looked after her as a father should look after a daughter. They went for long walks, though Rose grumbled most of the way out and all the way back. They swam in the sea in their brand-new bathing costumes, though Rose kept reminding her father that a woman in her condition might quite easily just roll over and drown, pulled under by the obscene lump in her stomach. They ate healthy, home-grown and home-made food, though Rose said it was making her fat and ruining her chances of eventual fame and fortune. The two, it seemed, went together in Rose's mind like biscuits and cheese. It was no use Arnold pointing out that fortunes could be earned in pot-banks or leatherworks; to Rose the only fortunes that mattered were made on the stage.

Arnold did not actually work the farm himself – he had an excellent man to do that – but he took a great interest in the work and was always expounding new ways to get their flowers to market.

339

'Ee'll make most of thy money in the spring, my dear,' Mr Caldicott told them. 'Then we'm likely to have daffy-down-dillies out weeks afore the rest o' the country, to say nothing of primroses and forsythia and jonquils and narcissus. And polyanthus. And iris.'

'And do we send all those flowers away?' Arnold asked, to receive a big smile and a nod of the head.

'Oh, aye, m'dear. Some as cut flowers, some in pots, but they all go off on the train to Lunnon.'

Rose, of course, took almost no interest in the flowers, but she wrote a lot of letters and twice during the early days of what she termed, tragically, her incarceration Granville Sinclair came to visit her.

'We miss you,' he said the first time, with such unflattering astonishment in his tone that Arnold nearly laughed out loud, but did not because he was too busy being disapproving. He had his suspicions as to who had caused Rose's downfall, though she was not at all helpful on the subject.

'I don't know how it happened; I've never done anything I shouldn't,' she said when he quizzed her. 'I've always kept myself to myself, so someone must have taken advantage of me.'

Arnold, with beautifully clear pictures of taking advantage of Lily long before Rose was born, wondered whether he ought to point out to Rose that a girl was rarely taken advantage of so thoroughly, when she slept, as to wake without any recollection of the event. But Rose's temper, always uncertain, was now such that Arnold hesitated to provoke it. In the end he just said, mildly, that she really should try to remember the name of the baby's father and left it at that.

The local doctor, called in to take a look at Rose, reported almost equal lack of success.

'She's clearly pregnant,' he told Arnold, 'but she refuses to discuss the birth or anything to do with it. I'd send the midwife up but your daughter more or less forbade me to do any such thing. Still, girls get fancies in her condition. I'll call later.'

Rose had also refused to wear the very nice, plain gold band that her father had acquired for her.

'I'm not married, so why should I pretend?' she said peevishly. 'And as soon as it's all over I'm leaving here, getting back to a proper city with a theatre.'

'She'll feel different when she holds the littl'un in her arms,' Mrs Shilling said. She was a motherly soul and kept house for Arnold and Rose. Arnold agreed with these sentiments, of course, or rather he paid lip-service to them, but in his heart he had severe doubts as to Rose's maternal instincts. He did not believe they existed.

'Are you ready to leave? You're so lucky, Nala,' Sven's eldest and prettiest daughter said tragically. 'You'll never come back, not once you've seen Paris – well, I'm sure I wouldn't. And you're really a

340

European, not just a little bit of you, like us, so you could fit in without any trouble at all.'

Nala looked lovingly at Gerda, who was her favourite amongst Sven's enormous brood. Gerda had managed to get the best of both worlds, mixing and mingling the good looks of both parents to perfection. She had hair as shiny and red as a chestnut fresh out of its husk and her skin was creamy-gold. Her almond-shaped eyes were a dark brown, not black, and her figure was long and slender, with small, pert breasts and almost no hips. She was sixteen and very conscious of her mixed race, though as Nala continually told her she was so beautiful and original that nothing else was of importance.

'Of course I'll come back, you goose,' Nala said reassuringly. 'Where else could I learn to use my skills the way your father has taught me? We are going to be famous, Sven and I, so I can't possibly remain in Europe and let my fame trickle away.'

'Well, perhaps you're right, but I still wish I was going,' Gerda said wistfully. 'If rich Frenchmen buy all our wares, then you'll want to come home and make some more very quickly, but Father was saying you're going to learn as well as to teach. What can they teach you and Father, Nala, about beautiful pots?'

'An awful lot, I fear. Remember, we only use the native clays and colours and our ware tends to be quite heavy, not light like the stuff made with bone-ash and china clay. Sven says he could make stuff like that easily, if there was a demand, but we hope that the foreigners will like our shapes and colours and glazes enough to order from us. And then, according to Sven, we'll rapidly become millionaires.'

'Yes . . . but Father says it isn't worth your going for less than two weeks . . . why can't you come back sooner?'

'We want to visit other people's workshops and see how they go on,' Nala explained. 'And we want to make sure that everyone possible sees our ware, otherwise the trip will be wasted. Your father even talked of visiting Sweden, Norway, and possibly even England, to try to get orders.'

'And will you? If so, surely you'll be away for even longer than a month?'

Nala shrugged. She was terribly excited at the thought of the trip and trying to be blasé and bored by it all; not an easy task when one is just seventeen and about to visit Paris for the first time.

'Let's leave it that we may,' she advised the older girl. 'But if this does put our pottery on the map, Gerda, your father says we'll definitely move the workshops – and your home, of course – nearer to Shanghai. So you see you'll see almost as much as me very soon. Shanghai's an international port. You'd like that, wouldn't you?'

'I don't know. But what about you, Nala? What would you do about the Ellises?'

'I'd visit them in my holidays,' Nala said a little uneasily. 'They've been so good to me, but no one can stay at home for ever, Gerda. They wouldn't want me to . . . look how good they've been about my living here during the week.'

'Yes, I suppose you're right. Things are very different in the West – Father's told us so often. There, you move away when you marry, all of you, whereas here we simply build another house on to the compound for the newly-weds.'

'I don't know very much about it,' Nala said truthfully. She did not want to talk about English habits because that made her think about the old old man in the old old house and that was upsetting. Sometimes she had dreams . . . she had never seen the old old house so of course her dreams were pure fantasy, but nevertheless she knew in her heart that she should not have cut herself off from her grandfather. Her mother had loved him dearly; her father had been fond of him and had deeply respected him. But if I were to get in touch now I might just make him unhappy over Mother all over again, Nala told herself. And anyway he might easily be dead, which would make me unhappy. By and large, the best thing to do was nothing. Just leave it. Forget about the old old man and the old old house.

'Will you send me some postcards of Paris?' Gerda said anxiously. 'I wish Father would send me abroad . . . I know I can't go to the exhibition really, because I'd be useless to him and you are very useful, but he might just send me away . . . I'm never going to get married here, you know. They all think I look odd!'

'You don't look Chinese,' Nala agreed. 'But in Shanghai you'll meet all sorts of people, including Swedes like your grandmother I expect. Don't worry, Gerda, you'll find a man to appreciate you.'

Gerda sighed and drifted out of the room as Nala checked her luggage again. Her ordinary Chinese clothes, a special European dress with silk stockings and high-heeled pumps, in case she and Sven were invited to some sort of reception. Then she looked round her room, shared it is true with three Han-ti girls but still somehow very much hers. It had whitewashed walls, a large communal bed-platform and a number of brightly coloured quilts, with a washstand to one side and a big, modern dressingtable so that the girls could see themselves as they brushed their hair and washed. The french windows led out on to the girls' courtyard and was ringed around by other, similar rooms shared by the Han-ti daughters.

I would miss it if I never saw it again, but I'd miss the workshops and the kilns more, Nala told herself and knew it was true. Every girl she knew, even the Han-ti, longed for marriage and a man of her own. Nala herself was the exception. She did not want a man or marriage, she told herself. She wanted to succeed with her pottery and to make a name for herself. Then and only then would she do a number of things. She would buy a nice house in the country somewhere and have a riding horse of her own, or perhaps even a motor car. She would employ a kindly old woman to keep house for her and a nice old man to do her garden. And she would paint beautiful pictures and make lovely pots and buy as many of the masterpieces of the past as she could afford . . . lovely old palace bowls in the blue and white china which were made in the 15th and 16th centuries, delicate wine-pourers, tiny figurines made of soapy green jade or delicious, yellowing ivory.

This idyllic picture would be completed by having her very own little cat and two nice big dogs who would love her and obey her and her alone.

Ouyang could come and stay with her, and bring his wife and their children, she supposed, for she knew, of course, that though she herself was unlikely to marry, Ouyang must certainly do so. He was her dearest friend, closer to her than anyone else now – for Kei and she had grown apart and the Ellises, dear though they were, belonged to her grandparents' generation – but close friends, when they are of different races, can be nothing more.

For Nala was coming to terms with her loneliness, though had she been questioned on the subject she would have laughed the idea to scorn. How could she be lonely, she would have said, surrounded all day by the Han-ti boys and girls, by the pottery workers, by neighbours, friends, acquaintances . . . how could she possibly be lonely?

But she was.

# CHAPTER TWENTY-FOUR

'What a place! Oh, Sven, I'm scared!'

Nala clung to Sven's sleeve, holding back, trying to hide behind his extremely ample proportions.

They had reached Paris the night before, just in time to fall, exhausted, into two single beds in two single rooms in a small hotel somewhere in the back streets of Montmartre. But now, after a breakfast of hot rolls and excellent coffee, they had braved the streets and arrived at the exhibition centre.

It was a huge place, echoing, vast, and it was also complete bedlam. People were darting about with packing cases, stands, lengths of velvet drape and huge notices. The din was indescribable.

'I thought it started today,' Nala said faintly, then had to repeat the remark, her mouth only inches from Sven's ear, in order to be heard.

'No, exhibitors arrive today,' Sven bellowed back. 'Today we set up our displays and get ourselves ready for tomorrow, when the press first and then the public will be allowed in. Did you not notice how careful they were being on the doors? Only badge-holders are being admitted. They don't want a member of the press worming his way in and giving all the secrets away a day too soon.'

'Secrets? Will there be secrets, Sven?'

'Bound to be, with all these big, famous potteries sending work to put on display. Now, Nala, we aren't here to be over-awed or to gossip and stare. Look for packing cases with our mark on. What a good thing I thought to mark them specially.'

There were packing cases everywhere and more being delivered by the minute, but Nala could not help thinking to herself that it was unlikely that more than a few would come from China. Most potters she had come across in that country produced in a small way, unlike Sven. He is big and he thinks big, she told herself as she rooted amongst the packing cases.

'Here they are!' Sven called presently. 'The people who run these exhibitions have promised me a counter and some display cases . . . I did not think to provide myself with drapes, however, or flowers, or . . . look around, Nala.'

Nala obeyed. As soon as she did so she saw why Sven was looking harassed, because almost without exception those displaying their china were doing so in a very fanciful way. Some of the vases were almost hidden by the displays of flowers in them, others were laid out on swathes of silk or velvet . . . someone had brought a stuffed lamb with a garland of flowers around its neck and the little thing was being stood on a piece of vivid artificial grass and the grass scattered with china cups, saucers and plates. They were rather pretty, the china itself garlanded with flowers, but privately Nala thought it a shame to take the eye from the china in such a fashion. Clearly, though, Sven did not share her feelings.

'We'll have to find some stuff,' he said distractedly. 'Nala, pop out and buy something suitable.'

'I don't speak French,' Nala pointed out. 'And what's suitable, Sven? I think we ought to set up the show-cases and the counter and get our ware out of the packing cases. Then and only then should we think about display.'

'You don't like all that velvet,' Sven said acutely. 'But you're only a girl, you may be wrong.' There was a short silence whilst he thought about it. 'On the other hand, you may be right. At least we will do nothing until we're sure.'

'Good enough,' Nala replied. They were speaking in Chinese and she noticed that the people at the next stand were glancing at them curiously. Their packing cases had their name and address on so she glanced at it and immediately addressed them in English.

'Good morning, may we introduce ourselves? We are the Han-ti Pottery and you, I see come from Great Britain. I'm Nala and this is Sven. I'm

English myself, though I was born and bred in China, and Sven is half Swedish. How do you do?'

The couple thus addressed immediately became wreathed in smiles. They were both women, both quite tall and similar enough in feature for Nala to guess that they were related.

'How do you do?' they said in chorus, and the younger of the two added, 'We're Phoebe and Edna Frobisher, from Chester, in England. We run a small pot-bank there – with a good deal of help from our workers, of course. We're sisters.'

After that, everything seemed easier. The sisters confided that they, too, had come unprepared for silks and satins and agreed with Sven's suggestion that they should all wait and display their goods first before rushing out to buy fripperies which might well prove unnecessary.

'We have a good deal of very subtly coloured and decorated ware, which could easily fade into insignificance if the material used for display was too rich and colourful,' Sven told them. 'What sort of kilns do you have in Chester?'

This was a good subject and very soon all four of them were chattering away as fast as they could go and exclaiming with admiration as the cases were opened and the contents reverently brought forth.

'This is celadon ware,' Sven told the sisters, taking the delicate, jade-coloured dishes and containers out of the straw in which they had been packed. 'No decoration is needed with this ware – the colour and the line say everything.'

The sisters murmured admiringly, then produced their own favourites.

'This is our country line; we call them Country Class,' Edna said, showing them some beautiful green-glazed pottery with a nice shape, comfortable to hold in the hand. 'We have our Sea Class as well . . . what do you think?'

'It's nice stuff,' Sven said. 'It is good that you've not made the Sea Class blue, but grey-blue. Unusual. And the white design breaking around the top of each piece . . . foam on the surf, of course. Very nice, very imaginative.'

'The sea around our coast is more often grey than blue,' Phoebe said, smiling. 'Do you admire the process of dipping a piece of reddish ware into a white slip, letting it dry to the consistency of leather, and then cutting a pattern on the white slip so that the red clay shows through? We use it sometimes. It's simple and quick but can be very effective.'

Silently, Sven pulled out a piece which had been so decorated. Both sisters clasped their hands and showed pleasure over the sketch, which was a lively horse rearing up with a young man a-tiptoe at its head. Nala had done it in a moment with a few quick, well-chosen lines scratched through the slip.

'That is very fine; ours is only fish.'

They produced a set of fish dishes, each one fish shaped and decorated

345

by scratching through a creamy-white slip so that the darker colour of the clay showed through. They were beautifully finished and the fish themselves were drawn in some detail.

'They are very fine too,' Nala said at once. 'Which of you did them?'

'Me,' Edna said without pride. 'I usually decorate; Phoebe is the one to throw a difficult shape . . . we have a couple of young men who do the glazing and firing, and they decorate too, sometimes.'

'We both do everything,' Sven said. 'But Nala is becoming a very fine artist. Presently we will undo the packing case which contains her tiles. You will like them, I think.'

They did. And Nala was pleased to notice that it was not only the sisters who appeared to admire their ware. Very soon people were strolling up from all over the huge hall, walking past, whispering, and then coming back and introducing themselves. Du Courtair from France itself, who specialized in bone china. A tall, skinny Belgian who was interested in salt-glazing and wanted them to try his formula for fruit-skin finishes. There were potters from all over, some from huge factories, others from tiny potteries with one small climbing kiln who were producing perhaps no more than a couple of dozen exquisite works of art a year, although they made and sold large quantities of more mundane ware.

When at last all their ware was on display, Nala felt justly pleased that she had persuaded Sven not to go buying silks and satins. The ware was its own best advertisement, she considered. It glowed with good workmanship and fine decoration, and the tiles made a background for the more delicate pieces, the strong, definite colours she had chosen adding to, rather than stealing from, the whole effect of the display.

When it was all in position she and Sven left the sisters to keep an eye on both exhibitions and went wandering themselves. Nala really enjoyed seeing so much beauty, and Sven did as well, she could tell, though he did his very best to appear indifferent.

'Look at that! Oh, Sven, that's so delicate . . . do you think we could make one like that?' Nala's whispers brought smiles to many a face, for everyone had brought their best and everyone longed, as indeed did Nala and Sven, for compliments and admiration.

'We can't go right round the whole hall,' Sven said at last, when they had spent an hour away from their own place and had not seen a fraction of the ware on display. 'Besides, everyone isn't here yet – the stall beside the sisters is still waiting for the workers to start opening their packing cases. Did you see? They were labelled with an English address so at least we'll be able to converse when they do arrive. I'm truly thankful that I learned English and taught it to all my children; you need a second language when your first is Chinese.'

'Yes, I'm glad as well,' Nala said. 'What was the name of the people next to the sisters? I didn't notice.'

'I can't remember the name, but the place was Langforth,' Sven said, having given the matter some thought. 'They've taken a double stand so they're probably in quite a big way. But you know what, Nala? I haven't seen anything yet to compare with our display, not for delicacy of colour, strength of line or beauty of design. And I'm not just saying it because I'm prejudiced; I think it's true. Wait until the press come in tomorrow . . . I think they'll make straight for us once they've looked round a bit.'

'Would that be good?' Nala asked rather apprehensively. 'I don't fancy being asked a lot of questions about how we do things and how we get our effects.'

'Questions? The press? They'll ask questions all right, but they won't be *that* sort of question,' Sven chuckled. 'They're more likely to ask you what you had for breakfast and whether you want to marry a Chinese or a European than how you came by that cracked celadon effect. Anyway, I'll deal with 'em. You just look pretty and take orders when they start giving 'em. And don't forget, you've got to decorate the stuff they buy, so don't promise what you can't perform . . . in other words, keep an eye on what's being ordered and when you get more than a couple of months' worth of work call a halt, tell 'em there'll be a delay. I can throw the pots quickly enough, but they all have to be fired, slipped if they need it, coloured, painted, glazed, fired again . . . you know how it is, it takes time.'

'I didn't know the press would order stuff,' Nala said rather confused by so much rhetoric. But Sven gave a bark of laughter and told her she had got hold of the wrong end of the stick again.

'The press won't want to buy but the public will,' he said patiently. 'And when the press have had their turn tomorrow then the public will be allowed in. The press will be useful because they'll make sure we reach a wide audience. Art critics will tell their readers to come along to the exhibition and take a look at the Han-ti display, talk to the potter and the artist, that sort of thing. But it's the public who pay over their money, so they're the ones we're most interested in.'

They returned to their own stand, to see the sisters packing up. They did not put away their exhibits, of course, having gone to so much trouble to set them out, but they did swathe everything in large dust-sheets and lock up the most valuable stuff in the only lockable showcase before leaving.

'We're going to have a meal in our hotel tonight,' Edna told Nala as the two of them worked at making their display as safe as they could. 'Another night we'll wander round the city and have a meal somewhere a bit more adventurous, but tonight we think we'll need all the rest we can get. And tomorrow we're bringing sandwiches for lunch. What will you and Mr Han-ti do?'

'I think we'll get bread and cheese and some fruit,' Nala said. 'It wouldn't do to leave the display with the public wandering in and out, and

I don't fancy eating alone in the city. I don't speak any French at all, you see.'

'You could always come with one of us,' Edna said cheerfully. 'If we have to eat separately that would be one solution. But tomorrow it's sandwiches for us until we see how things go.'

When they were on their way home Nala told Sven what the sisters' plans were, and Sven agreed that for tomorrow, at least, they would follow suit.

'And tonight we'll dine in our hotel too,' he added. 'I'm very tired, and I dare say you are as well.'

'I'm quite tired, but I would like to see something of Paris,' Nala said wistfully, but Sven shook his head at her.

'We'll have time enough for that when the exhibition's over,' he reminded her. 'For now, we'll need all our strength to keep going day after day, with only the two of us to do everything. Besides, I dare say the hotel food will prove to be quite good.'

It was. They had beautiful onion soup with cheese floating on the top, followed by steak in a cream sauce, asparagus and a green salad, and then a pudding which was all nuts, cream and chocolate.

'European food is *good*,' Nala said, scraping her plate so energetically that Sven warned her she would remove the pattern. 'I never expected to like it this much, though the Ellises made a very delicious steak pie, and I liked the way they did potatoes as well.'

'Now bed,' Sven said firmly when they had finished their meal. Nala pouted but went to her room as she was told. One of these nights, she vowed, she would sneak out and really take a look around. Outside her hotel window Paris seemed to grow more wakeful and exciting as the evening wore on, but very soon she was asleep, the long day, the hard work and the strangeness proving as efficient a sleeping draught as any poppy drug.

'Paris is a beautiful city,' Nala said next morning, as she was dragged at a fast trot through the streets. They had once more breakfasted on hot rolls and good coffee, and had then emerged into a street full of sunshine which smelt of baking and flowers. Sven hurried her along, though, not even allowing her to glance into the fascinating shops, so that they arrived at the exhibition hall before it was open.

'I want some of those little pretty flowers which smell so sweet,' Nala said hopefully as they passed a street vendor surrounded by posies. But Sven was anxious for his ware, and would not stop even for a moment, so Nala was rather cross when they were let into the hall at last and hurried over to their stand. All was well and they were the first people in, though others quickly followed.

'The chaps from Langforth have arrived,' Sven murmured to her as she dusted her precious china. 'See? They're late, though; they're rushing like anything . . . gracious, look at that!'

'What?' Nala turned and craned her neck but could see nothing out of the ordinary, let alone anything interesting. She turned back to Sven. 'What?'

'There . . . the young men from Langforth.'

'I can't see *anything*,' Nala said after a lengthy pause whilst she stared. 'They've left the dust-sheets up over their display cases so even if they've got good stuff inside them you can't see it.'

'Precisely! They've got something unusual and they don't want it on display until the press arrive. That's why they didn't turn up yesterday. They weren't late getting here; they simply didn't want their ware seen too soon.'

'Well, I think that's silly,' Nala said, immediately on the defensive for their own ware. 'What have they got that the rest of us haven't?'

They were soon to discover. The press arrived, jaded-looking men and a couple of women, strolling around appearing more interested in each other than in the displays. Some person of importance performed the opening ceremony and then the press and the dignitaries began to mingle with the exhibitors and to make their way from stand to stand.

Nala did not realize, at first, what made the press suddenly turn almost as one man, and make in their direction, but she was gratified to see the urgent interest, the sudden keenness, on more than one face. She turned to comment to Sven . . . and the press swept past, to converge on the young men's stand. Nala turned to look . . . and the breath was momentarily suspended in her throat.

'Oh . . . Sven! Whatever is it? Oh, that burning, glorious colour!'

The gentlemen of the press were pushing and shoving, holding cameras above their heads, shouting questions, clicking, flashing . . . and for the first time Nala got a good look at the young men.

One was ordinary enough, with brown hair and eyes, horn-rimmed spectacles and a thin, pleasant face.

It was the other who caused her to stare so hard, a slight frown creasing her brow. He had thick, shining brown hair, lightening to blond on top where the sun had caught it, and dark brows and eyelashes. His eyes were brown too, and there was a surprised, amused look about his mouth and he had a square, determined sort of chin.

She knew him. How she had no idea, but his face was as familiar to her as though he had lived next door all their lives.

Nala shook her head and looked again. Of course she did not know him; she had never seen him in her life before. She dragged her eyes away from the young man and looked, instead, at the ware he had brought all the way from Langforth to this place, to show it to the world.

And she had no doubt, now, that he was showing it to the world, nor any doubt that the world wanted to see it and was intrigued and impressed.

No one, Nala thought dolefully, will be interested in our work now, not with that . . . that rainbow of beatuy almost next door!

She could hear names being bandied about now, by the young men's stand. The other exhibitors, attracted first by the press's descent and very quickly by the blaze of colour, were deserting their own stands and crowding round the latecomers. One of them, the thin-faced one, was putting up a notice in bold black letters. *Haslington Pottery, Langforth, Great Britain*, it read. Again a little tremor of what appeared to be recognition passed through Nala, setting the hairs on her arms and legs tingling erect. A goose walking over her grave? Perhaps. But a strong feeling that somewhere, at some time, she had known the name Haslington well.

'Well, I'm afraid no one else will get much press attention now,' Sven said, but his tone was not as gloomy as Nala would have expected. In fact he sounded downright jubilant. 'This is a piece of luck!'

'Luck? To have them getting all the attention, all the orders?' Nala's voice was tart. 'I don't call it luck, Sven, I call it a disaster.'

But Sven, with a chuckle, shook his head.

'You're wrong, my dear, I'm happy to say. Those young men will get heaps of publicity, far far more than we could possibly get for our beautiful, graceful designs, because they've discovered something rare and extraordinary. I've never seen colours like that in a lifetime of experimenting with pottery and following the exhibitions all over Europe. And because people will flock to see the Haslington Pottery stand, they'll also see ours. You see, our stuff is ready to sell, we're eager to find buyers, but unless I'm very much mistaken those lads are still experimenting. Oh, they can produce those colours and shapes all right, but my guess is that they're very expensive indeed to produce, which means that only museums or really rich collectors will actually buy the pots. The customers will come to stare . . . and will remain to buy what they can afford, which will be our stuff.'

'I hope you're right,' Nala said doubtfully. 'But at this moment we're not even getting a glance in passing; they're all rushing straight over there and clicking their cameras . . . I'm terrified, Sven, that we shan't sell anything!'

'Trust me,' Sven said, a big smile on his face. 'Just trust me.'

It was an hour before the reporters dragged themselves away from the Haslington stand, but then several of them came over to the Han-ti display. And it was the young man from the Haslington stand who brought them, furthermore. He walked over to them and smiled straight at Nala.

'Good morning. I'm sorry we seem to have stolen your thunder a bit, but the excitement will die down and you'll get the attention you deserve . . . I haven't introduced myself, I'm Philip Haslington.'

'This is Nala Chang,' Sven put in, a hand on his protégée's shoulder. 'Can we help you, Mr Haslington?'

'You can; I wonder if I might borrow Miss Chang for a few moments? And the pot she would most like to see in the newspapers tomorrow morning? You see, the fact is the press want photographs of our ware but black and white photographs scarcely do it justice; so I suggested that to give the pictures more . . . more immediacy, it would be a good idea to have a lovely lady standing behind our display holding one of these exquisitely painted dishes in one hand and one of our jugs or vases in the other. Then the reporter has said he'll describe the colours of our ware and the reader can see for himself the beauty of the designs on your ware. Do us both a bit of good, what?'

'Suppose they think you made my dish, Mr Haslington?' Nala said rather coldly. She found his presence so close to her disturbing, almost exciting, and resented the fact.

'Oh no, I'll make sure a mistake like that doesn't occur. I'll suggest the caption is something like *Haslington colour and Han-ti design* – would that do?'

Nala found that she wanted to quibble, to argue, to do anything, in fact, but give in gracefully and thank him for giving her work a share of his publicity, but Sven was not so small-minded, she realized ruefully.

'You are very good, Mr Haslington; Nala will be delighted to oblige,' he said cheerfully.

Nala picked up her favourite dish, the one that would photograph best, she thought, having learned a thing or two already from Philip Haslington's comments on black-and-white photography. She chose the dish with the boy and the horse on it, and went over to the other stand.

'Keep quite still, Miss Chang,' a photographer shouted. 'Hold your left hand a little higher . . . higher still, if you could. That's perfect; now look at the piece with the horse on it and smile . . . no, lift your chin . . . perfect!'

The photographic session lasted half an hour, in the end, because the gentlemen of the press took a sudden, inexplicable liking to Miss Nala Chang and were absolutely delighted to find that she was not just selling pottery but had actually designed most of the artwork herself.

'What a pity we haven't got a wheel here,' one of the reporters lamented, but Nala could only be glad; she could throw pots when pressed but she knew very well she was by no means mistress of the art. Sven far excelled her there.

Mr Haslington was most attentive as well. He insisted that she sit down on his chair for the second photo-call, because she must be tired with so much standing about. He went and fetched her a drink so that she could toast their work . . . the photographers thought it would make a good picture . . . and finally he suggested that he and his partner would look after the Han-ti stand whilst father and daughter got themselves some lunch.

Father and daughter indeed!

'We aren't related,' Nala said quickly. 'Sven is the potter and I'm the artist. It is his business; I just work for him.'

'Lucky Sven,' Mr Haslington said and Nala very nearly threw the pot she was holding at him because she did not want to like him and she did not want him to like her. He worried and disturbed her . . . she found herself looking at him and thinking that his hair was too fair, though what she meant by it she could not possibly have said. Indeed, when Sven suggested that she might like to take her sandwiches and go outside for a little with Miss Edna, she was only too glad to do so.

'What a *kind* young man,' Miss Edna said as the two of them perched on a low wall down by the river Seine eating their sandwiches and watching a man painting a picture of the river with improbably coloured trees hanging over the water. 'He admires you very much, my dear, as we both saw.'

'He liked our ware,' Nala corrected at once. 'I wish . . . I wish he'd leave me alone! I'm going to get lots of orders for our work, then we'll be happy. I don't want to have to hear all about his wretched colours night and day.'

'His colours are wonderful,' Miss Edna pointed out. 'And he made sure that you shared the limelight, Miss Chang. I cannot but feel that your attitude towards him is a little unfair, perhaps?'

Nala sighed.

'You're right, of course. He confuses me. It's ridiculous, but I keep thinking I've met him before . . . do you know, even the sight of him walking towards me . . . it upset me in an odd sort of way.'

'You'll soon see he means you no harm,' Miss Edna said. 'I'm thought to be a very good judge of character, with almost psychic abilities in some spheres, and I felt no bad vibrations at all, none at all. Quite the opposite, in fact.'

'Yes, I'm sure you're right,' Nala said, and adroitly changed the subject. But she had not been exaggerating when she had said that Philip Haslington upset her; more, he frightened her. There was something about him which both attracted and repelled, and she was not used to feeling the tug and battle of strong emotions. Why should it be, she thought distractedly, whilst carrying on a normal conversation with Miss Edna about the beauty of the sun on the water and a potter's inability to cope with the density of water at all save with what the older women called 'suggestive swirls'. And presently they got up and went back in to the exhibition and Nala saw Philip Haslington's head above the crowd and immediately her stomach clenched and her heart started to beat unevenly.

I won't go near him, I won't even speak to him, she vowed to herself. He frightens me.

'She's a broth of a girl, that Nala Chang,' Frank observed that evening, as he and Philip settled down over a meal in a very large, very expensive restaurant. 'You liked her too, didn't you, Phil?'

352

'Yes, she was all right,' Philip said cautiously. 'But kind of prickly, if you know what I mean. She kept looking at me as though she didn't like me at all . . . anyone would have thought I was going to jump at her and bear her to the ground.'

Frank laughed.

'Nonsense, I spoke to her a couple of times and she was perfectly friendly, though these Chinese girls must find us very strange, I suppose.'

'She's not Chinese – well, she doesn't look it. And the fellow with her, Sven, isn't Chinese either. He was telling me his mother was a Swede; I suppose the girl is some sort of mixture like that as well.'

'Well, I liked her,' Frank said obstinately. 'And I thought you did, too. What shall we do this evening? Want to go to the *Folies Bergère* whilst we're in town?'

'Might as well,' Philip said rather listlessly. 'Wake me up a bit. I'm half asleep. Excitement, I suppose. We certainly made our mark, didn't we, Frank? The papers will be full of us tomorrow.'

Next morning, all the exhibitors were buzzing over the coverage given to the Haslington discoveries. People were still coming in in droves, but not merely because they wanted to see beautiful china. They came because they had heard about the new colours and textures and wanted to see them for themselves – and stayed, as Sven had prophesied, because there was other work, less spectacular perhaps but just as beautiful, which they could afford to stock in their shops and stores, or display on their shelves at home.

'We've taken a lot of orders for the celadon ware,' Nala reported excitedly halfway through the afternoon. 'And some of my designs are going well. You were right, Sven, the Haslington stuff hasn't spoiled business at all . . . are they selling much, do you know?'

'Go and ask,' recommended Sven. It was clear that he approved of Frank and Philip and could see no reason why his young assistant should fight so shy of them. 'It would be good manners, Nala, if nothing else.'

'I will . . . in a moment or two.'

But in the end it was not until the stallholders were closing up their stands for the night that she approached their neighbours. She walked carelessly along, as though bound for somewhere else altogether, and then stopped by Frank.

'Hello . . . have you taken lots of orders? We've done pretty well . . .' she began. Frank turned from the big ledger he was filling in and smiled at her.

'We've done all right, I think, but Phil's the man to tell you just how we stand . . . Phil, Miss Chang's asking after our sales.'

Philip must have been crouching on the floor at the back of the stand, packing some china up in paper shavings. At any rate he now stood up, a handful of paper shavings adhering to his dark trousers, and smiled at

Nala. No matter how she might fear or dislike him, he had a very nice, open sort of smile.

'Oh, hello . . . we're doing most awfully well, thanks, though of course it's mainly one-piece sales to museums and collectors. But we've had a lot of interest in mass production, once it starts. And you?'

'We've done well, too,' Nala said, trying to sound as natural and friendly as he had but hearing, in her own tones, that stiffness and coolness which she was trying so hard to hide. 'We're finishing now, though. I don't think we'll sell much more today.'

'Same here,' Philip said, gesturing to the packing case at his feet. 'Some of our colours get packed away each night because we aren't too sure what effect the air will have on them. They shouldn't be affected of course, but if something awful happened, like a fire, even if it didn't reach our exhibits, they might easily change colour. One thing we discovered when we started our experiments,' he added, falling into a conversation as naturally as though Nala were not so clearly poised to move on, 'was that the degree of heat can change a colour to an amazing degree. Why, when we first used . . .'

'Don't bore Miss Chang,' Frank reproved, grinning across at Nala. 'She's an artist, not a scientist.'

'A potter has to be a bit of each, though, don't you think?' Sven struck in. 'I know we use artists in the bigger potteries who only paint and draw, but in the smaller places, like ours, you've got to be able to do a bit of everything.'

'True,' Philip said. 'Look, I'd like to continue this conversation . . . are you two dining in your hotel tonight or could we interest you in sharing a meal out? It would be our pleasure to entertain you,' he added formally.

'I'm afraid . . .' Nala began, just as Sven said, 'It will be a pleasure.' She covered up with a cough and smiled brightly at Frank but dismay almost overpowered her natural good manners. To spend a whole evening in the company of a man who made her feel most acutely uncomfortable! Sven knew she didn't like that Philip fellow. Why on earth had he accepted their invitation so promptly? Though of course a free meal . . .

Nala, getting her things together behind their stand, chided herself for a most uncharitable thought as well as an untruthful one. Sven was a generous man. If he accepted a meal tonight from the Haslington Pottery he would most certainly offer one to them the following night, and be upset if they refused. This made Nala realize that she would have to live through two such experiences, and despite her resolve to be good and sensible she groaned aloud.

'What's the matter? You've not broken the flask?' Sven sounded so horrified that Nala had to laugh. He was not a drinker so rarely frequented the bar set up at one end of the exhibition hall, but he did enjoy frequent cups of coffee from the huge flask he had brought all the way from home.

354

'No, it's all right. Shall we go home first, Sven, to our hotel, so that I can change?'

She was wearing her working clothes – not the sort of thing she would have worn to make pots in, to be sure, but the simple white tunic and trousers with navy and red embroidery which she wore to sell their ware.

Sven raised his brows.

'Change? Into what? You look quite charming, my dear. But I'd like to go back to the hotel myself and get rid of the bag and the sandwich wrappings. Go and tell Mr Haslington that we'll meet him wherever he suggests in about two hours, can you?'

Fate was obviously determined that she should be cured of her dislike of Philip Haslington. Nala squared her shoulders and walked over to the other stand. She gave the message in a rather flat little voice, agreed to meet in the foyer of their hotel, and returned to Sven to tell him what she had arranged.

'That's fine,' Sven said at once. 'I wonder if they'll tell us how they got their colours, Nala? It's probably quite technical, but I'd like to produce ware in that deep yellowy-orange colour no matter what it cost.'

Because of all the impedimenta they seemed to get landed with after a day out, Sven and Nala took a taxi-cab back to their hotel. There Nala changed into a cream silk European dress and put on her first pair of high-heeled shoes. They were not too bad, she considered, trotting across her bedroom in them. It was similar to wearing the big cloglike sandals with a strap across the toes: you had to concentrate a bit to keep them on at first.

A long look in her mirror convinced her that the dress suited her; she picked up a handful of her hair, which she had worn all week in a plait at the back to keep it out of her way, and decided to pile it all up on top of her head, a style which would give her height and perhaps a degree of sophistication. Most women now bobbed their hair, but that meant frequent visits to a hairdresser to keep it trimmed and Nala could not see herself bothering once she was back in China and working hard again. But this way, with her hair up, you could see the line of her neck and she looked older, more in command.

It was odd the difference it made, but by now she was late and in a hurry. She patted her nose with a powder puff and flew down the stairs.

Sven, Frank and Philip were already in the foyer, no doubt discussing where they should eat. She came swiftly down the stairs, not troubling to make an entrance, and they all looked up; two of them immediately smiled and looked away again, to continue their conversation, but Philip stared, a frown creeping into his eyes. He looked not cross but puzzled.

'Good evening, Nala. When you came down the stairs just now you reminded me of someone . . . no, it was stronger than that. I thought for a moment you were someone I knew . . . had known . . . for a long, long time. It must have something to do with your hair, and seeing you in a dress instead of your tunic.' Philip was smiling now, but was that unease in his eyes? Nala thought it was and was glad of it. So it was not just she who felt instinctively that they had met somewhere before! The feeling of revulsion towards him was not so strong now, but she still felt happier out of his company than in it.

'We're going to the Restaurant Bon Nouvelle, on the Boulevard St Michel,' Sven said, turning to her. 'You chose well, my dear; that dress looks very pretty. Do you feel self-conscious about showing your legs?'

All three men laughed and looked at her indulgently. It was true, of course, that Nala never showed much of her legs in Chinese dress save when she rolled the trousers up to allow her to paddle or to keep cooler, but then she quite often wore European clothes when she was at home with the Ellises because they thought it nice for a change.

Now, she laughed as well and felt a lifting of the discomfort in Philip's company which had oppressed her. It would be all right – he was just a fellow-artisan, after all.

'No, it feels very nice and much cooler. How do we reach the Boulevard St Michel?'

'It's a fine evening, so we'll walk,' Philip said. 'It isn't far.'

The four of them made their way out on to the pavement in a group, but then Sven fell into step with Frank, leaving Nala with no option but to take her place beside Philip. They walked along in silence for a few minutes and then Nala stole a glance at her companion, to find him stealing a glance at her. He was frowning, still clearly wondering about her, but when their eyes met the frown cleared and he laughed.

'It's all right, Miss Chang, I won't eat you . . . it's just so puzzling that I should seem to recognize you. Were you ever in England? Or for that matter in Arabia? Yes, I suppose that must be it . . . I was in the army during the war and went to the Middle East . . . could I have seen you there?'

'Wouldn't it be nice if that were the answer,' Nala sighed. 'But I've never visited England and never been outside China, expect when I lived in Japan for a short time. Anyway, it's very much more strange that I should think I recognize you, because I know very few Europeans; indeed, I could count them on the fingers of my two hands, I suppose.'

'Do we all look alike to you?' Philip asked teasingly. 'I'm ashamed to admit that whilst I was in Arabia fighting the Turks I frequently saw the same man twenty times in ten seconds. I put it down to the things they wear on their heads, but it isn't that at all, really. It's seizing on a salient feature, which in the case of a Turk is usually colour, I suppose, and letting the rest merge into one's subconscious. And so when you try to recall a face, colour comes out first . . . and you promptly "recognize" a man merely because his face has the colour you are looking for.'

'But Turks aren't black or even brown,' Nala pointed out. 'I admit they usually have dark hair and moustaches . . . well, black then . . . but their skin is white, surely?'

'Yes, you're right. And when I think about it logically, it was the Arabs we saw most of, and they are often very dark indeed. But do you see us as all very similar?'

'No, not in the least,' Nala said promptly. 'But neither do I see the Chinese as all alike. They are as different, to me, as people can be. I'll grant you that colour can be similar, though there are very dark Chinese and very fair – the Manchus have very pale skin – but noses are different, eyes are set at different angles, some are narrow, some almond-shaped, and mouths . . . Chinese people have large and small mouths, mouths with pouting lips, almost no lips, heavy lips, almost negroid lips . . . people are all different.'

'You're right, of course. Perhaps it's the artist in you,' Philip said after a thoughtful minute. 'Don't you think that the majority of people never really *look* at faces? Most of us, if challenged, would be at a loss to say whether someone had brown eyes or blue, thick or thin lips, good teeth or bad. And as for ears . . .'

They both laughed.

'And ears are so important to a potter,' Nala reminded her companion. 'Handles are nearly all ear-shaped, aren't they? I often want to scream when I see a beautiful, natural shape completely ruined by the addition of a handle in just the wrong place or a spout which is too low or too high for symmetry. Yet a man who can create the shape in the first place, and must know the pleasure such a shape brings to the eye and to the hand as well, doesn't seem bothered when another man spoils his work with the addition of a badly placed appendage.'

'Perhaps he's bothered, but has no influence to stop it happening,' Philip suggested. 'Certainly in the big pot-banks, in England, a thrower might easily find that he never sees the additions which are put on to his original ware until it is complete, right down to the firing and glazing. In that case, all he can do is have a word with the man who attached the handle, and see if the fellow can put it higher or lower another time.'

'That must be frustrating,' Nala observed. 'I wouldn't work like that, it would drive me mad.'

'Yes, well, you're an artist,' Philip said. 'Artists like to follow a pot right through. I've noticed it in our pot-bank, and if you want good work from an artist then you have to let him have his own way over things like that. Do you do much casting at the Han-ti workshops?'

Almost without realizing it, Nala was beginning to relax, and by the time they reached the Boulevard St Michel she was chattering away to Philip feeling quite natural and friendly towards him. They had an excellent meal in very good accord with one another and then took a taxi-cab back to their respective hotels.

'You must come out with us to dine tomorrow evening,' Sven called, as the taxi-cab carried Frank and Philip out of the quiet little square in which their hotel was situated. 'See you in the morning!'

\* \* \*

357

'You seem to have got over your dislike of young Mr Haslington,' Miss Phoebe murmured slyly on the last day of the exhibition, as she and Nala were packing their ware away side by side. 'I told you he was a pleasant fellow and I felt good vibrations; was I not right?'

'Yes, you were. He's very nice,' Nala admitted. She could scarcely do less since he and she had reached a point where they usually chose to go out together to eat their sandwiches down by the river and spent a great deal of time during the day, heads close, discussing their art, their lives and their ambitions. Philip was ambitious, there was no doubt about that. He thought the Haslington Pottery was the finest in the world and intended to prove it by new experiments which would bring even more startling results.

'Iridescent lustre,' he would say yearningly, and Nala would laugh and tell him he must go to China and dig about in the museums and see if he could discover the secret that way, for it was assuredly in the hands of the ancient craftsmen in China once, but had been lost.

'No, I'll do it our way, by experiment,' he said. 'You've no idea, Nala, how exciting it is to work like that; the thrill when you bring a saggar out of the oven and see something different has been made by you, out of your own skill and daring . . . no, not daring, but your own determination to try something no one's thought it necessary to try before.'

'Except the ancient Chinese,' Nala reminded him, but Philip said they must have found it by chance and not by experiment which, he seemed to feel, did not count in quite the same way.

So the days passed pleasantly in warm friendship and Nala quite forgot how Philip had affected her at first.

Until the day the exhibition closed, leaving both of them with a few days to enjoy Paris before they, too, took the homeward voyage.

'Frank's going back today,' Philip told Nala. 'There's a lot to do at home thanks to our sales. He'll be met by the press, of course, and he'll have some good stories for them – our ware will be in at least three royal palaces by the time the month's over.'

'Boasting again,' Nala teased him, but she was thinking that it would be nice to have Philip to herself without Frank.

'What shall we do tomorrow?' she asked as they wandered out of the great hall. 'I'd like to see the shops!'

'Yes, I'd be interested, too,' Philip said. 'I'd like to see what they're selling and for how much. But first, there's something I've been meaning to ask you.'

Nala's heart began to beat a little more quickly. He was so shy, that was the trouble! She had decided she was unlikely ever to meet a young man she liked better, but he had never intimated, by word or look, that he shared her feelings. Was he actually going to ask her to marry him? Or at least to suggest they continue to meet?

'Oh, really? What's that?'

'I wondered if you'd consider working for me? At the Haslington Pottery, of course. We don't have an artist of your quality, your work is stunningly good, and I think that your designs on our background glazes and colours might do very well indeed.'

Nala stopped in the middle of the pavement, causing several people to mutter rude things to her, fortunately in French. She stared at Philip as though he had gone mad . . . and indeed, she wondered!

'Me, leave Sven and come to work for you? My dear sir, what would be the point? It would merely mean changing workshops and methods of work and I'm very happy where I am – and quite successful, too, in case you hadn't noticed.'

Philip, she was glad to see, was thrown by her frank reply. He opened and shut his mouth several times but nothing came out. Nala was reminded of a golden carp and very nearly said so, but contented herself, instead, with another reminder.

'Besides, what about my paintings? I've sold quite a few of them since we've been in Paris, and they're nothing to do with Sven.'

'Oh . . . oh, I've offended you.' Very perspicacious, Nala thought angrily. 'I – I'm sorry, Nala, I didn't mean . . . you see, to me working at the Haslington Pottery is pretty good, because we've got so much going for us. I thought . . . I thought you'd be better off. Sven's place is a lot smaller than ours, and you'd have many more opportunities . . . you could sell your paintings in your spare time, of course.'

Nala's bosom swelled with righteous wrath; in her spare time, indeed!

'Art isn't a spare-time thing with me, Philip. When I design a pot and then need to paint a picture I just do it – Sven doesn't mind.'

'I wouldn't mind either,' Philip said hastily, clearly not seeing at all why Nala had suddenly become so furious yet so cold. 'Really, Nala, if you'd just give us a try . . . whatever Sven pays you I'll double.'

There was a sore aching feeling at the back of Nala's eyes and her chest felt as if it had been punched. He liked her work, but for her as a person he had nothing but indifference, that was quite clear!

'I think we'd better forget it, Philip,' she said evenly. 'I'm not for sale!'

'Oh . . . no, of course not. I didn't mean . . .'

She walked away from him, too hurt and furious to care what she was doing to him. He was a great, six foot male anyway, who could take care of himself. Let him go home to his *marvellous* pottery and see if he could bribe another artist of her quality to work for him! Never a thought for Sven, who had befriended him, taken him out for a meal, shared many a laugh. All he thought of was his damned, damned, *damned* pottery!

Behind her, she heard Philip call her name. For a moment his voice sounded small, lost. She nearly glanced over her shoulder, nearly turned back, but then pride stiffened both her spine and her resolution. She was not to be bought, and particularly not as a mere employee. Not a word had he said about Nala designing what pleased her, demanding the sort of pot which fitted a particular scene. Oh no, that was not how he saw an artist! He saw an artist as subservient to the main business of producing the ware . . . she would no doubt be allowed to decorate only his plainer colours. He would not want an artist to draw her brush across that brilliant sunburst orange, which needed no design to get customers gasping and clamouring; she would be set to decorating pots which would not, otherwise, get a particularly good reception.

By now she had worked herself up into quite a temper; she went back to the hotel, pleaded a headache when Sven suggested going out to celebrate, and put herself early to bed.

Once there, she told herself that it was best to know what he was like. Shamingly, she had wanted his friendship, with a view, she knew, to a stronger relationship in time. Clearly he did not feel like that. Well, thank goodness you know before you had a chance to do anything stupid, she told herself, cuddling down the bed. At least this way you haven't made a fool of yourself. Imagine if you'd assumed his proposal that you should work for the pottery was just a tactful way of saying he wanted to keep you by him . . . then you'd have left Sven and arrived in England, only to find that his interest had been purely economic.

I've had a narrow escape, she told herself as the minutes and then the hours ticked by and sleep still eluded her. Suppose I'd thought I loved him, then I'd have been *really* miserable; as it is I know now that it was simply the first man who's ever paid me any attention, the first Englishman I've every really known, apart from Father. And he's shallow, self-interested, not worthy of the sort of affection I could have felt for him.

She did not fall asleep until the birds were dawn-chorusing outside her window, and next day, when she went down to breakfast hollow-eyed and pale, Sven said he wanted a word with her.

'Look, Nala, if you get any offers of employment from the big potters, don't turn them down on my account,' he said. 'The way the ware's gone, I'm going to be doing a lot of moulded, repetitive stuff. If you were a bit older I'd tell you to set up your own shop, and I could use you for my finer pieces, but as things stand I mustn't be selfish. If you have a better offer . . .'

'Thanks, but I'll stick with you,' Nala said, though she had hard work to stop her lips from trembling. She felt rejected all round! 'I'm going to start saving for a place of my own, though, and I'll keep on sketching and framing and trying to sell the drawings because they do seem quite popular.'

'That's grand,' Sven said. He reached across the breakfast table and picked up the last roll. 'Do you mind if I have this one?'

'Not in the least,' Nala said, and stood up to leave the table.

Back in her own room, she stared at herself in the mirror, watching the slow tears trickle down her cheeks. Philip wanted her work and Sven, when it came down to it, didn't want her at all! She was hurt and cast down as only a seventeen-year-old girl can be. She wanted to run away and hide, and she wanted to hurt the people who had hurt her. Most of all of course she wanted someone who would love her for herself.

She was glad when their time in Paris was over and she could say goodbye to the city and to Philip. She shook hands with him when he came to the station and was brisk and sensible, telling him with her mouth that she had no quarrel with him and with her eyes that she no longer cared for his company. It was Philip who looked lonely as she and Sven waved from their carriage window. But it was Nala who, in the privacy of the lavatory compartment, cried.

'I asked her to come back and work for us, and she wouldn't even think about it, wouldn't consider it,' Philip told Frank as they drove back from the station, for Frank had an old banger of a car now which he loved almost as much as he loved his Martha. 'She made it sound as though I'd mortally insulted her – she said she wasn't for sale!'

He sounded so aggrieved that Frank nearly smiled, but then took a quick glance at his companion's set, white face and refrained.

'You must have put it awfully badly,' he said mildly, instead. 'She was a nice girl; I really took to her. And I thought she took to you as well, Philip.'

Philip shrugged, then shook his head.

'Women don't care for me much,' he said wryly. 'They never have, I don't know why. There must be something about me . . . something unlovable, I suppose. But I was offering her a *job*; I never let her see that I was rather keen on her! Why on earth should she turn down a job?'

'She thinks a lot of Sven,' Frank pointed out. 'And she enjoys the work she's doing for him. Why didn't you ask her to come back to England as your guest, to see how she liked it? And then, if she wanted, you could have said, she could work at the pottery, or even do some designs for us whilst working for herself.'

Philip turned and stared.

'It didn't occur to me, that's why! All I thought of was how she loves her work and how beautifully she draws, and how much, how very much, I wanted to keep hold of her, having once found her.'

'You told her that?'

'No! How could I? She would have turned me down then for sure.'

'Philip, you're mad – you never gave the girl a chance. What makes you think she didn't like you, anyway? Freda likes you.'

'Freda was talked into going out with me by you and Martha,' Philip said without mincing matters. 'She enjoys having fun; it doesn't much matter to Freda who she's with, so long as she's enjoying it. I like her, but I don't kid myself that she fell for my charms, man!'

'Well, write to Nala,' Frank advised. 'Keep up the connection; who

361

knows, one day she may come to England and then you can speak to her again.'

'I don't have her address,' Philip said mournfully.

'So what? Write care of the Han-ti Pottery; that'll find her.'

'Well, I might.' Philip leaned back in his seat and stifled a yawn with his hand. 'I'm damned tired, old fellow.'

On his arrival at the Hall he wondered whether to write at once, then shook his head at himself. Why ask for a snub? He would lie low until the exhibition next year and then try his luck again.

# CHAPTER TWENTY-FIVE

Rose gave birth to the baby at the end of September and Granville came down to visit her and asked her to marry him. Rose refused.

'But why, Rosie?' Granville asked, though at first he had been so stunned by his mad foolhardiness in asking and her insanity in refusing that he had simply gaped at her. 'Why? I thought you rather liked me.'

'I do . . . but I don't like this baby,' Rose said with what Granville considered to be unfeminine frankness. 'You'd expect me to look after it and so on, but I'm not staying within a mile of it once I'm up and about again. If Father wants it he can jolly well have it – I'm going back to the stage.'

'You're unnatural,' Granville said. 'Don't you have any normal motherly feelings?'

'No, I don't think I have. At any rate, not if you mean do I want to feed it and change its smelly napkins and so on. I didn't want it to begin with, remember, so it's just like an uninvited guest. The sooner it and I are parted the better.'

'You're very hard,' Granville said, not altogether accusingly. 'Well, if that's how you feel . . . want to rejoin the Jolyons?'

'I wouldn't mind, just for a bit. Is that Ames woman with you still, though?'

'Yes, of course she is. We're a tight little community and Peggy's one of the best.'

Rose sniffed.

'Huh. It depends what she's supposed to be best at,' she said nastily. 'I've been in bed six whole days, you know, since it was born . . . I think I'll be leaving in another two or three days.'

'But you can't leave just like that; what about the baby's feeds and so on?' Granville asked, really rather shocked. 'It has to eat, Rose . . . what sex is it, anyway, and what have you called it? I can't keep referring to the child as "it".'

'Why not? I do. But it's a girl. I'm not interested in naming it but Father keeps calling it his little Bud . . . Rosebud, you know.' She shuddered convincingly. 'Honestly, men! Anyone would think it was his instead of mine the way he carries on about it.'

'Well, I'm off later this afternoon; if you decide to join us the Jolyons are in Bristol again, and we're rehearsing the panto in a fortnight's time. You've got money?'

'Sure.' Rose still had the necklace; if all else failed she was quite prepared to pawn it to get money for her train fare out of this God-forsaken place. 'I'll probably be seeing you quite soon, then.'

Bud, as Arnold called his granddaughter, was bottle fed, so when her mother simply disappeared when she was nine days old, leaving a note pinned to the cradle to say that she had returned to the stage and would be very much obliged if Arnold would put the baby out for adoption, it was not the desperate business it might well have been. Nevertheless Arnold did not find it easy explaining to doctors, midwives and visitors that his grandchild's mother had simply gone back to her interrupted career.

So there was Arnold, forty-five years old, with a tiny granddaughter who had not even been properly christened, a flower farm about which he knew virtually nothing, and a story to concoct for the folk back home . . . if he should decide to return.

He decided, not unnaturally, to stay in Devon for the time being at least. But he wrote to Philip and asked him to come down for a few days. And Philip, who had attended the exhibition and done marvellous business there, who was becoming famous for his discoveries and who had sold ware to a good many of the crowned heads of Europe, decided to take a few days off and joined his father on the farm.

'So Rose was pregnant – I should have guessed,' he said as he and Arnold stood side by side, staring down into the cradle at its tiny occupant. 'A little girl . . . where's the proud mother?'

'Gone,' Arnold said lugubriously. 'Disappeared. Left a note telling me not to look for her . . . she's gone back to the fellow who was responsible for Bud, if you ask me, and back to the stage, of course.'

'Typical,' Philip said shortly. 'What are you going to do, Father?'

'Do? What, with Bud? I'm going to keep her here, I think. It's a wonderful place for a child to grow up, and then when she's old enough I'll start thinking about bringing her back up north so that I can earn a crust or two.'

'The saddlery seems to be going on all right under your manager,' Philip said carefully. 'And the pot-bank's doing awfully well. Do you know what I think you ought to do?'

'No; what?'

'I think you ought to find Mama. Rose didn't really try, though she had a very good lead. Why don't you get in touch with Rose and tell her that either she gives you all the clues she can about Lily or you'll . . . you'll leave the baby with her.'

'I couldn't do that,' Arnold said, shocked. 'She'd neglect the child, or give her away or something. Rose can be very hard, Philip.'

'You don't have to tell me that,' Philip remarked. 'But it's only a threat, Father, a sort of moral blackmail. You go and say that to Rose and I guarantee she'll hand over any information she's got within five minutes.'

'Well . . . but what then? Your mother's stayed away of her own accord for years; why should she be interested in us now?'

'Because perhaps she's waited, all these years, for someone to run after her,' Philip said. 'Perhaps she'd like to meet me again . . . she might even be interested in her granddaughter, you never know. If you discover where she's hiding, though, you could find out.'

'I'll try,' Arnold said. 'She's probably married again, mind; that'll be why she hasn't got in touch. But I bear her no grudge. I was in the wrong, not she. It would be fine to see her again . . . fine!'

'Then search for her,' Arnold advised. 'I love this place, Father, it's a dream. I'll come and stay with you again when I need to unwind. And you're very welcome to come back to the Hall whenever you want to do so, whether as a guest or as the owner. Remember that.'

And for a few days Philip really did enjoy himself. He climbed the cliffs for gulls' eggs, he roamed the beaches and swam in the sea even though the long autumn was merging into winter at last. He arranged for the baby to be christened and they called her, after much thought, Lily Adeline, after a girl Arnold confided in his son that he had once loved and after his wife.

'Adeline . . . was that Addy, Unk's daughter who went to China?' Philip asked, and was amazed at his father's nod. How many things you don't know about the people you're closest to, he thought. How many things they don't know about you!

He had never breathed a word to anyone about Nala, save to say that there had been a talented artist who had refused his offer of a job, but that did not mean to say he had forgotten her. Indeed, he would willingly have done so – the girl had turned down, flat, the chance of working with an organization which was heading for stardom and the top of the market as inexorably as . . . as the girl herself was heading for obscurity. But she was always in the back of his mind, tantalizing him with her artistic ability and, if he was honest, with her wide, dark blue eyes, pointy-chinned little face, and the smile that tilted her mouth up at the corners, giving great sweetness to her unusual, almost exotic looks.

But he knew full well that he could not expect her to come to England for *him* – when had any woman shown that he mattered one jot? His mother had run away and left him, had never attempted, in any way, to find out if he was alive or dead since. His solitary love-affair had been organized for him by his best friend, and the girl, Freda, had made no secret of the fact that she was out for a good time and prepared to accept almost anyone who was willing to spend money on her and enjoy their friendship. Anything other than friendship, however, had never been offered, and Freda had made it clear, without putting it into words, that she wanted no strong emotional relationship with anyone, probably least of all the boss.

But I offered Nala the biggest compliment I could offer anyone – a job working on the new sort of china that we're developing, Philip told himself in anguish. And even that, even the biggest bribe in my armoury, she turned down. How can I think of her? How can I not? I ought to be glad she's half a world away. I've got my own life to lead anyway and who needs women? But she was never far from the forefront of his mind in those months directly following the Paris exhibition.

'Did you fall out with Nala when she said she wouldn't work in England?' Frank asked once. 'I thought the pair of you would have exchanged letters, at least.'

'We didn't exactly fall out,' Philip said guardedly. 'But I couldn't see much point in continuing a friendship with half the world between us, so I didn't write. And she must have felt the same, because nor did she. It's better, probably. Perhaps we'll meet next year, at Brussels, if she's still with Sven. If she's gone solo by then I don't suppose she'll be able to afford to exhibit.'

'Things are extremely fraught in China,' Frank told him when Christmas was only days away. 'Do you keep in touch with the news there? They say the Communist Party is flexing its muscles to try to take over the government. A European could easily get caught in the middle of the sort of affray which might result.'

'If you mean Nala, she's scarcely a European,' Philip said cruelly. 'And if you mean Mr Warburton's granddaughter, I think she must be dead, since there's still been no word.'

'It didn't occur to you to ask Nala if she knew the Sawyer girl? But I suppose that was the first thing you said to her.'

Philip, who had fully intended to ask any and every Chinese potter he met about the Sawyer girl, blushed to himself, though he was sure his complexion did not change outwardly.

'She wouldn't know her; she and Sven have this tiny workshop some- where in the back of beyond . . . still, I ought to have said something, perhaps. If they come to Brussels next May I'll ask them then.'

'I'm getting exceedingly sick of cranes and bamboo,' Nala said, taking a big batch of celadon ware, thus decorated, across the workshop to be packed up. 'I never thought those orders from Europe would keep on coming in the way they have. I never thought I'd get bored with painting, either, but you were right: you can have too much of a good thing.'

'I told you so,' Sven said. 'Never mind, Nala, we've done so well I'm getting a copyist in.'

'To copy my drawings? Oh, but . . .'

'Well, we could put them on transfers, I suppose, but then I wouldn't be able to put "Handpainted" on the invoices, and to tell the truth your signature means a lot, or is beginning to do so. Once we've got all these orders out, though, we'll think seriously about going for one exclusive design, which you can do yourself, each piece an individual, and another line which the copyist can do for us.'

'Oh . . . well, all right.' Nala glanced round the workshop, walked over and put away some paints which she had left standing on her table, and then went to the door. 'I'm off now, Sven, if that's all right; it's Friday and I'm having the weekend with the Ellises.'

'Good girl,' Sven said abstractedly. He had just opened his kiln and was examining rather anxiously the ware which he had just taken out. 'The glaze could be better,' he observed. 'It's a nuisance when you don't get it quite right . . . wish I'd taken more notice of what Philip was saying about heat and glazing last June.'

'Mm,' Nala agreed. 'You could always write to him. Just care of the Haslington Pottery would find him.'

'Yes, I suppose . . . you don't write yourself, then?'

'Me? No, why should I?'

'I thought the two of you were quite close, that's why,' Sven said. 'You certainly seemed friendly.

Nala felt the warmth rise in her cheeks but she noticed thankfully that Sven was too interested in the uneven glazing on his pot to glance up.

'We were both youngish, both with similar interests, I suppose,' she said in as neutral a voice as possible. 'But it really was just ships that pass in the night; there was no real interest to keep a relationship going.'

'Mm; then I'll write, when I get time,' Sven said. 'Have a good weekend, Nala.'

Nala replied suitably, let herself out of the workshop and shut the door gently behind her. Sven was supposed to leave about now – there would be a meal waiting for him at home – but she knew very well that, with the glazing not firing right, he would probably be there until midnight. Never mind, it was his business; she had a perfect right to go off and enjoy her weekend.

But it was impossible, of course, as she packed, as she bade the family goodbye until Monday morning, as she ran for the 'bus and sat aboard it, that she should not think about Philip.

She had really liked him by the time the exhibition was over, more than she had ever liked a man before. But all he wanted was her artistic abilities and she simply wasn't prepared to give up her own chance of fame in order to make his more certain. Now if he had spoken to her on a more personal level, if he had said that he felt just over a week was not long enough for two people to get to know one another, that the strong attraction he felt – if he had felt it – needed more time, a deeper acquaintanceship, and that he was therefore offering her a job in his pot-bank . . . well, that would have been different.

But the truth was, he had not been interested in her as a woman at all, just as an artist. And a good artist can get work without having to abandon her country and the people who love her, Nala reminded herself severely. What was more, she had not lied when she said she wanted to have her own place one day. It was true. Though now it no longer seemed the ideal goal it once had; it seemed a lonely sort of thing, to have a business and no man of your own, not even a family. The Ellises were very dear to her, very dear indeed, but they were also extremely old. And they loved each other so much that their affection for herself could not compete – nor should it, of course, there being no tie or blood or even adoption between them.

Furthermore the conviction had grown upon Nala that she would never marry whilst she remained in China. The nearest she had ever come to knowing and loving a Chinese male was her relationship with Ouyang, which was still one of the best things in her life, but Ouyang was destined to marry a rich man's daughter, someone who would bring to the Te Ku compound many lands and a large dowry.

Kei was still her dearest and best friend. But Kei had her beloved husband and her little children, their farm and their house and a host of step-children, all of whom now loved her as if she had indeed been their mother. Nala never felt left out, precisely . . . but she knew herself to be an outsider.

But with Philip, it had been quite different. She had *known* him – perhaps it was just his Englishness she had known really, but she had felt she had known him always. And they had talked the same language quite literally, for she found, in his presence, that her excellent English came straight from the heart, the right phrases, little jokes, small talk, being instantly available because it was Philip to whom she spoke.

But he had not cared about her, not in the right sort of way, and no wonder, for a week's acquaintance cannot be sufficient. There were times when she found herself wishing that she had not given Philip such a definite no, when she thought it would have been more sensible to have said 'perhaps', and left it to fate to decide whether they would ever meet again, for if he had been really keen . . . on her work, of course, not her company . . . he would have kept in touch and perhaps, by keeping in touch . . .

But they would have no opportunity to work together now and it was time she took her mind right off Philip Haslington and began to think seriously about her future. She knew that Sven had been right and that his workshop was not the place for her. Now that he was becoming well known the work would be much more stereotyped, the pieces less original, and the copyists he talked about would be a fact and not something vague, for the future. His own children, in fact, would want to come into the business, perhaps in some capacity other than, as at present, merely kiln-fillers, packers and fettlers when Sven cast pots. There would be, very soon now, no place for Nala in the workrooms, though Sven would never turn her out. He would just hope that she would see she had outgrown him, as she knew, in her heart, that she had.

Unaccountably, tears had welled up in her eyes. Nala turned and stared out of the 'bus, forcing the tears back, keeping her face solemn and straight, not allowing it to twist with the sorrow she felt inside. She would do all right! Very well, she would have to do all right alone, but that was no bar. Other people managed . . . other people had no relatives, no help, and they became famous, sometimes. What was more important, of course, was that they were happy and fulfilled, and made enough money to keep themselves so that they were a drag on no one.

When the 'bus reached the village Nala jumped off, her little case in her hand, and went straight to the Te Ku compound. She needed a few moments before she arrived at the Ellis bungalow, for Mrs Ellis was far too shrewd. She would read Nala's sadness and something perilously close to despair no matter how hard Nala tried to hide it, unless she had a breathing space first.

'Where's Ouyang?' she asked the old porter in the gatehouse. 'I'm home for the weekend . . . I thought I'd have a chat to him before I go up to the bungalow.'

The porter was the very same old man she had first met when she and Kei had applied to the family for a job when they arrived in China. He smiled stiffly, creakily, at her.

'Well, if it isn't little Nala Chang! Do you want to see the Old Mistress as well, or just Ouyang?'

It would be impolite just to ask for Ouyang, though Nala longed to do so. Thank heaven he had not yet left for America, for his term would not start until the autumn; at least she would be able to talk to him, let him see that her heart was a little cracked, though of course it was by no means broken.

'Both, if you please. Will you tell them I'm here?'

'I'll walk up to the bungalow with you,' Ouyang said, when Nala at last rose to leave, bowing rapidly in the direction of the Old Mistress. 'It will give you a chance to tell me your latest plans.'

The Old Mistress cackled.

'What a girl she is, eh, my boy? Always some mad scheme . . . first she says she'll be a potter and we tell her girls don't make pots, not in China. So she becomes a potter. Then she says she'll go to Paris with Sven Han-ti and we say nice girls don't go off halfway across the world and return as nice as they went. Once more, she proves us wrong. What will it be this time, I wonder?'

'I'm thinking of starting my own little business, when Sven moves to Shanghai,' Nala said. 'I'm not ungrateful, Honourable Old Mistress, but soon there will be no place for me. The children are growing up and I need to paint the things which long to come forth from my mind, not endless white cranes and bamboo thickets.'

The Old Mistress laughed and flung both hands in the air. They were thin and yellow and twisted with age, yet they were still beautiful and the rings which glittered on her fingers were priceless.

'You see, Ouyang? Always a new idea, always an outrageous one; yet Nala makes outrageous ideas into reality until one is in danger of thinking the ideas commonplace. Goodbye now, my child. Come and see us whenever you're in Pentai.'

Nala and Ouyang made their way out of the village. It had been snowing and the sun shone faintly through a bank of thin cloud on a white landscape. As they went, Nala was reminded of that first time she had visited the Ellis bungalow, expecting to meet teachers but finding friends instead. She smiled at her companion.

'Do you remember the first time I went to the Ellises' place, Ouyang? It had snowed . . . you came to meet me with your sledge and we rode all the way down the hill in grand style!'

'How could I forget? What a funny little thing you were then, Nala-san!' The old Japanese title, which had once made her feel a stranger, sounded like a love-word now. 'I remember everything about you,' Ouyang continued. 'You were great fun then as you are now, with your Lion-dog face and your Lion-dog eyes.'

'My eyes don't pop,' Nala said, thinking of the little dogs that Westerners call Pekingese but which are Lion-dogs to the Chinese. 'And my nose doesn't turn up, either. You're just jealous because I had a good time in Paris.'

Ouyang put a finger under her chin and turned her face towards him. He stared down at her, smiling slightly.

'Your eyes are big and round, just like the Lion-dog's. Your nose is quite respectable, but there can be no doubt that you're a *yang kuei-tzu*, Nala, even after ten years or so of trying to be Chinese. And as for enjoying yourself in Paris, that isn't all the story. What went wrong?'

'Oh . . . I learned that I don't belong in Europe with Europeans any more than I belong in China, with the Chinese,' Nala said a little flatly. 'It's a sad thing when you first realize you don't belong in either world.'

'Not belong? What rubbish. You're a silly little Lion-eyes,' Ouyang said, squeezing her, an arm about her shoulders. 'Nala, has it never occurred to you that I don't belong either? My family and all my friends are well-to-do, and they would be shocked and deeply hurt and upset if they knew I had Communist leanings. So although we're both of China, we are, in a way, both foreign devils, I because I believe in a Marxist regime for my country, you because you cannot quite accept the Chinese viewpoint. But who made you feel a foreigner in Paris? Not Sven, surely?'

'No . . . it was nothing much . . . there was a young man, Philip, his name was. He was very nice, very friendly, and I thought he was interested in me as a person – do you know what I mean, Ouyang?'

Her friend nodded, his face and eyes equally serious, for once.

'Well, he wasn't,' Nala admitted. 'He was only interested in my abilities as a potter and a painter. He asked me if I'd go to England and work for him. Not with him, even, for him!'

'And you said no? But Nala, things might have changed if you were working for him. Didn't it occur to you that he might have wanted to say something more, but felt he didn't know you well enough?'

'Oh yes, I *wondered*,' Nala said gloomily. 'But it was his whole attitude . . . he kept going on about how my designs would make his pottery famous . . . anyway, I said no. I want to draw what I have in my head, Ouyang, not what someone else wants me to draw. So I'm going to open up my own place just as soon as Sven goes off to Shanghai.'

'We're a couple of misfits,' Ouyang observed. He put his arm round her waist again, drawing her close. 'I can't even consider marriage, you know, because at the moment a Communist has to be prepared to drop everything and fight for what he believes in. If the crunch comes then a wife and family can be hostages for a man. Tell you what, Nala, we'll be celibate together, shall we? After all, you're the only person apart from my friends at university who knows what my plans for the future are.'

'We'll be special friends for each other, as we've always been,' Nala said. 'It will be a long and lonely year for me, Ouyang, whilst you're away in America.'

'Yes, and for me. Nala, I'm going to tell you a secret. My parents and the family think I have a job down in Shanghai this summer. I go in a couple of weeks, but in fact I'm going to join the Communists up in the mountains. They will teach me, amongst other things, to be a soldier.'

Nala's hand flew to her mouth.

'Oh, Ouyang, why must you do these things? I shall be so frightened for you!'

'Why? Every man must fight for what he believes in, little one, and I believe totally in Communism. It is the way forward for China; I'm convinced of it in my heart. You believe in something far simpler, yet far greater, in a way, because it is unique. You believe in your own talent and you're going to back your belief by working for yourself. Good luck to us both. I shall write to you several times a week, even from the camp in the mountains. And when I reach the States you may write back.'

'I will, I promise,' Nala said. They were crossing the bridge over the stream, the wooden boards echoing hollowly beneath their feet. 'You are so good for me, Ouyang. You put things in perspective. Take care of yourself, whether in the mountains or on the sea or far away in America, for you are dearer to me than the brother I never had could possibly be.' They stood on the bridge, facing one another. 'You'd better go back now; I'm within sight of the house and if you're going off to Shanghai – or the mountains, rather – you'll have lots to do in the compound.'

'Yes, I am quite busy.' Ouyang took her face between his hands and kissed her, very gently, on both cheeks, on her nose and then, as lightly as a butterfly's wing flutters against a leaf, on her lips.

'Goodbye, little dog's eyes.'

'Take care of yourself, oh friend of my childhood,' Nala said with quaint formality. 'Goodbye, Ouyang!'

'Goodbye, Nala.'

Mrs Ellis was in the kitchen, baking. Nala called through the open doorway, and then went right into the room, put her arms round the older woman, and kissed her cheek.

'Dear Auntie Sarah . . . how odd that you should be baking! The very first time I met you – remember it? – I came up from the village through the snow and walked into this very kitchen and there you were, baking bread. It's like turning the clock back.'

Sarah Ellis turned and surveyed the younger woman with a smile, rubbing her nose and leaving a smear of flour behind.

'You've changed a lot, my dear,' she observed. 'You're very much a young lady now. And what's your latest news? I had word that Sven is seriously talking about moving to Shanghai now that his workshop is becoming famous. You'll go with him, of course . . . but dear Nala, we'll miss you so much, Hamish and myself.'

'I'm not going,' Nala said. 'When Sven goes he'll leave a number of things behind because he can't take them with him – his climbing kiln, for instance. I haven't asked him yet but I'm going to suggest that he lets me buy his equipment, a bit at a time of course, so I can stay in the village. If I did that, I'd still be able to see you for two days each week.'

'Oh, you lovely girl!' Sarah stood back, clasping her floury hands. 'Hamish is very slow now . . . we're both most awfully old . . . and having you here once a week has been more of a joy and a comfort than you could possibly know. It's what you want, isn't it? You aren't doing it for . . . for . . .'

Nala laughed and put her own hands round Sarah's floury ones.

'I almost wish I could say I was doing it for your sake, and get myself some credit, but it wouldn't be true. I'm doing it for what Hamish would call my artistic integrity. Sven said last summer that I'd grow tired of drawing and painting the same things over and over and he's right, I am tired of it. I want to paint the pictures in my head, I want to make a pot in a different shape, and put a strange glaze on it. He agrees that I should do that, and sell my paintings too, not just those on pots but on canvas and paper as well. It'll be hard because I won't be able to employ anyone else, but it will be fun and very good for me.'

'Yes . . . but Nala, my dear, you are young and you are English, or mainly English.'

'All English,' Nala reminded her. She had told Mrs Ellis as much of the truth as she thought politic some time ago but Sarah was forgetful now, in her late seventies, and although she could remember every detail of her early ministry in China, and things about her own youth in Great Britain, she did forget things she had only learned in the past two or three years.

'Yes, of course. All English. What I'm trying to say, Nala, is don't you think it might be a good idea if you were to consider going back to England, at least for a short visit? The political situation here is uncertain, the Communists are gaining ground all the time and eventually they are going to tackle the War Lords and their forces. If they win, they'll try to rid the country of all foreigners; if they lose and the War Lords overrun the provinces they'll simply kill, indiscriminately, anyone who stands in their path. I would feel more comfortable knowing that you had somewhere to go in time of trouble.'

'I come here in time of trouble,' Nala said, a little surprised to hear her old friend talking so seriously of war. 'Anyway, Auntie Sarah, there hasn't been any real trouble for foreigners since the Boxer Rebellion, nearly a quarter of a century ago. If there's trouble I'll come to you here and we'll lock the doors and the gates and chop down the bridge over the river and be snug as bugs in rugs until the trouble has passed us by.'

'If the peasants fight, they'll fight anyone with a grain of rice more than they have themselves,' Aunt Sarah said with sadness but conviction. 'My dear girl, I've spent more than fifty years in this country and I do know something about the Chinese. There are many honest and true men and women, but the vast majority have a streak of cruelty and ruthlessness in their natures, a positive pleasure in watching suffering, which must repel all Christians. It is they I fear, they I want you to guard against. In a year or two you will be a successful young businesswoman. If there is trouble, Nala, you'll not escape it.'

'But others are successful,' Nala cried. 'Oh, Auntie Sarah, you're being unnecessarily pessimistic. There won't be a war or a revolution or whatever it is you fear. I'll be all right. The Chinese have always treated me as one of themselves, and they won't change just because the balance of power changes!'

'Hmm. I wish I could be as sure. Will you at least take a Chinese into your workshop, so that enemies cannot say the place is in the hands of a foreign devil? It's a small precaution but I think a wise one.'

'If I can afford to do so,' Nala began, to be promptly put in her place by a snorting Aunt Sarah.

'Afford? In China? My dear child, you don't want a great strong man with muscles like water melons, you want a young girl, like yourself! No, younger . . . one of the children from the convent, a little orphan, would suit you admirably. Find one who is good with her hands, feed her and clothe her, and she'll work harder than many a coolie pulling a rickshaw, and for love, what's more.'

'But it's taking advantage . . .' Nala began, to be promptly and firmly contradicted.

'Taking advantage? It's being a practical Christian, helping those less fortunate than oneself. Kei would have died for your mother, I dare say, and then for you. This girl that you are to employ will be the same.'

'Yes . . .' Nala hung her head. She could never forget the story her father had told her of the girl for whom she had been named. Yenala had died because she had been with a white woman at the time of the Boxer rebellion. 'Right, Auntie Sarah; I'll go up to the convent tomorrow morning and see what they say.'

'And I'll go with you,' Sarah said firmly. 'They know me . . . there will be no thought of palming you off with a thief or a half-wit if I'm around!'

Nala looked at the older woman with real love; she was smaller, thinner, more fragile than ever, but her grey eyes were clear and bright and her mouth was firm. She had never been beautiful, but the beauty of her soul showed more and more as she aged.

'Of course, I couldn't tell for myself if the girl was a thief or a half-wit,' Nala mocked gently. 'Oh, Auntie Sarah, it's a long walk up to the convent. Are you sure you wouldn't rather simply advise me?'

'No indeed; it will do me good,' Sarah said. 'We'll take Hamish as well; he enjoys a walk.'

It was not difficult for Arnold to discover where the Jolyons were playing, so he drove into Bristol on a winter's evening when the snow was whirling dizzyingly in front of the windscreen and the lights were on all along the main streets.

He went straight to the theatre and along to the stage doorkeeper's room. He asked to see Granville, gave his name and was led through to the manager's room. Granville was sitting at a desk filling in forms, but he got up as Arnold entered the room and held out his hand with a boyish smile.

'Mr Haslington, this is a surprise. Do you want to see Rose? She's . . .'

'Not yet. I want to see you first, Mr Sinclair. I believe Rose first came to the Jolyons because she thought her mother was with the company. Tell me, is it true that Lily Rivell had been with you at one time?'

Granville looked hunted.

'Ye-es,' he said slowly. 'That's certainly true. But as you know, Rose didn't wish to pursue the matter any further, and so I thought it best to say nothing.'

'I can understand that,' Arnold said patiently. 'But I, Mr Sinclair, would very much like to contact my wife again. I should be most obliged if you would give me the means of getting in touch with her.'

'Well . . . I can't be *sure*, of course, that she's still where I heard of her last . . . this wouldn't go back to Rose, would it? I mean I wouldn't like her to think . . .'

'I don't suppose my daughter will mind if I contact her mother, so long as I don't bring Lily down on her or decide to let her bring up her own child,' Arnold said mildly. 'Please, Mr Sinclair. If I am lucky enough to find Lily no mention of the part you have played will pass my lips. How does that satisfy you?'

'Very well. Four years ago, Lily was down in Devonshire, at a little town called Barnstaple. She was with a theatre, of course, playing leads or supporting roles. But whether she's moved on or not I couldn't say.'

'Barnstaple!' It was too good to be true! In the very same county where he and Rose had fled so that she could have the baby without the whole world knowing, and a town, furthermore, not so very far away from his present home.

'That's right,' Granville said, mildly surprised. 'D'you know it?'

'Well, yes. Do you remember coming to visit us on the farm?'

'Of course.'

'Barnstaple's only a few miles away.'

Granville smiled.

'Really? Well, I've never actually visited the place, you see, but Lily went there and wrote to me a couple of times – Christmas cards, that sort of thing – but she hasn't been in touch for two years at least. Tell you what, Mr Haslington, you go and look around Barnstaple and if you find she's moved on, let me know. She's a real trouper is Lily, the sort of player a manager's always glad to find. If you have no luck then I'll put the word about on the grapevine and we'll find her, I've no doubt of that.'

'Thanks very much,' Arnold said with more warmth than he had previously shown. 'And now I'd better go and see my daughter!'

'Yes, of course . . . Umm . . . Mr Haslington?'

'Yes?'

'Not a word, eh? Stay mum.'

'Not a word,' corroborated Arnold.

It was pleasant to be driving back to Devonshire, this time with definite news of his wife. Arnold hummed as he drove, and then actually burst into song. It would be good to get back to the soft air of the country, to smell the sea on every breeze and to stroll out into the snow and down to the cliffs where they grew the best of their bulbs to see whether they were showing yet.

It hardly ever snowed, the locals told him, but it had been a harsh winter everywhere. Never mind – the winter that had lasted, for Arnold, ever since he had lost Lily looked like easing up at long last. Of course I don't expect her to forgive me, or to come back to me or any romantic nonsense like that, Arnold reminded himself. I don't deserve it, and anyway things like that just don't happen. She's been married, she'll be married still. But I'd like to let her know I've missed her dreadfully all these years and tell her how Philip longs to see her again. Because he does, though he'd never admit it to a living soul. And . . . well, I'd like to tell her how sorry I am, how it was all my fault it went wrong, and how I've regretted my behaviour every day of my life since she went.

It was a long drive from Bristol but Arnold had started at the crack of the winter dawn so he arrived before darkness had fallen. He drove up the main street, chose a pleasant little hotel and booked himself in for the night. Then, on foot, he strolled out to take a look around, as he phrased it. I'm not going to rush into anything this time, I'm going to take it easy, look about me, see how the land lies, he told himself . . . and headed straight for the theatre.

The company were doing a comedy . . . *The Importance of Being Earnest*. Arnold eyed the cast, looking at the wrong end of it first and being surprised, stupidly, that neither of the ingénues was played by Miss Lily Rivell.

She was playing Lady Bracknell. Well, I'm not going to rush in and spy on her, Arnold vowed, walking into the booking office and buying a ticket for that night's performance. I'll just sit here and enjoy the performance and see if I recognize her, he told himself as he took his seat in the front row. She'll probably have changed out of all recognition – she must have done if they've cast her as that old battle-axe of a Bracknell woman!

She came on. She had not changed at all. She was far too beautiful to play Lady Bracknell, Arnold considered; she put the rest of the cast into the shade, especially the young things playing the ingénues. And her acting – superb was the only adjective. He had never seen a high-born lady better played, unless it ought to have been over-played, for Lady Bracknell must be an exaggeration. Halfway through the play Arnold wondered whether he had ever seen Lily playing Lady Bracknell before, for many of her actions and mannerisms seemed strangely familiar. In the last act, he suddenly recognized what he was a watching: a first-rate imitation of his late lamented mama, in full fig and doing her best to depress any pretensions around. He laughed more heartily than ever after that . . . how furious his mother would have been, but to what excellent use Lily had put her years of misery at his mother's hands!

When the entire cast came on for their curtain call, Arnold decided that it would not be fair to go round to the stage door now; it was too soon, too precipitate. He would go back to his hotel, have dinner, go to bed, and then decide tomorrow what he should best do.

The cast were heartily clapped and cheered, the lights went up and they came forward for their last bow.

Arnold leaned forward in his seat and waved, at the same moment calling, 'Bravo, Lily my dear!' in the loudest voice at his command.

If he was petrified, so was Lily. She stopped in mid-curtsy and her face, beneath the greasepaint, went quite white. Then she recovered herself and looked straight into his eyes. And smiled.

An enormous, unbelievable happiness flooded through Arnold. He smiled back and kissed his hand, then stood up and kissed both hands. And then, without waiting for the performance to end officially, without waiting for the orchestra . . . one man with a violin and another on the piano . . . to begin to play 'God Save the King', he left his seat, plunged recklessly out of the theatre and ran like a boy round to the stage door.

He was halfway down the corridor, with the stage doorkeeper still gibbering behind him, when he saw a figure approaching. It was Lily. Running.

They ran, quite literally, into each other's arms. And hugged and hugged, breathless, speechless, bemused.

Then they kissed . . . and it was the most wonderful thing that had happened to Arnold for years and years. He held Lily in his arms, a scented, weeping, trembling Lily with her golden hair coming down and her costume cumbersome and boned like armour, and knew that this was the culmination of all the harsh years in between, all the unhappiness over Rose, all the worry with the baby. This was the real homecoming.

'Lil . . . oh, Lil!' he muttered against her hair.

'Arny! Oh, Arny, I never thought I'd see you again!'

'Nor me. This is a miracle . . . I've found you! God knows I've searched, advertised, tried my utmost . . . but I've done it at last, I've found you!'

In the dusty, dimly lit corridor, locked in a fierce embrace, they muttered and exclaimed and wept a little. And cared not at all for the stage doorkeeper, or the rest of the cast, or for anything but each other.

# Part III

## *Addy's Girl*

# CHAPTER TWENTY-SIX
## 1926

'Come along, Bud darling, we've got a long journey, you know.'

Lily called up the stairs of the farmhouse to the small figure, lugging an armful of assorted soft toys, who was beginning to descend towards her. Not hurrying. Lily Adeline, always known as Bud, was annoyed at being torn away from her beloved home, even though a Christmas at Haslington Hall with aunts and uncles and a score of cousins should, Lily felt, have been a high treat.

'I'm coming, Mummy; is Daddy ready?'

'Daddy has been sitting in the car for ten minutes, young lady, as you very well know,' Lily said. 'Darling, you've already packed a multitude of toys; don't you think they were sufficient?'

Bud did not bother to answer; surely the state of her arms, forced out at an uncomfortable angle with their burden, was answer enough?

'All right, jolly silly question,' Lily said, as her adopted daughter reached the foot of the stairs. She and Arnold had decided to adopt her when it became very clear that so far as Rose was concerned, the child might not exist. Adoption, Arnold felt, kept Bud safe, and Lily, knowing real joy, was making up for the participation in her own daughter's childhood which she had lost.

'Can I sit in front?' Bud said, as she always did. And as she always replied, Lily shook her head.

'No, darling, you've got much more room in the back and Daddy needs me in the passenger seat to direct him with the maps. But we'll have a fine time; we'll stop for coffee at eleven o'clock . . . you can have milk and biscuits, or orange juice for a special treat . . . and then again at lunchtime, and I dare say we'll have a nice high tea somewhere as well. Uncle Philip's awfully busy at his pot-bank, you see, and because he has no children he doesn't have a nanny or anyone who can get nursery tea ready, so until we're settled in it will save him trouble.'

'And will Auntie Bella and Auntie Dotty and all the cousins be there when we arrive?' Bud asked, struggling with the doorhandle of the Rover. 'My favourite is baby Suzanne. When baby Suzanne's big she has to call me auntie!'

Lily laughed and opened the car door so that Bud might hurl her armful of toys on to the back seat and then climb in with them, showing a great deal of the seat of her frilly pants.

'They don't arrive until tomorrow, I don't think,' she said. She saw Bud settled then shut the door firmly, and got into the passenger seat. 'Sorry we've been so long, love, but Bud had a few more toys she wanted to bring along.'

Arnold swivelled round in the driver's seat and stared despairingly into the crowded back of the vehicle.

'Oh, Bud,' he said reproachfully. 'If Santa Claus brings you more toys, whatever shall we do with them? There won't be room in the car to bring them home; you'll have to leave them at Uncle Philip's place.'

'Couldn't we ask him to deliver them to our real home?' asked Bud hopefully. 'He's got the sledge, after all.'

In the face of such an obvious solution both adults were momentarily stunned into silence; then Arnold mumbled that probably they could send them by train and Bud settled back, obviously considering the subject closed.

'When can we stop for our elevenses?' she asked as the car swung on to the road. 'Is it nearly time?'

'If you could tell the time I'd buy you a watch,' Arnold groaned. Bud's favourite remark was to ask the time.

'Little girls of four can't tell the clock,' Bud said patiently. 'But I nearly can; Miss Hetheridge says I'll be telling the clock by Easter.'

'Miss Hetheridge knows her stuff,' Arnold admitted. 'Now, Bud, how about you seeing how many blue and white cows you can see as we drive along? A prize for the first person to reach five!'

'There's no such thing as a blue and white cow,' Bud said placidly. 'What's the time?'

Lily sank back in her seat as Arnold began to expound to the child the respective positions of the large and small hands and to quiz her to tell him the time. She was tired. It is not an easy thing to suddenly find oneself first a wife and then a mother at the age of fifty, and as she got older Lily found it grew more difficult and not less.

But she would not have changed either state for the world. Of course it had not been easy, such things never are. That first night, when she had smiled at the audience and suddenly recognized Arnold . . . she could remember the shock, the feeling that the world had started spinning backwards, and then, in his arms, the sudden, incredulous joy, the *rightness* of her position.

But then had come the difficult part, the explanations, the catching up, and the fact that within two days Arnold had wanted her to go through another marriage ceremony with him and return to the farm, leaving her job and her company behind with as little fuss as she had done on the first occasion.

But she was older now, and the circumstances, as she pointed out, were very different. Now, she would be letting people down by such an action and she had no intention of doing that.

They had strolled, that first morning, down Butcher's Row, over the High Street, down Cross Street and to the banks of the Taw. It had been a beautiful morning, the sort of morning that means spring will not be long delayed. Arnold had helped Lily down on to the actual beach beside the mighty river, and they had found little pink shells embedded in the sand and smelt the good smell of the sea, for the Taw is a tidal river . . . they found little crabs, too, and skirted fishing boats, tarry-bottomed, pulled up above the tide mark.

And they had talked. How they had talked! Seventeen years' worth of living had been done since they had last met and Arnold was determined, this time, to admit to his faults, to tell Lily all about his fateful liaison with the horrid Edith Wragge. He went further: he told her about Adeline.

'So you see there was someone else,' he ended. 'A nice girl, Lily . . . you liked her yourself when you met . . . and one who had the good sense not to marry me. I made her into a reason for being unfaithful to you; I told myself Edith Wragge was just like Adeline, but the truth was I wanted a bit of excitement, a bit of naughtiness. Perhaps Adeline was right and I married too young, I don't know, but I let you down as badly as a woman can be let down and I want you to know that I've spent the last twenty years regretting it. So will you marry me again? I know there have been others and I don't blame you for it . . . but will you become Mrs Haslington and try again?'

'Well . . . no,' Lily said apologetically, and saw his ruddy handsome face whiten. 'Look, Arny, the truth is I never married those others, not one of them. I was married to you, wasn't I? So I just lived with them. So far as it goes, I'm as much Mrs Haslington as I ever was.'

'Oh, Lily!' He had hugged her then, and kissed her too, and they had clung, sinking into the sand and not caring a bit, like young lovers again.

He had stayed in Barnstaple a week and then he had gone back to the flower farm, but Lily had gone with him. She had coached her understudy into the part, paid all her debts, said goodbye to all her friends and left because she knew very well that this was the sort of second chance granted to few people on this earth, and she intended to grab it with both hands.

Arnold had done a lot of apologizing over the flower farm, and over the hitherto unexplained presence of their grandchild, but Lily had been delighted by both. His suggestion that they should send the child to live with some loving and responsible person such as his sister Bella or even one of her children, recently married, had been treated with the scorn Lily felt it deserved. The child was a darling, pretty, intelligent, charming, and she, Lily, was the very person to bring the little girl up.

'I'll see she doesn't become a selfish little madam, as our Rose seems to have done,' she said. 'And as for the flower farm – it's like heaven, Arny; much nicer than that dull old Hall so full of sad memories for me. We'll make a new start in a new place, and I'll work like a demon to make a go of it this time round.'

They had both worked like demons, and they had made a go, not only of their marriage, but of the flower farm as well. Lily, a real city girl, had taken to country life like a duck to water. It was she who, trowel in hand, had first planted masses of daffodil bulbs on the actual cliff-face itself, and a rich reward they had obtained by having the earliest blooms for miles around. Out in all weathers, getting tanned, with her hands like a navvy's and her nails torn and split, Lily was happier than she had ever been; and Arnold, too, grew to love the work as well as the place.

'Not that I'll ever enjoy digging in the rain,' he had warned her. 'I didn't make a lot of money to end my life doing *that*; I'm employing people to do the rough work whether you approve or not.'

The only slug in the ointment, Lily mused now, using a turn of phrase natural, she told herself, for a farmer's wife, was Philip. She had adored her son; it had broken her heart to leave him all those years ago, and she had contemplated getting in touch with him many times but had never quite dared to do so. She had constant news of the family through one of her maids, Meg, who had married down in Bristol but who kept in touch with her parents back in the village. She knew, therefore, that Arnold had not married again and that he was bringing up the children to the best of his ability. To appear, like a phoenix, to her son and perhaps to spoil his relationship with his father was not fair and Lily wanted to be fair. She knew, of course, that Arnold had given it out that she was dead and this had been a further pain to her, making it impossible for her to see either child without proving their father a liar.

Rose had been charming to her . . . but it was an absent-minded sort of charm, without any real meaning. She was delighted to find she had a good-looking, presentable mother and there it ended. Unless she had some need of Lily, she would not bother with her.

Philip, from whom Lily expected a much warmer response, had been polite. He had said all the right things, smiled whenever their eyes met – and she had felt his antagonism like a sword-thrust through the heart. She had tried to explain to him that she had not wanted to leave him . . . and he had said it was quite all right, he understood already and most certainly did not blame her for what she had done.

'But . . . Philip, I had no money, not even a few shillings,' she had said desperately. 'I couldn't take either of you, it wouldn't have been fair.'

'Of course not. Why should you, indeed, when Father could look after us here with dozens of servants and all the money that he needed? That is what children want, after all.'

His words were spoken so coldly, yet with such apparent understanding and sympathy, that she had been silenced. And ever since, whenever they met, it had been the same. Outwardly he had been friendly and forthcoming, talking about his experiments at the pot-bank, his successes and failures. Inwardly, she sensed the iced lake of his dislike and disapproval.

Yet Arnold, who loved her, noticed nothing, denied that Philip was even slightly antagonistic towards her.

'He adored his mother, and he loves you very dearly still,' he said indulgently. 'But a man of twenty-six is a very different kettle of fish from a little boy of five, my dear. You mustn't expect him to climb on to your knee and tell you he loves you; he is naturally reticent, now, about his feelings.'

Now, sitting in the car and heading once more for a Christmas which, for her, would be made miserable by Philip's dislike, Lily wondered desperately what she could do to mend matters. If she could just get through to him once . . . the only person who truly understood her position was old Sidney Warburton and even from him she had failed to get any practical help.

'The boy was desolate when you left,' he said the first time she had a chance to tackle him about Philip. 'I was pretty miserable too, Lily. My daughter dead, you gone . . . I was pretty damned unhappy. And you never sent word, not so much as a card. I knew you'd forgotten me and why not, an old codger at the wrong end of his life, but Philip was younger, more easily hurt. I doubt he'll ever get over it, ever see you as his mother. You've changed a lot over the years, my dear, but Philip's changed more. Arnold didn't like him much as a lad, he's only grown fond of him as he's matured, and Philip had to put up with all that on his own. Rose was no help and Arnold adored her and pushed the boy aside. You shouldn't expect him to forget, perhaps.'

'No . . . but he's punishing me for what wasn't my fault,' Lily said desperately. 'What could I have done? Taken him with me, to starve, perhaps?'

Sidney shook his head reprovingly.

'Starve, indeed! A woman of your talents need never starve, Lily. You could have come to me, instead of walking right out of our lives.'

It silenced her because it was true. But she had chosen to go to young Tony Harcourt-Jones, who adored her. It had been balm to her wounded pride, her shattered self-image, that he had wanted her with such wild abandon that he had been willing to hide her for weeks and then to take her to London on a tour of the theatre companies until she found someone who would take her on.

And that small action had lost her her son. Well, she would have to accept that she and Philip would spend the rest of their lives in a state of armed truce. Better that, she supposed, than open warfare. At least they were both masters of pretence, for no one had ever commented on a difficult atmosphere when they were together.

'Is it eleven o'clock yet, Daddy?'

Lily turned in her seat to survey the child in the back. She was not pretty; she had somehow managed to miss out on the fair beauty which was Lily's and she was nothing like Arnold either. She was very tiny and very dark, with a small, screwed-up monkey-face, little bright eyes and sticklike limbs. But no child could have been dearer to Lily than this one. Not now. Once, Philip had been dearer than any other person could possibly have been . . . but Lily dismissed the thought as irrelevant. That Philip had died twenty years ago, when that Lily had died. The new models had no common ground and were better apart, but family convention said that Christmas must be spent, by everyone, at Haslington Hall and family convention could not be ignored just because she, Lily, found the fortnight painful.

'No, love, it isn't eleven o'clock. But the little hand is on the nine and the big hand is on the three, so what time do you think it is?'

Nala walked round her immaculate selling area, with her arm linked in Aunt Sarah's. Uncle Hamish, despite careful nursing, had died a year before and it had not taken much persuasion to get the old woman to move in with Nala. Not that they had sold the bungalow; nothing had been further from their thoughts. They spent every weekend there, unless something more important came up, and Aunt Sarah lived there during the week as well in summer, when Nala could drive over two or three times a week during the light evenings.

But now, with Christmas close and the snow blanketing the land, it was easier and more convenient if Aunt Sarah shared the small compound which Nala had retained when Sven sold the rest of the property. It consisted of a kitchen, a bathroom, a small bedroom and a graciously proportioned living area, all attached to the workshop so that Nala could come and go as she pleased without having to step outside her own property.

'Do you like those drawings there, Auntie Sarah? I was pleased with them when I first hung them but now I'm not so sure.'

The two women stopped in front of the drawings. They were all studies of peasants, drawn with clear, sure strokes, in black ink on white parchment. They were simply framed in a pale wood and looked very modern and clean.

'I like them there; you can see each face, and I recognize every man and woman without effort,' Aunt Sarah said. 'Why? What's wrong with the position?'

The drawings were hung on a whitewashed wall and beneath them the long bench was covered with delicate celadon ware. To Sarah, they clearly looked all right, but Nala was shaking her head.

'Too much white,' she said. 'You know that screen-printing on silk I did last summer? I know most of it was sold, but wasn't there some dark blue left? And some poppy red?'

'Yes, I think so. Why?'

'Because I can hang a swathe of the poppy red behind the drawings, on the wall, and that will help to make them show up. And it will do the same for the celadon. Now that I've got a proper show-room I really must make more of an effort to display things properly.'

'You work too hard already,' Aunt Sarah said. 'I do hope, my child, that you aren't going to try to work in here as well.'

'No, of course not. I couldn't bear to waste time in here when I might be working in the room at the back, and anyway, I very soon wouldn't have anything to sell if I did that. But young Mienga will sell awfully well. She's so pretty and polite that people will buy just to oblige her, I'm sure.'

Aunt Sarah laughed and they moved on, to examine, this time, a wall half-tiled with Nala's best tile-work, this time in a deep royal blue with Chinese characters drifting down as though they were leaves in autumn.

'Clever,' Aunt Sarah said after a moment. 'That's an unusual colour. How did you attain it?'

Nala looked rather guilty.

'I didn't. I . . . I sent away for the tiles, which were dreadfully expensive, and then I did the decoration straight on to them, fired them again, and that's the result. Only of course I lost a good twenty per cent through breakages.'

'Mm. Well, they're beautiful. But will they sell at the sort of price you're going to have to ask?'

'I hope so. But it's just an experiment. I'll see how they go and whether I need more.'

They moved round the room again, but Nala's mind was no longer on the scene before her. Instead of the oil paintings of harvest scenes she saw again the letter she had sent to the Haslington Pottery, and the reply.

She had asked for the tiles to be sent, explaining that she had her own small business now and wanted to see whether one of the new colours, decorated with her art, would sell in China. She had waited weeks, breathlessly, for a reply. It had been the first time she had done anything to remind Philip Haslington of her existence and she was both horrified at her own sudden forwardness and afraid that he would snub her.

She need not have been afraid. A letter came back, with her order, from someone she had never heard of – a Roger Trewin – in which he said they were honoured to receive her business, that the tiles were herewith, and that he hoped to hear from her again in the future.

She often met Sven, because she used his pots when she was too busy to make her own or when she wanted something special, and told him about her experiment with the tiles. He had looked at her long and hard.

'Really? And what did Philip say?'

'Oh, nothing. The letter came from someone else, not even Frank, someone I'd never heard of. Trewin his name was, I think.'

'Well, what did you expect? When do you think your letter reached England?'

'Oh, about August, I think. Things take so long.'

'Philip will have been holidaying somewhere then, I imagine. August's a dead month in England. Probably he doesn't even know they've supplied you with tiles.'

It had been a relief in a way and now her hands were tied. She could not write for more supplies until she knew whether these tiles would sell and very few people came to buy in winter, with the snow disinclining her customers to travel right out of the village to take a look at her stock.

'Are you going to make the effort to come to Belgium in the spring?' Sven asked her before they parted. 'You're doing so well now, Nala, that it might pay you to come. Tell you what – if you will, I'll share the cost of a stand with you, and we can travel together as well. You remember my daughter Gerda? She's coming with me this time.'

'Well, I might,' Nala conceded. 'Will the Haslingtons be there, do you suppose?'

Sven chuckled.

'If they've cracked the secret of iridescent lustre nothing would keep young Philip away,' he said. 'They didn't come last year . . . in fact they've only been once since our first exhibition . . . but I think they'll be there this spring. How about it?'

'I'm awfully fond of Gerda . . . yes, Sven, it's a deal, provided everything is all right here, of course.' They were standing in her workshop whilst the two girls she now employed worked round them. 'Give her my love, anyway. No young man yet?'

'No. She's too European-looking, poor child. No man yet for you, Nala?'

Nala shook her head.

'Tell Gerda it's the same for me,' she said, smiling. 'I'll keep in touch, Sven.'

'The harvest scenes are awfully good,' Aunt Sarah remarked, breaking into Nala's thoughts and bringing her smartly back to the present. 'I should think they'd go down well with the folk back home . . . is that what you're hoping for?'

'I'm hoping the buyers who buy for the big companies in Europe and America will see them and take a chance on some,' Nala admitted. 'Then . . . yes, then I think foreigners will buy more than the locals.'

In fact she sold more to local people than she had anticipated, for the rich Chinese may like antiques and rare objects, but businessmen buy what is good and Nala's delicate, beautifully decorated ware and her paintings were good by any standards. But because of the fact that her outlook was different she frequently realized that she had a view of a particular scene or happening which was not shared by the local Chinese . . . she would draw a corner of the marketplace which local artists knew so well that they never even considered immortalizing it, yet it was, on parchment or paper, outstandingly strange or beautiful.

'One day you'll be famous,' Aunt Sarah said now. She had picked up a tall vase with pine trees laden with snow and dripping with icicles depicted on it. 'Whatever made you draw that? Yet it's beautiful, I see that now.'

'Yes, it's lovely,' agreed Nala, taking no credit for the beauty, for had they not both seen those very pine trees, day after day, on the bank of the stream opposite the bungalow? 'I'm going to use that design on a tea-service for one of the Kuomintang. I can't remember his name but he's an important man. I told him it would be expensive and he just waved that away as being irrelevant. I hope he pays, when it's finished!'

'One of the Kuomintang, eh?' Aunt Sarah shook her head. 'There'll be trouble one of these days between them and the Communists. Chiang Kai-shek is a strong leader, and he's got all south China under his thumb; he's bound to challenge the Communists in the north one of these days.'

'Oh, I don't know; being a Communist isn't like being Chinese or Japanese, or black or white . . . there are Communists in the army and others in our village – why, a Communist can drink with you at the inn and you none the wiser. It's really a way of thought, and ways of thought are difficult to fight.'

'Communists should live in Russia,' Aunt Sarah said crossly. 'I don't know any, but if I did that's what I'd tell them – go and live in Russia, I'd say. We don't want Communist rule here; it just means Russians.'

'You're old fashioned,' Nala said. 'Communists in China don't need Russian backing, they're Chinese through and through. Now, to change the subject, do you like my new sales area, or shop, or whatever you like to call it?'

'It's delightful,' Aunt Sarah said, moving back towards the door which led into the house. 'Shall we discuss it over tea? Your young Mienga has a way with toasted muffins and I made a batch yesterday.'

'Yes, let's have tea now,' Nala said. 'But to go back to our previous discussion, I sometimes think I'm a bit of a Communist. They believe in equality, and when I go out and see beggars starving in the streets and children dying of malnutrition during a drought then I really do think that Communism could help China in some ways at least.'

Aunt Sarah snorted but allowed herself to be led back to the house and a plateful of toasted muffins.

'If you'll come to tea on Christmas Day then, Unk, you can see us all together . . . and remember, we did ask you to luncheon and you said you couldn't manage it and we asked you to dine and you said no, so the least you can do is come to Christmas tea.'

'It's good of you, Philip.' Sidney and his godson were sitting by the study fire, smoking, or at least Sidney was smoking; Philip was just sitting, one leg cocked up on the other knee, watching the flames paint roses on the old fireplace. 'But the fact is, Christmas is an unhappy time when you're alone and missing . . . people. I think about Addy's girl more at Christmas than at any other time . . . wonder what she's doing, who she's with, whether she's happy, that sort of thing. I know so little about the Chinese, too. Do they celebrate Christmas or does is just pass like another day? Most of them are Buddhists – those that have any religion at all, that is. So what does young Adeline do?'

'She'll celebrate,' Philip said. 'Bound to . . . she's a missionary's child, after all, and she loved her father very much, you said so. She wouldn't abandon his religion.'

'Perhaps she wouldn't. I don't know. I can keep it under all the rest of the year, but at Christmas, which is a time for families, it all comes flooding over me and I miss the little girl I never knew.'

'Then come to us . . . you'll forget how lonely you are and you can watch the kiddies . . . come to us,' Philip urged. 'There's no call to nurse your grief and loneliness, Unk, not with a whole houseful of Haslingtons so close.'

'I thought, once, that your father and my Adeline might make a go of it,' Sidney murmured, almost under his breath. 'I didn't want that; thought he wasn't man enough for my Addy. If only I hadn't interfered, brought John here . . . things might have been very different.'

Philip looked up sharply, then down at the floor. Unk did not know he had spoken aloud, so he would not let on he had heard.

'Then you'll come? For Christmas lunch? The kids would love it, and you know that's true – I don't have to make things like that up. Say you will, Unk; I can't bear to think of you here by yourself on Christmas day.'

'Perhaps I will,' Sidney said on a sigh. 'Yes, perhaps I will. Lily's the only one who knows what it's like to spend Christmas alone, when what you want most in the world is the feel of a child's hand in yours, the sight of that child's pleasure making your life worth living.'

'Lily knows? My mother?' All Philip's careful defences crumbled. 'Oh no, Unk, not my mother. She went her own way, left us . . . she doesn't know what loneliness means. It means sitting in the nursery after lunch on Christmas Day, six years old and with a lump of misery in your chest big enough to choke you, whilst your father gets down on the floor and plays horsie in the night-nursery next door with the baby, then goes off downstairs with the littl'un in his arms and clean forgets he's got another child, sitting by himself looking out over the rainswept park.'

'Philip, my boy . . . if you feel like that it's your father you ought to blame, not your mother! She thought she was doing her best for you when she left you in a warm home with servants and a father who loved you both. She had no conception of what Arnold must have felt for you . . .'

'I don't blame Father for loving Rose more than me. Why should I? Rose was a lovable little thing; I clearly wasn't. If I had been my mother would have taken me with her, not just abandoned me. Anyway, it's all behind me, all past. But Mother doesn't remember any of it, she doesn't even remember that I knew all about her lover, young though I was. Oh yes, I put two and two together when I was no more than seven. I'm not blaming her exactly, but I just knew she loved that young army officer more than she loved me . . . why not, indeed? . . . and went off with him, leaving me with Father.'

'Which young army officer?' Sidney said.

'I don't know his name, I just know there was one,' Philip said dully. 'Forget it, Unk; it's part of the past. But don't expect me to sympathize with my mother's loneliness, because I don't believe it existed.'

Later, making his way home through the rain-soaked dusk, Philip strode out and dug his hands in his pockets and turned up his coat collar – and wished he had said nothing to Unk. It was not fair to upset the old boy. It was no fault of his if Philip had discovered young that he was not a lovable child. The hard thing had been to accept that his mother, who had given every appearance of loving him very much, had in reality been indifferent. Now, of course, he knew better than to accept at face value any demonstration of affection. He was just not the sort of bloke people loved. He was lucky to get friendship and liking; that should be enough.

Christmas day passed successfully, with lots of presents, lots of food and endless games and charades. Sidney came to Christmas lunch and appeared to enjoy both the lavish spread and the children's attentions, for he was every bit as popular as Philip had intimated with the younger ones.

Boxing Day was not quite so easy; a cold lunch had been planned with hot soup first and hot pudding to follow, but children who have had an exciting Christmas Day with too many presents and too much food tend to be irritable and touchy within twenty-four hours.

Dorothea had seven-year-old twins, a nine-year-old and an eleven-year-old. Just when the grown-ups were gathering the young together for lunch a twin smote an elder brother upon the nose with a judiciously swung steam-train. Whilst only a model, it was very heavy and packed quite a punch. Blood flowed, screams rent the air and when Auntie Bella smacked the offending and aggressive twin the other one bit Auntie Bella in the hand and left tooth marks and drew blood.

Dorothea had brought a nanny with her, a sensible woman who had taken all the children under her wing, realizing that once the adults got together little notice would be taken of the younger ones. Now she tried to sort out the twins and their brothers, to rescue little Bud whose fingers had been trodden into the carpet in the fracas and whose yells rivalled the victim of the steam-train, and to persuade Bella's Josephine, a plump, managing child of twelve, that it was not her place to batter her cousins, no matter how richly she might think they deserved such a fate.

Lily and Philip, not together but one shortly after the other, entered upon this lively and indeed startling scene. Children shed blood and howled, other children howled and hit, still more children lay on the floor and wailed, whilst others simply wandered about, demanding their lunch and threatening each other's most precious possessions.

There were actually only eight children present, but they gave the impression of being at least twenty-eight.

Bella, nursing her injured hand, turned and heaved a sigh of relief at the sight of reinforcements.

'They're being *devils*,' she cried vivaciously. 'Lily, do take Bud away before she gets trodden on again! Philip, my dear, can you grab the twin with the train before he brains anyone else?' She turned to the twin without the train. 'Which one are you? Simon or Peter?'

'I'm Peter,' the twin said sulkily. And untruthfully, as Bella instantly divined.

'Really? Well, I shall call you Simon,' Bella said, causing both twins to glare at her with unalloyed hatred. 'Philip, take Peter up to the old nursery, would you? He can cool off there for ten minutes whilst we sort everyone else out.'

'Come along, Peter,' Philip said. He seized the hot and grubby hand of his small cousin and led him to the stairs. Lily, in her turn, picked Bud up off the floor and cuddled the child in her arms. Bud laid her hot pink cheek against the cool silk of Lily's dress and sighed blissfully. She was not used to so many children and though she enjoyed their company enormously, she also found it very tiring. She wanted nothing more, at this moment, than a quiet luncheon, a wash and then a nice long nap.

But even as Lily left the room with her child in her arms, the remaining twin – Peter? Simon? – rushed past her like a whirlwind and made for the stairs.

'Watch out, that one bites!' Bella shrieked and so Lily hurried off to her own room and handed Bud over to her maid, a local girl whom she could not remember at all.

'Madge, my dear, would you clean this little person up, please, and then take her down to her daddy? He'll be in the study having a pre-luncheon drink, I dare say. Tell him I think she's had enough for one day and had better have a quiet snack with us and then a lie-down.'

Madge took the willing Bud, and Lily ran for the stairs which led up to the nursery wing.

It was a long time since she had been up here – twenty years, she realized with a little shiver. The day she had left Arnold she had come up here, talked to Philly, held him against her heart for a hug and a kiss – and had then walked out of his life for ever. No wonder the poor fellow didn't care for her now – but how could she have known? She had honestly believed she was acting in his best interests; she had had no idea that Arnold's deep love for his little son would simply transfer itself to the daughter, leaving nothing left over.

Sidney had told her and her shame had been such that for two or three days she had avoided not only Philip's eyes but his company. He had only to enter a room for her to scurry out of it, and this had suited him well enough, or so it seemed. But now she was deliberately seeking him out because she did not feel it fair to leave him with two homicidal twins on his hands, she told herself, and for no other reason.

Halfway up the stairs she realized she was still holding bunny, the earless, eyeless, almost furless pink rabbit which was the love of her child's heart. Knowing Bud, she doubted that she would consent to so much as wash her hands without Bunny watching, and was about to retrace her steps when she heard a scuffle above her, a roar, a defiant shout and a thump . . . and then a twin came streaking past her, or at least trying to streak past, whilst from upstairs came a wrathful shout that boded ill for Simon. Or Peter.

'Less of that, young man,' Lily said briskly. She grabbed the twin's arm and hauled him, kicking and scarlet-faced but providentially silent, back up the stairs and into the old nursery.

To her astonishment, a fire burned in the grate behind the big old brass fireguard and the curtains were fluttering slightly in the breeze from the big old sash window, open slightly at the top.

She looked enquiringly across at Philip, who had trapped his twin between his knees and appeared to be lecturing him.

'Why is the fire lit and the curtains up, Philip? I thought it would be deserted.'

Philip looked up at her. The amusement which had filled his eyes gradually died out as he saw who it was. But he was very polite. Of course.

'Oh, Mother. I'm sorry, I didn't realize you were going to come up here. It's being used, that's why the fire's lit. Whenever Dorothea brings the children she takes over the nursery wing – they sleep here and in the night nursery next door. See?'

He indicated two single beds which Lily had not immediately noticed.

'Oh . . . well, I suppose it's better to keep it used and aired,' Lily said uncertainly. Her son frightened her.

'Yes . . . and there are bars on the windows and the kids can make as much row as they like without disturbing anyone else,' Philip said briefly.

'Of course.' Since her twin was now letting his wrist lie in her grasp without struggling Lily released him. To her relief he did not immediately run away but turned and stared ruminatively at the child still gripped between his cousin's legs. And then, before she could stop him, the boy . . . Peter? Simon? . . . had grabbed Bunny from her hand and was holding him over the fireguard.

'Let us both go, or the slug'll burn,' he said briskly. 'Let Simon go, Philip!'

'Don't be melodramatic and stupid, Peter,' Philip said calmly. 'I'm not hurting your brother, I'm simply telling him that a boy of seven who bites Auntie Bella isn't big and brave and terrible, he's simply acting like a spoilt kid, and if this sort of thing is going to happen again, it can happen somewhere besides my home; understand? And any more cheek from either of you and you'll go hungry this lunchtime. Is that clear?'

For answer the pink rabbit, Bud's dearest favourite, sailed over the fireguard and landed squarely in the middle of the fire.

Lily screamed, she could not help it, and dived for the fireguard, but someone else was quicker. Philip was past her, dragging the guard back, falling on his knees in front of the flames and grabbing, with quick, short grabs and jabs, protecting his face with the other hand so that he could get closer.

The .rabbit, burned but still whole, rolled out of the fire and Philip picked it up, still smouldering. The twins, realizing in a moment the enormity of their action, were but two pairs of receding footfalls echoing up the stairs.

Mother and son stared at each other, then at the pathetic, charred object in Philip's hands.

Lily reached for the rabbit and took it away from Philip, taking his hand as she did so and turning it palm up.

'Philly, darling, your poor hand!' she said, her voice throbbing with concern. 'Oh, my dear boy, just for an old rabbit, to take a chance with your safety like that . . . you shouldn't have done it. I can always buy Bud another rabbit . . . but another you is a different matter altogether.'

She was still holding his hand and Philip made no effort to withdraw it.

'What did you call me?' he said a trifle stiffly. 'What did you just say, Mama?'

'Why, Philly, of course. I always called you Philly when you were a little boy, though I dare say you don't remember.' She traced a line across the palm of his hand with a gentle forefinger. 'Do you remember your cuddy, and how you went into the fire after it and burnt yourself? And how you came running out into the rain to find me?'

'Yes . . . I didn't think you did, though.'

'Oh, yes. Why, Philly, for years and years and years all I had of you were my memories of those first five years. I knew everything we'd done together, every word you'd ever spoken to me, by heart! I'd lie in some miserable little bed in some run-down terraced house in Leeds or Birmingham or the east end of London, and go over in my mind how you'd sat on my knee in the row-boat that time we had a picnic on the river, and tried to row with me, your little hands on mine . . . and how your poor little head got stuck in the gates after you lost your cuddy and got burned trying to rescue it. A soldier came by . . . do you remember that? . . . and you wouldn't call out to him because you were so sure I was near. And when you were ill that time and I sat by your bedside all night in my cream satin evening dress and crystals . . . oh, I remembered everything.'

'Mama . . . why did you leave me, then?'

'Because . . . Philly, I went to a young man who had said he would take care of me if I had to leave Arnold . . . your father. He was a nice young man but I wasn't in love with him; I'm afraid I just used him. He kept me for a few weeks, and then I went up to London and got myself a job in the theatre. I never would have done it if I'd guessed for one moment how Arnold was going to change towards you, but how could I tell? You were the apple of his eye, he adored you; he'd shown no real interest in Rose, but left her to the nurse most of the time. Oh, Philly!'

She took him in her arms as openly and lovingly as though he had still been her little boy, and he went to her easily, hugging her tight, taller than her, broader, stronger, but just for that moment a child again.

'And . . . and you never forgot me? You really did love me? Just as you said?'

'Just exactly as I said. More than anyone in the world; more than I loved Arnold by then, because I knew he was unfaithful to me and had fallen out of love with me. Did you miss me, love?'

Philip sighed and gently held her away from him. He tried to grin, to make light of it, but his eyes were full of tears.

'Yes. I missed you,' he said simply. 'Mama, I'm so glad you're back.'

# CHAPTER TWENTY-SEVEN

Spring in China is very beautiful and Nala always awaited its coming eagerly. It meant changing into lighter, cooler clothes, being able to swim in the mountain lakes, and eating her meals out of doors in the little courtyard with the willow and the pine tree.

But this year there was a strange spirit abroad in China and it made everyone wary. There had been too much fighting, too many battles. The War Lords in the north had been finally crushed, they said, but now Chiang Kai-shek was too big for his boots, too full of his own importance. He had been issuing threats of what he would do to anyone who supported the Communists and his troops had killed peasants and others who did not immediately fall in with his ideas.

Shanghai was no longer a good place to be. Sven came back to the village and told Nala, his face heavy with sadness, that he was frightened of his fellow-countrymen for the first time for many years.

'Chiang has made it clear that he won't stand for Communists who simply seize the goods of rich men and say they will give them to the people,' Sven told her. 'I'm afraid that there will be a pitched battle in Shanghai and, whoever wins, anyone with two *cash* to rub together will be massacred and his property taken. Whether it is given to that amorphous mass called "the people" by the Communists, or goes into Chiang Kai-shek's coffers, it won't save my life.'

'What will you do? Where will you go?' Nala asked, but Sven said he'd think about it and would probably flee, with his entire family, by sea if the worst came to the worst.

'There's always Japan . . . or Korea,' he said. 'They appreciate potters there.'

After he had left, the thought he had planted was still there; if by some trick of a cruel fate a potter has to leave China, he (or she) will be appreciated in Korea. Or Japan.

The weekend came, and Nala went back into the hills and spent her two days with Aunt Sarah at the bungalow. The old lady was frailer than ever, but indomitably cheerful. 'I shall spring clean this place now that I'm back for the summer, she said, as she waved Nala off on the Monday morning. 'And then when you next come it will be clean as a new pin. Take care of yourself, and don't go into the city, not for a little while, my dear.'

'Why not?' Had rumours of war reached Aunt Sarah in this remote spot? But the older woman had many Chinese friends who would have visited her to welcome her back and they must have warned her to tell her young friend to take care.

'Why not? Because Chiang Kai-shek hates the white people, he hates all foreigners. He says it is just the Communists but friends tell me that if he wins he'll rid China of all the *yang kuei-tzu*, and that means us. Oh, I know they say he'll simply insist that we get aboard ships and go home, but . . . the Chinese can be a strange, cruel people. They hold life very cheap.'

Nala returned to her workshop and began to fire a new type of pot. It was to be made especially for the *la-mei* blossom, for the blooms, so sweetly scented, so rare and clear a lemony-yellow, come out almost first of the flowering trees and they come upon branches still bare with winter, flowering before a leaf has so much as burst its buds.

She threw the pots first, then fired them. After that they would receive their first coloured glaze, and they would be fired again. Then they would have their design painted on, before being fired for the last time. She meant to draw and paint the *la-mei* blossom on the pale green and creamy white vases, so that the design would echo the beauty of the blooms the vase had been created to hold.

It was a slow job but a pleasant one, and she was only halfway through the work when she heard that Shanghai had fallen to the forces of Chiang Kai-shek – and that he was massacring Communists in that city.

A few vases later she heard that the Kuomintang were on the march once more . . . and that there were dead Christians amongst the victims of this new revolution. Later still, that the Kuomintang troops were flooding the country, killing foreigners, anyone who might be a Communist, and those who did not immediately join their ranks. A rich family was not safe, but neither were poor peasants for many of them were suspected, rightly or wrongly, of being Communists.

She was finishing off the *la-mei* design on the biggest vase of all when a friend from the next village came into her workroom. He was also a potter, making very beautiful, sturdy pots which Nala quite often bought in and decorated to sell. Now he was out of breath, wild-eyed.

'Nala . . . you must go! Quickly, quickly, my dear, you must leave this place!'

'Why, P'ei? Is it Communists or Kuomintang?'

'It's the Kuomintang . . . they're killing the whites and the Communists! They took the city last night and they say the streets are running red with blood this morning. Now they're marching this way . . . you must run, Nala, you must hide!'

'They're coming from the city? Then I'll go to the bungalow,' Nala decided. 'I'd have to go back for Aunt Sarah anyway, so I might as well go that way as any.' She put down the vase regretfully, for the order was almost complete. 'Will you get someone to take over here, P'ei, until I come back? If they see it is in the hands of an ordinary Chinese perhaps they won't wreck the place.'

'We'll do our best,' P'ei said, his face reflecting the worry he felt. 'Do go now . . . go, go, go!'

'Are the 'buses running?' Nala picked up a quilted jacket from where she had flung it down across a chair. 'Can I catch one, do you suppose?'

'No . . . I don't think they'll be running since they start in the city. You'd best borrow a donkey or a mule, and go by the quiet ways. Here, wear this.' He picked up a straw coolie hat and put it on to her head. 'It would be safer.'

'Very well.' Nala could not take the threats seriously, but then she had never seen violence or war, she told herself, leaving her home behind without a backward glance and going straight to the nearest farmer who would loan her a mule. He was worried too, she saw the way his eyes flashed white at her presence, but the horror had not yet struck the village. Nala agreed with the farmer that the mule should be collected by one of his sons in a day or two, and mounted the sturdy beast. Friends waved her off, wished her good luck, and soon enough she was in open country, with only farmers' cottages along the way and the rice fields and the grain fields still flat and empty, waiting for the crop to appear.

She rode hard, or as hard as the mule would consent to go, and arrived at the bungalow before darkness had fallen. Aunt Sarah welcomed her but Nala could see she was worried.

'Come in, my dear . . . I'm very glad to see you,' she said. 'You're safer here with me. We'll bar the gates and keep within the walls for a few days and hope the danger moves on without affecting us.'

They stayed in the compound, in the end, for almost a week whilst news, rumours and tales of dreadfulness abounded.

At the end of the week, however, Nala decided that she simply must find out what was happening.

'Stay here, keep the gates locked, and I'll go into the village and round to the Te Ku compound and see what I can find out,' she said. 'Take care of yourself!'

Aunt Sarah frowned.

'I ought to go instead of you,' she said. 'But I doubt I'd ever reach the village. I'm not so steady on my pins as I once was!'

'I'll be all right,' Nala said, with a confidence she was far from feeling now that it came to the point. 'I won't take any chances, I'll keep my coolie hat on and my head down. But they won't bother me, they'll just think I'm a peasant girl making for the fields. Don't worry about me, Auntie Sarah.'

'I don't,' the older woman said unexpectedly. 'You're a sensible and courageous girl and you've been brought up in this country. I don't think anyone would hurt you. But they may send us packing, my dear . . . or we may decide it's the only way to stay alive. If so, we'll go together.'

Aunt Sarah's mule was old, like its owner, but it was a stolid, reliable animal with no desire to leap and bound – or even to trot – but the ability to keep going at a steady pace for mile after mile.

Nala was in the act of saddling it and slipping the bridle on over its large, meek head when one of the neighbours came into the stable courtyard.

'Missie Nala, my son has come, he is in great distress. The soldiers are close, they will come this way, he says you must go and hide in the village, you and Missie Ellis. This is known to be a white woman's home . . . you must go!'

'History's repeating itself,' Aunt Sarah said placidly, bundling herself into a warm jacket and heavy clogs. 'Did I ever tell you how Hamish and I fled before the Boxers during the revolution in 1900? We had a teaching school then, with our mission, and we took all our little girls and boys and tramped nearly a hundred miles until we reached safety. But now you and I have nowhere we can tramp, so we shall have to hide until the revolution moves on.'

'Yes . . . but we must go now,' Nala said urgently. 'The neighbours will say we left long ago so they won't search for us. You ride the mule, Auntie, and I'll walk beside it.'

They set out. The countryside was rich with spring, the trees snowy with blossom, the grass beginning to gain its deep summer colour. Birds sang, little animals rustled through the undergrowth, and when they passed a stream its splashing note was enough to lift the lowest spirits. In the rice fields the new grain was pushing out of the water, tiny green spears which would presently grow high and strong, bringing a good crop. The peasants were working on their fields but they did not wave or greet the two women and Nala hurried the mule on, chatting inconsequentially to Aunt Sarah, bent on reaching the village and finding someone who would hide them for a few days or a few weeks.

'There are the soldiers,' Aunt Sarah said presently, from her superior position on the mule's back. 'Dear me, they are actually heading for the village . . . now what should we do?'

'We'll have to keep on; we'll make for the Te Ku compound as we'd planned,' Nala said and then saw someone approaching fast, on foot. It was Ouyang, with a child swinging from his hand, chattering to him, whilst Ouyang answered and hurried towards them.

'Get off the mule,' he said as soon as he was near enough for them to hear his voice. 'I'll take it. Get into the nearest paddy field and start weeding. Both of you. Go on! They won't stop a couple of peasant women up to their knees in mud and water, but a woman on a mule is a traveller, and travellers are suspicious when things are in a turmoil.'

'Right,' Nala said. She helped Aunt Sarah off the mule and the two of them, without more ado, plodded into the nearest paddy. 'What shall we do when darkness comes?'

'Oh, then you can come to us, since all the field workers will be wending their way home. I'll stable the mule.'

Hastily he picked up the child and put it into the saddle where it beamed down at Nala and Sarah, proud as a peacock with its sudden elevation from a walker to a rider. He was a very young child, no more than three, Nala supposed. He was still wearing his baby-trousers, with a slit in the back so that he could squat and urinate or defecate without soiling his clothing.

'Ouyang . . . what will you say when the soldiers question you?' Nala called softly.

'The child ran away from the compound to follow a servant to the fields. I went after him,' Ouyang said. He smiled at Nala. 'Don't worry, little dog-eyes, you shan't have my death on your conscience.'

'I hope you're right,' Nala murmured. She bent over the water and began conscientiously to weed. 'And I hope this won't be the death of you from rheumatism, dear Auntie Sarah.'

'Rheumatism is less deadly than the loss of a head,' the older woman said drily. 'Besides, I've always been fond of gardening.'

She bent to her work.

The troops passed by. They spent a considerable while in the village and longest of all, probably, in the Te Ku compound, but then they went on their way – and their way went via the bungalow. As the sun was beginning to sink Nala smelt smoke. She glanced quickly at Aunt Sarah, then returned to her weeding, but a surreptitious glance back towards the mountains confirmed her guess; they had fired the bungalow.

To keep the older woman's mind off her home she began to suggest that they should turn for the village now; to start walking slowly when you were with an old lady was natural, not suspicious. But Aunt Sarah was not listening. Eyes closed, hands clasped, she was praying. Nala watched the old lips move for perhaps two or three minutes, then Aunt Sarah unclasped her hands, opened her eyes, and spoke.

'Well, I've done my best. Now we'd better return to the village.'

But Nala knew that, inside her mind, Aunt Sarah would still be praying, and with as much conviction as though she spoke aloud.

'I've recently come home, first from Nanking and then from Shanghai. The first rush of rage has cooled and white people are being sent away from China on any ship which will carry them away from here. They may take no possessions with them and only a few *cash* in money, and they are warned not to return here save as traders, for China is one nation now, and one nation is stronger than a dozen little factions all fighting each other. You must leave, Nala.'

Ouyang and Nala were in the courtyard which adjoined the room she had been given, standing under a plum tree white with blossom. Ouyang had been gone a week and had come back to state calmly that with the Communists now the main cause of worry for Chiang Kai-shek, she and Aunt Sarah were less likely to be killed by terrified peasants or military personnel simply because they were white.

'But it must be a straightforward journey to Shanghai, preferably on the train and still in peasant disguise,' he warned her now. 'It's absurd, but you'll be safer in a city which is becoming used to sending white people off over the sea than in a smaller community where people act quickly, frightened that by not acting they may bring danger and trouble down on themselves.'

Nala chuckled.

'You mean they'd chop our heads off in case they were suspected of harbouring whites and then repent at leisure when the authorities called it murder. Yes, I understand. We'll make for Shanghai then, and take a ship to . . . oh, to somewhere safer.'

'That's it. But my dear little one, I can only accompany you if my presence makes you safer, not if I become a danger. Do you know what I mean?'

'You mean that you're a Communist, and Communists have a price on their heads,' Nala said at once. 'What will you do, Ouyang? Where will you go? I don't want you to put yourself in danger for us.'

'My face is not well-known so for the time being, at least, I shall behave like any other student. But when high summer comes I think I shall go to the mountains and find Chou En-lai. I would have gone at once except that I think I'll be more use here than in hiding.'

'And Chiang Kai-shek is doing just what you wanted to do, making China into one strong nation,' Nala reminded him. 'Does that ease your conscience a little, make it perhaps seem more sensible to do as your parents wish and take a post in the city, using your languages?'

Ouyang smiled at her and drew her close so that they could speak without being overheard.

'I'm afraid my idea of a strong China and Chiang Kai-shek's don't necessarily mean the same thing,' he said. 'The Nationalists – that's what they're calling themselves now, instead of the Kuomintang – have acted wrongly by our creed. They have taken from the rich all right, but they've kept it for themselves. And in other cases they've let rich oppressors continue to oppress, provided they pay money into the Nationalist coffers. So there is a battle still to be fought and won, little dog's eyes, and I'm going to be there when it matters. Chou En-lai is a great man, but Mao Tse-tung will be greater. He is in the mountains, training an army of workers and peasants, and I'll join him when he calls. But in the meantime, I'll take you through to Shanghai and see you on to a safe ship. If you write to me at the Te Ku compound I'll get the letters some time. And I'll write back when you give me your new address, so we shan't lose touch. And one day, I'll send for you to come back to our new China, where all sorts of things will be possible which would be frowned on today.'

'If you're sure you'll be safe, then thank you,' Nala said. 'You are the best friend in the world, Ouyang.'

'I'll be true to you as you would be true to me,' Ouyang said. He took her hands, squeezed them, then smiled and turned to leave the courtyard.

Nala stood still for a moment, trying to tell herself that Ouyang was right; he would do more good helping the Communists into power than he would by working in the city. But she had little faith in the Communists; they were too quick to kill and maim anyone who did not agree with them. It seems, she told herself ruefully, as she turned back into her room, to be a trait of the Chinese character that they don't argue with those who hold differing opinions to their own, they just wipe them off the face of the earth!

But Ouyang was different; he was a true friend. Only a friend, because that was all he could ever be to a foreign devil with dog's eyes.

Philip had been working so intensively all day that when there was a knock on his office door and he looked up, he saw double for several vital seconds. He blinked and rubbed his eyes. They had done it! Iridescent lustre had become a reality, and not merely a reality, but a commercial reality! He had slogged away at the figures, paring things down, economizing by bulk buying, keeping the cost as low as possible, and the latest tests proved that it could be done. So the eyes he turned on his secretary, though blinking and bleary after seven hours of solid bookwork, shone with triumph.

'Yes, Miss Withers? We've done it, by the way, these figures prove conclusively that we can produce the new ware commercially, and at prices which will have buyers flocking, what's more.'

'Oh, good, Mr Philip. There's a gentleman to see you, he . . .' Miss Withers's small, black-clad figure lurched as someone pushed impatiently past her. It was Sidney Warburton, waving a newspaper.

'Philip? Have you seen this?'

'It's all right, Miss Withers, Mr Warburton and I are old friends,' Philip said as Miss Withers, bristling, showed a tendency to surge forward and drag his godfather by the scruff of his neck back to the foyer, where he belonged. 'Come in, Unk, and sit down. Now what's all this about?'

'The Chinese . . . there's been a massacre . . . thousands killed, they say . . . it's that bloody Boxer Rebellion all over again, only this time it's the Commies and some other lot . . . Kuomin . . . something or other, I can't say it . . . and this time it's young Adeline who's mixed up in it, Addy's girl!' Sidney's voice was raised, strident. 'I'm going over there. I won't stand for this . . . an innocent child, mixed up in this bloody business . . . I'm going to fetch her out of it!'

'But Unk . . . you don't know where she is . . .' Philip began and in the same instant his own blood ran cold.

Nala! She was out there, she looked completely English, she was clearly white. Horrible pictures flickered across his imagination; Nala raped, tortured, dead. He pressed the heels of his hands into his eyes. He could not bear it – why on earth hadn't he acted months ago . . . no, years ago? He should have gone over then, told her he loved her, demanded that she come back to England with him!

'Unk . . . there's a girl I met . . . why should they hurt English people, though? If the fighting's between the Commies and the whatsits, why should Addy's girl get involved?'

'Because they've always hated foreigners, missionaries in particular if you ask me, and why not? Marching in there changing a religion which had satisfied the country quite well for . . . oh, I don't know, a couple of hundred years? A thousand? Well, anyway, this lot are killing whites . . . read the paper, boy, for God's sake!'

Philip took the paper and read, the colour draining from his face.

Sidney was right; the victorious troops, so the report said, were killing anyone even suspected of Communist sympathies, and white people, regardless of their standing in the community, were being slaughtered along with the rest. It's a purge, the newspaper said; China is ridding herself of foreigners and traitors in her midst, she will become one strong young nation, a colossus of the Far East.

Philip, almost hypnotized, read on. The Communists under their leader Chou En-lai had threatened industrialists and rich men with instant sequestration of goods and wealth should they get into power. This had had the understandable effect of making the rich and the powerful throw in their lot with Chiang Kai-shek. Not, the report went on, that this was likely to save them or their wealth. If Chiang Kai-shek could see no advantage in sparing them, their money would undoubtedly be filtered off into Nationalist pockets, instead of going to support the omnivorous Communist peasant population.

'I see,' he said at last, reaching the end of the piece. 'So you plan to rush off to China, at a time when the mere sight of a white face is enough to bring on an attack of blood-lust, and try to search for one small white girl amongst the millions? And you think I might go with you; is that right?'

Sidney stared at him for one moment. Then he sat down in Philip's visitor's chair, sank his head in his hands and burst into tears.

'I won't go. I'm too old, too tired.'

Aunt Sarah faced Nala across their room, her loving, humorous mouth set in a determined line. Nala sighed and crossed the room in a couple of strides, putting both arms round the older woman's shoulders and dropping a kiss on her lined brow.

'Darling Auntie Sarah, I won't go without you.'

'Nala, you must! Ask the Old Mistress; they can keep me safe here, to live out my days in peace, those days that are left. The long journey down to the coast would very probably kill me, and if I survived it I'd die on the sea voyage to England. This is my home, dearest; to dig me out of it is to dig a snail out of its shell and we all know what happens to snails treated in that way. Let me stay here, there's a good girl.'

'It wouldn't be fair to the Te Ku family,' Nala said urgently. 'Think of what would happen to them if they were found to be harbouring a white woman, when the order has gone out that all white people must either die or leave the country! I mean to leave the country, but even so I cannot make my way down to the coast openly; Ouyang says I might easily be killed by some over-zealous soldier or even a frightened peasant. We will have to hide, and lie, and be terribly careful until we reach the comparative safety of Shanghai, where the government is gathering all the white people together and shipping them overseas.'

'Well, I won't do it,' Aunt Sarah said obstinately. 'Ask the Old Mistress . . . please, Nala, dearest, ask her!'

In the end, Nala had little choice, and the Old Mistress was reassuring.

'I am old, and Missie Ellis is old,' she said in her high, cracked voice, her bright eyes fixed on Nala's face. 'I shall say Missie Ellis was a servant to the missionary on the hill, the one who has gone to England. I shall say this woman was left homeless by the soldiers who burned down the bungalow, and I took her in. I shall say we are both old, both tired. Who would hurt a woman as old as I? And they would have to hurt me before I would let them touch Missie Ellis.'

'But the risk . . .' urged Nala, only to see the Old Mistress's mouth curve up into a very sweet smile.

401

'Risk, Nala, my child? You should know better! Who is more respected, more loved, in China, than the old? Not one person in this whole village would raise a hand against a woman of my years, nor a woman as old as Missie Ellis. Do you think others are different? We shall be safe, believe me. And Missie Ellis is right when she says such a journey might kill her; it would certainly kill *me*.'

'Then we'll leave together tomorrow morning,' Ouyang said, when she told him what had transpired. 'Poor Nala, to have to leave your dear friend behind. But it is for her sake; you are doing what is best for her and what she wants. And when you get to Shanghai you may fall in with Sven, or another of your friends.'

'Yes . . . but they can't make up for Auntie Sarah,' Nala muttered. 'I'll never see her again, will I, Ouyang?'

'Not in this world,' Ouyang admitted. 'Will you meet me in your courtyard at dawn, then? We'll travel on the railway as far as we can. I don't think they're keeping a watch on the trains – not the ones going to Shanghai, at any rate. But if we see soldiers, or if we're challenged . . . you'd better say you're my wife.'

'In no circumstances,' Nala said promptly. 'It's bad enough that I should let you risk your life by coming with me to Shanghai; I refuse to let you court death by claiming to have married a *yang kuei-tzu*!'

'We'll see,' Ouyang said, 'See you at dawn!'

It was hard to leave next morning. Nala wept as she crept from the pile of quilts, kissed her companion's brow, and dressed in the half-light. She wept more when, just as she was about to creep out through the door, a voice from behind her said, 'Goodbye, my dear, and good luck; think of me!'

She flew back to the bed-platform and hugged the frail figure sitting up amidst the quilts and then, not trusting her voice, she went, looking back only once.

Ouyang was waiting for her. He glanced approvingly at her clothing – the sensible peasant cotton, the clogs, the coolie hat tied under the chin with a thin black lace.

'All set? We'll get O'ai Chin to drive us to the station.'

It was going to be a fine day; as they drove the mist began to lift from the paddy fields in delicate, drifting scarves and the sun lit up the distant hills, gilding the mountain tops. The air smelled fresh and sweet and the mule's feet and the iron wheels of the cart clattered across the dry bits of the track and sloshed through the muddy patches. Somewhere a cock was crowing, and as if it had been a signal other cocks answered. A dog barked thinly and a thread of smoke rose through the roof-hole of a little cob-cottage, still otherwise looking asleep, with its thatch pulled down over its eyes.

I shall never forget this, Nala found herself thinking. Whether I'm in

Japan or in England, or whether I am about to die, spitted on a soldier's sword, for the rest of my life I will remember this quiet, misty morning, the steam rising off the mule's back as it hurries along the road, the dew glittering on every bush, and the sun inching its way up into the pale yellow morning sky.

She glanced sideways at Ouyang. He was glancing sideways at her. Their eyes locked, then parted. Nala looked down at her knees in the faded blue cotton. We are dear friends who must part, she reminded herself urgently. Dear, dear friends.

'Get on the train, get right into a corner of the third-class carriage, and I'll join you presently,' Ouyang hissed at her as the train drew into the station. 'We'll need food – besides, it'll look more natural.'

'You . . . you wouldn't leave me?' Nala's voice trembled despite her resolve to be brave. Ouyang squeezed her hand.

'Never – not until I have to. Do as I say.' He let go of her hand and gave her a little push. Nala climbed obediently into the nearest coach. It was already packed with humanity – and not humanity only; crates of hens, a small but noisome pig, several gaunt dogs and a couple of geese were already in residence. Nala settled·herself in a corner, on the straw, as Ouyang had suggested . . . or commanded, rather. Then she waited.

Others crowded in. A girl of Nala's own age or thereabouts came and squeezed down next to her. She glanced at Nala, then smiled. With the coolie hat well pulled down and her hair cut so that it hung shaggily over her face, with her skin darkened with some sort of concoction that the Old Mistress had produced and with her eyes kept half-shut, Nala must, she imagined, have looked quite authentically peasant-Chinese at a first or even a third glance. She did not intend anyone to look at her for long, though. Presently she rolled up her sleeve and scratched her arm. It was blotched and speckled with what looked like some hideous skin disease, or possibly measles. Actually it was red paint but it would serve, Nala hoped, to discourage close scrutiny. And it certainly seemed to work now for the other girl drew back a little and turned to gaze out towards the platform.

Presently, there was a disturbance in the doorway and Ouyang began to push and shove his way through the crowd, apologizing cheerfully, using language she had never heard him utter when someone trod on his foot and being the image of an anxious young man parted from his wife or betrothed.

'I left her . . . went to get something to eat,' he was saying as the train jerked into sudden movement. 'Ah, there you are, Li!'

Ouyang reached her side, squatted down and winked, a quick flutter of his right eyelid.

'All right? Feeling quite well? Good, good. I've brought you melon seeds to chew and some cakes and noodles in a bowl. Eat now, eat and you will stay well.'

'Thank you,' Nala said, trying not to grin at him. She took the bowl of noodles, however, and realized within seconds of scraping the bottom of the bowl clean that she had indeed been very hungry. They had been sitting on the station platform for almost a whole day before a train had come along bound for Shanghai, and in all that time she had not dared eat or drink because it meant leaving the platform and perhaps missing the train. Or at least that was what she told Ouyang; what really worried her was that she might have to relieve herself as a result of eating and drinking. If the train had come then she would have missed it and she found herself loth to take such a journey through hostile country without Ouyang's support and help.

'It is a long way to Shanghai,' the girl next to her muttered presently. 'Are there many stops?'

She was addressing the man on her further side and Nala listened eagerly to his reply.

'A great many. But whether the train will stop for long, as it's so fully laden and cannot take on more passengers, I cannot tell.'

Ouyang bent forward.

'But some of these people will have to get out in the smaller stations, won't they?' he asked reasonably. 'Surely it cannot be that everyone on the train is bound for Shanghai?'

'No,' the man admitted reluctantly. 'But most of us are, I dare say. Where are you and your woman bound?'

'Shanghai; to visit relatives,' Ouyang said carelessly. 'She wants to live near her family, so we're taking a look at the city.'

'It's a great city, but a dangerous place,' someone else chimed in. 'I wouldn't want to live there but for the work; there's always work to be had in Shanghai. Even the beggars are rich there.'

There was a laugh at that, and before long the entire coachload of people were chattering away as if they had known one another for ever. Nala smiled to herself. Ouyang was clever; if anyone was to poke their noses into this coach they would never guess that, until the train started, not one person on board had so much as spoken to the others. They appeared to be neighbours and friends to a man.

'Have a drink of goat's milk,' the young woman nearest said to Nala. 'Don't be afraid that you'll need to piddle as a result; we all shall! They say one of the planks in the corner there comes up and you can use the gap.'

'I bet it's draughty,' Nala said, giggling. The other girl giggled as well.

'Better a draught than a burst pipe,' she said, and everyone within earshot laughed. A warmth of shared experience seemed to rise like a physical thing in the confined space. Ouyang took Nala's hand in his and squeezed, smiling at her. She knew what he meant; they were in it together now, not just he and she but every person in the coach. If the soldiers came no one would cry out against another; community spirit is a wonderful thing. I wouldn't be surprised, Nala found herself thinking, if we reached Shanghai safely after all!

The train did stop everywhere and several times they got out on a lonely little country platform to stretch their legs, relieve themselves and buy food or drink. But they always took care to climb back into the same coach and were speedily enveloped in the fellow-feeling which Ouyang had so cleverly exploited.

In fact, Nala was actually enjoying the journey when the first soldiers came.

They were at a tiny country station, all crowding round a seller of vegetable stew with dumplings, when a raucous voice shouted at them to 'stand back and keep still'.

Impossible though it may seem to obey two such contradictory commands at one and the same time, everyone endeavoured to do so, and apparently succeeded, for the backward surge from the seller of stew was accompanied immediately by a frozen stillness as an untidy group of soldiers appeared on the platform.

'Keep back, keep back,' their officer shouted, still in the hectoring tones of one addressing not people but rather pigs or sheep. 'I need room on the train for my men . . . move over there . . . move over.'

The soldiers all had guns with fixed bayonets and they all looked dirty, sleepy and extremely young. Danger appeared to have passed them by, or perhaps they had looked dangerous once, when they were fresher. Nala found it impossible to be seriously scared of them once she'd taken a good look at their tired young faces and apparently the rest of the company felt the same, for instead of keeping back, moving over or doing any of the other things the officer was shouting about, there was a concerted rush back to the train. No one, it seemed, was going to relinquish his or her place in the coaches to a member of the armed forces . . . particularly a member so young and so patently tired!

'Out . . . out . . . out!' the officer screamed, rushing impotently up and down the platform and gesturing with his swagger stick and an out-thrust fist. 'Come on there, these men must get through to Shanghai . . . out, a dozen or so of you!'

No one answered, but no one moved either. Someone, braver or more foolhardy than the rest, shouted out, 'We've paid for our tickets – have you?' but fortunately for him at that moment the train began to move forward and the passengers grabbed at the doors and pulled them closed.

They could hear the officer shrieking after them, commanding the driver to stop, his voice threatening, cajoling and finally fading as the rattling roar of the train built up to full steam.

'So that's the Nationalist Army,' Ouyang said thoughtfully, under cover

405

of the racket. He put a lazy arm round Nala's shoulders and pulled her until her head rested in the hollow at the base of his neck. 'Not very impressive, were they? Perhaps it won't take as long as I thought to get rid of them. But sleep now, Nala-san, whilst you have the chance. I'll hold you so you don't fall over and lose your hat.'

He chuckled and Nala laughed too, then relaxed against him. Very soon, she slept.

# CHAPTER TWENTY-EIGHT

Philip was on deck when the first sign that they were approaching land came up on the horizon. Another businessman, also heading rather apprehensively for Shanghai, leaned on the rail beside him.

'That's it,' James Fryer said, pointing to the low, greyish cloud against the blue of the sky. 'Well, I wonder what sort of a reception we'll get?'

'I was told in London that we wouldn't be able to leave Shanghai unless we had an escort,' Philip said, pulling a face. 'I need to be able to move around freely . . . I wonder how long the embargo on foreigners will last?'

'Not long; they need to modernize, and this fellow, Chiang Kai-shek, admits and acknowledges it whilst kicking whites out of his country as fast as he can,' his new acquaintance said. 'It's not trade they want to discourage, anyway, so much as dumping – and the missionaries, of course. You don't make a firmly united country by letting foreigners in to corrupt your young people with a whole new ideology, which is what Christianity must look like to them.'

'What do you mean by dumping?' Philip asked. 'I thought we took from them, I didn't know we dumped!'

'Didn't you? Well, we used to do just that. Made them buy inferior Indian and even English products at high prices, whilst making them sell decent stuff to us for peanuts. Oh yes, the British haven't got much to be proud of in their dealings with the Chinese in the past. But now it's a different story. There's competition, for one thing. If we offer them say guns for one price, we're liable to lose the deal if our competitors can offer them the same thing for less. Keeps us on our toes, and johnny-Chinaman is no fool when it comes to playing one European country off against another; he sees how it benefits him to keep his cards close to his chest and shop around.'

'Well, I'm buying anyway, not selling,' Philip said somewhat mendaciously, since his first reason in coming to China at all was to find Nala and persuade her to leave with him, and his second to find Addy's girl and persuade her to go back to Sidney. 'I'm interested in china, pottery, stuff like that. D'you think they'll let me trade?'

James shrugged.

'You never know, but they like money. It's the one attribute common to the lot of 'em that I've managed to discover. Offer them enough loot and they'll murder their own mothers.' He laughed, took a last drag on his cigarette, and threw the butt into the sea; daylight was fading now and Philip followed the arc of the little orange glow until it was doused in the lazy swell of the ocean. 'Well, might as well get some shut-eye. We'll dock in the early hours but they won't expect us to go ashore until it's full daylight.'

He headed for his cabin and Philip, after one more lingering glance at the horizon, followed suit. It would be a long and probably difficult day tomorrow, he reasoned. Best get some rest whilst he could.

But once he was in his cabin and had climbed into his bunk, the enormity of his task almost overcame him once more. He had not intended to come here himself, he knew it was a fool's errand whether one was searching for Nala or Addy's girl, but the sight of his godfather, a man he both loved and respected, in floods of tears . . . only a selfish swine could have refused to come. Besides, if he had not said he'd go to China Sidney would have gone himself – and by himself if necessary.

He had wanted to accompany Philip, but the plain truth was that at nearly eighty his health might easily have made him more of a burden than an assistance. Philip had left him, in fact, at the flower farm with Lily and Arnold, sure that he would be well looked after there.

'I'll fuss him and fatten him and make him take long walks,' Lily had promised, her eyes tender as they rested on her old friend. 'They're a long-lived family, the Warburtons; he should be good for at least ten years yet if what he and Arnold between them told me is true. I do wish you luck, Philly, dear, both with your own search and with the search for Addy's girl. I hope you find them both, but I'm going to *browbeat* God for Addy's girl; Sidney's suffered – and waited – enough.'

Philip, heartily agreeing with her, could only hope too . . . but Addy's girl was a stranger to him, Nala was not. Despite their brief aquaintance he knew there was no one in the world to whom he would more willingly hand over his freedom. Blow her brilliance as an artist! Blow her ability as a potter! It was Nala herself he wanted and he should have had the courage to tell her so long since.

In his study back home he had one of her paintings. He had bought it quite soon after meeting her, seeing it hanging up in a little gallery in Paris, priced fairly, nicely framed. It made him think of her and he often looked at it and imagined the slim, clever hand holding the brush, the swift, positive movements, the way her head would turn to glance at him over her shoulder . . . all Nala was there in that little painting.

He had wondered whether they would allow him to travel to Shanghai so soon after a revolution, but when he had visited the Consul in London the man had been quite optimistic.

'It seems they're going to allow foreigners into Shanghai quite freely provided they are legitimate traders,' he said. 'You won't be allowed to roam the countryside, not this time, but they may give you a military escort if you want to visit one particular place or they may simply let you send a Chinese representative. We're not worried for the lives of those we send to Shanghai – the Nationalist Government wants to make a good impression on the rest of the world – but we have to warn people that they can't any longer wander at will.'

So Philip knew, already, that he might well find himself confined to Shanghai, but even if he was, at least he was within a few hours' travelling of Nala's workshop. He had taken the trouble, before he left England, to check her address, and also Sven's. He had them both in the lid of his suitcase – not that he needed the reminder, since he knew both addresses by heart.

Then there was the idea of sending Nala a message. He could do that if all else failed. And once he had Nala, he felt that finding Addy's girl would be very much simpler. He did not know why he felt this, save that Nala spoke the language and knew the people, but he felt it, nevertheless. So he did not fret himself now with worrying over Addy's girl. Nala would find a way.

The second lot of soldiers came at a larger station; they were already there, in fact, when the train pulled in. Ouyang, who had poked his head out of their coach to have a look around, came back to Nala, his face grave.

'We won't either of us get out for food here, Nala. Too many military. We'll just stay quiet and hope they don't interfere with us.'

It seemed they were searching the train for someone, however, for Nala could hear them going to each coach in turn, asking questions, shouting, pulling people out.

'What'll we do if they come here?' she whispered.

'When, you mean. We'll just brazen it out . . . I'm glad my hair's grown longer, lately.'

Ouyang grinned at her; but it would not be he for whom they searched of course, but she. Nevertheless they both stayed put in their corner.

The troops came in, shouted and yelled, turned half the occupants out on to the platform and glanced – cursorily, it seemed to Nala – into each face. Then they moved on to the next coach.

She and Ouyang relaxed and Ouyang said that since the army had seemed satisfied he would wriggle through the crowd in the coach and see if he could attract the attention of one of the food sellers on the platform. He did so, and was buying just as the train began to move out, so that he had to hurl money, laughing, into the man's little cart even as the man, laughing too, hurled the food into Ouyang's arms.

Nala was keeping well back, out of sight, but even so she heard a shout, then several more, and then a voice, raised in a bellow, commanding the train to stop.

The train, gathering speed, was deaf to the cries from the platform and charged on its way, and Ouyang, with both hands full of fruit and rice cakes, made his way back to her side, squatted down and handed her half the provender he had bought.

'Here we are,' he said cheerfully. 'Nala, my love, it's possible that I may decide not to come all the way into Shanghai with you – will you be all right if I leave the train before we reach the city?'

Nala's heart sank; she would have to approach a ship, find the captain, and see if she could get aboard, all whilst endeavouring to look as Chinese and innocent as she possibly could. But she nodded emphatically. If Ouyang had to go then he had to go. She knew he would never let her down if he could possibly help it.

'I'll manage very well, really I will,' she said. 'You go, Ouyang; it wasn't fair of me to accept your company even this far . . . you have work to do which is far more important than I am.'

'Nonsense . . . and probably I'll come all the way with you and see you on to a ship,' Ouyang reassured her. 'But just in case . . . so that you don't feel I've run out on you, I thought I'd better prepare you. It's possible, though unlikely, that there may be another attempt to search the train at the next station, and if so, since I know the countryside there well, I'll just slip quietly away before there's trouble.'

'All right,' Nala said. She wondered what the soldiers would do to her if she was discovered, but on that score at least Ouyang was reassuring.

'Everyone is saying that the English are being repatriated and that the feeling against foreigners has died down,' he reported after a chat with someone on a wayside station. 'Whites have been given so long to leave and we're well within the time, you've got weeks yet.'

In due course they reached the next station, which was in well-wooded country. Nala suggested that Ouyang might like to get off there anyway since he knew the area but he rejected her suggestion scornfully.

'No indeed, I'm with you all the way now,' he assured her. 'But listen to me, Nala-san – if I'm taken for some reason you mustn't linger to find out what happens; it'll all be one of those beaurocratic muddles which are so typical of the army. Just go on and get out of the country. All right?'

'But why should they take you?' Nala asked, puzzled. She lowered her voice to a murmur. 'Your politics aren't written on your forehead, dearest Ouyang!'

He laughed and squeezed her hand.

'Silly little dog's eyes, of course they aren't! I'm being over-cautious.

Just forget all about it; I'm coming to Shanghai with you and I'll see you safely on to the ship. Don't worry about it.'

But she did, of course. She trusted him implicitly, though, so if he said the danger no longer existed once they were past the wooded countryside with the small station set amongst the tall, graceful beeches, then he must be sure of himself. So she tried to put any danger out of her mind and concentrate on what she would do when they got to the Bund; should she get aboard a ship for Japan, as she had at first intended, or should she take the plunge and go to England? That was what Aunt Sarah expected of her, she knew that. But it was a big step. If only she could be sure of her welcome there, but her grandfather was bound to be dead and his heirs might not want her at all. And then there was Philip . . . he was probably married with a family by now. Her heart lurched into her clogs at the thought; she would go to Japan, where at least she could be independent of everyone.

But at last the train drew in to Shanghai and she and Ouyang and all their new friends prepared to depart and go their separate ways. Fond goodbyes were said, those returning on the train in a few days promised to look out for each other, and Nala and Ouyang made their way out of the station and set out to walk to the Bund, where the ships would anchor, waiting for passengers.

It was a bright day and rather too hot for comfort. Nala took off her quilted jacket and slung it round her waist, tying the arms about her, but kept the coolie hat on for shade now as much as for disguise. She saw policemen, black, brown, yellow, and some white faces, too. Everyone seemed in a hurry, impatient even with each other. Ouyang stopped once and bought them both a length of sugar cane; with the cane to chew on, he explained quietly, their faces were less obvious to a casual observer.

Ouyang knew Shanghai well, so he threaded his way through the narrow streets until they found themselves on the Bund, then they walked until they came to the part where the large ships were docked. They were examining the names of the huge craft, trying to find one which looked as though it was about to depart, when another put down a gangplank with a rattling roar. Nala and Ouyang, who had been strolling slowly along the Bund, dodging beggars, food vendors and the masses of rickshaws and pedestrians which crowded it, stopped to watch.

'The people on that ship must wonder at the shipping on the water,' Ouyang remarked. 'Sampans, dhows, junks . . . at this time of day you don't need to get your feet wet, you could simply jump from vessel to vessel and go miles!'

'It's very busy,' Nala admitted. 'I've not been on the Bund since I was a very young girl, when we arrived here from Japan. I don't remember much about it then, to tell you the truth, and when I've come in with Sven we stay in the city itself; usually on Nanking Road, in fact.'

'I don't like it much; I prefer Nanking, and I like Peking best of all,'

Ouyang said. 'Oh look, the passengers are beginning to disembark. When they are off we could just slip on board and see when the ship sails for England again.'

'Yes . . . oh, look, soldiers!'

'Yes, I see . . . give me your arm.'

Uncomprehendingly she did so and felt Ouyang's fingers close firmly but gently around the soft muscle.

'Now let's walk on . . . keep looking at the ships, ignore the soldiers.'

They began to walk slowly along the Bund.

'Have you ever seen anything like it?'

Philip and James Fryer were standing by the rail, waiting for the rush of passengers to leave them a clear gangplank. Looking over the landward side of the ship was astonishing enough to one who had never visited China before – the great hotels and stores which line the Bund, the imposing palaces and temples, were all foreign and exotic enough, but it was the masses of people who caught Philip's attention. Beautiful little Chinese girls, faces painted, hair piled high, wearing tight skirts and Western blouses, tittuped along on high heels, giggling together. Beggars in rags and filth limped or dragged themselves along or lay in the dust, begging bowls held out whilst they whined at the passers-by for alms. Men strode out, ancient crones tottered alone on tiny, bound feet, schoolgirls passed, and the never ending stream of rickshaw coolies tugging their vehicles, barging, swearing, kicking up a dust, added to the colour and innate foreignness of the scene.

'Yes, I have, because I've been to China before, though I admit it's a fascinating sight. But what about the shipping? We're in the mouth of the Yangtse here, of course, so you get the boats coming down from the inland waterways as well as sea-going craft. Look at that woman with her washing on lines all over the junk . . . odd to think she's probably spent her entire life on board a boat and will bring her children up just the same, don't you think?'

'Yes, it's a life I can't really begin to comprehend,' admitted Philip. 'Oh look, soldiers!'

There were a great many soldiers, idling along the waterfront; or were they idling? It occurred to Philip that they were in fact scrutinizing people's faces as they passed by. He leaned over the rail, watching the men nearest him. One of them suddenly stopped as if he'd been shot. He said something to the man next to him and both heads swivelled as if on the same pivot. They were staring at a young couple, the girl with dark swinging hair and a coolie hat and the young man with his hand gripping her upper arm, their heads close.

The soldier shouted something ahead of him, up the untidy straggling column of men, and the officer at their head shouted too, some sort of command, Philip thought.

411

In a moment, there was wild confusion on the waterfront below the ship. Whatever the officer had shouted it clearly held a threat not only for the soldiers but for the ordinary people as well. They began to run, apparently away from the docks, women and children, men and rickshaw coolies, bumping into one another, crying out, falling over. And then Philip saw, with horror, that the soldiers were armed and that they were levelling their weapons . . . at the young couple directly below the gangplank!

He gave a shout, echoed by James, and the two of them made for the gangplank at a run. Whatever was happening – how could the soldiers even contemplate firing with so many people around? Someone was sure to get hurt, probably killed. The proverbial innocent bystander could be multiplied many times in the conditions on the dock.

Philip and James reached land just as the salvo rang out. People screamed, a man shouted, other people, near enough to hear the shots but too far to know what had happened, began to run towards the incident whilst others ran away. It had been confusing before but now it was like a scene from an earthquake disaster. People ran in one direction and then another, women lost their children, coolies had their rickshaws dashed from them by the press of people. Someone fell into the water, pushed by the crowd which surged to and fro, half of them eager to escape from the threat implicit in the sound of the shots, the other half even more eager to see what was happening.

The soldiers ran forward. There were eight or ten people lying on the ground but Philip was inclined to think that most of them had been knocked over by pressure from the crowd, for although a man was clutching his leg and another his shoulder, all the blood came from one source.

It was the young man with the girl in the coolie hat; he was lying on his back, where the force of the bullets had knocked him, and blood was pumping out of a great hole torn in his cotton jacket. Philip pushed through the crowd of watchers and bent over the youth. The girl was on her knees beside him, crying with shocked, tearing sobs, speaking to the young man in a shaky, imploring voice. Philip could only guess from her tone what was being said but after a moment the young man's head moved on the bloodied earth and he spoke a few words in a thin rattle and then he moved his head again and blood gushed from his mouth, splashing up on to the girl's hands and arms. As he watched, the young man suddenly seemed to slacken all over, as though every muscle in his body had ceased working at once, and Philip knew he was dead.

A soldier bent over the girl and grabbed her arm. Philip said, 'That's enough of that!' and James said something similar, Philip imagined, in Cantonese.

The girl put small, blood-speckled hands up to her face and through her sobs she said that she would be all right in a moment.

It took Philip several seconds to realize why he could understand her so well; she was speaking English!

'Stop that man! It's Ouyang Chin, a Commie cell-leader from the north!'

Nala heard the words but it took her a second or two to realize they referred to her Ouyang and to understand his danger. When she did so she dragged at his hand, urgent for him to flee.

'Run! They're after you, Ouyang! Run!'

It was too late. They had been seen and identified. Ouyang had not taken two steps when the salvo of shots rang out and he fell. For a moment Nala thought she had been hit too, but she had been knocked sideways by Ouyang's body, so that they both landed on the ground at the same moment.

She was on her knees in a flash, bending over him, trying to pull him to his feet, crying to him to go, run, for the awful guilt made her ignore the blood, the hole in his jacket. She had let him come here, to this! She bent over him.

'Can you get up, Ouyang? Darling Ouyang, you must run or they'll catch you! Ouyang? *Ouyang!*'

The last word was less a word than a scream of mortal agony; she had seen the blood pumping out of the hole in his chest and knew the significance of it at last.

Her enemies were all about her; she could see feet and legs, some of them in army uniform, but she knelt by him, desperate for him to understand that she knew, now, what he had done for her.

'Ouyang? Dearest one, friend of my childhood . . . you saved my life with your own . . . I shall never forgive myself, never!'

It was as if the impassioned self-accusation had some power to bring him back for a second from that lonely journey upon which he was all but embarked. He turned his head a little; his eyes opened.

'Nala? When I called you dog's eyes . . . it was a love-name, little one. You were . . . dear to me.'

'And you to me, Ouyang,' Nala said steadily.

'It was . . . no fault of . . . yours,' the rattling, gurgling voice continued unsteadily. 'Mine . . . the fault. Only mine. I love you, Nala Chang.'

'And I you, Ouyang Te Ku.'

He moved his head again and blood gushed out of his mouth so suddenly that the hot flood engulfed Nala's hands and tunic before she could possibly have moved back, even had she wanted to do so. She put out a hand and touched his cheek . . . and knew he was dead. No one could have survived that rush of blood.

Someone was talking above her, someone was defending her; a soldier seized her arm and then dropped it as an English voice spoke hotly, bidding him desist.

Nala wept then, scrubbing at her eyes with her dreadful hands, more

413

lost and more alone than she had ever been before in a life which had
been a lonely one, of late.

A hand touched her shoulder; a kindly hand. A voice asked her where
she lived, whether he could take her home.

She looked up.

It was Philip Haslington.

She had longed to see Philip but now it no longer mattered, she was
almost unaware of him even though she stood within the circle of his arm.
Death had struck too quickly and savagely for her to understand her
suddenly changed circumstances completely. As they led her away she
kept telling herself that this was a nightmare, just a vile dream; Ouyang
was so *alive*, so full of his plans for his country's future. He could not have
been snuffed out in a second by that bullet.

Yet some part of her mind knew; she gave instructions that Ouyang's
body was to be returned to her village to be buried there; she said no word
about the Te Ku family because she knew that Ouyang's first thought
would have been to keep his parents and family right out of it. If trouble
was to come as a result of his death it must not come to those he loved.

In a dream, she heard Philip asking the soldiers just what the man had
done; heard, too, the reply.

'He was seen on a train heading for Shanghai,' the officer said. 'He
trained with the Communists, was a cell leader, an important man. We
have vowed to wipe out all Communists from our land.'

So that had been it; despite her comment his Communist leanings had
been marked on his forehead. A glance at his strong, handsome face and
his enemies had known him instantly.

'And how was he recognized? By a man who was himself a Communist
but has changed his coat?' Philip said coldly. 'Your men fired into the
crowd without a thought for anyone else, of course.'

'I'm not translating *that*,' James muttered, beside him. 'Come on out of
it, old boy, we've done the best we could. Let the girl deal with the rest.'

A soldier stepped forward. Philip got between him and the girl with the
bloodstained hands.

'No; this is the girl I've come here to find,' he said firmly. 'She's coming
with us.'

He had no idea whether he was doing the right thing or not but he
turned on his heel and went up the gangplank again, on to the British
ship, pulling Nala behind him. The officer called after them and James
translated.

'They say they need the girl . . . you have no right to take her on the
foreign ship and would you please take her down on to the quayside again
immediately.'

'Tell them no,' Philip said briefly. 'Remind them that she's English.'

414

'I'll go down and talk to them,' James said. 'And then I'll go to my hotel. Do I take it you won't be coming ashore then, old man?'

'Not yet . . . no, I don't think I shall,' Philip said. 'I'll take care of things here, first.'

He put his arm round the unresponsive Nala and turned her towards the nearest companionway. James watched them go, then descended the gangplank on to the quay once more. He walked over to the soldiers, who were already showing signs of moving off. No one had yet touched the body as it lay on the hard-packed earth.

James glanced back at the ship, at the soldiers and then at a nearby rickshaw. He beckoned the coolie over. Not altogether to his surprise, for he did know China, the soldiers did not seem particularly interested in the young man's body. Killing him had been their aim; he was dead and so the incident was over. The coolie approached cautiously.

'You heard what the young lady said? That the boy's body was to be buried in her village?'

'Yes, me hear she.'

'Can you arrange it for me? I'll pay you of course.'

The coolie nodded and hefted the already lightened body on to his vehicle. With James following he hurried off the wharf, heading for the crowded streets of the city.

'You never said why you were there.'

Nala and Philip sat opposite one another in the small cabin which Philip had just vacated and now intended to book for the return voyage.

'I was worried about you, Nala. About your position with a revolution raging. It said in the English newspapers that they were killing whites. So I came.'

'For *me*?' She looked across at him, for the first time with some feeling in her expression. 'All this way just for me?'

'Ye-es . . .' but perhaps it would make her think him a besotted fool or a liar or possibly even both. Better to tell the truth. 'For you and another young girl who's alone over here. My godfather has a granddaughter he has never seen but he loves her very much. I told him I'd keep my eyes open for her, too.'

The light died out of her eyes. She nodded dully.

'I see. Do you still want me to work for you, then?'

Philip hesitated. She was in a state of shock, useless to tell her now that he wanted her for herself, not for her talents. And anyway, if he once said that and she turned him down, reiterated her disinterest, he would never get over it, never dare to speak again.

'Yes . . . yes, I do. And of course there are other reasons . . .'

But she had turned from him and was looking, with increasing distress, at her bloodstained hands and clothing.

'Can I wash?'

She seemed not to realize that she had interrupted him in mid-sentence. He was glad all over again that he had not taken this opportunity of telling her that he thought he loved her. After so many years he could scarcely announce that he *did* love her; she would want to know why it had taken him so long to declare himself, and that was fair comment. Useless to try to explain to her that he had thought himself unlovable, had not even considered that she might feel for him what he thought he felt for her.

'Wash . . .? Oh yes, of course.' He sprang to his feet and ran the taps into the little basin in one corner of the room. 'Can you manage in here? I'm afraid all my soap and flannels and things are packed . . . Heavens, they've probably been taken to the hotel I booked . . . but the company provide towels. I dare say you'll manage.'

She began to wash.

'So we are going to England?'

'That's right, Nala. After all, where else would you have gone? You have no one, isn't that right?'

'No one,' Nala repeated. She was looking out of the porthole as the Bund slipped away and the big ship ploughed through the sea of tiny craft and coffins which bobbed down the Yangtse to the sea.

'Well, then? You intended to come to England, didn't you? Wasn't that why you came on to the Bund?'

'Ye-es. Or Japan. Sven is in Japan.'

'Sven's a married man with God knows how many children,' Philip said, his voice hard and angry. 'What would be the point of joining him in Japan?'

'Aren't you married, Philip?'

'Good Lord, no! Nala . . . what was that chap to you? The one who was killed?'

'Ouyang? We were like brother and sister.'

He thought her voice lacked conviction but had too much sense and too tender a heart to say so. He supposed, miserably, that they had been lovers. Well, why not? But he would have to let her get over that affair before he told her what he felt about her. In the meantime, he must remind her that his entire pottery was at her disposal.

He reminded her. She thanked him and looked, if it were possible, even more miserable than before.

During the course of the voyage he tried over and over to tell her about the Haslington ware and how she would have a completely free hand, she might decorate or not . . . if she wanted to do a series of landscapes on tiles that would be wonderful, if she preferred tiny little pastel figures to be put on the pottery that would be wonderful too. He bent over backwards to show her that he wanted her on any terms, she could turn the pottery back to front and over and over if only she would stay with him. She was beautifully polite and thanked him over and over but in a small, cool little voice which told him that her mind was elsewhere.

Towards the end of the voyage he hardly spoke at all, he was too miserable. They walked on the deck or sat in their cabin or ate in the dining-room and seldom exchanged more than a few polite nothings. Both of them had longed to see the other again and now that they had they were too inhibited by recent events to say what was in their hearts.

Nala could see that he did not really like her at all, not particularly. But he needed her to decorate his wretched pottery. How could she be with him there, day after day, and never show what she felt?

They were, in fact, both firmly grasping the wrong end of the stick, but neither knew it and they were extremely miserable, and Nala's blindness to the way he looked at her, the tones of his voice, was due to her guilt over Ouyang, which threatened, at times, to completely overwhelm her.

How could she have been so blind, so stupid! Ouyang had died because she had not realized that a man who had spent over two years drilling Communist recruits up in the mountains must be recognized, from time to time, for what he is.

So Nala hugged her guilt and her conviction that she did not even deserve love and must certainly not look for it from Philip, and Philip decided she had been deeply in love with the young communist and could not even spare a thought for him, let alone a glance.

Together all day and all night as well, because they had separate bunks in the same cabin as Nala was terrified, now, to be alone, they might still have been a thousand miles apart. Each was turned inward, each suffered in a way that neither could have believed possible of the other.

# CHAPTER TWENTY-NINE

It was high summer here, Nala reflected, watching the strange land whizz past the train. She admired the train, perhaps partly because it reminded her of trains at home; it was made of highly polished wood with lots of brass, and the carriage in which she and Philip found themselves was upholstered in dark red plush, with pictures of seaside holiday resorts underneath the rope luggage racks above their heads and a glass door leading into the corridor.

She admired the countryside, too, in a way. It was very soft and many-coloured, the grass greener than she had ever imagined grass to be, the crops more colourful, the very houses with their warm red bricks or golden thatch pleasing to the eye after – it must be confessed – the sameness of the Chinese landscape.

She had yet to see a great plain stretching to the horizon or a great river like the Yangtse, but she supposed that the English had such things somewhere in their lovely land. She thought it very beautiful and sat with her nose almost pressed against the glass, staring, staring.

She liked the bread, too. It reminded her of Aunt Sarah's bread, which was so delicious and so much nicer than its Chinese counterpart, and the butter was grand. They ruined tea, of course, but she drank it to please Philip.

They had docked, travelled to London, taken a cursory glance at the capital city of which even a young Chinese would have heard, and then got on another train bound, Philip told her, for Langforth. The name had stirred faint bells until she remembered that she had sent to Langforth for the tiles which Philip made. She had never mentioned them to him, never asked why he had not responded to her order himself. It no longer mattered. Somehow, she had ruined their tentative relationship. He talked of nothing but his wretched pottery and she, for her part, talked scarcely at all.

The train journey was only marginally less miserable than the voyage had been, but now she had fright at her shoulder as well as guilt and loneliness. She was afraid. She was going to a strange town, to meet strange people, she would have to find lodgings, she would have to buy food and get herself clothing more suitable to England than her tunic and trousers. Philip had bought her a grey linen dress with a little jacket to go over it and some brown walking shoes but she could not wear these things for ever. She would need clothing and she had no money and no idea how to get some or even what money was worth.

She thought about running away before Philip found out that the energetic, self-reliant Nala was dead and a miserable, uncertain idiot stood in her shoes; but even running away needed courage and Nala had none. She had lost it all on the Bund in Shanghai; it had simply flowed away from her as Ouyang's blood had flowed away from him.

But the train was pulling in to a big station and Philip was standing up, getting her small case and his own larger one down from the rack above their heads.

'We've arrived, Nala,' he said. 'I ordered a taxi to meet the train rather than one of the family. I thought you'd prefer it.'

He means I look a mess and I'm not fit to meet anyone, Nala told herself, and he's right, I wouldn't want anyone I knew to see me now.

She followed Philip off the train, then looked curiously round the platform. It was a drab but busy station and when they climbed into the taxi-cab she saw that they were in a drab but busy town, though it was too dark to see details clearly.

They drove for some miles, then the car stopped before a huge old

418

house. Trees clustered all about her and the house-lights shone brightly, welcomingly.

'Here we are,' Philip said bracingly. 'We'll go indoors now, Nala, and Mrs Parton will have a meal waiting for us, then you can go to bed and have a good night's sleep. Everything will seem easier to face in the morning. I'll introduce you to everyone then.'

Nala followed him into a lofty hall. The staircase had wide, low treads and a graceful curve. Something stirred in the back of Nala's mind, some recollection, but she ignored it, too lost and lonely to heed a vague feeling. But she smiled at Mrs Parton, a small, fat woman in her fifties who had once, long ago, been Philip's nursery-maid, so she informed the newly arrived guest.

'So I've known the family . . . both families . . . all me life, you could say,' she said comfortably, taking Nala's thin and rather shabby jacket. 'Just you come along o' me and you'll find a good fire in your room, hot bottles in the bed, and a meal on a tray just waiting for the word. Poor dear, you're wore out, I can tell, but a good night's sleep will see you right.'

Nala, who suspected that Philip had planned a more formal dinner, was glad to go to her room with Mrs Parton and be clucked over, fussed and helped between the sheets. She ate her supper sitting up in bed, then slid gratefully between the covers and slept at once.

'Did you have much difficulty finding her, Mr Philip?' Mrs Parton asked, as she served Philip's supper on a tray, later. Philip took the tray from her, eyeing its contents with satisfaction. Mrs Parton certainly knew how to feed a hungry man – a big roast ham sandwich made with her own good bread and surrounded by pickles was just what he would have chosen. He gestured the housekeeper hospitably to the chair opposite his own.

'Sit down, and I'll tell you all about it. It was rather odd, actually, I barely had to disembark from the ship! As the ship was docking she came on to the quayside with a young fellow, they were clearly looking for a ship to escape on, and some soldiers fired at the chap and shot him. He died at once, poor bloke, and I ran down the gangplank to see if I could help, and it was her!'

'Isn't that romantic,' Mrs Parton said approvingly. 'And did you recognize her at once?'

'Well, not quite at once,' Philip admitted, remembering those first few incredulous seconds. 'She was covered with blood and pretty dirty, and she was wearing local clothing and a big straw coolie hat. But I knew her pretty fast, as you can imagine!'

'And you brought her to safety,' Mrs Parton said dramatically. 'Poor little thing, she was so exhausted and bewildered I scarcely said more than ten words to her. She fell asleep before I left the room, you know.' She shook her head and got to her feet. 'Well, this won't get the pots cleared away and washed up, and I see you've got rid of that great sandwich without any trouble. Do you want another mug of coffee or will you take that one up to bed with you?'

Philip knew he was being dismissed and smiled to himself but got obediently to his feet, nevertheless. Mrs Parton would never go off to bed until all the work was done and the rest of the staff dismissed, but it was late and no doubt she was longing for the day to be over.

'I'll take this up with me, thanks,' he said, saluting her with the now half-empty mug. 'Can you wake me at eight-thirty tomorrow? You can leave the young lady until tennish, I should think.'

They reached the hall and crossed it. Mrs Parton slipped through the green baize door into the staff quarters, the empty tray with its used crockery held in one capable hand.

'Yes, I'll see you're woken,' she agreed. 'As for the young lady, I'll wake her myself. Nice girl, and so like her mother!'

'Thanks,' Philip started, then turned, startled, to stare at the house-keeper's departing form. 'Like her mother! Oh, but Mrs Parton . . .'

But the door swung silently; Mrs Parton was pattering off towards the kitchen, the tray held martially before her.

Philip made his way up the stairs, a frown on his brow. Like her mother? But what on earth would make Mrs Parton say such a thing? She could not know whether Nala was like her mother or not . . . or was it just an idle remark, the sort of thing, a semi-platitude, which women say? Like her mother, pretty as a picture, just comfortable little sayings which are taken for granted when the subject of the remarks is a young girl.

He was actually stripped off and washing in the bathroom when a thought struck him like a thunderbolt.

Mrs Parton thought Nala was Addy's girl! And worse than that, he immediately wondered whether he had ever put into words which of the two he had found when he wrote home! His frantic cablegram saying that he was returning with 'her' was scarcely explicit . . . yet surely he had told Unk, at least, that the girl he was bringing back was Nala Chang?

He spent an increasingly anxious ten minutes wrestling with his suddenly blank memory before the exact wording of that cablegram to Sidney Warburton came back to his mind.

*Found my girl; will come back and search for Addy's later. See you soon.*

Philip relaxed. He might not have told Mrs Parton or any other member of staff which girl he was bringing home but he had most certainly told Unk, and also Frank. He remembered writing a short but ecstatic letter to Frank, giving him a cut-down version of their reunion. Philip heaved a sigh of relief and shrugged the covers up over his shoulders. He would sleep now, and forget Nala and their troubles for a few hours. After all, they had the rest of their lives ahead of them to sort out their differences. Poor girl, she must think him a strange fellow to bring her all this way and never declare himself, but in the morning he would tell her how he felt and ask her to marry him. If I don't take my courage in both hands and speak, before I know where I am she'll be working for me in the factory and marrying someone else, he told himself, just because I haven't had the courage to tell her I love her!

Nala woke early. She climbed out of bed and padded across the floor. There were curtains at the window, dimming the bright dawn-light. She tugged them back impatiently and looked out. It was a shimmering day, the pearly sky reflecting the mist which lay in every hollow, hung in long, soft, gently swirling veils over the lower ground where, Nala was suddenly sure, a river must flow. She stood on tiptoe and peered to her right, seeing a tall tower standing amongst trees, the tops of which already seemed to glow with a sunrise that Nala could not see.

For the first time since Ouyang's death, Nala felt refreshed and excited. She glanced approvingly round her bedroom, at the large, comfortable bed with its peach satin bedspread, at the dressing-table, the wash-stand, the little chairs upholstered to match the bedspread and at the carpet, which was white but garlanded all over with flowers and ribbon bows. She wondered who had owned the room, whether it was Philip's mother's or his sister's, and then she turned to the window and found that the room no longer mattered.

Outside the window, grey dawn was brightening into day and the sun was soon to climb over the distant hills. She must get dressed and go out, she decided, for now that she was properly awake all the strange feelings she had felt when she first saw Philip were coming to life again. She knew this place! The trees, the formal garden, even the wood on the skyline . . . and the tower! She would go and take a look at the tower as soon as she had some clothes on.

She dressed quickly in her blue cotton tunic and trousers, for it was early – not even the servants would be about yet – and her grey dress was crumpled and dirty. She looked at herself in the glass and borrowed a comb off the dressing-table to tidy her hair, splashed her face with cold water and rubbed it into rose with a rough towel which hung beside the wash-stand, and then headed for the door.

It was very early, she realized as she stood on the upper landing. There was not a sound, no one stirred in the big house. She stole down the stairs, then tiptoed across a huge hall, marble-tiled, which she supposed she must have crossed the previous evening, only she had been in such a daze of tiredness that she had not even noticed it.

She did not go to the front door but to a small lobby where she found a side door which only needed unlocking and unbolting. She dealt with it, opened up and stepped out into a side garden.

It was a misty morning. Nala crossed an odd little garden with small beds divided up one from another with little green box hedges. She glanced at the plants and recognized some of them . . . thyme, sage, marjoram. It must be a herb garden, and very pretty it looked in the early light. She bent and rubbed the leaves of one or two plants to get the scent, then moved on.

A rose garden came next. Nala loved roses but found she had no desire to linger here. It was the tower she wanted, and the river beyond it. The river? How did she know there was a river? But she shrugged the thought aside and continued on her way, crossing two sloping meadows and walking confidently into the trees. She glanced ahead and saw the outline of the tower, continuing to thread her way amongst the tall trunks of beech, elm, ash and oak.

She reached the tower and stood with one hand spread out on the stones, a puzzled frown on her face. She had been here before . . . but that was totally absurd. She had never even visited England, let alone this particular spot. She shrugged presently and moved away from the tower, down to where she was sure she would find a river.

It flowed calmly, eddies forming where the bank protruded out into the water, its little beaches strewn with sand, its quiet stretches rich with riverweed which flowed like mermaids' hair in the current. It had high banks on the further side; cows grazed in one meadow, sheep in the next. The beasts stood up to their fetlocks in a white early morning mist which swirled as they moved and would soon dissipate as the sun came up. The air of peace which overhung the scene seemed to enter Nala's very soul. She breathed deeply and smelt the unfamiliar smells of the English countryside. Even the smell of the sheep and the cows was different, a richer, warmer, slower sort of smell than the smell of Chinese cattle.

Pulled by what thread she knew not, Nala turned to her right and began to walk along a narrow path by the river. She dreamed on her way, the peace bringing with it happiness and even a sort of forgiveness for the dreadful way she had brought Ouyang to his death. Here, it was not her fault, though she could not have said why this should be so. She just knew that she was not blamed, not by Ouyang himself, not by Philip, and not even by Nala, who had done the deed in complete innocence of the dreadful consequences.

She reached a stile and climbed over it. She was being led, she was sure of it now. When she cleared the trees further along the bank she turned right again as one in a dream. She saw a house, more like a castle, dreaming as she had earlier dreamed, pressed into a hollow in the grounds around it, perfect, more beautiful than any house she had ever seen or imagined. A rich profusion of plants, flowers and trees grew close to it. She walked up the meadow which separated her from the house and cows – or bulls – came over to her and breathed softly at her down their noses and dogged her footsteps until she turned to look more closely at them and then they turned and ran, jostling and pushing like schoolboys, so that she laughed and turned away from them, pretending not to notice as they immediately began to follow her again, big eyes curious, strings of saliva dangling from their gently chewing mouths.

There was an orchard, the trees lush with green apples, the grass long and sweet. Nala brushed through its dew-heavy length and felt the blades cold on her ankles, soaking the ends of her trousers and drenching her shoes, but she continued. Through the orchard, the house smiling at her now above a yew hedge. It did not occur to her to wonder how she knew it was a yew hedge; she just did. It had been cut formally, squared off at the top but allowed to grow up into a high arch so that one left the orchard under the arch and entered the gardens proper.

She stopped for a moment under the arch, simply staring. It was so beautiful! There were roses everywhere, and great bushes of lavender, a hedge of what she seemed to believe was veronica, purple and lush, and dianthus sending wafts of their clove-scent towards her on the breeze. The grass-paths all led through the garden towards the house, so she followed them. Columbines, heavy with dew, brushed against her legs and delphiniums the colour of a summer sky reared against the mellow red-brick wall. She could see a peach tree, espaliered, and a pear, too, grown for their beauty as much as their fruit.

She was almost through the garden, seeing the big circular carriage drive separating her from the house, longing for the moment when she should reach it, when a figure came out of the front door and stood, for a moment, at the top of the steps. It was a man, smoking a pipe.

For a moment Nala stood stock-still; she knew . . . no, of course she did not, could not possibly . . . she *knew* that man! She moved a step nearer and he saw her.

He pulled his chin in to his chest and then he seemed to grow several inches, as if he was actually putting on a spurt to see her better over the intervening shrubbery and flowers. Nala took another step, uncertain. Who was he? Why should she feel she knew him when she so patently could not?

He was coming down the steps towards her, his hands held out, a beatific smile on his face, but she could see tears making two shiny marks down his rosy, wrinkled cheeks.

'Addy's girl!' he said, and Nala knew that normally his voice would be a good deal louder and more self-confident. 'It's Addy's girl! Oh, my very dear child! He found you!'

Nala ran the short distance between them and found herself clasped in arms which seemed to fit round her naturally, into whose strength it was second nature to burrow. She said, 'Addy? That was my mother,' and the man nodded . . . she felt the nod though her head was buried under his chin . . . and then said softly, 'And my daughter, my very dear daughter,' and hugged her as tightly as he could hug.

Nala hugged him back, and far away she heard Kei's voice in a sing-song.

'An old old man and an old old house . . .' Kei was saying, giving the small Nala the choice between that and herself. Well, she had chosen Kei and she had thought it was too late for that old old man, that old old house, but now she knew that she was being given a second chance, even a second life.

'I should have come long ago,' she said softly, as the old man held her back from him the better to see her. 'But I was afraid . . . I was only small when my father died and left me alone. It seemed easier to stay in China with Kei and to forget all about you. Only I never quite could.'

'I've never stopped thinking about you,' the old man said. 'I did try to find you . . . but Philip managed it, eh?' He chuckled. 'The young scoundrel, telling me he'd managed to find his Nala but would go back later for my granddaughter!' He put an arm round her waist and led her back towards the house. 'Come in now, we'll have some breakfast and tell each other what we've been doing these past dozen or so years. But did Philip tell you I'd have come if I could? Only he was afraid I'd be a hindrance, you see . . . too old. Poor lad, I suppose he's in a state about his Nala.'

'His Nala? I don't understand.'

'No, I dare say he didn't tell you. He's not easy with women. But the fact is Philip fell in love with a young thing he met years ago at an exhibition of fine china in Paris. He never could bring himself to tell her – no self-confidence with women – but when he heard about the revolution and the fighting and the communists killing people he said he'd have to go to China to tell his dear love to come home with him so that he could look after her. Only I suppose he found you and decided to come back here straight away. I'm old, you see, and it worried me that the years might slip away and by the time you came home it would be too late for me.'

'I see,' Nala said. A little smile touched her lips and her eyes, which had been shiny with tears, were shiny with joy. 'I'm Addy's girl . . . what was her name, Addy's Father?'

He laughed then, and hugged her, and opened the front door to lead her inside.

'Oh, you've got two names and I can only pronounce one of them – Adeline – so I've always called you Addy's girl. But the other one . . . Yenalda, was it?'

'Yenala. But I'm just as happy being plain Addy's girl.'

Philip woke later, when the sun poked long gold fingers through the gap in his curtains and the light found out his face and spoiled his sleep. He had told Mrs Parton not to wake him until eight and it was only seven but he was thoroughly awake. No point in trying to sleep; he might as well get up.

Washing and dressing did not take him long and he decided he would go along to Nala's room and just peep in, see if she was awake. If not, he would leave her to sleep but if she was awake they might have a bit of a talk. It was time he told her how he felt about her, he knew that, and here, on his own ground, perhaps he would not feel quite so unsure.

He went quietly along the corridor and tapped, very gently, on Nala's door. He listened, but heard no sound. Equally gently, he turned the handle and peeped in.

He saw that she was gone immediately and flung the door wide. Early sunshine bounced off the window panes and streaked the carpet. She had pulled the curtains right back and re-made the bed, and he was relieved to see that her little suitcase was still on the chair and her pyjamas lay in an untidy pile in front of the dressing-table. He smiled to himself, turning away from the room, closing the door behind him. She was getting better, more like herself! She had obviously decided to go out early and explore, either in the grounds or around the house itself. Wherever she was he would soon find her, and as abruptly as he had decided to search for her he was suddenly sure that the moment had come to tell her he loved her. Earlier, he had been unsure because he knew she was not ready for such a declaration. Now he was certain that she was perfectly capable of either accepting him or rejecting him, and for the right reasons, what was more. If she said no, then he would persuade her to work at the pottery until she had enough money to set up for herself. If she said yes . . . joy flooded him; a big, stupid grin spread across his face, meaninglessly since no one was in sight. How painful and demoralizing was unrequited love, how comfortable and confidence-building was its opposite!

He hurried down the long flight of stairs to the tiled hall.

Ten minutes later he knew she was not in the house; one of the maids, a funny little thing with frizzy hair and protruding teeth, said that she had seen the lady . . . or at least a lady . . . making her way down through the meadows towards the river.

'I were coming to work,' she confided. 'I were early, too!'

Philip congratulated her, gave her a shilling tip and hurried off whilst she was still stammering her thanks. He went to the tower, then to the river. And then, because he thought it likeliest, he turned to his right along the river bank.

He had no idea why, but he was suddenly sure she would have gone to the Manor. Haslington women have been running to Unk for years, he told himself with grim humour. Why shouldn't this one follow suit, even though she isn't a Haslington woman yet?

He went along the river path, over the stile, up the meadows and through the garden without meeting a soul, however. At the house he hesitated, looking up at the windows. He could see no one, but perhaps she had gone round the side or the back.

He walked around the house, or as close as you could get because of all the flowers, shrub and creepers which grew so prolifically here. He was

425

halfway round when he heard voices from above his head and stopped for a moment to try to identify whence they came.

A window was open; the voice came from there and it was definitely his godfather speaking.

'This will be your room,' Unk was saying. 'Your mother slept here when she was a girl; she only moved into the room next door, which is bigger, after she married. The child of the house always sleeps here. If you look out of the window . . .'

Philip stepped back, the better to see. The window was already open and now Nala leaned out. She was following the direction of Sidney Warburton's pointing finger and did not immediately realize that she was being observed. She looked quite beautiful, Philip thought, with her hair tumbling forward over her shoulders and her big blue eyes fixed on the middle distance.

'Over there is the Hall, where the Haslingtons live,' Sidney was saying instructively. 'When Addy was young she and Bella Haslington used to signal to each other with their lights. There isn't a young girl of your age living there now, my dear, but no doubt you'll find friends quickly enough.'

'I'm sure I shall,' Nala said. She was looking down.

Philip stepped close to the wall.

'Juliet?' he said.

Nala frowned, then the frown cleared. Mrs Ellis had made sure that her education was not entirely neglected.

'Romeo?'

'That's right. Will you marry me?'

Nala primmed her mouth at him, but her eyes were sparkling.

'Marry you? I thought you wanted me to decorate your china at the pottery?'

'Only if you won't marry me. Nala?'

'But you don't even know who I am! You haven't even asked what I'm doing here, in this house.'

Philip sighed.

'I don't care who you are, and I care less what you're doing in the Manor – it sounds as though you're thinking of buying it! Will you marry me?'

'Yes, of course I will! Shall I come down or will you come up?'

'You will?' Philip, who had been marshalling his arguments to persuade her to agree, stared up blankly, the wind completely removed from his sails.

'Yes, I will. I ought to ask my grandfather's permission first, perhaps, but I've been managing my affairs for so long that I don't think it would be fair.'

'Your grandfather? But you've not got a grandfather; your parents died long ago, and . . .'

426

A second head appeared beside Nala's at the window, with a Cheshire-cat grin almost bisecting its face.

'My dear Philip,' Sidney Warburton said, 'you don't mean to stand there and tell me you didn't realize you'd found Addy's girl?'